NEW YORK REVIE
C L A S S I C S

A FORTUNATE MAN

HENRIK PONTOPPIDAN (1857–1943) was born in Fredericia,
Denmark, into a family with deep roots in the Lutheran church. He
rebelled against the pious atmosphere of home by moving to Copenhagen
and studying to be an engineer. In 1879, he abandoned those studies to
become a schoolteacher, a journalist, and a fiction writer. His first
novels, inspired by the ideas of the realist critic Georg Brandes, focused
on social issues of country and village life, but increasingly his work
took a psychological turn, culminating in what is widely regarded as his
major novel, *A Fortunate Man*. He is also the author of *The Apothecary's
Daughters*; *Emanuel, or Children of the Soil*; and *The Promised Land*.
He was awarded the Nobel Prize in Literature in 1917.

PAUL LARKIN is a journalist, filmmaker, critic, and translator from
the Danish and other Scandinavian languages. In 1997 *The Gap in the
Mountain . . . Our Journey into Europe*, the six-part film series he wrote
and directed as an independent production for RTÉ, won him the
European Journalist of the Year Award (the overall award and the film
director category). In 2008, he was awarded the Best International
Director prize at the New York Independent Film and Video Festival
for his Irish-language docudrama *Imeacht na nIarlaí* (The Flight of the
Earls) starring Stephen Rea. His translation of Henrik Pontoppidan's
The White Bear and *The Rearguard* and Martin Hansen's *The Liar*
are also published by NYRB Classics. He lives in a Gaeltacht area of
County Donegal, Ireland, where Irish is the predominant language of
everyday use.

FLEMMING BEHRENDT is a Danish journalist and literary critic
who has written extensively about the work of Henrik Pontoppidan.

A FORTUNATE MAN

HENRIK PONTOPPIDAN

Translated from the Danish by
PAUL LARKIN

Afterword by
FLEMMING BEHRENDT

NEW YORK REVIEW BOOKS

New York

THIS IS A NEW YORK REVIEW BOOK
PUBLISHED BY THE NEW YORK REVIEW OF BOOKS
207 East 32nd Street, New York, NY 10016
www.nyrb.com

Library of Congress Cataloging-in-Publication Data
Names: Pontoppidan, Henrik, 1857–1943, author. | Larkin, Paul, translator.
Title: A fortunate man / by Henrik Pontoppidan; translated by Paul Larkin.
Other titles: Lykke-Per. English
Description: New York: New York Review Books, 2025. | Series: New York
   Review Books classics |
Identifiers: LCCN 2024017171 (print) | LCCN 2024017172 (ebook) |
   ISBN 9781681379272 (paperback) | ISBN 9781681379289 (ebook)
Subjects: LCGFT: Bildungsromans. | Novels.
Classification: LCC PT8175.P6 L913 2025 (print) | LCC PT8175.P6 (ebook) |
   DDC 839.813/72—dc23/eng/20240415
LC record available at https://lccn.loc.gov/2024017171
LC ebook record available at https://lccn.loc.gov/2024017172

ISBN 978-1-68137-927-2
Available as an electronic book; ISBN 978-1-68137-928-9

The authorized representative in the EU for product safety and
compliance is eucomply OÜ, Pärnu mnt 139b-14, 11317 Tallinn, Estonia,
hello@eucompliancepartner.com, +33 757690241.

Printed in the United States of America on acid-free paper.
10 9 8 7 6 5 4 3 2 1

A FORTUNATE MAN

I

IN THE years around the time of our last war with Germany, there was a Christian minister by the name of Johannes Sidenius who lived in a small provincial town in east Jutland. The town lay at the bottom of an overgrown fjord and was hidden from view by the surrounding green hills. This priest was a pious and austere man. His outward appearance and, indeed, his whole way of life placed him sharply at odds with the rest of the town's inhabitants who therefore regarded him for many years as an intruder whose peculiar ways prompted various reactions, ranging from a simple shrug of the shoulders to downright indignation. Whenever he walked—tall and severe in demeanor—through the town's winding streets, dressed in his long, gray and rough-spun coat, big dark blue spectacles perched on his forehead and his hand firmly gripping a large umbrella with which he struck the pavement in tack and tandem with each step he took, people on the street would instinctively turn and stare; while those who looked on from behind window panes and lace curtains would smile at the scene, or scowl, as their mood took them. The town's elders, the old estate and cattle merchants, never deigned to offer him a greeting, even when he was clad in his vestments. For, despite the fact that they themselves were wont to appear in public wearing clogs and canvas smock coats, sucking continually at their pipes, they held it at as a shame and disgrace upon the town that they had got such a wretched cleric who appeared amongst them dressed as some lowly bell ringer, and who, to boot, obviously could barely provide for himself and his brood of whelps. One had been accustomed to a quite different sort of clergy here—to men attired in fine black cloth and a collar of the best white cambric with its attendant brilliant chest piece; men who also by their very name had spread a luster over the town and its church; men who would go on to be archdeacons and bishops within the diocese, but who were never arrogant in their piety, or felt themselves to be above the town's worldly affairs and took a full part in the citizenry's functions and festivities.

Indeed, the large red vicarage had previously been a byword for hospitality, where, once any religious business had been concluded with the minister, there was a standing invitation to retire to the drawing room. Here, the lady of the house and her young daughters would be in attendance and over coffee, or (when a better class of folk was present) a small glass of wine and homemade cake, one could gossip about the latest news and events in the town. But now, people avoided the rectory, unless some pressing reason drove them there, and these days one got no further than Pastor Sidenius's funereal study, where the curtains were usually half drawn because his eyes could not tolerate the reflected glare from the walls on the other side of the narrow street.

Moreover, this pastor then usually left visitors standing in this place, never offering them a seat, dealing with them in a curt manner and showing no apparent interest in them. He was, in fact, least hospitable to those who believed themselves to be most deserving of special attention. Even the families of the town's civic officials no longer paid a call to the rectory, given that Pastor Sidenius—instead of offering them refreshments—had taken it upon himself to question them on their spiritual inclinations and generally addressed them more like candidates for the rite of confirmation standing before a bishop.

He had aroused particular animosity when officiating at burial ceremonies for the town's more illustrious citizens—where the populace would form a procession in pomp and ceremony, holding garlanded guild banners aloft to the accompaniment of a brass band and with civic officials in gold braided uniforms and plumed hats also in attendance—all this, it was averred, being a fitting way to offer thanksgiving and spiritual inspiration following a light wine reception in the home of the deceased. However, in place of a glorious send-off, with the obligatory eulogy in memory of the deceased, this Pastor Sidenius restricted himself unbendingly to the recital of a prayer more befitting of unchristened children and the lower classes. Not a word on the decency of the dearly departed and the fruitful furrow he had diligently plowed throughout his life; no mention of the fact that the town's rising prosperity had made his name, or of his selfless devotion to its Pavements Department, or communal water provision. In fact, the deceased party was barely mentioned at the graveside, and then only with additional comments such as "this poor heap of dust" or "this worm fodder," and the greater and more refined the gathering which he addressed, the more flags and banners that snapped in the wind swirling around the graveside, the shorter the prayers became and the more miserable was his description of the remains which people had come to honor, so that mourners left the scene with an anger which was more than once audibly expressed, even in the hallowed grounds of the cemetery.

The only townspeople who were regular attendants at the rectory were a pair of small, shriveled old ladies from the spinster fraternity and a pale, long-bearded Christ-like figure who was an itinerant tailor. There were also a number of "saved" people of no means, who in Pastor Sidenius's home had found a long sought-for refuge in a town whose thoughts otherwise rarely strayed from temporal considerations. However, the fact alone that Fru Sidenius, the pastor's wife, was of a very weak disposition and had been confined to bed in recent years meant that there was no suggestion of any kind of social circle having been established. Indeed, it should be said that Pastor Sidenius himself was in no way disposed to social engagements and his acolytes sought his counsel on matters of faith alone. On the other hand, they would meet up every single Sunday in the church, where they would occupy their chosen place immediately below the pulpit and then provoke the ire of the rest of the congregation by, in a most ostentatious manner, singing even the most interminable of psalms without once consulting their church hymnals.

Pastor Sidenius belonged to an ancient dynasty of clerics, which traced its lineage right back to the Reformation. For more than three centuries, the call to spiritual works had gone from father to son—yes even to daughters as well, in as much that these had in many cases married their fathers' curates, or their brothers' student friends. It was from this deep well that the conscious authority in the pronouncement of the Lord's word, for which the Sideniuses were renowned, had sprung from olden times. There was hardly a parish in any part of the country where at least one family member had not been present, at some point in the passage of the centuries, to remind people of the need for obedience to Church Law.

Of course, among such a large number of servants in the Church, not all would prove to be equally zealous in the commission of their vocation. There had even been the odd family member whose passions lay more in the direction of decidedly secular affairs—people in whom a lust for life, which ran as a suppressed but powerful undercurrent within the dynasty, had suddenly broken out in rather uncontrolled ways. Thus, in the previous century, there had been a priest in Vendsyssel, "Mad Sidenius" by name, who was said to have led the life of a wandering hunter in the great forests around the Jutland Ridge. Here, he would often be seen carousing in the taverns and imbibing schnapps in the company of the local peasantry, until finally one day, in a drunken rage during the Easter celebrations, he struck down his sacristan so violently that a spurt of blood desecrated the very altar cloth.

Despite events such as this, the vast majority of the family had been upstanding champions of the Church and several of them were also very well read. Indeed, they were theological scholars, who in their rural isolation had sought respite from the gray blandness of each passing year via the interior workings of the mind, a deep investigation of their own inner world, in which they would eventually discover the greatest happiness in life, its greatest rewards, and the ultimate goal underpinning everything.

It was this inherited disdain for the value of all things secular which had been Johannes Sidenius's buckler and shield in the cut and thrust of daily life, and the thing that had kept both his back straight and his mental resolve undaunted, despite the strain of dire poverty and the many reverses he had suffered. But in this regard, he had also received great support from his wife, with whom he enjoyed a deep and contented union; for all that they were so unlike each other. She too was of a deeply religious disposition, but—in contrast to her husband—she possessed a doleful, fervent nature, for which life engendered constant agitation and dark anxieties. Due to her family background, she had once lacked conviction in her faith. However, because of her husband's influence, she became first a true believer and then a zealot, for whom the daily struggle to make ends meet, combined with so many childbirths in quick succession, served to confirm her by now passionately jaundiced view of life's travails and the need for Christians to strictly observe their daily duties. And then there were those many years, since her last child had arrived, where she had remained bedridden in her dark room hoping to regain her strength; and, to cap it all, the recently concluded and disastrous war and the hostile confiscations of property and money, the bloody humiliations—all this had hardly helped to make her view of life any more hopeful.

Though her husband would reproach her severely for it, she could never really banish these anxieties from her mind. For, even as she admitted that this displayed a sinful lack of trust in God's providence, she just could not refrain from ceaselessly reminding her children that strict moderation in all things was their duty both before God and man. She would react as if having witnessed a shocking crime whenever she learned of the lifestyle of her fellow townsmen; of their parties which boasted extravagant menu selections and several kinds of wine; of the silk dresses the ladies wore and the golden jewelry displayed by young girls—yes, she even found it difficult to forgive her own husband when, every so often, he would return home from a walk with some modest gift, which he, not without a certain quiet gallantry, would present at the foot of her bed—a pair of roses arranged in a posy, some nice fruit, or a jar of ginger preserves to help her night cough. Of course, she was both happy and touched by his small gestures. Yet, she could not refrain from saying, as she kissed his hands tenderly: "Heavens dear, you really should not have done that."

A brood of pretty but rather sickly children grew up in this house;

eleven in all, five boys with clear blue eyes and six equally bright-eyed girls, all of whom were easily recognizable amongst the town's other youths, partly because of an unusual neck collar they wore, which made the boys look rather girlish and made the half-grown girls rather manly in appearance. The boys, moreover, wore their brown hair long and had curls flowing almost to their shoulders, while the girls wore their hair plastered to their skulls and had just a plait at each temple that ran in a hard little curve in front of their ears.

The relationship between parents and children, as with the over-all tone presiding in the home, was thoroughly patriarchal in nature. During the frugal, indeed meager, mealtimes, which always began with a prayer, the head of the household would sit at the end of the long, narrow table with his five sons arranged according to age on one side and the five daughters in a corresponding sequence along the other; while, in the absence of her mother, the eldest daughter, the scrupulous Signe, took pride of place at the other end of the table. It would never have occurred to any of the children to speak without first being invited to do so. On the other hand, their father spoke to them frequently—about their educational progress, about their friends and their classes at school, and thereby came to tell his own story. In his own didactic way, he would explain conditions and events from his own youth, describe how school life was at the time and recall life in his father's and grandfather's mud- and wattle-built rectory, and much more besides. And sometimes, when he was in just the right mood, he would even tell amusing anecdotes from his student days in Copenhagen, from his time in the renowned residential hall, and the madcap capers the students would get up to with the town's watchmen and the constabulary. But, having in this way raised the humor of his children, he never failed at the end to give a cautionary twist to his tales and a warning to them to turn their thoughts away from frivolity and attend instead to the Lord's bidding.

This large flock of children, and especially the fact that it had done so well—firstly at school, then in the wider adult world—had gradually become a source of great pride to Pastor Sidenius, and at the same time caused him to give thanks in humble gratitude that the Lord had clearly blessed his home. For there was no doubt that these youths, genuine Sideniuses all, were eager, and inquisitive, and, more than anything, had developed a strict sense of duty as they had grown up one after the other to become a mirror image of their father. They had even inherited all the little quirks in his appearance and deportment—right down to his proud bearing and the measured almost military gait. There was only one of the children who caused his parents sorrow and distress. This was one of the boys in the middle ranks whose name was Peter Andreas. It was not just the fact that he was disruptive at school, and thus provoked a stream of complaints from that side, but also the fact that he had already, at a very young age, begun to defy the customs and practice which prevailed in the home. He had not even reached the age of ten when he first disobeyed his parents outright, and the older the boy became, the more he showed a reckless defiance, which neither chastisement, coercion, nor even the strictures of the Lord himself, were able to quell.

Pastor Sidenius would often sit at his wife's bedside discussing what they should do with this wayward son in whom both of them saw the specter of the degenerate Vendsyssel priest, whose ill repute was forever etched into the family's bloodline. And, instinctively affected as they were by their parents' jaundiced view, his brothers and sisters began to look upon the boy as a stranger in their midst and exclude him from their games.

Now it is true that the boy had come into this world at an unfortunate moment, namely at a time when his father had been moved from an isolated and sparsely populated parish up on the heath to the region's market town—a move which involved a substantial commitment and expansion of his ministry. In this way, and purely by chance, Peter Andreas had become the first of all the children whose earliest rearing had been left to his mother. However, in the years when Peter Andreas was small, she had always had her hands full looking after those even smaller than he was. This meant that when she was finally consigned to her sickbed and sought to gather all her children around her, Peter Andreas had grown too big for her to keep a proper eye on his behavior and whereabouts.

Thus it was that Peter Andreas became almost from birth, so to speak, a stranger in his own home. The first years of his life were mostly spent in his sisters' playroom, or, as he grew bigger, he was often to be found in the outhouse where an old woodcutter plied his trade, and whose rough and ready observations on life and events around them had an early influence on the boy's view of the world. He then graduated to what became, in effect, a second home within the environs of the large merchant houses in the neighborhood with their accompanying timber yards. Here, too, amongst the yard boys and shop apprentices, he absorbed a profoundly temporal view of the world and its many bounties. At the same time, all this fresh air and physical tumult encouraged his physical development and imposed a ruddy glow upon his broad features. In fact, as young as he was, local youths and the timber yard boys soon came to fear him because of his physical prowess and he finally set himself up as the leader of a small gang of rogues, which roamed and harried about the town. Before anyone in the house realized what had taken place, he had grown into a half-wild street urchin. It was only when he got older, and especially when at nine years of age he entered the town's grammar school, that the boy's volatile tendencies became obvious to all; and both parents and teachers alike then frantically sought to remedy the initial neglect.

But by then it was too late.

One day, in late autumn, a scion of the town's petit bourgeoisie was to be found in Pastor Sidenius's study with the intention of booking a christening for the coming Sunday. He had completed his business with the least ceremony possible and now stood on the brink of departure with his hand on the door handle when, after a moment's deliberation, he turned again into the room and—in quite a provocative manner—said:

"While I am here, I may as well use the opportunity to request that the good pastor restrains his son and keeps him away from my garden. He and some other boys are very fond of my *calvilles* and, to speak bluntly pastor, that is something I will not stand for."

Pastor Sidenius, who sat bent over his writing table with his large dark blue spectacles pushed up onto his forehead while he wrote the name of the prospective godparents into the church register, lifted his head up slowly at these words, shoved his glasses back into place and said sharply: "What are you saying? Are you suggesting that my son..."

"Yes, that's exactly what I am suggesting," the man replied assertively, his hand on his hip in a stance which suggested no little satisfaction in his triumph over this self-righteous man of the cloth. "The son of the pastor himself—Peter Andreas is it not?—who is now some sort of captain, d'ye mind, for this little band of pirates which goes crawling over people's garden walls and fences. And the law must be observed, even by a child belonging to a church minister. Otherwise, I'll be forced to bring in the constabulary, and that might have him over the birching chair at the courthouse before you know it. And heaven knows what kind of effect that would have on the good pastor's standing in this town."

With a slight quiver in his hand, Pastor Sidenius put the pen to one side and rose from his desk.

"My son..." he repeated, as his whole body shook.

While this drama was being played out in the rectory, the little devil himself sat in a classroom and concealed his guilty conscience, from teacher and classmate alike, behind a large pile of books. For, on his way to school, he had already encountered this raging denizen of the town who had shouted angrily at him from across the street: "Just you wait my boy! Because I'm going up right this minute to have a little word with your father!" Peter Andreas rarely worried about facing the wrath of his father but, on this occasion, he felt that he had done something that was rather beneath him and his unease grew with each moment that brought the time to go home nearer.

With his ears on red alert, he slunk through the gateway to the rectory and passed the hall window where his father would normally await his arrival and then call him in for a dressing down after he had committed some misdemeanor or other. However, this window was firmly closed. Nor was there any sign of his father in the yard that led round to the kitchen. Peter Andreas began to breathe sighs of relief. "That man was probably just trying to scare me," he thought to himself, as he bowled into the kitchen in his normal manner to find out what was for dinner. Then, gripped by a sudden recklessness, he even ventured into his mother's bedroom to say hello. But here he was stopped dead in his tracks by a bleak stare emanating from the dark confines of the bed. In a hard, almost alien voice, his mother said: "Go into your room! I couldn't so much as look at you."

The boy stood hesitantly at the door for a moment. He could see from her face that his mother had been crying. "Do you hear me young man? Stay in your room until you are called." Upon which, the boy stole softly away, crestfallen.

Sometime after that, the house's one-eyed maid appeared to tell him that dinner was being served. His brothers and sisters were already sat in their places around the long table, waiting for him. As soon as he appeared, all conversation stopped and from this and their muted demeanor, he understood that they knew what had happened. In an attempt, therefore, at indicating a superior air he threw himself noisily into his chair and stuck his hands into his pockets, but nobody paid him any attention. Only one pair of eyes followed his movements. His sister Signe, with her large, bright thoughtful eyes, watched him from under a darkly knitted brow.

But then came the sound of footsteps from the adjoining room. Per gave a slight jump when his father pushed open the dining room door. Contrary to his normal practice, he gave no greeting as he entered. In silence, he sat down at the table, bowed his head and clasped his hands together.

But instead of offering a prayer, he began to speak. Something, he said (as his eyes closed behind his dark glasses), was troubling his mind—a serious matter, which he wished to discuss with his dear children before they began to eat. After this, he confirmed what most of them already knew concerning their brother's fall from grace.

"What has happened can neither be ignored, nor excused in any way," he continued. "Just as it is God's will that all that is born in darkness will one day be revealed to the light, so has this deed come to light to receive its judgment. Peter Andreas has chosen not to heed God's will and commandments. Just as he has ignored the warnings of his mother and father, so has he turned away from the word of the Lord, which says: Thou shalt not steal. Yes, my son, I am afraid that your sin must be called by its rightful name. But you must also know and understand that it is out of love for you that your father, your mother, and all your brothers and sisters, be they large or small, appeal to your conscience through the words coming from my mouth. This is because we can never lose hope entirely that, at some point, we may succeed in finding a path to your heart, so that you not will not end your days like that wretched brother upon whom the Lord pronounced his judgment of doom: Thou shalt be banished and without peace wherever in the world thou art."

All around the table, the children's small, red-and-blue-checkered handkerchiefs had begun to quiver. All the sisters were crying. Even the older brothers were greatly agitated and found it difficult to hide their emotions as their father concluded his lecture with the words: "Now, I have spoken. And if Peter Andreas will commit these words to his heart and truthfully seek out the forgiveness of God and man for the sin he has perpetrated, then this issue will nevermore come between us, but will be forgotten; it will be dead and erased from our memories. Therefore, my dear children, let us join together in prayer to the good Lord in heaven that he will take thy straying brother into his hands ... pray that God will soften his obstinate spirit and guide him away from the servitude of sin, away from the path to perdition. Grant this Oh Lord, thou who art in heaven, that not one of us will be lost to you, when on the final day of resurrection your children are gathered around your glorious throne! Amen!"

There was just one person upon whom the whole scene had a completely opposite effect to that which was intended and this was Peter Andreas himself. His father was rarely able to make much of an impression upon him any longer. For he had been a much too willing understudy to the yard boys and shop apprentices who were far from respectful when speaking of his reverend father. At the same time, up until this point, he had not been able to inure himself entirely to the flow of pious utterances and ominous biblical rhetoric with which his parents had perpetually sought to sway his conscience. Indeed, it was true to say that when on Sundays he saw his father kneeling at the front altar in his white vestments, or standing under the resonating carved vault above the pulpit, even he would sometimes feel himself gripped by a momentary feeling of awe.

But on this occasion, even words from the Good Book itself could not exert any influence over him. It was true, that in the very first moments of this unusual form of reprimand he became subdued and uneasy, but the fright was short lived. As far as his simplified school-boy sensibilities were concerned, there was a ridiculous disparity between the solemn invocation of Our Lord and the pathetic question of a pair of apples he had snatched from across a garden fence; and the more his father went on pronouncing, and the more the yammering of his brothers and sisters increased all around him, the more becalmed and unaffected he became by the whole scene.

At this moment, a kind of seismic shift took place in the mind of the eleven-year-old boy. For he now found that he could look upon the others with a feeling of innate superiority. Even when the two small twins, who thus far had just stared blankly at the distress of their older brothers and sisters, began a pitiful whimper, he found it difficult to suppress a smirk.

But these high spirits were not without an element of compulsion. This was inevitable given that the attempt to shame him into submission had struck at his most sensitive place: his sense of honor. The color in his cheeks had also gradually disappeared. As his father had brought his speech at the table to a close, a terrible agitation stirred in the very depths of his consciousness, a dark, skulking thirst for revenge, which rose up to blind his eyes in a shimmering mist.

The memory of this mealtime gathering would, henceforth, assume a momentous importance in the boy's life. In those moments, his hitherto carefree mind became possessed of an implacable hatred of his entire family line, a defiant sense of isolation from it, which became the heart and soul, the motivating instinct, in his future life. He had, from a very early age, felt a sense of abandonment—as if he were homeless while being under the same roof as his parents. Now he had begun to wonder whether he really did belong there, or whether he might actually be a latchkey child whom the parents had somehow adopted. The more he brooded over this, the more likely he felt that this was the case. Everything, right down to the increased wariness his brothers and sisters showed towards him from this day on, simply served to confirm his suspicions. Had he not also been told a thousand times that he was not like the others? And had his father ever caressed him, or given him a kind word? And his appearance? Whenever he looked at himself in the mirror, he noticed that he was darker than his brothers and sisters, had ruddier cheeks and strong white teeth. He also now recalled that the neighbor's yard boy had once, apparently in jest, called him a street rogue and a gypsy boy.

This thought, that he was not born of his parents, had haunted him throughout his childhood years and in the end became his reality. For not only did it give him an explanation regarding his awkward status in the home; it also satisfied his boyish pride immensely. He had always felt it somewhat humiliating to be the son of an old, half-blind man without a tooth in his head, who was the laughing stock of the whole town. He was also deeply ashamed of the poverty in which the family was enmired. He had not reached much of an age before he was happy to starve the whole day at school rather than bring himself to eat the homemade bread and dripping in front of his friends. Once, when his mother had requested that one of his father's old cassocks be made up into a winter coat for him, he could barely bring himself to put it on as the shiny material revealed all too clearly from whence it came; and when his mother tried to assert her will, he came close to tears, tore it into shreds and flung it to the floor in a defiant rage.

He would escape into proud dreams of having been abandoned as a child by some troupe of wandering gypsies—one of those nomadic families of the night, of whom the old one-eyed nanny had so often spoken, and who, of course, were to be found out there on the barren heath where his own parents had once lived. He imagined that his real father was, in truth, a great chief with a blue-black mane flowing down his back and a rich cloak slung over his shoulders, a staff of oak in his strong brown hands, an all powerful sovereign, a king ruling over the dark heath's great expanse—the place where freedom and wild storms reigned.

Peter Andreas was at that age where dreams take real shapes and the wings of fantasy can finally take flight. And now, when all avenues of possibility seemed to have opened for him, his powers of imagination ran riot. With regards to his own life, nothing seemed impossible anymore. His reveries would often transport him to the highest reaches of adventure land. He convinced himself at last that he was the son of a king, who, like the hero in a story they were reading at school, had been abducted by tinkers and then sold into slavery—the slavery that his father's rectory represented for him. So convinced was he by his dreams that he sometimes felt that he could recall certain things and events from the time spent in the happy world of his childhood home—a great room, for example, with marble columns and hundreds of black-and-white-checkered floor tiles upon which his small feet could glide, a blue lake between high mountains, a monkey in a golden cage, a tall man wearing a red cape who lifted him onto a horse and sat him up front as they galloped through large dark forests.

Gradually, both his parents and the teachers at his school became aware of the gloomy reticence which had enveloped the child and which, on occasions, bore the character of a monomania. At home, he would wander noiselessly from room to room—apparently indifferent to all and sundry. Outside the home, meanwhile, he would frequent places known only to himself. His father could not, so to speak, get a word out of him. Even with his mother—who was previously able to claim some form of intimacy with him, and in whom, when it came to the bit, he had always found most understanding and indulgence—there was now a wall between them, which grew higher with each passing year. It was true that in the gathering gloom of evening when he knew her to be alone, he would sometimes go in to her and sit by her bed and freely ask if he should rub the knotted veins in her afflicted legs. But never did she receive any reply, other than yes and no, whenever she sought to delve into his world and draw from the well of his brooding mind.

Despite this, both mother and father contented themselves with the notion that his taciturn manner was a sign that he had begun to repent of his former ways. But then something happened which snuffed out those hopes for good.

One winter evening, at around nine o'clock, the family was gathered in the sitting room, waiting for the town's night watchman to pass by in the street and proclaim, in his singsong voice, that it was time to retire for the night. In her usual motherly fashion, Signe sat knitting on the horsehair sofa by the mahogany table. Her hands worked with practiced speed, while at the same time she read aloud from a copy of *The Fatherland*, which lay spread out in front of her under the drowsy light of an old oil lamp. Her father sat in his time-honored evening seat—a stiff old-fashioned high-backed armchair, which had been covered with the cheapest kind of material and bore a flowery pattern. He sat there tired and crumpled, his head bowed and his arms across his chest. His large green eyeshade served to hide more than half of his pallid, wrinkled, and beardless face. As he dozed, he heard—yet did not really hear—the monotone recitation of the four columns of news from abroad. Pastor Sidenius was a morning man. Even in the depths of winter, he would rise in the morning when the church clock struck six. It should also be said that he did not have much time for newspapers and that kind of worldly literature, which he regarded, at best, as a useful sedative with which he could lull himself to sleep after his midday and evening meals.

Two of Signe's younger sisters were also sitting at the table, dressed in their large checkered cotton smocks and—despite their eyes being red with fatigue—bent conscientiously over their crochet work. In appearance, they were exact copies of their older sister, had the same slightly old maid facial expressions, the same small, hard plaits by the side of their ears, the same bright, almost cavernous eyes under a determined brow. The door into the bedroom was open, and within the half-light surrounding their mother's bed, another one of the smaller children could be seen rubbing mother's tortured legs.

Peter Andreas was also in the room. He stood apart from the rest of the group by one of the windows and every other moment stole quick glances up at the clock on the secretary. By this stage he was fourteen years of age with a big boned and solid frame, which had outgrown the clothes he wore. His two older brothers were now adults and had left home to take up studies at the university in Copenhagen. As the home's eldest son, Peter Andreas had inherited their room— a small gable end attic, where he spent most of his time when he was in the house.

As soon as Signe had finished her reading session, he grabbed the opportunity to say goodnight and slip away, but his father stopped him as he got to the door by asking why he was leaving their company with such haste and he offered the pretext of a school essay that was still to be written.

As he left the room, his father turned to the others—"is there anything else in the newspaper?" he asked, still groggy from having dozed.

Straight afterwards, their mother's weak voice could be heard from the bedroom—"what time is it children?"

"It's ten minutes past nine," the two youngest girls piped up simultaneously, as they turned from looking at the clock.

Then all was quiet for a while. They all knew that the night watchman would soon pass their door. Some people passed by in the street. The only audible thing was their voices. A new fallen layer of snow served to muffle their steps.

"Shall I read some more, father?" Signe asked.

"Ah, I think that's enough," he said as he rose, removed his eye shade and proceeded to promenade backwards and forwards across the floor in order to shake off his lethargy prior to evening prayers.

Nor was there long to wait before a deep drone was to be heard outside in the street. It was the old watchman's "song." It was like the sound of a drunken man having an animated conversation with himself. The two small girls immediately began to pack their sewing kits together; and Signe also began to clear up for the night. Then the two maids were called from the kitchen and Signe sat herself down at the piano.

Once more their mother's voice could be heard from the bedroom.

"I think this evening we should sing 'Praise the Lord, for he is near.'"

"That would be nice Signe," her father said. He had positioned himself behind the large armchair and placed his folded hands on its backrest.

Signe had an expansive and quite appealing soprano voice, which she used with an unrestrained gusto that was quite out of character with her otherwise subdued utterances. As she sat there with her hefty fingers reddened by too much work, stroking the piano's yellowed keys, her gaze soaring towards the heavens, she revealed the nature of the faith, hope, and love which had encouraged a girl, who was still not twenty years of age, to sacrifice her youth for the sake of the home and her small brothers and sisters. This, however, was no romantic euphoria, radiating from her small round face while she sang—no heavenly ecstasy, where paradise was revealed and her soul was transported by celestial visions. As the full-blooded Sidenius she was, she had absolutely no inclinations towards Catholic mysticism. No, the inner conviction which shone in her countenance and lent an uncommon fervor and power to her voice sprang from a quite sober and unfailing conviction that she was one of the chosen few who followed the narrow path of righteousness and whose true inheritance awaited her in heaven where eternal joy would be the just reward for life's troubles and privations.

In the middle of the psalm's second verse, her father suddenly stopped singing and lifted his head as if listening for something.

"Quiet!" he cried, and all singing stopped.

At the same time, their mother called out from the bedroom: "Someone is ringing at the gate," she said.

Now the others heard the weighty tones of the night bell being rung down at the other end of the house and this sound, which disturbed the peace of the evening, was at once frightening and alien to them.

Their father hurried, via an adjoining room, into his own room, which was located by the side of the gate, and threw up the window.

"Who is it ringing at this hour of the evening?" he called out.

In the sitting room, they could hear a man's voice coming from the street. While the two youngest girls, who were in some distress, looked at each other and then at their sister Signe who had remained at the piano, their father maintained his harsh tone: "Your child is sick you say…What is your name, and where do you live? Krankstuegyden…I see…How old is the child? A year old! Isn't it strange how the people of this town suddenly turn to their minister for help as soon as trouble arises. Otherwise, they see no need for God's presence in their daily lives. Why have you waited so long to have the child baptized?…Yes, of course I will come. You must go home and get things ready, so that there are no delays when I arrive. And be sure there is a light on the stairs," he called after the man, who had already disappeared.

When the pastor returned to the sitting room, he inquired as to the whereabouts of Peter Andreas.

"I'll call him now," said Signe, who was aware that her father, because of his weak eyesight, was reluctant to venture out unaccompanied on such a night, where all was slippery underfoot.

"Boel can fetch him," the pastor said turning to the old maid as he did so. He then went into the bedroom to dress. "You, Signe, will have to stay here and help me into my vestments."

The pastor's wife had lit the night lamp in the bedroom.

"Be sure to wrap up Johannes," she said in her usual rather dispirited tone. "I would say that it is a cold night. I could hear it earlier, the way the church clock rang out. Signe, fetch your father's lined vest. It is hanging in the press."

But at that moment, old Boel came back in with the news that Peter Andreas was not in his room and nor could she find him anywhere else in the house.

The pastor rose instinctively from his chair, in which he had only just sat in order to facilitate the insertion of a pin into the rear of his collar. He then went very pale. And from the maid's worried expression, he could see that she knew more than she had revealed. He closed in on her and spoke with a commanding urgency: "What is it?...Speak out!...You are hiding something from me."

Shaking in fear before the pastor's anger, she confessed all and explained that, as Peter Andreas's room was up in the loft, she had heard him creeping about in the night on several occasions recently; and as she had just then found his window wide open she proceeded to investigate further and discovered that the window in the hall was ajar and that there were fresh footsteps in the snow outside.

In the bedroom, the pastor's wife was making efforts to rise from the bed. But then she slumped back into the bed again with a plaintive cry and put her hands to her eyes in the manner of a person attacked by dizziness.

The pastor hurried in to her and grabbed her free hand.

"Now mother...don't fret!" he said, in spite of the tremble in his own voice.

"May God give us strength this night!" she cried.

"Amen!" the pastor said with great emotion and still holding her hand.

Peter Andreas, meanwhile, was to be found on the steep slopes just north of the town, where an animated group of callow youths had taken to sledding in the moonlit nights which prevailed at that time. It was the king's own provincial highway they had chosen as their sledding lane—a broad, even roadway which swooped in one unbroken curve from the top of the hill right into the town itself. Indeed, if one had built up sufficient speed and had no fear of the night watchmen, it was possible to career down Nørregade's steep incline and almost reach the town hall without stopping.

The descent into the town offered the most open and panoramic view of the whole area: firstly, across the snow-clad town itself with its glowing red street lamps and roofs bathed in moonlight, then across to the frozen fjord and meadows that were just sheets of ice; then finally in the distant countryside lay the outlying villages, forests and fields that were blanketed in drifts of snow. And above all this, the heavens flowed in an immense vault, where the moon and stars seemed to play hide-and-seek behind the clouds—as if these ancient globes had been smitten by the high spirits of the youths below.

Hallo! Amidst screams, whistles, and hearty shouts, the railed sledges hurtled downwards along the frozen surface, steered with the help of a long spiked stick which trailed behind and served as a rudder—hopping and bouncing over small stones, sailing over every possible hindrance as easily as a boat riding the waves. Here and there along the way down stood small clumps of servant girls, their heads wrapped against the cold and their hands wound into their aprons, which they sought to use as a muff. When, every so often, one of the contestants became unseated and fell backwards like some toppled knight of old, and the empty sledge sped on with increasing speed down the hill, the shrill peal of female scorn would ring out from this female chorus and was augmented by the gleeful cries of other boys who just happened to be racing by at that point.

The boys from the grammar school, "The Tadpoles," who were in a definite minority, fared worst of all in the event that just such a disaster should befall them. Peter Andreas's greatest vitriol, therefore, was aimed at those who had shamed the standard by allowing such a defeat to happen.

He himself steered his new and handsome long sledge with supreme authority. He had procured it on hasty credit from one of the town's wheelwrights, had painted it deep red and dubbed it "Blood Eagle." During the day, he kept the sledge out of sight in one of the timber yards in the town. He flew effortlessly, and almost silently, through the air, his sledge riding on English bar-iron, as he let out sudden shouts: "Make way there!" He was eager for battle and his round cheeks glowed in triumphant excitement. Occasionally, he would raise himself up athwart the sledge rails as he sped along, swing his spike above his head, as a warrior would his spear, and cry: Whoo-hoo! The raging torrent, all that reckless, honor-seeking, youthful vitality he had been forced to suppress at home and at school, would burst forth in such moments as this and manifest itself in a haughtiness which made him appear slightly ridiculous even to the best of his friends within the group.

Then, suddenly, a loud warning shout would be heard from the foot of the hill. In an instant, all the sledge racers had peeled off to the edges of the slope, careering down into deep gullies as they did so. At the same time, those who were on the return journey upwards hurried to places of concealment provided by snowdrifts and bushes. Only the girls remained standing, tittering and leaning into each other conspiratorially.

Down below, at the entrance to the town, the night watchman came into view. There he stood at the edge of the dark streets in his greatcoat with its upturned collar, the tin badge on his chest reflecting like a star in the moonlight. All sledding sports on the country roads were strictly forbidden in deference to market-bound farmers and their horse-drawn transport. For this very reason, the boys had posted lookouts along the hill to avoid being caught by surprise. Now, the dreaded "Wolle" was down there looking up at them along the suddenly deserted roadway, while from the ditches came half strangled cries of "cluck cluck" or "miaow" followed by muffled laughs and giggling, at which he raised his truncheon in a threatening manner before turning around and disappearing into the streets of the town again.

Shortly afterwards, the lookouts called the all clear. And within minutes, the whole slope was once more alive with playful activity.

Then one of the bigger boys, an apprentice, managed to coax one of the girls on to his sledge, a sight that stoked the jealous fires in Peter Andreas's breast. About halfway down the hill, therefore, he pulled up by the side of a knot of high spirited lasses and offered the tallest of them a tour on his sledge. After some hesitation, she yielded to the temptation, straddled the sledge and sat herself in front of him. Peter Andreas then brazenly slung his arms about his captured treasure and "Blood Eagle" soared once again into the night.

"Make way there!" he roared with all the might his lungs possessed; for the world had to know of his triumph.

"Was that not Peter Andreas? Yes, that was Per all right!" he heard from a couple of friends as he shot past. They were making the upward journey, dragging their sledges behind them. He felt that his heart was ready to burst. For there was no mistaking the unbidden admiration in their voices.

Even his female escort—a dark-eyed, raven-haired tinker child—turned approvingly to him as they sped on, and her laugh revealed a large red, half-open mouth that brought a fire to his cheeks. Familiar dreams were stirred once again in his emotions—dreams of living by night on the great heath, dreams of being the wild rover, where a tent or sunken redoubt was his home. He would be at one with the stars and the racing clouds.

The sledge only came to a complete stop when it reached the edge of the town, at which point the girl made to rise in order to return to her friends. But Peter Andreas prevailed upon her to remain seated. He had no intention of letting his prize go and thus proceeded to drag her and the sled back up the hill. Foot by foot, inch by inch, he toiled up the hill with his heavy burden. He imagined himself to be a warrior, a Viking, returning in triumph from exotic lands with war booty and a beautiful woman in tow, a captured princess who must now satisfy his every whim up there in his timbered longhouse, which lay deep in the woods, and he stamped the depth of his fantasies into the ice-covered slope with such fervor that beads of perspiration broke forth from his brow.

When they had reached the crest of the hill, and as he once again positioned himself at the back of the sledge in preparation for the next descent, the girl turned around to him and said: "I heard them saying that you are the pastor's son. Is that true?"

Her question was such a jolt back to reality for him that he literally blanched in response.

"No. It isn't!" he replied through gritted teeth and with a vehemence which exploded from the depths of his soul. And "Blood Eagle" flew down the slope once again and with such speed that its iron rails sang across the ice and snow.

And in truth he had never felt so strongly that he did not belong down there in that gloomy and oppressive dwelling, where his father, brothers and sisters doubtless now sat and sang psalms together and uttered their pathetic prayers amidst all the fairy-tale wonders of this winter night. Like underworld trolls, they were blind to life's bright splendor and too paralyzed by fear to embrace its beauty. He felt that he was a million leagues apart from them, in another part of the heavens entirely, where he was at one with the sun, the stars, and the ceaselessly changing firmament.

Hush—what was that! All at once, he heard a sound that had followed him throughout his early youth ... the tolling of the church bell. Like a herald from the underworld, it rose to meet him through the frosty, gossamer air ... eleven somber, brooding strikes. How he hated that sound! From all of the wind's four corners and at all hours of the day it sought him out and mocked his hopes and dreams ... always warning, always calling. There was no place on earth to which he might flee, where it would not find him. Like an invisible spirit, it pursued him, regardless of which forbidden road he chose to make his escape. In springtime, when he would steal away into the meadows with his huge kite "Hero," or in the summer when he took a small boat out on to the fjord to catch perch, the sound of this phantom would come to his ear with its stifled incantations.

"Hallo!" he cried in an attempt to drown out that sound while, with even greater passion and defiance, he threw his arms around the tall young woman in front of him. She turned to him smiling and gave him a look which sent sweet shivers of goose bumps down his spine.

"You're pretty," he whispered into her ear. "What's your name?"

"Oline."

"And where do you live?"

"In Smedestrædet ... Riisagers Yard ... And where do you live?"

"Me?"

"Yes. If you are not the pastor's son, who are you then?"

"Who am I? ... Me? ... I can't tell you that. But do you want to meet up tomorrow evening in Voldstrædet, when it gets dark?"

"Aye! We can do that surely."

Without realizing the danger, Peter Andreas had left the outer limits of the town behind him and was now traveling at full pelt down Nørregade itself. However, he had not traveled much further down the street when a large figure leaped out from a street corner and roared a thunderous "Stop!" as he planted the curved end of a staff in front of the sledge. Emitting a frantic scream, the girl ran off, while Peter Andreas found himself being bodily lifted by night watchman Ole's huge fists.

"Now I have ye, yer little bastard! I'll teach you bleedin kids to play sport with the night watch. Let's have him in the courthouse! . . . And no backchat! . . . Which whore's family do you belong to then?"

Peter Andreas understood straight away that he had to be as cute as cute could be to get out of this dilemma. In a trice, he adopted a breathless pose saying: "Thank God you are here watchman! There's a huge scrap going on up there between two gangs of boys. That big apprentice who works for Iversens has pulled a knife! You should hurry, sir . . . He's off his head."

"What's that yer saying?"

"Quick, hasn't he gone and stabbed Alfred . . . the mayor's son! May God spare him and keep him from all harm. He is up there, lying in a big pool of blood."

"Jesus! The mayor's son!" the night watchman groaned and released his grip.

"I'll run on and tell the family and call for doctor Carlsen," said Peter Andreas, quickly grabbing the reins of his sledge. He was gone before the night watchman regained his composure.

The town's clocks were just about to strike the midnight hour when, after crawling over the neighbor's fence, Peter Andreas crept in through the hall window, which he had left ajar on leaving the house. He had removed his boots while still standing in the snow, and now made his way in all stealth towards the stairs leading to the attic. Before he knew it, the door to the study was swung open. Now his father stood in front of him, holding a lamp aloft.

For some time, father and son stood opposite each other without speaking. The only thing that could be heard was the clink from the hood of the lamp in Pastor Sidenius's shaking hand.

"You come and go like a thief in the house of your own father," said the pastor finally. "Where have you just come from?" he added, in a voice which was so low it was as if he could hardly bear hearing the answer to his question.

Peter Andreas explained exactly where he had been, without evasion or any attempt at embellishment. At that moment, his contempt for his father was so complete that lying was just not worth the effort. And since he had gone the length of a full admission, he also admitted the purchase of "Blood Eagle" and the debt he had incurred with the wheelwright.

"So these are the depths to which you have sunk?" his father said, without revealing to his son that, in truth, his worst fears had been assuaged. He was well aware that there were boltholes in the town which led to places of ill repute and a dread had come upon him that his son had been lured to just such a place. "Get to your bed!" he continued. "You are, and will ever be, a slave to sin! . . . We will discuss this further in the morning."

Early the next day, when Peter Andreas was called down to attend morning prayers in the sitting room, he steeled himself for a repeat of the hide-branding ceremony to which he had been subjected as a result of his apple-pinching exploits. Signe sat by the piano, where just one light burned brightly. The rest of the large room faded away into darkness and it was so cold that plumes of moist air rose from their mouths as they sang.

However, both the first and then the second psalm was sung from beginning to end and then the Creed was proclaimed without any reference being made to the previous night's events. Nor was anything said to him about it throughout the course of that day. Pastor Sidenius had, in fact, spent the whole morning sitting by the side of his wife's bed and his parents had finally agreed that it was a waste of effort to try and influence the boy's attitude by way of persuasion. The only hope now was that time and the general hardships of life would, by the grace of God, bring about some change in the situation. The only preventative action they agreed to take was to add a row of spikes to the top of the neighbor's garden fence and that from now on his father would personally ensure, every evening, that the boy was in his bed.

Peter Andreas could not have cared less. None of the domestic arrangements involving him, for good or ill, had any impact on him any longer. The time had passed where he would lay plans, via some childish fiction—an open revolt or secret escape—to bring his torture to an end and set off into the great world outside so that in some hit and miss way he might reach that kingdom which his dreams had promised him. He was now both old enough and clever enough to realize that the quickest and surest way to reach that precious goal of his own independence was by patiently completing his studies, and it should also be said that it was not long before he discovered other ways to cock a snook at his father's newfound vigilance. When all in the house had settled down for the night, he would use a rope end to slip down from his gable window onto the half roof of the hall and from there skin down the drainpipe to the street. Thus, he was still to be found on many a moonlit night out in the fjord with his beloved fishing rod and, on his return, he would bequeath the whole of that evening's catch to the night watchman in order to purchase his silence as to what had transpired.

He had also managed to renew his acquaintance with the dark-eyed Oline from Riisagers yard. They had arranged night-time assignations on a couple of occasions in one of the town's large timber yards; but in truth they had just as quickly grown apart from one another. The downright brazenness of this little hussy's expressions and manners had embarrassed him, and when on one occasion she made a blatant assault on his virtue, he cast her aside in shame and never sought her company again.

He held an abiding love, however, for the harbor and the comings and goings on the quay, such as they were, between the coal boats and the small Swedish timber steamers. Here, he had made the acquaintance of a ship's chandler who ran a small provisions shop and he would often spend his free time there so as to listen to the stories the sailors told about their adventures in foreign countries, about the huge ocean-going steamers that could carry up to a thousand people, and about life in the big ports with their massive shipyards and docks.

However, the life of a sailor held no attractions for him. He had bigger fish to fry. He wanted to be an engineer. For he felt that this profession was precisely the one that offered him the best chance of realizing his dream of leading a proud and free-spirited life, full of adventure and exciting experiences. Besides which, by opting for such a purely practical career as this, he would, in the clearest way possible, be signaling a stark rejection of his family background and a break with its so cherished ancient traditions. His choice was a conscious challenge, especially to his father who would normally speak in extremely derogatory tones when referring to the popular euphoria over technological advances. Thus, on one occasion, when there had been a whole commotion amongst the citizenry following a proposal for the revival of the town's declining shipping trade by a widening of the entrance to the fjord, he had spoken with the utmost disdain about the whole affair. "These people with their constant concern for all other things than the one that really should be occupying their minds," he had said. From that day forth, Peter Andreas knew that he wanted to be an engineer.

Furthermore, he received an added stimulus in this regard from a scholarly quarter. While most of his teachers, influenced by his parents' own view of him, had already come to the conclusion that he was someone who would never manage to make anything decent of his life, Peter Andreas had gradually gained a friend and patron in the guise of his math teacher. This person, an old military man, had even gone out of his way to praise his abilities to his father when, as happened a number of times, the pastor had lost all patience and proposed that the boy should be taken out of the school and immediately placed in some trade apprenticeship. It was almost as if the old soldier had adopted his stance out of a basic empathy with the boy and took pleasure in reducing the dictatorial reverend to silence with his words of high praise.

This issue aside, feelings in the town towards Pastor Sidenius and his family were actually undergoing a sea change. Changing times and conventions played their part, by gradually introducing a more conciliatory atmosphere. Added to this was the fact that several of the old merchants and cattle breeders, who had previously dominated public opinion in the town, had passed away in the intervening years and—more significantly—had been shown, for the most part, to have assumed an authority in the running of the town which was not commensurate with either their trading prowess, or their private wealth. They had been old school traders, who in their rustic arrogance were not willing to acknowledge that times had moved on without them and who poured scorn on the new-fangled developments in the means of exchange and the new customs this had brought about in business life. Several of the town's most illustrious families, who had lorded it on the basis of inherited wealth, were reduced in the years after the Schleswig Holstein war to the margins of poverty. And as the previous prosperity declined, so the need for the succor of religion gained ascendancy. Pastor Sidenius's grave pronouncements on the vanity inherent in temporal concerns and the promised land that was to be found in poverty and loss began to find an audience amongst the people, and most of all amongst those who had been his fiercest opponents. The flock of disciples who would gather to hear him preach on Sundays grew unceasingly, to the point where none of the town's citizens found it prudent to avoid greeting him as he passed in the street—or at least not when he was clad in his vestments.

It was as these events unfolded that the hour of liberation finally arrived for Peter Andreas. Thanks to the old math teacher's insistent representations to his father, Pastor Sidenius had finally agreed to allow his son to travel to Copenhagen so that he could continue his studies at the National College of Engineering. He was now sixteen years of age.

One beautiful autumn evening, as the weekly passenger boat to the capital slowly steamed out along the still overgrown and curving banks of the fjord, Peter Andreas was to be found standing on the afterdeck, a bag over his shoulder and looking back towards the town, which adopted an ever darker hue against the amber tones in the evening sky. He had shed no tears on taking leave of his family home. Even the last moments with his mother were free of any great shows of emotion. And yet, as he stood there in his new tailored jacket, which carried a hundred Rix dollar note stitched into the lining of his jacket vest, and looked at the serried mass of roofs and the church's heavy brick tower melding into the luminous heavens, he was gripped by angst, and his heart was moved by vague feelings of gratitude. He now felt that he had not taken leave of hearth, home, and his parents in the proper manner, and almost wished that he could turn back in order to enact the ritual of departure once again. And even if it was the distant sound of the church bell at eventide, drifting out to him across the meadows as a final salutation and note of caution from home, the only feeling it now aroused in him was one of reconciliation.

This capricious frame of mind lingered with him during the first phase of his stay in Copenhagen. It even became gradually stronger as he fell victim to that particular sense of loneliness which always crowds in on a country person who moves to a large town with its utterly strange and indifferent array of faces. He did not know a soul in Copenhagen. As yet, none of his school friends had moved there because they had stayed on at school in the hope of going to university. He suffered frequent bouts of utter misery in the first few weeks and he would often go down to the bridge at the Exchange to see whether a ship laden with apples had come in from his home town, in which case he could get news from the town and have a yarn about mutual acquaintances. The only thing that remained unchanged was his attitude towards his father. If he wrote home at all, he wrote to his mother.

As for his older brothers, one of them, Thomas, had already completed his studies a year earlier and had been appointed as a curate somewhere down the country. It was true that the eldest brother, Eberhard, still lived in the city, but he was out of town at that moment; and even on his return, there was hardly any contact between the two of them. Eberhard was of a cautious and apprehensive disposition and had turned his back on the world from sheer terror that he would otherwise encounter somebody or something that might be injurious to his social standing. Thus, he was irritated in the extreme by this demeaning little brother who had rushed over and wanted to make a show of himself about the place, without so much as getting into university.

In the first few months, Peter Andreas lived in a wretched rearward facing attic in the center of the town, which offered a view of hundreds of red tiled roofs. He subsequently moved in with an old couple in Nyboder.

As winter settled in and the Christmas period approached, he began to put money aside for a trip home by train and then ferry. Thus, he would avoid having to ask his parents to pay for the journey. The evening meal and fuel for the oven to heat his room were the only two areas where his belt could be tightened any further. In the end, his only form of sustenance was bread and coffee.

On the day before Christmas Eve, he set off for home after having first announced his imminent arrival in a very brief letter.

On the daylong, interminable journey through Zealand and Funen, and at the sight of the hordes of high-spirited Christmas travelers thronging the carriages and enacting joyous reunions with friends and relatives at the various stations along the way, his own sense of anticipation began to grow, until finally his own mood had become positively festive. Memories of home came to him and the air of expectation that always accompanied the return of his elder brothers; how the lamps would be lit in all the rooms and the evening meal delayed until the arrival of the train so as to make their welcome home even more of a celebration. And he then began to think about his old friends who possibly already knew that he was on his way and would, perhaps, be there to greet him at the station.

The carriage gradually emptied on the way up through Jutland until, finally, he was the only one left. Darkness had descended and the lamps on the train had been lit. A storm was imminent and rain pelted the windows. And yet, he still had an hour and a half's traveling ahead of him. So he stretched out along the bench and soon fell into a doze.

He awoke to the sound of the train going over a bridge. His heart missed a beat. He knew that sound. It was Skærbæk bridge. So there was just five minutes to go.

He jumped up to the window and wiped away the condensation... yes, there was the river... and the meadows and the Skærbæk hills! And now the track began to curve and the first lights of the town could be seen through the mist and rain.

His sister Signe stood on the platform waiting for him and he felt an immediate sense of unease when he saw her. There she stood, slightly round shouldered, in an awful, old-fashioned coat that was too short for her, wearing black woolen gloves and the skirt of her dress inadvertently raised, so that her long thin ankles could be seen above a pair of clumpy feet shod in galoshes. It annoyed him that she had presented herself in such a way, leaving her unfortunate physical shape as a hostage to public ridicule. He had been certain that his two younger brothers—the twins—would also be there. The very fact that it was Signe alone who met him aroused his suspicions, given that she was, of all his brothers and sisters, the one he liked the least.

On the way home through the streets, he was soon given to understand from what she said that his parents were not exactly overjoyed at his return. In fact, they found it inconsiderate of him to have taken a holiday so soon. There was a lot of money involved in making such a journey, she said. In any event, he should first have asked permission from his father.

Even before they reached the rectory gates, Peter Andreas's initial excitement had gone into decline. And as he walked into the sitting room and saw his father sitting there in his customary evening place in the old faded armchair, with the green cardboard screen covering his eyes, he was already regretting ever having left Copenhagen. It was now also obvious that it was only with a certain conscious effort that his father bade him welcome and stroked his cheek. The door leading in to the dining room was closed and Peter Andreas could hear that the floor was being scrubbed; and when he saw a tray containing a small *smørrebrød* buffet on the table, he understood that the others had already eaten. His mother, as always, lay in her bed.

Her welcome was not lacking in either sincerity or warmth and she had kissed him emotionally on both cheeks, but Peter Andreas's heart had turned to stone.

He was too young to understand that he had not suffered any greater injustice than would normally be visited on one of the smaller offspring in a large brood of children, where the eldest had already harvested the first and best crop of their parents' affections. Though this affection may never diminish, it does change its character—it loses the luster of revelation, which burns so brightly at every small step forward made by the older children. At bedtime, when Per was left to his own devices up in his old room in the loft, he began to laugh. He was, at heart, more irritated than deeply offended. He had made a laughing stock of himself. He ridiculed his own crass sentimentality, which had led him to pine for this so-called home and swore a binding oath that never again would he allow himself to be deceived by such sentiments.

And when the days of Christmas were upon him, with the eyes of the pious turned to heaven and the constant traipsing to church and wave after wave of psalms, he himself remained firmly aloof and just counted the hours until he could escape back to his freedom and independence in Copenhagen. Even the reunion with his old friends had brought nothing but disappointment. Some of them could hardly bring themselves to acknowledge him, influenced as they were by their parents. Of course, due to the fact that his father, and the rest of his family, would only speak of him with some reluctance, people in the town had soon got the idea that he was someone who had fallen by the wayside. Besides, several of his friends had begun to make much of their imminent elevation as academics amongst the citizenry. He had paid immediate visits to all of them but not one of them had asked him to come again.

Thus, as soon as the new year came in, he returned to Copenhagen.

2

ONE OF the best known and most respected inhabitants of Nyboder, during the period in which this tale is set, was an old pensioner, Senior Boatswain Olufsen, who lived in Hjertensfrydgade. Every morning, just as the tower clock in Saint Paul's church struck eleven, his tall, thin, slightly pitching figure was to be seen stepping out from a low door in the compact two-storey dwelling whose upper floor he occupied. Then he would pause for a moment in the quiet, empty street, as a sailor would—taking in the weather, looking up to the skies and running the rule across the rooftops as if inspecting a ship's tackle and rigging. He was dressed in a somewhat faded but diligently brushed overcoat, whose buttonhole boasted a fluttering emblem in the red and white of the *Dannebro* flag, which denoted his long service in the Danish fleet. His white head was covered by a gray cylinder hat, and on his left hand, which he used to lean against his umbrella as he walked, was an old, shriveled leather glove.

Thus arranged, and with his right arm placed behind his back, he would shuffle carefully along the uneven pavement. At the same time, his wife's reflection would appear in a street mirror which had been affixed outside the sitting room window on the first floor from whence she would continue to observe her husband's progress until he had successfully navigated the gutter channel at the corner of Elsdyrsgade. There she would stand in their crow's nest, decked out in her nightgown with its pattern of large flowers and her head festooned in paper curlers, enjoying the cut of his smartly attired figure with no little pride and self-satisfaction, as if she herself had invented him from top to toe.

At the very point where Senior Boatswain Olufsen passed Nyboder's guardhouse with its high gantry, which housed the alarm bell, he would shift the umbrella over to his right hand in order to be able to give a salute with his gloved hand in the event that the watch crew should oblige him with a military salute—something he set great store by and always observed. From there he would turn down Kamelgade and head for the square at Amalienborg Palace, where he would present himself on a daily basis just as the changing of the guard was about to commence. After listening to the martial music for a short while, he would go back over Store Kongensgade, through Borgergade, and then on into the town center itself.

Here, where he was outside of his former area of operations—where nobody knew him as Senior Boatswain Olufsen who had received the order of the Dannebrog from the king's own hand; where, to put it bluntly, he was just an ordinary civilian out for a stroll and was therefore at the mercy of people who were wont to bump and buffet him—his upright bearing would involuntarily shrink as he tentatively nudged his way on tender feet amongst the rushing populace. He never went any further than Købmagergade. Anything that lay to the other side of this street was, as far as he was concerned, not part of the real Copenhagen but rather a kind of suburb, which was so remote that he could not fathom how anybody would want to live there. By his charts, Adelgade and Borgergade were the town's main thoroughfares, and along with the triangle formed by the streets of Grønnegade, Sværtegade and Regnegade, as well as the area around Toldboden and Holmen, they encompassed his entire world. As soon as his daily stroll had taken him as far as the brushmakers in Antonistræde, or he had called in to Miss Jordan's booklenders on Silkegade so as to swap a book for his wife, he would turn around and head for home.

However, a couple of hours would normally have passed before he finally got back to Hjertensfrydgade. It was, you see, his habit to station himself at almost every street corner on the way home to observe the passing confluence of people and carriages. Moreover, and despite his eighty years and rheumy eyesight, he still retained a weather eye for any approaching maid or servant girl and particularly for those whose arms were exposed to the elements. On the occasions that such a heavenly body would come so close as to brush past him, he would declare his undying love for her in a soft whisper and then hurry away with a bowed head and a chuckle on his lips.

Another contributory factor was that he was obliged to stop for a moment outside a large number of shop windows in order to look at the goods displayed there and learn the prices off by heart for everything ranging from the underwear in the woolens boutique to the diamond jewelery in the goldsmiths—not by any means because he intended to purchase any of these things (severely hindered as he was in this regard by the fact that his wife, being all too familiar with his weakness where females were concerned, never allowed him to cruise anywhere with money in his pocket); but his empty pockets notwithstanding, he gained a great deal of satisfaction from simply going into the shops and partaking of the shopping etiquette, requesting permission to inspect the various goods on show, inquiring about the price of the costliest items, and then shuffling off after saying that he would "call back at a later date."

Senior Boatswain Olufsen always spent the early afternoon at home in his sitting room—"the parlor," as it was called in the Nyboder vernacular—a low slung cabin-like room with a series of small windows looking out onto the street. Here he would sit for hours by one of the windows in his shirt sleeves, and a skull cap on his head, watching the legions of half-tame crows over at the little green as they took flight and squawked over neighboring rooftops, or were to be observed squabbling amongst the rubbish bins, which at that time of day were still standing in the quiet, empty street. Occasionally, a kind of milky film would cover his failing eyes, his head would slowly sink down to his chest and his mouth would fall open.

"There you go again cooking peas, wee man," his wife would say in reference to the distinctive buzzing noise which Boatswain Olufsen would emit whenever sleep was just about to overpower him. The woman of the house had her own habitual afternoon spot in the form of a low chair by the side of the stove, where she sat and knitted. At the same time, she would read one of her tattered old novels, which she would perch on her knee, turning the pages with her elbow so that her knitting could proceed without interruption. Meanwhile, in the adjoining room, a young blond-haired girl could often be seen sat in a corner with her sewing. This was their foster daughter, Trine, and the door into her room, which looked out over the inner yard, was invariably left ajar. There was also a canary in a cage in this room. The cage was hung up by the side of the window and the bird would spend all day hopping up and down on its perch.

Madam Olufsen herself was nearly as tall as her husband and the effect was compounded by her horseguard stature—not to mention the hint of a fine gray moustache which now graced her upper lip. Moreover, her habit of pottering around in the morning, still in her nightgown with the flowery pattern and her head covered in curlers fashioned from old newspapers, could not be said to be her most attractive trait. However, by lunchtime, after she had donned her whalebone corset and her Merino dress of fine Spanish wool, and had also covered her partially bald pate under a lady's cap with gaudy stripes, from whence peeked the, by now, carefully arranged curls at her temple, she presented a rather coquettish figure to the world. In fact, adorned in this manner and with her cheeks, which had still not completely lost their bloom, one could better understand the reputation she had always enjoyed in the Nyboder quarter as a former beauty of considerable note.

There was no doubt that they had always been regarded as a handsome couple, herself and Senior Boatswain Olufsen. They had also always been a very happy couple. And if it was the case that the old boatswain had not always strictly observed the commandment governing liaisons with unchaste women, his good lady had, on the other hand, been loyal for both of them, despite the fact that she had never wanted for admirers seeking to lead her astray. Indeed, if the strong and persistent rumor was to be believed, one of the Royal Court's most dashing young princes, whose habit was to prey on the young married women of Nyboder while their menfolk sailed distant seas, once passed by our heroine on the corner of Haregaden and, after having presented himself, made a gallant proposal to her, as was his wont. Madam Olufsen curtsied and shyly cast her gaze downwards and then proceeded to follow him down one of the dark, lonely alleyways which skirt the town's keep. But here, where pure solitude reigned, she suddenly threw his little, deflated Highness across her knees and gave him a right royal spanking, which perhaps was not the first chastisement the appalled prince had received from an affronted Nyboder woman, but it was certainly the most painful.

The social cachet enjoyed by this aging couple was of long standing and their home continued to be regarded as a favored meeting point for Nyboder's most auspicious inhabitants. Few Nyboder dwellings could match the conviviality over which these two veterans of Hjertens-frydgade presided. For, quite apart from the usual religious feast days and holy days of obligation which are celebrated the length and breadth of Christendom by the consumption of rich foods and warm punch, they also held a range of incessant family celebrations and annual commemorations to mark events of a more private nature. Thus, there was the annual celebration marking the admission of Peter the canary into the family, then there was the commemoration of the day many years ago when Senior Boatswain Olufsen lost part of his big toe due to a severe bone infection. But pride of place in the celebratory canon belonged to Madam Olufsen's blood-letting day, which always occurred well into the spring season when heat had begun to permeate the air. This ceremony was always initiated with a substantial lunch with a chocolate theme, where the barber who was to carry out the operation was the chief guest.

On these august occasions, the assembled company always consisted of the same seven or eight old friends, who had, for more than forty years, come together to celebrate all the significant moments in the history of the family. These were by name: Retired "Master Carpenter" Bendtz from Tulipangade, retired Quartermaster Mørup from Delfingade, Chief Ship's Artillery Officer Jensen, and Riveter Fuss from Krokodillen, all accompanied by their ladies. Nor had the rituals which governed these festivities undergone any kind of significant change, despite having been in place for more than a generation. Once all the guests were assembled in the back room, Senior Boatswain Olufsen would open the door into the parlor, where the table had been laid and call on the guests to be seated with a time-honored witticism that it was now time for them to "stuff their faces." Once the guests were seated and the hostess had set the steaming goose or fowl on the table, Fuss the riveter would also follow tradition by feigning great shock, throwing himself back in his chair and declaring: "My word, Madam Olufsen, that must have been some egg you hatched!"—whereupon she would berate him as an old rascal and then invite all the guests to treat her abode as if it were their own.

At precisely this point in the proceedings, a curly haired young man would sometimes walk into the room to the general delight of those present. These veterans would all respectfully rise and offer their hand as little Trine—the foster daughter—whose face had suddenly gone scarlet, would scamper off to fetch a chair from the side room, set a new place at the table and bring a warm plate from the kitchen.

This youthful stranger was the Olufsens' lodger, the twenty-one-year-old engineering student Per Sidenius who had, for some years now, lived in the downstairs room with its accompanying tiny backrooms facing into the yard, all of which formed a part of the Olufsen residence. Here he enjoyed the status of favored guest, and as the serving dishes gradually emptied, and the schnapps glasses were filled and refilled, the atmosphere became merrier and more boisterous.

There was only one person who remained quiet and subdued—this was little Trine whose task it was to serve the guests. She filled the glasses, brought in more bread, changed the plates, polished the lamps, rooted out the salt cellars, retrieved lost serviettes and handkerchiefs and brought water for the ladies on the occasions when a sudden spasm or hiccoughs came upon them—all done so unobtrusively that her presence never registered with the guests. It was as if an invisible sprite moved amongst them. It has to be said that she was easily overlooked given her slightness of build, which belied her nineteen years in this world. The older people within the fraternity regarded her as still being a child, a very restricted child who in reality was somewhat lacking in mental alacrity. She had been an abandoned orphan whom Senior Boatswain Olufsen had plucked from dire straits. However, where she had originally come from was a mystery to all. It would never be said that she was beautiful and even for the youthful Hr. Sidenius she was nothing more than an invisible implement who brushed his boots and collected his linen for washing.

At last, when the punch bowl and sugar-strewn apple puffs had been brought to the table, the guests took this as a prompt to sing various party pieces and patriotic songs, whereby Madam Fuss excelled herself by singing a song in a *treble clef*, which, truth be told, was more admired for its power than its beauty.

As the song commenced, and after ensuring the guests had no more requirements at the table, Trine quickly made good her escape. Once out in the kitchen, she lit a lamp using one of the embers from the open hearth and descended the narrow and steep staircase—a kind of ship's ladder—in order to get Hr. Sidenius's rooms ready for when he retired for the evening. These were two small dark and damp rooms, which were very poorly fitted out with a small bench upholstered with oil cloth and a folding table, upon which an assortment of books, drawing implements, and large rolls of paper bearing pencil marks was strewn.

Trine set the lamp down on the table, opened a window and stood in a momentary reverie with her hand on the window sill looking out across the tiny garden, which was guarded by a fence and an outdoor toilet and was bathed in a romantic sheen from the full moon in the skies above. But then she gave a start, in the manner of one whose own thoughts had been the sudden cause of extreme consternation, and she began the work of Sisyphus in bringing order to the chaos that continually reigned in these chambers. She lifted various items of clothing which had been abandoned across the furniture and hung them up behind the screen in the corner of the bedroom. She then tidied the books on the table and placed the myriad little drawing tools into their respective, and carefully arranged, compartments and cases. Despite the fact that her young gentleman had never bothered himself to give directions in this regard, she knew exactly where each article belonged, and where he would expect, nay, demand, that they be housed. With that instinct which love engenders, even amongst more simple souls, she had assimilated all there was to know, intuited his habits, divined his wishes and doggedly worked her way through the labyrinth of his moods and unpredictable impulses until she had mapped the path which led to the core of this young man's will. Once, and once only, had he let it be known to her—and here he had lifted his finger and adopted a terrifying countenance— that she must regard her service to him as her life's primary and solemn duty, the conscientious fulfillment of which would be weighed and adjudicated by God himself on the Day of Judgment.

For this reason, it was with a genuine sense of being the guardian of a Holy Grail that she moved around down there in his small chambers and busied herself with her master's possessions. And it was with a particular sense of devotion that she lingered in his modest sleeping quarters, while she fussed at his bed, righted his slippers so that they both faced inwards, and then neatly placed the matchbox by the side of the lamp bowl nearest to the bed. When, finally, she took his precious pillow into her hands in order to bump up the filling, she clasped it to her heart for a moment and closed her eyes in pure bliss.

Up above in the "parlor," meanwhile, things had become more and more animated. Riveter Fuss had brought out his guitar and, despite the many objections from the ladies present, proceeded to sing a notorious music hall ditty—"The Bandy-Legged Hag of Gammelstrand." The men were fit to be tied with laughter. The young Sidenius was equally enthralled and the eighty-four-year-old Master Carpenter Hr. Bendtz chuckled and wheezed like one of his old lathes. The ladies, however, rose in indignation and retired to the back room, where coffee was now being served accompanied by sugar candy and blackcurrant liqueur.

It was only as a new day dawned that the company broke up, and the various couples shuffled contentedly homeward in that state of enervated elation which encourages public displays of affection, kisses, and embraces, even in the middle of the street.

This band of merry veterans, who defied their aging bones and receding hairlines by drinking with such an unrestrained gusto from the cup of life that they could nearly see its very dregs, provided Peter Andreas with his first refuge in life, a temporary haven on the way to that Land of Luck and Happiness of which his dreams had foretold. Here he encountered for the first time a willing indulgence of that part of his nature which at home in the rectory they had sought to suppress and hidebrand as the mark of Cain and the Devil's own work. He had been particularly grateful for this sanctuary in his first lonely year in Copenhagen and, indeed, for the cheerful and rather idyllic Nyboder area itself, which was like a hidden province from bygone days lying in a quiet corner of the capital city. While it is true—as his circle of friends in the city gradually increased—that his relationship with the old pair and their social circle took on a more fleeting character, it was never entirely broken and his aging guardians continued to dote on him, almost as if he had been one of their own sons. They were not long in noticing how poor he was, even though he had made great efforts to conceal this from them, and there was more than one occasion when he would have gone to bed on an empty stomach but for Madam Olufsen tactfully inviting him in to "sample" a new cheese, or "give his opinion" on a newly cooked side of ham.

For all that, they never managed to gain any real insight into his background. As lively and talkative as he might sometimes be—he would never broach the subject of himself and his dreams, though he would often lead them along by answering their questions by saying that he was studying to be become a "man of the cloth." In the same manner, he maintained an obdurate silence with regards to anything that touched on his home and his relationship with his family, though Madam Olufsen in particular never tired of sounding him out on the subject. He had firmly resolved to treat his former life as something forgotten, something dead, which even as a fading memory would not be allowed to haunt his new life. He had fought with might and main to transform his inner being, to expunge every bitter and humiliating memory residing in his soul, so that he could be left with an untarnished tablet of marble upon which he himself would inscribe his life's victories and coming good fortune. For this reason, there was not so much as a portrait on his table or wall that might remind him of—or describe to others—the home he had left behind, and which he never wanted to see again before the time when he could return as one who held people to account for their actions and apportioning his judgment upon them. Were he to suddenly drop dead, a search of his most secret hiding places would not reveal even a letter, or note, that might give a clue as to his antecedents. Even his very name had been changed as much as possible so as to avoid the slightest memory of his past. For he no longer signed his name as Peter Andreas but simply as "Per," and it was a matter of regret to him that he could not also procure a more appropriate surname.

Gradually, the sum of his connection to his parents was reduced to the short letters he sent, whereby on a quarterly basis he acknowledged the financial support he still (and without any great scruples) accepted from them, but which, of course, was completely insufficient, particularly because of the huge expense of lectures, books, drawing and painting tools, etc., which his studies demanded of him. From the time he had reached his eighteenth birthday onwards, and in order quite simply to survive, he had been forced to teach mathematics at a school for boys and copy technical drawings for a master tradesman. Nor was he in contact with any of his former school friends, most of whom had been students in Copenhagen for some time by this stage. He almost never saw them. Their honor offended as it was because Per had occasionally had the cheek to make fun of their bourgeois academic pretensions, they had quickly learned to avoid him and now showed that same formal reserve that his brothers always displayed towards him.

Per, for his part, chose to turn a blind eye to all this. Yet, his apparent indifference was often more feigned than genuine. For the truth was that he had frequent bouts of quiet despair. His constant sense of humiliation was not just on account of his poverty, and especially his enforced role as a tutor in a kindergarten, which he never mentioned to anybody else. Worse still was the fact that his studies, and the future prospects they appeared to offer, now seemed more like a crushing disappointment. When, four or five years ago, he had seen the engineering college for the first time, he had approached its portals with a heightened anticipation bordering on veneration. He had imagined it as a temple of the arts, a profound place of discourse and thought, where newly liberated mankind's future success and prosperity would be forged amid lightning bolts and thunder beneath the ark of the new world covenant—he found instead a grim and insignificant building stuck in the corner of an old bishop's residence and within its shoddy walls a collection of dark and depressing lecture rooms which bore an all pervading smell of tobacco and remnants of packed lunches, and where an assortment of youths were to be found standing over small tables covered in paper, while others sat reading study notes and drawing on long pipes, or surreptitiously playing cards. His soon to be lecturers he had imagined as firebrand preachers of the holy faith that was the natural sciences, but what he met instead in the lecture rooms was a group of withered schoolteacher types who could barely be distinguished from the schoolmasters to whom he had only recently bidden a relieved adieu. One of these types, who bore the demeanor of an entombed mummy and whose voice during lectures would constantly fade away and could only, apparently, be revived by the imbibing of some sort of medicine from a hip flask, delivered his lectures from vague memories of Hans Christian Ørsted's days and the early experiments in electromagnetics. Another lecturer—Professor Sandrup, who was actually the designated lecturer in engineering—had the custom of always wearing a white tie and looked more like an aging theology graduate, or minister, than a science teacher. He enjoyed a certain reputation as being theoretically well versed but was, in fact, a pedant, who, in accordance with his pedagogical scruples, had compiled a set of lengthy technical specifications which found the need to use a mass of scientific jargon to describe even the simplest of tools, such as an axe and a wheelbarrow. He then demanded that students should learn these lists verbatim as part of the examination procedure.

Thus, from every source of academic instruction, Per received the same basic message—that a competent engineer was not (at least not any longer) the proud, globetrotting heroic adventurer of his dreams, but actually a simple pen pusher, a conscientious counting machine, a living set of calculus tables chained to a drawing board. The vast majority of his fellow students—and more precisely those who were regarded by teachers and students alike as being the most gifted— dreamed of nothing more than at some future point achieving a secure position (however humble that might be) within the civil service. Once this pinnacle of achievement was reached, they could settle down to a comfortable life as masters of their families, with a small parcel of land, a small house and an equally small garden—all of which could be rounded off after forty years of diligent service with a modest pension; and if fortune was particularly kind, some sort of public recognition of the contribution they had made, and perhaps even an appointment as a Justice of the Peace.

But this kind of prospect was pure anathema to Per. He knew that his destiny lay far beyond the realm of everyday concerns and medi-ocrity. He felt the blood of one who was born to rule coursing through his veins and nothing but a place at life's top table, in the company of the world's highest freeborn men, was good enough for him.

He had even identified a means by which he could achieve a proud and independent social status for himself. For, at the same time as he, on a more or less regular basis, attended lectures and worked on practical course projects, and without neglecting his humiliating but necessary spare time jobs so that he could continue to put bread on the table, he had in all secrecy begun to make draft plans for a huge watercourse project, in effect a fjord realignment, which he had conceived as early as his first year as a student in Copenhagen. The seeds for the idea were actually sown even further back in time—right back to his early youth, in fact in that period when there had been so much talk at home about resurrecting the declining shipping trade on the fjord by dredging and regulating the navigation channels and rebuilding the port. In other words, the very undertaking his father had criticized so vehemently because of the stir it caused amongst the townspeople, and which was then abandoned. Even at that young age, he had dreamed of being the one who would turn that huge plan into a reality—that he would be the one to bring the tang of the high seas and the bounties of world trade to the town's pathetic and moribund harbor. And this dream, of becoming the actual benefactor for the very town which had borne witness to his daily humiliations, had never really left him since. The disastrous visit home that first Christmas as an exile had only made these dreams all the more urgent for him. It was a thing that nagged him in his loneliness. It became an obsession, the realization of which eventually took on the form of a kind of religious conviction. It was not just a temporary goal but the thing that would dictate the path his future life was to take.

He began working on the project as soon as he had learned how to draw canal profiles in accordance with contour line principles set out in admiralty charts, and had now been working on his master plan for three years. Day in day out, he had beavered away, cutting corners from his quota of night sleep so as to gain time for the calculation of land areas, the strength of sea currents, draw in fascines and fittings, design embankments, and set pier heads and mooring poles. And year by year, he made his plan more ambitious, added new things, turned it increasingly into a monster project. Influenced as he was by a group of German technical journals, which he had managed to procure, the notion had grown on him that the expanded and deepened shipping lanes could be continued on the other side of the town, in the form of a canal, or set of canals, in the manner of those built in Holland. In his mind's eye, he could vaguely make out his final and colossal objective—no less than a fully developed network of waterways which linked all of Mid-Jutland's larger rivers, lakes and fjord inlets to each other and joined the now cultivated heath, and its profusion of new town developments up there, with the sea on both sides.

Yet, every time his thoughts soared towards those dizzy heights, his nerve seemed to fail him. A raft of demons would descend upon him as he worked at his desk, leaving him impotent and pouring scorn on his dreams. You are mad! they would scream. In this benighted country, you have to be old and gray before they let you anywhere near a decent project, where it's regarded as the height of presumption for a young man to have any greater ambition than to grow a humpback while chained to an office chair and where an engineer, who wants to retain the respect of his fellow citizens and confidence of his superiors, will not push things any higher than expressing a hope, perhaps, of one day achieving a post as an inspector of his Majesty's highways. Have you forgotten already how your venerable mentor, the noble Professor Sandrup, admittedly in a grim but fatherly way, put you to rights that time when during an oral examination you began to reveal all that new stuff you had learned from your reading (at nobody's invitation) of those modern German periodicals: "Young man, you really must try to resist that unfortunate trait you have of wanting to be different from the rest." Was it not in those tones that it was put? Words borne of experience! Words of hope!

However, he rarely allowed the poison from such bitter thoughts to eat into the inner core of his being. He was too young for that, and his moods too capricious. A brisk walk, the admiring glance of a pretty girl, a lavish feast laid on by the Nyboder veterans, or an evening spent in the company of friends at a café—nothing more was usually required in order to banish the dark furrows of doubt from his brow. Women proved increasingly to be the most effective distraction when the threat of a turn in his mood loomed on the horizon. He was now twenty-one years of age and his attraction to the opposite sex was beginning to dominate his imagination and provide new vistas into which his mind could tumble.

One evening, along with a friend, he entered an old-fashioned Swiss café, which at the time was a favorite meeting point for the town's substantial artistic and literary demimonde. With a look which shone with pure excitement, his guide pointed out some of the most hotly debated artists and authors who could be spied amongst the throng. However, Per, who was not the slightest bit interested in that kind of thing, had fixed his gaze instead on a young girl who was standing behind the counter—a tall, slim figure with a glorious mane of strawberry blond hair.

"That is Red Lizzy," his friend explained. "She's the one that was the model for Iversen's *Venus* and for Petersen's *Susanne*. She is not bad, eh? Look at that skin!"

From that day forward, Per was a regular guest at the café, especially at those times of day when things were less frantic. He had become quite smitten by the young girl, and when it became apparent that this attraction was reciprocated, a path was very quickly cleared towards a more intimate kind of relationship.

His pride in his own appearance had grown apace as he stepped into manhood. He was now broad shouldered and powerfully built, had a proud forehead, framed by dark curly hair, and light blue eyes which sat below a manly brow. The hint of a moustache had begun to appear above his full lips. Yet, thanks to Madam Olufsen's motherly care, he had retained much of his boyish vigor and his cheeks still bore a brick red and unmistakeably rural tinge. In public, and without even realizing it himself, he would often be seen to have a smile on his lips, and this constant, slightly empty, gesture was often a source of disappointment for those who did not know him well; for it led them to assume that he was in essence of a childish disposition, moving through life in blissful harmony with the world around him. He had not completely been able to shake off the image of being the provincial blow-in. However, when he was dressed in his best clothes, he was imposing in stature. He held his head high and there was a dignity in his deportment. In spite of his frequent bouts of penury, he would never allow a decline in his sartorial standards. Or at least this was the case whenever he showed himself on the street, where he would always have the appearance of being newly groomed and polished. Even by this stage, he had garnered enough experience to realize that there were moments in life when a white shirt front and an impeccably tailored coat might do more for a young man's future than years of toil and self-sacrifice—in other words that nothing was completely lost as long as appearances were kept up. At home, on the other hand, he took a far more devil-may-care approach and, in fact, found a certain pleasure and comfort in pottering round in his old clothing.

The café which, more than any other, came to enjoy his patronage, and where he squandered more time and money than he cared to admit, was the so-called Cauldron, which was a watering hole for a radical clique of artists, the Liberationists, a circle of young and not so young aesthetes—indeed, a very gifted circle, but all to some extent stunted in their development, either because of a lack of creative growth, or because they had flowered too quickly. There, of an evening time, sat the highly controversial seascape painter Fritjof Jensen, a beefy Viking-type figure sporting a sailor's peacoat and tousled hair and beard—an inspired and brilliant artist, a roguish Falstaff type with a foaming ale tankard never far from his reach, bereft of principles and as mercurial as a boy suffering the first pangs of puberty. There, from noontime onwards, and year after year sitting in a pose of morose contemplation, was the sickly poet Enevoldsen, polishing his glasses, attending to his nails, fiddling with his cigar, or otherwise engaged in a myriad of other petty occupations which he set himself while he composed his vibrant and vivid verse, masterpieces in miniature, which set a new tone in Danish poetry. There sat the young naturalist figure painter Jørgen Hallager, with the face of a rabid dog—rebel, anarchist, insurrectionist, artistic revolutionary, the man who wished the demise of all educational institutions and the execution of all academics, but who also made a good living working as a colorist for a photographer. And there was that old cynic, the journalist and comedy writer Reeballe, a small, bandy-legged dwarf who always wore a wig and boasted one eye that stared glassily from his head, while the other appeared to gaze forlornly down at his long straw-white goatee, which partially covered his stained shirt front— the perennial butt of the cartoonists in the city's satirical magazines. A well chewed cigar stump in the side of his mouth, and with one or both hands hidden behind his back, below his waistband, it was his wont to drift in a usually drunken state around the tables, set himself down here and there, often amongst people completely unknown to him, and involve himself in their conversations in the most disruptive manner possible. He too saw himself as a reformer, but in a classical sense of the word. He claimed Socrates as his role model. His philosophy, he averred, was that of the clear, sober rationalist. In his most befuddled moments, he had the habit of beating his breast and declaring himself to be "the last of the Greeks."

Although Per was so much younger than this group of men and had not himself made any overtures towards them, he had achieved the distinction of being invited into their circle—as Fritjof Jensen once put it—because of the "painterly redness of his cheeks." More important, however, was his relationship with Lisbeth—the apple of their collective eye and mind, whose vivacious silky hair and translucent skin tone had helped to bolster the artistic careers of so many in the group, which favor they repaid by always welcoming her latest admirer into their fold, even where said admirer had no connection with the artistic fraternity.

Nonetheless, Per continued to feel like an intruder amongst this group. Nor was it modesty alone that deterred him from taking a more active part in their conversations. His inability to appreciate the merits of painting mirrored his lack of feeling for poetry. Indeed, he found that his studies provided him with all the material he needed to spark his imagination. Thus, his creative energies were so wrapped up in his hugely ambitious plans for the future that the arts never got a look in.

At the same time, he could never have been described as a neutral observer. Privately, he was highly amused by this curious group of people, whose members could suddenly go into a frenzy over a particular shade of color, or disappear into the deeper realms of ecstasy because of four lines which rhymed in a certain way, as if the very existence of the human race depended on their correct interpretation. He enjoyed such histrionics as a kind of comedy of manners and would frequently laugh to himself on noticing how even Lisbeth had been gripped by this melodramatic fever and—proud as she was of her body's significance for the arts—wished for nothing more than that her life might be regarded as being joyfully devoted to the glorification of aesthetic beauty.

There was one person within this group who sought to indulge Per as much as possible, a man who likewise would always stand on the fringes of the circle and who, generally speaking, was not even welcome there. This was a certain Ivan Salomon, a young Jew, son of one of the city's richest men—a small creature who was fleet of movement in the manner of a brown-eyed squirrel, always smiling, ever seeking to please, and entranced by the fact that he could spend time in the company of so many famous artists. This young man's abiding ambition was to one day discover and then promote the cause of a new genius. Thus, he engaged himself in an endless search for some hidden or misunderstood talent, whose patron he would then become. Every physical peculiarity—a pair of deeply set eyes, a powerfully prominent forehead, or perhaps just an unkempt hairstyle—he took as a sign of rare ability and many an amusing story had been told regarding the disappointments he had subsequently suffered because of this.

It was obvious that he had now placed all his hopes in Per, who for his part felt most uncomfortable at being the subject of such attention. Even his flattery was contrary to Per's true nature. He felt great unease, for example, when Hr. Salomon—in quite open references to his rapid conquest of Lisbeth—smilingly told him that he was an undoubted Aladdin figure, Fortune's child, upon whose imperious forehead one could discern a winged message from the Gods: I came, I saw, I conquered! The words themselves, Per found, had a certain ring to them and stirred his innermost, secret emotions to fever pitch. However, it was painful and embarrassing in the extreme that he should first hear these hopefully prophetic words from the mouth of an obsequious Jew.

One evening Per entered the Cauldron at around midnight and walked straight into a riot of a party. It was that giant of a man Fritjof Jensen—known by everyone as simply Fritjof—who was standing the drinks in celebration of the fact that he had just sold one of his eight-foot canvases, *Hurricane in the North Sea*, to a butter merchant. In the middle of the floor in a room, which was separated from the other sections of the café by a corridor, a number of small tables had been joined together and some twenty people sat around two garlanded bowls containing champagne punch.

At the upper end of the row of tables—partially obscured by the swirl of tobacco smoke—sat Fritjof himself, holding court like a god on Mount Olympus. In front of him was his colossal private trophy bowl, the so-called "Abyss," and from his slurred speech and wall-eyed countenance it was clear he had made manful efforts to drink his bowl dry. He had spent a whole day carousing and had seen the sun go down and rise again in an oyster house, fraternized with ladies of the night, roamed around in the woods and raided wine bars, and gradually accumulated a band of friends, and acquaintances of those friends, whom he had happened to meet along the way.

A series of speeches were delivered. At one point, a pale young man with Mephistophelian features sprang up onto the seat of his chair and called a raucous toast to a certain Dr. Nathan of whom Per had heard much comment in these surroundings and always in tones of reverence and joy. This Nathan was a literary critic and popular philosopher who was regarded by a particular group of younger academics as a spiritual leader, and who—also unhappy with the way things were in Denmark—had moved to Berlin. Other than this, Per knew very little about him, despite the fact that one could hardly open a newspaper or satirical magazine without seeing his name— "Dr. Satan," as they invariably called him. That the man was a Jew had contributed to the fact that Per had never felt the urge to find out more about him. He did not even like this strange race of people and had, besides, very little time for literary types. And this particular doctor of letters had even held a series of high-profile lectures in the university itself—that place of sanctimonious utterances which played wet nurse to the whole gang of academic philistines who, in Per's eyes, were the worst blight on the country.

The pale young speaker standing on his chair, and gesticulating with his arms in such a triumphant fashion, was a writer by the name of Povl Berger. With roars of approval from his inebriated confederates, he first described Dr. Nathan as his "Hero," then his "God," and finally his "Savior," and after emptying his glass, crushed it in his hand as a mark of honor with the result that blood ran freely down his fingers.

Per was stunned and sat there open mouthed. He had the feeling of having been transported to a madhouse.

In the run of the evening, the size of the company was swollen by a constant stream of new arrivals. In order that room could be made for the newcomers, more small tables were added to the original configuration but this time to either side of the main body of tables and in this way the shape of a cross was formed. But then there came a sudden roar and a hammering on the table. It was Fritjof who was shouting: "Are we going to sit here like a bunch of damned disciples around a cross! … What's all this pious formality about? It's enough to turn a man's stomach! … Let's form a horseshoe instead! We'll make a pact with the devil by venerating his footwear! … Move round will yez shipmates!"

And once his will had been done, and everyone was seated again after the disruption, he lifted his refilled trophy bowl and cried: "Praise to you Lord Lucifer! Holy Liberationist! Great champion of freedom and happiness! God of all the little fiends running round! … Long may you bless me with a steady stream of fat butter merchants and I swear I will build thee an altar from oyster shells and empty champagne bottles! … Hey, waiter! … Hominus Minimus! … More wine here! … A sea of wine! … A baptismal font full of wine my friends! … Hey! Is there anybody listening out there!"

The proprietor, a short Swiss who always wore a pullover, appeared at the door leading to the main part of the café, which had long since been closed up and its lights extinguished. With frequent shrugs of his shoulders and hands raised in apology, he bade the indulgence of the good gentlemen for he dared not provide any more service that night. The clock had struck two some time ago and the obliging night constable had already given him a warning knock on the window with his baton.

"Clock? … Clock!" Fritjof roared. "Are we not gods, Hr. Minimus? Clocks are for tailors and cobblers!"

"Yes, and for café propryters also I'm effrayed!" the little man answered, his head resting on one shoulder and his hands placed in supplication on his breast. And on noticing that his little witticism had been successful, he added with a smile that he looked forward to a return visit by the gentlemen again the following day, bidding them to come as early as they wished. "We are opening at seven."

But at this Fritjof lurched back in his chair and thrust his hand into his right trouser pocket. "Wine I said!" he roared, strewing a handful of gold coins across the table as he did so, where they rolled and clinked across cutlery and plates, some landing on the floor. "Here's some butter! ... Do you want some more! ... Drink, shipmates! ... Leave that shit where it is! ... We are not grubby little philistines!"

However, his adoption of the high moral ground was an Olympian step too far for the other guests who suddenly became quite sober as they busied themselves retrieving the gold coins from the floor, while Fritjof continued to roar: "Wine! Wine and girls is what we want! Wine, I said!"

Yet these protests were to no avail and the revelers gradually drifted away from the tables and into the night. The proprietor had a quiet word with each departing guest, imploring them in gracious tones "on account of the Poleece" to leave quietly by the backdoor. Only Fritjof was unrelenting and continued to bellow and shout.

In the end only Per remained at the scene. But when he too made moves to leave, Fritjof grabbed him by the sleeve and threatened, implored—in fact begged him with sobs emanating from his throat, to stay.

Per finally relented and sat down once again. He found that he could not, in all conscience, leave a man alone like that when he was in such an overemotional state of mind. After promises were made with regards to keeping good order, coffee and cognac was brought to the table, after which "Hominus Minimus" retreated with much shaking of his head back to his small office behind the bar.

Fritjof planted both elbows onto the table and placed his bearded head between his hands. He had suddenly become quiet and cast his half closed eyes downward.

Per, who was sitting on the opposite side of the table, lit a fresh cigar. A solitary, partly dimmed gas lamp burned directly above their heads. The rest of the large room was just about discernible through a silvery veil of fine, swirling dust and tobacco smoke. All around them was a confusion of empty tables and chairs, just as the guests had left them. The tables were strewn with cigar ash, champagne corks, and broken glass. But all was deathly silent now...so conspicuously silent after the bedlam that had gone before it that it was as if the slightest noise might call forth echoes from every corner.

Given that Fritjof had still not said anything, Per assumed that he had fallen asleep. So, in the end, he knocked his glass against that of the artist's and said "skål!"

But instead of offering a toast in response, Fritjof began to speak in doleful tones about death. As he looked uncertainly across at Per with glazed eyes reminiscent of a blind man, he asked him whether he had ever got the shakes thinking "about that—you know—the other side of the grave."

Per, who was not prone to such nervy preoccupations, and in any case was still too engaged with the present life to worry about what might come afterwards, initially believed that the question was a joke and started to laugh. But then Fritjof gripped him by the arm and, in words that carried both a threat and a sign of his deep angst, said: "Be still man! You never know what's round the corner!...You young pups don't think twice about your health. But just wait till you see the first gray hairs sprouting at your temples. Then you'll start feeling those prickly heat rashes on your body when you start to think that your ever so well groomed person is going to be served up as a special dish for hundreds of hungry maggots. Think! Just a bit of surplus lard around the heart and bang—gone! A pillow filled with wood shavings to rest your pretty head, eight screws for the coffin lid and—there you go boys—dinner is served!...I'm telling you boy... you never know what is round the corner! Maybe there's more up there beyond the stars than our new fangled Jew prophets actually care to dream about. And if that's the case...what then? Do we not all then face a final Day of Judgment?...We kid ourselves that we are so much cleverer now. Oh yes! But happier?...Cheers!"

Per's eyes widened. He stared at this bearded wild boar, this lusty high priest of bacchanalian pleasures, who had now suddenly revealed himself as being kindred in spirit to his mother and father—yet another underworld troll, whose deepest soul actually resided in a phantom world, where everything revolved around the grave and vengeful God waiting on the other side—shunning the forces of light he himself had invoked in such an arrogant fashion only minutes previously.

And this was not to be the only time that Per received a startling insight into the inner world of these "Liberationists" and thereby discovered suppressed heresies—a night side, the never entirely discarded remnants of former selves, who in unguarded moments would spring to life and make a grim mockery of their new personas. Be it Reeballe, "the last of the Greeks," who, on the rare occasions he was sober, was known to torture himself in trying to live with his conscience, and then Lisbeth who would regularly produce her confirmation psalm book from her commode as soon as the pains in her lower back would start, or if she feared that she might be with child. Gradually, he began to perceive the central thing that sapped the human will and rendered the world into effectively nothing more than one giant poorhouse. Just as one person sought comfort in the depths of a bottle, another invoked his "inner voice" with immature verbosity and schoolboy pranks, a third, in self-imposed artistic isolation, withdrew into his shell like a snail responding to thunder, while a fourth lost himself in futile dreams of a future anarchistic brotherhood of men—this was how people behaved all over the world as they fought their respective demons, while life, hale and hearty and with a smile on its face, simply invited them to partake of the abundance that was all about them. Of course! He had seen all this before in his own home.

And now he was overwhelmed by a dizzying sensation, a feeling that he was, in fact, a breed apart, an exception to the rule, who already as a child, by some fortunate twist of fate, had sprung the chains against which even the freest spirits of the day still chafed. Ivan Salomon's description of his having the luck of Aladdin and the god-like signs written on his brow, now suddenly took on a far greater import for him. In essence, the will to act and to ruthlessly and recklessly desire was the simple key to everything—and then the full glory of life was his for the taking!

So it transpired that he did, after all, come from a regal line. He had in fact been crowned with the emperor's laurel wreath. At least one person had already bowed before its shining majesty and had read its inscription: I came, I saw, I conquered!

3

ONE DAY, following a long period of deliberation, Per placed a number of rolled-up drawings and calculation sheets under his arm and went in search of Professor Sandrup in his private chambers. He had decided to invite the professor to study his channel and fjord realignment project and pronounce his judgment on the plan. The professor's eyes widened on hearing the request; he placed his spectacles quietly and precisely on his long nose and then emitted a series of small grunts to signal his irritation. And with that disquieting gift, which is the preserve of veteran teachers, to unerringly detect the weak points in a piece of work, it was not long before he discovered an error in Per's waterflow velocity calculations.

Per, for his part, could deny neither the presence of the fault, nor its significance for the plan as a whole. Instead, his face turned scarlet and he made no attempt to defend himself.

The professor then removed his spectacles. And, after acknowledging that Per had demonstrated great enthusiasm and no little application in developing his grand plan, he urged him to cease wasting his time on such pointless exercises and devote himself, instead, to a meticulous and systematic study of the prescribed examination subjects.

When Per arrived back home, he took out the papers and studied them thoroughly once again. But it was to no avail. The error was irrefutable. It had crept its way into his calculations from the start and its rectification would, as the professor had quite rightly pointed out, imply that the projected mean water level at the river's lowest stretch would bring the water table below sea level. In other words, the whole plan had been built on a false premise and was therefore useless.

His face reddened with shame once again as he witnessed the complete and irresistible collapse of his proud kingdom. For over an hour he remained in the same position, sat bent over his table with his head in his hands without moving so much as a muscle.

But suddenly he rose and with a devil-may-care attitude stuffed his drawings, calculations, and estimates into a draw in his commode, lit himself a cigar, and walked into town, where he spent the rest of the afternoon in a billiard hall. Exchanging banter at the top of his voice, he strolled around the hall in his shirt sleeves and accepted the challenge of anyone who fancied their luck against him. He was unusually confident in his stroke action, winning game after game. No one would be allowed to see that, on that very same day, he had suffered such an ignominious defeat.

Towards evening, he met an acquaintance who offered to sell him a spare admission ticket for an artist and student carnival taking place that same evening. The ticket was on offer at half price. Per bought it immediately.

The following evening, he was to be found, the collar of his coat turned up, standing and waiting in one of the dark and quiet corners of Vor Frue Plads. It was snowing heavily and even though the square was usually a busy thoroughfare and offered access to Vor Frue Cathedral, there was not a soul to be seen. The ground in front of the cathedral was blanketed by a thick layer of snow, which was completely devoid of footsteps. The two statues at the entrance depicting Moses and David were now adorned with two large white hairpieces and this new headgear, along with their black cloaks, gave them the appearance of two law officers from the age of enlightenment.

The cause of his lingering there was a female, a youngish married lady, whom he had met at the carnival and with whom he had danced half the night. He held out no great hope, however, that she would turn up. This was his first adventure in love with a real lady and she had been very clear that she would make no promises. In fact, a more accurate description would be that she had tried to laugh off his bold request with a shy wave of her hand.

The bell up in the tower of the cathedral had struck nine some time ago and he had just begun to think about going home when he heard a polite cough from behind him. It was one of the town's messenger boys who inquired of his name and then handed him a letter.

Per hurried to the base of the nearest available lamppost and, as his nostrils took in the violet perfume emanating from the scented paper, he read: "Not coming—of course. Will, however, try to get you an invite for Manufacturer Fensmark's party, which is next Sunday. I believe they have a deficiency of gentlemen who like to dance." The letter was unsigned. There was, however, a postscript, which said: "I am actually quite cross with you. I do hope you are at least slightly ashamed of yourself."

Per placed the letter in his pocket and smiled contentedly. Then his thoughts turned to Lisbeth. At last, he had a good reason to dump her. The fact was that he had felt a growing distaste for this kind of brassy slut with their coarse manners and continual cadging, as well as their dirty rooms that were nothing more than flea pits. Now was the time for a more expansive love life. In his imagination, an alluring distant horizon beckoned full of noble and uplifting experiences: risky assignations, secret trips in horse-drawn carriages, the furtive squeezing of hands under tables, stolen kisses from behind quivering ladies' fans, timorous admissions of love.

He had just come through Skoubogade and made to turn into Vimmelskaftet when he roused himself abruptly from his reveries with a severe oath. For there, walking directly towards him, was a diminutive figure clad in a sable overcoat and carrying a large umbrella. Despite the fact that the umbrella hid the whole of his upper body, Per immediately recognized him because of his rapid foot movements. It was none other than Ivan Salomon.

In an attempt at avoiding the need for a conversation, he jumped quickly across the gutter and made for the opposite side of the street but it was too late. A cry, a shriek of delight: "Hr. Sidenius! . . . Is that not Hr. Sidenius?" stopped him dead in his tracks.

"If you are on the way to the Cauldron," said Salomon, "I would advise against it. I have actually just come from there. I am afraid that tonight the place is just mind-numbingly boring. There's nobody there except Enevoldsen; but our precious author is sitting there in his own little world, polishing his spectacles and clearly having difficulty producing so much as a comma. No, good sir, let's go somewhere else. You will do me the honor of dining with me this evening? You are free, are you not?"

Per knew that he might as well give up all ideas of resistance—try as he might, there was no objection or excuse that Salomon would not be able to beat down in a trice.

And the truth was that he was of no great mind to go home to his lonely abode, and thereby ruin his good spirits, by being reminded of the thing that lay in a drawer in his commode. Sleep was out of the question. And now that this man had more or less insisted on having his company—well, a one-off occasion could do no harm.

Shortly afterwards, he was sitting on a wine-colored velvet sofa in a newly built hotel restaurant, which was the preferred haunt of the landed aristocracy and of the military officer classes while they were on their travels. An expensive Brussels carpet adorned the floors of the restaurant, the walls were essentially huge mirrors, the service was provided by formally dressed waiters who glided silently about, and conversations amongst the clientele, which included several ladies, were conducted in subdued voices.

At first, Per felt slightly intimidated. He was not used to frequenting such distinguished establishments. But he was especially uncomfortable to find himself in such a place with Salomon. For young Ivan had immediately attracted attention to himself, which was by no means favorable, by dint of his rather boisterous and intrusive behavior.

There was one particular guest—a gentleman sitting alone, whom Per had not yet seen—that had looked up in great irritation from his newspaper. This man was in his forties, a tall, skeletal being with a certain slackness about him whose head was bald to the point of being naked. His face was haggard and was dressed by a long, drooping moustache above which a gold pince-nez hovered. He had shot a baleful glance at Ivan Salomon; but when he noticed Per, a slight reddening appeared in his pale yellow cheeks and he had quickly hidden himself so completely behind his newspaper that the only thing now visible to the other guests was a pair of crossed legs.

"What do you want to eat? Oysters perhaps?" asked Salomon, as he pulled off his russet gloves and placed them in between the two lowest buttons on his front vest. "I presume that you have completely fresh shellfish on the menu this evening?" he said, addressing the waiter who gave his reply with a rather slapdash bow.

Per could not bring himself to say that this particular exclusive dish did not appeal to him in the slightest. But on the other hand, he was not going to turn his nose up at a solid evening meal. The long wait in the cold frosty air had brought a great hunger upon him. Meat was what he needed, cheese and eggs—lots of eggs.

"Oysters are fine," he said. "But I'll tell you straight out sir: I'm as hungry as a wolf."

"Bravo! Excellent!" Salomon exclaimed, as he clapped his hands together in excitement, while the other patrons of the restaurant—including the ladies—turned in consternation to look at him. The gold pince-nez sitting on the nose of the unaccompanied gentleman also came momentarily into view as he peered enquiringly over the edge of his newspaper.

Oblivious to all this, Salomon continued to address the waiter: "Now, do tell us good man . . . what else is there on offer tonight?"

The waiter then proceeded to reel off a list of dishes.

"Very good, we'll take the lot!" he exclaimed, seized as he was in complete and utter euphoria, while he waved his arms in swimming movements across the table. "Load her up! *En grand souper* my friend! . . . And no hanging around there! We are as hungry as stock brokers in a bull market."

Per, who very quickly perceived the supercilious air now adopted by the waiter, could see only one way to conquer his own embarrassment and that was to throw in his lot with his companion and let the rest go to the devil. With great deliberation, he selected a toothpick from the container on the table, leaned back into the corner of the sofa and proceeded to flash challenging glances across the restaurant at anyone who looked his way.

The "shellfish" was now served, arranged on a bed of ice cubes and accompanied by a bottle of chilled champagne. Next came the wildfowl, the asparagus, an omelette, various cheeses, celery and then the fruit bowl. Per attacked everything that was put in front of him with gusto. He justified himself by saying that, as he had been landed in this situation, it was as well to make the most of it. It was also the case that he had never before in his life beheld such regal culinary splendor.

As for Salomon, he had merely picked at the first course but had, on the other hand, maintained a barrage of chat. For he had started upon his favorite topic—the Renaissance. "Ah the great age of Man," he said, "when writers, artists, inventors, all the great talents lived like emperors, were feted as kings, were adored by queens; while our present day geniuses sit half starved in their garrets and must beg for the leftovers from the table of polite society. That's why their creations so often lack that majesty, that gigantic power which is not to be denied and carries all before it. I referred earlier to Enevoldsen. And, with God as my judge, I have the utmost admiration for his talent. For example, I regard his 'Creation' as a lyrical masterpiece. And yet—is this not also true?—He works in filigree, bewitching tricks of the mind, beautiful statues instead of great monuments. I mean, for three days he will sit and worry his head over an adjective. The problem is that he has never really seen the world in all its epic scale and splendor. That is the heart of the matter! . . . Ah to be rich . . . to be rich! . . . to have riches!"

Now Ivan also eased back into the sofa, placed both hands behind his head and slid one of his feet underneath the opposite leg, thus revealing a red silk stocking.

"Rich? But I thought you *were* rich," Per remarked drily—more for something to say than anything else.

"Oh, rich! . . . No, I'm talking about having millions to play around with ... mountains of gold sovereigns to get rid of as and when you pleased! The geniuses in our midst should be lauded and garlanded as minor deities; they should hold court, go hunting and stage masked balls, take lovers ... Think of Rubens! Think of Goethe! Think of Voltaire!"

Salomon leaned across the table in order to fill up Per's glass once again. He then attempted to extricate more information from his dinner guest about himself and his plans for the future. For he had discovered from a mutual acquaintance, who was an engineering student at the College of Engineering, that the common view amongst Per's fellow students was that he was engaged in developing some great technical innovation; and it was to Ivan's great sorrow that he had been unable to prize any information from Per in this matter, so that he might have a pretext to offer his support.

But now, more than ever, Per was of no mind to be on such intimate terms with his host. Instead, he simply pretended that he did not understand where the conversation was going. When he had eventually finished eating, he simply lit a cigar, puffed smoke rings into the air, and gave up any pretense of actually listening to his dinner companion's utterances.

Per's thoughts, goaded by the good wine, drifted away in search of the woman he had met at the carnival. Fru Engelhardt was her name. As his eyes followed the whirls of smoke from his cigar, the shapes evolving therein transformed themselves into profusions of flowers, then a fine billowing alcove curtain through which he was offered glimpses of her full figure in all its naked splendor. With a start, he realized that he was completely smitten. If he was to be completely honest with himself, he mused, his feelings for her up to that point had been no different to those he usually felt when in the presence of beautiful and full-bodied women. The only thing which had cooled his ardor slightly was her age. Yes, she was a young wife, but not exactly a girl anymore, although his guess was that she still had not reached her thirties. But so what? The glance from her dark brown eyes, soft and deep as perfectly formed chestnuts—her audacious stature in that gorgeous columbine pattern dress, her sculpted shoulders and that little button nose with its flaring nostrils—all this betrayed a youthful ardor, an inherent drive to abandon herself to her passions, which rendered the question of age and years meaningless.

Suddenly his gaze fell upon the gentleman with the gold pince-nez who had finally put his newspaper to one side and was calling the waiter to pay for the bill. As their eyes met, both men rose slightly out of their seats and gave ceremonial greetings to each other.

"My God, that's Neergaard!" Salomon exclaimed. "Do know you him?"

"Actually no ... I met him by chance at the carnival."

"What? Were you there too? ... I didn't see you."

"Well the place was absolutely jammed. So you were there too Salomon?"

"I was indeed. Playing Hamlet! You obviously didn't see me, or recognize me."

Per could well remember having seen a little man dressed in black who was in the company of a lady dressed as the Snow Queen. She, for her part, had aroused no little indignation amongst the other ladies present, partly because of her daring décolleté arrangement and because of her ostentatious show of diamonds, which hung like hoar frost within her white veil, reflecting all the colors of the rainbow as they played in the light.

"You were in the company of a lady?" Per ventured to ask.

"Yes—my sister!"

"Ah ..."

In the meantime, the gentleman with the gold pince-nez was putting on his overcoat, assisted by the waiter. It was with no little envy that Per observed both the attention to detail in his sartorial elegance and the man of the world superiority with which he allowed the waiter to bring his hat and cane before concluding the little drama with a flourish of his hand to signal his need of a light for his cigarette. During the previous evening's festivities, Per had only managed to exchange some common pleasantries with this man. Shortly after his first dance with Fru Engelhardt, the gentleman had suddenly appeared by their sides and introduced himself. After that, the man had kept a watch on them from a distance, to the extent that Per finally took him to be a fellow suitor for the lady's hand.

In order to make his exit from the restaurant, Hr. Neergaard was obliged to pass the table occupied by Per and Ivan Salomon, at which point Salomon flapped his hand in a familiar gesture and shouted: "Good evening, Neergaard ... Good evening sir ... how's life treating you?"

Hr. Neergaard's eyebrows were raised in an expression of complete surprise at this overfamiliar outburst. He then gave a patronizing smile and acknowledged the greeting with a careless nod, without even bothering to extract the cigarette from his mouth. On the other hand, he greeted Per with an almost exaggerated politeness, who was thereby in turn obliged to give an acknowledgment.

"What kind of fellow do we actually have there?" Per asked after his departure.

Salomon shrugged his shoulders.

"Don't really know what I should say ... I basically don't know him that well. Only really meet him at this or that ball or function. He was, at one time, quite a distinguished personage. He is a law graduate, is always spoken well of and has excellent connections with people that matter ... in short, has been presented with many outstanding opportunities to make a big fish of himself in our relatively small pond. In fact, there was talk of a position being opened for him in the diplomatic service ... at the London embassy I believe. The Prince of Wales himself is supposed to have suggested that this would be to his liking. I don't know what it was that upset the apple cart. But the bottom line is that he declined the offer of a position. He is without doubt something of a rare breed. Now holds nothing more than a modest position in one of the ministries."

The very next day, Per received the invitation to the ball promised him by Fru Engelhardt and he now busied himself with improving his wardrobe so as to ensure that he might stand comparison with the finest of his fellow cavaliers as he made his entry into Copenhagen's high society circuit. Thus, there was nothing else for it but to obtain the necessary funds via a credit arrangement. To this end, one of his acquaintances from the Cauldron introduced him to a retired farmer who had the habit of feathering his equity nest by lending to young people at sixty percent interest, with security being demanded in the form of their life insurance policies, books, furniture, birth and vaccination certificates, all augmented by a solemn, witnessed declaration of good intent on the part of the prospective debtor, and with his hand placed on the Bible.

Madam Olufsen's eyes were as large as saucers when she saw the many new things arriving daily at the house from the town's most eminent department stores. She and her husband had long discussions about all this "to-ing and fro-ing" and their conclusion was that something was definitely up. Per himself kept his own counsel. He had overall been quite reticent in the last while and, apart from that, was hardly ever at home.

The only one who could have shed some light on events was the even more reticent Trine. With the heightened perception that comes with the thousand eyes of love, this girl—as far as her limited understanding of these things went—established very quickly what was afoot and, with increasing regularity, she would retire to the outhouse privy, which was her place of retreat when she could no longer ignore her sore heart or stop the tears from flowing.

Despite all this, it was perhaps with even greater care and a clearer sense of devotion that she pottered about in his small rooms and attended to his personal belongings. Her loving care was especially bestowed on all the newly purchased items, which she took to be his betrothal finery. It was as if her own future happiness depended on it. She sewed labels onto the fine linen garments, on the handkerchiefs and on the waferthin silk stockings and also placed clean paper in the unlocked bottom drawers of the commode, where they were all to be stored. When the evening of the ball arrived, it was also Trine who was obliged to tie his white cravat, button his gloves, tell him whether his new coat tails were sitting correctly at the back, and reassure him that his machine-clipped hair really suited him. And when the clock struck half past eight and the carriage that had been ordered failed to appear, it was of course herself who was branded a fool, and herself who had to venture out, bareheaded and without a shawl, into the dark sleety evening, all the way down to Adelgade to call a replacement.

The dance had already begun when Per entered the ballroom itself. A dozen or so couples were dancing around the floor with an air of ceremony about them, while a similar number either stood or sat along the walls of the room. It was amongst this latter group that he quickly spied Fru Engelhardt. She was dressed in fire-red silk and was fanning herself with a large fan, which had feathers at its peaks. A gentleman sat by her side. He was completely bald and could be seen rocking his collapsible cylinder hat on his knee—Neergaard.

The sight of this man, and more especially the pangs of jealousy which he then felt, the fact that this man's presence might also be due to Fru Engelhardt's enticing correspondence, completely ruined his mood. In the first quarter of an hour, he would not even grace the ballroom with his presence, preferring a decampment to some adjoining rooms where a group of older gentlemen were playing cards. Only towards the end of the first waltz would he deign to go in again. He then bowed stiffly to her as an invitation to dance. At no point did he establish eye contact with his fellow cavalier. She seemed at first reluctant to acknowledge him. At last, however, she rose, gathered her train about her, and with a somewhat motherly mien swept her bountiful body into his arms.

"My what an ungrateful so and so you are," she said, in her un-apologetically strong Copenhagen accent, when they had danced a couple of circuits without a single word emanating from Per's lips. "You don't even thank me for getting you the invitation. And it was no easy task let me tell you."

"I am extremely grateful to you Frue!"

"My, aren't we formal! Has something upset you?"

"Yes—slightly."

"And what might that be . . . assuming you can tell a lady?"

"Why is that man Neergaard here? I don't like him. You would be doing me a great service by refraining from dancing with him."

"Well, really! ... You are certainly not slow in setting your stall out."

She laughed, but at the same time leant her full weight into his body.

Then it was Per's turn to laugh. This clandestine token of intimacy, the fragrance from her hair and her partially exposed bosom resting against his chest, set him momentarily on fire. They danced around the ballroom for several more turns and by the time he led her back to her seat, Neergaard had disappeared. He saw him sometime later standing at the other end of the room, courting the attention of a quite young girl with long, corn-blond plaits down her back.

The ball then proceeded at a sluggish pace, and without much apparent enjoyment, other than that shown by the house servants who were occasionally allowed to peek into the ballroom from behind a door. It was only after the assembled gentlemen noticed that certain liquid refreshments had been laid on for them in some of the side rooms that the occasion began to find some spark.

It should be pointed out that the gentlemen in question were something of a mixed bag and quite lacking in the finer social graces. This is very often what happens when otherwise cultured families, having no sons of their own, must press ball gallants into service via friends and friends of friends without any guarantees as to good breeding other than the address of the individual concerned.

These invited gentlemen felt no obligation towards their hosts. They were at liberty to behave as they pleased, yawn, criticize alleged shortcomings, and generally be as demanding as they would be in a public place of entertainment.

The host, a small white-haired man who even himself did not know the names of his guests, moved in a state of angst around the rooms as if he were the greatest stranger of all. With a forced "society occasion" smile on his lips, he persevered with the prime duty demanded of him by the lady of the house and her daughters, namely to get the ball cavaliers to "work the rounds." Whenever he found a gentleman standing at his ease in front of one of the paintings in the sitting room, or tarrying too long at the refreshment stand, he would sidle up to him and begin a conversation, which always started in a quite innocent fashion with some remark on the visual arts, the theater, or whether it was cold enough for skating on the canals, but without fail ended with his charge being led back to the dancing room where he was then presented to one of the older female patrons of the house who was bereft of a male consort.

Fru Engelhardt had promised to keep the evening's final dance, the *cotillion*, for Per. But after he had eaten and the dance had begun, he sought her both in the ballroom and the adjoining rooms without success. He found her finally in a small dimly lit alcove, which formed part of a hexagonal turret room on the other side of the sitting room. She was sitting all alone in the corner of a sofa, which was arranged in such a position that it was concealed from view, unless one actually entered the room itself.

She received him with a gentle but tired and melancholy air, saying that now he would no doubt be cross with her, but the fact was that she could not face any more dancing and she could not, of course, demand of him that he too should quit the ball in order to sit there and entertain her. That kind of sacrifice she just would not accept ... he must not under any circumstances feel beholden to her.

For all his inexperience in the mores of high society, Per was not so stupid as to misunderstand her intentions. He shoved a chair alongside her, and for a while they both sat quietly while the music and general hubbub from the ballroom washed over them—softened substantially as it was by having to pass two or three large rooms on its way to them. Then Per suddenly took her hand, which had been left at liberty on the arm of the sofa, and when she offered no resistance he declared his love for her in very frank and direct words and repeated his previous request for a romantic assignation. At last, she promised to submit to his wishes and he bent across her white arm and placed kisses, once, twice, three times above her elbow. He had, in fact, assumed that she would rebuff these premature and audacious advances and she did, in truth, give a warning that she would be extremely cross with him if he tried that again—but the bright sheen of joy in her eyes and the palpable animation in her ample breasts served to contradict the words coming from her mouth.

But just at that moment, footsteps could be heard in the outer room. Per just managed to fling himself back in his seat when Neergaard's long shape showed itself in the door opening. He gave a polite and apologetic bow, but remained standing there with his hands behind his back, as if pondering the wisdom of entering the room.

"Do come in," Fru Engelhardt said.

"Are you in need of company?" Neergaard asked, in a manner which Per did not like—it was almost gruff in its delivery.

"Ah, not really I suppose, but if you have some entertaining tale or ditty to recount, we would love to hear it."

"Well, given that you and Hr. Engineer Sidenius are obviously so lacking in entertainment . . . quite abandoned by the world you both are."

"Yes," she said, as she waved her fan listlessly and leaned back into the corner of the sofa. "It is a pain I admit . . . tiredness overcame me . . . I came over all faint, what with the dancing and all those people. But you Neergaard? Why are you not dancing? After all, you've not wanted for potential partners."

"Ah no Frue, on the contrary," he said—as he finally took the decision to move into the room—"I believe that I too should retreat into this kind of atmospheric gloom and get used to the idea of not being part of the dance anymore. May I?"

He wheeled a chair over to the sofa from the opposite side of where Per sat. In this way, the two men came to sit face to face without even having greeted each other. At which point, Fru Engelhardt suddenly found her tongue. She launched into an attack on the guest list, but waxed lyrical about the supper provided, before then moving on to the varying standards of "toilette" and "etiquette" shown by the ladies that evening. Per simply sat there, observing Neergaard and saying nothing. Neergaard was equally taciturn. He had bent forward slightly in his chair so that his face was no longer visible. His elbows now rested on his knees and his long hands—which betrayed a slight shake—played with the gloves which he had removed.

"My God Neergaard, you really have turned into such a bore," she suddenly exclaimed, breaking off from the flow of her own conversation. "You, of all people, who was always the life and soul of the party. Come on, do tell us the secret. What has happened to you?...I take it that there is a lady involved."

"You may be right there madam."

"Ah, I bet it's that Frøken Holm! Sweet little thing she is. Of course! She is just up your street sir. It's only fair to enlighten you Hr. Sidenius. Hr. Neergaard was once honest and entertaining enough to admit to me that he finds any blond and blue-eyed beauty quite impossible to resist. And to cap it all, this particular one is from the country," she said, turning again to Neergaard. "She is the essence of daisies and clover, summer sunshine and full cream milk...the perfect dairy maid you have always wanted sir. When can we expect to hear wedding bells?"

Hr. Neergaard, who had lifted his head during this repartee, now leaned back in his chair, placed his hat over his stomach and then his hands on top of it and, with an almost breathless sigh, said: "The wisest thing, perhaps, when you get to my age, is to face the fact that you have at least one foot in the grave. All that remains is to ensure that you have a decent burial."

Fru Engelhardt laughed.

"Oh come now...what a bleak view of the world! What would we poor ladies do if every man carried on so? Look at Hr. Frick, the retired captain in the cavalry. He is sixty-two and still dances like a young lieutenant. And I have no doubt that he is still something of a conquistador with the ladies. Ah no, men of your age still have things to look forward to."

Neergaard bowed his head in acknowledging her words.

"I thank you Frue for your kind words despite the fact they have the ring of a graveside oration. Of course, I am aware that nowadays the skill in preserving the bloom of youth has been developed—by both men and women—into a fine art so that even those of an advanced age can seem strikingly fresh faced—just in the same way that we have learned to conserve peas and asparagus and other vegetables. But, to me, the thought of an old, desiccated cavalier on his horse is an abomination. No, a timely exit is the only option, give youth its day, and thereby avoid constant humiliation. And a thousand humiliations await those of us who achieve my vintage. Gout, poor digestion, old man's gruel, kidney stones, the trials of the operation table—this is the reality of life for anyone on the wrong side of his forties."

"But the memories," Fru Engelhardt said softly. "All those great memories you have Neergaard . . . have you forgotten them?"

"Memories? Hm! Are they not also in a kind of petrified state, brought down from the shelf to provide some meager sunshine in the winter of life—a reminder of the summer that disappeared so quickly? No madam, please do not talk to me about memories! They are just something else to plague the spirit . . . memories are the very thing which make us feel that all of life's subsequent events are but more evidence of a vanishing tide, a wearisome and fading recurrence of what once was."

"My dear Neergaard you are simply impossible tonight. But I forgive you. You are obviously out of sorts . . . there's some kind of kink there. You really should see a doctor. He will almost certainly recommend a trip to the hot springs at Carlsbad to get things back in line."

"Perhaps madam. Or perhaps some of those world-renowned lead tablets . . . a revolver full at a time. Nothing beats them where pain killers are concerned."

"Oh for God's sake! I am not talking to you anymore. You just won't take anything seriously!"

As if watching a tennis match, Per had shifted his attention backwards and forwards between the two speakers throughout the whole of their verbal exchange. The convivial tone of their discourse had once again left him slightly uneasy as he mused on the relationship that existed between them; but he reassured himself by recalling that Fru Engelhardt had already told him on the night of the carnival that she and Neergaard had known each other since childhood. Besides which, her whole attitude towards him—not to mention the sarcasm underlying her recommendation of a stay in far-flung Carlsbad—clearly pointed to one thing, and one thing only, and that was how his obdurate behavior had annoyed her immensely.

At this point, however, the adjoining rooms came alive with the sound of breathless dancing partners throwing themselves down onto the chairs by the refreshment tables. The ball was coming to an end. That said, there were still at least three or four couples who were too in love and caught up in the occasion to let the music stop and they danced to its frantic tattoo in an ever quickening tempo so that dust whirled from their feet.

Outside, the carriages began to maneuver up to the front entrance. Fru Engelhardt then went round bidding farewell to everyone with her arm linked to her husband's. This man was a tall and stout wholesaler with a jovial demeanor who had spent the whole evening at one of the card tables. When they passed the place where Per was sitting, and to his extreme consternation, Fru Engelhardt actually stopped and introduced the two gentlemen to each other. Her husband shook his hand and passed a few polite comments. Per, for his part, felt extremely uncomfortable and could not bring himself to make eye contact.

Why, for heaven's sake, had she done that?—he wondered anxiously, just as he overheard her speaking to her husband in a deliberately loud voice amongst the throng of departing guests: "Is it not next Tuesday you're off to London darling?"

The wholesaler answered this point in the affirmative. And Per reddened visibly and smiled. It was a smile that got ever broader as he turned quite pale and his wide-eyed gaze followed her white Amazon shoulders framing that fire-red silk dress. Ah yes. Life was now really beginning for him in earnest!

As the clock struck three, Neergaard and Per made their way home in the moonlit night. Per had no wish to be accompanied, but when the two men took leave of the ball and Neergaard had asked him where he lived—and did it not make sense to go home together given that they lived so near to each other?—he was hardly in a position to say no. And at least he had the pleasure of accepting this offer as a final acknowledgment of his victory in the battle for Fru Engelhardt's favors—a white flag. There was also the undeniable fact that he had been overwhelmed by the urbane politeness his erstwhile opponent had at all times shown him despite the huge age gap between them.

Neergaard began talking about the party, and about social events in general, but Per was too wrapped up in himself and the events of the evening to really take in what was being said. In spite of the sharp frost and the long walk that was ahead of them—Neergaard was already staggering slightly—Per had thrown open his coat. His conquest and subsequent feelings of superiority had made him positively hot. With a contented smile on his face, he blew out smoke rings into the clear air as he walked.

They turned away from the canal at Holmen's bridge and then proceeded along the left side of Kongens Nytorv. They then passed the National Bank, whose imposing contours rose before them into the sky like some great ancient tomb. A sentry in a red cape guarded the entrance to this grave yet elegant monument to mammon.

Shortly afterwards, Neergaard stopped in front of one of the old, narrow and dilapidated houses, which lived on borrowed time along this broad and distinguished thoroughfare.

"Well, here is my humble abode. Would Hr. Sidenius not consider honoring my home with his presence and partaking of a glass of wine? It is not that late after all."

Per hesitated but then said yes. He wanted the night to live on for some time yet and was in no mood to return to his quarters. From that day, when he had locked his drawings into the upper drawer in his commode, he had moved around in his own rooms with a feeling of dread, as if he had buried a corpse under his own floorboards.

Soon he found himself comfortably ensconced in the corner of a sofa, which lay behind a large table. A high-necked lamp with a green silk screen burned upon the table. While Neergaard rummaged in the adjoining room in search of suitable drinks, Per ran the rule over what was obviously a very well-appointed and elegant bachelor apartment. He could not help but make comparisons with his own tiny and impoverished home. How on earth was he supposed to entertain a lady like Fru Engelhardt in such a place? He noted that the room was completely carpeted. His inquisitive eyes also took in the carved mahogany furniture, the vases and gold-plated candelabra. There was no doubt that these things had been handed on to him as part of an inheritance. And across the dimly lit room, on the opposite wall, he could discern a set of small and large pictures representing a veritable army of portraits: paintings in gilt-edge frames, daguerreotypes, engravings, small ivory pendants, lithographs, hand-drawn likenesses and modern photographs ... a long cortege depicting the dead generations of the Neergaard line.

This funereal air was emphasized for Per when, on closer inspection, he noticed that everything in the room bore the mark of a growing neglect. The carpet was nearly worn out and the furniture covers faded beyond repair. There were also a number of cracks in the glass panes of the large beautiful book cabinet, which contained an impressive range of bound books.

Neergaard then appeared to curtail his musings. He was carrying a long-necked bottle and two large green goblets. He sat down in an armchair opposite Per and took great care in pouring out two measures into the glasses.

"I am delighted to have made your acquaintance," he said, as he lifted his glass. "Allow me the honor to toast your health, Hr.... Hr. lucky Per! The Fortunate Man personified indeed."

Per shot him a glance. He was taken aback and slightly annoyed at this direct allusion to the evening's events. But given that the intention was to crown him as Victor Ludorum, he was reluctant to reveal his displeasure. He grabbed his glass and gulped down the wine.

"I am, however, obliged to hold up my hands and admit that your not particularly witty nickname is not my own invention," Neergaard continued as he proceeded to polish his glasses. "It is actually one of your friends that I am quoting ... that little fellow Salomon whom I saw in your company the other day. He is a great admirer of yours. My own view is that the appellation can be a double-edged sword. There is an old saying that good fortune is the preserve of fools. And an esteemed Latin author wrote that luck is the begetter of sorrow."

Aye, Per thought to himself: Seek ye your crumbs of comfort! They are yours to keep!

"But for the fact that it sounds like an abominable paradox," Neergaard continued, "I would say outright that the miserable seem to me to be the most fortunate of all. After all, they have the satisfaction of being able to damn their fate, insult the good Lord himself, hold providence to account and so on—while they whom, as they say, Lady Luck smiles upon may only bemoan their fate when their luck occasionally deserts them."

"But why would anyone want to be the victim of misfortune?" Per inquired, smiling to himself, as he watched the smoke from his cigar.

"Why?" Neergaard asked, whose whole tone was tinged with a tone of soft pity, even though Per was not receptive to its particular timbre. "I believe you don't quite grasp my point, Hr. Engineer! My belief— despite my aversion to paradoxes—is that luck itself is actually the greatest turn of ill luck that could ever affect a human being because . . . well, because we human beings in nine hundred and ninety nine cases out of a thousand lack the ability to make sure that our great fortune does not do us more harm than good. In our day and age, we are no longer instructed in the art of handling the magic that life has to offer us—that's the truth of it. Lady Luck invites us to a sumptuous feast but we decide we'd rather be peasants at the king's banquet. When all is said and done, we all prefer homemade porridge and our little mother's pancakes, regardless of the dazzling delights that confront us in Aladdin's Cave. I presume you know the tale of the young swineherd who wins the princess's hand and half the kingdom with her. It ends, in my opinion, just at the point where it starts to get interesting—at least where we adults are concerned. We should have been allowed to follow this clodhopper in his velvet slippers and brocade waistcoat as he went round and became progressively paler and scrawny from his pot of good luck. We should have seen him lying in the princess's silken sheets, whimpering in his longing for Daisy the milkmaid and the thought of her hefty arms around him. For there is no doubt that this is the way that things would have ended up. Not one hour would have passed without heartache for him, until he once again stepped into his farm clogs and abandoned his crown and scepter in favor of his father's manure fork."

Neergaard had put his glasses on again and sat back in his chair, the fingers of his long hands folded beneath his chin. His lackluster eyes rested on Per with a look that was at once inquisitive and engaged and yet bore a slight angst, as he continued: "For all our celebrated Danish fantasizing, we all retain an immovable partiality for the tried and tested. Regardless of how fervently we, in our young days, rush to embrace the magic and all-encompassing wonder of life . . . the moment that wonderland opens its gates to us and the king's daughter beckons to us from her balcony, we become filled with doubt and turn to look back at that familiar seat by the stove."

"You are probably right," said Per. He was still studying the depths of his cigar smoke with a smile on his lips. "That's probably the way things will turn out for most people. But there are always exceptions to the rule."

"Not one in a thousand, Hr. Engineer. Perhaps not one in ten thousand! One day you yourself will discover the kind of dark power that the force of habit and the echoes of home exert upon us, even though we might perhaps hate them at the same time. For example, look around you right here sir! There we go, plodding on through life and dragging with us an accumulation of remnants left to us by our ancestors, all of which stacks up around us like the Great Wall of China, but we just cannot face the idea of parting with any of it. We make ourselves cozy in a mausoleum full of family heirlooms and, in the end, we have no other feelings left to cling on to, save those of filial piety."

"Well, perhaps—but that cannot be true of everybody," said Per. "I for one could hardly be tempted by that particular devil. Because the things that I can drag around with me from my past would just about fit in my breast pocket."

"Then I congratulate you! But then, what help is that really? The power of the spell that family and home holds over us is not just about material things. For we allow our possibly long dead father's meaningless exhortations, or a simple mother's prejudices, to influence our actions right up to our own old age. And then on top of that we have our dear brothers and sisters and fretting uncles and aunts."

"But for my part anyway, I happen to be quite fortunate in that regard as well, because with my background I will never be caught in that situation."

"Well then, I must once again congratulate you. But, with respect, you must have come from some kind of home . . . and presumably one of those famous Danish vicarages which are so renowned for their coziness. Actually, I must admit that I am drawing this conclusion from your surname—if I am not mistaken?"

Per let this last remark pass by as if he had not heard it and said that he did not know—and had never known what was commonly called next of kin.

"No, really! Are you, perhaps, a—."

"Yes," said Per, deliberately cutting across him. "I stand alone and on my own two feet in this world."

"Well, I never!" Neergaard leaned forward with his hands on the chair's armrests and stared at Per in wonder and astonishment. "So little Salomon has a point after all. There really is the sense of mystery and adventure about you. No family worries! No brothers or sisters to plague you! No well-meaning uncles and busybody aunts. Free as a lark in the clear air!"

Per's refusal to comment was simply confirmation that this was indeed so.

Neergaard sank once again back into the armchair, and a moment's deep silence followed.

"You really do seem to have been blessed by providence Hr. Sidenius. Were I not so old and decrepit, I might even be tempted to envy you in all your good fortune. Not only free but carefree in all matters of family and society. And with a hunger for life's bounty that's as urgent as a blackbird in a cherry tree. Yes, that's just how it should be! But then? What help is it? Even if we are not born with chains, we seem to feel an urge to make chains for ourselves as life progresses. We are, and will ever be, a band of slaves. We only ever feel really at home when we are in chains and shackled—what would you say to that now?"

"To be honest, I can't quite follow your drift," Per said, as he looked up at the clock on the book cabinet, which told him that the time was beyond half past four. He had begun to tire of the monotone nature of the conversation. He had also begun to fear that he had let his tongue run away with him in his replies.

Another short while passed before Neergaard answered. Still, he maintained his preoccupied and tense gaze while looking across at Per.

"My drift? The drift of my thoughts?...Hah, we acquire friends and habits and, as time goes on, allow ourselves to be hamstrung by all kinds of commitments and obligations. That is before we even begin to touch on the stuff that binds men and women together, which we prefer to glorify by calling it love, affection, our natural instinct, or whatever you will. Even such a free spirit as your good self must admit that women have arms which, in spite of their softness, can wrap themselves around a man like an iron vice."

"Ah now, not to the extent that it would annoy me," said Per, who laughed out loud. "And least of all when you are in a really tight clinch with them."

"Yes, you are young yet. But stay with my point—see if by some chance it should befall you that some woman or other whom you desired purely physically, even though you at the same time possibly hated her...a tart perhaps, or some big bosomed Bessie, who you in the innocence of your youth had kissed...in short, a creature to whom you felt attached out of pure habit or fond memories...see now if this woman were to betray you in a particularly coldblooded fashion, behind your back. How would that free spirit react in such circumstances?"

Where is he going with all this? Per thought to himself. But out loud he said: "What would I do? Why, just go and get another one."

"Very good! But what if the new one should prove to be less than satisfactory—and you have to admit that there's always that risk—what then?"

"Well, I'd just take a third, a fourth, a fifth...for God's sake Hr. Neergaard, there's no shortage of women in this world!"

"Yes, that is true!...That is so true!"

He went on repeating these words, closing his eyes as he did so as if he had discovered the secret of the Holy Grail itself.

Per stirred himself in order to signal his imminent departure. The conversation had become a bit too personal for his liking. It was also getting very late. A couple of bakers' wagons had already been heard dashing along the street outside, heralding as they did so the breaking of a new dawn.

But Neergaard became suddenly gripped by a strange exhilaration. He refilled Per's glass and begged him to forget about the lateness of the hour.

"I count myself truly fortunate to have made your acquaintance Hr. Sidenius. You really are a breath of fresh air and also very enjoyable company. I hope you will not be offended if I raise a certain issue with you—a proposal if you like."

What now? thought Per.

Neergaard explained that though this issue might, on the face of it, seem rather strange, from what he now knew of Per he was sure that he would accept the whole thing in the right spirit. All this was to do with one of his friends, a close relative, who was dying. He was terminally ill ... his time was very short ... he was sick both in soul and body. Never mind that. That wasn't the heart of the matter. A long story short then: This man, who had never married, was in a quandary as to what he should do with his worldly remains—which, by the way, amounted to no more than some furniture, a pair of poor paintings, a few books ... in fact not unlike what you see around you here. One thing was sure—he was not going to hand them on to his family. He did not want them put in places where they risked becoming objects of veneration. He has made it explicitly clear that the whole kit and caboodle should be put up for auction and sold—spread to the four winds. This had now become an obsession with the poor man and, given that his own people were well to do, and besides which were more than likely to oppose his wishes, because most of what he owned was inherited, he had then begun to talk about leaving it all to someone who might benefit from it more, or at least enjoy some fleeting moments of pleasure thereby.

"Now it occurs to me . . . may I not propose your name to him? I am convinced that, if he knew you, the same thing would occur to him. You are precisely the kind of person he so often wanted to be himself. Free and frank and without a care in the world. No, please . . . as long as you have no objections to my proposal, please don't say anything. It's agreed and there won't be another word about it. As I say, the whole thing doesn't amount to much . . . it is probably no more than a few thousand crowns, that's after debts and other obligations have been reconciled."

He must be drunk as a lord, thought Per, who felt that raising any objection to the idea was just not worth the bother. Instead, he made a joke of the whole thing.

"Well—I suppose it's better than a slap in the face!" he said. "Money always comes in handy, wherever it's from. But I really must get home sir. Thank you for the entertainment!"

"Ah no Hr. Sidenius, you are not leaving? Stay a bit longer! . . . it's so stuffy in here. We'll let some air in. That's it!" Neergaard rose awkwardly and threw a window open, allowing cold air to stream into the room, which immediately aroused the glow in the glass lamp. A long smoky tongue of flame briefly illuminated the whole room. "Do sit down again! I know that we've sat here and all the talk has been so melancholy. But the bottle is not empty, and it's good wine, you have to say."

But Per would not be persuaded a second time. He had begun to feel a slight unease at his host's rising agitation. He also noticed for the first time the pallor in his face and how clammy his hand was—a hand that shook slightly as they took leave of each other.

So many strange people in the world! Per mused to himself, as he finally escaped into the street and, with a freshly lit cigar in his mouth, struck up a steady pace through the town, which was now truly coming to life. Thoughts came flooding back to him recalling the night-time scene in the Cauldron with the larger than life Fritjof. As soon as they get you on their own, they can't wait to tell you about some great dread that hangs over them. They already have one foot in the grave. And then they deliver their own graveside sermon, damn them!

Here and there in the gray morning mist, men could be seen lifting rubbish and sweeping the streets. Small licensed premises in cellars and down stairways were opening for business, along with a single tobacco kiosk. All the street lanterns were now extinguished, but soft lights spilled out onto the street from all the baker's shops and the aroma of freshly baked bread filled the air, tempting passers-by to stop and gaze at the large display windows. Outside one such shop, Per himself stopped for a moment and became witness to a scene just unfolding between a sweet little bakery maid, who was perched up a stepladder easing some cake plates onto a shelf, and a half-naked apprentice baker who sat below her on the counter, his legs dangling to and fro. Per could not hear what passed between them but the apprentice's wide grin and the feigned indignation of the young girl, who was using her foot to fend off his hands, made all words redundant.

Per smiled, while his own thoughts tangled with Fru Engelhardt in exactly the same way. Yes, the night was over now. Life was waking to a new day and yet the urge to love, and be loved, could banish thoughts of breakfast and breaking bread. Then the factory horns began to blow. He stopped and listened with the air of a worshipper being called to prayer. At first there was just a couple of blasts coming from the direction of Nørrebro, then one started in the docks at Christianshavn; eventually the sound was coming from everywhere—a cock crowing with a thousand voices, an Evangelium for a new age, which one day would drive away all the dark forces of spookery and superstition—never to return!

4

ABOUT a week later, on a gloomy, foggy evening, a thin gentleman in gray apparel alighted from a tram at the corner of Grønningen, went past Husar barracks and proceeded to walk across the lengthy, triangular square leading to the Nyboder quarter. With one hand behind his back and the other gripping the handle of an umbrella, with which he forcefully struck the pavement at each stride, the gentleman moved with vigor and a steady rhythm through the streets of the area. As he walked, the man would stop for a moment and scrutinize each new street sign, which was illuminated by the feeble glow from a street lamp.

With each row of houses in each street completed, without finding the name he was looking for, and when in this desolate place there proved to be not a soul that might help him on his way, the gentleman turned a corner at random and quickly found himself completely astray in the warren of tightly knit and identical streets for which Nyboder was renowned. All the windows in the low-slung sitting rooms facing on to the street had their shutters in place. There was nothing more than a small round, or heart-shaped, peephole in each shutter, and street lights were even fewer than those found on the outer square. That said, life behind these shutters was lively enough. For there was a general hubbub of conversation to be heard, as well as the cries of children and, here and there, music from a harmonica. Indeed, every word that was uttered within was clear to any passer-by. Of a sudden, a door might be flung open and a housewife clad in her nightgown would empty a chamber pot into the gutter, or a little dog would be let out. Cats also ran by and performed courting rituals or struck up a chorus.

Eventually, the gray-suited man happened upon a solitary individual with whom he could make inquiries and thus make his way to Hjertensfrydgade, where with the help of matches he read the numbers above the doors in the street until he reached the house in which Per lived. At first, he fumbled with his hand looking for a bell wire and when this was to no avail, he set about the old-fashioned door latch, finally worked out how it opened the door and stepped into the house's tiny lobby. It was so dark that he could not see his own hand in front of him. With the intention of alerting the house's occupants as to his presence, he gave several exaggerated coughs.

At this point, the door leading to the downstairs living quarters was opened. A young ship's carpenter and his family lived here. A fledgling housewife, who carried a baby at her breast, looked out into the lobby. The light from a lamp in the room shone above her severely combed head and threw the stranger's facial features into stark relief. He had a young, but rather long and pale face with red-rimmed eyes and a small clump of whiskers below his ears.

"Am I right in saying that Hr. Sidenius lives here?" he asked, without prefacing his question with any kind of greeting.

"Yes that's right, sir—he lives there in the back chambers. But he is not at home."

"I see!...would I be talking to the mistress of the house?"

"No. He's renting from the Olufsens up above...I'll call up to Madam."

At that moment, the steeply inclined staircase began to creak under the weight of a ponderous step, and Madam Olufsen, who had been standing and listening from behind the door up above, revealed herself on the landing with a small tin lamp in her hand.

"Does the good gentleman wish to speak with Hr. Sidenius?" she asked.

"Yes, but I presume he is not here," the stranger replied in a tone which suggested that he held her personally responsible for his wasted journey. "Is there any point in waiting for him, in your view?"

"No, I'm afraid not. It's not that long since he left."

"What time of day is most likely to find him indoors, in your view?"

"Well now, see, he doesn't spend much time at home just at present. But I would say that early evening is the best time for catching him at home."

"Thank you. Goodbye."

"Who shall I say called?" Madam Olufsen asked.

But the stranger had already turned and disappeared through the door. The sound of his steady footfall and the smack from the tip of his umbrella as it hit the pavement could be heard gradually fading as he moved down the street.

"He had the cut of a priest," said the diminutive ship carpenter's wife with no little concern in her voice. "Why is he looking for Hr. Engineer Sidenius d'ye think?"

But on this occasion, Madam Olufsen was in no mood to discuss the affairs of her lodger. She gave a short "good night" and returned to her own chambers.

Here, the Senior Boatswain was to be found with a pair of large silver spectacles perched on his nose as he read *The Runaway Negro Slave, or Shipwrecked on the Coast of Malabar*, a novel he would bring home with him each winter from Miss Jordan's booklenders and which he would scrutinize with the same wonder and excitement as in many other winters gone by.

"Sounded like someone looking to speak with Sidenius," he asked, without lifting his eyes from his book.

"Indeed and it was," Madam Olufsen answered, pulling her shoulder shawl tightly round her, as if responding to a sudden chill in the air, and shoveling some scraps of turf into the stove. Then she sat down in her armchair to set about knitting. There had not been much mention of Per between them of late. However, they both privately acknowledged that their lodger had drastically changed his course in the last while and that he was steering straight into a rough headwind. Yes of course he had always been one for cutting loose; but these long bouts of gallivanting, which at one time he had passed off as a bit of a laugh, had never gone on for more than a day or two. Now, though, he had hardly been home in three weeks, and when they did see anything of him, he was taciturn, abrupt and surly to boot. He had even talked about moving out. Nor could the company he was keeping be so choice if it was true, as he had let slip one day, that he had known the senior civil servant, whose name had been all over the papers after he had shot himself.

Then, on top of that, they had another reason to be vexed with him. For not only was his rent in serious arrears, but they were also tortured by a daily stream of irate people coming to their door waving bills from tailors and shoemakers who were owed money. "Who was it exactly down below who wanted to talk to Sidenius?" Senior Boatswain Olufsen finally asked.

"I didn't know him at all. But now that I think on it, I mind seeing him before. A long time ago. If I am not wrong, at that time Sidenius told me it was someone from the New World. But he doesn't look American to me."

As this conversation unfolded, Per was waiting for Fru Engelhardt in the same dark corner of Vor Frue Plads where he had previously stood watch in the hope that she would come. On this occasion, he had better grounds to believe she would actually turn up. While it was true that he had not seen her since the evening of the ball—she had strictly forbidden him from greeting her in the street or, indeed, from attempting any other form of contact with her—but today was the day that her husband was to travel to London, and the previous day he had received a signed note from her saying "Tomorrow Evening." His assumption, therefore, was that the rendezvous point and time would be the same as the last arrangement.

He had, however, received other correspondence that very morning which had animated him to an almost greater degree than this long-awaited tryst. The correspondent was none other than Neergaard's solicitor, who, to his great consternation, informed him that Neergaard had, in a letter to be opened after his death, "bequeathed a certain sum," which would accrue to him "by way of the proceeds from a public auction of the deceased's property, fixtures and fittings, in accordance with said deceased's last will and testament." This will, the letter went on to point out, was not strictly valid in legal terms, as it had not been set out in the prescribed manner; but given the fact that the deceased's two sisters and sole legal beneficiaries were married and of prosperous means, there was no reason to believe that these parties—who at the moment were both domiciled outside of the kingdom—would not consent to the deceased's last wishes. Thus, in his capacity as executor of the deceased's estate, the solicitor requested an interview with Per at a convenient moment when his business affairs brought him in the vicinity of the solicitor's offices.

Per could not decide what his best approach should be to this turn of events. His initial feelings were of embarrassment. For all his fatalistic belief that his star was hitched to Lady Fortune's wagon, and even though money was being thrown into his lap at a time when he could not have needed it more, he just could not bring himself to believe that this final capricious gesture on the part of a suicide represented some kind of heaven-sent succor. On the other hand, he felt that he could hardly refuse such a substantial sum, which would set all his hardships to rights for the foreseeable future. Very little remained of the loan he had raised and yet, despite this, most of his equipment was still not paid for.

But then a closed carriage rolled up besides him from a side street. A hand, adorned by a bright glove, motioned at him from the gloom beyond the window frame and, in one brisk set of movements, Per stopped the carriage, flung the door open and shouted up to the jarvey, giving the name of a restaurant famous for its view across Kongens Nytorv. He then stepped in.

What he experienced during the short carriage journey paved the way for a series of crushing disappointments that night. He had hoped to find his liaison nervous and ill at ease—to observe that under her fur cap she was blushing and quivering from sheer angst and mortification. He had even prepared a few phrases that might conquer her shyness, but he was never given the opportunity to show off his skills in the art of seduction. For Per had barely taken his seat and thanked her for gracing him with her presence when the lady threw herself up on to his lap, like some courtesan, pushing into him with such a violent gusto that he was left almost completely winded.

It has to be said that she did allow her veil to drop over her face as they mounted the brightly lit staircase leading up to the restaurant; but when they were escorted to one of the discreet dining alcoves by the *major domo* and their table waiter, she immediately threw off both cape and hat without showing the slightest deference to the presence of these strangers. Moreover, while Per's actions were stilted and awkward, in what for him was a completely new situation, his dinner partner seemed to feel quite at home there, arranging her hair and cushioning her curls in front of a mirror, pulling off her gloves and plumping her full figure down in the middle of the sofa behind the immaculately laid table.

Per, meanwhile, quietly took his seat on the opposite side of the table. It was obvious to him that this was not the first time she had partaken in this kind of rendezvous. In fact, he was fairly sure that he had seen a knowing smile spread across the face of the bewhiskered waiter when they had first entered the establishment.

"Why are you looking at me in that funny way," she asked, once they were alone, placing her head to one side and pouting in the exaggerated manner of a flirtatious school girl. "My God, you are actually running the rule over me sir! Does my look displease you?"

She looked down at her breasts, which filled the square-cut bosom part of her dress to overflowing. Her look was black and strictly tailored, thus emphasizing her ample upper body and the cut of her waist, which was as slim as a young maiden's. "Well say something then! You are a terrible man altogether. You are like a moody bull or something... Ha ha... let's see if I can get a bull's eye then!"

As she began to pluck red berries from the centerpiece table decoration, to obtain the necessary projectiles, Per's attention was drawn to her hands. His mouth pale and tight with sudden passion, he gazed at their healthy firmness, the soft, dexterous fingers, the clear, lustrous nails like stunning pearls and the little dimples which, as her hands moved, revealed themselves around her delicate knuckles like tiny pink buds only waiting to be kissed. He caught one of the berries she had thrown in midair and captured her hand in the same movement. He was just about to draw her hand across the table to his mouth when the door was thrown open and the waiter and his assistant marched in with the first course.

The champagne was poured and the dishes were presented for their delectation. Once they were left to themselves again, Per smiled and lifted his glass in homage to her. A few more glasses were consumed, by which time his circumspection was completely dispelled. For God's sake, he said to himself, why should he worry about her past? The main thing was that she now belonged to him, was his property, his conquest.

By the time the dessert had arrived, he had begun to speak of Neergaard's suicide. Per offered his considered view that the man was mentally disturbed and finally began to describe their late-night tête-à-tête at his home and Neergaard's frazzled state of mind as he revealed his veiled intentions with regard to his earthly remains. He also pointed out that he could not have known the fatal dynamic that was at play in their conversation. Per then prattled on about certain rumors of there being a woman in the background. For example, an acquaintance of his who hinted that he had gleaned this intelligence from Neergaard's landlord had spoken of a certain lady who for many years had been a regular visitor to his home. Her face was always covered by a veil, and it could be reasonably inferred that this was the same lady who, on the evening before Neergaard's burial, had gained access to the funeral parlor and had strewn a veritable cascade of roses across his coffin.

As Per spoke, Fru Engelhardt sat in a meditative pose with her elbows on the table, while her little finger continually ran around the edge of her wine glass. Her face revealed a half-distracted demeanor. She looked for all the world as if she were listening politely, but without any great interest, to a tale that was a bit too long in the telling for her liking. When Per then went further and began to delve into Neergaard's past and pass on the gossip that told of him turning his back on a promising career as a diplomat, she began to show clear signs of impatience. She took a grape from the fruit bowl, dipped it into her wine and proceeded to suck on it. Then she interrupted him apologetically with a question relating to some other matter entirely, which had suddenly "occurred" to her; almost simultaneously she asked him to ring for the waiter and have the coffee brought in. Finally, when it became obvious to her that Per was still not of a mind to drop the issue, she rose demonstratively from the table, said "the meal was lovely thank you" and went over to the piano.

"What shall I play for you?" she asked after testing the instrument by performing a few quick scales up and down the keys. "Do you know this?" she asked, as a barrage of flat tones was thumped up from the depths of the piano. "Waldtraum!" she declared during the performance, clearly happy herself with the din she was creating.

But Per had once again become withdrawn and taciturn. He could not help but notice the lack of concern she displayed in the fate of this poor soul, even though he had been part of her social set, had worshipped humbly at her feet; indeed, had he not been her escort to the ball the night before he took his own life? Then a vague suspicion flitted across his mind like some dark dread emerging from the shadows: what if Neergaard had been more than that? Was her indifference all a front? But he was given no time to do any more than grab at the thought as it came and went. For, disturbed by his prolonged silence, Fru Engelhardt had abruptly canceled her impromptu concert and stood up. She now approached him from behind and placed her arms around his neck, forcing his head backwards as she did so in order that their eyes could meet. No, it is impossible! thought Per, as he regarded the playfulness dancing in her gaze. And now soft, becalming kisses rained down on his brow, his hair and eyes until her lips finally sought his mouth in a sudden fervor, a signal of her urgent and insistent desire. Then she whispered something into his ear and he rose forthwith. Without waiting for coffee to be served, she scorned any attendance and threw her cape around her while Per paid the bill, after which they hurried downstairs to the waiting cab. Closely entwined and with lips constantly seeking lips, they were conveyed to a hotel, whose guest book would record them as a Hr. and Fru Svendsen from Aarhus.

However, in the long night that followed, as Per lay awake in the half light of the hotel room, his dread suspicion reared up again and again until he finally succumbed to the grip of a terrible waking nightmare. His thoughts flew once again to the time spent in the dead of night in Neergaard's chambers, echoes of the words they exchanged came back to him, words he had dismissed as being of no consequence. And with a grim clarity, the reality of how things stood dawned upon him: that woman who lay sleeping by his side was also part of the estate which Neergaard had bequeathed to him, to have and to hold in perpetuity—indeed, she had been Neergaard's very "lodestar" and her casual indifference to him had driven him over the edge.

And he, yes he himself, had been her willing accomplice!

His overwrought mind conjured forth lurid images of the deceased. Wherever he looked in the room his bare skull would emerge from the shadows and stare balefully at him, as if in mocking pity. And there she was, by his side, the murderess, who had sneaked in like a thief and bestrewn his coffin with roses. There was no other way of explaining it. She slept the sleep of an innocent child in its cradle, her breath rising and falling in long contented drafts. At the very same time as her husband was being tossed about in his bunk on the high seas, and even before her lover's corpse was cold in the grave, she had sought the joys of someone else's embrace. And he, yes he himself, had been her willing accomplice!

Per became gripped by feelings of self-loathing and disgust, a sheer horror, that drove him out of the bed. He had to get up. He would leave right there and then.

At that moment, Fru Engelhardt turned slowly in the bed, threw an arm above her head and spoke in a drowsy voice: "Are you up?"

He gave no answer. Even the sound of her voice made him shudder. She tried to force her eyes open, but the effort was too much for her. And, after a weak attempt at a smile, she turned back into her dreams.

Per, for his part, moved quickly to make good his escape. In all silence, he would disappear without bidding adieu. His plan was to leave a note with the porter down below. One word would suffice by way of explanation: Neergaard.

However, by the time that he stood at the end of the bed with his overcoat on and his hat in his hand, ready to steal away, his gaze could not help but linger once more on the partially exposed figure, which lay in a position of complete abandon. Yes, there she was, lying on her back with both hands under her neck and one knee raised. Those very fine shoulder straps that were meant to keep her underwear in place had slipped down so that the ample, creamy flesh of her breasts was revealed in all its glory. Her dark hair, meanwhile, flowed across the pillow in a frenzy of disarray; her head was slumped down and her face pale and drawn from the night's exertions.

Per felt his heart thumping against his chest. His knees buckled slightly. For he just could not wrest his gaze from the sight before him. The truth was that for all his fear and distaste, he was once again irresistibly drawn to her white, outspread arms, the soft tremble from her breasts, her partially open lips, still blushing from the passion of their embraces. More than anything, perhaps, he was shocked at what he now saw in himself. He, for whom any talk of contradictions and dual personality in human nature had hitherto been a non-issue; he, for whom women in particular had simply been harmless playthings, now stood shaking as he was confronted by the hidden forces which roll their thunderous dice and toy with the will and fate of man as a storm blows dust and chaff where it will along a country road. For the first time in his life, he felt himself to be at war with demons in whom he had not even wished to believe, whom he had scoffed at with a superior air. Deep down, he heard his father's commanding voice pronouncing half-forgotten words about "the power of the Dark One" and "Satan's snare," words that made him turn pale. But then Fru Engelhardt opened her large brown eyes, as if she had become conscious of his unrelenting gaze. Groggy with sleep, she threw her hair back from her face and sat up in the bed.

"My God! Are you up and dressed already?"

He gave no answer.

"Is it morning already?"

Still, he gave no reply.

"What's going on, for God's sake? Are you sick, or what?"

"No . . . at least not yet."

"Not yet?" What are you talking about man? And why are you looking at me like that? Tell me what's wrong with you!"

"What I am saying is … I am trying to make sure that I don't catch a sickness … a terminal sickness … the way Neergaard did."

A spark of understanding flashed across her face like lightning in the gloom. But a moment later she was smiling again. For all that her countenance was now pale and drawn, she maintained a measured, even tone as she spoke: "What utter nonsense you come out with sometimes! What on earth has your … ahm … your friend's ill health got to do with you? Come on, calm down and be nice to me again—there's a good man!"

"I'm glad to hear that you avoid the mention of his name in this place. But at the same time it shows you up for what you are and you will forgive me madam if I now speak more bluntly. While you slept, I worked out, in what way is no concern of yours, that you were Neergaard's mistress, and that it was your deceitfulness and downright treachery madam that led him to take his own life. Now do we understand each other?"

As she listened, she bowed her head and bit at her quivering lips.

"Go!" she said softly, but with no little pride, as she flung a corner of the bed sheet across her bosom. "Go, I said! A country bumpkin you are, and a country bumpkin you will always remain!"

Per took a step toward the bed, jutted his head forward and was on the verge of casting the words "whore's bitch" into her face, but thought better of it. His own feelings of having been complicit in the affair strangled the words in his mouth and he turned silently and left.

Once down at the concierge's booth, he woke the night porter and settled the bill. As he totted up the amount to be paid, it occurred to him that there could now be no question of his accepting Neergaard's bequeathment. He went home in great haste through the dark, deserted streets.

It was at that hour when the footsteps of those few souls who are abroad in the dead of night echo backwards and forwards across the empty streets and houses. The last diehard patrons of the bars and cafés have made their uncertain way home and the night constables stand chatting at the junctions of major thoroughfares. Only thieves and the notorious shadow dwellers in the back lanes and alleys were abroad.

Another gentleman, with coat upturned and his hat pulled down over his eyes, hurried past him, having emerged from just such a mean passageway into the glare of a streetlight. Per was normally wont to find a measure of entertainment in these sinners slinking homeward with their at once haughty yet shameful demeanor. Now, though, he turned his head away to avoid the sight and wondered how he must look to other people. He did not have the nerve to look into the mirror of his soul and behold his own degradation.

Per got home to Hjertensfrydgade and, standing once again in his own small rooms, which he had tried at all costs to avoid just lately, he was immediately comforted and felt a hitherto unknown sense of security. He quickly threw off his clothes and in jumping into bed was minded of his feelings when, as a child at home in the rectory, he had pulled the bed quilt up around his ears after sitting in the dark and hearing the old one-eyed nanny telling one of her ghost stories.

After a few hours of troubled sleep, Per awoke to the sound of a starling whistling in the garden. The bird's glad tones told him that the sun was shining. For all that, he remained in bed and had no inclination to get up. He was tired. And why shouldn't he just stay where he was? After all, there was not a reason in the world to get up.

Then, in his semi-conscious state, he stole a quick glance over at the upper drawer in his commode. He then turned to the wall with every intention of finding sleep again.

This, however, proved impossible. The moment his thoughts had turned to these cursed drawings, he was immediately wide awake. Thus, for an hour he lay with his hands behind his head staring up at the soft, low wooden ceiling and its myriad threads of resin, which could be studied to eternity. In the clear light of this bright new morning, he went over the events of the night before and could not help but feel a certain embarrassment at the way he had behaved. It occurred to him now that he had betrayed a certain lack of maturity. It had to be said that a lady of Fru Engelhardt's style and substance deserved a modicum of deference. By the time he had risen from his bed and taken his morning coffee, it was absolutely clear to him that he had behaved stupidly. He had been far too sanctimonious, that was for sure, too edgy over the whole thing—perhaps a case of having drunk more than his sufficiency?

Nevertheless, the singular delight of simply being at home remained with him—a feeling he had not felt for a long, long time. He had lit his pipe and sat, rocking slightly, in his poor wreck of a chair, while his gaze tarried at one of the small houses in the neighboring street, whose first-floor windows he could see across the fence. In one of the windows, a pair of children with ruddy cheeks could be seen along with their mother who was darning socks, while on the outside wall, which was bathed in sunlight, a linnet was chirping and hopping around in a green painted cage. He could not decide what exactly it was in the scene across the street that captured his imagination so vividly. After all, it was just the same everyday image of home comforts that he had observed year in and year out. But on this particular morning, it was as if something new had entered the frame, as if he was really seeing it for the first time.

A knock at the door gave him a start.

It was Madam Olufsen, who then entered to let him know about the gentleman who had been there asking for him the previous evening. "What class of gentleman was this?"

"Well, I don't really know, but I can say that I didn't like the cut of him. And, if I am not wrong, he was here once before, the same man."

A debt collector probably—Per thought to himself, and thoughts of Neergaard's inheritance came unbidden to his mind and disturbed his newfound equilibrium. Could he actually contemplate turning his back on that money, of which he was in such dire need?

Madam Olufsen's tall, big-boned figure remained standing at the open door, blocking nearly all the incoming light. There was more she wanted to say to Per.

"While I am at it, Sidenius, I wouldn't mind knowing how the land lies. Were you not talking about moving out?"

Per smiled sheepishly.

"Ah, that was a bit off the top of my head kind of talk, you know yourself. No, of course I want to stay on here Madam Olufsen! That's if you still want me here?"

"Oh . . . of course . . . if ehm . . ."

"I can see there's something on your mind . . . Ah, I know what it is. I have been a bit distracted this last while. But let's not talk about that. And gracious me, Madam Olufsen, there I go again—do forgive my inattention. For there you are in all your finery so early in the day! Is my good landlady gracing a church with her presence today?"

"No but, well, did you not know, Sidenius? Skipper Mortensen arrived in town the other night. And we are paying him the courtesy of a visit this afternoon."

"Count me in good madam! I'm joining the ship's muster. I've actually been longing to see that old sea dog again."

"I'm sure that's just your talk, Sidenius. You've moved on in life and our little gatherings are not really for gentlemen like you."

"Oh Madam Olufsen, what nonsense, if you don't mind me saying! Oh come on, it's not like you to dig your heels in with me. No, it will be as I say—the old crew is reassembling! And let's hear no more about it!"

Madam Olufsen could not resist a smile, in spite of her, in truth, heavy heart. She could never stay cross with him when he was in this kind of humor.

"Well Hr. Sidenius," she said. "You know that there will always be a welcome for you where Mortensen is concerned. He is never as glad to see anyone as when you walk through the door. I would go as far as to say that he is a little taken with you."

Skipper Mortensen was an old friend of the household. He lived in the Dano-German port of Flensburg, but brought his ship to Copenhagen on regular twice-yearly visits to sell cheese, butter and smoked foodstuffs to some of Copenhagen's larger pork victuallers, individual customers and acquaintances. When, on his daily and meticulous inspection of the Ships and Harbor List in the *Telegraph*, Senior Boatswain Olufsen saw that the sloop *Karen Sofie* had passed through the customs boom and was moored at the Exchange, he could not settle before the day and hour of a courtesy call was decided upon and Trine dispatched into town to warn young Didriksen—this being another friend of the family and the driver of a hackney carriage who lived in Brøndstræde and who had, for many years now, willingly placed himself and his carriage at the old man's disposal on such auspicious occasions.

Thus, on the very stroke of three, Didriksen was to be found outside the Olufsen abode—his carriage all spick and span and with its roof down, as if attending some merchant's wedding at Vor Frue Church. Following a short lull in proceedings, the veteran couple emerged before the waiting crowd, which included some dozen curious children who had gathered by the carriage, and many more older neighbors who watched the triumphal procession from door and window. Madam Olufsen was clad in a Vienna shawl and a cluster of light purple grapes danced merrily on her hat. The Senior Boatswain, meanwhile, wore his stiffest funeral collar with the twenty-five-year service medal and silver cross glinting in the sunlight from beneath his unbuttoned overcoat.

These gallant decorations aroused no little public attention as they drove through the streets. As he sat there—his hair brilliant white and exuding a ceremonial air—with both hands as still as statues on the horn of his umbrella, Senior Boatswain Olufsen could have passed for an old admiral from the turn of the century, and there was no doubt that he would have invoked a respectful response from the curious onlookers commensurate with his image were it not for young Didriksen's habit—proud as he was to be in such company—of turning at every other moment to carry on a conversation with his esteemed passengers in loud and familiar tones.

They first did a tour of the whole of the old town quarter, examining the large new buildings that were rising up everywhere and the remnants of the old ramparts, which were being torn down. They also marveled at the new, far too big and clumsy, omnibuses coming in from the direction of Frederiksberg, which amongst the human hordes in Østergade bore the resemblance of elephants plowing their way through a forest with riders on their backs. From Kongens Nytorv, they turned down towards the canal, stopped for a moment outside Holmen's Church, where fifty-two years ago they had been joined together in matrimony. Finally, the veteran couple in their carriage drew up alongside the quay by the Exchange.

Per had already arrived. He called a greeting from the railings of the *Karen Sofie*, where he—rather disheveled in appearance—sat and took in the heat from the spring sunshine, while Skipper Mortensen himself—an older man sporting a graying full set—left his vessel to welcome the new arrivals.

Deep in the ship's open cargo hold, *Karen Sofie*'s belly so to speak, which was accessed by a ladder running down from the main deck, a shop of sorts had been set up, whose dark interior was bejeweled with large hams, sausages, smoked joints of lamb, and millstone-size cheeses. It was a veritable provisions grotto holding a treasure trove of foodstuffs. With Per and Skipper fore and after of her, Madam Olufsen was maneuvered down the ladder, followed by Senior Boatswain Olufsen who, here in his natural maritime element, was keen to show that he had not lost his sea legs and jumped around like an old jack tar, spurning each and every offer of assistance. However, he stumbled as early as the first rung of the ladder and would have undoubtedly broken his neck but for Skipper Mortensen's life-saving arms. Be that as it may, he still managed to give young Didriksen a tongue lashing when the young landlubber, as the last man up above, chose to crawl down the ladder with the utmost care, securing his footing at every step of the way. "Look lively there! Why man, you are like a louse crawling through a head comb!" he bellowed, using salty turns of phrase that had first been used in the Danish fleet in the 1600s and the reign of Christian IV.

After an hour of meticulous searching and sampling, weighing and haggling, a deal that pleased everybody was struck and the purchased goods were brought up on to the main deck. Then the event took place which was repeated year after year with the same predictability as one of Riveter Fuss's jokes—namely that Skipper Mortensen would open the door to his cabin and invite his guests inside for light refreshments, at which point Madam Olufsen would insist that she could never bring herself to abuse a good friend's hospitality in that manner, even though such surprise invitations always gladdened her heart. Senior Boatswain Olufsen, too, was chivalrous to a fault in absolutely refusing to take up any more of their friend's time, while young Didriksen, who was all too used to these initial formalities, calmly extracted the plug of tobacco from his mouth and stowed it away in his jacket pocket.

It was not long, however, before the guests were benched in front of a splendidly laid table and all thoughts of careful politeness were quickly forgotten.

Per still felt completely at ease amongst these plain, unassuming people. In the same way that he never ate more heartily than when dining from tables such as this with its solid fare of pork cuts, schnapps and beer, he still found the unaffected and jovial banter of common folk more to his liking. In this company, he was not—as was the case in the Cauldron—reduced to being a withdrawn and caustic spectator; he threw himself with heart and soul into the various discussions, offering his own opinions on the weather, the prices at the food stalls, the ferry services, and military matters affecting the city.

Once everybody had eaten their fill and tea and rum was served, the conversation moved on to reminisces about the war years and the difficult times that followed. The only thing that Per remembered from the war was the first seizure made by the enemy when they took over the rectory and the courtyard and the sudden flood of soldiers and horses, which forced the evacuation of the whole house—except, that is, for the upstairs quarters, where the large family had to cram itself into a couple of small bedrooms. At that time, he was just seven or eight years of age and had found the whole thing highly entertaining. He just could not fathom why some people got so upset that they started to cry. For a South Jutlander like Skipper Mortensen, however, events surrounding the war went much closer to the bone and he described with colorful relish the atrocities he had witnessed, both in the invasion of 1864 and also in the "Three Years' War" along the Danish border which preceded it. He even had the satisfaction of seeing Madam Olufsen put her hands to her ears, declaring such stories to be unbearable and war generally an abomination.

But this aroused Senior Boatswain Olufsen's ire—his fighting spirit being easily inflamed under the influence of drink. He was already retired by the time 1864 had come around and, as he had had no involvement in the border war some fifteen years earlier, because he had been in hospital for his bad joints, he began to belittle these "German skirmishes" and the alleged misfortune they had brought on the country. In no way, he insisted, could this be compared with the wars against the Englishmen, which he himself had witnessed in 1801, 1807, and 1814. "At that time we were forced, if you don't mind, to give up both Norway and the whole of our fleet. See, now that was a proper war!" In order to outdo the Skipper, who described the defeats at Dybbøl and Fredericia in detail, the Senior Boatswain began to speak of the bombardment of Copenhagen and the sea battle, which he had seen with his own eyes as a five-year-old boy from the vantage point of the Customs House. Here he had watched the injured being brought ashore in a rag tag of boats that were "as full of gristle and gore as a butcher's carving board."

However, that was enough for Madam Olufsen who would not hear a word more about it and, given that night was beginning to descend, demanded to be taken home forthwith. Unfortunately, it now transpired that young Didriksen had fallen asleep, such was the impression made upon him by the tales of his country's humiliation. There he sat, open mouthed and his head thrown back. When attempts were made to revive him, his upper body simply slumped forward and he slept on undisturbed as his head and arms crashed onto the table, despite the fact that his impact knocked over a glass of beer, the contents of which poured onto his upper legs and knees. After a moment's silence, as the whole spectacle was taken in by those around him, Per lifted the bottle of rum and established beyond doubt that said bottle had been quietly nipped at until the rum was no more. Thus, it was ascertained that the young man was blind drunk.

Madam Olufsen took this as a mortal assault on her dignity. Outside on the quay, their carriage awaited them, its knock-kneed steed having stood patiently and munched at an empty feedbag; but it was clear to everybody that there was nothing else for it but to let the young man stay on the ship and sleep off his intoxication. The great day out had ended disastrously. The two old timers were forced to shuffle off down the quay in all their finery, each carrying a wrapped-up parcel of ham under one arm and with sausages and joints of meat sticking out of their pockets.

Per followed them as far as Holmen's bridge, where he managed to get them onto a tram. He himself had no intention of going home. Some air and space was what he needed after all that entertainment and heavy drinking. He then took the measure of himself in a shop window before continuing down along the canal and up towards Højbro.

It was at that hour when the slant of the sun's rays begins to fan across the rooftops and sets the church spire of Helligaandskirke aglow, while the streets down below came alive with the evening crowds as they moved between the bright lights coming from the shops and stores. Daylight still lingered in the open square. The sparrows still hopped around, fussing at the street detritus and the newly lit lanterns burned with pale spectral flames within their glass casings in which the setting sun also flickered. Per walked slowly into the heart of the city via Østergade, which was alive with people. The sight of such crowds brought a feeling of melancholy upon him. Despite the chill in the evening air and the red noses of passers-by, a hint of spring was abroad. The sense of expectation could be seen in the hopeful glances of the young and could be heard in their voices. Shoppers stood clustered around a dressmaker's large window display to inspect the new spring fashions. And any fashion-conscious gentleman that was out for his evening stroll wore a small spray of violets in the buttonhole of his coat.

Per had come to walk behind a courting couple who moved so closely beside each other, and in such harmony of rhythm, that it was as if they were conjoined at shoulder and heel. He stole a glance at the young girl's eyes and how she gazed at her beloved in such free and obvious devotion; his thoughts then turned to the pleasures of the previous night and he became more and more dejected. He could not stop his recriminations over what he now described, without any hesitation, as his immature indignation. In particular, he remembered one thing which completely rekindled his ardor for the passionate Frue Engelhardt—the way in which she had covered her bosom as he was about to leave. Her gesture had been quite touching. And those roses on Neergaard's coffin. She must have really loved him. And, after all, what was there to get so worked up about? When push came to shove, human life paid no heed to small, piddling concerns. It demanded space to freely express itself and where it rose up in all its majesty, all society's conventions were as nought. In fact, there was something rather noble, almost spiritually uplifting, in such an unbridled zest for love, which vanquished all those pettifogging tribulations of the heart—yes, could even vanquish the horror of death itself. That kind of undaunted, all-consuming abandon to nature's laws was perhaps the highest expression of humanity. The "dark forces" which had gripped him so violently when standing at the end of her bed—despite his qualms of conscience he had still been incredibly drawn to the soft luminance of her embrace—yes, they represented the very essence of his nature; the shackles binding the very center of his elemental urges were being sundered after generations of repression! Yes, that was it! There was no such place as Hell, other than that place which human beings themselves created in their superstitious fear of life's pleasures and the sovereign power of the flesh and its delights. And heaven was to be found in the physical coming together of a man and woman, wherein lay the soothing amnesia for all life's sorrows and absolution for all sins—where two souls met in guilt-free nakedness, just as Adam and Eve had done in the Garden of Eden.

There were some half-forgotten words, a vague recollection, which suddenly came to him in an image of flaming letters. It was Neergaard's mocking description of the peasant boy in the fairy tale who had ventured out into the world to win a kingdom for himself but who continually looked back, and—when the wonderland for which he yearned was suddenly there before him in all its enchantment—fled home again to his seat by the cozy fireside and the familiarity of his mother's apron strings.

He reddened with shame. That's how utterly pathetic he had been when, for the first time, life had tested his courage and convictions. But could not the damage that had been done be undone? If, for example, he wrote a letter to her, explaining everything and asking her forgiveness?

He had reached his home in Hjertensfrydgade. The ship carpenter's wife in the downstairs living quarters opened her door and told him that there was a gentleman inside who had been awaiting his arrival.

"It is the same gentleman that was here last night ... I'd say he is a man of the cloth. He has been sitting in there for over an hour."

The visitor proved to be none other than his brother Eberhard. He sat in the rocking chair by the table; the lamp was lit and the shadow of his head was thrown across the bare wall like that of some ancient troll. He had kept on his overcoat, and his hands, kept warm by a pair of woolen gloves, rested on an umbrella stationed between his knees.

"I had almost given up the hope of ever meeting you," he said, after they had exchanged a handshake. "You are aware perhaps that I was here yesterday evening?"

Per made no reply. His heart thumped in his breast. He understood that his brother must have had some message of a serious nature to impart to him if he had sought him out two days in a row. Nor was it difficult to ascertain, judging by Eberhard's countenance, that he himself was aware of the import of his visit. His whole demeanor was clearly designed to make an impression upon Per; but it was precisely for that reason that Per marshalled all his inner forces together and, with great effort, managed to give off an air of complete indifference.

"How about a cigar?" he asked, while at the same time being on the verge of fainting, and all the time thinking: Has mother died?

"I will not be smoking thank you," Eberhard replied.

"A beer maybe?"

"I have turned my back forever on all forms of alcoholic beverages. I find that suits my disposition entirely. And I might add that, as a matter of principle, I never partake of meals or refreshments outside of mealtimes."

Per smiled. And while he felt no craving whatsoever for alcohol, he brought a bottle of ale from his cupboard in the corner and opened it.

"Well, my own view would be that it would equally be a sin to deny a man's thirst, regardless of the time of day," he said.

Eberhard sat for a while, twisting his umbrella back and forth, while his large pale eyes regarded his brother, who had seated himself at the other side of the table and now quickly emptied his glass.

"You seem to be more conscientious in that regard than is necessary," he remarked finally.

"Have you come all this way just to say that?" Per retorted in an immediately aggressive tone of voice.

Eberhard made a slight, dismissive movement with his hand.

"You are well aware that I do not involve myself in your affairs. The reason for my visit lies in another direction altogether."

Per did not wish to inquire any further—in fact, he dared not. His own reactions had taken him aback—he did not understand how even the very idea of some kind of bad news from home had made him so agitated. He had believed that the days when those kinds of feelings could still affect him were long gone. The fact was that, in recent years, the people at home had been as good as dead to him, and the close proximity of his brother had not exactly given him great longings to return. Quite the opposite. As Eberhard sat there, his hand locked to his umbrella and watching him with sidelong glances from his billy goat eyes, all the hostility that had been buried in his past was aroused once again. The arrogant tone of censure in his bearing and the air about him, the silent demonstration of wounded family honor, the whole stultifying and self-righteous atmosphere which Eberhard exuded from his tightly buttoned deportment brought back the memory of the ordeals of his childhood so vividly that the hated and all-pervading reek of the turf fire at home in the rectory became personified in the shape of the brother who sat in front of him.

And yet there was in the gaze with which Eberhard beheld him an expression of genuine sorrow, of real brotherly attachment. The small cellar-like room with its second-hand furniture, the bare floor and sparse walls, the sad, empty space which—in spite of all the care and attention little Trine lavished upon her shrine—was the very picture of a rootless existence had evoked his sympathies and he awaited just some little signal that would allow him to speak from the heart.

But Per gave him no such opening and so they sat for some time without a word being exchanged between them.

"You might as well know that I have just returned from a short journey," Eberhard began, as if feeling his way towards something. "I was at home for a few days."

"Oh really, they are keeping well I take it?" Per ventured.

"Oh no, I could not exactly say that. Father has failed somewhat in the last while."

"I see."

"In fact he is actually quite bad."

"Bad with what?"

"How can I put it... before my return, I spoke at length with Doctor Carlsen, and he confirmed what I had already suspected for some time based on the letters from home—in other words that father's condition raises the most serious grounds for concern. To speak bluntly, we must prepare ourselves for the time, very soon, when he will no longer be with us."

Per, who was aware that his brother's eyes were watching him like a hawk, betrayed no change of emotion, even though his heart hammered against his chest. However, he felt no sorrow on hearing this news, not even sadness nor remorse. No, the unease which had gripped him came essentially from a vague sense of disappointment. It had never occurred to him that his father or mother might die before he had completed his life's work—that they would never witness the triumph that would vindicate him. And now this news had arrived at just that point when his great hopes regarding his project had been shamefully dashed to the ground.

"In all probability it is cancer we are talking about," Eberhard continued. "Doctor Carlsen did not exactly use that word, but it was clear from what he was saying that he had no doubts about it. Though father is still up and about and performing his duties...you know yourself his strict sense of duty. But a few months more, perhaps less, will see the end of that and I believe he is fully prepared for the end. Of course, mother is stricken with grief, but—strangely enough—it is as if her concern for father's condition has given her a new lease of life. She has even begun to get up from her bed to spend more time with father; but I believe that this wonderful grace that she has received, grateful as she is to have been blessed with it, is also a portent that God will soon call father to his side."

Though Eberhard was not a theologian by profession, he was wont to express himself in biblical language. He was a lawyer and was viewed by his peers as possessing an extraordinarily clear and sharp legal mind. Despite his relative youth, he had already attained a high level of social esteem. This was exemplified by the stir he had caused after the publication in a journal of an essay he had written about the prison service and its educational role. He actually had a position at the headquarters of the administration section for prisons and, given that he was a paragon of diligence and duty, was held in the highest regard by his superiors.

"It was my view that you should be informed in good time of the way things are," he continued, as Per had still not uttered a word. "I did not want you to be ill-prepared should the catastrophe come upon us with greater speed than expected. We—for here I am speaking on behalf of all your brothers and sisters and after consultation with them—believed that once you were apprised of father's condition, you might feel obliged to...I mean, feel moved to seek a reconciliation with him before it is too late."

"I don't understand...what are you talking about?" Per asked brusquely, but without being able to look his brother in the eye.

"As I have already pointed out, I have no wish to involve myself in your affairs. I simply meant it as well-intentioned counsel to a brother—your own conscience must now decide whether the attitude you have adopted towards your parents for so long is defensible ... other than that, I have nothing more to say. However, what I do find necessary to clarify, even at this stage, is that father's death will, of course, have a significant effect on fiscal matters at home. I am aware that father has hitherto—and without any form of acknowledgment from your side—provided you with a regular subvention, which, while perhaps not being a huge amount, did—and I can say this with complete confidence—stretch him over and beyond his limits. And he has done this so that he would not censure himself for showing indifference to your studies—or whatever term one might use to describe them—in spite of the fact that he has never been afforded the opportunity to assess your abilities, or the progress you have been making."

"I am well aware of that."

"This support will, of course, not disappear overnight should father leave us. But mother's situation will be modest enough, and the greatest thrift will be required in all areas."

"Where that is concerned, you need have no worries for my sake," answered Per, who had now determined that he would after all accept Neergaard's inheritance in order to gain complete independence from home. "I had actually intended to write home to say that from now on I was fully able to get by on my own two feet. I have no need of any kind of assistance in the future."

His brother's eyes widened. But as Per did not provide any further information, he adopted a solemn air and held his counsel for a time.

Eventually, however, Eberhard's curiosity got the better of him.

"May I ask ... exactly how you intend to—," he began.

But Per cut across him.

"I really feel, in all honesty, that you should be as good as your word and keep out of my affairs. I have also told you before that it annoys me."

Eberhard rose. He was pale, and his mouth with its low-slung lantern jaw was stiff with indignation.

"Well, I can see that it is a waste of time trying to speak to you. I think it would be best if we do not take this any further."

"As you wish."

Eberhard took his hat in preparation for his departure. But when he got to the door, he turned again towards Per, who had remained sitting at the table, and said: "There is one more thing I have to say to you Peter Andreas! Even though you—given your obvious disposition—would perhaps have difficulty understanding this, you should bear in mind that at this moment in time there is nobody who father thinks more about than you. When I was at home just recently, not one single day went by without him speaking about you . . . and the same goes for mother as a matter of fact. Of course, the time has long gone when they believed their words might have some influence upon you. They have been left with the hope that life itself would make you think again and that you would come to understand how great your debt is to them. Now it looks like father's time with us will soon be up. Beware, Peter Andreas, that you don't commit a sin which you surely—sooner or later—will come to bitterly regret."

For some time after his brother had left, Per remained sitting with his hand under his chin and looking gloomily down at the floor.

"Think again" . . . "bitter regret" . . . "sin" . . . "grace" . . . How he knew all those lectures so well! The whole demonic catechism repeated yet again! And how typical it was—a genuine characteristic of the "Sidenius" clan—to use sickness and death as a pretext for renewed attempts to panic him back into the embrace of home and the Church—invoking death itself as a recruiting sergeant for the black-clad guardians of the cross. For what did they really want from him except that he bowed his neck in obedience, to be chastised in the name of his forebears? Where did all their concerns actually lie? Was it for him as a person, in the way that mother nature in one of her bright, joyful moments had created him? No, it was his subjugation they demanded with such impatience. It was his humiliation that was required so urgently now that his father was about to die. He knew them! It was for the sake of the turmoil in their own souls that his lust for life had to be extinguished. Their piety could not bear the sight of a straight back and a raised head where "grace" was not present.

He looked up and shivered uncontrollably. It had become so strangely cold and gloomy in his room after his brother's departure. Why could they not just leave him in peace? Had he not, with his own hands, buried the grim, old feelings from the past and hammered a stake through them all? Why come now and stir them up again? As for his father? Yes, let him die! There was no debt of love there. In fact, he it was who owed Per a number of years, which he preferred not to think about. But now he, in turn, had wiped him from his memory. They were quits.

He emptied his glass. Then he jumped up, as if trying to shake off the memory of an evil dream, gathered himself, and went up to the old couple to talk himself into some kind of equilibrium.

5

EBERHARD'S visit and the tidings relating to his father's ill health did have one particular consequence for Per. It put an end to his aimless gallivanting around town, by which he had hoped to put his defeat at the hands of Professor Sandrup behind him. That very same evening, he took out his drawings and calculations from the drawer of his commode and then spent the whole night sitting at his table, head in hands, studying his papers intensely, until the lines and markings began to dance before his eyes and his head sang with five-figure numbers humming in his brain like bees in a hive. And on that same night, he made a solemn vow that from then on he would not rest until he had either become completely convinced that his plan was unworkable, or he had overcome all its obstacles and had pursued his vision through to a final victorious vindication.

Not too many days after this, by way of a revaluation of his channel lines, Per actually succeeded in rectifying the fundamental error discovered by Professor Sandrup. Moreover, in order to avoid being deceived by yet another fault in his calculations, he then carried out a detailed validation test on his flow-velocity estimates, and when he found that his results concurred exactly with his base-line estimates, all the tension which had built up inside him was released in a deafening roar of delight. At last, he felt that he was standing on solid ground once again. All his hard work, in other words, had not been squandered; the thousand and one nights he had spent hunched over his desk had not been in vain. Ha! Perhaps even at this late hour, victory could not only be achieved but be seen by his father to have been achieved before he closed his eyes forever at home at the rectory.

Per now quickly settled the acquirement of the Neergaard inheritance without succumbing to any further bouts of scruples. There was no point in being squeamish, Per said to himself. Life was a bare knuckle fight for any man from his kind of background who wanted to force his way to the top. Besides which, it had transpired that the amount in question was not as large as expected. On visiting the solicitor, he was told that the property had been "somewhat indebted." Per digested this news in silence and it did not occur to him to question an officer of the law on this issue. The solicitor also sought to ease any doubts Per might have by reassuring him that he would, at least, get a few thousand crowns once the outstanding dues had been settled—in other words, he could work in peace and financial security for at least a year. Thus, without further ado, Per requested an advance on the sum in question so as to clear his debt. The solicitor was only too happy to accommodate him in this regard.

Per then terminated his teaching duties and the other side-line job he had been forced to take on, so that he could devote himself entirely to his *magnum opus*. Like an impatient young bear emerging from its first winter hibernation, he shook off the indolence that had settled upon him and fell to his work. As autumn asserted itself across the country, bringing dark clouds with sunlit haloes and ice blue showers of hail, Per was to be found sitting at his desk in his cramped quarters, sometimes for the whole day and much of the night—a solitary figure bent over his papers, deaf to the calls of the starlings amassing in the evening sky, and oblivious to the rose-red petals from the apple tree falling like soft snow showers outside his window. He was woken every morning by the peal of the bell from the Nyboder watch that roused people from the area to a new working day, and he would already be sitting at his desk by the time Madam Olufsen presented herself to the outside world in her night gown with its big flowery pattern. The good lady had the morning habit of carrying the chamber pot out into the garden, discreetly hidden between her night gown and shift, which she would then use to water her assortment of primulas.

Despite the relative prosperity he now enjoyed, Per made absolutely no changes to his way of life, which if anything was now even more characterized by his innate and long-practiced frugality. On the other hand, he procured numerous, and rather expensive illustrated, manuals and other technical journals which he needed in order to develop his studies and work plans. For the same reason, he took out subscriptions in specialist periodicals from both Germany and America. Henceforth, he would never again set foot in the College of Engineering. He suspected that his former student colleagues had gotten wind of the reason for his visit to Professor Sandrup's chambers and also of its aftermath. Besides, he regarded attendance at the interminable lectures he was forced to suffer there as a complete waste of time. They were nothing more than platforms for boring pedants waffling on about the need to be practical at all times, like cripples, thought Per, giving instruction on the best way to dance.

Fru Engelhardt he never saw again. Of course, the possibility of a reconciliation sometimes crossed his mind, but he had demurred at taking any positive steps towards that purpose. No matter how embarrassed he continued to be over his behavior that night, the experience had still left him with a residue of wariness with regards to the life of amorous adventure so highly praised by others. He had asked himself whether the many hoops through which one had to jump, the playacting, and more especially the great costs involved, were actually worth all the trouble. Every time he became tempted to renew his acquaintance with this seasoned lady, he simply called to mind the sinful heap of money she had cost him in the run of just one evening—at which point an undertaking to forget all about her and return to his channel profiles and water-level calculations was never too difficult to make.

Whenever the sun shone down from the heavens, Per would fling open his windows to the world outside with the result that butterflies and bumblebees would often blunder into his room. However, this never occurred to him as being in any way a romantic or lyrical interlude. At most, his cheerful mood might lead him to whistle out loud, upon which Senior Boatswain Olufsen would stick his head inside the window (adorned as it invariably was with a brightly colored calotte) in order to express his pleasure at Per's great spirits, or Madam Olufsen might place a cup of steaming coffee on the window ledge and bid him take a "moment's rest to catch his breath." And if Per's venerable landlady had ever feared that her favorite lodger had been seriously led astray, her worries were now directed in the opposite direction entirely.

"Take you that drop of coffee while it's still nice and hot," she would say in the commanding tone she often adopted to conceal her motherly feelings towards him.

Then Per would cast aside his fountain pen, or drawing implements, light his little shag pipe and lean against the window chatting with the two pensioners as they pottered around in their small patch of garden. Space was at such a premium in the garden that the two of them could barely bend over without bumping into each other with that part of the lower back Senior Boatswain Olufsen would call "the part that was slapped on using the bits that were left over" (a blasphemous reference to the Old Testament and Genesis).

However, it was never long before a nagging restlessness would invade Per's mind once again. And soon he would be sat brooding over his drawings whose sheets and pages conjured visions for him of pickaxes and shovels flashing in the sun, huge earth embankments being leveled, marshes and small lakes reclaimed. Sometimes he would also imagine he heard the soft whump of excavation charges, which shook the very depths of the world just by a simple push of his finger. Once again he had revised and expanded his project. For now—in complete harmony with his proposed network of canals—he had drawn up an outline plan for a new, large-scale harbor facility on Jutland's west coast, which would be able to compete on equal terms with Hamburg and Bremen. Nor did he stop there. As he wrestled with his ambitious project, the idea gradually dawned on him that he might be able to harness the huge energy potential offered by the incessant waves coming in from the North Sea, which, by means of large buoys constructed from iron plates riveted together, and positioned along the surf line, would transfer the energy via cables linked to onshore industrial facilities. Wind power was something else he imagined could be utilized by means of motors that were able to gather and process the energy. If this were to happen, the conditions could be created that would transform Denmark into an industrial manufacturing power of the first order.

On balmy evenings when facts and figures hammered in his head after a full day's work, Per had formed the habit of joining Senior Boatswain Olufsen on a bench that had been constructed from two planks and attached to the timber fence that surrounded the garden. An old piece of sail cloth acted as a canopy. This was the so-called gazebo, which, according to the old man himself, afforded the best view of the various gardens in the area. Often there would be other visitors who counted as old friends of the house—be it Hr. Bendtz, the moss-grown veteran carpenter, who would come rocking along on his cane, all the time complaining about his lumbago, or the perennially cheerful Riveter Fuss with his cherry-reddened face and white gorilla beard. Madam Olufsen was often on hand to dispense rum toddies for all who came and Trine would then have to run down to Krokodillegade to fetch Riveter Fuss's guitar. A musical ensemble could then be put together because in the first-floor apartment of the house behind them was a young artillery gunner who was able to play some lovely airs on a drone pipe. Every evening he would sit by his open window with the long homemade instrument in front of him and when Riveter Fuss began to accompany him on his guitar, the whole thing became a veritable concert, which brought joy to the whole Hjertensfryd quarter. All around the place people would lean out of windows and doors to listen to what was being played and children would stop their games and clamber on top of fences to see what was going on—indeed, even the sparrows which were beginning to settle down for the night in the trees above would swoop on to the roofs of the houses and remain there with their heads cocked to one side, as if in veneration of what they heard.

On one such evening of music and song, Per espied a delightful young girl standing by an upstairs window in one of the neighboring houses. Her hands were crossed lightly behind her lower back and she gave the odd glance upwards to look at the drifting clouds in the evening sky, as if her mind was attuned to nothing more than the concert that filled the air. However, the sudden bashful glow from her cheeks betrayed the fact that she was not entirely unaware of the bold, decidedly masculine gaze being directed at her from the vantage point of the Senior Boatswain's gazebo.

The house in question served as the official residence for one of Nyboder's most esteemed personages, a Master Jacobæus by name, whose wife was at all times addressed as Madam, at least by the master's underlings. Per discovered from Madam Olufsen that the young lady was this man's niece and that she had recently moved to the city to learn dressmaking.

From this evening onwards, Per chose to join Senior Boatswain Olufsen and observe the setting sun from the garden bench on a much more regular basis. Here he could monitor the windows of the neighboring house, and, almost without fail, the young lady would appear in one of them, busying herself at a flower vase, or the bird cage. She would also sometimes open a window, move a pot of herbs to one side, and lean out so as to gain a better view across the rooftops or down to the neighboring yard, or up to the heavens—anywhere, in other words, except the most obvious place to look, which was the Senior Boatswain's garden.

For all this activity, no direct eye contact was ever established between them, no matter how much Per applied himself to the task of opening a communication line of unspoken romance across the timber fence. And then one morning, just as he closed the front door behind him and walked into the street, he saw her for the first time outside her house. As luck would have it, she had chosen just that moment to return from the corner bakery just opposite her own abode—wearing green canvas slippers and carrying a wicker basket in her hand. Per could not resist a smile when he observed her crushed demeanor, indeed her indignation, that he should find her on the street in such a shameful state, but her mortification simply made her all the more attractive to his mind, and he made so bold as to raise his hat in greeting. The young lady, however, simply acted as if she had not seen him and she would, in fact, produce a brilliant riposte

to the events of the morning that very same day. Per was just returning home from one of his short, sharp "constitutionals" along Lange-
linie when she came out of her uncle's house dressed in a chic, bright
spring jacket and with a large silk scarf under her chin. She also wore
a hat which was graced by a veil. She stood for a moment on the
doorstep so as to fasten the last button on a pair of new and shiny
black gloves, whereupon she slowly made her way down the street in
the direction of the city walls. Both her hands were ensconced in her
jacket pockets and she gave not so much as a glance in the direction
from which Per advanced. But even at this, Per could not resist a
smile. For he had just fleetingly caught sight of her face up in the
street mirror by Master Jacobæus's house and had guessed that she
had seen him going out earlier and had timed her exit, in all her
finery, to coincide with his return.

But Per now had the bit between his teeth and resolved to take a
bolder approach. He got Trine to ferret out information regarding
the dressmakers shop where the young lady was being taught and the
times when she would normally depart from said premises—and then
early one evening, at around seven o'clock, he surprised her near
Nørrevold, just as she stopped to look in a shop window.

He greeted her with the utmost decorum and inquired as to
whether he might introduce himself, and to his great surprise, she
took no offense whatsoever at his audacity. It seemed that, with a
lack of guile so typical of those from the provinces, the young lady
found it quite natural that two close neighbors who had the fortune
to meet in the maze of streets in a big town should hold a conversation
and accompany each other along the footpath. However, her openness
was not entirely without artifice. The young lady revealed this herself.
For, as they came closer to Nyboder, she suddenly stopped and announced that he could not accompany her any further. And Per, who
knew that Master Jacobæus was the kind of man who was well aware
of his responsibilities where his young niece was concerned, and who
also guarded his interests jealously, required no further explanation
and bade her adieu with a stated wish that he might see her again
"very soon."

From then on, they would often meet in the same way and walk the same route homeward together. However, by unspoken agreement, they changed their route on the grounds of prudency so as to take in Kongens Have and Rosenborg gardens, where there was less chance of meeting any of Nyboder's residents. Per also extended the route slightly on every subsequent meeting, without any objection on her part.

Francesca (for this was the young lady's name) was of middling height, slim, almost thin, but with an ample bosom and hips. The most noticeable thing about her was her gait, which gave notice of something proud and "secure" in her character. Whenever she walked along the pavement with her hands in her jacket pockets and her youthful bosom thrusting boldly forward, people would instinctively make way for her and Per was amused by the stolen glances sent her way by the menfolk who passed by. Her pale facial tones, which still bore a ruddy glow about them, often bore a petulant expression and her brow was usually drawn and somber—all of which did not really mean very much, it was just her way of asserting herself in these new and strange surroundings. Her challenging demeanor, in other words, was meant to let the good burghers of Copenhagen know that country people could be just as sophisticated.

Likewise her, on the face of it, rather daring association with Per could be explained by the exact same fear of being regarded as nothing more than a yokel who had just arrived on an apple cart from the country. Per, for his part, did not misconstrue her apparent boldness. For this mirrored his own need to assert himself as a young man born and reared in rustic Jutland.

The fact that they both hailed from the provinces had, in a very heightened way, the effect of cementing their understanding and appreciation of each other—indeed Per's strong attraction to her (even though he did not think of it in this way) could be traced back to memories of his youth, as her particular type of beauty, her manner and non-Copenhagen dialect aroused echoes of his first erotic awakenings and his attraction to the blond and blue-eyed Valkyries from his own area.

The capricious and artful gods decreed that a period of settled weather should be produced at just this time, with a series of extraordinarily beautiful summer evenings with big, bright skies full of vibrant color—as if purposely designed to set a stir in two young and free hearts like theirs. Their by now regular promenade had gradually extended so as to take in the necklace pearl of city lakes and they always chose to make their way home via the romantic gardens lying behind what remained of Copenhagen's eastern ramparts. Here they would stroll backwards and forwards along the elevated laneway with its broad crowned trees; making several turns before finally accepting that it was time to part.

And of what did they speak about during these meanderings? Well, about the weather, about people they encountered along the way, about mutual acquaintances in Nyboder and the news of the day—and never, ever about love. Per never even broached the subject. In the beginning he refrained from so doing because he did not want to scare her. Thereafter, he avoided the subject for his own sake—out of fear of the power she increasingly exerted over him.

Per's original overtures to her were made without any clear goal in mind. It had just been a question of a young man seeking a diversion by having a bit of fun with a young woman. Per had been so completely engrossed in his work that his keyed up mind had become awash with adrenaline, which in turn had left him physically enervated. Thus, he had instinctively sought out that well of sustenance which generates such erotically charged momentum in all youths. But it was the very fact that, contrary to his usual practice, he sought nothing from the relationship, and then there was this bright festive air which Mother Nature had lent to everything night after night, this radiant glow which—just as they met each evening—transformed the city and its environs into a fairy-tale landscape. The culminating spices that were added to this heady mix were the clandestine arrangements which, for Francesca's sake, had to be observed in order that they could meet, and the attendant apprehension and agitation she could no longer hide from him when it was time to go their separate ways—all this had gradually lent a previously unknown, in fact undreamed of, sense of magic to everything—until one day Per remarked to himself that he had never before really understood what being in love was actually like.

And he was right.

He really was in love now for the first time. He, Per Sidenius, who in certain regards was so far ahead of his age group, had lived the life of an innocent, or a caged animal, where the realm of the senses was concerned. Now he walked around with an almost overwhelming feeling that he was experiencing some kind of birth in his inner self—that a completely new world was revealing itself to him. Per, whose way with woman had otherwise been to make the distance between words and action as short as possible, became the epitome of courteousness in his dealings with this young lady. For example, he was so anxious not to offend her that it took him a long time to raise enough courage to ask for a kiss on taking his leave of her. And when she yielded to this request and he saw the crimson blush firing her cheeks, he almost regretted his temerity, and he felt that he was committing a sacrilege by touching her innocent mouth with his own and stealing the warm glow from her lips.

Towards the end of the summer, Francesca went home to her parents for an extended visit. Despite the routine they had established in their most recent meetings, and the sense of indiscretion they now indulged by choosing to stage their increasingly more tender departure scenes in the direct vicinity of Nyboder, there was still no one who was aware of what was going on between them—nobody, that is, except Trine. With the almost clairvoyant state possessed by this simple-minded girl in affairs concerning Per, she had known everything for a long time. Besides which, Per had once felt obliged to bring her into his confidence in order to bring a letter across to Francesca's house—an awkward task, not without its risks, that she performed as if she were the bearer of divine tidings. Using the self-conceived pretext that she needed to fetch a clothes peg that had blown over the fence, she gained access to Master Jacobæus's fortified redoubt and successfully conveyed her secret message into the right hands. But directly afterwards, when Per had left her again, she crept around in such a ghostlike fashion, and sought the refuge of the outhouse with such frequency that Madam Olufsen assumed she was sick and finally ordered her to bed, placing a powerful poultice in the form of a mustard plaster on her stomach.

When Francesca returned to Copenhagen in October, the feelings which she and Per felt for each other soon reached such a pitch of intensity that something had to be done. Per was beset with apprehension. The thought that he might allow his feelings to run over into full-blown seduction he rejected out of hand. On the other hand, he could not, in the cold light of day, see any way in which he might transform their situation into that of an official engagement; but this, without doubt, was the outcome which Francesca desired. Indeed, she awaited Per's next move with no little impatience. She had on a number of occasions—completely unsolicited—made him aware of her family background, even going so far on one occasion as to make a passing remark relating to her father's considerable wealth. But to marry a saddlemaker's daughter from a small town on the island of Funen was completely at odds with the great aims in life which he had set for himself. Every time he felt tempted by the thought, he saw Neergaard in front of him and recalled his words about the swineherd who became a prince, words which had already, on another occasion, revealed themselves in an aura of blazing letters, a Mene-Tekel—"counted and counted, weighed and divided," an admonishing Biblical scripture on tablets of fiery stone.

Then something happened which brought matters to an unexpected but decisive conclusion.

Master Jacobæus had, for some time, entertained suspicions regarding the veracity of his niece's explanations for her increasingly late arrival from the dressmakers and one day he decided to investigate matters more thoroughly. This led to an interrogation of the young girl under which she was eventually forced to confess all.

The very next day saw Master Jacobæus stride into Per's quarters where, without so much as an introduction, he bluntly asked him whether it was now his intention to make a decent woman of his niece. Per's immediate reaction was to talk his way out of the situation, ask the gentleman to take a seat, and let on that he did not really understand what was going on. But the angry man snorted and threw his head back, demanded that Per desist from blackguarding him and that he give a straight answer to a straight question. A yes or no was all he wanted.

Still Per hesitated before replying. He weighed the fact that, were he to say no, it was more than likely that he would never set eyes on Francesca again—and his heart sank at this thought. He saw her standing in front of him, just as she was probably pacing the floor in the house across the street at that very moment, clenching her hands in anxiety and tension as she waited for word of what had transpired. And in truth, at that moment the thought crossed his mind like an epiphany in his soul that he might cast all his dreams of greatness to one side and hold tight to this bird, this lucky sparrow he held in his hand, and turn his back on the majestic birds which soared above the roofs and vertiginous mountain slopes. But, once again, Neergaard's gleaming skull emerged from the depths to mock him. And he drew himself up and said—no.

A scene now took place which Per could never thereafter think about without biting his lip in shame. With both hands in his trouser pockets, as if trying to control his urge to strike out, Master Jacobæus stepped so far into Per's personal space that the hair on his bushy gray beard tickled his face. And then this complete stranger in his room proceeded to denounce him as nothing but a pup, a lout and a corner boy, and left him in no doubt that if Per should ever again in his life approach his niece, he would be thrashed unmercifully and turfed out of Nyboder like the mongrel cur that he was.

Per's face had turned chalk white with rage; but not a muscle did he move, nor did he attempt to answer in kind. Though it was not this man's threats that reduced him to silence. This was not the first time he had been confronted by balled fists, and there is no doubt that his first thought as the man closed in on him was to grab him by the throat and slam him up against the wall and pin him there until the madness had flailed its way out of him. But when he stared down into this pale, contorted face with its quivering mouth, which far more clearly than any spluttering speech showed how seriously the whole affair had affected him, how grief stricken and embarrassed this man was, a profound sense of guilt was bestirred in Per's heart, a guilt that kept his hands down and his mouth shut.

It must be said that in the aftermath, when Master Jacobæus had left, Per did ask himself what sin exactly he had committed. After all, he had not meant to cause Francesca any harm. If he had known from the beginning that they would end up falling in love, he would simply have avoided her; but the truth was that at no stage had he abused the trust she had placed in him. God knows, the kisses they had exchanged in all innocence could hardly cast a shadow over her future life. So what harm exactly had been caused?

It was nothing more than his own "conscience" come spooking him again—this vague, eerie phenomenon that was wont to suddenly place him in a hall of mirrors, in which he saw himself reflected in horrible distortions. Per, who believed that he had been liberated from all thoughts of black marks and shadows on the soul, now stood there like a fool, burning with shame—and in the end it was more his annoyance with himself that helped him to almost completely forget both Francesca and their abrupt separation.

As things turned out, Master Jacobæus's threats proved to be quite needless. For, acting on her own initiative, Francesca returned home to Funen the very next day. Two days later Per received a small parcel with certain gifts he had given to her on different occasions. She returned everything without a single accompanying word of either explanation or reproach. However, every single article had been carefully wrapped in rose tinted-tissue paper. And as Per now stood there holding these objects in his hands, a new humiliation enveloped him. His eyes began to moisten. He was simply unable to avoid it. Indeed, had he not hurried to stuff the whole package down into his drawer, an even bigger embarrassment could easily have befallen him, as he was just about to burst into a flood of tears.

And yet, and yet, Lady Luck had not in fact deserted him. Not long after these traumatic events, something happened, which not only led him to forget his sudden banishment from Aphrodite's hallowed halls, but almost appeared to be an uplifting nod from the Fates themselves—a reward for his refusal to yield to a momentary weakness. If he had many times felt that his ship had lain becalmed in endless dog days as he waited for a favorable wind to carry him further on his adventures, a storm of events now began to swirl around him that would bear him along into new and open seas.

A good while previously, Per had made such great strides in the work on his project that he had decided he could once again submit his plans to a recognized authority so that they might be adjudicated. On this occasion, he had made an approach to the chairman of the Royal Institute of Engineers. This was a retired military engineering officer with the rank of colonel, whom he had often heard described as a shrewd, open-minded, and very influential technocrat. The colonel was also the editor-in-chief of the institute's highly respected monthly journal. Per had sent him a synopsis of his project, along with a letter signed "P. Sidenius, Engineer," in which he had also provided a précis of his ideas in general and boldly expressed the hope that the colonel would feel himself in a position to acknowledge the importance of the ethos underpinning his proposals and recommend that they be published in the institute's monthly journal.

For several weeks he had waited impatiently for a reply and had finally given up hope of receiving any kind of answer. But the colonel had chosen that very moment to write to him, stating that he had read the outline proposals with "great interest" and invited him to call in to his office at a convenient time; he should also bring with him the detailed plans that had been referred to, so that they could discuss the issues involved in greater detail.

As soon as Per was done racing through the letter, he knocked on the low ceiling with the back of his hand, a signal for Trine that her presence was required downstairs.

"Tell their royal highnesses that we are having a trooping of the color!" he commanded.

He then took out a bottle from the bottom of his clothes press which held the remains of some Swedish punch, set up three glasses in a line on the table and filled them up.

"What's all this about Per?" Madam Olufsen asked as she stuck her curler-bedecked head into the doorway. The Senior Boatswain, meanwhile, could be heard lurching stiffly down the stairway.

"A great turn in the tide of life Madam Olufsen! Come in and congratulate me!"

"My God, Hr. Sidenius, have you gone and got engaged?"

"No you're wrong! Guess again Madam Olufsen, as Rumpelstiltskin once said."

"Have you won the Lotto then?"

"Well I suppose you could call it that . . . Anyway, it doesn't matter! I raise my glass to my old, steadfast friends! And give my thanks for the kindness you have always shown me! Cheers Senior Boatswain Olufsen! . . . And may ye not get a heart attack if you see my name in lights very shortly!"

The very next day Per was to be found standing outside the colonel's home-cum-office with his drawings rolled under his arm. A young lady opened the front door and, after being forced to wait some time in a kind of hallway while the girl delivered his business card, he was led in to a large studio-type room with a three-bayed window. The windows allowed bright and airy light to flood in from a nearby garden. A small flushed man with tight frizzy hair got up from a large writing table and bustled towards him. He held a pince-nez in one of his hands. But halfway across the floor, the man stopped in mid-stride, perched his glasses and pince-nez on his nose and looked Per up and down, giving all the indications of a man who had received an unpleasant shock.

"Good God in heaven!" he exclaimed. "Are you, I mean . . . the engineer Hr. Sidenius, is it not?"

"Yes, the very same, sir."

"Well—I never!—You're nothing more than a pup."

"Ah," said Per in a slightly hurt tone. "Well I'm twenty-two, so not quite a pup."

"Yes but . . . well I mean . . . all this must be some kind of—"

It was clear that the colonel wanted to say "misunderstanding" but thought better of it as he turned on his heels like someone who was peeved with himself because he had committed a gross error of judgment and was at a loss to decide the best way to conceal his embarrassment.

"Well, ahem...take a seat then," he said, quite reluctantly. "I suppose there's no harm in having a very brief chat about this matter." And, after throwing his hand out to indicate that Per should be seated in a small wicker sofa at the side of the writing table, then seating himself in a wide armchair facing the sofa, he continued in the same tone of voice: "As I explained in my letter to you, I did—in amongst a whole mountain of absurdities, not to say downright insanities—find one or two elements in the plans you submitted which—possibly—deserve further consideration. It goes without saying that your idea of a major canal facility covering a large part of Jutland and the auxiliary components you say are required, I find—to put it mildly—almost childlike in its naiveté. So...we're happy to kick that into touch. On the other hand, I must admit, where the idea of a major realignment of the easterly fjord inlets is concerned, there is no doubt that the idea has a fairly sound basis...and similarly the way you envisage the plan might be realized is indeed innovative and does contain new observations."

As he spoke, he turned a ruler slowly round in his hand and observed Per with a sharp eye from behind his pince-nez, which was perched almost horizontally on his ruby-tinged nose. The colonel's tone of voice had by turns become less dismissive. Per's robust, broad-shouldered figure clearly appealed to his military mindset. And then he suddenly stopped in the middle of what he was saying, placed both hands on the armrests and exclaimed with renewed surprise: "But—may God strike me dead and send me to that big parade ground in the sky!—how could a young man like you come up with such a mad idea like this project? It cannot be because it would make any practical difference to your own life. You look, if you don't mind me saying, more likely to have young nubile women on your mind and all that carry-on rather than logarithms and land-mass calculations."

Per's head told him to laugh at this remark, even though in his heart he was not amused by it. He then proceeded to give a full and frank explanation as to how he had toiled at his plans for several years, and how these ideas had really occupied his thoughts since he was a young boy. Once he had found the flow of his story, his eloquence increased accordingly and he began to describe with unbounded self-confidence how significant the project was. While making references to relevant facts from abroad to support his case, he declared it his absolute conviction that the authorities at home had, since the beginnings of the railway building program, to an unforgivable degree neglected the development of the country's natural transport network: the waterways, which almost everywhere had been allowed to fall into disuse and were thus on the verge of choking to death. All this, of course, was to the detriment both of the country's prosperity and the wellbeing of the people.

After this final fusillade of words, the colonel, whose face during Per's pronouncements had shown the hint of a smile, broke out into spontaneous laughter.

"Well I swear—there's no doubt!—you don't lack for courage! And do you not think that I am aware that your project represents a challenge to all us old men with our wigs and arthritis who have so shamefully, as you say, neglected the nation's honor ha ha! And then, on top of that, you demand the right to criticize and lacerate us in our own journal. I have to say that the whole thing is simply *le comble*—it just beats the band! Are they the detailed plans you have with you there? Let me see them for heaven's sake!" One by one, Per rolled out his drawings and spread them out on the colonel's writing table.

"Heavens above send down a dove!" the colonel cried in alarm. "There's enough here to cover my old mess room! How could it have ever entered your head to do all this, a young man like you? This is bordering on sheer madness my dear man! ... And yet with all this I still don't see the outline proposals for the fjord realignment that I mentioned. There is no point in denying that it is this that interests me more than anything else."

Per rolled out his final drawing, an enormous sheet that nearly covered the whole table. A sheet of paper, furthermore, that represented a full six months of dogged industry. It contained outline summaries and cross sections of parallel embankments, land spurs for current control, fascine coverings, support walls, etc.—everything carefully, indeed meticulously, set out, right down to the scale symbols and the handwritten headlines that were so neat they resembled printed script.

The colonel fixed his pince-nez more securely on his nose and took a calliper compass out of its holder.

"As you are possibly aware," he declared after a silence, which signaled his reluctant admission of how impressed he was, "as you are possibly aware, some ten years or so ago there was actually talk of widening this very fjord inlet and also the reconstruction of the harbor. At that time, I myself was actually consulted about the whole thing . . . and it's possibly because of the memories that were stirred in me by your project that I . . . that I . . . Well, anyway, take that chair and sit here . . . then explain to me how you see the whole thing working."

For well over an hour the two men sat beside each other, engrossed in measurements and calculations. Time and again the colonel threw his callipers to one side and declared the whole thing to be the work of a madman, but a moment later would see him expressing a warm acknowledgment of some pleasing discovery, a shrewd use of the terrain, a well-executed foundation method and so on. Per maintained his composure throughout. He was, in contrast with the old campaigner, the epitome of cold-blooded reason. Showing clever tactical awareness, he was happy to cede ground on all minor points so as to heighten the effect when sticking to his guns in the face of any major attack on his work. This lengthy battle of wits gradually developed into a kind of duel between the upstart prince and the old, venerated knight, and on more than one occasion the master was reduced to silence or, indeed, was betimes forced to give way to his callow opponent. In fact, the old colonel finally became so persuaded by Per's arguments that the canal project, with its projected network of locks and sluice gates and large port on the west coast (that he had dismissed so perfunctorily) was now taken up for renewed and detailed study.

Then, his face puce with the strain of it all, the colonel suddenly brushed all the papers to one side and said: "Let me hold on to this stuff for around a week. We have to get it knocked into some kind of shape . . . separate the wheat from the chaff, and believe me there's a lot of chaff! Before there can be any talk of it being published in our journal, the whole thing has to be summarized and made ready for battle. I'll see what I can do. I grant you that now I have a better understanding of your underlying philosophy, but the plan really needs to be presented in its entirety to do it full justice. Seen as pure hypothesis, there is no doubt that it has much to entertain the mind and the obsessive technicians amongst us will have a field day with it. You have no shortage of ideas young man! How old did you say you were again?"

"Twenty-two."

"Oh happy youth. God, to be alive and be twenty-two! As I say, come back to me in a week's time."

As Per made to leave, the colonel gave a hearty handshake, which also signaled his collegial respect.

"My word, your eyes are like cannon fire young man," he said suddenly as he continued to hold Per's hand. "Where did you get them from, eh? You look at people like a hungry wolf. Well—good hunting is all I can say!" he concluded with a smile, once again taking his hand in a final goodbye.

When Per stepped out onto the street, it seemed to him that the whole world was transformed. The air was so gentle, the heavens had been raised to new heights and people looked so peculiarly small.

Time to calm down, Per thought, forcing himself to look at his position with clear-headed analysis. Good God—what had happened was only what he knew was bound to happen, sooner or later. He was not even going to send the journal to anybody once it was published, not even his parents or other family members—they would no doubt get copies of it at some point. And besides, at the moment the whole thing did not amount to much. He had merely taken the very first, and tiny, step on the way to fame and fortune. That was all. What mattered now was to harness all his energies for the next and even greater step. For this involved the far more difficult task of bringing his ideas to a wider audience, to create a positive atmosphere around them, to draw supporters to his banner from amongst the governing elite and the broader populace.

In the days that followed, Per once again frequented the billiard halls, both in order to kill time and to dampen his impatience until he could legitimately pay a visit to the colonel. One evening he walked into a café on Kongens Nytorv and ran into Fritjof, whom he had not seen since their post-debauchery conversation in the Cauldron, when the shaggy, unkempt giant had revealed himself to be more like an altar boy, a shorn and quivering lamb, than a lion amongst men. Now he was once again in his artistic pomp, holding court amongst a circle of young, submissive worshippers of beauty, who were all, just as Fritjof was, dressed in evening wear and drinking mineral water and cognac. The scene represented the aftermath of a dinner arranged by an art dealer. Fritjof had pushed his large gray Rubens hat back on his head and the palms of both his hands rested on a bamboo cane of monstrous proportions, which was firmly planted between his protruding legs.

"Well raise the skull and crossbones me hearties! If it isn't Salomon's young Aladdin!" he almost roared as Per entered, offering a greeting as he did so in the way of a gracious raising of his hand. "Where has that genie in the lamp been keeping you for so long? Come and join us man!"

But Per was in no mood to get stuck in that kind of company and instead chose a seat at a nearby table. In reply to Fritjof's repeated questions as to why he had been off the scene for so long, Per answered briefly that he had been working non-stop.

Fritjof let out a roar of laughter of Olympian proportions.

"Of course! You are another one of these new-fangled functionaries whom Nathan has begun to idolize. You can have it! You've probably been working night and day to see how you can extract a drop of water from one of our poor little lakes, eh? Or you've worked out how to blow the cliffs at Møn to smithereens so that you can use them for mortar?

Or, tell me, in what way have you served the cause of progress and contributed to the beautification and improvement of our great fatherland?"

Per looked out across the faces of the young artists, who sat in solemn torpor, their arms lolling over the backs of chairs, in an attempt to give the impression that they brooded over some imminent artistic revelation. As he lit a cigar, he leaned back in his chair and threw out his riposte: "Maybe it is just as well that we can't be all geniuses, able to create heaven on earth—on little pieces of canvas."

"No, of course not! Long live the captains of industry! Let's have more and more stinking chimney towers, and may God bless our sewers! And tell me another thing young man, have you ever really thought what this brave new world that has been brought to us by machine power actually looks like? Do me the service one day of taking an hour of your precious time to accompany me down one of the back alleys in this town where you will observe the deathly pale faces of the brood that lives there, festering like maggots in a dead corpse. Or we can dander on up to where the thieves and bandits live, the millionaire Jewboys with their fat-assed madames . . . putrefaction and decay wherever ye care to look my friend! Oh, God help us! And you call that progress! That is the great dawn of science that we are all waiting for! God help us I say! No, I'm sorry, but I'd rather bow down before some carrot cruncher out in the sticks who couldn't care less about making the world a better place and is happy to sing a song and plow his fields till the cows come home. He is more of a real person to me than all of them damned Rabbi heads babbling on about progress put together. What do you say?" He turned to his supporters seated around the table, who responded with a chorus of supportive mumbling.

Per was not in the least surprised by Fritjof's outburst given the man's rather befuddled state. His sentiments were not dissimilar to those he had expressed during the evening they had spent together at the Cauldron. But what he could not fathom was Fritjof's repeated and scornful attacks on Dr. Nathan, given that he had previously been such an outspoken champion of Nathan's cause. However, he felt that any attempt to continue the conversation was just not worth the effort and so with a shrug of his shoulders he turned back to his newspaper.

At that very moment, the entrance to the establishment was thrown wide open. A seemingly endless procession of people then flowed in from the street, comprising ladies obviously dressed for the theater and accompanying gentlemen with their overcoats slung across their shoulders. In no time at all, they had taken every available seat in what moments before had been an almost empty café. An opening night performance had taken place at the Royal Theater that evening and it was as if this tide of people had brought with them the emotion and catharsis they had experienced in the final act. The playwright's name and that of the actors involved were bandied about, roles were discussed and the essential meaning of the piece aroused passionate debate like bushfires erupting at various tables. But the presence of Fritjof and the other artists, of whom a goodly number had gained widespread fame despite their youth, provoked increasing attention and comment amongst the well-heeled guests. All about the tables, people put their heads together, pointed and spoke in whispers, or with their hands covering their mouths. Sitting alone in a corner, one young pale man in particular attracted a flurry of quick glances and comment with his Mephistophelian aura. This was the author Povl Berger, one of the great Enevoldsen's many protégés and widely viewed as his literary successor, following the recent death of this much venerated man of letters who had literally dropped dead in mid-sentence. Per overheard some ladies at a nearby table speaking in animated tones about Berger's poetry. This same young man now came into Per's mind from Fritjof's Bacchanalian night at the Cauldron. Povl Berger it was who had jumped up onto a chair in order to propose a toast to Dr. Nathan's name and who had finally crushed his glass in his hand in an idiotic display of reckless euphoria.

And with that a deep sense of despondency came over Per, as he sat and observed the Bedlam taking place before his very eyes. He could not help but reflect on the fact that, no matter how much he succeeded in making a name for himself in his chosen field of expertise, he could never hope to achieve the kind of celebrity enjoyed by a two-bit rhymer whose name was on everybody's lips. Even when his ideas were finally in the public domain, his own name would still hardly register outside of a narrow circle of engineers and technicians. While the press was willing to devote a mountain of column inches to the latest tacky romantic novel, his own creative monument would presumably receive no more than a passing reference in a side column. Yes, if he had only written a poem about the sea, or painted a quiet, moonlit canal instead of toiling over a canal project.

As he rose from his seat to leave, he could not resist turning to Fritjof and saying: "It seems that you precious artists have little reason for complaint in this country of ours. You can see for yourself the commotion that a piddling little theater piece can stir up. Within a week the whole town will be tongue-tied about this great event in our lives."

"And what man? What else do you want people to talk about in this country?"

Fritjof's choice of words seemed to hit home. For a moment he looked at the scene around him without saying a word.

"Maybe you are right," he said at last. And as he gave a final scathing look at the circle of artists before him, as if to offer a challenge to each and everyone of them, he gave his parting shot: "But just wait— things are going to change!"

"There he goes! Yet another self-deluded lunatic!" Fritjof cried when Per had gone. Then he drank heartily from his glass. His table confederates automatically raised their own glasses and uttered more mumbled noises of support.

Per was unable to reign in his impatience for any longer than precisely the week the colonel had requested for his further deliberations. But when, eight days later, he found himself once again in the colonel's study, he encountered a completely different man to the enthusiastic colleague from whom he had taken his encouraging leave only a week before. The colonel neither offered his hand in greeting, nor invited him to take a seat. With a blustering bluntness—which quite obviously was an attempt to conceal a measure of embarrassment—he returned Per's papers to him without standing on ceremony, except to remark that on closer inspection he had in fact found the proposals unsuitable for inclusion in the journal.

"The whole thing suffers from a marked lack of mature reflection. And, besides, you are just too young to attempt this whole thing by yourself... I mean, you have not even sat your exam yet... you have not even gained your master's degree from what I gather?"

Ah it's like that is it? Per thought to himself. He has decided to watch his back and has been asking around about me... he's possibly even been to see Professor Sandrup. Here we go!

In the meantime, the colonel had positioned himself by the side of a large stove at the other end of the room. From this vantage point, he ran a mistrustful rule over Per, his bearing and apparel, right down to the cut of his boots—in fact, he even inspected Per's hat, which Per had left on a chair by the door when entering the room.

"Your name is Sidenius," the colonel said after an awkward silence. "Are you by any chance related to the line of pastors of that same name?"

As always when Per was confronted with this question, he contracted a momentary deafness. He then began, in quite provocative language, to mock the colonel's sudden change in attitude with regards to his work. But the colonel broke him off curtly, and with a hint of nervousness in his voice, by saying that any further discussion was a waste of time and completely pointless. His views on this issue were now set in stone, and that was that.

It was clear that he wanted to be rid of Per as quickly as possible. It was as if he wished to deny him the right to speak—for fear that he once again might turn in his favor.

"I must apologize," the colonel said finally, and in a more sympathetic tone, taking a few steps forward as he did so—"I must apologize in the event that my words last week should have aroused a sense of false hope on your part, but I am in no doubt that this rejection is in fact in your best interests, given your undoubted commitment. I do not deny that you have ability, but at this stage you must first and foremost learn to acknowledge your deficiencies. A young man like you of twenty-two years of age should not have any ambition other than to listen and learn. Our journal has never been an outlet for young people who simply want to publicize their first faltering experiments."

After these words, he turned back to his desk with a dismissive wave of his hand as if to signal that the audience was at an end.

But Per remained standing where he was.

"Exactly how old and decrepit does the colonel believe I should be before he will deign to give my work the acknowledgment it obviously deserves?"

His face as red as an angry crab, the veteran soldier rounded on Per with such haste that the carpet cut folds at his feet.

"Why you impudent whelp. I'll have you...!" he exclaimed, but faltered at the sight of Per's quivering, death-white countenance. He saw that there was a real danger of fisticuffs and, from fear of a scandal taking place, he sufficed by stating once again that any attempts to discuss the matter further would be futile. He had nothing more to say.

"Yes, but I have something to say to you oh mighty colonel," said Per. "You will live to regret that you have shown me the door."

"Am I hearing you right? You dare to threaten me!"

"Make what you will of it. But the next time we meet, it will be because you, sir, are looking for me! You have just committed a grave mistake Hr. Colonel...You have underestimated me and I have overestimated you. Had I known you better, I would not have put you through so much trouble. We will meet again but on my terms next time!"

During this dressing down, the old soldier had seethed with anger. But he gave no reply. The truth was that he was torn by an inner conflict. When the door banged shut with Per's departure, his whole body shook, as if he was jolted into calling him back. But with a "by Christ, that young fellow—" he turned and went back to his writing table, where in his indignation he started to root around amongst his papers.

Some minutes later, his quite terrified wife ventured into the office from the adjoining sitting room and said: "Who was that person you had in with you just now? Dear me! He slammed the front door so hard after him that a big piece of the picture rail fell down."

"No doubt he did! Aye, wait till you see. He will come to cause more damage than just a bit of falling ceiling plaster that boy!"

"Who was he?"

"You probably know just as much as me! A lunatic, I presume. Or better still a chancer! . . . Or maybe he's a genius! . . . Only time will tell my dear."

6

ONE SUNDAY morning in the beginning of April, a spring day with quiet weather and high, drifting clouds, Per was sitting outside the restaurant at Langelinje promenade observing the unending stream of day-trippers who, after attending church and partaking of lunch, had come out there to take in the sun and fill their lungs with the fresh sea air.

His outward appearance had changed somewhat over the preceding months. He had lost a good deal of weight (which was by no means to his detriment), and the so-called imperial goatee beard, which he had grown around his chin with the express intention of developing a more mature look, gave his face more character and depth. Nor did his general demeanor carry his former devil-may-care attitude. As he sat there with his hand under his chin, staring out over the passing crowds dressed in their Sunday finery, it was not difficult to discern from Per's slightly troubled gaze and his puckered eyebrows that here was a young man upon whom life had visited its first serious moments of distress in his adult life.

The fact was that he had sustained a crushing defeat. He who up until then, and during the whole period of his scheming and assembling for the future, had possessed a determined patience that was underpinned by utter confidence and self belief—he who had been so eagle-eyed, so controlled, at times so cleverly calculating—had now quite lost the run of himself following his clash with Colonel Bjerregrav. Thus, with the motivation of gaining revenge on the colonel and Professor Sandrup, or whoever it might be that had presumed to block his advancement at any point in time, he had not only sought out a number of the city's foremost men and shown them his work, he had also visited the editorial offices of the daily newspapers, seeking to get articles published about his ideas. In fact, he had even requested an audience with the minister for home affairs himself in order to impress upon him the urgent need for a complete restructuring of the country's waterways, ditto the Department of Maritime Works. And everywhere he went, he had just encountered the same wry smiles and shoulder shrugs—where, that is, he had not simply been shown the door without further ado.

It was Per's great misfortune to be forced to suffer this time of adversity in complete isolation, without any connection to another human being in whom he might confide his disappointments and who might prove a sounding board for his utter indignation. A wounding bitterness was not long in taking hold of him, causing him to shun human contact and fostering dark ruminations in his mind that he was the victim of a planned and conscious campaign of persecution. His former fellow students at the College of Engineering he chose to avoid wherever and whenever possible. He had convinced himself that every last one of them believed him to be mad (and in truth there were a good number of them who actually did think this way). Nor had he set foot in the Cauldron for over a year, despite his awareness that Lisbeth had long since found consolation in the arms of another man. Per had got to the stage where he felt a downright disgust for all artists, the country's spoiled little brats who practiced a similar hysterical idolatry with nature as the clerics did with their talk of the life to come, and who therefore also enjoyed a status as favored beings—"instruments of the divine" bringing revelations from on high. At the heel of the hunt, these worshippers of canvases and atmospherics, for all their ridiculousness, were not as innocent or benign as he had believed. They too had played their part in undermining the belief in man as master of the earth and absolute ruler.

Overall, in these days of constant buffeting headwinds, the dire torturous feelings of loneliness, which had dogged him since his childhood days at the rectory, were aroused in him once again. Just as he had once felt himself to be an orphan amongst his parents and brothers and sisters, he now felt that he was a wandering stranger in his own society. In his compatriots, he saw nothing but massed ranks of self-righteous Sideniuses, who, like the Pharisees before them, covered up their petty bourgeois timidity with an arrogant contempt for this world's delights and splendors, and it often occurred to him how blessed the Roman Catholics were that their priests never married—that all the spiritual debilitation that was inbred within the Church's false humility was not allowed to go any further, whereas in the Protestant countries this laming debility was passed on from generation to generation. A debility, in other words, which took root amongst the population, proliferating in all directions and turning all natural conventions upside down—creating a grotesque kingdom of humpbacked underground trolls who shunned the bright light of life, where the poor were counted as blessed, the meek exalted and death was the only glorious salvation—an upside down land where small things were deemed to be big and the crooked declared straight.

There was also the fact that he had other demons to contend with, amongst which were his financial worries. Despite the fact that he had lived as thriftily as a poor student in his garret and had frequented the cheapest possible cellar restaurants in the Borgergade area, where he ate cheek by jowl with carriage jarveys and messenger boys, the Neergaard inheritance was all but spent. He had worked out that the money available to him could not be stretched any further than another couple of months. And what then? Was he going to go back to being someone whose only real function was to whip young recalcitrant schoolboys into line? Or take out the begging bowl, perhaps—wending his way between factory owners and craftsmen pleading for copy work?

To compound things further, Per was afflicted by love troubles in as much that he just could not shake off the memory of Francesca. He would sometimes find himself simply sitting and staring, with no little emotion, at some small memento of hers that he had kept: a dried and pressed flower she had once fastened to his buttonhole; an Easter greeting from her as his secret admirer containing a snowdrop and written in mirror script; a ribbon of blue silk he had sequestered from her neck one evening. Yes, the truth was that when, as daylight faded and he betook his usual lonely evening stroll, and saw other young men who the heavenly and earthly powers had blessed, in all the best connotations of that word, enjoying the sunset and the early spring air, arm in arm with their sweethearts, there would be moments when his old fallibility would come back to haunt him and he would ask whether or not he had sacrificed his future happiness and good fortune on the high altar of a delusion—whether, indeed, he might not sooner rather than later forget all his haughty, unrealistic notions and settle down like everybody else did. Was it not time that he learned with good grace to take up his appointed seat on some hard office chair so as to finally tie the knot with Francesca and become a pillar of society, a happy father with a happy family in that inverted kingdom where to be mediocre and shun the light was the highest call?

Nor was this the end of his troubles by any means. As if all the powers that be had conspired to test his steadfastness, he had, only a few days before, received an almighty shock following a horrible turn of events at home in Hjertensfrydgade with the sudden death of Senior Boatswain Olufsen. The old man had taken his usual mid-morning constitutional over to Amalienborg Square, then on to Borgergade before turning into Antonistræde, and was on the home-ward leg of his journey when, at the corner of Gothersgade and Adelgade, he promptly collapsed and there remained lying on the pavement. He had still just enough wits about him to mutter his name and address as he was carried through the throng of curious onlookers to a closed carriage, which brought him back to his own door. His wife was just at that moment standing in the upstairs room watching the street mirror in anticipation of his return when the carriage stopped outside the house. As soon as she saw the arm of the police constable being thrust out of the window to open the carriage, she understood what had happened and hurtled down the staircase. Per, who was in his room at the time and heard the sudden commo-tion, ran out into the hallway to investigate and from this vantage point was able to watch Madam Olufsen as she forcefully shoved the constable away from the carriage door and moments later entered the house again with the body of the Senior Boatswain dangling in her arms. Completely on her own, and refusing all offers of help, the seventy-three-year-old woman of the house carried her dying husband up the steep stairs, while the police constable, with a dignity befitting his official capacity as an officer of the law, followed behind carrying Hr. Olufsen's gray cylinder hat and brown cane. As soon as a message was dispatched, in all haste, for a doctor to come, and while the quite shattered wife of the ship's carpenter down on the ground floor had run off on her own initiative to look for a local clergyman, Per and the constable helped Madam Olufsen to convey her husband on to the bed, where he then, some minutes later, breathed his last with his head sinking on to her breast.

From that day forth, Per had felt ill at ease in his quarters. This had been his first real brush with death. The image of that stiff, stomach-turning corpse, with its gaping mouth, lying up there above his head, had kept him awake at nights; and during the day when he sat at his table with his head between his hands, staring vacantly at his drawings—those five or six ill-starred sheets which had cast a spell on him and robbed him of his will and reason—it was as if the deathly quiet that reigned over the house, that chill from the crypt that pervaded his room from the ceiling above, mocked all his own tribulations by reminding him how worthless and pathetic even the greatest of lives were when faced with death's dominion; how minuscule, in fact, the length of even the longest surviving human life when compared with the eternity of oblivion.

In fact, he had actually stayed away from home for a whole night and day. In order to harness his wandering thoughts, he had drifted between cafés and billiard halls and then spent the night in the company of some strumpet or other, one of the angels of the street who at least knew how to dispense some sort of comfort; and now here he sat outside Langelinje Pavilion with an empty glass in front of him, hounded out of the town itself by the sound of church bells, the curse of his childhood that had been at his back the whole morning with its unending invocations. Never had he felt so alien in the world, never so lacking in hope and despondent as he had been on this supposed Day of Rest, as he walked through the streets with their long rows of shuttered shop windows and observed the parks and walkways full of cheerful citizens clad in their Sunday best. Here, for example, came a thick-necked gentleman with his nose in the air and hands behind his back, a lawyer (he supposed), a loan shark maybe, a swindler, who had gained absolution for his week's worth of sins in some church or other, and now he was out and about airing his born-again soul with a Havana cigar jammed between his teeth. And here was another fat-necked gentleman on the march, who could have been a twin of the first, with a luxuriant blond woman attached to his arm and a delightful little girl holding his hand—the happy family-type father personified, who had found his call in life by being a sales rep for tin buttons, or had perhaps set himself up for life by opening a lucrative toilet paper business. And here came the students and soldiers, the laughing young girls and doddering old ladies with their crab apple smiles, all parading their own cozily arranged snail shells, which for them was the center of their whole world. Modest people! Happy people! Honest, fine upstanding Sideniuses all!

A shrill blast from the horn of a passing steamship made him jump. A massive freighter was just at that moment steaming away from the harbor, driven on by thundering piston strokes. The sun's glare gave a sheen to its black-painted hull and smoke billowed out over the edge of it's funnel, like a phalanx of black wool. The captain was standing on the wing of the bridge with his hand on a signal bat. A red ensign fluttered at the ship's stern, telling the world that this was a ship of the British merchant marine.

On seeing this, an immense feeling of wanderlust came over Per . . . to get away and start his life anew in another corner of the world entirely, to live amongst different people altogether . . . to try for America, Australia maybe, or even further afield, to some remote unknown country where pious clerics and church bells were unheard of.

The thought was in no way strange to him, the temptation not a new one. And what was stopping him really? He knew nothing of the pull of hearth and kin that, for example, had laid Neergaard low—the curse he had talked about on that night of nights like some baleful charm that was sure to drag you down. Besides, with the imminent collapse of the old order at his home in Nyboder, he would almost certainly lose his only safe haven in the country. Moreover, was it not simply futile to expect any kind of future in this run down land—a land upon which the Fates had obviously pronounced impending doom? In recent days, following the Senior Boatswain's death, he'd had occasion to dwell on the old man's vivid descriptions of his many experiences during his long life, stretching right back to the famous sea battle with Lord Nelson himself on Maundy Thursday. This had taken place at the anchorage right in front of where he was now sitting. The old seadog had witnessed all that as a child in his mother's arms, and then came successive humiliations, a complete national dismemberment without precedent, which had been presaged by the barrage of cannon fire that fateful day. So why cling to a country that was nothing more than a sinking ship? A country that within the course of a single lifetime had fallen to wrack and ruin, had been reduced to nothing more than a flaccid and shriveled stump that barely registered on the bulging map of Europe.

A new life! A different land, a different sky! It was as if new energies were called forth in him by just thinking of what might be. While his eyes continued to follow the receding shape of the steamer, all his youthful fantasies of living as a lusty freebooter rose up once more, hammering in his blood. He told himself that it was out there maybe— far, far away—that great fortune and triumph awaited him. There in the great beyond, that was where his childhood dreams of winning the golden fleece might be realized. He might yet win a princess and half a kingdom out there—even though the princess might be black as ebony and the kingdom nothing more than a palm-bedecked oasis in the South Pacific!

At that moment a shadow was cast across the table. A small, fashionably dressed man now stood in front of him, lifting his hat and with a delighted smile on his face—Ivan Salomon no less. "Well, I was sure it was your good self and I was right! . . . That really is a turn up! It's so long since I have seen you! I must say, I believe you are avoiding your old friends. How are you keeping Hr. Sidenius?"

Per half rose from his chair and mumbled something by way of a greeting. He was not exactly enamored with the idea of having to meet someone in this way, but he invited his surprise interlocutor to take a seat.

Salomon sat down on the opposite side of the table, using the handle of his cane to give a few sharp raps on its metal surface in order to call a waiter's attention.

"Is there something I might offer you?" he asked. "I see that your glass is empty. An absinth perhaps?"

"I don't want anything, thank you."

"Not even a small glass of beer? Or a glass of wine . . . A glass of English Port, say. You won't be tempted? The stuff they sell here really is first class you know."

"As I say, many thanks. I don't want anything," Per repeated, with much more emphasis this time, while also reflecting with melancholy that here at least was one friend, one admirer. He recalled from somewhere a saying, that he had either heard or read, that no king was so lonely that he did not have at least one fool for company.

Salomon ordered a glass of iced water for himself and proffered a cigarette from a silver case.

"Of course, I know that you have been up to your ears in work Hr. Sidenius! Your great plans and inventions! That's the reason you sought peace and solitude, am I right? That's exactly what I had assumed. Well, when are you going to set off the dynamite and amaze us all? Can the world expect some revelation or other someday soon from that mind of yours, which has been blessed with such gifts?"

Per answered this with a simple shrug of his shoulders.

"I may as well say that great things are expected of you. Expectations tinged with a great yearning for the tide to turn. I always say to people who complain about the fact that nothing of any great import happens in our country anymore—just wait, I tell them, a new generation is emerging in our kingdom. They will light the flame of revolution."

Per still refused to engage in that particular discussion. Salomon's sycophancy left him ill at ease, not least because his words laid shamelessly bare his own thoughts and aspirations—thoughts he himself hardly dared admit to harboring.

"Have you read Nathan's latest essay in *The Beacon*? Have you not heard tell of it? Ah, you must read it! It is manna from heaven for someone like you! Quite superb I tell you sir! The way he exposes to their shivering bones what he calls our anemic aesthetes here at home and calls bold men of action and initiative to arms…wonderful stuff!"

Per looked up in surprise.

"Dr. Nathan?" he said.

Of a sudden, he recalled his last café conversation with Fritjof and how the artist had made repeated references to this Jewish writer in ways that he, at that time, neither understood nor even bothered himself to understand. But now these further remarks by Salomon had made him curious to know more. He asked what this doctor at the university had actually written, to which his table companion responded by immediately offering to lend him the article in question.

"Ah don't put yourself to any trouble," said Per dismissively. "I doubt whether I would ever get around to reading it." And, after leaning back in his seat, he added as a throwaway remark: "It half occurs to me that I should take off somewhere."

"You're not thinking of leaving us?"

It sounded almost like a fearful cry.

"I'm considering it. Yes."

"For good?"

"Perhaps."

Little Ivan Salomon threw his gaze downwards and sat, for some time thereafter, without saying anything.

He had, from other sources, heard certain rumors regarding Per's project and about Colonel Bjerregrav's and Professor Sandrup's negative attitude towards it; but he could hardly believe that it was possible in these new times that somebody like Per could be subject to such a blatant lack of appreciation.

"Well, yes," he said. "I can understand that you perhaps feel the need to get away from it all. There is not exactly—at the moment—

what might be called favorable soil here for you to plow and sow. I am minded of the expression you once used to describe our noble cradle of learning—the College of Engineering. You called it 'a breeding ground for office bureaucrats.' I find that description quite superb. And it is beyond question completely accurate. In the times in which we live, everything is geared towards the encouragement of mediocrity. There is no longer any room for idiosyncrasy, no appreciation of, nor even a perceived need for, the exception to the rule, for excellence, for trailblazers. It is just as Dr. Nathan has described it when he writes that for too long we have indulged in fairy tales rather than engaging with reality and, because of this, the nation has been sapped of its willpower to a significant extent."

"Is that what he wrote?"

"Oh yes—and much more besides. But you will permit me to send the article anyway? Oh you simply must read it Hr. Sidenius! Are you thinking of going far away, once you leave?"

"I don't know. I haven't really gone into that much—."

"Ah but you will be back I would wager. Yes, you will soon be back amongst us sir! I have no doubts at all about that! Denmark's future will, at some point, lie in your hands! But perhaps it's not such a bad idea, trying to think tactically, to disappear for a while. It could even be a smart move. A period spent abroad always lends a certain prestige to one's curriculum vitae. Say you were to gain a position with one of the big English or French engineering companies—Blackbourn & Gries for example—the company that deals with large bridge-building schemes. As it happens, we have had occasion to do business with them. But perhaps you have other plans?"

Per muttered an evasive response.

Salomon sat quietly for a while, fiddling with his gaily patterned silk handkerchief. During this whole conversation, he had burned to ask Per a question but had not been able to summon the courage to force it past his lips. His question referred to Per's travel costs. Salomon was far more aware of how things stood with the young engineer than Per himself realized. He knew, for example, quite a lot about Per's financial hardships and it grieved him sorely that Per's attitude towards him had thus far precluded any offer of friendly assistance from his side. Now Ivan's hopes were raised that he might finally get the chance to perform the kind of service for Per that he simply loved to perform for anyone whose talent and future potential he recognized and admired. And this generosity of spirit was by no means simply a case of satisfying his own vanity. For despite his many slightly ridiculous traits, little Ivan Salomon was at heart an unselfish person with a childlike innocence and a basic sympathy for his fellow man. His natural disposition was to be helpful, his natural drive was to find things to worship and his only passion was to help ensure that his idols were apportioned their proper place in life's pantheon.

Suddenly he jumped from his seat as if he had been tipped out by some mechanism in the chair.

"I'm sorry but I am going to have to take my leave," he said. "I've promised my mother and one of my sisters that I'd go with them to our place out in the country—and I can see the carriage approaching."

Down in the narrow, deep-set roadway that separated the restaurant from the walkway, which was traversed by an arched bridge, a lavishly equipped luxury coach came into view. A coach driver and attendant dressed in blue livery were enthroned behind a pair of large brown horses whose reins were embellished with silver trappings. Two silk parasols could be spied at the rear of this spectacle—one was white and the other was a lilac color.

"Would you care to be introduced to my family?" Salomon asked. "Both my mother and sister would love to meet you."

Per made a number of excuses as to why this was not a good idea. He had absolutely no desire to be dragged from his seat and made a show of under the gaze of so many people. But Salomon had already motioned to the driver and moments later the coach eased to a halt at the foot of some steps that led from the restaurant down to the roadway below.

Two ladies could be seen beneath the parasols, one of whom—the youngest—immediately caught Per's eye. Nor was this the first time he had seen her. However, on the last occasion, she had been wearing a ball mask and he had been unaware of who she was. That was the evening of the carnival that had taken place over a year ago. The same night, in fact, that he had met Fru Engelhardt for the first time. He could not help but now recognize this young lady from that night, as mysterious as a décolleté Snow Queen in her white silk dress that shimmered with diamonds. Since then, on the few occasions she had crossed his mind, he had imagined a whey-faced Jewess, showing off her finery and trinkets like some merchant advertising her wares. However, now what he saw in front of him was a decidedly young girl, hardly more than eighteen, nineteen years of age whose Jewish ancestry could never be denied, but who had a fresh, regular face with a rosy complexion that was framed by a lustrous mass of curly hair. She wore a short, narrow-cut velvet jacket that was lined with fur and caught the eye immediately but, at the same time, showed no little discernment in taste. Her head was covered by a little hat, from which flowed two large brightly colored silk bows, like oversized butterfly wings. Directly beneath these wings sat a pair of lovely ebony eyes, full of life and devilment. And these eyes observed him with undoubted interest, a bold curiosity that almost had him bewildered.

Their mother on the other hand had returned Per's greeting with a brief and measured nod.

"So that's what you look like then," she said. "My son has often spoken of you. You are an engineer. Isn't that right?"

Per answered mechanically—he had not averted his gaze from the young woman, which gaze she returned with full favor, albeit that it became more and more concealed behind her long, delving eyelashes.

However, the encounter was soon over with. Ivan ascended into the coach, and after Fru Salomon had let it be known that any of her son's friends were always welcome in his home and final formal salutations were exchanged, the attendant took up his place on the driver's bench and the carriage rolled away.

A warm glow rising in his cheeks, Per walked back into town.

He could not dismiss from his mind the boldness of those jet brown eyes. And he suddenly saw this young maiden quite clearly before him, just as he saw her on the night of the carnival as she eased past him through the throng—half-naked, a golden crown on her dark hair, like some mythical shepherdess with her long, undulating veil of sparkling diamonds.

And it was as if the voice of the Great Tempter himself whispered in his ear: "The black princess . . . and half a kingdom awaits!"

True to his word, Ivan Salomon sent Dr. Nathan's controversial essay to him that very same evening, and, given that he had no other task with which to occupy his mind, Per began to browse through it straight away. However, his mild curiosity was quickly transformed into a captivation with its language and tone, to an extent that surprised him. The article brought certain books to his mind that were of a similar nature—Martensen's *Ethics* for example—from which he had been obliged to read aloud for his father as a young boy on his free afternoons—a task which had been an undoubted influence on his attitude to literature outside his own area of specialty. Here now, in black and white, and expressed in clear and authoritative language, he was able to read something that expressed what his own experience had taught him about life and human beings, and his heart rejoiced at the witty, yet utterly excoriating, attacks on all those things he himself hated about life in Denmark. First and foremost, the whole pack of petty, self-righteous clerics, typical Sideniuses to a man, whom Dr. Nathan also viewed as the country's greatest misfortune and shame.

Per was particularly taken by the conclusion to the long essay, where the author, as a response to the attacks which his campaign had provoked from many quarters, offered his impressions in evocative prose of his return to his homeland following a study period abroad that had lasted several years. He described how, following a journey in an express train across a resurgent Germany with the cacophony of noise in its great cities, and then on through the bustle of Hamburg and the newly created Kiel canal, he arrived by steamship one tranquil morning at Korsør harbor, and even as the ship made its approach to the little town's quiet and forlorn quay, he had been gripped by a feeling of having been transported to a different world, a dreamlike, ethereal realm. Nor had this impression in any way abated when, with the sun rising at its back, his rickety, rumbling train pressed on through the countryside and eventually rocked all the other passengers to sleep. The train, moreover, stopped at every quarter of the hour at every little country station along the way, where a pair of farmers, followers of Grundtvig with their spreading pilgrims hats and large tobacco pipes, were invariably sitting and waiting—not for the train that had just pulled in but for another that was due in another hour or so. It was as if he had arrived in a country where a clock was of no use to anyone, where everyone literally had the whole of eternity ahead of them. And this feeling stayed with him when he reached Copenhagen and walked its narrow streets. Nothing seemed to have changed in the intervening years. The pavements were still in the same rag order, the shops just as provincial, the carriages were the same old snail-house conveyances as before, passing the same old theater placards extolling the virtues of the same childish poetic chivalry dramas as were playing the day he left. The overall impression was that life had stood still here, whereas out there in the great beyond that was Europe, huge changes had taken place in all aspects of life—a revolution in ways of thinking that had transformed societies and presented the populace with far greater and audacious goals to aim for.

Finally, Dr. Nathan concluded, he had arrived in the vicinity of the student halls at Gammelholm and coincidentally at that time of the day when, in his days as an undergraduate, he had taken his afternoon coffee along with some of his fellow students at the university. When it occurred to him that he might yet bump into one or other of these old acquaintances, he went inside the building. The sight that confronted him there astounded him. For here he saw almost the exact same company, gathered around the exact same table in the exact same corner, as had been there when he had sat amongst them all those years ago. They had all aged considerably since he had last seen them. One amongst them had already turned gray, others had become thin and gaunt but the majority were now decidedly fat, and from both their facial expressions and bodily movements, and more especially the self-satisfied drawl of their speech, the early onset of intellectual decrepitude was laid bare. All that aside, they sat there just as they had done year in year out, as if they had been rooted to the spot. Indeed, their conversation, to which—unrecognized as he was—he had listened while sitting at a neighboring table, consisted of the same exalted theological and philosophical meanderings with which they had leavened their imbibing of coffee and tobacco in the days of yore. A conversation, moreover, which revealed the fact that not a single iota of what had been thought, produced or composed throughout the length and breadth of Europe had managed to breach Denmark's borders. And with that he understood exactly where he found himself. He had been transported to the land of Sleeping Beauty where time stood still and where the pallid rose of fantasy and the impenetrable briars of speculation furtively concealed the decay that reigned in the kingdom at the heart of the forest. But at that same moment (these were Nathan's last words in the essay) he understood his call, his true vocation. For just like the man in the fairy tale who, upon returning from a great and lengthy adventure, tore the hunter's horn from the sleeping watchman to rouse the country's champions from their deep slumbers, Nathan had sought to bestir those who still had fire in their hearts; first and foremost the country's youth, and amongst these more especially the strong and battle-ready who had the courage to clear a new path and tear down the unyielding tangle of fantasy forests and fables, the overgrown and petrified tomb in which the nation's spirit had been embalmed.

It was this final call to arms in particular that stirred Per's blood and brought a gleam to his eyes. He felt that these rousing, inspirational exhortations were directed at him personally—in fact, that they had been personally dedicated to him. Per slammed his hand down on to the table and, as if to confirm his inner thoughts, he called out loud: "Yes! Yes!" He recalled how the old colonel on that fateful day had mockingly described his project as a throwing down of the gauntlet to the aristocracy of Danish engineering. So be it! That's exactly what it would be! For he now understood that he had been brought on this earth to herald a new and bright dawn, that he was indeed the trailblazer who would rouse this slothful nation with its progeny of clerics and sacristans. Little Ivan Salomon was right. Great things were indeed expected of him. Him, Per Sidenius, and no one else.

He rose from the table. Oblivious now to the corpse of Senior Boatswain, which still lay in the room above him, laid out in its garment of sugar paper, he walked backwards and forwards across the floor with brisk, firm steps. And suddenly he pushed his fist to his forehead, while he repeated again and again his affirming mantra to himself: "Yes—yes—yes!"

Then Ivan's sister, the young and nubile Miss Salomon, came to his thoughts. He saw her dark doe eyes, full of curiosity and boldness, and then (behind the veil of her eyelashes) the almost deliberate temptation in her gaze.

Never before had it occurred to him that he might further his ambitions by marrying into a rich family. He had always relied too much on the sufficiency of his own abilities to think of anything like that—and, besides, there was something about that way of thinking that disgusted him. Now he confronted the fact that, in the battle for the prized goal, it did not pay to be too precious about the means by which that goal was achieved. A Jewess? Yes, why not? And anyway, Frøken Salomon was also young and beautiful. Indeed, she was (as far as he could see) extremely well endowed. It was about time he abandoned all that kindergarten stuff about happiness being something that landed upon you out of the blue, in the way that people won a lottery prize. For there was no doubt that there was no such thing as unfailing or one hundred per cent happiness and good luck, other than that which human beings themselves wrenched from the hands of fate. Just like a wild animal, a saber-toothed beast, or Gyldenbørste the sparkling Golden Boar of Norse legend, Lady Fortune had to be hunted down and captured . . . like a hidden treasure trove reserved for the quickest, the strongest, the bravest!

A few days later, the funeral of Senior Boatswain Olufsen took place with all due ceremony. His corpse had been removed to the church on the previous evening and all the old friends of the house then gathered on the day of the burial to partake of a subdued lunch before he was committed to the soil. At twelve o'clock precisely, young Didriksen pulled up his carriage in the street below and Madam Olufsen accompanied by old Bendtz descended her stairs and stepped on board. As the carriage departed, covered in wreaths, the rest of the mourners made their way on foot to Holmen's cemetery.

A summer warmth seemed to pervade the air on this spring day. The small bushes dotted around the graveyard were already green of hue and gaggles of birds tumbled over the gravestones as they played a joyful mating game of catch if catch can. The small, quiet cortege of old and decrepit figures that moved slowly and haltingly along the pathway in the cemetery in their faded and outmoded ceremonial dress—and borne upright by walking canes and umbrellas—could have passed muster as a procession of revenants in the clear sunshine. Only Per, who walked at the very rear of the procession, seemed to be in tune with the living, bursting vitality of the natural environment around him. Yes, he too was moved by the solemnity of the occasion, but Death's hold on him had been broken. When he joined the other mourners around the grave and watched the sun-kissed coffin gliding down into the dark, narrow, and cold hole in the ground, he felt, for his part, a certain sense of elation mixed in with his feeling of dread. Innumerable days of life and sunshine still lay ahead of him. His coursing, youthful blood still sang its rich, hopeful promise of tomorrow in his ears. Young still—young still!

After the burial, Per went home to change clothes. He intended to pay the Salomons a visit.

However, a great surprise awaited him back at Hjertensfrydgade. A visitor's card had been left on his table—a card which bore a noble crown and the name Baroness von Bernt-Adlersborg on it. At first, he assumed that it had been delivered to him by mistake; but then he noticed that a short message had been written on the back of the card. In courteous, almost humble language, the baroness requested an "interview" with him and gave a time when on that same day and the following day she could be found at the Hotel d'Angleterre.

Then the wife of the ship's carpenter came in to tell him in a quite breathless fashion how an extremely refined lady had turned up outside in a proper coach and horses and had asked for Per personally. She had given her a "note," she said, and had asked her to put it on his table.

Per looked at the card again.

Baroness von Bernt-Adlersborg! Never on this earth had he heard that name before!

"It has to be a mistake really. Are you sure it was me she asked for? She mentioned my name?"

"Did she what? As I am standing here she did. 'Hr. Sidenius,' says she. And she was more than a bit peeved that she didn't find the good sir at home if I may say it straight out."

A range of audacious images raced through Per's imagination.

"What did she look like?" he asked. "Was she young?"

"Well... I suppose you could say that. Though she was around twice my age," said the carpenter's wife.

"And it was a lady you say... a real lady, I mean?"

"Oh Lord above she was! She had a big fur wrap in her carriage."

Per consulted his watch. There was no time to lose if he was going to meet this mysterious baroness that very day. And there was no denying his impatience in wishing to solve this sudden conundrum. Thus he dismissed all thought of visiting the Salomon household, dressed himself in his choicest finery and set off from the house.

A hotel porter with long, thick sideburns approached Per in a somewhat supercilious way as soon as he appeared in the lobby of the hotel, but when he heard who it was that Per was looking for, he bowed deferentially, opened the doors leading to the stairwell for him and simultaneously rang a bell, which summoned, in a matter of seconds, a waiter and housemaid from above. Displaying an air of ceremony (or so it seemed to Per), as if he were a king come to service his lady queen, the two flunkeys led him up the wide, carpeted stairway and on through a long corridor, at the end of which he was handed over to a Swedish-speaking chamber maid who took his card from him and led him into a room, a small salon, which was equipped with the usual— but for Per very imposing—hotel elegance: some brilliantly red velvet furnishings and a cut-glass chandelier hanging from the ceiling.

Though he was not generally someone that was easily put off his stride, at that moment Per felt slightly uneasy. For it suddenly occurred to him that he had walked into a trap. That this whole rigmarole had been set up by one or other of his enemies who wished to get one over on him.

He did not have long, however, to ruminate on this issue. Almost immediately, a tall lady entered the salon via the side room.

Young she was not. The word pretty would have been an even greater distortion. Her face had withered and her nose bore signs of an ominous ruby reddening. Her coal black dress, moreover, gave Per a hint of parsimony. All the same, it had to be said that she was obviously a lady of some standing in the world. There was, in her bearing and deportment—not least the way in which she gave him her hand and thanked him for coming—so much that spoke of a fine and gentle grace, as well as a certain tact, mannerisms which cannot be learned but are the preserve of the more refined classes.

"It has not—I hope—been too much of a surprise for you Hr. Sidenius that I should wish to see you and have at least a brief conversation with you," she began as they made to sit across from each other in a pair of the plush red armchairs that were a feature of the rooms. "You were, after all, my dead brother's last real friend and confidant. There is also the fact that you were, I suppose, the person to whom he gave his last goodbyes in this world—"

Everything now fell into place for Per. At once he remembered what the solicitor who had administered the estate had told him—that the deceased was survived by two sisters, one of whom was in a prosperous marriage with a Swedish landowner.

The baroness continued: "I have, for a long time, been moved by a desire to meet the man with whom my only brother felt such a strong bond. In fact, in whom he saw a kind of younger version of himself—that's the way he put it in the letter he left behind to tell us of his wishes concerning his will. But my beloved husband was bedridden for so long that I was forced to remain in my home faraway. I was not even afforded the opportunity to come home and attend my dear brother's interment."

The baroness's strange way of expressing herself, along with her rather odd facial movements, betrayed a permanently nervous disposition. Her last words were followed by a bout of heavy sobbing and the lady then sat for some time dabbing at her eyes with a lace handkerchief.

Per felt extremely ill at ease and remained silent. He was simply unable to put aside the sense of discomfort he felt on being reminded of his relationship to her brother Hr. Neergaard, the eccentric suicide.

"Yes, indeed, I have not had my sorrows to seek," the baroness continued, upon recovering somewhat from her bout of weeping. "That's why you must give me leave to weep. As you may be aware, the Good Lord has now also seen fit to call my noble husband to his side and I am left quite alone."

Per found that the best way to signal his sympathy was by bowing his head.

"Now what I wanted to say to you Hr. Sidenius is that I have often thought of writing to you—on my sister's behalf as well—in order that you would not believe us to be indifferent regarding your welfare. But I simply could not face doing it. And I am sure you would prefer to avoid correspondence with a lady who is a complete stranger to you and, perhaps, of no great import."

Per forced himself to mutter a quick objection to this very thought.

"Yes, indeed ... In all honesty, I would probably not have disturbed you even today by paying a visit to your home were it not for ... no, I just cannot escape from referring to it ... when I went to the cemetery today and saw those lovely, and quite fresh, flowers on my brother's grave, I saw at once who it was; the person who had in such a beautiful way chosen to mark his first anniversary and I felt an irresistible urge to see you and convey my gratitude to you because you have in such a loyal manner and—dare I say it?—like a loving and dutiful son honored the memory of my poor brother."

Per stared down at the tip of his boots and went very red. Fru Engelhardt's name emerged from the recesses of his mind. He himself did not even know where Neergaard was buried.

"But now let me look at you properly sir," the baroness continued.

She felt more and more taken with this quiet and shy young man, whose natural modesty even precluded admission of the kind and loving deed he had performed. "My word, how strong and fresh you look! Ah, I can see you are not one of these modern young types who fritter their youth away in utter frivolity and immorality. How old are you Hr. Sidenius?"

"Twenty-three."

"Ah, so young! May God grant you great fortune in your life! If I may say so, I'm aware that you had it hard as a boy. My brother wrote to us about that. You lost your mother early. And your father ... well, you have never known your father."

The velvet cover of Per's chair began to burn underneath him. He moved quickly to change the subject.

"So you are just passing through baroness?" he asked.

"Unfortunately—yes!" I arrived here last night and will be setting off, God willing, from here tomorrow morning. I am on the way down to my sister. Her proper title is Dame Prangen. She has—as you are probably aware—been living in southern Europe in the last year on account of her health. Just imagine Hr. Sidenius, I have not seen her in more than a year and we three siblings could never bear to be parted. For many years, my only regret was that I had to live away far away from my own dear country. And Alexander was just the same. He too loved his home with all the great love he possessed in his warm heart. Hr. Sidenius may well have heard that His Royal Highness the Prince of Wales was so gracious as to take a personal interest in my brother, and because of this the matter of his taking up a position at the embassy in London was raised. Under such patronage there is no doubt that a brilliant career beckoned for him. But despite all the things that might appeal to a man like Alexander on being presented with such an opportunity, he decided that he should decline. My blessed mother still lived in Copenhagen at that time and my sister had not got married. And Alexander loved Copenhagen so much and he adored the family home. He could not thrive very well outside of the places he knew and loved. I believe it was from that period in his life, after mother's death, may God have mercy on her soul when he was left stranded amongst all those memories, that his melancholy came upon him. Then of course in his final time he was actually quite ill . . . but still! That he should do that of all things!"

The recollection of her brother's final and bloody end sent the handkerchief once more up to her eyes, and Per grasped the moment to rise and signal his departure.

The baroness, who remained seated, took his hands between her own with a motherly warmth and said: "How very glad I am to have finally met you! May it never be as long again till we meet once more. Will you promise me faithfully that you will come to visit me when I return, God willing, from abroad? It's more than likely that I will spend the coming summer with my sister and brother-in-law at Kærsholm, and I have no doubt that they too will give you a most hearty welcome."

"Well, I can only express my deep gratitude . . . I mean I wouldn't want to be the cause of any inconvenience," Per stammered in his embarrassment; this was the only reply he could muster.

"Not at all young man! Remember Hr. Sidenius that you are now, in a way, part of our family. That, at any rate, is how I would interpret my dear brother's last wish. My sister, I have no doubt, would feel the same in that regard. Keep well, really well! And many thanks, once again, for thinking of Alexander with such affection—on this day of all days."

Per walked slowly, in the end almost hesitantly, down the stairway of the hotel. Only now had it really dawned on him how significant this new acquaintanceship was (or might prove to be) for him—if, that is, he was able—without having too many scruples as to the way it had come about—to exploit it energetically and shrewdly. By some magical turn of Fortune's wheel, a path had been opened up, which had led him to people with enormous influence. If his memory served him correctly, the Master of the Hunt Prangen's ancestral estate actually lay in the area in which he planned to put through his Mid-Jutland canal link, something that obviously would give this man particular grounds for considering his plans with interest. At the very least, it was crucial that no opportunity be left unexplored. In the high stakes game he was now playing, he could not have too many trump cards in his hand.

The thought struck him at that moment that there was now perhaps no need for him to nurture further contact with the Salomon household. Regardless of how attracted he had been to that young woman, he was not exactly entranced by the idea of marrying into a family of Jews. And who knew what might happen? Who knew what kind of opportunities, including the matrimonial kind, that might open up for him in aristocratic circles?

On the other hand, with the Salomons, he would presumably come into contact with the real bull traders on the stock exchange, bank executives and the city's industry magnates—put simply, the small circle of money men who, at the end of the day, were society's real decision makers. Leaving aside all speculation regarding marriage, it would be of great importance for him to be able to fraternize with such people and have the opportunity to curry their favor to the benefit of his great project. Besides, the baroness was now traveling abroad—and time was of the essence. That very day, the next day, or at least within two to three months, he had to have procured the magic wand which would give him power over people and which, in his hands, would be transformed into lightning bolts.

He had now emerged on to the square and looked up at the clock on the high corner building. There was still time to call out to the Salomons and he decided that this is what he would do. However, Per was still somewhat shaken by his encounter with the baroness and he felt the need to sit down in a café for a moment and take a glass of beer in order to compose himself and almost get a second wind prior to this new visit that lay ahead. Never before had he set foot in a Jewish household and he had heard so much about the importance that was placed on maintaining the old customs and etiquette amongst such families. It was crucial that he made the right impression and he was anxious to avoid causing offense in some way.

However, he soon returned to his previous thoughts. He could not help but wonder at the fact that the words he had let slip so flippantly that night at Neergaard's house could have had such far-reaching consequences. For it was clear from the way the baroness had spoken that it was that particular throwaway remark about his background, or lack of one, which had made an impression on her brother. He remembered that he had immediately regretted his frivolous words but that rectifying his mistake was not worth the effort. Now he wished that he had in fact done just that.

Dammit!—he emptied his glass—what was done was done! Dubious actions could sometimes lead to positive results. At any rate: he who wished to go forward in life should never look back.

Wealthy merchant Philip Salomon's residence stood out as one of the few places where a large family occupied a whole house right in the heart of the city. It was located in the Bredgade area, was of an older vintage with two storeys, and was not at first glance terribly impressive when seen from the street, especially as it was surrounded on both sides by apartment dwellings. However, on closer inspection, it became obvious that an aura of refined dignity prevailed over the house. From the high, black tiled roof with its blue sheen and the ample dimensions of the window stanchions, it was clear to see that the house had a distinguished history. Older people in the area still called it the "Palace." It had belonged to a bankrupt family of the nobility, from whom merchant Salomon's father had bought it at the beginning of the 1830s. From the gatehouse, one proceeded via a modern glass door to a hall that was so high and mighty that it gave echoes of any footsteps that should sound therein. Its walls were hung with armor, old bronze artifacts and exotic weapons from the Orient. The visitor was left with the feeling of having entered a museum. In the distance, a double-winged staircase with gilded banisters led up to the rooms on the first floor.

The maid who accepted Per's card led him into a kind of library room and bade him take a seat, at which Per sat down in one of the leather armchairs and promptly began to cast a careful eye on his surroundings.

Heavy silk curtains at the windows in the color of red wine, an inch thick, luxurious carpet over the whole floor, gilt leather tapestries, an octagonal table in the middle of the floor with silver and mother of pearl trimming, expensive, bound volumes of books on the shelves, paintings on the walls, an old inscribed candelabrum hung from the ceiling. An antique, richly carved wooden surface ran along one of the walls and served as a display shelf for old silver—in the form of tankards, mugs and beakers. Amongst these last items there was also a pair of old altar chalices.

But for his visit to the baroness and the impression this had made on him, all this splendor would have had an even greater effect on him than it already had. At the same time, he was still very deeply impressed. Almost in spite of himself, he was smitten by this un-ashamed homage to the power of money. A shiver of secret pleasure crept through his soul at the thought of this elemental power that had pressed the ancestral treasures of so many foreign peoples, yes, even vessels used by the sacred Church itself into service as items of decoration in this very much Jewish abode.

Per smiled rather sheepishly to himself. There was no use denying it—it was not little princess Salomon's beauty alone that compensated for the fact that she was "black."

The door to the side room was opened. Then a diminutive gentle-man with a repulsive appearance stepped into the room and performed a deep bow. Despite being around sixty years of age, he was dressed in the height of modern, not to say youthful, fashion. He wore a short, bright overcoat and a monocle dangled at the front of his chest. In his hand he carried a shiny silk hat.

"My name is Hr. Director Delft," he said, with the hint of a foreign accent in his tone of speech. "I am the uncle here in the house."

Per felt at once that this man's exaggerated politeness was a perfect complement to his horrible gorgon head.

"My name is Sidenius."

"Ah—the yong engineer I take it? My nephew has spoken much of you sir. But please I beg you to sit! Fru Salomon—my sister—is with a seamstress engaged. She will soon be at your service. Please I beg of you! Make yourself comfortable!"

Per sat down again. The uncle meanwhile chose a seat at some distance across the room.

"May I be free to inquire...have I had the honor of seeing Hr. Sidenius here in the house before?"

"No. I met both the Frue and her daughter for the first time just the other day."

"Aah yes, my niece Nanny...I believe I was told about this."

A short pause ensued, after which Hr. Delft, with a smile and a tone that would have made anyone other than Per suspicious due to his inflated politeness, threw out the remark: "My niece is rather lovely. Do you think? Do you find so Hr. Sidenius?"

There is no doubt that Per was taken aback by this. However, with a patronizing smile he looked directly at this queer little man and said: "Miss Salomon, sir, is absolutely stunning. An all round beauty."

"Jah, indeed! I suppose you could not say that she can count as, what can one call it, conventional. But I can assure you Hr. Sidenius that she brings a queue of young men here to the house all the days of the year. For what cannot beauty do! And youth! Furthermore, also...my brother-in-law is of course not without resources."

The man is clearly a bit damaged—Per thought to himself and turned slightly away to end the conversation. But his interlocutor went on regardless: "If Hr. Engineer should honor the household by visiting more frequently from now on, you will certainly get the chance to find some amusement and make most curious observations in this regard. For—will you agree Hr. Sidenius?—money is a big magnet. Ah jah jah. These little round pieces of metal bring out the deepest human feelings...bring the heart's most noble emotions out into the light of day. Deference, friendship, love. Am I right?"

Per was now in serious danger of completely losing his patience with the man. Fortunately, however, the maid returned and as she held the door into the adjoining room open, she asked him to go inside.

Per ventured into a room, or rather a whole floor, which, to a far greater degree than either the lobby or library room, gave him the sense of having entered a truly authentic fairy-tale world—a millionaire's world—a land of ever-flowing milk and honey. The vast room with its magnificent, slightly domed stucco ceiling in the Rococo style, from whose corners plump cherubs blew their gilded horns to pronounce the judgment of Solomon, had once been the old palace's function and ballroom. Here, where a line of slender chairs along the walls and a pair of high ornamental mirrors had presumably constituted the sum of furniture in the room, there was now a surfeit of modern furniture and decorative objects. Deep sofas and large yielding armchairs, tables, footrests, bear skins, expansive plant and foliage arrangements, columns with statues, bric-a-brac and whatnots —and then yet more armchairs and easy chairs, small and large tables and more plant pots and artworks including a portrait on a painter's easel. A concert grand stood more or less dead center in the room. The sound of running fountain water and chirping birds could be heard from an adjacent room that had been turned into a conservatory with palm and rubber trees.

Eventually he observed Fru Salomon sitting on a soft ottoman beneath one of the windows, where she was doing some sewing with an air of settled domestic contentment. She received him in a friendly manner and reached out her left hand in welcome.

They had just exchanged initial pleasantries when Per heard a door being opened in the conservatory and then a cheerful humming, which quickly developed into the clear trills of a song. A moment later, Frøken Nanny was standing in the doorway dressed in outdoor clothing and a hat. On discovering that there was a visitor in the room, she abruptly curtailed her singing and, in mock horror, placed her sleeve across her mouth—as if to muffle a shriek.

Per rose and gave a bow.

Her performance had been executed so naturally that Per had not for one moment suspected that she had been aware of his presence all along.

"Are you still here in the house my child," her mother said. "I thought you had gone already. Ahm, I've no need to introduce. You know my daughter already don't you?"

Per answered with yet another bow of the head, while at the same time ensuring that his accompanying, and perhaps overly bold, stare transmitted the emotions to which he was subject just at that moment. Even before setting eyes upon her again—simply by hearing the sound of her singing as she moved through the scales, which to his ears were golden echoes—his mind was made up. She was the key to the promised land! It was here where the treasure lay waiting for him! And as she revealed herself to him there in the doorway, bathed in the sunlight emanating from the conservatory and bird song all about her, young and luscious as she was and tempting to watch like some eastern dancer in the temple, she seemed to him to be the embodiment of a fairy-tale princess flanked by a procession of nymphs waving palm leaves in adoration.

Nanny sat for a moment. She perched herself on the very edge of a stool and, thus, an opening gambit-type of conversation ensued—the kind in which mutual strangers take advantage of the occasion to investigate the counterpart's appearance, character and manners using the cover of a range of run-of-the-mill remarks and questions.

It has to be said that Per was no master in the art of conversation. He was far too wrapped up in himself and his own personal considerations for this to be the case. Besides which, he had no interest in the subjects that would normally be the meat and drink of conversation, knew very little about current events in the life of the city, in the theater, politics, or the world of literature. Nor did he even feel any obligation to be entertaining. On the occasions when, in spite of everything, he managed to make an impression upon a woman, this had happened by way of a well-calculated tiger leap from the lair of silence out into the most open and free declaration of his feelings.

Now here he was, sitting and listening while the young lady spoke, and making a stab at guessing the actual magnitude of merchant Salomon's wealth. His eyes stole round the room. And his mind became a whirligig at the thought that one day all this might be his.

Fortunately for Per, Nanny was more than able to cater for any entertainment that was required, without relying on a significant contribution from him. But at the same time as she sat there on the edge of the stool—adopting the most appropriate of postures, with her elbows tucked in at the sides and the small, tasseled velvet muff in her lap—and allowed her lovely red mouth to chatter on, her eyes were also busily, and somewhat audaciously, assessing Per's persona bit by bit—right from the tips of his thick curly hair, down to his ankles and his slightly rustic shoes.

At last, Fru Salomon became rather alarmed at her daughter's chatty exuberance.

"Dear child, you've obviously forgotten your music hour."

"Yes, I had indeed Mother, oops."

She got up immediately. And with a quick glance to her mother and a more lingering look at Per, which spoke volumes, she swanned out of the room.

Per made no pretense of hiding his air of distraction once Nanny had left the room. His answers to Fru Salomon's questions, who had steered the conversation towards his studies, were pure nonsense. He was completely enthralled by this young lady. Perhaps it had been her bearing and way of walking, the thing he had been least impressed with when she had first entered, because it had struck him as being slightly heavy and waddling. For as she left (and for exactly the same reasons) it had all been quite enchanting for him. He felt the marked sense of womanliness about it, so female—an unconscious mating dance.

But now he observed the appearance of a black clad-figure in the middle of the floor—a lady—who must have come in via a door behind him.

"My daughter Jakobe," Fru Salomon said by way of introduction.

Per was shocked. It had never occurred to him that there might be other children in the family, other than the two he had already met—and a flash of concern strafed his thoughts with regards to the millions which, in his imagination, he had already claimed as his own. Who knows, maybe there are even more!—his thoughts exclaimed in sudden alarm.

This young lady seemed to be some years older than her sister, had a taller and slimmer figure and was, in Per's eyes, frightfully scrawny. On the whole, she reminded him more of her brother Ivan, who also had markedly Jewish features—skin pale as wax, a large hooked nose, and a wide mouth framed by a short jutting chin.

If her appearance had already had an unpleasant effect on him, his first impressions were not improved by the tone of superiority she adopted—mutedly and at distance—when responding to his greeting. Shortly afterwards, Per rose from his seat and made a polite exit.

"So that was the natural genius and force of nature we have all heard so much about," said Jakobe, almost before the door had closed properly after Per. "He didn't come across as being exactly, shall we say, sophisticated."

"His upbringing obviously leaves a lot to be desired," Fru Salomon said. "It seems that he has always had to contend with very difficult personal circumstances, according to Ivan."

Her daughter shrugged her shoulders.

"Hah, of course, why wouldn't he have? They're all impoverished one way or another in this country. Would the good God in heaven not, at least once, send a talent amongst them that was born rich. Let's face it mother, there is something pitiful that marks even the best of them when they have that stamp of poverty about them. And then you couldn't even say that he was pretty to look at. To think that Nanny proclaimed him the other day as nothing more or less than the Danish Byron."

"Hm—pretty? Maybe not . . . but you have to say, Jakobe, that he is handsome."

"With those staring bug eyes! Mother, I found him positively hideous," her daughter said as she closed a book through which she had been browsing with a smack. "He gave me a horrible feeling like a . . . like a glass-eyed horse. And then he looked like a big brute," she add shortly afterwards, with an emphasis which suggested that some dark memory had passed over her soul.

"I believe that young man has upset you dear Jakobe."

"That's exactly what he has done mother. I don't know where men of today got this meat market way of looking at women from. It's as if, when they are looking at you, they are weighing up how many pounds of flesh they will get out of your body."

"Well I have to admit all right that I noticed he was a bit coarse in that respect. But you know, Jakobe, we can't just abandon young people like him," said Fru Salomon gently.

"Well you always say that. But I just don't understand why we continually get dumped with all of Ivan's failed geniuses. We all know what the end result is going to be—even with the pick of the bunch. Look at that Fritjof Jensen for example. He received nothing but kindness in this house—I know for a fact that father sometimes helped him out of embarrassing money troubles. And now there he is screaming about the Jews in all the newspapers."

"Ah now Jakobe, dear angel, let's not get into—"

"Do I smell the blood of a Christian in the house?" came a cry from a half-open door, where the uncle's terrifying face appeared around the door jamb.

"Is that you, you rascal!" said Fru Salomon. "Come right in. We are all alone now...is that the children I hear?"

"Here is the whole brood of them!" he cried.

And in stormed a mob of black-eyed children, still in their outdoor clothes, and ranging in age from twelve to four years—no less than five in number and all so fresh faced and vigorous in appearance that Per's remaining hopes would have been completely dashed at the sight of them. For a while the room was filled with a deafening racket emanating from the red throats of all these children, none of whom seemed able to stay still for a second. All had a tale to tell. First they swarmed around their mother, then their sister or the uncle, and all those dark eyes shone in eagerness to tell their own story.

When order was finally restored, the uncle piped up: "That's right. I forgot to congratulate the house on its new acquisition. I met here just a while ago Hr.—I seem to forget his name. It was not so noble a name. The son of a cleric, I am to believe?"

"Are you starting too now!" Fru Salomon cried. "Listen to me. I don't want to hear another word about that person. He is a friend of Ivan's.

And he came out to visit us today. Full stop. Are you staying for dinner, Heinrich?"

"Here? Lea, my sister dearest, have you ever tasted a kosher pork chop?" said the little wizened man, whose expressions, even for his closest relatives, were often a source of mystery as to whether they were meant to be taken in jest or seriously.

Fru Salomon started to laugh.

"I take it you have been mooching round in the kitchen. Oh, shssh! I hear Salomon."

Perhaps because of being overwhelmed by his impressions from the rich house he had visited and conscious of having made a significant decision, Per had not gone straight home. He had altered his route to take in side streets that were devoid of people, motivated as he was by an urge to be alone. He had now not only found his true path and ultimate goal but also the means to get there. "Philip Salomon's son-in-law"—they were the magic words that were going to open the portals of life for him and reduce people to being his humble servants.

And why doubt his good luck? If he looked back on all the strange things that had happened to him in his life, hadn't little Ivan been right in what he had once said about his having the luck of Aladdin? And was it not exactly like some lucky sign that it was Nanny's brother of all people who first interpreted the God-like scripture on his forehead: I came, I saw, I conquered!

7

A M O N G S T those men who each day at around two o'clock would come strolling through the arch of broad-crowned trees lining the approach to the Exchange, there were not many whom the door flunkey, all tassels and epaulettes, greeted with greater veneration than a tall, stout man who radiated a particularly ruddy glow from beneath his dark locks. A man, moreover, whose double chin was shaved as tight as a white drum over which sat a pair of extraordinarily thick and blood-red lips, all framed by the customary side whiskers befitting a powerful merchant. Hats were also lifted and heads bared as this man moved amongst the denizens of the opulent brown-walled trading hall with its imposing columns. His arrival would arouse most attention amongst the corn agents who stood in the window recesses facing the canal, and amongst the skippers seeking a cargo, who sat in quiet expectation along the bench to the left of the entrance door. This commanding personage was none other than the merchant Philip Salomon, the head of the trading concern Isaac Salomon & Son, and one of the city's richest men. Rumor had it that Salomon presided over a fortune that ran into many many millions.

Salomon's visits to the Exchange rarely lasted very long. As a rule, his business was already done and dusted, and he had returned to his own office, by the time the usher was executing his daily duty in ringing his bell as an ear piercing warning that share notations and trading had commenced. For Salomon was not one of those who regarded the Exchange as an exclusive club where gentlemen could gather after lunch in order to sift the latest gossip in town and pass judgment on current theatrical events. He rarely graced the theater with his presence and attended society events only when they could not be avoided. Salomon's life was divided equally between the world of commerce and his family; whereby he gave the former his cool and clear business head and the latter his solicitous and easily moved heart. And, as was often said about him—with an allusion to the fact that his office and his house were in the same street—he knew his way home.

Philip Salomon was the only child of Isaac Salomon, a man who had been the subject of much public comment in his day and in whose name the company had been founded. Isaac Salomon had proven to be a remarkable man in many ways, a genius where business matters were concerned, who, from being a lowly itinerant peddler of various wares, had dragged himself up to a preeminent position in Danish commercial life. So much so that a new title was bestowed upon him in ordinary street parlance—"Salomon the Golden Fleecer." In his day, Salomon the elder would often have a score of fully loaded ships at sea at any one time; he had been a factory owner and had run plantations in the West Indies. Moreover, with his innate business acumen, Isaac Salomon had opened up several new overseas trading markets for Danish industry in general. He had also, during the anti-Jewish pogroms of 1819, been one of those who had suffered most at the hands of the Copenhagen mob.

It was this very same Isaac Salomon who had bought the "Palace" and had furnished it with such overflowing munificence. Just as he was unperturbed by the outrage of the prim and proper classes and the attempts of the envious to hold him up to ridicule, Isaac Salomon had never shrunk back from cocking a snook at even the highest echelons of the aristocracy itself. He saw fit to travel through town in a full-blown coach and four and had been known, on certain festive occasions, to have two flunkeys stationed at the back of the carriage. He took on the role of a patron for the advancement of the sciences, established trust funds, and declared his home an open house for artists. All this he did despite being a feeble, humpbacked little man, who, there is no doubt, had by dint of frenetic self-learning gradually acquired a leavening of knowledge but absolutely no cultivation. A man, moreover, of whom it was said, on good authority, that he had purchased his wife for the sum of a hundred Rix-dollars from an impoverished Jewish widow in Jutland with whom he had lodged during his wandering about the country.

The collection of oriental weapons in the lobby of the Salomon "Palace" was a legacy from the old man's days, as was the hotchpotch of costly gimcrack articles which still festooned this grand house to overflowing. Indeed, the whole ensemble of artifacts, which lurched between pure ostentation and jumbled confusion, was nothing less than a museum that recorded the arrival of objects brought home in Isaac Salomon's ships from the far-flung corners of the world and which the son—more from filial loyalty rather than a question of taste or personal preference—had allowed to remain, more or less unmolested, ever since.

In general, a talent for business and hard work were the only things that Philip Salomon had inherited from his father. However, there was perhaps a direct connection between the old man's years of wandering and the unfettered joy Salomon the younger felt during his sojourns in the great outdoors. In the summer months, he would remain in his country retreat far longer than most other captains of commerce and for the rest of the year had the habit of driving out on excursions on any Sunday that gave even the slightest hint of tolerable weather. The whole family would be in tow and on the road almost from the cock's first crow. Philip Salomon himself would drive the carriage with his wife alongside him, while a swarm of their own children and assorted friends packed the rear of the Charabanc. It was only when they were well and truly in the countryside that they would pull up at an inn or the clearing in a forest. Fru Salomon and the smallest children would then guard the picnic basket while Salomon and a clump of children deemed old enough took off on an expedition into the interior of the region. With his large broad-brimmed hat shoved to the back of his neck and his overcoat draped over his arm, this much-feared king of the Exchange jungle would saunter cheerfully off as a pack of snub-nosed youngsters danced, shrieked and scrapped all around his feet with the ferocity that infuses city children, and especially Jewish children, when they are let loose in the countryside. And, of course, no hill could be approached without an assault party being organized, no farmer could be encountered without Salomon having to engage him in conversation, no shepherd boy would be left in their wake without being the richer by at least a Mark. But, above all, Salomon was an eager flower picker and never was he as glad as when, on returning from his country expeditions, he was able to present to his wife a huge bouquet of wild flowers, for which she would give thanks by smiling and offering her left hand for him to kiss.

Fru Salomon was none other than the legendary Lea Delft—or Fru Lea Moritz as she for a short period had been called—whose dusky eastern beauty had, at the start of the 1850s, provoked a stream of fashionable gentlemen to make their way to a small bespoke clothing and tailor's shop in Silkegade—a good number of these gentlemen subsequently being driven to amorous distraction, while visiting the shop. In fact, uncle Heinrich—Lea's brother—had always insisted that she had been the real reason why the new lunatic asylum Skt. Hans Hospital had been built. The shop belonged to her parents, who had emigrated from Germany, where she too had lived in the earliest years of her life. She was already married by the age of eighteen—the result of a burning passion for her cousin Marcus Moritz, a poor, consumptive German savant who was to become father to her eldest children, Ivan and Jakobe. The latter of these was not even born when he passed away and Lea then moved back in with her parents. Their state of penury notwithstanding, Lea's parents (who were also cousins) belonged to one of Germany's most distinguished Jewish families, a circumstance which made them both very proud. When, after several years as a widow, Lea got engaged to Philip Salomon it was almost regarded as a deliberate step downwards. For in the eyes of the bride's family, the groom's millions were scant compensation for the fact that his father had run like a camel from country to country with his wares on his own back. For the young widow, on the other hand, Salomon's financial status, and her concerns regarding the insecure future facing her two children, had settled the argument. As she had said often to herself: she had once allowed her heart to completely rule her head, now it was time for her head to overrule her heart. That said, there was no suggestion that she was engaged in a deceit. Her heart was bountiful enough to give common sense its rightful due without becoming scourged because of it. Any pangs of sacrifice were always eased by its overwhelming abundance. At any rate, she had subsequently bestowed generous recompense upon Philip Salomon for any possible absence of love that he had endured from his wife on their wedding day.

For twenty years now, they had lived together in a happy marriage. There was no doubt that Fru Lea—about whom one of her worshippers had once said that she possessed the most beautiful face in Copenhagen, the most delightful figure in Denmark and the loveliest hands in the whole world—had become somewhat matronly as the years had progressed, but she still, both outwardly and in her inner essence, retained the exotic stamp of "race," which the discerning eye would immediately recognize. The shape of her head with its hooked nose and triple chin—and not at least the way in which she held it aloft—carried a regal air that brought sculpted busts of ancient empresses to mind. Her heavy, black hair, which hung from a parting in two plaited ringlets flowing down over her ears, bore only individual strands of silver, while the rich, creamy complexion of her skin was smooth and unblemished; her teeth were in good health and order and her jet-brown eyes boasted a lustrous sheen. For his part, Philip Salomon was still so besotted with his wife that he would sometimes forget himself, even in the sitting room, and continue pressing his big lips against her hand or cheek, so that in the end she would be obliged to fix him with a hard stare to remind him that the children were present.

Indeed, Fru Salomon felt only one lingering cause for regret—a regret that seemed to deepen as the years went by. For the great swirl of life as it was played out in foreign parts had left such an impression upon her during her frequent visits to relatives, and in her first marriage, that she could never really feel at home in Copenhagen. And, though she was careful not to betray these feelings to anyone other than her husband, her heart still pined for the country she regarded as her real homeland. Thus, one of her greatest delights in life were the month-long family visits she would make to Germany each year. Moreover, it was still the case that when she wished to express herself with the utmost precision, she would have to resort to a word from her mother tongue.

It had also been Lea who had insisted that her two eldest children—Ivan and Jakobe—would for the most part be educated abroad. She was not—as she used to say in her, especially at that time, rather faltering language—going to have her children turned into "garden dwarfs" in the provincial town which Copenhagen represented for her. On top of this, there was, where Jakobe was concerned, another motivation. For Jakobe had always been a difficult child; so susceptible to the impressions life made upon her; so sensitive, above all, to any insult that referred to her Jewish identity. Thus, a mixture of Jakobe's delicate sensibilities aligned with her physical frailty meant that her childhood had been one long tale of suffering. She would often return home pale as a ghost if a boy had so much as shouted "greaseball!" at her in the street. Moreover, she would become sick with distress and vexation any time one of her small blue-eyed classmates humiliated her—as happened time after time—by rejecting her many attempts at securing a secret confidante, as all young girls aspire to do. But, despite all her previous bitter defeats, her passionate desire for understanding and a reciprocated affection led Jakobe to continually go back and simply suffer further derision. She had inherited her mother's exaggerated emotional propensities but not her happy-go-lucky nature, nor her sound mental equilibrium, nor for that matter her proud and patronizing smile, which she presented as a riposte both to the blatant prejudice of society's sophisticates and the rough tongues of the rabble.

Nor had Jakobe been blessed with Fru Salomon's conventional beauty, and even the natural bloom that lights up the early teenage years had more or less failed to materialize. Jakobe was thin and gaunt, had large unappealing facial features and could not even boast of that willowy grace which compensates most youths for other defects during their early years of flirting and courtship. Jakobe became even less appealing in the view of her peers by eagerly seeking redress for the humiliations visited upon her by her friends by outshining them in those areas where she was best able to assert her superiority. Given that she had a clever head on her shoulders and was a fanatically diligent pupil, she was always able to negotiate her way through examinations with a brilliance that was unparalleled for a girl of her age. Moreover, she often had the habit, in the depths of her girlish anguish, of seeking other ways of inflicting pangs of jealousy on others by recourse to her substantial funds of pocket money. She might, for example, turn up at school with a bag of the finest confectionary, upon which she would become the center of a short-lived and dearly bought form of attraction.

Gradually, the tension between Jakobe on the one hand and her classmates and teachers on the other became so fraught that the headmistress personally recommended that her parents remove her from the school, after which her education was completed at a finishing school in Switzerland. However, Jakobe's time at a foreign boarding school, coinciding as it did with her brother Ivan's placement at a German business academy, aroused no little indignation amongst people whose patriotic sentiments—so soon after the disastrous war—were still very much to the fore. For this reason, the Salomons declined to repeat the exercise with any of the other children.

Nanny came next in the row of siblings and in her nature this child was a warm summer's day to Jakobe's dark night. A sheer delight from the cradle onwards, Nanny radiated health and physical robustness and had grown up under a state of general worship, stroked and petted as she was, like a cuddly kitten and with no apparent damage done to her apart from a perhaps rather exaggerated charm and an inclination to melodrama. Her father called her his "little miss normal," because she had always seemed to be in a state of balance, had never been known to be sick; even toothache was an unknown thing to her. However, for all the truth in the above, Nanny was also the "whirlwind" in the Salomon household—constantly either just coming in, or getting ready to leave, and thus usually to be seen bustling around in her hat and coat. Her voice could be heard all over the house and at least ten times a day would signal her most recent arrival home. And should the sound of laughter and shrieks emanate from up in one of the girls' bedrooms, accompanied by the thud of heavy steps across the floor, then one could be sure that Nanny had taken a bath and was now, in her flowing white robe and hair flung back, in the midst of dancing a tarantella for her sisters.

There was also, it must be said, one other volatile character in the Salomon household; or at least he appeared there everyday, and this was none other than the aforementioned uncle Heinrich, Fru Salomon's brother. This small, wizened man, whose physical appearance was so markedly different from his sister's, was also in other regards living testimony to the uneven way in which family characteristics are handed down within Jewish families. Hr. Heinrich Delft was a bachelor and dubbed himself "Hr. Director" as Per had very quickly discovered. In his youth, he had fallen victim to a "mishap" involving a sum of money with which he had been entrusted. The aftermath of this saw him spending many years in America and also (according to his own account of things) periods in India and China as an agent, or traveling rep, for English companies. He had now returned to Denmark with a small amount of capital in his pocket, with which, even at his advanced age, he was still able to enjoy life's material indulgences without ever tiring of their being repeated day after day. Where his travels and experiences were concerned, and likewise with regards to his financial position, he maintained a reserve that was meant to suggest the existence of untold abundance. Even with his nearest relatives, he gave the impression that he was concealing some source of fabulous wealth, just as he continued to insist that he was still a co-director of an Anglo-Chinese steamship company. All that notwithstanding, uncle Heinrich lived in an extremely modest three-room apartment and approached any potential expense, that was not directly connected to his bodily welfare, with extreme caution. However, he made no little effort where his physical appearance was concerned, adopted all the new fashions sported by the young gentlemen in the town, suffered the daily attentions of a barber who would curl and perfume what was left of his dark hair and on festive occasions saw it as his sartorial duty to wear an ostentatious pin brooch, which would, he often averred, have "some queen of the ball swooning in his presence." Should a sense of devilment descend upon his nieces, they would resort to teasing their uncle Heinrich by saying that the brooch was a pure fake; he had once left the house in a violent rage, without returning for a whole week, because his sister- and brother-in-law had stooped so low as to question the authenticity of its stone.

Thus uncle Heinrich was hardly an easy going or pleasant person to have in one's company, albeit that there was a sense of half conscious tomfoolery in his permanent air of indignation. For in his self-adopted role of guard dog in his sister's home, the utter relish he displayed whenever an opportunity arose to chase after people who, for one reason or another, had inflamed his ire—especially when this concerned anyone who might be suspected of sniffing around his nieces' respective dowries—all this signaled his fixation with the idea that his true mission in life was to give counsel and protection to the young ladies of the house. If there was an ounce of real gravity in the man, it was contained in this personal crusade. Dark and private thoughts of his own were the catalyst for his desire to protect these much sought-after girls. For, hidden behind his boastful deportment, lay an acknowledgment of the shame he had brought down upon the proud name of his family and it was as penance for this that he now wished to play a providential role in the lives of his sister's daughters, so that the choices they made were not done on a whim but rather represented a good and, more importantly, a distinguished liaison for the family.

The Salomons had not, for many years, maintained any kind of large social circle. Copenhagen's orthodox Jewish community tended to avoid them because of their "irreligion," something which Fru Lea in particular quite happily acknowledged. On the other hand, the family as a whole had never felt any compulsion to throw itself into the town's Gentile social scene and had, therefore, been content instead to hold "open house" twice a month, and otherwise let it be known that all friends and acquaintances were welcome to drop by unannounced and at any time without fear of causing offense. And despite the fact that a change in this house policy was enacted when Ivan

returned from Germany and Nanny achieved adulthood, Ivan sometimes came close to realizing his dream of reinventing the Salomon
home in the style of a Renaissance prince's court, because a number
of the younger members of the intellectual avant-garde were now
regularly received in the family circle with authors and artists foremost
in their ranks.

During this period, Jakobe mostly lived abroad. She had found a
new home in her old boarding school in Switzerland, amongst whose
high peaks she sought a remedy for her delicate, and with each passing year, more sensitive physiognomy. She would spend the summer
months at home, during which time her parents decamped to the
countryside, but she would soon feel the urge to escape again whenever the cold, damp air began once more to take hold and the first
visitors in the winter social circuit began to appear. But one day—when
she was nineteen years of age—and barely a month after she had taken
off on her winter flight south, her parents received a rather confused
letter from her, in which, mixed up with various other things, she
issued a throwaway remark that she might give up her Alpine retreat
in favor of permanently settling down at home in Denmark. A few
days later, a new letter arrived that confirmed her imminent return.
Almost simultaneously, a telegram arrived to the effect that she was
already on the way home and was to arrive the following day.

Typical as this hasty enactment of a decision was for Jakobe, her
parents were still left in a state of unease by it all. They sensed that
something serious had happened to her and Fru Lea confided to her
husband that affairs of the heart were very possibly involved. During
the summer, Jakobe had spoken very animatedly about a young
lawyer from southern Germany who was also a well-known politician.
He was the nephew of the owner of the boarding school and had
visited his aunt on a number of occasions. Fru Lea knew only too
well her daughter's susceptible bloodline, which had already led to
some bitter disappointments. When Jakobe came home, it was clear
to see that her heart had been broken, but as she did not offer any
explanation as to the reasons for her return, other than that she had
on this occasion felt lonely amongst all the new boarders and became

homesick, nobody attempted to pressure her into any kind of admission—least of all her mother, who had always insisted that as far as she was concerned the secrets of the heart had to be respected. As a personal example of this policy, she had never explained to her husband exactly why she would not allow him to kiss her right hand. She had merely given him to understand that this was to do with a promise she had given the love of her youth in a moment that had become sacred for both of them.

Jakobe had now been at home for four years. She had reached the age of twenty-three and was still not engaged to be married. Not that this, in any way, meant she had wanted for suitors in the intervening period. Indeed, some of these had been of a most flattering nature. For in spite of her physical frailty, she had grown into a state that bordered on beauty. In particular, the more mature gentlemen felt themselves drawn to her pale and singular demeanor. In fact, some amongst them actually preferred these attributes to her sister Nanny's radiant but rather more conventional beauty. Set within her face, with its powerful hooked nose and its absence of chin—a face her admirers described as an eagle countenance and her detractors as nothing more than parrot features—were a pair of large somber eyes, where the whites struck a strong blueish tone that at times could almost appear black. There was no question that her nose was too big, her mouth too thin lipped and wide, but those eyes of hers boasted an unforgettable gaze, proud and shy at one and the same time and burning with loneliness and wide-ranging thoughts. Her figure was longer and taller than that of her brothers and sisters, a stature that was accentuated by her long slim legs and her curious way of walking with quick steps that never made a noise. Those rare mortals who had seen her truly smile, spoke of her beautiful teeth. Then, in general, there was over her desiccated and nervous figure this peculiar spectral grace, which suffering, longing, and loss can impart upon a delicate female form.

However, it was primarily her inner strengths that people thought of whenever Jakobe was discussed. She was widely famed for her intellectual capabilities, her will power and encyclopedic knowledge.

In her solitude, she found comfort in books, studied ancient and modern languages, history and literature, and ceaselessly sought out new fields of knowledge that might satisfy her impatient yearning for new vistas of learning. Fru Salomon had always said about her that she was the very spit of her sensitive father. However, it must be said that the majority of the young, or at least youngish, men who were the most frequent guests in the Salomon household at the time when Per made his first appearance were there because of Nanny. It was not just the fact that the vast majority of them simply viewed her as being far more attractive; there was also the consideration that as Philip Salomon's own physical offspring, Nanny would be much the greater beneficiary in terms of family inheritance—this despite the fact that Salomon had moved to declare his legal parentage of both Jakobe and Ivan while they were still very young children. Another consideration was that Jakobe did not exactly encourage the rituals of courtship. She was seldom to be seen about the house and her reticence often came across to strangers as cold hostility.

At the modest gentlemen's dinner, which Per attended as a first-time family guest, he met—apart from some more seasoned gentlemen from the world of business—the writer Povl Berger, a lieutenant Hansen-Iversen who was in the Hussars, a university graduate called Balling and a journalist by the name of Dyhring. Per had only ever met the first of these before, but the truth was that he had barely recognized him. Povl Berger, the fanatical, barricade revolutionary and worshipper of Dr. Nathan had, since he had last seen him, lost his Mephistophelian goatee and had allowed his sideburns to spread across his whole face. In fact, his facial demeanor was completely different. Berger now had the semblance of one of those currently fashionable pictures of the suffering Christ figure, which was precisely the visage he strove to achieve—as one of the other gentlemen, in all confidence, subsequently whispered to Per.

Berger had in recent days, his informant revealed, amazed his friends by distributing certain sanctimonious verses with which he both prostrated himself before Nanny's graces and favors and also looked forward to his own immortality on Denmark's Parnassus.

The person relating all this information was the ex-student Balling, who also considered himself to be a writer, but of literary history. Balling was a well over six-foot drainpipe of a man with a mane of hair above his dangling limbs and a face that bore all the expressiveness of a frying pan.

Subsequently, the poet and author Povl Berger, who had indeed now converted to traditional religious piety, drew Per into a corner and confided to him that Balling was nothing more than an idiot who had fallen under Dr. Nathan's spell and now wanted to become a genius and trailblazer. However, the only thing he had achieved thus far, Berger continued, was to study his way to chronic gastritis. There was no doubt that Balling was immensely well read, had indeed consumed whole libraries of books and was so full of quotes that some witticism would escape from his lips on the flimsiest of pretexts. He was, in short, that kind of bookworm who clamps himself onto the literary canon as fiercely as a leech and proceeds to gorge on its very lifeblood, but for all that is forever doomed to be lacking in substance.

The year previous to this, Balling had succeeded in getting a book on classical tragedy published and, given that it had received some favorable comments in the press, Ivan had immediately moved to secure his attendance at the gathering of intellects in his home. Per, who beforehand had been slightly uneasy at how he would compare against his potentially rival suitors, was utterly reassured once he actually caught sight of them. Even the presence of the lieutenant in the Hussars did nothing to shake his confidence; though he granted that this man was turned out superbly and boasted a pair of bold blue eyes framed by light, rakish sideburns in a face that had been kissed by the spring sunshine.

Where the journalist Dyhring was concerned, Per was not even sure that he could in any way be regarded as a future rival. His slap-dash deportment amongst the ladies of the house suggested the opposite. For reasons that Per could not fathom, Ivan had been extremely keen to bring them both together. As soon as Dyhring arrived, they were introduced to each other and, once the meal was over, Ivan was at pains once more to initiate a conversation between them, where Per could explain the great project he had in mind.

But Per was in no mood for common-sense conversation. His thoughts were far too occupied with Nanny's presence for that. Her low-cut dress of raw silk and the red roses in her black hair were both tempting and lovely to behold. Per had been given the honor to lead her to the table and this privilege, the pleasantries at table and the, for him, unexpected delights of the cuisine set before him, emboldened his spirits to the point that he became completely overwrought. Indeed, in the postprandial smoking room, where the gentlemen were served coffee and liqueurs, Per teetered on the brink of causing genuine scandal as uncle Heinrich, full of malicious glee and displaying a sly, diabolical mien, continued to fill his glass to overflowing. Per gave a country slap to Philip Salomon's shoulder, praised his wine cellar and gave a veritable speech in praise of the ladies of the house.

Some of the veteran visitors to Salomon soirees gradually gathered around Per and proceeded to engage in some playful baiting of this young man who was so obviously in polite company for the first time in his life. At the same time, Fru Salomon and Jakobe were in the sitting room entertaining a middle-aged, fair-haired gentleman who did not partake of tobacco. This was a certain Hr. Eybert, who was one of the town's more significant factory owners and, moreover, a well-known politician of the liberal—or so-called "European"—persuasion. In other words, a well-educated man, lacking in prejudice and commanding widespread respect.

Within the inner sanctum of the Salomon family's social circuit, Eybert was quietly mentioned as Jakobe's future husband. Being in his mid-forties, he had gone beyond his best years, and was also a widower with two children. His love for Jakobe was an established fact. He made no attempt to hide this, either from her parents, or from Jakobe herself. For their part, both of them looked favorably on the idea of a match; Hr. Eybert was a proven friend of the family and on top of that was a very affluent man who could never, therefore, be suspected of entering into a gold-digger marriage. For lots of reasons, they wanted to see Jakobe married; and in this regard they were subject to the constant urgings of the family doctor, a Jewish professor who quite forcefully declared that the "child would simply be destroyed entirely if she's forced to live life as a bloody nun in a silent order."

With the sort of suspicion that perpetually rests in the bosom of an older suitor the moment a new, and young, male face suddenly appeared in the Salomon household, Hr. Eybert immediately steered the conversation round to Per and asked about this young man whose voice levels had steadily increased in volume as the meal had progressed.

"That is a Hr. Sidenius ... one of Ivan's friends," said Fru Salomon in a tone that she ensured carried something of an apology on behalf of the hosts.

"Yes, indeed. I have him—a Sidenius! Is he not supposed to be a bit ... you know ... ?" As he spoke, Hr. Eybert made circular movements with his index finger at his temple.

"Ah, I don't think so," Fru Salomon replied with a slight laugh. "But there's no doubt that he is somewhat temperamental."

"Well if that's the case, we can put it down to a family trait."

While thus far seemingly being unengaged with the conversation, Jakobe raised her eyes from a book that she had been leafing through.

"He is the son of a pastor, you say?" she asked.

"Yes, indeed," the manufacturer remarked. "The family seems to have produced a veritable rash of clerics. And it is presumably for that very reason that the seed throws up a deviant strain from time to time. I mind that one of my uncles, a large estate owner in Jutland, once told me of a Vendsyssel priest—obviously now long dead—who went by the name of 'Mad Sidenius.' By all accounts, this epithet was well deserved. If the words of my old Jutland uncle are to be believed— and I have to admit that this was not always the case—this man was more of a highwayman than a 'priest' who thought nothing of resorting to fisticuffs in the most dubious of hostelries roundabout. I also remember a story about a parish clerk in the same locality ... by all accounts, and in utter inebriation, the Mad Sidenius ... well, without wishing to impose upon the modesty of two ladies—didn't he drag the clerk's breeches down and proceeded in the name of the Father,

Son and Holy Ghost to give him an almighty shellacking that rang through the church and was witnessed by the whole congregation. I suppose you might call it a kind of religious awakening! But the upshot of the whole affair was that the good pastor was finally defrocked and locked up."

While Fru Salomon had smiled at this story, Jakobe had listened with an increasingly gloomy countenance, and it was precisely this darkening of her mood, expressing as it did a vehement disgust, that had inflamed this wealthy manufacturer to, for him, otherwise unknown heights of eloquence—indeed, led him to flesh out the tale so as to render it all the more terrifying.

From within the gentlemen's smoking room, Per's voice could be heard booming out. Jakobe almost visibly jumped. The sound of this voice chilled her to her very marrow. She picked up the book once again and began to browse its pages for distraction, while a particularly bitter memory filled her mind.

The time was four years ago and the place was one of Berlin's large railway stations. She was on the way to her lodgings in Switzerland, and this was actually the last trip she was ever to make there; for it was shortly after this event that she had surprised everybody with her sudden return to Denmark. In Berlin she had arranged to meet with a female friend coming from Breslau with whom she would continue the journey south. She was ill at ease and nervous. For she knew that very soon her gaze would once again meet that of the lawyer who had taken her heart and she believed that he too felt the same way about her. It was for this reason she had been unable to settle at home that summer and had departed even earlier than usual. As she now entered the large railway concourse and stood beneath its glass arch, she saw something further along the platform—a flock of pitiful scavengers. These creatures were surrounded by a circle of gawking onlookers who were held at a slight distance by a couple of police constables. Because of the motley nature of the clothes they were wearing and their southern European appearance, Jakobe assumed at first that it was a band of gypsies whom the authorities were deporting to their homeland. In her agitated state, she turned aside to go to the opposite end of the platform in search of a waiting room. On her way there, she encountered two men carrying a stretcher and on this—covered only by a cloak—was an old and haggard man who looked about him in bewilderment. His eyes were bulbous and blood-shot, gleaming with an obvious fever. Completely disconcerted, she approached a railway guard and asked where the waiting room could be found. The man looked at her, offered an impertinent smile, and remarked that she ought to be able to smell her way there. All she had to do was follow her nose, he said. At that, she turned her back to him and moved on.

Outside a set of double doors that again was blocked by police-men, there was another assembly of curious people who were lifting their heads and standing on tiptoes to look at something going on inside. Jakobe could only make her way through the throng with great difficulty and then suddenly she was confronted with a sight that stopped her dead in her tracks. Beyond the doors, on the floor of a large, dimly lit waiting room, another group of people were sit-ting or lying on the ground. They were the exact same kind of out-landish creatures she had seen on the platform except that here they numbered in their hundreds: men, women and children, gray old men and suckling babies latched on to their mother's breasts. Some were almost naked; many had bloody bandages wrapped around their heads or hands. They all had a deathly demeanor, were exhausted and filthy, as if they had been wandering for an age in a desert of blistering heat and dust. It was immediately obvious that this huge ragbag army, in which only the white headscarves worn by the women gave any hint of uniformity, had grouped themselves according to family origin. Thus, they were gathered around the head of the fam-ily, who for the most part were small, black-eyed men, dressed in long kaftans with belts around their waists. They all carried staffs and some kind of drinking vessel on their belt. These seemed to be the only possessions that most of them had. However, a small num-ber had cooking utensils with them and, here and there, tied bundles could be seen, which obviously contained family possessions and were jealously guarded by the children.

In the first moments, Jakobe simply stood nonplussed at the scene that was being played out before her. Then her heart froze. In the dim interior of the room, she glimpsed a number of Jewish men who had white marks on their arms. In the company of some women, these men were walking around distributing clothes and food. In a flash, she understood everything. Now gripped by dizziness, she realized that what she was looking at was one of the small armies of outcast Russian Jews, who in the past six months had been pushed through Germany before being shipped off to America. All summer long, she had been reading newspaper reports about these legions of refugees and the shameful acts which the mob had visited upon them—either to the indifference of the authorities or even with their outright collusion. The newspapers described how Jewish homes had been set alight with the families still inside; Jewish families had been robbed down to the very clothes they stood in; their women had been violated and abused; old Jews and children alike had been stoned to the point where the gutters ran with blood. All this she had read about every day of the summer but had reassured herself with the thought that the reports were just typical press exaggerations—that such bestiality, perpetrated against a friendly and hard-working race, was simply an impossibility in this century of freedom and common humanity.

"Achtung!" came a cry from behind her.

It was the two men with the stretcher who had now returned and, with some difficulty, were pushing their way through into the room in order to carry away yet another of the many sick and wounded who were to be found within. In their wake, a pair of uniformed senior police officers appeared and, with the undeniable air of statutory authority, took up a position at one of the doors. For a moment they observed the depressing scene and then they moved on, their sabers rattling in time as they progressed down the platform.

Jakobe did not dare to watch any more of it. She recognized the angry flashes, like red lightning in front of her eyes, for what they were. Gasping for breath, she staggered into an adjacent first-class waiting room. The windows in the waiting room looked out on to a public square where people were strolling about, having conversations and laughing. Trams hooted and dogs ran about in the summer sunshine. She was forced to grip the window ledge so as not to faint. And this was no dream! This was reality! These blatant outrages could take place right before Europe's eyes, without one powerful voice to speak out against what was happening! And the church bells rang out God's peace over this town, and its priests preached from their pulpits on the blessings of Christianity and the victory of Love Thy Neighbor in a country where crowds could with coldblooded curiosity—in fact a downright malicious glee—observe this mass of homeless wretches who had been herded through a succession of countries like some pestilential plague and abandoned to privation and destruction. All in Christ's name!

She gave a start.

Out on the square, she could see the two senior police officers. There was no doubt that both of them were the very cut of Prussian lieutenants with their precise hair parting, full-length sabers that almost dragged along the floor, and silver epaulettes on their broad shoulders. Her hands clenched involuntarily. With their autocratic insouciance and utter arrogance, these two officers of the law seemed to Jakobe to symbolize the whole brutal, self-satisfied smugness of Christian society. To her, they resembled more a nest of Pharisees and she praised her great fortune in not having a lethal weapon ready to hand, given that these officers were so close to her. In subsequent hindsight, she had become convinced that she actually would have been able to kill them with her bare hands.

The truth was that Jakobe's directly ensuing disappointment in love had affected her equilibrium so much precisely because this soul-destroying event had taken place immediately prior to her own personal disaster. The one humiliation worked itself in upon the memory of the other. Indeed, her impressions of the two events gradually merged in her mind and gained a fateful power over her.

Amongst many other decisions she made at that time, she resolved never to bind herself to a man ever again. A fellow Jew she would not marry. She would never see her children going through what she herself had had to suffer because of her unhallowed antecedents. But starting a family with a Christian was just as unthinkable. Thus, she developed an implacable hatred of this society, which down through the centuries had been nothing more or less than a pitiless executioner of her kinsfolk. Moreover, even the people themselves terrified her and seemed to pose a constant threat. The sight of such a thick-set blue-eyed bull of a Viking such as Per quickly aroused her memories of those two broad-shouldered, power-mad officers. Even after several years had passed, she could not think of them without feeling a murder lust beginning to wring at her fingers.

Then there was also the fact that she was starting to feel old. She had basically lived life as an adult since being eleven or twelve years of age. She had experienced deep feelings of love and equally deep feelings of rejection as early as her thirteenth year. Thus she felt that her heart wanted nothing more than refuge from the whole thing.

The fact that her old friend Hr. Eybert was fond of her and wanted her as his wife, she had long been aware of. For her part, she set great store by the conversations they often had. For all their personal differences, they had many common areas of interest—both political and literary—and they looked at events, both at home and abroad, with almost the same level of circumspection. Essentially, she really liked him. This diminutive, gentle man, with his wispy beard and fair hair that was always wet-combed to his head, had a positive and calming influence upon her; nor did he remind her in way of that bulldog brutality which so often terrified her in her encounters with other men. It was true, on the other hand, that not one scintilla of his persona was able to arouse her basic female instincts. Except, that is, when he occasionally spoke to others about his two small children who were bereft of a mother. In these moments, something would move deep within her heart and she would briefly feel the blood rising into her cheeks. Indeed, there were fleeting moments where, in her yearning to have a role in life and sacrifice herself for some cause, she would allow herself to be gripped by the notion that she might be a mother figure for this lonely man's little innocents.

*

One day, as evening quickly descended, uncle Heinrich was to be found slumped in a deep armchair in the library, lost in his own thoughts and a cloud of smoke drifting around him from one of his aromatic, after dinner Manila cigars. He had been sitting there for some time when Ivan came into the room and pulled up a chair opposite him.

"Uncle—there's something I'd like to discuss with you."

"Then you've chosen a most unfortunate moment to do it young man. You know very well that it discommodes me to hold conversations after I have eaten."

"But uncle, you don't like speaking while you are eating either— you always say that, so how am I supposed to know when we can have a chat?"

"When I'm asleep boy. Well then, what is it anyway?"

"Will you do me a favor, uncle?"

"Ivan, you know very well that, as a matter of principle, I never do people favors. So let's talk about something else."

"All right, let's call it a business transaction then—or whatever you want to call it," said Ivan as he adopted his favorite sitting position with one foot tucked up underneath him. "The thing is, that there is a young man who interests me greatly...this is a person who—"

"Basically, Ivan, one of your so-called geniuses. Next point!"

"Yes but this time I am completely certain, uncle! We are talking about a major talent. One day he will come to achieve something groundbreaking within his field of expertise. But he is penniless."

"Penniless? Yes, that seems to be the primary condition of your geniuses, as far as I can see."

"And it goes without saying, uncle, that he is not being given the chance to make his mark here at home. That, of course, is the fate of all our most gifted people. But I tell you that I'm not worried. His name shall be in lights. I have spoken to Dyhring about all this and he has promised me that he will interview him sometime soon and do a big piece on the great innovations our friend is working on at the moment."

"In other words, Ivan, this person you are talking about is none other than that arrogant whelp with the upstart nose who was here the other day and made a whole show of himself—him with the ridiculous name. What's ye call him again?"

"Sidenius."

"Herr Gott von Mannheim! To think that any poor soul could have a name like that!"

"Well, uncle, that poor soul is seriously thinking of leaving the country, at least for a while."

"He's come into money then?"

"No uncle. That's exactly what I wanted to speak to you about. You see, I want to provide him with the necessary travel expenses that I know for sure he doesn't have himself. But he is very proud by nature. And so sensitive about that whole area that—yes, well— I am almost certain that he would refuse me, if I just simply went to him and offered the money. He would look upon it as an insult. That's just the way he is."

"Well if that's his damn attitude Ivan, don't waste your money on him is what I say."

"Ah stop, uncle! It is precisely that kind of person who needs help most. And you are going to find a way round it."

"Me? Are you mad?"

"What I thought is that you might play a kind of decoy role for me. And I know you will, good uncle Heinrich, as I'm asking you with all respect. You see, this money has to be offered to him in such a way that it could never cause offense . . . and absolutely anonymously; otherwise he'll never take it. Of course you are more than capable of coming up with some device—you can say that some friends and admirers wanted to show their appreciation of him before he sets off . . . or you can offer him a loan, whatever you think's best."

Uncle Heinrich raised his bushy eyebrows and considered things for a moment. In principle, he was not opposed to the idea of acting as a benefactor, as long as it didn't cost him anything. Moreover, he did have at least a smidgen of goodwill towards Per, as someone who, amongst all Nanny's suitors, might actually have the gumption to really get on in life and become an appropriate match for her.

"And by how much were you thinking of indulging this rogue?"

"Basically whatever he needs to get where he wants. I had thought of say five to six hundred crowns. Maybe more. I have not set a limit. He'll be assigned an account with Griesmann and then he can withdraw from me via him."

"My sister's son is a lunatic! You are just like your mother and father, and all your brothers and sisters. The whole damn family is stark raving mad!"

"Who's got a light?" came a voice from the door leading into the sitting room. It was Nanny.

There she was standing with her hands on her hips, sticking her upper body forwards. An unlit cigarette jumped up and down between her lips. Her uncle pulled a face.

"Here she is now with her substitute dummy! Haven't I said to you before that it is a disgusting, stinking habit for any real lady?"

"Are you in bad form uncle? What a shame. Because there was something I wanted to talk to you about."

"You as well! Talk away young lady! My after dinner repose has been destroyed anyway."

"I've a bone to pick with you, little uncle dearest."

"Pluck all ye want! And have done!"

"I think you could show a bit more discretion than walking down Strøget with your damsels at a time of day when more refined folk are walking about there too. Or, at least, you could show due regard to your family by choosing a less frightening class of female escort than that horror bag I saw you with both today and the other day. We shouldn't have to suffer for your awful taste in women, uncle."

Nanny had positioned herself behind his chair, on whose back she now rested her arms, while sending cloud after cloud of cigarette smoke tumbling down over his half-bald pate. Despite his irritation at what Nanny was saying, he did not move, but preferred to stay where he was with his eyes partially closed, indulging in the pleasure of feeling the hot bursts of breath from her young strawberry lips.

"I have also said to you before, Nanny, that it is horrible and disgusting to listen to a young woman using such lewd language. And anyway that young damsel you are referring to—"

"What young damsel uncle?"

"Herself. The one you have perhaps spotted me accompanying; on just one occasion, and one occasion only I might add—that is my landlady's daughter, a very educated and most respectable—"

"I'm not talking about any young lady. I'm talking about what looked more like an old buzzard with red flowers on her hat and red sauce slapped on her cheeks. And I'm telling you uncle—you really ought to be ashamed of yourself."

"And my reply to that, you little hussy, is that you are the last person in the world to be talking about shame—yes you! Or what else are we to make of the class of person you drag to this house with your coquettish flirting? A certain Hr. Sidenius d'ye mind! An utter carrot cruncher if ever I saw one who has just about learned enough manners to know that he's not allowed to wipe his nose with his fingers anymore. And as for the phizog on that fellow! He literally looks like his mother was an ale house wench and his father a jack pudding."

"Well I think he's a fine thing."

"Yes, a fine thing, you say," her uncle snapped at her. "But I'll tell you this Nanny! If you marry one of those pagan Christians—especially one who does not even possess a hint of blue blood, or a title ... well then—"

"Well then what uncle?"

Uncle Heinrich flashed a terrifying stare up at her from the depths of his chair and said with slow and deliberate emphasis on each word: "Well then, you will not inherit my brooch pin when I die."

"But you've promised that to Jakobe anyway, uncle. And Rosalie told me that you've promised it to her as well. Ivan too, I think."

He shot up in a rage and charged out of the house, crying: "You are all lunatics in this house! I will never ever set foot inside this house again! It's a malignant hole! That's it. I've had enough."

Ivan and Nanny looked at each other with an air of being slightly stunned. As was usual with their uncle, they weren't really sure whether his words had been expressed in deadly earnest, or whether he had been half joking. Then Jakobe appeared at the sitting room door.

"What did you do to poor uncle Heinrich? He was completely beside himself."

"Not a thing," Ivan replied. "You know very well that he doesn't like my friends—and now he's turned against Per Sidenius. Other than that, not much really...You see I told him that Sidenius was thinking of going off abroad somewhere and I asked him to do me a small favor where that's concerned—that's the top and bottom of it."

"Is Hr. Sidenius thinking of leaving Denmark?" asked Nanny—and there was something in her tone that made her sister standing at the door to study her more intensely.

"Well he's thinking of it, yes," Ivan said.

No more questions were forthcoming from Nanny. As if distracted, she moved across the room and threw her half-smoked cigarette into a bronze bowl that was on the table.

"I think Nanny is really casting a heavy line out for Hr. Sidenius," Jakobe said to her mother later that evening. They were alone in the sitting room both sat around one of the table lamps.

"And how do you come to that conclusion now?" Fru Salomon asked rather sharply—as if that very same thought had slowly but surely been working its way through her mind and unsettling her slightly. "Hr. Sidenius is like a bull in a china shop. And Nanny is not that stupid. Besides, I believe he is leaving the country and if that's the case we won't have to worry about him anymore."

"I've a feeling, mother, that this so-called trip abroad might become a bit of a drawn out saga," said Jakobe after a moment's silence. She leaned back into the corner of the sofa and away from her mother—staring straight ahead of her and lost in her own dark tribulations.

"Dear child! What would you know about any of this?"

"Ah mother, I'm not blind! From the moment I set eyes on that man, I knew what he was about. And from the look of him, once he sets his mind to something, there's no going back. Ivan says that himself anyway. Whatever else you might say about him mother—and there's a lot of ground to cover!—he's a bit of a character. There's no doubt about it."

Fru Salomon smiled to herself. "I think you might be changing your mind about him, Jakobe."

"No, mother I'm not … and I would never be able to. His whole personality is far too different from my own for that to happen. But it seems to me that he still has a lot to learn. Who knows what way he might turn out if things go well for him. Maybe one day he really could prove to be the best man for Nanny. At any rate, I almost think I would prefer Per Sidenius as a brother-in-law than, say, the likes of that Dyhring fellow."

"Well Jakobe, you've turned into a proper little matchmaker all of a sudden," Fru Salomon cried. "The other day it was Olga Davidsen's future happiness you were sorting out, and now it's your own sister you want to marry off."

Jakobe's cheeks suddenly became hot and flushed. To herself, she had to admit that her mother's reproach had hit the mark.

"Mother dearest," here she bowed her head slightly to conceal her mortification and laid a hand on her mother's arm, "You know very well that that's just how we old maids carry on."

In these spring months, Per became a frequent guest in the Salomon household. It was true that, primarily, it was still Nanny's presence in the house that attracted him there; but it was also true that the new and exotic style of family life to which he was now exposed was a point of pure fascination for him. One evening, just after he had left, Jakobe could not help but throw out a question: "God knows what Hr. Sidenius is really thinking about when he sits there like that, just staring straight ahead and not saying a word?"

In fact, Per had been sitting there thinking of his childhood home. He saw the living room in front of him in exactly the way it had become lodged in his memory—those long winter evenings when just a single dim lamp burned and smoked at the table in front of the horsehair sofa, and his father dozing in the stiff-backed armchair, the green cardboard eye shade partially concealing his face, while Signe read aloud from one of the newspapers; the smaller sisters meanwhile were sitting bent over their sewing chores, regularly stealing quick glances up at the clock to see whether it was soon time for the night watchman to pass by and declare the day over and time for bed. Once again he heard the small sighs that would emanate from the bedroom next door, where his mother lay bedridden and giving occasional vent to her anguished heart. He heard the quiet rattle from the oil lamp, and smelled the turf burning in the stove, a smell that was always tinged with the tang of polish or medicine.

However, it was not the disparity between the opulence all around him and the domestic wretchedness of his early youth that most struck him. It was much more to do with the difference in tone—in the degree of empathy in the conversation, the life temperature in the two homes. Here, when he heard the children of the house, with their helter-skelter chatter, speaking to their parents almost as if they were friends; when he heard Fru Salomon discussing the new spring fashions with her daughters, seeking their views on the colors and styles that suited them best, in fact, directly prevailing upon them that it was their duty to be well turned out; when he continually found their minds enthusiastically engaged in what was happening out there in the big wide world but with never a mention of that mysterious "hereafter," which like an open grave had permeated his own home, where the routine morning, noon, and night was to turn a collective back on the world so as to pray and sing psalms; yes, his own home where to be well dressed and pay attention to one's appearance was tantamount to a desecration of all born-again souls—then he felt a deep sense of gratitude that he really had found right there in his capital city what he had thought would only be found in foreign climes—Children of Nature, whose heads had not been turned by thoughts of Heaven and Hell.

All that said, his attachment to the Salomon household meant that he had come to revaluate the concept of wealth. Prior to this, and in true bucolic fashion, Per had always viewed money like some kind of weapon with which—in the manner of an assassin—a man could battle his way through the dogfight of life. Now his eyes had been opened to the influence a good and secure standard of living actually had in securing the healthy spiritual growth of a person—the composed and free development of a person's character. He began to understand the reverence that Jews were supposed to have for hard currency and which all right-thinking Sideniuses were scandalized by. He remembered his father's contemptuous words about "those who worship Mammon," and his religion teacher, a pale and worn out theologian who—as he stroked his pupils' hair with a hand stinking of the contents of his pockets—earnestly exhorted them never to yearn for the kind of treasures that moths and rust could eat away in a matter of months. Per pondered on the way that, in this dirt poor country, generation after generation had been browbeaten into a philistine contempt for all "earthly goods," and how spiritual enervation, pettiness, and slovenliness had, at the same time, spread throughout the whole of society. He felt a defiant urge to shout out across the land: "Show respect for money! All hail Mammon...the people's champion and savior!"

However, Per was also well aware that the sheen of gold still provoked a slight sense of fear in his very blood. As he looked around at the lavishly decorated rooms, he could still feel the remnants of his innate troll-like nature stirring within him. Indeed, every time he sat in this veritable Palace of the East, he would think back to his own young life—those days of meager joys and the horrors of a tortured conscience—and he sensed with shame that he really was what his father had always called him, "a child of the night," an underworld troll—a true Sidenius.

Life in this rich, very grand and sociable merchant's home, where so many freeborn and confident people were gathered, was for him more like looking at a mirror into his own soul, which challenged him to renew his search for self-awareness. For the first time in his life, he had encountered people to whom he felt inferior. Even when speaking to the young girls or their friends, he had been forced to use all kinds of deceptions in order to conceal the deficiencies in his own cultural awareness and the huge gaps in his general knowledge.

In all haste, and discreetly as possible, he set about obtaining what he lacked in terms of erudition and discernment. In particular, he threw himself into the study of Dr. Nathan's books, which in these circles he had so often heard described, discussed and disputed. Per also sought to improve his woeful language skills so as not to appear like a complete numbskull in a house that received so many foreign visitors, and where even the younger children spoke the three main European languages with great accomplishment.

Thus, despite the fact that he mainly went to the house because of Nanny, Per sometimes gained more pleasure from simply sitting and chatting to Fru Salomon and Jakobe, whose interests and topics of conversation he found to be most enlightening. His respect for Jakobe, in particular, had grown immensely. With consummate ease, she was able to discuss anything from the old Greek philosophers right up to the new developments in Bismarck's policies; but at the same time she was no raving suffragette. The disagreeable impression she had first made upon him, notwithstanding, and despite the fact that she sometimes seemed to throw barriers up against him, he enjoyed talking to her about what he had been reading or intended to read.

For her part, and almost in spite of herself, Jakobe gradually yielded to Per's keen interest in Dr. Nathan, a man whom she saw as the country's greatest leading light and the herald of a new dawn. In Nathan, they had found a source of common interest, a deep well from which, in their different ways, they could draw up the emotion that ran deepest within them—hatred of a Church which had cast a blight over their childhood lives. And Per made no effort to hide what lay in his heart. He gave vent to his feelings with the kind of naive openness that gradually won, if not her sympathy, then at least her forbearance. In fact, the truth was that it was Jakobe during this period who was overseeing Per's development, far more than even she herself realized. Nor was Per fully aware of the influence that her dominant personality was gradually working upon him. So despite the great respect for her that he clearly had, Per did not fully comprehend the extraordinary esteem in which Jakobe was held. This manifested itself, for example, at the large-scale evening receptions held in the house, where the cream of the Liberal party's leadership was to the fore.

While Nanny would flit like an effervescent elf from room to room on such occasions, with literary aesthetes like Balling and Povl Berger in train, Jakobe was the exact opposite. For in spite of her naturally reserved, or even at times dismissive, comportment, the leading lights at the party would always end up gathered around her chair. These included the truly famous university professors and the many distinguished doctors who constituted such a significant part of Copenhagen's already extremely influential progressive political movement.

At one such gathering, Per overheard a man in this same group complaining over the fact that a woman of such obvious intellect and with so much ability didn't seem to be able to make some man happy by settling down with him. "But then, who would?" the man had rhetorically asked himself. "I mean a woman like Jakobe, who has so much of a queen about her, should at the very least be wooed by a prince. That old bore Eybert is hardly going to light her candle."

These words, though said in jest, had a serious impact on Per and, bit by bit, also began to affect the way he viewed Jakobe's physical appearance. He had to admit that she carried herself in a particularly proud way, and that her facial profile really was more redolent of an eagle than a parrot. His eyes were opened to the beauty in her light, yet purposeful, gait with its strangely silent, predator-like footfall. Per noticed the imperious way she eased herself into an armchair—yes, she even managed to make blowing her nose look like a graceful act. One evening, and by complete chance, they came to be alone together in the study. Nanny was attending a dinner party and was not expected back for another hour. It was for this reason that he had sat down so as to await her return. Per and Jakobe were sitting on their respective sides of an octagonal table inlaid with mother-of-pearl buttons. The lamp stood between them, throwing the shape of its yellow silk shade on to its dark surface. Jakobe sat with her hand under her chin, leafing through a picture album. They had remained silent for some time when she suddenly asked how it had actually come about that someone like him, who came from a long line of priests, had decided to go down the technical route and become an engineer.

"Does engineering not appeal to you then?" he asked by way of a diversion.

"Yes, of course—why shouldn't it?" she asked before going on to speak with great passion on the important role that the great engineering companies would one day have in the liberation of humankind, in that by reducing the distance between countries via railways, telegraph systems and steamships, they contributed to a leavening of national differences and thereby had already taken the first step towards finally realizing one of man's oldest aspirations—brotherly understanding between all races of the earth.

Per stole quick glances over to her a couple of times as she spoke and his face reddened somewhat. He had never looked at his own efforts from that viewpoint but felt an extraordinary attraction to the idea that his canal project might be seen as working towards such superior ideals. His mood took on a veritably regal air.

In general, Jakobe always seemed to have that effect on him. Her words and Dr. Nathan's books were all of a piece. At times they had the power to illuminate the far shores of certain remote and mysterious thought processes, with the result that they seemed more like a series of alluring revelations. My God, she's bright! he often thought to himself when he sat opposite her and observed her striking Sphinx-like features, and he would then sometimes experience the amazing sensation that he was sitting face to face with nothing less than a young Sibyl. In such moments, Jakobe became a force of nature—the inscrutable guardian of wisdom's fathomless depths.

"I wish, Frøken, that we had met a long time ago."

Though he had tried hard to inject some levity into his tone of voice, he could hear how corny his statement sounded. And the way that Jakobe smiled in response let Per know that she was by no means flattered. But, undaunted, he plowed on: "Yes, I know that was a stupid thing to say. But it is true for all that—I really am, for the first time in my life, walking around with the sense that I'm becoming a fully rounded person. And like it or not, if I may say so Frøken . . . Jakobe Salomon has played her part in that process."

"And what kind of creature does Per Sidenius think he was prior to all this?"

It was a while before he gave a reply: "Do you recall your Danish lessons at school and the reading book that told the legend of the mountain troll who crawled up through a mole hill so he could live amongst human beings but got terrible fits of sneezing whenever the sun broke through the clouds? Ah, I could tell you a long tale that would explain exactly where that legend comes from!"

And as they sat there, Per began to reveal to her some of the most intimate aspects of his being. Ambushed by a sudden need to confide in someone, he spoke—albeit using a partially humorous tone—about his childhood and his estrangement from the parental home. Jakobe had already heard something of this from Ivan. This sudden outpouring made her cautious and she gave him no encouragement to continue.

However, they were soon interrupted anyway by uncle Heinrich who came into the room from the hallway. The old lecher rarely missed a chance to scrutinize his nieces when they were in *grande toilette*. Naturally, therefore, he first inquired as to Nanny's whereabouts. At that very moment, they heard the carriage roll into the forecourt and moments later Nanny swept into the room. As she caught sight of Per, she stopped abruptly and with no little calculation allowed her white fur stole to fall slowly down so as to reveal her shoulders. Per had stood up and was confused by what he saw. Of course he saw a beautiful female form in front of him, dressed as she was in a white, very low-cut silk dress; still flushed by the party's conviviality and her eyes sparkling with festiveness. And yet when he allowed his gaze to settle back on her sister's black-clad figure, as she sat there deep in thought with her hand under her chin and bathed in the soft light from the lamp, it occurred to him that Jakobe came out well from the comparison. Feeling strangely ill at ease, he took leave of the Salomon household and walked slowly homeward. And in the middle of the street, he stopped dead in his tracks and spoke to himself in a kind of half terror as he pushed his hat back from his forehead: "My God—could it actually be? Is it really Jakobe that I love?"

8

IN ORDER to advertise his name to the wider world, and thereby promote his plans within the Salomon household, Per had for some time mulled over the idea of publishing a small pamphlet. This would be his riposte to Colonel Bjerregrav, and it would be pitched as a direct challenge to that whole shower of "Engineer Clerics" in Denmark who had wanted to cut out his tongue and banish him forever to some dark and obscure place. Those particular gentlemen would soon see that there was at least one rebel who still had fire in his belly.

Amongst other things, he would stress the urgent need for a complete overhaul of the country's transport system. Using estimations that would probably suffice as a rough guide, he would show how ridiculous it was for a small country, devoid of fuel resources and surrounded by the sea, to favor the development of an expensive railway network instead of working to create a huge canal system that would bring even the smallest of towns into direct contact, so to speak, with the mighty oceans. First and foremost, this approach would enable him to sing the praises of his own project, which would be comprehensively described in the booklet and be accompanied by drawings and cost estimates.

Moreover, he also intended to reveal a more philosophical side to his arguments. Egged on by Jakobe's words that evening, when she had talked of the cultural battles that lay ahead and the natural position of leadership in modern society that fell to the engineering sciences, he had decided to bolster the book still further with some general, but forceful, introductory words regarding the momentous tasks facing the country.

Per then sat down to compose the document that would be his personal battle cry. Unused as he was to literary expression by means of a pen, and even though spelling and punctuation were not his forte, he boldly threw himself into his "publication." In a style and tone that was heavily colored by the impressions he had gained from Dr. Nathan's writings, he began by alerting his readers to the fact that the "the philistine academic elite" had plunged the country into an abyss during the course of the preceding century. He then painted a bleak picture of the irredeemable destitution the country would finally suffer if, in spite of all good sense and the experience of other countries, it continued to worship at the false and outmoded altar of butter and pork and did not set out with determination to source new forms of income for the people. As a counterargument, he sketched a vibrant picture of the kind of wonderland that would arise, relatively quickly, if powerful industries were to be created to transform the country. As his pen rampaged across the paper, Per envisaged heavily laden freighters plowing full steam ahead towards his canals, which calmly awaited the raw materials coming from far-flung corners of the earth. He saw proud factory chimneys rising up alongside his flowing, meticulously controlled, waterways and heard the sound of humming flywheels and roaring turbines. On that barren Jutland heath, which had so dominated his thoughts and dreams since childhood, he now saw urban settlements overflowing with people; newly built towns bustling with activity; places where no church bells rang out in the midnight hour to bestir phantom spirits in the minds of the people, but whose electric road lighting chased the dark and its evil spirits away.

One day, as he sat at his desk, positively glowing with inspiration, he received a surprise visitor. His door was given a couple of smart raps by the top of a walking cane and none other than "Director" Delft revealed himself in the doorway. He wore a bright suit in the Parisian style, was heavily pomaded and perfumed, and boasted a blue-tinted monocle for his one good eye that was the victim of a vicious squint.

"Good God Sidenius! This is where you have been hiding," he said, without even the slightest pretense of an introduction. He then cast a calibrating eye on the surroundings in the small, dark backroom that was overflowing with papers and rolls of drawings. "So it's here where you've been hammering at that false gold for a future that is never going to happen! Well you could not have picked a better dwarf's cave to batter out a rake of bad shekels eh? Sorry! My apologies! Have I come crashing in on you just when you're in the middle of running off a few thousand? Ha, ha, ha!"

By now, Per was only too aware of uncle Heinrich's extremely blunt way of expressing himself to take offense. At the same time, Per's smile was somewhat forced. He could not warm to this ugly little man and was put out by his sudden appearance. What does this old scoundrel want with me? he wondered.

"I hope it's not a great shock to see me?" Hr. Delft asked with an exaggerated show of concern once he had settled himself into the one-armed rocking chair that Per had offered him. "I've been intending to come out to you for some time Hr. Sidenius, but my business commitments have just not allowed me to do so until now. The troublesome situation in China, you know, and complications in India are causing incredible trouble in our company. I spend the whole day sending telegrams. Well, here I am now sitting here and able to have a cozy chat with you—about everything and nothing as we might say."

At this point, uncle Heinrich gave a short pause with the obvious intention of heightening Per's curiosity. But Per merely offered a calm and watchful disposition and no question passed his lips.

Thus, a somewhat lengthy pause ensued, during which Hr. Delft once more proceeded to subject Per's tiny little room to close inspection through his monocle.

"Were you ever in China yourself, Hr. Sidenius? India perhaps? Well, you must have been to America? Oh! All young men should go there, so they can really learn the art of taking this bull of a world by its horns."

Yet another silence, after which Hr. Delft's tone was altered and became more cautious.

"Do you, Hr. Sidenius, happen to recall a brief conversation we had on the first occasion I had the honor of meeting you in my brother-in-law's house? You were good enough to offer some affirmative words regarding my niece, for which I expressed my deep gratitude. On that occasion, I took the liberty of drawing Hr. Sidenius's attention to the enjoyment that was to be gained by sitting back and studying the many ridiculous characters those young women attract to that fine house. Well, am I not right in what I say? Is it not, dear sir, very often a complete spectacle? In they come those young men, like strutting roosters without so much as a bad penny to their name and with faces as soft and innocent as a newly scrubbed baby's backside."

At this point it occurred to Per that had it not been for Jakobe, the old codger would have been pitched headfirst into the street by now.

"And it is such a Danish thing to do...do you not think?...as Danish as pigs," Hr. Delft continued unabashed, as he threw yet another pitying glance about the room and all its wretchedness. "In other countries this would simply not happen...why the very thought would not even be entertained! In America for example—"

Hr. Delft then began to speak of the experiences he had in the company of a young man in New York who "*machte* a great career" and snapped up a millionaire's daughter from right under the noses of blue-blood barons and counts, even though he was, in truth, a poor devil who ate his dinner in a downtown saloon.

"That young man was called Stadlmann, an Austrian. He was the kind of man whom people either praised as a genius or cursed as a shyster. One of his schemes was to make full-cream milk and butter out of prairie grass but without the bother of it going through a cow in the first place. Wonderful idea! Nothing to do but go to a laboratory where he tried some experiments and got to know a son of Samuel Smith—I'm sure you have heard that name before Hr. Sidenius—one of the great matadors of the stock exchange on Fifth Avenue. Why, the man is worth seven or eight hundred million—that's dollars, you understand! And Samuel had an only daughter who was twenty years old and, may God help us, doesn't she go and become *verliebt* in this here good for nothing and wants to marry him. Now what do you say to that, sir! Of course, the next is that this fellow goes headfirst into a trash can. If a man of Samuel's stature had just given his daughter away like that, he would have been the laughing stock of the whole union of states. But, at the same time, there were a few of us who were aware of what was happening and had followed each step of the affair, as one might say. Well, there we are sitting in our club one day and we all quickly agree that there might be some business to be made out of this story. So we set up a limited company."

"A limited company? Trading on what?" asked Per, who had begun to listen.

"On what? On the young man of course ... on his chances I mean. We all put up some share capital ... first it was five, then ten thousand dollars so that he could set himself up as young rake about town in New York—rent himself a swish apartment on Broadway, keep a servant and a riding horse, invite journalists to supper and get gossiped about in the newspapers ... long story short, within two months he was the talk of the street. So off he went one day and asked Samuel for his daughter's hand."

"Ah. And he got her?"

"Not a hair on her head did he get. Samuel was betting on a different horse altogether where his beloved daughter was concerned. He himself was the son of a midden and cess pit cleaner and nothing would do but to get his daughter married into nobility."

"But what happened to your limited company then?"

"It went very well. We got a return of about two hundred percent."

"I don't understand. When the father would only give his daughter away to an aristocrat—"

"Yes, it goes without saying that we had to provide the young man with a title. That cost us four thousand dollars. But we are talking about one of Europe's most ancient and proudest names. The whole thing went like clockwork. The young gentleman supplied us with the name and address of an old widowed Countess von Raben-Rabenstein who lived in the area where he was reared. She was as poor as a church mouse and her only means of income came by way of leasing part of her property as a boarding school for young girls. We sent her a long letter, along with a return ticket to New York, and requested the honor of her presence at the ceremonial opening of a new children's refuge, which we, as concerned philanthropists, had set up in the city—these unfortunates were three street urchins and a drunken old black woman that we hired for three months—but this was never mentioned to the good lady of course. We explained that this sanctuary was going to be named after her highness and was particularly dedicated to helping children of Austrian parents . . . how could she refuse! The whole thing was a priceless comedy! Upon her arrival by steam packet, the lady was received by the full complement of partners in the company and she was garlanded with floral bouquets before being driven in a coach and four to a gala dinner at the Hotel Netherlands. Once there, she was presented to the already assembled journalists as Hr. Stadlmann's flesh and blood aunt—this news could be read in all the newspaper the following day. Then we showed her a legally drawn up document of adoption and, at the same time, sort of waved a thousand-dollar check under her nose until she swooned into our arms. Six months after that, the newly baked Count von Raben-Rabenstein's marriage to Samuel Smith's daughter was celebrated with all due pomp and ceremony and was attended by the who's who of the entire aristocracy of the United States Union. I can speak as a witness to all this because I too was one of the select group of invited guests and actually had the honor of leading another kind of aristocrat, the new duchess of Catania—born Simpson—to the banquet table."

Per was crumpled forward in his chair, nervously twirling one end of his moustache. Hr. Delft had hit him right in his most sensitive spot with this story, namely his pecuniary shame. At that point, he was just about able to keep his head above water with regards to his personal necessities. How then was he going to be able to get his book published? He had wrecked his head over that question.

He had sat with a forced smile on his lips and listened to the whole long drawn out tale, a tale which otherwise was just like a lot of the after-dinner bandits and robbers stories Hr. Delft was wont to recount in his brother-in-law's house. But Per had swung round to the belief that it might be a clever move on his part to humor this old goat.

Indeed, he now wondered whether this change of tack might be used to procure some sort of loan on not unreasonable terms. With that, he leaped into the breach.

"I suppose," Per said, "that it's not such a bad idea—creating a limited company based on a young man's prospects. In fact, if I may say so Hr. Director, you should introduce that kind of approach here at home. I have only one objection to it. Why stop at speculating on the chances of a marriage? If I may say so sir, you lean towards the more unpredictable end of business affairs. Why not take a chance on one or other of the many opportunities that can present themselves to a very bright, energetic young man? What would you say for example to an engineer with one or two good ideas ... say, a brilliant hydrotechnical project?"

"I'll be frank with you sir," Hr. Delft replied with a merciless smile, "the actual name and purpose of the venture is not what counts, as long as it has a certain ring to it. Take that limited company I've just told you about. Its name was 'The Land of Milk and Honey Company.' A marvelous name don't you think! On the strength of it, we got a couple of gullible subscribers from the meat and butchery trade to stand as guarantors."

"What you are saying is that it might be possible to form a similar kind of consortium here in Denmark if, for example, the right candidate were to provide the necessary details for a program of work and was able to show that his project—if it were pursued with the requisite energy and enthusiasm—could at some point earn millions for the shareholders?"

"Yes, why not?"

The surprising bluntness of the reply made Per suspicious. He is trying to lure me into a trap, Per thought. He's aware of my plans and now he wants my head on a plate so that he can scuttle off and reveal to Jakobe and her family that I was nothing but a mercenary from the start.

He withdrew into his shell and said no more. But for all that, when Hr. Delft lifted his hat as a signal that he was about to leave, Per became extremely perturbed. He told himself that he had no choice but to take some kind of drastic action in order to get money, and he decided to push the boat out, at least a little further into open seas. However, at that very point, an overwhelming lethargy took the wind from his sails. He felt himself sullied and demeaned by his unending financial woes. His indignation rose at always having to act like a sneak, to fawn over people, and even lie in order to get the things he needed in life. But in the next turn, suddenly seized by a quiet desperation, he broke free of all these scruples and said: "Hr. Director— is it not time we put our cards on the table? I can assume from what you have said that you are aware of my interest in your niece, and I grant you that it is somewhat reckless of me, given my present position, to have any hopes at all with regards to a lady who possesses so many outstanding advantages—both personal and social."

"A gallant speech. And well put young man."

Per pushed on. "Well, then, given that you, sir, have raised the question, and by doing so have given me some justification in putting to you the following straightforward question: Will you, Hr. Delft, make moves on my behalf so as to form the kind of business venture we have just discussed?"

"Me?" the little man exclaimed as he jumped from his chair in sham outrage.

"Yes, you precisely!" Per continued undeterred. "I admit that I'm in a very awkward position just at this moment. I have to get money from somewhere . . . and money I will get, even if I have to steal it."

Hr. Delft, who was still of the belief that Per's plans revolved around Nanny, had now arrived at the point he had been working towards. Per's last outburst had appealed to him. It strengthened his conviction that Per possessed the determination and wherewithal to build a career for himself and gain the kind of position in society that was commensurate with the standing held by his sister's daughter.

He suddenly began to laugh with obvious pleasure.

"You are by no means the worst of them. If I'm not mistaken, you are proposing that we cut a deal for the procurement of my own niece's hand. Well, I respect your sentiments. But I no longer involve myself in private arrangements. Not even where young ladies are concerned.

But now I'll tell you the real reason for my visit. I have confidence in you young man! I think you have a future ahead of you and I want to help you. You need money. And money you shall have. But I should explain. We're not talking about interest payments or anything like that. This is not a business transaction you understand, so you can call it what you will. Do you know Hr. David Griesmann, the barrister? He can be found in Klosterstræde. You can draw down what you need for the moment via him, with the security being—well, ehm, the expected profits from your extraordinary inventions of course. But I want my name kept out of it. If anybody asks me whether it is my good self that is bailing you out, I will deny all knowledge of it. Just so that we are clear on that point!"

Per was struck dumb. But Hr. Delft's dismissive tone and ill-befitting deportment as a benefactor made all thoughts of accepting the transaction impossible. And how could he be sure that this all too generous offer was not a devious trap?

So when the "Director" once more took his hat, Per made no effort to delay him further. He simply smiled, and in order to give some kind of explanation as to his hesitancy, said: "Yes, I will, of course, look upon your offer as some kind of humorous diversion that you dreamed up. Hopefully you will also understand that my own words were meant as a joke. Your tale from America certainly got me into the spirit of things."

At first Hr. Delft looked at him with no little surprise. Then he offered his most withering and merciless smile.

"Heaven forbid, Hr. Engineer! You have all too little trust in my powers of perception. I can assure you that they want for nothing sir. Believe me I understand, shall we say, the lay of your land. In the meantime . . . should you wish to continue with this, ahm . . . joke, as you call it, you now know where Hr. Griesmann has his chambers. His office hours are between ten and four. And I can assure that he also has a very highly developed sense of humor . . . loves a good joke that man! I bid you good day!"

Delft was already standing with his hand on the latch when he once more turned to Per, who had remained standing at his desk.

"One more thing Hr. Sidenius! You have previously mentioned a certain eminent widow to my nephew Ivan. A Baroness von Bernt-Adlersborg; isn't that right? Forgive my presumption in asking such a question...do you know anything more about this lady?"

"No. I had a passing acquaintance with her deceased brother. But why do you—?"

"Sorry! This would be an older lady would it? And no doubt a bit...well, soft in the head?"

"Possibly. But I have to ask—?"

"And you received a letter from her the other day...a friendly letter that came from abroad. Ivan told me this. In the letter she asks you to pay a visit to her home in the summer and apologizes for the fact that she's at a health spa at the moment and cannot return until the winter. True or false?"

"Devil take you man!" Per exclaimed as he banged his fist against his desk. "Why are you throwing all these meaningless questions at me?"

But without being the least intimidated, the grim little man moved his gnomelike figure right in close to Per, lifted himself on to his tiptoes and spoke into his face: "You see—I should really point this out to you—there may be people in this country as well who would only consider giving their daughters away to men whose name has a noble ring to it. Adieu!"

By the end of May, the Salomon household had already moved out to Skovbakken, the family's holiday villa, which was an hour's coach ride from Copenhagen. Per enjoyed his Sunday excursions to the villa whenever "open house" was declared, but he would also show up at other times, under the pretext of wanting to consult with Ivan with regards to book publishing and similar issues affecting his manuscript. Nor was he perturbed in the slightest by the fact that not everybody in the family was equally pleased to see him arrive. Nanny in particular usually preferred to turn her back to him, once it dawned on her that she had been ditched. From the moment Per had gained the conviction that it was Nanny's sister he cared more for, and that to follow his predilection was hardly likely to harm his future prospects, it was exclusively Jakobe's company that he sought.

However, a corresponding increase in Jakobe's feelings for Per had not unfortunately taken place. Quite the opposite. The sense of unease that had overcome her at their very first meeting was once more aflame in her heart. The root cause of this was their night time conversation in Copenhagen, in which he had confided to her the true nature of his relationship with his parents and brothers and sisters. As genuine as her hatred was towards Christianity, Jakobe was still taken aback by the apparent ease and lack of sensitivity shown by Per when describing the whole issue. In her Talmudic reverence for the home and ancestry, such implacable hostility to blood relatives made her fearful.

Moreover, a new turn in his behavior had taken place, and this too made her uncomfortable. As he had gradually overcome his insecurity in social gatherings, which had hitherto dampened his natural self-confidence, he had developed, amongst other things, an unfortunate tendency to intervene in conversations, not only when it was warranted but also when keeping his counsel would have been the better option. After having read a handful of books by Dr. Nathan and like-minded authors, he clearly felt that he could speak with some authority and would launch himself, with the brashness of a provincial, into any and every discussion that might arise on the great issues of state and human emancipation. This was particularly the case when family and guests retired after dinner, during which he partook of the wine with a particular relish. He would then proceed to expound, actually to preach, the gospel according to the natural sciences and the Great Age of Man that was about to dawn—all in a way that would often cause his audience to smile discreetly, or look away in embarrassment.

He seemed to feel honor bound to excel at everything. On walking tours in the forest, he would jump over every road barrier and challenge the other gentlemen in the company to try the same thing. On rowing tours, he would immediately grasp both oars in order to show off his arm strength. Per's sense of style was also a source of irritation. Strictly following the current rough-and-ready French mode, his suits were cut very tightly and, to an almost lewd degree, accentuated the powerful curves of his muscular frame. On top of this, for part of his summer wardrobe, he had opted for a type of linen shirt with a very open collar that not only revealed his bulging neck muscles but actually revealed the upper part of his chest. To the eyes of others, this gave him an inappropriate likeness to the kind of gadabout who pimped off street girls in saloons and taverns. Nanny did nothing but gloat after Per had visited. One of her favorite expressions was: "My fear is great that when, one fine day, he finally bursts with his own self-importance, it will be his backside that goes first."

Despite everything, Jakobe felt almost sorry for him. But as it gradually dawned on her that it was herself and not her sister that was the focus of Per's attentions, and that it was in order to impress her that he was acting like a bull in a china shop, she was at a loss to know how to deal with him. Jakobe sought to ensure that she would never more be left alone with him, and she spoke to her brother Ivan about making good the suggestion that Per might take a trip abroad. It was just not possible for him to continue his visits—at least until he himself came to appreciate his lack of social finesse, and she had no doubt that a period spent experiencing foreign cultures and philosophies would be the quickest way of helping him.

Finally, the awareness of Per's intentions became an unbearable worry for Jakobe and, on one particular day, her worst nightmares nearly came true. It was the beginning of July. The whole family was sitting outside on the graveled terrace in front of the villa, enjoying the cool of the evening after a sweltering day. The dinner table had only just been cleared and coffee served. Dressed in simple white shifts, and still wearing broad brimmed sunhats, the small, and even very small, children ran or crawled on the immense double staircase. This was made of marble and was flanked by thickets of rosebushes that eventually led down to the strand and the edge of the sea. Everything was in full bloom. The assorted bushes were a riot of color, and each zephyr of wind wafted a floral perfume across the coffee table and mingled with the aroma from Philip Salomon's Havana cigar.

There were no strangers present, other than longstanding confidante of the family, Hr. Eybert, who the day before had returned from his yearly trip to a spa resort. Hr. Eybert sported a modest hairpiece to cover the top of his head, which he had bought in the Rue Gossec in Paris. As he sat there, resplendent in his south of France tan, recounting his Alpine excursions and mentioning mutual friends whom he had met on different parts of his journey, Hr. Eybert actually cut quite a youthful figure. Philip Salomon, who had edged himself away from the table so as to inspect the evening papers, offered an occasional question, or informed Ivan of some news item or other coming from the stock exchange. With an apparent nonchalance, Philip Salomon was able to follow two or three different conversations at the same time as he was computing multiples of five-figure numbers in his head, before committing the conclusions to the giant accounts book he kept in a particular part of his memory bank. And yet, there wasn't anyone in the assembled party who in a more conscious fashion enjoyed the peace of the evening, the smell of roses, and the whole atmosphere of wellbeing and joy that permeated this family occasion.

Nanny was not at home. She had left as soon as dinner was over so that she could take in a summer concert at Klampenborg along with a female friend. The journalist Dyhring had provided her with the invitation.

At around eight o'clock, Per suddenly arrived. He was in an awful mood. Forced by desperate need, and not actually expecting any positive result from it, he had that morning sought out the barrister Griesmann whom Hr. Delft had so mysteriously recommended to him. To Per's amazement, and on the spot, he received a significant sum of money, simply by the fact of providing his name and a receipt. However, despite the fact that he was now, and for the foreseeable future, released from the one real source of acknowledged grief in his life, he returned home in an unhappy and agitated frame of mind. Filled with feelings of having sold his honor, he had stuffed the packets of notes into a drawer in his commode, without even wishing to count them.

Now the sight of the newly returned, and reinvigorated, fellow suitor, who sat by Jakobe's side, increased Per's agitation tenfold. In the uneven mixture of feelings that constituted Per's love for the young lady, vanity took pride of place, and even a slightly less suspicious eye than Per's would have immediately perceived that Hr. Eybert's return from abroad had enlivened her.

Thus, the calculated carelessness with which Per greeted his rival was executed in such an exaggerated way that it had the opposite effect to what was intended and raised a smile from Hr. Eybert.

"I believe I have the misfortune of having made an enemy of that young man," he said, speaking under his breath and in French to Jakobe who—in her outrage at Per's behavior—declined to reply.

Unfortunately Hr. Eybert's words were also picked up by Per, whose face blanched. In spite of repeated requests for him to take a seat, Per remained standing. Even when Ivan shoved a chair right underneath him, he refused to sit down. He simply placed a hand on the back of the chair and, in this position, continued to stare with a studied insolence at Eybert. A certain uneasiness arose amongst those who were witness to this. But fortunately more visitors arrived at the very same moment and a scandal was averted.

However, for the rest of the evening Jakobe could not free herself from the effect of these moments of excruciating apprehension. She had actually started to shake. And she promised herself that she would no longer indulge the presumptuous arrogance of this immature upstart. She had clearly given him far too much leeway as it was. If he should dare to behave like that one more time, she would ask her father to ban him from the house. What a stupid, stuck up little pup! What must poor Eybert think?

When these last two visitors had left, Jakobe and her mother had sat alone for a while on the terrace without a word being exchanged between them. The mother then began to talk about Eybert.

"I think he began to feel a bit anxious over his little Astrid. She is probably a bit off color again."

"Oh," said Jakobe, who began to blush slightly. "I've not heard him say anything about that mother. I hope it's nothing serious?"

"Ah, I don't think so, but that's probably the reason he went home early. He doesn't have much confidence in his housekeeper you know. He is really in a bit of a tight corner, poor man."

Jakobe gave the impression of not having heard this last remark. She leaned back in her wicker chair with her hands gathered in her lap and looked out over the Øresund, whose waters were perfectly still and shone in a milky glow. The huge evening sky was empty of stars. Over on the Swedish side, the coastline was peppered with windows reflecting the burning embers of sunset.

Of course, she was well aware that her parents' greatest wish was to see her marry Eybert. This was no secret, and especially in most recent times, her mother had not shown any restraint in pushing her in that direction—something which, by the by, had got her back up to some extent. Was there any need to push so forcefully at an open door? In the last month or so, her thoughts had automatically turned towards him more frequently than ever before in the long time they had known each other. During his absence abroad, she had for the first time seriously missed his company. Her longings had been an almost daily occurrence, not just for their intimate exchange of opinions on all the disheartening events taking place around the world, but also for his actual physical presence, his bright smile and intelligent eyes. She longed also for all the serenity that pervaded his personality and had such a beneficial effect upon her. The fact that her cheeks had become flushed was because of the strong effect the news of his little daughter's illness had had upon her. At that moment, and with no little bashful confusion, she had perceived that she already looked upon herself as something of a mother to the child.

The fact that she was not in love with him in the way she had fallen for others was all too clear to her, but she spent no time distressing herself over this. Now in the maturity of her early adult years, she preferred the security she felt when at his side to the feverish passions that had scourged her heart. If Eybert was not, she would argue with herself, that proud and wonderful standard bearer of truth whom she had once, in her youthful haughtiness, dreamed of drawing to her breast to bestow sanctuary and joy, he was at least a man of serious principles and conviction. And if it was true that he was no longer young, at least he did not call shame upon his head by the kind of puerile behavior and lack of male courtesy that so often made young men so unappealing.

And then there was always such a clean and wholesome smell about his person—something that meant a great deal to her, as she could not be in the company of others without receiving a set of very definite olfactory sensations from each person present. These, furthermore, and to her continued annoyance, would follow her and sometimes trigger unbearable sensations in her long after the event. She could mark Per's arrival while he was still more than a body length away from her. This was due to that stink of poverty, which came from the damp and musty storage, lack of washing and remnants of tobacco that always hung about his clothing.

At the end of the day, Eybert had one sovereign advantage, which had occupied her thoughts long before he had in any way become dear to her. He came from a well-respected family, and with his excellent financial standing and academic background (being a political science graduate), he had very quickly become one of the leading lights in the quickly burgeoning liberal scene in Copenhagen, with a seat in parliament and a not insignificant influence on policy within the party. Those who found entertainment in compiling lists of potential ministers for the—hardly likely—scenario that free-thinking policies and politicians might gain representation within the government, often mentioned his name within the first ranks; and it was this prospect of social esteem and the wielding of power that proved so strongly alluring to her. That indifference to social rank and superficial marks of merit, which she showed to the world, was not quite Jakobe's true nature. It was a necessary refuge, forced upon her by her own shrewdness and pride. In fleeting moments, she would still dream about achieving an uprising, in the very chambers of the Royal Court itself, that would make good the humiliations she had endured, and with the might of king and emperor behind her she would finally triumph over those who had besmirched her bloodline. At these thoughts, she would raise her head proudly and her cheeks would begin to glow. Were it not for the fact that her sober judgment would return very quickly to convince her of the folly in such thoughts, there is no doubt that poor Eybert would not have had to wait for so long, and in vain, for an answer from her.

As far as Per was concerned, his clash with Eybert led to a decision to ask for Jakobe's hand as soon as was humanly possible. Now that he had serious money in his pocket, he would of course turn thoughts of traveling abroad for a year into reality. Per envisaged that his studies during his sabbatical year would take him to both Europe and America. But before that he wanted to make Jakobe his own. He simply could not run the risk that Hr. Eybert, or some other sly old fox, would snap her away from him during his absence.

The fact that Jakobe was not exactly encouraging him, but rather was clearly avoiding his company, did nothing to dampen his hopes. He had known from the very start that his approach would have to be conducted with all due caution; that he would, so to speak, have to conquer her bit by bit. His own clear opinion was that he had already made such inroads into her heart that he could hear its very beat. The increased shyness that she now showed whenever he was near, he took as a good sign. Now he had to show a bit of caution, give her peace and time to think, before he made the decisive move.

On a subsequent day, Per received an express delivery letter from Ivan, who informed him in high excitement that the article Dyhring had promised to write about his ideas had now gone to press and would more than likely appear in *The Falcon* the very next day.

"Now would you indulge me somewhat," he wrote, "by paying Dyhring a courtesy call. I know that he would appreciate the gesture. Be mindful of the benefits that might accrue to you by conquering any possible unwillingness you may feel in doing as I suggest. Dyhring is someone who can be of great use to you, both now and in the future. As I have had the presumption to point out before, my dear Sidenius, obtaining the backing of the press is, in this day and age, a necessary evil!"

Per hardly slept that night. A week previously, Ivan had once more brought him to meet the respected young journalist, and on this occasion Per finally gave in to the pleadings of his friend and revealed his ambitious plans. The fact was that he himself saw the wisdom in paving the way for the launching of his project manifesto and he was now on tenterhooks to see his name and thoughts revealed to a curious public for the first time.

But cold reality soon reduced his aspirations to regret and disappointment. Instead of the front-page coverage he had expected, he found a side column on the newspaper's third page, printed in brevier type and signed off with one of Dyhring's all too frequent petty flourishes "S'il vous plaît." In his animated state, Per did not even notice that the article had been written in a slightly humorous tone. Indeed, even the headline "Millionaires sought," he took completely seriously. On the other hand, he became highly displeased on discovering that his name was nowhere to be found, and that right through the article he was described as "the young, talented inventor," or some such moniker. Moreover, he was deeply offended by the superficial way in which his cost analysis had been treated. Worse, he became incandescent on noticing the incorrect placement of a decimal point; a slapdash fault, which, in his opinion, would completely distort his vision of the work's character and significance.

A courtesy visit to Hr. Dyhring, so as to express his gratitude, had been the furthest thing from his mind; he felt rather that if there was any thanking to be done, it should be Dyring thanking him for providing such marvelous material for the article. But now he regarded it as his solemn duty to reconcile himself to this visit in order to ensure that the insidious decimal point could be corrected as quickly as possible. Thus, that very same morning, he sought out Dyhring at his private residence—an elegant bachelor apartment in one of the most exclusive parts of town.

Though it was past midday, Dyhring was still not dressed. This fact led his housekeeper to deny that "master" was even at home; but the door leading to Dyhring's sleeping quarters was then opened a touch and the journalist's gold-blond head peeped forward into the corridor. Silk paper curlers protruded from the tip of each end of his waxed moustache.

"Ah Sidenius. It's you!" The tone was one of slight disappointment— "Well, indeed, ahm, just go straight in. My hair stylist is with me at the moment. I shall be at your service shortly."

Per then had the opportunity to inspect Dyhring's rooms at his leisure. These were the source of many wild rumors with regards to their opulence and ostentation. There was no gainsaying their elegance. Silk coverings on the furniture in the study, Jean Gobelin wallpaper, paintings, stacks of books and subscriber periodicals strewn around the chairs. There was a veritable harem of portraits on his writing desk, showing various women in various poses. The door of the adjoining dining room had been left ajar and Per was able to gaze upon a sumptuously laden table that had been set for lunch. The table cloth was blinding white and there was a wine carafe, flowers and fruit.

Per could not help but contemplate the difference between this place of abode and his own quarters, with his two small, dark chambers—and he found himself gripped by a, for him, unusual type of irritation. It was not in any way that Per could feel jealous of a person like Dyhring, who in his eyes was a somewhat contemptible fellow— a kind of pimp acting for that great whore the "Town Scandalizer," or the views and opinions of the rabble more generally. But it cut him to the quick that such a wastrel, newspaper scribbler like Dyhring had already achieved the type of independence and position of influence that he could only dream of.

At last, Dyhring appeared: small and livewire—walking on tiptoe—dressed in chocolate colored trousers, slippers of Moroccan leather and a short, madder-red smoking jacket that was embellished with black silk cuff lining.

"Now. How can I help you Hr. Sidenius?" he asked, in the manner of someone who was used to receiving petitions and requests. "Please be seated."

The two young men now sat down opposite each other and leaned back into their respective sky-blue, silk-covered armchairs, crossing

their legs over as they did so. All other obvious differences notwithstanding, the life experiences of Per Sidenius and Otto Dyhring were
not dissimilar, and this went beyond the fact that they were almost
the same age. Just like Per, Otto Dyhring had no emotional ties to his
childhood home. He was the son of a hopelessly indebted and dissolute
military officer, who had sent his wife to an early grave and had then
taken his own life. Dyhring was then thrown at the mercy of relatives
in the provinces before, at eighteen years of age, being sent to Copenhagen as a student. Exactly like Per, he arrived without a penny in his
pocket, but was fortified by fierce ambition and a determination that,
come what may, he would make his own luck and avenge himself on
a childhood that had been nothing but privation and humiliation.
With the cold-blooded single mindedness of a hunter stalking his
prey, and with an instinctive vision of the cave in which Aladdin's
lamp lay hidden, Dyhring worked his way into journalism just at the
right moment. For, in line with developments right across the world,
the press had broken the political mold and introduced a varied and
consciously literary way of telling the news. Without ever displaying
any particular talent as a writer, but with the shrewdness of a dispassionate tactician—and assisted by a visage that pleased the ladies—he
very quickly attained a position of influence at one of the most trend-
setting newspapers in the capital. Once he was ensconced within the
portals of the new power broker, Dyhring exploited his position quite
ruthlessly and with complete disregard for the howls of outrage he
would often provoke from a scandalized ruling class. Even by the age
of twenty-one, his yearly income was approaching that of a government
minister. Theater directors fought with each other over the chance to
stage his French farces, book publishers bought his patronage by
purchasing his translations (ghostwritten by some down at heel language teacher or other); actors and variety singers, young poets and
graying socialites; purveyors of alcoholic beverages and circus impre-
sarios . . . all courted his approval and showered him with favors. Where
women were concerned, such favors were preferably provided in kind.
Like a young god basking in his own insouciance, and untroubled by

scruples, he looked down from his throne on his minions below—worshipped and loathed, envied and despised—and feasted on mankind's own stupidity, vanity, cowardice, and hypocrisy.

Dyhring had only written the article about Per's project as a small favor to Ivan Salomon, who would sometimes help him in placing an investment. Per Sidenius did not interest him in the slightest, and in order to be rid of him as quickly as possible he promised that he would publish the necessary corrections in the next number of *The Falcon*. However, once Per began to talk about his work, it proved very difficult to get him to shut up. Dyhring was thrown into despair and finally resorted to openly yawning behind his womanly white hand. He found this squawking peasant unbearable. Besides, he was expecting a lady. In the same issue of the newspaper that had carried the article about Per, he had also composed a lyrical panegyric for a ballerina who, at that time, was dancing in a circus review—thus he awaited his quid pro quo tribute.

At long last, Per made good his departure and Dyhring went into his dining room, whose door had been closed by an invisible hand for the duration of the visit. As he entered the room, he almost fell over in shock. There on a chair directly in front of his laid table sat Nanny Salomon. She was crowned by a broad-brimmed hat of white lace and held a half-savaged radish in her hand. The petite and slightly twisted figure of Olga Davidsen, Nanny's perennial female companion, was standing at the window. Olga's face glowed red in sheepish exaltation.

"May I ask how in the name of God did my darling little cherubs manage to sneak in here unannounced? I didn't hear the bell ring."

"And why should we ring the bell? I have the key to your porch entrance for heaven's sake," Nanny replied, with a studied audacity that left her friend Olga speechless. "Anyway the door was wide open...your Madame was sweeping outside. She told us that you were, ahm, entertaining; so we asked her to show us into this room. My my Dyhring, you do have a better class of radish."

Nanny judiciously picked out a new victim from the plate, dipped it into the salt bowl, and snapped her shining white teeth into it.

"You really are so saucy Frøken Nanny! Are you actually aware of who it was that I was entertaining, as you put it—and who has literally just left a second ago?"

"Of course. That was Hr. Sidenius. One wouldn't mistake his voice for anyone else's."

"And you say that without batting an eyelid. Imagine if you had come a couple of minutes later—you would have run straight into his arms."

"Well now. That might have been quite enjoyable."

Dyhring smiled and wagged his finger at her in mock admonishment.

"Bold, frivolous, delectable little miss Nanny! What is this wonderful performance trying to tell me?"

"Ah—" she cried, as she ran a discerning eye over the assortment of food on the table. "The discerning Hr. Dyhring should construe that Nanny Salomon is ravenous with hunger and that she is sorely tempted to join him for lunch . . . all these delicious things. Mm . . . goose foie gras! My favorite dish. But enough of all that, let's cut to the chase," she said, interrupting herself. She then wiped her mouth with one of his napkins and stood up. "Are you aware, sir, that today is the last day that Bakken will be open this summer? And do you not, sir, feel at least a tinge of shame in the fact that you have not, not even once, offered two young and innocent girls the security of being our chaperone up there? You know, of course, that our moms won't let us set foot in such a place while unaccompanied."

"Good Lord! Why would you want to go up to Bakken?"

"Why would we want to go there? . . . Olga! Did you hear that? Hr. Dyhring is playing all naive with us! He's asking us why we want to go up to Bakken! To have fun of course! We want to listen to the barrel organs and ride on the carousel, eat hot waffles, watch the fire eater and see the fat lady—"

"Ah I see. And I'm sure there are other things you'd like to do."

"Well now that you mention it, we want to listen to the cabaret singers and dance on the open air dance floor. But more than anything, I want a screaming balloon. A really horrible, big red screaming balloon that goes Brrrrrreeeeeeeeeeeee! Don't you know!"

Dyhring had drawn very close to Nanny as she spoke, observing through half-closed eyes that her bountiful breasts and white arms could be glimpsed through the light summer material of her bodice. He now spoke in a half whisper so that Nanny's friend could not hear him: "It really is great foresight on your part dear Frøken Salomon that you are always accompanied by a life guard. You are madam so ridiculously seductive in that dress that I—"

At which point he was cut off.

"Olga," said Nanny, turning to her friend. "We are leaving. Hr. Dyhring has started being naughty again . . . call the maid!"

She pulled the skirts of her dress out with two fingers and gave a curtsy. She then flounced out of the room, her arm around the waist of her companion.

However, at the doorway, she stopped, looked back over her shoulder and said: "Is that agreed then? We meet at seven o'clock at Klampenborg station? But I'm telling you Dyhring. If you should start blabbing to Mama about our little visit here today, I will simply denounce you as a liar and you will never more be allowed to kiss me—on my cheeks."

"My God Nanny, you are sailing close to the wind today," her friend whispered as she quickly pulled her out of harm's reach.

While Dyhring enjoyed a solitary lunch, he emptied his sherry glass a few times and fell into serious reflection. His tactics regarding a future marriage arrangement had occupied this young blade's mind in the last while. He had recently spent a morning totting up his income and investments and the balance sheet told him that it was no longer prudent to delay making a suitable match. Out of the assortment of rich men's daughters with whom he had initiated a somewhat laissez faire set of dalliances, Nanny Salomon did not carry the same weight in gold as some of the others and was not, therefore, the one he had coveted most. On the other hand, she was without doubt the most beautiful, the brightest, the boldest—in short, the one who reminded him most of how difficult it would be to finally stop consorting with her type of female free spirit.

Then his doorbell rang again. And even though he had given his maid strict orders that she should admit no one, other than a certain circus lady with flaming red hair, he heard a loud man's voice out in the hall, along with the sound of an umbrella being thrust into the umbrella stand. The dining room door was pushed open and there stood an older gentleman, who was flushed and severe of countenance—Colonel Bjerregrav.

"I knew you would be here. No. Please remain seated. I can see that I've interrupted you in the middle of some obviously pressing and vital piece of work."

"Ah! Greetings dear uncle! Will you do me the honor of joining me for lunch?"

"I'm afraid I must gratefully decline young nephew. You know very well that I don't like eating for free. Besides, I had my lunch less than two hours ago."

"A glass of wine then?"

"Don't put yourself out in any way young man. Entertainment is not exactly the reason for my visit."

"I thought as much uncle. You've obviously got something to get off your chest, given that you have bitten the bullet and decided to come here in person."

"Your perspicacity amazes me nephew! A sudden longing to see you again was not, to say the least, what brought me here. So, to the point: just by chance this morning, while I was waiting for my hot towel and shave, I happened to lift a copy of that rag you write for and came across an article about a so-called canal system project ... an article you might know something about ... or at least, if I am not mistaken, it smacked of your amateurish way of putting things. May I ask what the devil you are playing at, writing such a thing? Since when, at any time in your life, have you ever bothered to consider serious issues, and that includes the Department of Maritime Works? And even though I don't doubt that, as a general rule, you are happy to scribble on subjects about which you have not the foggiest notion, I have my own very good reasons for warning you against continuing this particular line of laughable journalism."

"Yes. In fact I've already been made aware of this ... that a few mistakes may have crept into the piece," said Dyhring smiling.

"Mistakes? Why the whole thing is a colossal wild goose chase my friend, and a chase you'd better not get caught up in. You are also way off beam if you think you are doing that young man any favors in writing such guff. The only thing you'll achieve is to give him more mad bees for his bonnet than he already has."

"So you know him then?"

"Know him? I know him better than I know you! This fellow had me under siege in my own home with his ridiculous project. He is like an escaped animal!"

"So you're saying he's all bluff and bluster?"

"Now I wouldn't go that far. No. I wouldn't say that. But he's very immature and doesn't have the patience to learn his profession properly. But that doesn't stop him from believing he has the right to lash out at everyone else, oh no . . . or that he has some kind of call as a great innovator. Nobody else is good enough! And now he's going to publish a pamphlet you say."

"Did I say that?"

"It's the obvious next step! Raise the roof, get everybody up in arms! It's this Jew doctor I'm telling you that has our young people all stirred up. Give us air to breathe he says with his typical melodrama. We need reform, revolution everywhere—"

"But tell me this uncle, do you not think that's exactly what we do need? I seem to recall that you would often launch your own tirades and denounce us a nation of sleepwalkers and describe our home-grown engineers as seriously lacking in backbone and gumption. In fact—am I not right?—you yourself once issued a pamphlet that was quite barbed in its tone."

"That was completely different . . . and I would ask you, young man, to refrain from making those kinds of comparisons," Dyhhing's uncle said as his face took on an even redder hue, all the way up to his bald forehead. "The complaints that I saw fit to make against the administration, and only after lengthy reflection and an examination of my conscience, were fully justified and well grounded. At that time, let me tell you, the political opposition was not just an expression of some juvenile urge to cock a snook at our elders. No. It was informed by a serious and patriotic concern on the part of we young Danish men for our country's future. And therein lies the difference my boy!"

"And do you believe that you were looked upon in that way by our rulers?"

"Yes, actually, I do believe that . . . but I have absolutely no intention of entering into a discussion with you about these matters. I just wanted, for your own sake, to warn you against lending your weight to this perennial project maker, who will simply make you and your august organ a laughing stock in the eyes of all those who actually know about these things. You are well aware that I'm not exactly an admirer of the career you have chosen for yourself, but I have to say one thing in your favor though—up until now at least you have never made a complete and utter fool of yourself. And—since I am here and have your attention—I'll mention something that I've always meant to say to you, something that occurs to me every time I read an article of yours. It surprises me Otto that, with your sharp eye and your—may I say—particularly clever type of journalistic nous, it has never occurred to you how you are standing in your own shadow by working for that scurrilous newspaper."

"Do you, perhaps, have something better to offer me uncle?"

"Well, I am not at liberty to say exactly. There might be something. You know, of course, that Hr. Hammer, the newspaper proprietor at the *Dannevang* is a very good friend of mine. We have had not a few conversations about you. Like me, he acknowledges that you are not without a certain talent and style but cannot bear the fact that you place these at the service of such a disreputable cause. I wouldn't be at all surprised . . . in fact I think I can say with some certainty that a favorable position at the newspaper might be offered to you if you were to show, shall we say, a more considered approach in your scribbling."

"*Dannevang*! But that's nothing more than a reactionary old foghorn uncle! And on top of that, its blindly jingoistic, warmongering and sickeningly holier than thou. I hope you are not asking me to change my convictions?"

"Your convictions! Listen here, my boy, it's Bjerregrav you are talking to now, so you can drop that whole masquerade. I know you! And I'm now going to tell you something else. But I'll start by making an admission. Some time ago, you chose a career path with the kind of foresight that deserves great credit. Journalism really does appear to be the new springboard for those with ambition in our society. I'm sure you have seen that Editor Lille has been appointed as our Washington envoy. Then there was another journalist recently who was elevated to County Governor d'ye mind. For better or worse, it is now a fact that the government has given its imprimatur to the quality end of the press, and that kind of patronage also encompasses appointments to state offices for anyone worthy of such a role—without fear or favor. It seems to me, Otto, that you might want to ponder your brain on that! Bear in mind that in any situation where your colleagues may have a chance at advancing their position, you will usually be in an even better position. You have a name that still commands respect in the army, and that also means in the treasury and at the Royal Court. The fact that I am your uncle, who is happy to stand shoulder to shoulder with you in any honorable endeavor, might also be of some use to you. And finally, you yourself of course possess attributes that might be of benefit to you—in the diplomatic corps for example. Who knows? Perhaps it's all up to a choice that only you can make my boy whether at some point you become Hr. Lille's replacement as envoy in Washington."

Dyhring, who had begun to smile to himself during his uncle's speech, threw his head back slightly, narrowed his eyes and spoke aloud, but to no one in particular: "Washington? Yes, why not? American ladies are reputed to be most enticing. And the cuisine, at least amongst the upper classes, is no doubt on a par with London, or even Paris. I shall certainly consider it uncle."

At this the colonel had heard enough. He positively exploded; his face afire with rage.

"And that's how you dare to answer me!"

"Yes, I'm sorry uncle. I'm just not the sort that takes life all that seriously."

"No, that's true," said the old military man after a short pause—his voice breaking with emotion. "You cannot take life more seriously. For you and all your selfish, godless, and rootless friends, life is either a good or bad joke, depending on your whim. The great difficulties our country faces, the needs of our people, political disasters, war, pestilence and fire—for you and your ilk, it's all one big game, stuff to fill your column inches, just more victims for your mercenary pen. No, none of you can take life seriously. But in that case life will not have any use for the damned lot of you. You can be sure of that! Life will turn its back on you . . . spit you out like dust. Dust to dust, ashes to ashes! Mark my words!"

Dyhring remained seated with his legs outstretched and his thumbs in each pocket of his smoking jacket. He continued to stare into empty space with his tight, chameleon-like eyes.

"Only time will tell, uncle! Only time will tell!"

Out in the country at Skovbakken, Jakobe was the only one who was at home that afternoon. After lunch, Fru Salomon had taken the youngest children on a forest excursion and Nanny was still in town. Recently, Jakobe had barely moved from her own room. She was once again enduring one of her periodic bouts of anguish and despair, suffered blinding headaches and lay in bed night after night with her eyes wide open; she was kept awake partly by her physical afflictions and partly by her agonizing over thoughts that were fomented by an unending mental tapestry of degrading, carnal desires. Exhausted after one such all-night vigil, she had curled up on her chaise longue and remained there, her eyes lightly closed and her hands under her cheek. Her room was on the first floor and her open balcony door offered a prospect of tree tops and an expanse of blue sky where clouds scudded like feathered down. The deep stillness around her that was interwoven with the soft sighing of leaves from the garden lulled her into an occasional but nervous half slumber; the kind where the body sleeps but the mind remains alert. At the slightest noise, she would open her eyes and be wide awake.

"Jakobe! Are you up in your room? In heaven's name. Is there no one at all in this ghost house!"

It was uncle Heinrich's voice coming up from the garden. She rose slowly, sat still for a short while with her hands pressed to her face, and then she went downstairs. She found her uncle in the garden room. After complaining in his usual hysterical way at having to wait for some attention, he produced a slim packet of papers from his breast pocket and threw them down onto a table.

"Now you have it!" he said.

Jakobe's tired face suddenly brightened.

"You bought them!"

"I did as I was bid Jakobe. I'll say it only once more: Don't get me involved! I've warned you often enough that they are not worth the paper they are written on. Rubbish at the end of the day."

"I can hear from your voice that they've gone up again uncle. What did I tell you?"

"What did you tell me . . . you tell me?" he spat at her. "I swear, women are mad! You get lucky on one occasion and you think you are queens of the stock market. Though your sister has a more level head than you do, at least she will sometimes listen . . . doesn't keep losing her marbles."

Jakobe shrugged her shoulders defiantly, lifted her papers—some shares in sugarcane—and stowed them safely in her pocket. Both she and Nanny, in all secrecy, were dabbling on the stock exchange using their clothes allowance and uncle was the trusted go-between in all the necessary transactions. Both sisters indulged their speculations with no little passion; but while Nanny's sole motivation was profit, even if this meant only a modest return on diligently placed invest-ments in solid bonds and stocks, Jakobe's main impulse came from the risk that was inherent in the game itself, as well as her feeling of triumph when, despite her uncle's warning or wagging fingers from newspapers, she dared to venture into the madness of a bull market and lived to tell the tale.

In the meantime, Hr. Delft had lifted the day's edition of *The Falcon* from the clump of newspapers that lay on the table. He stood for a couple of moments browsing through its pages and then said: "I suppose you have read Dyhring's article about this Sidenius? I swear, the young man seems to be making a name for himself!"

"Ah, the truth is uncle that Dyhring has turned it into more of a joke than anything else."

"Joke—hm. Do you know what, my girl, that little joke could turn serious some time soon. He has the feel of luck about him that boy! They've already started talking about him at the Exchange."

This last statement was pure fantasy; but Hr. Delft had taken every opportunity just lately to lionize Per within the family. Once it had dawned upon him that it was actually Jakobe's hand that Per sought, Hr. Delft's esteem for him had rocketed because of the ambition that it implied. From then on, he had resolved, in his own inimitable way, to give Per his full support in such a daunting venture. Then there was also the fact that he harbored a particular loathing for Eybert, whom he had not, despite strenuous efforts to blackguard his name, managed to dislodge from the bosom of the family. The mere thought of finally seeing this man humiliated was enough to have his eyes spinning in his head out of sheer malice.

At dinner that evening *The Falcon* article once again became a subject of discussion, raised this time by Ivan, who had just returned from town and was full of fantastic notions about the clamor it had raised. On the way to the railway station, he had called into Dyhring's editorial office and Dyhring had—without giving any specific names—described his uncle's visit and generally let Ivan know that he had really taken great risks in fighting Per's corner on this issue and, therefore, hoped this huge favor would be returned as and when the opportunity arose.

"Ha! All the old duffers are starting to get worried now!" Ivan cried gleefully across the table. "They want to crush Sidenius by muzzling the papers! But they won't succeed! And once his voice is heard properly! Then, by God, they really will start squealing!"

Neither Philip Salomon, nor Fru Lea, said anything in response to this; the latter had of late chosen to maintain a noticeable silence whenever Per's name was mentioned. Nor did Jakobe offer any kind of response, as she apparently busied herself in helping one of her much younger siblings by her side. However, she was neither as indifferent, nor unconcerned, as she outwardly appeared. In fact, for a moment, her brother's account of the apparent threats made against the editorial team at *The Falcon* prompted a rush of blood to her cheeks. She could not even listen to talk of any type of coercion or persecution without flaming up. But then Ivan's completely overblown acclamation of his new champion soon cooled her ire, which was eventually turned to outright disgust by his triumphalist, preaching tone.

As they sat at the post-dinner coffee table out on the terrace, they received a visitor in the form of Hr. Eybert. Uncle Heinrich disappeared in the same instant. He would not—as he was wont to say with the usual spiteful invective he reserved for Eybert—"breathe the same air as that walking laxative." Very soon after, Nanny left the table in order to go to the train station and Ivan followed quickly on her heels, in his case, dying with impatience to find out whether the evening newspapers were carrying anything on the article in *The Falcon*.

Eybert had rented a summerhouse close by and was, therefore, an almost daily guest at Skovbakken. Despite this, his visit took Jakobe somewhat by surprise. When she heard the dogs start to bark, she had been convinced that it was Per who had excited their attention. Ever since she had read the article about him, she had expected his arrival. She refused to believe that he would let a whole day go by without appearing like a Victor Ludorum bedecked in laurel wreaths— she had already suffered extreme discomfort at this prospect and felt pity for him. With this welcome surprise, she returned Eybert's greeting with an unusually warm handshake.

Indeed, it was no wonder that this aging suitor bore an optimistic mien at just that time. With each day that passed, Jakobe gave him increasingly persuasive proof that their engagement was almost a done thing. Amongst other things, she had begun to wear an oriental ring Eybert had once given her as a birthday gift, and which she had hitherto declined to place on her hand; and when his two little girls came visiting, Jakobe would often send the nanny home and spend a half day out in the garden with them.

They now walked down to the strand, where they chatted as they walked up and down a path that ran along the raised breakwater. As was so often the case when they were alone, they began to talk about politics. This time, it was the colonial expropriations on the part of the great powers, and the associated arms build-ups, that they fell to discussing. Hr. Eybert expressed the hope that Denmark would have enough sense to refrain from any kind of adventurism. As an acknowledged statesman, he was proud to represent the cautious wing of Danish politics, and in spite of his social standing and cultured upbringing, felt himself naturally aligned to the broad mass of agrarian reformers who had always expressed the most common-sense approach to the nation's affairs. However, in his conversations with Jakobe, he preferred to give his words a bolder, more revolutionary twist, in order to cover the differences in their respective natures. The fact was that in all areas of life, Jakobe tended towards the more extreme viewpoint. Thus, she believed it unwise for the country to prematurely abandon all attempts at competing with the giants of trade and industry. Denmark's areas of trade and commerce in countries offering long-term development markets had to be secured before neutrality could be adopted. As she often made clear to Eybert: a minnow like Denmark was in itself a ridiculous proposition—such a small and poor country was, at the end of the day, impossible to sustain. What she dearly wished to see was the rise of a movement at home that could persuade people of the fact that only by the possession of wealth, indeed an abundance of riches, could a small state secure its existence in the world and gain the respect of the great powers.

By now it had begun to drizzle. As the sun sank in the west, the heavens took on a somber hue and they were forced to seek shelter indoors. Some lamps had been lit in the garden room and, at Fru Salomon's express request, Eybert sat down at the piano and played a number of "Lieder ohne Worte"—her favorite music. Amongst his many other excellent attributes, Hr. Eybert had a fine ear for music.

His playing was not only executed well, and very properly, but also with great feeling. On this evening in particular, his interpretation of the music was so affectionate that his underlying intentions were not to be mistaken.

In the meantime, Jakobe was to be found leaning against the door leading into the garden, where she looked out at the sheet rain. Jakobe had no innate love of music and very quickly acquired a state of detachment whenever it was played. In other words, Hr. Eybert's attempts at imparting a subtle declaration of love upon her person fell on deaf ears. Jakobe stood and mulled over the fact that Per actually hadn't appeared that day. The truth was that on this occasion she had done him an injustice. This now made her feel slightly ashamed of herself. It was also true that all the glorification of him that day had not exactly passed her by without effect. She asked herself whether she might have failed to give him his due, and perhaps had therefore cast a too hasty and damning judgment on his idiosyncrasies and character. Maybe Per Sidenius really was a force of nature, who would one day sweep all before him and rouse the people for the battles to come. At the very least, he seemed to have the natural leader's capacity to draw an army around him. To think he had even managed to chain uncle Heinrich to his triumphal chariot! Well, she herself was not oblivious to the unnerving power that emanated from his eyes that were as bright and cold as the sea. And he was no coward. She would not easily forget that Sunday dinner, when he had put the fear of God into everybody by engaging in a daredevil escapade in the sea. She had, quite by chance, been standing by the very same door, looking out across the water. She could clearly hear the university graduate Balling's juvenile screaming and splashing around. These sounds carried from the area near the beach hut, which was hidden by the sea. Then she suddenly saw Per's dark head, far out amongst the extremely choppy waves. At first, she did not even consider the possibility that it was a human being out there, never mind Per Sidenius. Only when she heard the shouts of alarm from the beach hut did she understand. And she could still feel the pure terror she felt, like ice cold lightning striking her in a flash from head to toe.

There was no doubt that the heroes of the future she had always envisaged were made of more pristine and noble stuff. She had dreamed of a reborn aristocracy, a nobility of the spirit, that would bring about the liberation of mankind by elevating the virtues of justice and beauty. But perhaps it was broad shoulders and manly arms that were needed just at that particular historical moment. Perhaps there was no escaping the need for a terrible rending asunder of the criminal and hypocritical society in which they lived, a vengeful apocalypse that would purge the world in blood and fire.

9

BY THE month of August, Per had completed his literary call to arms, his manifesto, and soon after he read the whole thing out loud to his friend Ivan Salomon. Jakobe's brother was unable to follow very much of what he heard but his face blanched with euphoria and he immediately took it upon himself to pay for the printing costs.

Thus, Per could now begin preparing for his long journey. He had already been attending language classes for quite some time, based on a "Grammar Made Easy Method"—and overall felt that his departure was only a matter of weeks. But before that, and in accordance with his master plan, he had to propose to Jakobe. His decision was that he would do this on the 3rd of September, which was a Sunday. His tailor had promised him that the first items in his new wardrobe would be ready by that time. Per had requested that his new clothes be styled after the English mode, because Jakobe had recently—and as if on purpose—made a remark in his presence that she preferred the more ample cut of the English style to the tight severity of the French look.

His original idea had been to wait until his book had been published and discussed in the press; but he had very quickly begun to champ at the bit and felt a great urge to put an end to all his restlessness and angst regarding how his marriage suit might be received. It had become almost impossible for him to sleep at night. He had gambled his whole future on this throw of the dice and had recently almost boiled over in a café where he had met Lieutenant Hansen-Iversen. In blunt language, the lieutenant had insisted that Jakobe's engagement to Hr. Eybert was a settled matter.

On the appointed day—a glorious Indian summer's day, with crowds milling about at every railway station—Per set out for Skovbakken and Jakobe as early as was acceptably possible. His fervent hope was that he could speak with her before the usual flood of Sunday guests began to arrive.

However, his strategy went awry from the start. For the day he had chosen proved to be ill timed. When he arrived at Skovbakken, he encountered a house that was already alive with visitors. The family's third eldest daughter—fifteen-year-old Rosalie—was celebrating her birthday, and a number of female relatives who had come to offer congratulations were augmented by a crowd of the young girl's friends who whooped and swooped about the house like a swarm of parakeets. A number of general acquaintances were also in attendance. Amongst the latter was the despondent graduate, and inveterate bookworm, Balling who—after pursuing Nanny to no avail—had now decided that Rosalie was the one who should bask in the reflection of his coming literary glory.

There was another gentleman present whom Per had met before—another academic and seemingly half-decrepit bachelor who was now a locum teacher. This was Hr. Israel who was related to the family on the Salomon side. He was a small, humbly clad man, tentative and nervous in his movements. He had the perennial habit of stuffing his hands into his coat sleeves, as he turned his balding scalp and turkey neck, first left then right. It was as if he stood in permanent dread of being in someone's way. Unless he chose to speak (and he much preferred to listen rather than hold forth) nobody would suspect that this was that same Aron Israel who, in certain circles, enjoyed a standing equal to that of Dr. Nathan himself—that he was in fact a quiet and reflective intellectual who possessed a vast knowledge across a range of subjects. And yet his brilliance was not the first thing one thought of when his name was mentioned. The thing which had secured his great reputation was his utter selflessness, an altruism of a particularly heightened kind that is particularly prevalent amongst Jews. His many friends were wont to say that his soul was as pure as his pockets were dirty.

Aron Israel had been offered a great number of prestigious posts at the university—all to no avail. He could not even be tempted with an associate professorship, as he felt that there were always others who needed those kinds of positions more than him. He was actually a man of substantial means but lived a frugal and inconspicuous life, while all the time secretly giving away large sums of money, especially to poor students. Along with two sisters, who likewise had never married, he lived in an old-fashioned apartment in Sværtegade. His modest sitting room, which was packed with books from floor to ceiling, was a rendezvous point for many of his former students and other young academics who came to seek his guidance, borrow books from him and in a myriad of other ways abuse his generosity. However, for all the above, Hr. Israel could not be said to be an original thinker or teacher of men. Only those people who tended to judge a human being on the basis of character could place him alongside a revolutionary spirit like Dr. Nathan. Aron Israel himself had huge admiration for this controversial figure and would often—abandoning his usual reticence—jump into the fray to defend Nathan against the kind of pedantry which people displayed when disparaging his activities. Nor was this criticism confined to the Gentile community, with many Jews—partly from cowardice and partly from jealousy—pronouncing judgment upon him. Of course, the more they criticized Dr. Nathan, the more they engaged in the kind of—admittedly often comic—petty sermonizing that is so often directed at those who carry the spirit of the age. Israel liked to compare Nathan's detractors with court jesters and bell-ringing page boys who carried the purple train of a great monarch.

In short, Per had allowed himself to be unduly influenced by Hr. Israel's unimposing exterior. The truth was that he did not possess the necessary prerequisites for appreciating Aron Israel's true worth and had, therefore, always been somewhat arrogant in his dealings with him. Despite this, the little man had never shown him anything but courtesy and would listen intently when Per, his tongue loosened by a good dinner and post-prandial liqueurs, began to hold forth in loud and lecturing tones on what the future held in store. Nor did it take long, on this occasion, for Hr. Israel to quietly approach Per and begin a conversation with him about his studies.

Of Jakobe there was still no sign. She had remained in her room and only revealed herself once most of the earlier visitors had left. She had no wish to be the subject of inquiring glances, or perhaps even intrusive questions, from people who awaited the final declaration of her engagement to Hr. Eybert—not least because the crucial words in this drama had still not been uttered.

It was Jakobe herself who had contrived to avert the final question from Eybert's side. Her hope was that she could put off the decisive moment until Per had left the country for foreign shores. Plagued by a hot shame, she had been forced to admit to herself that he had, for quite some time, occupied her thoughts more than was appropriate at the very moment when she was supposed to be yielding to another man's advances. In her most recent bout of sleepless nights, she had tortured herself in her efforts to avoid thinking about him. However, she was convinced that, on the very day she received word of his departure from Denmark, the debasing mastery he had gained over her fantasies and imagination would disappear forever.

As she now set eyes upon him in his new English tailoring, she instinctively sought a hiding place. The resolute and probing gaze with which he demanded her attention immediately gave Jakobe an intimation of the decision that Per had reached. For that very reason, she chose at first to avoid him; but when she realized that avoiding his formal proposal would be impossible, and given that she too wished to put an end to an intolerable situation, she resolved that it was as well to let the whole thing come to a head as soon as possible.

She went down into the garden and ceaselessly traversed one of the paths that lay closest to the house. She had every expectation that it was here that Per would seek her out as there was little chance of any private exchange being witnessed.

She was right. It was not long before she heard his rapid footfall in one of the adjoining paths. In the same breath, a laming dizziness came upon her. She had to cease walking, but then took some more faltering steps towards a large stone vase, as if this might provide some sort of refuge. The vase had been placed behind a bench and was about midway along the heavily shaded path. The column upon which it stood was overgrown with ivy. She tried to give the impression that she was busy fixing some vine creepers that had become snagged on the stone, but her hands began to shake and, as his footsteps came closer, her heartbeat became so violent that the sunspots in the gravel started to dance before her eyes. Now she heard him directly behind her. She spun round to face him with a stare full of hatred and fear.

"What do you want with me?" she almost roared. "Why do you persecute me so Hr. Sidenius?"

He bared his head with a noble gesture and requested permission to speak with her for a moment.

She bade him make his point as briefly as possible, something he promised to do with yet another deep bow of his head.

"My word, Frøken Jakobe, you look shattered! Would you not take a seat for a moment."

He gestured to the bench under the stone vase with its back to the supporting column. Once again Jakobe requested that he should not detain her there unduly, but the truth was that she could barely stand and was forced to follow his lead.

When she had taken her seat, Per sat by her side but was careful to keep a respectful distance between them. Two minutes later, his proposal of marriage had been made.

Per was well aware of the speech that was required on such occasions and shaped his words accordingly, but he also added: "You must, surely, be aware Frøken, that I would not have approached you in this way if I had been in any way able to remain silent. Nor must you think for one moment that this is just some kind of passing summer infatuation, which you may be thinking given the relatively short time I have been lucky enough to know you. For that admittedly short period has for me at least, and in many ways, signaled a decisive shift in my life. I have already told you that, from the very day that I walked into your parents' home and saw you, a new life began for me. Frøken Jakobe! People say about me that I am not without talent—and I firmly believe that myself! I even have the gall, do you mind madam, to believe that Denmark has great need of my abilities. But at the same time I know that without you I will never really achieve what I want. I am well aware, in other words, of exactly how much you have already influenced my development. So it's not just my own personal happiness and good fortune, but my whole future and general wellbeing that hangs on the answer you are now going to give to my request for your hand."

She had let him speak out. In fact, she could not bear to interrupt him; because she now had to admit to herself that she felt a demeaning desire to hear him speak his words of love—that this was what had driven her to seek this final conversation with him. There was also something in his actual voice that made her weak. That deep, strong male vibrancy it carried overwhelmed and deafened her to all other considerations. Despite the fact that Per had unconsciously let slip more than he intended with his last remarks, it had escaped Jakobe's notice that he had essentially been more concerned with himself than with her.

Unnerved by her continued silence, as well as her dark and motionless facial expression, Per chose to plow on: "Of course, I understand that it is quite audacious of me to presume that I am worthy of approaching you in this way Frøken Jakobe. You do not want for suitors; you are beautiful, intelligent, and very wealthy—and here am I, a poor engineer, whom nobody has heard of, with only his future prospects to bring to the table. But please don't see this as a demand for a final and decisive answer from you. For it is nothing of the sort. All I ask of you is simply some small hopeful sign . . . even the hint of a promise that I can carry in my heart as I venture out into the world. Trust me Jakobe! There is no torment I would not be happy to endure . . . No task I would not willingly carry out if I thought that it would win your favor!"

While the first part of his speech had been very well rehearsed, Jakobe's determined silence impelled him into this spur-of-the-moment speech with its rash set of pledges. But Per was at a loss as to what to say next. He bowed his head as if to signal to Jakobe that he was ready to hear his fate.

After a long pause, Jakobe drew herself up.

"I suppose I should really express my gratitude, Hr. Sidenius, for your good opinion of me. Though I should say that I'm quite convinced you are overestimating your own feelings for me. Nevertheless," she cut in very quickly when Per made to object, "all further explanations on my part are superfluous because I have to tell you that I am already engaged to be married."

"So it's true? . . . and with Eybert of course?"

"I'm afraid, sir, that such questions are not your prerogative," she said abruptly, upon which she rose and left. In the manner of someone who had just suffered a brain seizure, Per remained seated on the bench staring at her departing figure.

Out on the terrace, Fru Salomon was to be found sitting with Aron Israel's two small, richly rotund and jolly sisters. They called out to Jakobe as she passed by, but their niece gave the impression of not having heard them and went straight up to her room. As soon as she was in the door, she pulled off her right glove and pressed the back of her hand against her cheeks to feel how much they burned. Her breasts were heaving and her knees threatened to buckle. That she should have to endure such an ordeal! She felt like someone who had just escaped, by the skin of her teeth, from some mortal danger. With frantic movements, she threw off the other glove, her hat, and summer jacket and dumped them onto her bed, as if liberating herself from something that had defiled her. Completely enervated, she collapsed into her armchair. Praise be that it was all over. She would never see him again! The room began to revolve in front of her. She closed her eyes and placed her hands across her chest. Ah, her bulging hammering heart! That same terror as before! All those storm-ridden hours and the tattoo of sweet distress it drummed out once again from the depths of her memory!

She stayed sitting with her eyes closed and allowed herself to glide into a dream state, which soon conveyed her to that sacred mausoleum where her former hopes of a Great Love were now embalmed. In her writhing self-mortification, she sought to exculpate her obsession with this man, who was strange and objectionable to her, by saying that it was not himself but purely those latent emotions he aroused that left her in disarray. In order to chase away the recurring images of Per Sidenius, she yielded to the fervor of past feelings that still flowed in the core of her being—invoked all her old passions right from that first time in her early adolescence when she had been gripped by the painful throes of lust pulsing beneath her left breast, all of them again and again flinging her forwards to that final and fateful defeat—the ultimate disaster which had locked her heart as tight as a fist that forms when an open hand is rejected.

But then the gong sounded for dinner. She gave a start and looked at her watch. Had she really been sitting there for almost two hours? And she was not even dressed for dinner yet! Well it couldn't be helped. She was so deathly tired. And Eybert, waiting down there for her no doubt! Jakobe put her hand to her forehead and stood still for a moment. Not once, in all that passage of time, had he entered her thoughts!

Very few of the lunchtime visitors now remained. A scattering of the birthday girl's young friends were still there, along with the aesthete Hr. Balling, Aron Israel, and his two sisters. Balling was circling around Rosalie, his mane of writer-manqué hair flowing freely. For her part, Rosalie stood in the middle of the living room hopping up and down with joy on alternate legs and holding Philip Salomon under his arm—ready to move into the dining room and, as Queen of the Day, take the seat of honor by her father's side. Hr. Eybert was indeed also in attendance. And, at the other end of the room, stood Per—engaged in an apparently casual conversation with Ivan.

A feeling of raging indignation fired through Jakobe when she set eyes upon him. But then it occurred to her that he had, perhaps, remained there so as to avoid the suspicions and grounds for gossip a sudden departure would have aroused. Thus, in her by now far more composed state of mind and regardless of how much being in his presence pained her, she could not but thank Per for this magnanimous gesture.

Nevertheless, when the seats were taken for dinner, Jakobe made sure that they were as far away from each other as possible, and overall went out of her way to act as if he were not there. But then she could not avoid noticing that, much against his usual behavior, Per hardly touched the wine carafes. In fact, she could have almost sworn that he was making a peculiar but obvious show of repeatedly filling his glass with water, which he then would tinge with some drops of wine. Finally, there was no mistaking his clear intention. He had some stunt or other in mind and did not want to stand accused of having acted under the influence of alcohol.

Once again, she was gripped by a desperate panic. What would this reckless madman do next?

However, the dinner came and went without incident and the assembled company decamped to the garden where the younger ladies fumbled with cigarettes and the gentlemen loosened their jackets and cravats and brought out their cigar cases. Soon, blue rings of smoke began to hang in the late afternoon air from dark and imposing Coronas, which carried a portrait of Bismarck on their vivid band. Fru Salomon, Eybert, Aron Israel, and his two sisters had ensconced themselves in a timbered pavilion where coffee was served by none other than the family matriarch herself. Jakobe had also just sought refuge here when the entrance to the double doors was suddenly darkened by Per's broad frame. His facial expression was carefree, and he offered a smile, but his whole demeanor carried with it a certain provocation.

"I beg your pardon Hr. Sidenius," said Fru Salomon, who in the last while had more and more begun to assert herself against her son's rather brazen friend. "We don't smoke in here. Ivan is probably down by the strand. Coffee will be served down there shortly."

As Per withdrew in silence, Jakobe fired a look of surprise across at her mother. As grateful to her as she was for ridding the room of his presence, her mother's tone had pricked her feelings. Was it possible that she knew? At any rate, it was not impossible. After all, her own eagle eyes had come from her mother's side.

Anyway, she had decided, once and for all, that if Per did not possess enough tact and decency to keep away from the house, she herself would inform them of his marriage proposal. For all the world and at any price, she now wished to be spared from being in his company. And as she laid her tired, aching head against one of the timbers in the pavilion wall, she briefly closed her eyes and was filled with a wonderful premonition of the peace and tranquillity she would enjoy once she was absolutely sure that she had seen the last of him.

At that very moment, she heard his name being mentioned. It was Aron Israel who, in all innocence, had begun to talk about *The Falcon*'s two-week old article on Per's ideas and spoke in high praise of the "visionary plans this young and bold engineer had for the country and its folk."

"Of course, I'm not … obviously … qualified to say … I mean, to give expert judgment as to whether the whole thing can actually be done," said the little man in his strange and halting way of speaking. "But Hr. Sidenius appears to be serious in his, uhm, assertion that we as a people—given our curious geographical situation and our … which we have to admit … hitherto unused … or … perhaps rather … hitherto ignored natural resources, actually have very favorable conditions for becoming a first-rate industrial nation; especially when the point is reached that these modern machines he speaks of … these wave machines and wind motors, or whatever name he puts on them … have reached their full potential. As I say, I would not be so, ah, reckless as to offer my opinions on the technical side of these matters, but there is something wonderfully appealing, to me anyway, in that young man's dream … to embrace superhuman powers that we have always regarded as a danger to us—forces come to destroy us and our land … the west wind, towering waves, all the elements of fire, air, and water … to harness them so that they become the fount of our riches, an inexhaustible treasure trove of power that would transform even our most backward areas into new, well yes, Eldorados. Why! It has the ring of a fairy tale about it."

Aron Israel's words spread a wave of alarm throughout his audience. Hr. Eybert had adopted a defensive position in his chair and betrayed a nervous smile. Fru Salomon quickly offered more coffee. Balling, who had entered the room in time to hear the whole thing, gave the speaker a pitying look. Even Israel's two steadfast sisters became aware that their brother had ventured far out into dangerous seas. A long silence had filled the room when his last words trailed away.

Hr. Eybert was the one who felt obliged to break the spell.

"Well, Lord knows, dear sir, we have no shortage of fairy tales in this country."

"Hear, hear!" came the lion's roar from Balling, whose blood always got up whenever he heard anyone but himself being praised.

Encouraged by this sign of support, Eybert pushed on: "Believing ourselves to be wild geese, when in fact we are little more than tame ducks, has unfortunately been one of our favorite delusions as a race; and there is no doubt that we have paid a heavy price—both politically and financially—for this strange obsession. Dr. Nathan has never written a greater truth than what he said in an obituary for a friend of his who had gone to the bad: in this country, we come into the world, live a life, and then die as complete and utter fantasists."

Aron Israel sat for a while and tugged thoughtfully at the wispy beard on his chin. Then he spoke up; almost by way of an apology: "Yes, indeed. But, with respect, isn't the very thing you are arguing a kind of superstition as well? I mean, do you not find that our young men ... almost without exception ... very rarely reach for the stars? As a tutor and lecturer, I have had the privilege of being in close contact with our young people and I have often been shocked by the fact that they rarely allow their dreams and ambitions to soar beyond anything but the most workaday confines of life. Nine times out of ten, they might aspire to nothing more than some modest position in society—an aldermanship, a lucrative doctor's practice, or perhaps a snug little rectory in the countryside. And that's why I find something ... something appealing, about meeting a young man like Hr. Sidenius who, there is no doubt about it, is aiming high ... there is something very grand and magnificent about it if you will—"

"With respect Hr. Israel, it is not my intention to split hairs with you about the meaning of this or that," said Eybert, unable to keep the caustic tone from his voice. Fru Salomon meanwhile once again sought to ply the guests with coffee and Israel's sisters made discreet attempts, via signs and gestures, to get their brother to change the subject. "Perhaps," Hr Eybert continued, "it would be even more accurate to describe us Danes as a race lamed by fantasies rather than a race which simply indulges in fantastic dreams. However, the consequences, dear sir, are—unfortunately—exactly the same."

Balling sought to bolster Eybert by firing an arrow from his quiver of devastating quotes: "Ah yes—'We are a fogbound folk, full of misty thoughts and empty oaths,'" he recited, but without revealing the source of his wisdom. On the other hand, he rolled his eyes for dramatic effect, as if seeking to force them into the shape of quotation marks.

Aron Israel remained in seated repose, modestly waiting to see whether any of the others present wished to contribute to the debate. Then he said: "Is it really so awful that a young man dares to dream? I mean . . . haven't the greatest amongst us become great because their glorious dreams pushed them on? Indeed, has any great champion ever performed a feat without first dreaming about it? In essence, reality is born out of the warp and weft of our fantasies, and—"

"God help us!" Eybert cried, attempting to inject a tone of humor into his outburst. "That's another thing altogether! I mean, when one not only dreams but actually understands what it takes to realize something concrete, then—"

"Yes, I'm not sure about that," Aron Israel retorted. "Where the essence of personality is concerned, at any rate, there is hardly any decisive difference between the two things. I mean . . . are dreams, just like our hopes and desires . . . not the father and mother of invention?—as one might put it . . . Intimations of that secret magic power that can get one's personality to expand far beyond what we may feel are the limits placed upon us by birth, upbringing, custom, lineage and other accidents of fate . . . and in that way . . . or so it seems from the evidence . . . blow apart nature's own restrictions. So even though, for example, Hr. Sidenius may fail in his attempts to turn his bold fantasies into reality . . . which is the far more likely scenario it has to be admitted . . . well, these can still be of the greatest significance for his own personal development, something that . . . in pure philosophical terms . . . must be said to be the most important thing."

"Excuse me, my gentlemen, for interrupting!" Fru Salomon intervened, with a hint of nervousness in her voice; she had sat all the while with her eye on Jakobe, who had listened to the debate with a pained expression in her eyes. "Please don't be offended, but we had intended to go for a ride in the carriage. It's waiting outside the porch this very moment. I can hear my husband cracking the whip."

Aron Israel became somewhat sheepish, and everybody rose at once. Jakobe also followed them out of the room, but more slowly and keeping her distance. When she had arrived at the top of the broad marble stairway and reached the terrace at the front of the villa, she chose to remain there for a moment with her hand resting on the parapet. Lost in thought, she looked out across the sea.

The carriage—a Charabanc—was parked outside the porch stairway and Philip Salomon himself had taken the reins and was accompanied by two of the half-grown children, sitting at either side of him. At the heel of the hunt, Rosalie and her friends preferred to stay at home and play croquet, which meant that Balling suddenly declined the offer of a tour. Then Aron Israel and uncle Heinrich both made their excuses for not going, pointing out that the light, in a Scandinavian summer, might well last longer into the night, but that didn't stop a chill descending in the evening. Nanny, whose whereabouts was now raised by her father, was found to have disappeared. She had, in fact, left the house as soon as dinner was over because she had summoned Dyhring to a rendezvous at the train station. Thus, there was more than enough room for both Per and Ivan—an outcome which was completely the opposite of what Fru Salomon had intended. Right up until the last second before departure, she made efforts to unseat them from the carriage by exhorting them to act like gentlemen by following Balling's example and remaining at the house. Rosalie would appreciate such a gallant gesture on the part of the younger menfolk, and it was her birthday after all. However, Per pretended that he had not heard Fru Salomon's entreaties and threw his large frame emphatically into one of the outermost places.

The sun had passed its zenith and was in decline. The evening sky infused the forest with a reddish glow and there was not a puff of wind. At first, they traveled along the coast road; then they turned into the twilight that was descending over the forest. Here Philip Salomon allowed his horses to plod their own leisurely pace along the sandy roads.

There was nonstop banter in the carriage. Hr. Eybert, in particular, was the height of entertainment. Per, on the other hand, did not utter a single word. He sat ramrod straight, without moving his head; only his eyes moved uneasily, as well as a tinge of color in his cheeks, which shifted constantly in tone. Since that morning—from the moment when Jakobe had walked away from him, and after the first effects of her answer had begun to assert themselves—he had repeated the same mantra to himself: "No. This is not the end of it." He had invested far too much in these hopes and dreams of his to give them up without a fight. Per felt that the whole edifice of his Great Project would collapse around him were his luck to desert him now. And yet, even concerns for his future had, throughout the day, been pushed more and more to the back of his mind by a simple sadness, or perhaps disappointment, over the bald fact that Jakobe just did not love him. He had not realized that she actually meant so much to him. Even though it was obvious to him that she was no real beauty, the thought that some other man was going to take her from him was intolerable. Self-interest and his wounded vanity had, in the intervening hours, goaded him to the point where he had convinced himself that he truly loved her. For the first time in his life, he believed that he understood the word "worship." As he sat there, he saw Jakobe in front of him with her narrow, pale face, framed by her waves of black hair. She was standing proudly before a primeval forest, where the trees were bathed in the flames of a red sunset, or plunged into the deepest shadow. She became a sacred being for him at that moment, and he lost all reason at the very thought that the clammy Eybert, or some other Hr. Fishblood would desecrate her beautiful, proud maidenhead—that anyone other than himself should induce the implacable Sibyl's gaze in those olive black eyes to yield to the earthly delights of human love! But that was never going to happen. Through clenched teeth, he repeated his incantation that this was not the end of it. His final answer to all problems in life, "I will," now faced its sternest test. There was no in between. It was do or die!

Exactly what action he might take in order to fight for, and retrieve, Jakobe's favor was still not clear to him. He would trust in the wheel of fortune and allow blind instinct to warn him when the moment to act was at hand. However, he had already caught a straw in the wind—a small triumph on which to cling in the whirlwind of his perhaps imminent defeat. Both at the dinner table, and now during this excursion, he had felt that Jakobe was irritated by Hr. Eybert's various chivalries towards her, and that she sometimes had forced herself to remain silent so as not to reveal her ire at the already overfamiliar tone he had seen fit to use with her. Per now made a new observation. As they passed one of the dust-red laneways leading into the forest, an old woman stood by the roadside offering flowers for sale; Eybert bought a bouquet and presented them to Jakobe with a gallant turn of phrase. Jakobe did indeed take them from him but without offering a word of thanks, and Per also noticed that she kept them drooped in her lap, not even bothering to smell their fragrance.

By this stage, they had reached Raadvad and emerged out of the forest. For a while they traveled along Lundtoftevejen, but then Philip Salomon turned the carriage to the left in order to reach home via Eremitagesletten.

The evening was already well advanced. Pockets of white mist were starting to form around the small ponds and hollows close to the roadside. All was becalmed. Not a sound was to be heard right across the broad plane on which they traveled, except for snatches of a song that was being sung somewhere in the distance by a group of other travelers as they too made their way through the forest.

The horses began to snort and sneeze and the ladies pulled their shawls more tightly around their shoulders. The conversation, which had momentarily entered a lull, became animated again as the carriage passed a herd of red deer that was grazing nearby. At the sight of the deer, Aron Israel's two old sisters were moved to recount a story about a Swedish student from Lund who had once made a bet that he could round up a similar herd of the king's finest game and actually capture one of its number. However, after an hour or so of reckless charging hither and thither in the forest the student suddenly dropped dead with an exploded heart.

"Do the ladies really believe that, with all respect, old wives' tale?" Hr. Eybert inquired, with a smile on his lips. "I recall hearing that story when I was a boy; but even then—and to speak the truth—I found it hardly credible."

Speaking across each other in their eagerness, the two elderly spinsters assured Hr. Eybert that the tale was indeed true. In fact, they had both, many years ago, read about it in *The Daily*.

"Again with all due respect ladies, I suspect that my doubts are well founded," said Eybert teasingly. "Even a half-mad Swede would hardly come up with such a crazy notion. Or at least he would have run his way to insanity long before his heart gave out."

For Per, who had felt himself personally touched by the story, Hr. Eybert's dismissive tone felt like a gauntlet being thrown down before him.

"I find the story eminently plausible," he said.

Due to his studied silence up to that point, as well as the defiant tone in his voice, Per's comment caused an immediate stir.

"Ah, so you too, Hr. Sidenius!, can be ranked amongst the gullible believers in this instance," Eybert retorted.

"I believe," Per answered, "that whatever a man with any kind of self-respect says he will do; well, he goes and does it—come what may!"

Placing his emphasis on these last words, Per's gaze sought out Jakobe, who, however, had constantly acted as if he were not even part of the entourage and who, at that very moment, chose to look away from him.

"Well all that sounds very grand and, I must say, very manly," Eybert replied, a smile on his lips as he turned to the ladies. "But cruel nature has unfortunately set certain incontestable limits upon us feeble human beings—limits that not even the greatest Hercules amongst us could break. Nor can we deny that the great God above has equipped the delicate and, yes, delectable deer species with four long limbs with which they can gallop away from we humans with our two pathetic sticks that are really only suitable for a much more modest form of perambulation."

"The point, Hr. Eybert, is not just about speed but also about utter determination to see something through. And it is the latter which ensures that great marvels are created in this world. As the proverb says Hr. Manufacturer, he who laughs last, laughs loudest!"

Eybert raised his eyebrows; he began to understand the hidden threat that lay behind Per's words. With a look of pity, he turned away, without bothering to offer a reply.

"Why that reminds me," Eybert volunteered as he once more addressed the ladies. "When I was younger, I myself experienced something that is rather similar to the fable about the Swedish student, except that this really happened and the denouement was much less tragic. I remember that some of my friends and I were on the way home from a day out in the forest. We had hired a carriage at Klampenborg, so that we could take the coast road on the way back. Well, what do you think ladies? One of our number who was fond of boasting about his strength and fitness decided to offer us a bet. He was, he said, going to run the two miles of our trip by the side of the carriage. He swore an oath that he would follow our route exactly and be in Copenhagen at the same time as us, no matter how much we worked the horses. Of course, we were only too ready to make the bet and when we got to Konstantia, our would be Hercules jumped down and began to run. We had a pair of arthritic carthorses; so it was nearly impossible to persuade them to break out of their normal speed, which was a trot. In other words, the race wasn't that uneven, but after running for about five minutes my friend started gasping like a pair of punctured bellows, and after ten he suddenly stopped and announced that he was going to stop running because, as he put it, he 'felt sorry for the horses,' at which point, he jumped back into the carriage and was actually quite pleased with himself. Why? Well because he had placed the welfare of dumb animals above his own concerns. He then proceeded to lecture us on the moral duty that was upon all of us to care for God's creatures. Now then!"

Hr. Eybert's fable struck home. The two old ladies laughed, and Philip Salomon turned around and said: "If that man is still alive, I will, in my capacity of director on the board of the Society for the Protection of Animals, recommend to the board that he receives a medal in honor of his kindness to animals."

Per's blood ran cold with rage. He was convinced that the arrow of the story was aimed directly at him, and while Jakobe had not joined in the general merriment, he felt crucified by this victory on the part of his rival in love. His only thought now was resurrection.

When the two old ladies had finally finished laughing, he said: "I must say Hr. Manufacturer that I pity you, because you have lost your belief in human willpower. And may I ask you, sir, whether there is any hope for you? I mean, if someone were to actually accomplish the feat which that friend from your distant youth once attempted. Would your faith be restored?"

Once more, Hr. Eybert had cause to raise his yellow eyebrows in surprise.

"What are you saying, Sidenius? I don't follow?"

"Exactly what I have just said, sir. Is there any hope that you might regain your faith in human willpower if some other person made good your friend's words? For, if that is the case, I myself am more than willing to take on that duty. Right now in fact."

Without waiting for any kind of answer, Per swung himself over the tailboard and began running by the side of the carriage.

Philip Salomon brought up the horses and called after Per in a tone that was unmistakeable: "Hr. Sidenius . . . it would be my firm wish . . . that you get back in the carriage."

But Per called back in unmistakeable exhilaration: "Hr. Merchant! I can assure you . . . it's actually wonderful to stretch the legs a little bit. And don't forget that there is a lot riding on this! Nobody can know what it might mean in the future for God, King and Country if the prospective candidate for Holbæk rediscovers his belief in the power of the will! As for my heart, you need have no worries sir. I doubt very much that it is going to burst!"

"Nevertheless, Hr. Sidenius," Salomon said, almost as a direct order. "I cannot have you running by the side of the carriage."

"No, you are absolutely right sir. And anyway, it's a good idea to get a head start!"

And as he pushed his hat down on to his head, Per took off at a furious pace. Even though Philip Salomon whipped the horses up, in order to catch him, Per soon disappeared from sight—into the mist that lay ahead.

"That is just madness, madness, utter madness," Salomon muttered to himself. There was real anger in his flushed face and he gave the horses yet another touch with the whip.

But Fru Salomon then called up to her husband.

"I don't think you need to rush the horses dear! It was obvious that Hr. Sidenius wasn't too comfortable in our company, so—after his own particular fashion—he's just grabbed the chance to get away from us. And don't forget that this is the quickest way back to the station if he cuts through the forest."

This explanation made a lot of sense, not least because, even though the horses were still going at a fair clip, Per Sidenius was still out of sight. He could not have taken any other short cut because they were fairly near to Skovbakken and, besides, the fence running the length of the deer park ruled out any other option.

The two old Israel sisters were shocked to the core by Per's behavior and could not help making comments to Fru Salomon from behind the back of their hands with regards to his lack of upbringing. Even Per's great defender, Ivan, found that this particular stunt was in very bad taste, while Eybert granted himself the pleasure of a smile and some rather daring rhetoric regarding the possible causes of Per's sudden "disappearance."

Jakobe sat quietly, watching the moon rising blood red above the Swedish coast. Her outward appearance suggested that the whole escapade had barely registered with her. The truth, however, was that she felt deeply sullied by Per's actions, but at the same time strangely liberated. So free, in fact, that she wanted to laugh out loud. As indignant as she was over Per's behavior, after it had dawned on her that the exchanges in the carriage before his "leap" were all part of his conscious and continued campaign against Eybert, deep in her heart she had felt almost exhilarated by the fact of just sitting there and waiting for the eruption of a man's unbridled passions. And now this "Force of Nature" had been unleashed in the form of a ridiculous schoolboy prank!

In the meantime, they had now reached Springforbi and were back on the coast road. Here at the sea's edge, the air lifted and brightened. The mist cleared and the huge swarms of midges buzzing around the heads of the sweating horses could be clearly seen.

They had almost reached home, when Philip Salomon drew up the horses with a sharp jolt.

"What's going on? Is that not Louise waving there? Something must have happened."

One of the maids was running along the road towards them. Even before she reached the horses, Philip Salomon began calling to her: "What is it girl? Has something happened?"

"Yes...indeed it has...it's...," the maid could barely speak for agitation. "It's Hr. Sidenius sir."

"My word. He must be at the house!" came the cry from several voices at once.

"Yes, and I think he's not feeling the best. I'm to run for the doctor, sir."

"God above. What's wrong with him Louise?" Ivan asked, his face as white as a corpse.

"I'm not sure, sir...Hr. Sidenius fainted, I think. Hr. Dyhring gave him some of Madam's drops, but I don't think he's come round yet."

Philip Salomon bit his thick lower lip in silence and then snapped the whip over the horses' ears. He too was deathly pale. Everyone now sat in grim silence as the carriage raced along the final stretch before home.

Even before they had got into the driveway, they were met by a flock of agitated young girls; and as they pulled to a halt at the steps leading to the porch, Aron Israel emerged from the house, along with Balling and Nanny. Dyhring appeared a moment later and then finally

Per himself stepped out. His face was still pallid, and his shirt was in disarray but he was smiling broadly and had the air of someone who was in the best of spirits.

"Now do you see Hr. Manufacturer, my deed was as good as my word!" he cried in triumph, even before the carriage had finally come to a halt.

"Was it a bet?" the young girls asked in a confusion of shouts as they swarmed around the carriage.

"And what was the stake—if one might ask?" said Nanny. She stood apart from the others on the lowest step and her cunning eyes flitted knowingly between Eybert and Jakobe.

Ivan sprang at once from the carriage and with an anxious gesture took Per by the arm.

"But dear God Sidenius—you took sick!"

"Ah, it was nothing. Just a bit of dizziness. That's all. I was stupid. As we can now see, I had no need to push myself as much as I did."

The other passengers now alighted from the carriage; still struck dumb by what had taken place. Philip Salomon, who was grim of countenance, merely gave a curt order to the stable boy as he threw the reins to him: "Tell Kristian to run after Louise. We met her on the roadway. Tell her that there's no need for the doctor to waste his valuable time coming here."

Within minutes, the whole party was gathered in the half gloom of the hallway. The younger element chattered excitedly about what had transpired and otherwise displayed the kind of animation that often arises in the happy conclusion of a frightening event. No one amongst the party was more ebullient than Ivan. He had suddenly become ecstatic over Per's great feat and, again and again, asked to hear the story of how Nanny and Dyhring, who were returning from a walk in the forest, had met him on the staircase, unable to talk, and how moments later he had passed out in the sitting room.

Along the passage by the coat rack, Eybert was helping Jakobe remove her outdoor clothing. His eyes studied her warily as he, with hesitant movements, removed the stole from her still-quivering shoulders.

"I think I got a chill as we were riding through the forest," she said, in order to explain the involuntary, nervous shivers that were running through her, making her teeth literally knock together in her mouth. Very quickly afterwards, she began to ascend the stairs leading to her room.

Even though Per's voice and laughter could be heard all over the house, as if he had no thought for Jakobe, he had never once let her out of his sight. In his desperate agitation, he had made himself a promise that he would speak to Jakobe again that very night, even if it meant breaking into her chambers by way of her balcony. And now, as he laid eyes on Eybert's bouquet, which she had placed on the windowsill and then forgotten to lift again, he seized this pretext to approach her once again.

"Frøken Jakobe! Your flowers!" he called after her.

And in two, three leaps, he was up the stairway, bouquet in hand.

However, he did not reach the very top. Jakobe had just reached the top step, from which she now—without even turning, never mind expressing her thanks—stretched out her hand for the flowers.

But instead of handing them to her, Per took hold of her hand and—after assuring himself that no one else was on the landing—kissed it repeatedly and passionately. Jakobe sank to her knees. She did not even have the strength to pull her hand away. And when Per sensed this, he was up and by her side in an instant and lifted her into his arms.

"You love me!" he whispered over her. "Don't you? You want to be mine."

Her inner fortitude was broken. A quiver of pleasure ran through her as she fell into his crushing embrace; nor could she stop her hands from reaching around him.

"You want to be mine," he said again. "It's true. Isn't it?"

"Yes, yes ..." she uttered in low moans, made wild by the smell of sweat from his still inflamed body, and her head sank down on to his shoulder.

"I'll come again tomorrow morning ... We can talk about things a bit more clearly then."

He crushed her in his embrace again and then, with no more than a few giant springs, was back down the staircase and standing amongst the other guests in the entrance hall.

The whole thing had lasted no more than half a minute. And from that very moment, Per, who was now sure that victory was his, had completely regained his composure. He engaged freely in conversation, as if nothing of consequence had taken place, and then followed the others down into the garden room, where tea was being served.

However, gradually the aftershock that followed the release of all his built-up tension began to hit him. Now that his death or glory leap had vindicated his belief in his own innate good luck, he could barely conceive how he had dared to do it. If he tried to think of his past life, everything just went black. If he tried to think of the road that was now ahead of him, he became gripped by a new bout of dizziness. He could barely believe that the deed had actually been done. Was it really possible that from now on, and for evermore, he would be free from all financial worries, that he—Per Sidenius, the son of a poverty-stricken, rural cleric—was now the prospective joint owner of millions and millions! Yes, that was the reality of it! He held the lucky wand in his hand! The world had now opened her doors to him and called on him to enjoy all her magical wonders!

Despite the fact that Per had done quite well in concealing his inner agitation, a number of those present, and in particular the older people within the company, had sensed that something decisive had occurred up on the stairway. Indeed, the fact that Jakobe had chosen not to reappear strengthened that suspicion. For this reason, the atmosphere in the garden room became more pressured and, in the end, quite uncomfortable. Hr. Eybert moved amongst them with an ashen face and, on a couple of occasions, made to approach Per, which caused extreme consternation. Only the perennial academic Balling strutted around, displaying his usual lack of nous, and speaking in a loud voice on matters literary, his hope being that he would then be asked to entertain the company by giving a reading.

At last, one of the maids came in and gave the long-awaited announcement that the carriage to the station now stood at the door;

everybody bade their farewells as quickly as possible. Only Eybert, who was not going to Copenhagen, remained seated. He still carried some hope that Jakobe might come down again, now that peace had been restored to the house. But after waiting in vain for over half an hour, he too rose from his seat and departed in silence.

"Now, Philip—" said Fru Salomon, when she was finally alone with her husband. "What do you have to say to me after all that?"

"You are right Lea. This cannot go on any longer. That young man really is a bit of a lunatic."

"What have I been saying for the last I don't know how long?"

"I'll talk to Ivan first thing tomorrow. He'll just have to accept that, from now on, we cannot possibly let that person come here any longer."

"My fear is great, dear, that we've closed the gate too late! Did you get a proper look at our Jakobe?"

As soon as the carriage had left, Nanny went up to her room. She had crept to Jakobe's door and pressed her ear against it, and on discovering that all was quiet within, had peeped through the keyhole and saw that no lights had been lit in the room. From this she assumed that her sister had already gone to bed—disappointed, she tiptoed back to her own room.

Jakobe, however, was far from being in repose. The door to her balcony was wide open and she was to be found standing in the moonlight, following the sound of the carriage that took Per away from the house. Her face had aged in the last hour to that of an old crone. She was dark of countenance and haggard. Like one of the stone columns in the garden, she remained standing there until the last rumble from the carriage was swallowed up by the forest.

She went inside and closed the door behind her. She walked backwards and forwards across the floor a number of times; then she sat down on her chaise longue and pressed her head down into her hands.

She remained sitting there like that for a long time—victim of her own shame and despair. So this was how it was all going to end! This was where her dearly won asceticism had led her! In this igno-minious way, and in such a perverse metamorphosis, the ideal image from her youth of a hero/lover was going to be utterly distorted and inverted!

She made no effort to glorify the feelings that had thrown her into Per's arms. Nor did she try to deceive herself into believing that she would be able to tear herself away from the aberrant sensual indulgence in which she was now engaged. She knew her own feelings too well for that: she was in his power. And yet her humiliation would be complete if she were, at the same time, forced to admit that she had yielded so meekly to him! There was no escape route to salvation in any of this. Her fate had been sealed. As utterly brief as their encounter on the stairs had been, she had rested in his arms, his lips had touched hers as they embraced, and an intimation of the ecstasy of love had thrilled her to her very core in the strength of his arms—at that point she already half belonged to him.

There was a soft knock at the door and Nanny popped her head in.

"Oops! Sorry! Didn't mean to disturb your moonlight fantasies!"

"What do you want Nanny?"

"My apologies . . . I could hear that you were still up. Could you lend me a few hair clips?"

"Go and look yourself and see if there are any there."

Nanny was in her night clothes. In her own cat-like way, she glided across the floor to Jakobe's dresser and started to root around in one of the drawers. But she suddenly turned to face Jakobe and sat down on the partly extracted drawer. The moonlight from the window fell directly on to her and made her fine night linen almost transparent, so that her whole body shape was revealed. Pushing her upper body forward in a provocative way, but with a slight anxiousness in her voice, she said: "May I ask . . . are congratulations in order?"

Jakobe reacted with a start and a shudder ran through her.

"What are you talking about?"

"Oh, I'm sorry Jakobe! It's obviously still supposed to be a secret? But if it is, I should say that neither of you are very good at concealing it."

"Secret? What secret? I haven't a clue what you're on about Nanny."

"Oh come on Jakobe. You can't play little miss innocent with me! It's only a couple of hours ago that you were on the landing out there with Per Sidenius. So what weighty things were being discussed, pray tell?"

The very sound of Per's surname provoked a wave of nausea in Jakobe. Sidenius! What a name! ... Fru Sidenius!

"And as for that challenge and the bet—well!" Nanny continued. "The minute I heard about it, I knew something was afoot."

Jakobe straightened herself up, as if coming to a decision about something.

"Very well. You might as well know this evening, as wait for to-morrow. It's true that I am engaged to that man you have just mentioned. That's the top and bottom of it, if you really want to know."

Silence descended for a moment.

"If I want to know? ... What do you mean Jakobe? Of course I am delighted for you."

"Delighted—are you really?" Jakobe asked.

"Jakobe! What a peculiar way to talk to your own sister? Is there any reason why I wouldn't be happy for you? ... Ah, now I understand! You think perhaps that I myself ... I remember that you once used to tease me about Hr. Sidenius. But where that's concerned, you should not worry yourself in the slightest. Of course, I won't deny that I have always had something of a soft spot for your fiancé; but I really do feel that you and he, in all probability, make a much better match."

Jakobe looked up with a spark of interest.

"Why do you say that?"

"Because it's true. It has to be said that both of you seem to look towards a kind of higher plane, whereas poor me, I'm just a frivolous, common or garden party girl—haven't you told me that yourself often enough? ... Well, well. Now people really will have something to gossip about! And poor Eybert!"

Jakobe rose suddenly, and with a flash of irritation.

"Come on Nanny, it's late. And you must be freezing sitting there like that."

"Am I getting on your nerves with all my chat, dear sister? May God forbid and far be it from me ... I'm going. I'm going this minute."

But she remained sitting there for another short while. And, again, there was a hint of stealth in the way she finally slunk across the floor in her bare feet. When at the at door, she turned once more and said: "God Jakobe, you are so boring! You never share anything of interest with me. I was really looking forward to a good old chat and Lord knows I could probably do with a bit of guidance from my older, and more experienced, sister. I mean, imagine if I were to land in the awful situation where I too might have to offer my precious lips to a man with a beard."

"Yes, I'm sorry; please forgive me. I am exhausted," said Jakobe who had already begun to undress for bed.

"Jakobe. Would you stop this Jewish martyr performance! And don't try to kid me that you are going to bed. You will, of course, write to him this very evening ... pour your heart out to him in the dead of night, shower your love with a torrent of ink and ten thousand kisses by first post. But I warn you my girl! Don't leave yourself wide open at the start! Rein him in a little bit! Can you remember our Rebekka, when she got engaged? She had to use lip salve, he kissed her that much. And if I know anything about men, your boyfriend is someone who will expect the whole menu. Good night. Lucky sister! And don't dream too sweetly!"

10

NOT MANY days had passed before it became obvious to Per that despite the "yes" he had wrested from Jakobe's lips, he had not, in truth, moved very far from his previous position. In the first place, both Jakobe and her parents—the latter insisting upon this "in the most adamant way possible"—made a request that the engagement should for the time being remain a secret—or at least it should only be revealed to the closest relatives. Then there was the fact that Jakobe's behavior towards him was marked by a capriciousness that often tested his patience to the limits of what he could bear. On far more than just one occasion, he would go out to Skovbakken only to find that she felt unable to personally greet him, but rather stayed up in her room under the pretext of not feeling well. It was little consolation to Per that, at other times—say, when they found themselves alone in the garden as dusk fell—she would respond with no little passion to his caresses and declarations of love. For his part, Per was by now enough of a connoisseur of women's ways to appreciate the connection between such unrestrained displays of affection, and Jakobe's subsequent bouts of injurious disdain, to see that his continued acquiescence was a perilous policy.

Thus, after a week or so he gradually began to change his own behavior towards Jakobe, a certain nonchalance was shown; his visits became less frequent and, in the end, he chose not to appear for several days.

"Let hunger tame the starving lioness," he thought. Here was yet another test that would prove whether his willpower was strong enough to subjugate others and bring them to heel.

On the first day, Per's failure to appear was like a liberation to Jakobe. The second day left her puzzled, and on the third day she felt the first pangs of anxiety. In the end, she resolved to write to him to find out whether he had fallen ill; but just as she had lifted her pen, she heard his voice down in the garden. In the same instant, her feelings were utterly changed. Yes, her heart had begun to beat against her breast cage, but she wished him a thousand miles away. She could not even bear the thought of looking at him. Her mother immediately told one of her smaller sisters to announce Per's arrival, but she stayed up in her room, deciding to use the sheet of paper intended for Per to write a desultory letter to one of her friends abroad instead.

It was to be another hour or so before she appeared in the rooms downstairs. Per received her with the most indifferent smile he could muster and gave no explanation whatsoever for his long absence. For most of the ensuing evening, he stayed in the billiards room with Ivan and uncle Heinrich, and by the sound of things enjoyed himself immensely. As soon as afternoon tea had been served and consumed he left again, without hardly a word having been exchanged between them.

The night that followed was decisive in determining her relationship with him. For hours on end she traversed her room, fighting with herself backwards and forwards. Now finally, she declared, she was going to break this unnatural and demeaning entanglement, which had not only upset her relationship with her parents and long-standing friends, but was also on the verge of destroying her last remnants of self-respect. As the dawn approached, she sat down at her bureau to inform him of her decision. But as she made to commit her thoughts to paper, it was as if her hand recoiled in protest at the very act. Her hot fire of love ran like a sudden flame in her blood. She flung the pen away from her, then remained sitting there, as still as a statue with her hands covering her face.

From this night forward, she fully embraced her misery in the manner of someone who finds a perverse form of relief in yielding to an inevitable fate. Per Sidenius was her lord and master. Per continued to come and go as he pleased. When he stayed away, he would sometimes send a letter with some half-apologetic lines; on one occasion the letter was accompanied by flowers, but in general he gave no explanation for his absences and Jakobe never asked.

One day, Jakobe was in the parlor, where her mother was sitting on the sofa doing her sewing. Jakobe herself had sat down by the window and was reading a newspaper. She had not moved from her room all morning; not even the delights of lunch had tempted her. Even at this later stage in the day, she was still taciturn and barely looked up from the newspaper, which she perused without the slightest enthusiasm.

"Was there not a letter from Sidenius this morning Jakobe?" her mother asked after one of the lengthier periods of silence between them. She then began to root for something in her sewing box.

"Yes."

"Is he coming out to you today?"

"I don't know."

There was yet another hiatus. But then, as if having come to a decision, Fru Salomon placed her hands in her lap, looked directly at her daughter and said: "Jakobe, sit beside me here my girl and let's have a proper talk together."

Jakobe raised her head to reveal a frightened expression. She then got up and warily crossed the floor to her mother.

"What is it mother?" Jakobe asked as she leaned back into the corner of the sofa, as far away from her mother as possible, and putting her hand to her cheek.

Fru Salomon took Jakobe's free hand and said: "If I ask you a straight question on a personal issue, will you give me a straight answer Jakobe?"

"And what do you mean by that?"

"There you go again . . . so quick to take offense! Jakobe it's not my intention to pry. Will you just—openly and honestly—answer one straightforward question from your mother: Are you happy?"

"What a strange question," said Jakobe, affecting an air of incomprehension, indeed making attempts to force a laugh—but her face had gone sheet white.

"Ah now child. It's not that strange. You are well aware that I don't normally ask my children to take me into their confidence where affairs of the heart are concerned. However, in this case I believe I have the right to ask in all honesty... and to receive an honest answer."

"Sometimes you amaze me mother! Was it not of my own free will that I got engaged? So obviously I'm happy."

"Well, if that's the way you are going to take it Jakobe, I'll speak a bit more bluntly. You see, about an hour ago, I was looking for you up in your room. I thought you weren't feeling well, given that you hadn't come down for lunch. You had just left the room for a moment and I happened to see that the letter from Sidenius was lying on your bureau. Nothing so peculiar about that you might say, except that one wouldn't normally leave that kind of letter just lying around. But. What did startle me, to say the least, was that the letter had not been opened."

"And what of it?" said Jakobe after a short pause, during which the hand still being held by her mother had become as cold as ice.

"What of it? What of it, you ask? Listen Jakobe—I may well be getting on in years, but I'm not that old that I can't remember what it felt like when I first fell in love. If a girl leaves a letter from her sweetheart unopened and unread from eight o'clock in the morning until two o'clock in the afternoon. Well, all is not as it should be."

"Mother. You don't understand! There's a particular reason for that, which I can't explain to you."

Fru Salomon looked doubtingly at her daughter.

"Well, Jakobe my child. It was not—as I have said—my intention to pry. If you will just tell me in all honesty whether you are happy or not. Are you?"

"Yes, of course!"

She spoke as if the words had been dragged from her mouth, pulled her hand away and stood up.

Jakobe's mother looked up at her searchingly but, at that very moment, Nanny burst into the room, still wearing her coat, and firing off the latest news from the world outside even before this was removed. Thus, all further attempts at conversation were abandoned.

Fru Salomon once again took up her sewing work and Jakobe went up to her own room shortly afterwards.

She had taken great offense, not only at her mother's questions, but also at her somewhat pitying tone. The whole scene had filled her with a new sense of unease. Pity. The last thing she wanted was pity—not from others and not even her own self-pity. Of her own volition, she had conjoined her fate with this strange man. So there could be no complaints.

She seized Per's letter, tore it open and sat down to read it. Telling her mother the real reason why she had not been able to do this earlier in the day had been out of the question. Nothing shamed her more than these vapid, slovenly and juvenile letters that Per sent to her. Even his spelling left a lot to be desired. She herself saw her disapproval of them as a sign of her great angst that they might contain allusions to those moments where, during her encounters with him, she completely gave in to her most animal instincts, moments which she always viewed afterwards with hot shame and disgust. But this was more a halfway house of self-delusion. For when she had read his letters, only to discover that they contained not the slightest reference to the thing she feared most, nor even a hint of gratitude or suppressed desires, she would often crush them in her hand, or tear them asunder, and throw them into the fire.

Likewise, on this occasion, the letter contained nothing more than a few words to the effect that he would not be able to get out to Skovbakken that day. But along with this dispatch, which had been written on the back of a business card, he had also sent some papers that proved to be a correction sheet for his manifesto, which Ivan had talked so much about, and trumpeted as a new world wonder. Reluctantly, she pulled the papers out of the envelope. What was the point of sending them to her? She had no confidence in his talents whatsoever, not least where his writing abilities were concerned. The man could not even write correctly in his own mother tongue!

However, she had not read many pages before she felt a tinge of heat in her cheeks. As alien as much of Per's subject matter was to her, and even though it was fairly obvious which role model he was using in terms of his writing style, it soon dawned upon her that there really was something new and fresh in what he had to say. And yes, his vision of how nature's forces could be utilized in the cause of cultural progress was indeed monumental. There were certain phrases she recognized from his pronouncements while in his company, sayings which—because of their verbose, lecturing tone—she had never been able to take that seriously. She was even able to trace some elements back to thoughts and insights she herself had expressed in their conversations on these subjects, but this was far from undermining her reaction—on the contrary, it was in these very places that her eyes were opened to the originality inherent in his abilities and the spontaneous force of his arguments. Expressions that for her had been nothing more than platitudes became transformed in Per's form of polemic and now took on a significance that amazed her. Her throwaway remarks, to which she had given no serious thought, had been transformed by him into palpable images and were projected as fully-formed visions of what the future might hold. The truth was that she could not fail to marvel at the boldness and persuasive power inherent in what he had set out on paper.

Once she had finished reading, she sat for a long time with her hand on his papers and staring straight ahead in contemplation. Who was he really, this person, this stranger, who had become her destiny? In essence, she did not know him at all, other than the highly unreliable testimony provided by her brother Ivan and Per Sidenius himself. What things lay hidden in his past? What, for example, lay behind that dark, cold hatred of his home and family, which he had once revealed to her?

Very often in recent days, she had felt an urgent need to speak to members of his family. She wanted to shine a lamp into all these dark areas that sometimes caused her great concern and humiliated her more than any other issue, not least because Per's own account just made things more opaque with each telling. Jakobe knew that one of his brothers was a state lawyer who worked at one of the government offices in the center of Copenhagen. Per himself had told her that he had bumped into his brother on the street just recently and had, in all confidence, told him of their engagement. As fearful as she was at the thought of presenting herself unannounced to a gentleman who was a complete stranger to her, she resolved to seek out this brother who, surely, could shed more light on things? Without further ado, the very next morning she went into town.

The Prison Board offices, where Eberhard Sidenius worked, were located in a large, foreboding, dirty gray building by the side of the canal. Jakobe got lost in a labyrinth of lonely corridors, but finally found a post room, where two lethargic men sat with their backs stuck to a wall, staring at the floor. In response to her question as to where she might find Hr. Secretary Sidenius, she received the desultory reply: "First floor, third door on the right."

She had hardly turned her back before the men began discussing her in unashamedly loud tones.

"What a conk."

"Aye, a Jew girl wasn't she?"

Up on the first floor, she found the stated door and entered a shaded room with two windows that looked out over an interior courtyard with green trees. Eberhard stood over by the window, where he was writing at a pine lectern, which along with a pair of wooden chairs and a shelf bulging with ledgers and protocols, was the height of furnishing in the room. He was clad in a three quarter length, tightly fitting black coat, buttoned up to his neck. Jakobe noticed that the back of his coat sleeves were shiny with wear and, after the morning rain, the bottoms of his trousers had been carefully turned up to aid drying. In this way, a pair of rough-spun, dark gray woolen socks were revealed to the world, where they sat above a pair of double-soled shoes.

Despite the fact that he had answered Jakobe's knock at the door with a "come in," he remained standing where he was without looking up and continuing his work regardless.

Partly because of this behavior, and partly because of his clothing, Jakobe assumed that he was a scrivener and, therefore, inquired as to whether she might speak to the secretary—the senior clerk. Only when he turned, laying his pen to one side with a ponderous dignity, and she met the gaze from his eyes, cold as an icy lake, did she recognize with a shiver the family resemblance to Per.

She gave her name and added: "I know that your brother—that Per—has spoken of me to you."

Eberhard made a silent, officious gesture in the direction of the chairs.

"The reason why I have sought you out will presumably be obvious to you, sir," Jakobe continued after taking her seat. Her voice betrayed a tremor, her heart hammered in her breast, and she sought refuge in these formalities so as to be able to at least say something. "Of course I am aware that your brother—my fiancé—has for some time been estranged, not just from you but the rest of the family as well. It is not—of course—my place to pass judgment as to what lies behind this bad blood. However, I hardly need to tell you that the situation really saddens me."

Eberhard had remained standing at his lectern, where he adopted a rather affected pose, his angled head resting on his splayed fingers, which provided shade for his eyes. He calmly allowed Jakobe to say what she wanted to say. Not one flinch in his face revealed his thoughts, but had the very skies fallen, he could not have been more shocked. He was well aware that his brother had gained an entrée into the merchant Salomon's opulent household. But he had not for a moment believed Per's story that he had become engaged with this man's daughter—in fact, less and less so with each entreaty that Per made not to reveal this event to outsiders. He had simply viewed this claim as barefaced bragging that was meant to cover up some defeat or other that Per had suffered. He knew, of course, that Philip Salomon's private fortune could be counted in many many millions.

His first conscious thought was that this connection had to be broken at all costs. Nor was malice the motivation for this thought, still less envy. For he recognized that the future prospects that now lay open to his brother would lead him still further down the path of damnation and any hope of his redemption would be ruled out for many more years to come. In the past number of years, and far more closely than Per realized, Eberhard had followed the course of his brother's life and just at that very juncture had firmly believed the moment was at hand when Per—schooled by shame and privation—would finally repent of his ways and acknowledge that he had sinned against his home and parents.

"May I ask you madam," he said when Jakobe had stopped speaking, "whether it is you alone that has sought this interview regarding my brother's relationship to his family?"

"Yes."

"Then my brother, perhaps, knows nothing about your desire to seek me out in this regard?"

"No."

"You are asking, therefore madam, exclusively on your own behalf?"

Finding his manner distasteful in the extreme, Jakobe quickly pulled herself together. Nor had his tone of cross examination gone unnoticed by her and this inflamed her further. Her answer was definite and dismissive: "As I have just said, it is me who desired this conversation, not Per."

"It is as I suspected madam. It is of course—unfortunately—only too true that my brother has for many years, indeed from his childhood days, turned his back on his own kith and kin. In fact, it is probably no exaggeration, madam, to say that he has consciously hardened his recalcitrant spirit over time and taken a perverse pleasure in spiting every consideration he ought to show to the very people who deserve his greatest gratitude and respect. This attempt at turning his face to stone has even gone as far as his Christian name. You have called him nothing but Per. You are perhaps even unaware that this is a made up name?"

"I think he has told me that."

"Nor do l wish to hide from you madam something that is a matter of conscience for me—and you obviously require an open response from my side—and that is that my brother's engagement to you has far more to do with his rebellion against his own home than anything else. It is a conscious denial of the spirit in which he was raised—."

Jakobe looked up at him, her brow darkening.

"I'm not sure I follow you sir," she said.

"Then I'll try to be a little clearer, shall I? It has hardly escaped your attention has it that Peter Andreas was brought up within a God-fearing Christian family? Peter Andreas, himself, is well aware that, for his parents, Christianity is their only shield and sword in this life, and that they acknowledge no form of happiness, no matter how enticing that may be on the surface, other than that which comes to us from piety and devotion in the risen Christ."

"Ah, now I think I understand!"

Jakobe bit her lip so hard that she felt a sting of pain. Behind Eberhard's calm and precisely weighted comments, she heard the voice of the mob, just as she had heard it outside the post room when looking for his office. The same voices that had persecuted her throughout her life.

She would have much preferred to get up and leave that instant so as to display her contempt for him. But her need to hear more about Per was too strong; she composed herself and remained seated.

"I was well aware that Per does not share his family's views on matters of religion," she said. "But I must say…that this does not diminish him in my eyes."

"That does not surprise me in the least."

"What I mean, sir, is that if this is the only issue upon which he has broken from his home, then I think he may be forgiven. The fact that he has adopted different views on Christianity can perhaps be explained without necessarily assuming malicious intent on his part. He has at least been open about it, instead of being a hypocrite—a game he often could have played to his advantage had he wished—that surely can only be to his credit."

"I believe, Frøken Salomon, that there is little point in entering into a debate on this issue. Let it suffice for me to tell you that my parents—for whom I speak as their advocate on this matter—make no concessions to any person who turns his back and closes his ears to the Word of the Lord—least of all, madam, for someone like Peter Andreas who has been reared in a home where that one voice of truth has been heard from the cradle onwards."

Jakobe made no reply to this. She had bowed her head; and, as always when her mind was in uproar, the color in her cheeks rose and fell with each beat of her heart.

However, Eberhard misread both her bowed head and her retreat into silence. In the prosecution of his arguments and that Sidenius urge to assert one's beliefs, he felt that his words had achieved their desired effect, which was to humiliate this proud millionaire's daughter, in whose gaze he had immediately perceived a mark of disdain; her silk dress and gaudy gloves, not to speak of the light-perfumed fragrance she had brought into his room simply egging him further in his evangelical zeal.

For this reason, he changed his tone slightly. Hinting at sympathy for her, he said: "Far be it from me to cause offense, madam, but I do regard it as my solemn duty to tell you that many other aspects of my brother's life bear depressing witness to his long fall from that place of moral grace upon which he once stood. It is, of course, nothing but a huge delusion to believe that the religious life is only concerned with the divine spirit and does not leave its mark on our whole being and our personal behavior. However, I shall not dwell on this point where Peter Andreas is concerned. There are certain things which can hardly be talked about in the presence of a, er, ahem, lady, so—"

"I think I know, sir, exactly what you are referring to. But it is, I would argue, precisely Per's unfortunate relationship with his childhood home and then his ready acceptance into that other world— perhaps partly for that very reason—which both explains and excuses a good deal. And, once again, leaving aside those issues, I believe that they do not entitle you to call such a severe judgment upon his head."

"You misunderstand me, Frøken Salomon. We do not condemn my brother per se, only his deeds and actions—his life as he now lives it madam."

"But his life and deeds show that there are many things that stand in his favor. Per has shown both great aptitude and serious determination in deepening his knowledge of his profession. And while struggling under what were obviously difficult circumstances, he has, as young as he is, come to the attention of his professional peers and is well on the way to cementing his reputation."

"I think that I can hear in your tone that you yourself, with respect, do not really believe that. Of course, I am aware that a newspaper has recently referred to some canal project or other and has attempted to attach some significance to it. I'm also aware that he regards himself as trailblazer, a Prophet for the New Age in which we allegedly live. At the moment, it seems that a need to cause uproar has arisen amongst a section of our young people, which would merely be cause for amusement if it were not for the unhappiness it creates amongst that very same gaggle of weak and immature souls. That's the most worrying aspect of the kind of spiritual whirlwind that is presently bewitching some of our Danish youth—that it is always the most frivolous and weak willed amongst them who—like the chaff being winnowed from the wheat—are sent spinning furthest into the air and are blown furthest away from the place where they belong. And where poor Peter Andreas is concerned, the bare truth of the matter is as undeniable as it is depressing. I refer, madam, to the fact that, after seven long years of study, he has still not sat his final exams, or in any other way provided satisfactory evidence of progress—progress, that is, that would reasonably answer to the great sacrifice that has been made on the part of his parents. Be that as it may—and I will say again—we neither condemn nor turn our backs on Peter Andreas, only his deeds and actions, his present life. On the contrary, we all feel the utmost pity in our hearts for him; and in spite of everything that has transpired, we will never give up our hope that good will eventually triumph over evil in the battle for his soul. Where the only road to salvation lies for him, as far as his family is concerned, I need hardly explain. And if it means anything at all to you madam— and I am still presuming that you have made this approach in order to obtain a full and frank answer—I can tell you now—and this will presumably hardly surprise you, or leave you in any doubt—that under no circumstances, as far as his mother and father are concerned, will any sanction or approval be forthcoming of his, ahem, relationship with you."

Jakobe got up. Partially turning away from him, as if ready to leave that instant, she nevertheless remained for a moment, standing behind the chair, looking down at the point of one of her shoes as she pressed the tip of her parasol against it. Then she suddenly lifted her head and looked over her shoulder at him. Her face was still flecked by the most violent agitation, though a slight smile played on her lips and there was a glint in her dark eyes of some newfound fortune.

"I came here in the hope of initiating a reconciliation," she said. "That—I now realize—was very naive of me. But at the same time, I am happy that I sought you out sir. For I have gained the very information that I lacked. And—I cannot refrain from being as frank as you have been—I leave a much happier woman than the one that came into this building to see you."

Uncertain as to what Jakobe actually meant, Eberhard made to offer a reply but she was already at the door and left without so much as a goodbye.

Once she found herself standing in the street again, Jakobe was gripped by such an overwhelming longing to see Per that, after a brief struggle with herself, she called a passing hackney carriage and traveled out to Nyboder. She felt that she would not gain peace of mind until she had made atonement for her lack of faith in him and begged his forgiveness for the treachery her visit to his brother (she now realized!) essentially was. Oh, how well she understood him now! How her bosom heaved at the thought of what he had endured over there in his father's vicarage! As Per's smug and self-righteous brother held forth, she had gained enough insight into that family abode to make her flesh run cold.

She arrived at Hjertensfrydgade minutes after Per's departure from that same place. Remnants of gray blue smoke whirls from Per's cigar were still clinging to the low ceiling in his tiny room. Jakobe had been escorted there by Trine who disappeared instantly when "Madam" asked to be left alone.

She stood in the middle of the room and looked about her. She studied the bare walls, the dilapidated rocking chair, the little black pouf made of threadbare oil cloth. For a moment, her shock at the sight of this dark, prisonlike hovel made her almost forget her disappointment at having just missed him. She could never have believed that her fiancé lived in such poverty—so abject and so sad! With renewed force, a bright, revelatory, and ameliorating light fell over Per and his reckless striving to reach life's sun-kissed golden peaks. Surrounded by such funereal penury and after such a mournful childhood, how could he have become anything other than a hunter seeking good fortune wherever he might find it? Now she felt a new sense of tender satisfaction in the knowledge that her wealth could make him happy.

She lifted some of the bric-a-brac which lay on his work table, and then put them carefully back in their place again after having perused them for a moment with that blend of veneration and curiosity which signals the first real bloom of love. She moved about the room, stopping here and there as new thoughts came to her. In her need to be close to him, she had to touch everything that was his. As she passed an old dressing gown, which hung on his doorframe, she ran her hand caressingly down its length; yes, she even laid her cheek against it when she passed by again, closing her eyes as she allowed the curious smell of his intimate person to envelop her, a smell which she now—just as she had previously loathed the smell of tobacco—sometimes longed for with a rampant passion.

But then Trine returned and Jakobe sat down to write a short note on a visitor's card: "Dear Fiancé! Why do I never see you? It's three whole days since you called out to me. I will expect you this evening. I have so much to tell you."

It was her first letter to him. She placed the card in an envelope, which she found on the table, and wrote his name on the front.

As soon as she had left, Madam Olufsen began knocking on her bedroom floor with her walking stick to give notice to Trine that she was wanted upstairs for a report on events below. The ailing wife of the late Senior Boatswain was now for the most part bedridden. After her husband's death, her Amazon body had collapsed and she now only moved about when absolutely necessary and then with difficulty. However, her curiosity overruled all else when she heard the voice of a stranger down in the hall, and a female voice at that, and she had immediately stood up and stumped her way to the kitchen door the better to eavesdrop. She then went into the sitting room and sat in front of the window mirror to follow the progress of the departing hackney carriage until its wheels disappeared around the corner into Store Kongensgade.

When Per arrived back a few hours later and read Jakobe's note, he smiled with satisfaction. The carrot and stick has done the trick, he said to himself. But it was still too early for any signs of indulgence. Keep the bit between her teeth for a while yet!

On two separate occasions in the late afternoon, Jakobe walked along the station road around the time when a train was due to arrive from Copenhagen. When she arrived, deeply disappointed, a second time back at the house she found a telegram waiting for her in her room. Per, in his now customary abrupt fashion, apologized for once again being unable to make it out to Skovbakken that evening.

Jakobe remained standing with the telegram in her hand and mulled the situation over. "There's more to this than meets the eye"— she suddenly said out loud. It could not possibly be his work that kept him away from her night after night.

She went pale. Was it all off? she wondered. Had she lost him? No, no! She would not let that happen! She would write to him, admit everything, explain the whole thing, beg his forgiveness for her distrust and lack of warmth towards him.

She sat herself down, pressed her head between her hands so as to collect her thoughts. No. She was not going to lose him! She had to win him back, even if she had to go on her knees and beg him.

Her crisis was interrupted by the door being pushed ajar. Her sister Rosalie popped her head in.

"They sent me to ask you to call down Jakobe. A gentleman's here to see you."

Eybert! The very thought of him caused her angst to boil over.

Her old suitor had again begun to make appearances in the house. Was it an omen? That he should come at that very moment!

Her first instinct was to refrain from going down at all; but then she considered the fact that her mother might get suspicious if she stayed in her room. It was also reasonable to assume that she was aware of the telegram—knew no doubt that it was Per canceling once again.

Down in the garden room where day had faded to dusk, she found both her parents accompanied by a gentleman whom she did not immediately recognize in the half light. He had just that moment taken his place in an armchair, which had its back to the door she had walked through.

But he now stood up and in her flash of recognition that it was Per, she screened her eyes with her hand as if blinded by a vision. After reading her short note once more, he had regretted his callousness and was lit up by the idea of surprising her. With a loud exclamation, Jakobe threw her arms around his neck. "Oh it's you darling. It's you!"

For the better part of a minute, she simply clung to his chest, oblivious to all else. But then she composed herself, embarrassed at revealing such extreme emotions in front of her parents. However, she maintained her fervent grip on Per's hand, as if she were afraid that she might lose him again. Finally, with smiles and brimming with tears, she took his arm and led him into the garden.

Philip Salomon and his wife watched them go and then looked directly at each other.

"Well now dear, we had better let fate run its course," he said.

Fru Lea nodded slowly in silence.

In spite of the decision to keep the engagement secret, it was not long before it was being widely and openly discussed. Jakobe was hard put to contain her feelings now that they had been released from the burden of shame. She went around like someone whose very existence had been hidden away, but who could now stand forward and reveal her true, happy self to the world.

Per also noticed that he had become a subject of interest in certain circles. He was now the patron of the more exclusive cafés around Kongens Nytorv, having turned his back for good on the less salubrious haunts of his past, and when he entered such establishments, it was not uncommon for some of the clientele to stick their heads together and begin whispering as he went by. Indeed, high society was in shock at this strange liaison. The most dramatic stories were already being bandied about regarding this buccaneer who had not only scooped up Neergaard's riches but had now seized one of Philip Salomon's greatest treasures.

Rumors of an engagement had also reached Per's former student colleagues at the National College of Engineering. The article about Per in *The Falcon*, and not least the announcement of his coming manifesto, had aroused huge expectation there. Per had neither been as isolated, nor as misunderstood, amongst his comrades as he himself had believed. Nor was it just those mercurial souls, who just like him had found the air in Professor Sandrup's lecture hall too oppressive, but also the laggards—those who would grab at any critique of the college as an excuse for their indolence—all of them had been waiting for that day when Per, in some dramatic fashion, would reveal himself to the world. On the other hand, Per's burgeoning fame had now created a number of implacable enemies amongst the ranks of the honest toilers, who until then had looked upon him with little more than disdainful pity. This was particularly the case with a certain Marius Jørgensen, the apple of Professor Sandrup's eye, and who Per, precisely because of that, had dubbed "Little Lord Logarithm." This up-and-coming pillar of society now set about plotting a vicious revenge on Per by, in all secrecy, preparing a savagely satirical review, to be published by *The Business Post*, once Per's call to arms was in the public domain.

The Salomon household gradually began to reconcile itself to the idea that Per was now a prospective son-in-law. Though, outwardly at least, uncle Heinrich gave the impression of being the one who took least pleasure from what had transpired, he still sought to present himself to Per as the paternal benefactor, despite the fact that Per had long since worked out the truth regarding his story about the mythical "marriage consortium" in America. In fact, Hr. Delft never let up with his private game of poker and the "nobility" gambit was the next card he wanted to put on the table. At any moment that proved to be propitious, he would take Per by the arm and once again make references to the widowed Baroness von Adlersborg; and Per, who now scented the possibility of yet another triumph, began to listen more closely to his quiet mantra and, without anything being expressed in words, signed up to the idea. From his encounter with her shortly after Neergaard's death, he knew that the baroness was still at a South German spa resort, and he intended to amend the itinerary of his great European odyssey so as to pay her a visit. However, his primary intention was still that of simply maintaining a connection with a distinguished lady who might in general be useful to him in terms of the opportunities she just might be able to put his way. Yet it was also the case that he would have nothing against the idea of abandoning the hated Sidenius name forever—that preposterous piece of Sexton Latin, that troll mantle, which followed him everywhere he went and betrayed the dark roots of his past. Baron von Adlersborg! Why not? Now there was a name that would look well on a visitor's card.

None of these grand aspirations were mentioned to Jakobe. He believed that she paid little heed to outward symbols of status or rank and therefore presumed that she would hardly approve. He was not aware that Jakobe's plans for him, and their future together, went much further and higher. One evening, and at her express wish, he read aloud his whole treatise for her, explaining certain elements as he went along. And now, with a responsiveness born of love, each sentence he uttered sounded to her like a rousing fanfare.

However, she was sensible enough to keep these impressions to herself for the time being. Her newfound adoration did not blind her to the many chinks in Per's armor, and she was well aware that much was needed to be done before he could be said to be fully equipped for the coming battle which, she now accepted, fate had decreed to be his destiny. That aside, she indulged with increasing intemperance her passion for Per himself. The exultant fount of tender love she bore in her breast, that burning need she felt to cut loose from all restraint—all the things that had caused her so many bitter humiliations throughout her youth could now at last be expressed to the full. Night and day, she thought constantly of Per. Each morning she would send him fresh flowers so as to bring some life to his morbid rooms. She overwhelmed him with all kinds of useless gifts and racked her brains daily to come up with something new that would please him. In the end, she even talked her parents into moving back to town earlier than normal, so that she could see him more often, expect his arrival at any time during the day, and at night be aware that he was only eight hundred and thirty steps from her side—she had measured the distance herself in all secrecy. But even this was not always enough for her. An hour after he had left her, she would feel the need to sit down and write to him, or send a telegram. There was always something she urgently needed to tell him, or clarify, something she had not explained properly, or had said that she now wished to take back, and beg him to forget entirely—in all, a partly subconscious pretext to tell him this one simple thing: that she loved him, and that she was only counting the minutes, not to mention each beat of her heart, until she saw him again.

"Bon jour, monsieur!" she wrote to him one morning, the sun lighting up her room through her open window. "I wonder will you grace me with your presence this morning? If so, I could have refrained from sending this latest missive. But Per you make it so hard to plan things! Why did you not come over to me yesterday evening? I waited until ten o'clock. Went to bed in terrible form and really hated you with all my heart right through to eleven. Today I forgive you because . . . well, because of this gorgeous sunshine darling. Could you not, just for today, put all those corrections and drawings back in their drawers and come over to me—say around two? At that point, only myself and my mother will be at home. Don't forget that we are soon going to be far away from each other, and when you have gone, I'm going to be the first Jewess ever to join a convent and I'll wait there in eternal suffering until you come back to me."

With all this care and attention, Per felt as if he were being carried through life like some enchanted pasha. Within the space of a few months, he put on twelve pounds in weight. But for all that, the erotic atmosphere in which Jakobe enveloped him sometimes became far too much of a sultry clime. He was, of course, himself liable to eruptions of passion, especially after dinner when they retreated to the quiet intimacy of the parlor room. But Jakobe's relentless fire of love was alien to him and in the end quite stressful. After a childhood ensnared by crippled emotions, cut off from all other passions than those that thrived in the shadows, or could find free rein on the blasted heath or rain-swept fjord, he was almost repulsed by her sun-ripened fervor. He would often sit, half-embarrassed, under the deluge of her affections and was, overall, a most awkward paramour.

One day, as they sat holding hands and dusk falling, Jakobe put her arms about his neck and said: "Has it ever struck you, Per, that you have never really told me that you love me?"

"But you know that anyway, Jakobe."

"Yes but just knowing it is not enough for me. I want to hear you say it. I mean ... am I not allowed at least once to hear what it sounds like when my very own love tells me that he loves me? Say it now, Per!"

"But, dearest girl, I really have said so many times that—"

"Not with exactly those words Per! And it is those very words, precisely, that I want to hear. You have to remember that it is those three words that women are just waiting to hear, day and night, waking and sleeping—from the very first time we attend a dance or go to a ball. Just say them Per. Go on! Shall I help you? Now listen—after me ... in that way it becomes a declaration by both of us at the same time. Ready? I—"

"I," he intoned.

"Love—"

"Ah now stop, Jakobe. That's just stupid," Per objected, his cheeks hot with embarrassment and putting his hand over her mouth as he spoke. And when she persisted in her pleadings, he feigned serious annoyance and pulled free from her arms.

Despite the frequent relief he felt when emerging onto the street and lighting a cigar, after yet another ardent leavetaking at the entrance to the Salomon household, he rarely felt the urge to rush back to his own place and continue his work, still less to cruise amongst the bars and cafés as was his wont in the old days. He had come to enjoy walking the streets, preferably when they were quiet and bereft of people, allowing himself to venture into new moods and dispositions, which he did not fully comprehend, just as in that first time, when he had inadvertently gained entrance to that paradise of the senses, he had an exciting, yet intimidating, awareness that his whole being was discovering a new realm of delights. But while that first real lovers' haven, into which he was led by the fine upstanding Francesca, had actually proven to be no more than a cozy little herb garden full of wild mignonette and wall climbers and pleasing rows of vegetable beds, Per felt that he was now staring into a glorious oasis full of tall palms that swayed in the warm, sighing wind—majestic to behold and as profound as a temple. During these night wanderings, he began to glimpse a higher form of happiness and good fortune, greater and more pure aspects to lust and earthly desires than those for which he had hitherto searched. He began to understand that life only truly became enriched when a man was ensconced in a woman's love, and that there was a deeper truth, than he himself had realized, in those throwaway remarks he had made about heavenly embraces being the soothing amnesia for all life's sorrows and the final absolution for all sins.

One night, on returning from just such a hour-long excursion through the streets, he wrote these lines to Jakobe: "In a kind of humorous way, a man once called me 'Lucky Per.' Now I have never exactly regarded myself as destitution's greatest son in this life. Perhaps in occasional moments of despondency, I've been found to complain about my fate, a fate that allowed me to be born in a land where, back in the mists of time, the priest's son Adam married the parish clerk's daughter Eve, and so gradually filled up the world with millions and millions of Sideniuses. But now when I look back on my life up to now, I feel that a guardian angel has always watched over me, and though I've often gone astray and sometimes forgotten that all that glitters is not gold. Well, I here I stand with the Golden Wreath of Victory in my hand: you, Jakobe, and your love for me.

"Now, as I look forward to a night's repose, I feel a great urge to pay homage to you and embrace you with my thoughts and reflections. You, dearest Jakobe, have been my guardian angel from that day when I entered your parents' home for the first time—that day, in other words, which represents the decisive turning point in my life. Those words you bade me express the other day when we were together—the words that were locked in my heart. I whisper them now, so that they can carry across the still night air to your bedside: I—love—you!"

When, the next morning, he reread the letter in his more usual sober disposition, he reddened with embarrassment and threw it into the stove. He then wrote a new letter, which dealt almost exclusively with his book.

"I'm sick of waiting for those printers. They are taking forever to get the job done. I would say that it is the drawings that are holding things up. They have to be cut as wooden blocks. Were you aware, by the way, that I'm thinking of changing the book's title? 'New Times' sounds so boring. 'Our Future State' is what I now want to call it. You have to admit, Jakobe, it has a certain ring to it. Does it not?"

The month of October had now arrived and Per's travel preparations were finally complete. His plan was to first spend some time in Germany and visit some of the most renowned technical institutes down there. After that he wanted to make arrangements to follow one or other of the massive hydraulic engineering projects being undertaken by the Anglo-American Conglomerate Blackbourn & Gries. His future father-in-law had promised to grease the wheels with regards to obtaining a suitable introduction. Apart from that, he wanted to go to Paris, London, New York, and a number of the other great cities in North America. Overall, he intended to be away for two years.

Even though Jakobe could not fathom how she was going to cope for such a long time on her own, she made no objections. Indeed, she had been the one who argued that Per should add another year to his original plan. Per himself had been of the view that half that time would be sufficient, but Jakobe had pleaded with him to make sure he didn't end up just rushing from one place to another and to take his time. In this argument she found an ally in her father who one day summoned Per to his office and handed him a credit note for five thousand crowns, and also pointed out that a new note would be issued on the expiry of the first year.

In the middle of all the bustle to do with packing final items and completing his somewhat ostentatious travel gear, Per received a letter from Eberhard. His brother wrote that news had reached him of his imminent departure abroad and that he simply could not refrain from apprising him of his father's state of health, where a catastrophe was to be expected at any moment. He himself was to depart in all haste so as to attend the death vigil, where all the other brothers and sisters would also presumably gather.

On receiving this letter, Per spent the rest of the day walking up and down his floor, tortured by indecision. The tone of the letter had been uncharacteristically considerate, and his own good fortune had made him well disposed to thoughts of reconciliation. None of them could think for a moment, he concluded, that he was returning as the Prodigal Son.

But wait! His triumph was not yet complete. If only his book had been published!

This letter too was burned in the stove, along with some old papers he had cleaned out of his commode. None of this was mentioned to Jakobe.

The next day he left for Germany.

II

But now let me tell you about my actual debut on life's big stage, Jakobe. It was not without its comical moments. Of course you know the journey to Berlin better than I do and it has obviously not become any more entertaining since you last made it. To be honest, I eventually fell asleep and didn't wake until the train roared into Stettiner Bahnhof. Then I stumbled out of the station into the arms of a jarvey, got my suitcase dragged out, and shouted the address up to him: "Hotel Zimmermann, Burgstrasse." This is the hotel your uncle had recommended. But he just stands there staring at me and then repeats in his thick Berlin dialect: "Bu'straasse? Bu'straasse?" Then he shakes his fat boozer's head and says: "Kenn's nicht!" More jarveys began to congregate, until in the end we had a veritable convention. "Bu'straasse? Bu'straasse?" they all chimed at once, shaking their equally fat heads. "Kenn's nicht!" Everybody just ignored me—I'm only the passenger after all! But then suddenly one of them sticks a finger in the air and shouts: "Ah!.... Burrrrrrgstrrrrrraasse!" And it was this urgent drumroll of *r*'s that really brought things home to me. Now I felt that I was actually in a foreign land and my first ever travel experience was the acknowledgment that even a dyed-in-the-wool Jutland man like myself must develop a far more refined palate for consonants if he's going to travel abroad.

But wait till you hear what happened next! When my carriage finally rolled up outside Hotel Zimmermann (which, by the way, is an old kip of a place with a tumbledown staircase that almost runs out onto the street) a hausknecht in a leather apron came out to greet me. And then what happens? He has barely got the carriage door open before he, quite beside himself, runs back into the hotel roaring at the top of his voice: "Hr. Zimmermann! Hr. Zimmermann! . . . A decorated gentleman!" Suddenly I'm a nobleman! The whole house was now in uproar and the proprietor himself comes rushing out, baring his head and bowing almost to the floor. Unbelievable! In the meantime, I chance to look down at the lapel of my coat and there, in the buttonhole, is the last remaining oblong of the rose you put there this morning as we parted. Jakobe, my darling, if you'd seen the commotion your last gift to me provoked amongst them all! And then you can imagine the change of mood once they all realized their mistake. But fear not. I was quick to reassert our honor! When I finally got up to my room, I made sure to ring down and complain about lots of things in the best traditions of a Knight of The Grand Cross, and when the bellboy came to me with the guestbook, I just could not resist placing a nice little "von" in front of my name. Now don't go shaking your head Jakobe! You should have seen how it greased the wheels for me! As I left the hotel, the proprietor came out into the lobby and gave another bow, as if he wanted to kiss my bootlaces. The proprietor himself, do you mind, then opened the door for me with an utterly servile "Hr. Baron!" on his lips. So this was my second travel experience on my first day away from home—a title in one's name is not to be sniffed at, something your uncle has already told me, it should be said. Yes of course I know that the whole thing is a sham and ridiculous Jakobe, but one of the ground rules for gaining influence over people is, without doubt, that one has to be bold enough to exploit their foibles and idiocies.

I have now had a chance to look around the Unter den Linden area and am right now sitting in Café Bauer writing these lines to you. The streets are alive with a roar and hum that leaves me in no doubt that I now find myself in one of the world's great powerhouses. I get the feeling that I am sat in the middle of a huge waterwheel. And what are these giant cities other than monster turbines gobbling up great streams of humanity and then spitting them out again once their energy has been spent? What a huge concentration of human activity and power! There really is something uplifting in the feeling that the very pavement beneath ones feet is shaking from the energy created by all these millions and millions of people. Imagine exactly what we will be able to achieve in the coming centuries when we have learned to harness all that creative value. The ideas and innovations we are wrestling with in today's world are kindergarten toys in comparison with what the future holds!

But that's enough for today.

17th Oct.

I have rented some rooms in Karlsstrasse 25 (Address: Frau Kumminach, zweite Treppe links). For the moment, I am going to stay here in Berlin. There is something about the life and noise of this place that electrifies me. I actually feel it on my skin when the air in this great metropolis becomes charged with thunder and lightning. Herrrrrrich! Jakobe, you can imagine the almighty and veritable tempest I feel like hurling across the Baltic Sea at our sleepy little cattle pens in Denmark! Seen from this part of Europe, people and conditions at home look ten times more provincial. The people here (even down to street cleaners) have a different cut about them altogether. Take those dandies in Østergade for example—there's still something of the "choirboy from the backwoods" about them. Or compare our army lieutenants with a German officer in his imposing greatcoat with those huge blood red cuffs—then you soon see that our version is more like some callow uniformed seminarian.

I paid Dr. Nathan a visit today. He lives handy enough to Königsplatz and seems—despite his occasional rather bitter outbursts—to be quite at his ease in his voluntary exile. He made me feel very welcome but I have to say Jakobe that I was not overly impressed with him. I tried to give him some sense of what I say in my book; but he clearly does not have the foggiest notion about technical matters. Every other minute he would interrupt me with the clumsiest of questions. He hardly knew what a turbine is or does. The whole conversation was me saying chalk, he saying cheese. I left his home with a feeling of great disappointment. Really Jakobe, the whole approach used by people like Nathan is so strange. They say they want to build a new, enlightened civilization upon the ruins of romanticism—yet they themselves do not have a damned clue what this entails. They remind me of that kind of academically trained architect who, in artistic terms, can do a probably very appealing drawing of a new building but doesn't worry himself about (or perhaps even looks down his nose at) the question of where the timber is going to come from, where the brick kiln for the building is going to be etc. I'm sorry but they'll just have to make way for the real innovators! Men like Nathan are blocking progress, not helping it! I remember in one of those books you lent me in the summer—could it have been one of Nathan's own?—the undoubtedly correct observation was made that the prerequisite for the Renaissance in the fifteenth century was the invention of the compass, which made the discovery of the Americas possible and facilitated the exploitation of already-known colonies. Thus, untold riches flowed into an impoverished Europe and reinvigorated its peoples who had previously been under the yoke of a cabal of priests and monks. Hope, vigor, and a sense of adventure were restored to public life. But in the exact same way, I believe, the forward march of mechanization is the prerequisite for the next great cultural leap and those who preach about progress without understanding this essential dynamic are merely blowing soap bubbles into the air. This serves no useful purpose other than providing entertainment for poets and other simpletons.

19th Oct.

No Jakobe, I have still not paid my respects to your mother's uncle. I decided to put it off for a while, until my German was a bit more respectable. I walked past his villa in Tiergartenstrasse the other day—more a castle than a villa of course. Rumor has it that the man is worth at least fifty million. Would you do me that service of instructing me as to my required deportment? What is a Geheimecommercienrath? I mean—am I supposed to address him as your Excellency? Also—tell me a bit more about the family as a whole. There is a wife (Gemahlinn??) and a daughter. Yes? Do they have more children?

21st Oct.

Today, when I walked into Café Bauer—who do I see sitting there with a pirate's bandana round his neck and a roughly made walking stick between his outstretched legs? Fritjof! You'll be surprised to hear that I barely recognized him; he has aged so much in the last while. His beard is spattered with gray and his eyelids are all puffy and red. But for all that, he still has the stamp of a proud lion about him, even here in Berlin he causes a stir wherever he goes. He is here because some of his paintings are being exhibited by an art dealer. He has prospered as an artist down here and he is in all the newspapers. I'm no expert in these things but he insisted on my accompanying him to view the paintings. I think he wanted me to sing his praises and I must say that some of them have been brilliantly executed. In particular, there was a pair of large canvases showing the North Sea—all huge waves and turmoil. While I stood there looking at them, I could not help but look to the future, towards a time when my thousand-ton iron pontoons (you will remember them I'm sure from my book) will form an engineer's garland around Jutland's west coast and—firmly anchored—will be riding the surf out there, constantly and steadfastly absorbing the energy generated by the sea. Then I asked Fritjof whether he had ever been saddened by the idea, as he sat on the beach painting those monstrous waves, that all that wonderful power and energy had gone to waste for thousands of centuries—lost forever to mankind and human culture. But of course he let loose with his usual tirade about the captains of industry, their black hearts and the way they defile the true spirit of nature. Then I asked him whether he really did not see anything attractive in the idea that all that wasted horsepower could be of benefit to society, that it could be spread right across the country by way of a cable network and shared amongst all the towns in Jutland; in fact go right into every home, so that a seamstress, for example, in Holstebro could keep her machine going forever if she wished, or a mother in Viborg could watch her child's cot as it gently rocked, courtesy of the waves crashing down on our shore from the sea. You should have seen his face, Jakobe! "What are you prattling on about man?" he roared, so that other people in the viewing hall turned round. "Do you scoundrels want to turn my precious ocean into nothing more than a glorified farm animal!"

He is completely incorrigible. I actually felt really sorry for him. When I looked at him standing there like an exclamation mark with his battered slouch hat, the bandana, the crooked walking stick, the ill-fitting tie, I said to myself: "The last of the rebel artists!" In twenty years' time, that kind of person will be thrown into a lunatic asylum, and when they die, their bodies will be preserved and stuffed so that they can be exhibited in zoological museums between ancient mammoths and three-humped camels, a rare but now extinct species.

23rd Oct.

I had a great day yesterday, Jakobe. A few days ago, I read in one of the newspapers about some trials on a new kind of river barrier that were to be carried out near a little town called Berkenbrück, which is a couple of hours from here by train. These trials were going to be observed by a number of specially invited engineers. Of course, I immediately wanted to be involved myself; so I went up to the Danish consulate, thinking they would feel obliged to arrange an invitation for me. But never have I seen two eyeballs that expressed such stunned surprise as those that stared back at me when I stepped up and made my request. The flunkey concerned had to literally fall back into his chair to get his breath back. He could recall, he said, that they had once obtained a seat for a traveling actress at the Royal Theater, and they had once facilitated, d'ye mind, some Danish scientists in gaining access to manuscripts at the national library—but this! An older man then appeared from an adjoining room (I've no doubt that it was the head of department himself). He surveyed me with even greater horror and then informed me in condescending tones that to expect such favors in a foreign country, most of all in

Germany, where they were least inclined to help foreigners, was out of the question. At the very least, the consulate would have to confer with the minister's department at home before getting involved in this affair, and I would therefore have to submit a written request in two exact copies, as well as the necessary recommendations, references, and examination certificates from the various educational establishments I had attended from the age of seven, etc. In short I felt that I had been suddenly plunged back into my dear old Denmark—the very Parnassus of rigmarole. So I just decided to trust in my own luck and initiative. Yesterday morning, I took the first train to Berkenbrück and sought out the chief engineer who immediately handed me an invitation card—in fact actually thanked me for my interest in the project and provided me with all the information I asked of him with regard to the engineering work and the necessary preparations.

I'll try and give you some idea of what I saw there, Jakobe. Now the job involves diverting and draining a stretch of the riverbed so that repairs to a bridge pier can be carried out. In the first instance, and in the normal way, attempts were made to put a cofferdam in place across the river, but the current was too strong and they were unable to close off the dam structure without putting in a channel diversion. This, however, was out of the question given the time and expense it would require. But then they came up with the idea (and this was the ingenious aspect to the whole thing) to let the current itself effect the closure of the dam. This was by way of allowing a colossal wooden box to drift into place at the opening of the dam structure. The box had been built to the exact dimensions of the dam entrance, had been weighted down with the appropriate ballast, and was controlled and steered from the shore. The whole thing went like clockwork. As the wooden box jostled into its place (and even a bit before that), you could hear very loud creaks and groans coming from the sidewalls of the dam, and the water levels rose significantly for a while, but the flow of the river really did channel the box nice and easy into place, and in the end, there it was, driven into the mouth of the dam like a cork in a bottle. It was a truly gripping moment. I would have loved you to be there, Jakobe. The overall effect was heightened further by the fact that, at the very same moment, explosions could be heard at a nearby bank excavation, which would give the swelling river levels a temporary release into the surrounding marshland and a connecting lake.

Afterwards, we were served champagne in a marquee that had been set up for the occasion and then there were toasts and speeches. Towards the end of proceedings (now don't fall off your chair Jakobe!) I myself raised a toast, specially dedicated to "German engineers, who had once again proved their brilliance and superiority to the rest of the world." It went down very well. Of course I'm not saying that I didn't struggle with the language, but where I couldn't find the right word or phrase I got by with gestures and hand movements. There were shouts of delight with my impromptu speech and then a whole scrum to shake my hand when I finished. Not only that. On the way home a newspaper reporter asked me to do an interview. You will see my name in lights if you can get today's edition of *Tageblatt*, Jakobe!

And by the way, I got to know somebody else while there—a Professor Pfefferkorn, who may also prove to be very useful during my stay here. He's a lecturer at Berlin's College of Engineering and it turns out—what a small world!—that he is a good friend of our own Aron Israel and in that way has developed a bit of an interest in what's happening in Denmark. As we parted company, he asked me to be sure and pay him a visit while in Berlin.

24th Oct.

You have expressed your displeasure dearest Jakobe at my comments about Dr. Nathan—almost feeling sorry for him and feeling the need to defend him simply because I feel unable to regard him as our guiding light and leader. And of course I should perhaps have added that I have much to thank that man for—I admit that wholeheartedly! But as the dyed-in-the-wool university man that he is, he will always be the out-and-out highbrow aesthete—lacking any real understanding, yes even interest, in the vital things that are needed out there in the real world. The other day, when I tried to give him at least some notion of what my project is about, he barely allowed me to speak. He just kept going on about some theater review he had read, the political situation at home, and God knows what else. The only thing he really had to say about my project was that "it sounds a bit like a fairy tale." Now I ask you! And I'm supposed to look up to this man as my cultural leader! In reality, he is no more of a visionary than Fritjof. He has no notion of the great wonders that the future is winging towards us, and that these wonders will stand the present world order on its head, including the political order of things. A fairy tale, says he! I'll tell you this, Jakobe. Living down here has simply reinforced my view that nothing would be more like living in a "fairy tale" at home if we—with all our natural resources—continue with our present angst-ridden and timid Cinderella syndrome. That pathetic philosophy, which our great rulers seem to think is the best guarantee for our national independence and the natural bedrock of our culture. I maintain that we (in our tin-soldier society at least) have only one way of asserting ourselves amongst the great nations that surround us: money. As I say in my article: "A Lilliput land like Denmark is in itself a ridiculous proposition—such a small and poor country is, at the end of the day, impossible to sustain in our day and age." The only way we can get respect as a nation and people is by having abundance in all things that are naturally ours. The solution to that problem is money, money, and then more money. That lustrous golden sheen, which Nathan and all the others talk so much about, that is going to light up our country will actually come from the glow of high finance, Jakobe. The culture of poverty we have at home is just constant manna from heaven for our backwoods clergymen.

I often think of Venice, which was once a place of no consequence, but then turned its fortunes round to become one of the world's great centers of power. In today's north European transport and communications nexus, towns in Denmark like Hjerting or Esbjerg have a similar geographical advantage to that which raised the former lagoon region to international prominence. While down here, I find myself daydreaming about a future Hjerting or Esbjerg where the palaces of merchants with their golden domes rise up above expansive harbors, while small electrically powered gondolas glide across the sparkling water in the canals.

25th Oct.

Just a few quick words today, dear Jakobe. I've just come from the home of the Commercial Consul and was asked to pass on family greetings to you. I met the lady of the house and the young Frøken while there, and I must say that I received a warm welcome. Your half cousin is quite beautiful and, on top of that, strikingly undemonstrative in her deportment—to the point of shyness I would say. But then she is still so young. Things were otherwise a bit too refined for my liking, Jakobe. There was a groom standing at every door I went through, and I was received in the conservatory, which you have seen for yourself. The conversation was mostly about your Danish branch of the family—though I naturally, and as agreed, didn't mention exactly how things stood between ourselves; I just presented myself as a good friend and frequent visitor to the Salomon household. The day after tomorrow, they are holding a very grand musical soirée, to which I have been invited. Around three hundred invitations have been sent out apparently.

By the way, I'm sitting here writing with my overcoat on, as I am off this minute to meet Fritjof. We've ended up spending quite a lot of evenings together and, despite of all our disagreements, we do get on very well. He really can be most entertaining, Jakobe. He has brought me into the company of some of his German artist friends— half-mad fellows like himself, but appealing and convivial people. But isn't it strange, Jakobe? A few times now, these people have remarked on the similarities between myself and Fritjof. One of them even asked me recently whether I was his younger brother. Now can you explain that to me?

27th Oct.

Once more a very eventful day. I think I've mentioned Professor Pfefferkorn before to you? He is a lecturer at the College of Engineering here and he asked me to call in to him. Well today I did just that. He lives out in Charlottenburg, right by the side of the college, which is more like a palace with columns and statues. Building the whole thing must have cost millions. Professor Pfefferkorn himself gave me a guided tour. I saw the lecture halls, the laboratories and some interesting research and experiment workshops that are linked to the school. What impressed me most, however, was a really brilliantly designed and executed collection of models that showed the most significant aspects of engineering work—bridge building, locks and sluice gates, foundation and excavation work etc. Jakobe, believe me when I say that the place is a veritable playroom and paradise for any engineer worthy of the name. Professor Pfefferkorn promised to obtain permission for me to study there—something that ordinarily is difficult to obtain. As you can imagine, I am thrilled at this. The place is nothing more or less than an Aladdin's cave! I'm actually thinking of attending a series of lectures down here. There is one person, a Professor Freitag, a younger man, who has already gained great renown because of his work on electric motors. Overall, darling, I won't be just resting on my laurels. The tips of my fingers are already itching to start running through logarithms and tables again. Seen against all this, my book is of no consequence or, at least, simply inadequate! But just wait! One, two, three and bang! That nit-picking pedant Sandrup and his petty band of limp-wristed office boys will soon have to run and hide. For I swear, Jakobe, in ten years' time, they won't recognize their own country!

The other day I stood, together with Fritjof, beside the flagpole up on top of the town hall. This is 250 feet above street level. The sun was just beginning to set, but the air was still clear, and I believe I could see for at least a couple of miles in all directions. And everywhere I looked, there were tall buildings and streets stretching as far as the eye could see. The street lamps were already lit and there were telegraph wires, chimney smoke, and soft electric lights illuminating the central railway stations as the trains sped off into the night—and towards the horizon could be seen an undulating landscape of factory yards and huge workshops, which lent an impression of infinity to the city's outer limits. Then it struck me that, just a few generations ago, there was little more here than a relatively unassuming town with train-oil lamps, sawdust pavements, stage coach facilities etc.; and I was gripped by such pride at the thought of simply being a living human being that I—much to Fritjof's huge disgust—started to swing my hat and cheer. Sweet Jesus, these people with their talk of "Art" on painted canvases! My view is that the sight of a railway junction yard like this one in Berlin, all lit up with electric light and flashing junction boxes is far more pleasing to the eye than all of Raphael's Madonnas put together. If I actually believed in some kind of divine providence—I would get down on my knees (even in my best suit!) every morning and say a prayer of gratitude that I was born in this proud century, a century in which man finally became aware of his all-pervading power and began to reshape the world according to his needs and desires— and in a grandeur of scale that no god could ever have dreamed of!

Once Per had left, and now that she was no longer directly influenced by his physical proximity, Jakobe suffered something of a relapse into despondency with regard to her feelings for him. As if the proposed yearlong absence had robbed her of her newly found raison d'être. As soon as she received his very first letter, and especially when she was then obliged to send a reply, she felt very keenly how alien he had once more become to her within the space of a few days. She had suddenly so little to say to him. The many faults she had once seen in him loomed large again and her emotional seizures had come back to haunt her. To read Per's letters, with all their immature bluster, was a humiliating torture for her. They contained nothing of conse- quence and precious little concerning his love for her. Nothing at all on any longing he might feel for her.

But then, after several weeks of this torment, her brother Ivan met Aron Israel by chance out on the street, and Aron showed him a let- ter he had received that very morning from an old friend in Berlin, Professor Pfefferkorn, who spoke in glowing terms about one Per

Sidenius. Ivan asked whether he might be allowed to hold on to the letter for a while and, after reading it out loud to his parents in the sitting room, sent it up to Jakobe in a large sealed envelope bearing the legend: "Vive l'empereur!" The letter said:

"I should mention that I am, at the moment, enjoying an intimate connection with your country via a young man—an engineer by the name of Per Sidenius, who I gather is a personal acquaintance of yours. Per is blessed with such an abundance of natural talent that the Danish nation may, I am sure, expect great things from him. I have had the pleasure of his company on a couple of occasions now, and have therefore been apprised of the ideas he is wrestling with, and I must say that I am greatly taken with his proposals. I have seldom met anyone with such a direct, fresh and vibrant engagement with the natural world in all its different manifestations. I would not exactly say that his overall philosophy of life appeals to me—it is far too worldly and material for my liking—but there is no doubt that his kind of outlook will come to dominate in the future and there is little point in we ancients lamenting that fact. Every historical age has its own set of ideals; and when I listen to your young compatriot as he, without fear or any feeling of inadequacy, grapples with the most outrageously ambitious plans for the transformation of society, based on a steadily growing conquest of nature's forces—well, I believe that I see before me a prototype for the decisive, hands-on man of the coming century."

It was with flaming cheeks and a heaving breast that Jakobe read these lines. And then something most unusual happened; she started to cry. She cried not only because of her sudden great joy but also in shame that she had gone around filling herself full of self-indulgent doubt and had once again betrayed Per with her dark deliberations. "A man for the coming century." Yes, that was precisely the right way to put it. The precise way to illustrate his inner contradictions, excuse his failings, explain his extraordinary power. He was like the first formless template for a coming race of giants, which (as he himself had written) would finally take possession of the world as its rightful rulers and masters—a world which they would then reshape to their own liking and needs. He was a portent, cultivated in the stifling confines of domesticity and burdened with the full gamut of pettifogging timidity, superstition, and subjugation and was, thus, unbending and scornful of all piety. For him, there was no belief in providential powers other than those which sparked a man-made turbine into life. And who could blame him? The nineteenth century's dream of a Golden Age—its beautiful vision of building a kingdom on the twin pillars of good fortune for all and social justice, a kingdom that would come about simply by dint of the spirit of the age and the power of reasoned argument—how withered and anemic that vision looked now!

Even before Per had left for Germany, Jakobe had made attempts to gain an insight into the mysteries of mathematics and modern mechanics, but at that point it had been no more than an impulse driven by her new-found love for Per, an expression of her need to travel all the paths in his life, but she soon found that the problems in actually understanding these disciplines were a great deterrent to any further attempts. However, at this new stage, she once more threw herself into the study of the natural sciences with all the dedication and energy for which the Semitic race is renowned. It soon became clear to her that, without a thorough awareness of the physical sciences, a person in the New Age lacked a basic understanding of modern society and the natural laws which governed its development. Where once the greatest works of literature overwhelmed her desk, and Enevoldsen's *Creation* more often than not lay open at a new page (with the writer's picture used as a marker), there were now textbooks and primers in physics, geometry, and dynamics. Her letters to Per contained regular and precise accounts of her progress and requests for explanations and guidance in her studies.

Thus their relationship had been stood on its head. Jakobe, who previously had regarded herself as Per's intellectual superior, and whose rather tiresome task was to coax her fiancé along in the quest to make amends for his lack of sophistication and upbringing, suddenly had the role of pupil—dependent on his advice and patient explanations. Just as in those days of love's first raptures, she had lifted her pen a dozen times in a single day in order to write to him—sometimes just to scribble a line, be that a joyful cry upon suddenly grasping some difficult geometrical problem, or a simple sigh provoked by his not being there by her side when she needed his help on some issue.

And yes, her love for him was still a large part of her ardor—greater even than she herself realized. Everything that happened to her in the course of a day, even the flightiest of thoughts that strafed her consciousness, she had to report to him, despite the fact that the letters Per sent back failed to reflect her own intimacy and tenderness. But she had gradually become reconciled to this state of affairs. She now understood that she had been demanding something from him which nature had not bestowed upon him. Indeed, she now felt grateful towards him because he refused to be a hypocrite and preferred instead to reveal himself as he truly was.

She also wrote to him about politics—one of her old favorites, especially regarding the various workers' movements, which found themselves at the sharp end of new technological developments. Prior to this, she herself had never really quite understood her abiding interest in this constant narrative of pay disputes and power relationships. For the fact was that they went directly against the grain of her aristocratic instincts. She had always felt a sense of danger at the loud rumblings emanating from this great mass of toilers, whose strident demands seemed to present a threat to everything that she held dearest about life. But through her slowly acquired understanding of Per, she had now gained a measure of clarity as to the reasons for her reluctant feelings of solidarity with the besmirched and downtrodden—that army of workers fighting for the joy of pure light and clean air to breathe. It would be these very people who would forge the new century. Men for the twentieth century!

In the meantime, the days flew by for Per down in Berlin, where he divided his time somewhat equally between his studies and the delights that are to be found in such a great and exciting city. Everyday, he made new friends and was well received in every instance. The pattern was exactly the same as in Denmark: his open, smiling facial expressions allied to a certain impudence, as well as his apparent lack of artifice, won over every heart that encountered him—sometimes also by giving a suggestion of appealing characteristics that were not, in fact, a part of his makeup. It was while in Berlin that Per first truly became aware of his ability to captivate people by way of his personality and, without worrying too much over its provenance or implications, used it with great adroitness. At the same time, he began to affect with great enthusiasm a rather more doubtful Man-of-the-World deportment and, as is so often the case with visitors to a foreign country, only escaped general disapproval at this by the fact that his own bad habits were ascribed to national idiosyncrasies on the part of Danes for which he could not be held personally responsible. Indeed they actually had the effect of increasing his immediate appeal by arousing a sort of ethnographic curiosity amongst his hosts.

At the grand musical evening at the home of the Commercial Consul, Per's presence was inevitably drowned out by the sheer volume of brilliant uniforms and the prominent display of medals and decorations on the dress coats that the gentlemen wore. There was, however, a moment when he did become the subject of general attention as, during a musical interlude, the lady of the house sent word that he should join her and then showed him the honor of entertaining herself with his conversation until the music started up again. This veteran of balls and concerts, who was ostentatiously low-necked in her chosen attire and also caked in make up, had a weakness for young men who could boast a well-developed physique and she did little to hide this particular penchant from her audience. However, Per himself only had eyes for her ladyship's daughter, a nineteen-year-old brunette who was everything her mother was not—a reticent, fine-boned, delightful slip of a thing, who betrayed something close to shyness at any point where a man seemed about to approach her. There was, however, one pleasing similarity with her mother in that she was gorgeously dressed and revealingly so, to a point beyond shame, but entirely in keeping with prevailing aristocratic etiquette. That said, she seemed uncomfortable with her semi-naked state and wherever possible would cover her bosom with a fluttering fan.

Per had enjoyed little more than the chance to bow before her on being announced on first arriving and he could not even be sure that she knew who he was. From then on, she had been continually besieged by uniformed and distinguished-looking cavaliers to the extent that he finally gave up any thoughts of trying to get near her. During the concert, however, he caught her out on two occasions as she attempted to sneak a glance at him from behind her fan; the fact that her gaze had not come to rest upon him by sheer accident was betrayed by her overhasty attempts to look elsewhere when discovered. Yes, Per was convinced that he had seen her blush slightly.

When he left the party much later in the night, and slightly giddy with champagne, his head was buzzing with the most audacious of thoughts. Might there really be a chance for him? He remembered uncle Heinrich's tale of the impoverished Austrian in New York, who had secured the hand of an American oil baron's daughter and was now one of the world's most powerful money oligarchs. This young lady was heiress to a fortune of some fifty million dollars. Fifty million and a gorgeous bride to boot! It was worth a try! Ah rubbish! Fool's talk! But then! Had his good luck and fortune not held in every instance where he had seriously willed a particular thing into being? The truth was that he had not, thus far, dishonored Ivan's prophecy: he came, he saw, and had indeed conquered!

Now it was true that there was Jakobe to be considered—he had not forgotten that—and that of course was a severe obstacle. But he had a right to ask whether a man ought to be bound for ever by past events in his life, when out of the blue such glittering prospects suddenly beckoned. Indeed, was it actually permissible to turn one's back on such a prospect? Could he defend such a decision in the light of that cause to which he had devoted his talents and powers? God knows, he was very fond of Jakobe. He understood that she possessed remarkable attributes that were fully deserving of his praise and appreciation, and the merest thought of having to leave her cut his heart to the quick. But all personal considerations had to be sacrificed to the greater ideal of the common good—Jakobe herself would no doubt understand that and accept it. Fifty million dollars! Wealth like that in a small country like Denmark would procure for her husband the ear of the king himself. What could he not achieve at home with that kind of money! What an enormous boon in the struggle for liberation, a struggle to which Jakobe more than anyone else gave her blessing and wished to promote!

He had no desire to go back to his lodgings just yet, so he strolled along Unter den Linden, whose bars and cafés were still alive with revelers. Per normally tended to avoid these elegant eateries, where to be noticed was the main point to dining out, and one received precious little in return for a rake of shillings. For all his desire to come across as a man of the world, he had a native reluctance to part with his money and the simple truth was that he was always most at ease in one of Fritjof's artist pubs, where he could get a half-pound steak and a fried egg, a round cob of bread as big as his two hands, and then a jug of ale—all garnished by a smile from the pretty waitress—for little more than two marks. But in the champagne atmosphere that pervaded this night, he cast aside all his own petty rules and went into one of the most select wine bars—a favorite haunt of army officers and their ladies, which lay in the vicinity of the city's main keep.

With a half bottle of ice-cooled "Vix Bara" set in front of him and the lively bustle of silk dresses and clink of sabers all around him, Per continued his attempts at self-persuasion. That idea of a baronial title, which uncle Heinrich had planted in his thoughts, was a particular source of head-wrangling. Now that would be a distinct advantage in this new situation! In the circles in which he was now moving, little could be achieved without some kind of auspicious title. But as a baron, he need have no fear of adversarial suitors. All right. It was true that at this point he had very little to go on—nothing more than a stolen glance. But had he started off with anything more? In fact, did he even have that to encourage him when he saw Jakobe for the first time? No. He just needed to implicitly and fearlessly believe in his pact with the Wheel of Fortune—and be true to his own personal battle cry: I will!

It was well past three o'clock before he got home, and in his preoccupied state of mind there could be no thought of sleep. He threw himself onto his bed, drank one glass of water after another, but could not get his thoughts to settle. Though it was not just these fairy tale-fantasies that kept him awake. Here, alone in the somber solitude of his rooms, other thoughts began to loom out of the darkness and set his blood racing.

During the whole of his time in Berlin, he had felt an abiding unease, which just like the fabled shadow, only fully revealed itself when he was alone and stillness had descended around him. It was the thought of his father, and the possibility that he had passed away, that he could not be rid of. That is to say: in the run of a day, when he was occupied with something or sat in a café with friends, this worry barely cost him a thought, but as soon as he was left to his own devices in this alien town, and especially in the evening, upon returning to his empty and cheerless rooms here in Karlsstrasse, the shadow would rise up to confront him. Every night as he stood by his bed in his night shirt and winding his watch, he would ask himself: "I wonder was it today that my father breathed his last?"

It was the same this night.

Towards morning—just as he was about to slip into the realm of sleep—he awoke with a start. From somewhere or other in the room, he had heard a sound; a sound that to his ears was like a sharp knock, repeated three times. He was immediately wide awake. And though he knew that he had cast off all forms of superstition, he could not but wonder whether his father had, at that very moment, departed this mortal coil.

In the morning he had dispatched a telegram home to Eberhard and around noon he received a terse reply: "Father dying." He looked at his watch. In two hours there was an express train to Hamburg. He could be home by the next morning and then be on his way again by evening time. It was an absence of two full days, nothing more—and at least his conscience would be salved.

He stood for one minute more with the watch in his hand. Then he nodded with determination and began to pack his overnight suitcase.

Per himself was not really sure exactly what it was that drove him homewards. It was not just the fear of one day regretting that he had not bade his father a last farewell, even though the chances of a true reconciliation were completely out of the question. In ways barely perceptible to him, his decision was linked to other partly diffuse deliberations that had occupied his mind the previous night and, once again, shades of unconquered phantoms had made their disturbing presence felt. Just like the first Viking Age heathens who converted to Christianity, but still made secret sacrifices to the old pagan gods before any momentous decision was made, Per too felt the need to appease the God his parents worshipped by making this oblation at the very moment when he was readying himself for the last do-or-die battle to win Fortune's golden crown.

A couple of hours later he sat in a train heading north to Denmark.

12

As per's train wended its way overnight through his native Jutland, his thoughts turned more and more to the ill-fated journey he had previously made through that very same countryside. It was almost seven years now since that Christmas trip home and he had never been back since. Yes, he still remembered his homecoming that dark winter's evening, right down to the tiniest detail—how a cold, yellowish fog made up of mist and rain droplets had enveloped the town and rendered the sluggishly burning street lamps even more lethargic. He saw his sister Signe standing there on the drenched platform in that old-fashioned cape that was too short for her, those big black woolen gloves on her hands and the dowdy, long skirt from which her big galoshes protruded. He recalled his father's displeasure at his decision to take a holiday without prior permission from his parents and, more than anything else, his own distress on arriving home and hearing that the dining room floor was being scrubbed—a sure sign that his family had not even bothered to wait for him before eating.

At heart, he was shocked that he still had such vivid memories of these events, which felt ancient to him now and had no significance in his life anymore. Or at least he would not admit to himself that his family home, with all its depressing memories, might still have a hold over him. As far as he was concerned, that time in his life had rarely occupied his thoughts. It was as if the whole thing had become submerged below the new horizons that had arisen in the intervening period.

It was quite early in the morning when he finally reached home. The little town was bathed in clear October sunshine.

Because of Per's mode of dress, he caused something of a sensation on the platform by the simple fact of alighting from the train. He was wearing a charcoal-gray travel coat with silk lining and long tails. The coat also had broad velvet trimmings at the collar and sleeves. On his dark, closely shorn head sat a Scottish beret and beneath the high-cut trousers—as the latest fashion demanded—a pair of light-gray puttees could be spied. His overnight suitcase, hat box, and other travel accessories were also top class and positively shined in their newness.

A pair of farmers dressed in homespun cloth quickly made way for him and then looked on with awe as he strode by. To Per's great satisfaction, he overheard one of them muttering in a low voice to the other: "What would ye give me on that being the young Count Friis himself."

Even though he had sent a telegram announcing his imminent arrival, there was nobody there to meet him. "All the better," he thought, "leaves me free to do what I want!" With that, he resolved to book in to a hotel—something that would be far more suitable from every point of view.

But just as he was about to step on board a hotel omnibus, which was waiting outside the station, he noticed his brother Eberhard approaching from a small park nearby. Per understood immediately that his brother, who was so fastidious where his public persona was concerned, had awaited the train's arrival from the vantage point of the park so that it would appear that he, almost accidentally, had been passing the station while taking a stroll. The newly arrived prodigal gave an involuntary shrug of his shoulders. That kind of superiority complex which previously would have sent him into paroxysms of rage, now simply provoked a feeling of pity.

When Eberhard saw Per standing at the omnibus and negotiating with the hotel concierge, a look of obvious concern flashed across his face and he quickened his step.

"You're not staying at a hotel are you?" he said, almost before they had exchanged greetings.

"I am indeed," Per replied. "Given the way the land lies. I think it best if I cause the least annoyance possible."

"But a room has been made up for you and it's not as if there's not enough space. I'm sure that mother will be very upset if you decide to stay at a hotel instead of with us."

"Well—if you put it like that—would you grab hold of a porter for me?"

These last words were directed to the hotel concierge. Then Per asked Eberhard how things stood with their father.

"Father has been asleep since yesterday evening. For the most part he just lies there in a kind of half doze. In the last few days, he has only really been fully conscious on one or two occasions."

At that point, one of the town porters appeared from the station building along with the hotel concierge who made a whole show of bowing and scraping his hat all the while held expectantly in front of him. Per threw a coin across to him and then told the porter the destination for his luggage.

In the meantime, Eberhard had stepped to the side slightly, the better to size up Per's choice of apparel without being too obvious about it. When he got as far down as his brother's puttees, Eberhard's face revealed positive astonishment.

"I would suggest that we go home along the back of the gardens," he said, as he made to set off down a path that eventually led to the rectory by running along the outskirts of the town—a route which very few townspeople would normally use.

Per immediately protested.

"Going that way makes a long hike of a short walk Eberhard—and I'm actually quite tired."

"All right, if you insist," Eberhard replied with that flinching cheekbone and tight mouth which usually indicated that he found it beneath his dignity to quarrel about such petty issues.

The two brothers walked side by side down the main street but without exchanging a single word.

Returning to the town where he had grown up did not, in the first instance, make any great impression upon Per. With its narrow, winding streets, its single-storey—or rarely more than two-storey—half-timbered houses, underlined as they literally were by a neverending series of gutter planking, the place appeared almost comically toytownish to him in comparison with the world metropolis he had just left. The town had gone the same way as the family home: it had slipped from his life as the years had gone by and no longer even featured in his consciousness. And Per suddenly started smiling at the thought that it had once been his life's ambition to be hailed as the great matador in this dung heap that had done nothing for him other than mutely witness his continued denigration.

For all that, he immediately recognized almost every person that they encountered along the way. Each one of the small houses with their often thickly painted walls and a street mirror in front of the sitting room window, each name over a shop front, each tradesman's sign over a gateway or entrance port, conjured up a particular memory for him. This was particularly so with the old grammar school—its broad gable wall and playground enclosure looming directly over him as he walked by. Playtime had just started as they passed and the phalanx of noise thrown up by the boys was so redolent of his own schooldays that a myriad of partially forgotten childhood memories began to dance in front of his eyes. And there, just beyond the town, lay those sloping hills, the joy of his early youth, and then glimpses of his fjord with the endless expanse of meadows on each bank. He was filled with salt air and water spray as he tumbled on its tides in his makeshift skiff—the first imaginings of his canal project coming to him like a dream as the wind off the fjord reminded him how he first grasped the significance of its power. There he was again releasing his giant dragon-kite "Hero" into the sky, and then attaching his cord to a toy wagon loaded with stones—his shriek of delight when Hero began to pull it down the meadow with the ease of a god at play.

Then Per was brought up short. The school gate was opened and out stepped a tall, stooped man, whom he recognized immediately as his old math teacher. Per tipped his beret, as a matter of course, and then struggled to master a range of emotions that gave a color to his cheeks. As this old doddering man passed him by, clearly oblivious as to who he was, Per was struck by the fact that this veteran schoolmaster in his frayed and threadbare coat had played a decisive role in his life—yes, in fact, his destiny. Without this person's constant and urgent appeals to his father, Per was certain that he would never have gained permission to travel to Copenhagen and study at the National College of Engineering. He would then have been forced to take up an apprenticeship, or forced to work in some grocer's store. And what would have happened to him then?

Eberhard asked him something about his journey, but Per had become lost in his own thoughts and barely heard the question. He burned with humiliation at his inherent, indeed undeniable, affiliation to this grubby little town and its yokel populace. Particularly galling for him was the fact that the relationship was in no way reciprocal. There was Hjerting, the bow-legged general store owner, standing outside the wide doors of his mart in his white khaki apron and wooden clogs, still smoking that same silver-framed Meerschaum pipe; next he saw the barber Siebenhausen, as corpulent and pasty faced as ever he was and—just as in the old days—head protruding from his open window so that he could follow the progress of maids and servant girls up and down the pavement; lastly, there was the town crier whose tinny drumbeat and fishwife voice Per heard coming from a side street—all these people laid claim to a part of him, but he meant nothing at all to any of them.

However, they had now turned into the side street in which the rectory was to be found. Per's first glimpse of its colossal dark walls and foreboding gateway, like the entrance to a prison, but even more so the sight of that paved pathway strewn with tree bark, set his heart racing. The bald fact that he would, within a matter of moments, once again see his mother's face and be standing by his father's death-bed had not really confronted him until that point.

His sister Signe came to meet him in the hallway. She was clearly very moved at seeing her prodigal brother again but merely offered her hand in silence and with her body partially turned away from him, as if some thing had entered the house with him, a thing which made her look away.

"Mother has gone to lie down for a while," she said, when they had entered the dining room, where Per found his two youngest brothers—the twins. They had grown into adolescents during his absence from the home, so much so that he barely recognized them. They accepted his handshake but avoided all eye contact. Signe continued her monologue: "She said that I should call her whenever you arrived, but I really feel, Peter Andreas, that it would be wrong to disturb her. She has watched by father's bedside the whole night through."

Though her father lay at the other end of the spacious ground floor of the house, Signe continued to speak in the kind of hushed tones that become the norm in a home where a family member is not long for this world. Per said that there was absolutely no question of disturbing his mother.

In an exact repeat of his homecoming seven years ago, a tray with *smørrebrød* had been set out for him. Signe poured him a cup of coffee and, in order not to cause offense, Per forced himself to eat something from the tray, even though his anxious state meant that he struggled to get the bread down his throat. From the other end of the room, the twins watched him with large curious eyes. Signe said: "I'm sure you want to go in and see father? He either sleeps or dozes now. He has not been awake since yesterday evening. The nurse is seeing to him just at the minute. I'll go in and ask when you can go in to him."

Signe walked quietly away from him. As she closed the door behind her, she used both hands to make sure that the door would not bang shut. Eberhard had already left the room and, in order to avoid being left alone with their strange brother, the twins also disappeared very quickly through the door into the kitchen.

Per stood up and proceeded to walk up and down the floor, without really being aware that he was doing so. Finally, he positioned himself at one of the windows that looked out onto the little lawn and some of the old crippled trees, which were the height of what the rectory garden had to offer. His heart pounded against his ribcage and his thoughts flew in all directions as he looked for ways to guard against what was to come.

But little by little, as he stood there gazing at the sun-starved patch of green, enclosed by those high defensive walls, he began to regain the courage of his convictions and his thoughts became lucid once more. He had found the vindication he had been seeking. The release from his mental torture came in the very fact of his indifference at once again seeing the first playground of his childhood. Here in this place there was not one person to whom he was beholden. Not one happy memory did he have; not one flash of childhood rapture gave him an empathy with these walls, behind which he had felt like a prisoner serving a fifteen-year sentence. No. It was worse than that! Now it struck him at that very moment—a feeling that, he realized, would not otherwise have been in his nature came quickly stealing over him, a raw and plaintive melancholy, keening the fact that the shadows from these walls had left a dark stain on his life and made bitter his cup of natural joy, and those falsely inculcated feelings had haunted him since.

He gave a nervous start. The door behind him had been opened softly. It was Signe once again.

"You can come in now. Come Peter Andreas. This way."

Per went through the half-empty closet and into the sitting room. The door at the far wall, leading into the bedroom, was ajar. Signe approached it on her tiptoes, pushed gently at it and led Per to the bottom of a bed that had been moved away from the sidewall and into the middle of the floor. It was almost pitch black in there and Per completely lost his bearings for a moment.

Gradually, however, he was able to discern the shape of a shriveled head that lay on its side with its eyes closed—plunged deeply into a large soft pillow—asleep in the way a corpse might sleep. An ice-cold tremor ran through Per's body, though his agitation did not extend beyond the natural sense of foreboding that the sight of human decay and putrefaction excites in someone for whom death is life's greatest horror. Indeed, the fact that his father's condition so clearly obviated any idea of an approach had a calming effect upon him. The thing he had dreaded most of all was the fervent wish on the part of his family that these final moments would bring about a reconciliation. As far as he was concerned, he had nothing to say to his father and anything that his father might have wanted to say would in all likelihood only have made the situation between them more awkward—possibly leading to further unpleasantness, a nasty scene even.

As Per's vision became accustomed to the absence of light in the room, the facial features of the prostrate body in front of him began to take shape in all their emaciated starkness. He saw that his father had retained his mass of hair, but that it had obviously turned completely gray during his long illness. But, the face had become so dark that it was like an ancient bronze figurehead, and this image was further asserted by its complete lack of movement, even as the two flies hovering above it actually settled on its forehead or cheeks. It was as if eternal rest had already descended upon those firmly closed eyelids.

The nurse, who had been standing over at the washstand rinsing out a sponge, carried the bowl of water out of the room, leaving brother and sister alone with their dying father. Not a word passed between them. Signe was sitting in a low armchair by the side of the bed. She sat bent forward, with her hands folded on her knees, gazing at her father with a look that was almost beatific in its expression of love and pain. Her large bright eyes were full of tears and the sides of her mouth were drawn tightly downwards. Every so often she would reach over and gently wave her hand above her father's face to drive the flies away.

Suddenly came the sound of shuffling feet from the far wall. A wallpapered blind door, which led into a guest room, was opened up and his mother's shrunken and crooked form appeared.

She remained there for a moment, as she steadied herself on her black walking stick, while her free hand fumbled at the door frame for support. It was some time before Per could actually grasp that it was her. His only real memories of her were as a bedridden invalid and he had never imagined that she was so small of frame. She had also aged beyond all ken in the intervening years. Not only was her hair nearly white and her features whittled down to sheer bone, the enormous psychological strain of his father's long illness had, in an almost supernatural way, held her upright, and had also now lent an unnatural severity to her countenance, especially in her deeply set eyes that carried a clairvoyant light.

Per's sense of shock overwhelmed him. And the gaze that fell upon him from those eyes, combined with the way his mother held out her hand as he approached her, more to stay his progress than to greet him, left him even more confounded. It was clear that she expected some kind of anguished declaration of repentance from him and, for what seemed an eternity, they stood opposite each other like two mute statues. In the end, though, maternal feelings asserted themselves. As tears ran down her cheeks, she took his head in her hands and placed a kiss on his forehead.

Signe, who had risen from the chair, then helped her to sit down by the bed.

"So you really have come back to us, Peter Andreas," she said. His mother was bent over and half turned away from him in the chair and her hand partially covered her eyes, as if she could still barely tolerate the sight of him. "Why did you not come before this? . . . Now it might be too late."

There was something in this outburst that made him listen. "Too late," he thought. They had actually believed, right to the death, that there would be a reconciliation. They had regarded his homecoming as an act of contrition.

His mother began to speak again, but, at that moment the nurse came in from the sitting room along with an older man.

It was the local doctor, who had come on his daily morning visit. At a sign from his mother, both Per and Signe left the room and the nurse closed the door after them.

Per saw nothing of his mother for the rest of that day and, overall, his return home did not cause the kind of stir it might have done had circumstances been different. Quite naturally, all thoughts were turned to his father's condition and, despite the enforced silence in the house, it was still a hive of activity. One minute there were new sheets and covers to be warmed, the next minute some medicine or other could not be found. Then there was the constant stream of townspeople, arriving at all hours, to hear how things stood with Pastor Sidenius. On top of that, the two remaining siblings yet to return home were due to arrive in the course of that day, namely the brother who was a vicar on the island of Funen and a sister who was married to a doctor with a practice in one of the small towns along the banks of the Limfjord. Rooms had to be made ready for these guests as well, so everybody had their hands full.

Per had been given his old room up in the loft and he spent most of the day there. This was partly so as to make a vain attempt at catching up on lost sleep after his long trip and partly because he wanted to write to Jakobe. He had taken the decision, purely for appearances' sake, to rescind his original decision and remain there until his father had passed on; the way things looked, that moment was not too far away. He was full of little anxieties and was in bad form. No, he did not regret having returned home, but yes he just wanted the whole thing to end as soon as possible. He had only ever seen a person die once before in his life; that was the day in Nyboder when old Senior Boatswain Olufsen had been rushed back from his morning walk. The awful memories he had of that sudden fatality—the blank terror in Boatswain Olufsen's face and the hellish trauma that visited the house that day—the whole thing haunted him constantly.

In the early evening, the remaining brother and sister, Thomas and Ingrid, arrived at the house, the latter accompanied by her husband. Thomas was a ruddy faced theologian, very set in his ways, but with an underlying maelstrom of emotions that were sometimes whipped to frenzy by vague notions that he might yet have a brilliant career. Ingrid was a compact and self-assured provincial wife, a full-blooded Sidenius, for whom her adopted town of Løgstør was a town of some substance simply by the fact of her being there with her husband and children.

The family patriarch had opened his eyes a couple of times during the day, and in those moments seemed to have full clarity of vision, but the few words he spoke were incomprehensible and he soon slipped into unconsciousness again.

The family doctor paid his evening visit and on emerging from the dying patient's room, he turned to Signe, who had followed him out to the hallway: "There's no point in pretending that your father will survive another night. He's very close. I will await word from you when my presence is required."

The doctor's prediction proved to be correct. It was just after two o'clock that night when everyone in the house was roused from their sleep—the final death throes had begun. Per, who was still travel-weary and disoriented after almost two full days of being awake, had fallen into a comatose sleep and could not immediately gain his bearings. He was still partially in a dream state, in which he was traveling through Berlin with Fritjof and some of his artist friends. The entourage had just landed, via a hackney carriage, at their favorite local tavern in Leipzigerstrasse, when the door of his room was opened and Signe appeared at his side holding a candle aloft and asking him to come downstairs.

In a flash, he understood where he was and the import of his sister's visitation. Even for Per Sidenius's ox-like constitution, the sudden switch from the carousing carousel around one of the world's great cities to his sister appearing as an angel of death was too much. Even after he had dressed, he still had to walk backwards and forwards in his room for some time in order to compose himself before going downstairs.

When Per arrived in the rooms below, he found all his brothers and sisters assembled in the sitting room; most of them had not even gone to bed that night, but had dozed in chairs and on the couches in order to be as close to their father as possible should anything happen. The room was fully lit and both wings of the door leading into their father's bedroom had been pushed back completely. Inside the bedroom, only a solitary night lamp burned. It was standing on a table at the top end of the bed and threw a weak pall of light along one side of their father's white shape, leaving the other side in complete darkness.

In order to ease his breathing, Pastor Sidenius had been raised up slightly and supported by pillows. He was fully conscious but could not speak; nor could he lift his blackened eyelids any longer. At that very moment, his children were saying their final goodbyes to him. Their mother called out their names as, one by one, they stepped up to the bed and took his hand, which lay flat and lifeless on the blanket. She was sitting in her low wicker chair by the headboard on the opposite side from the lamp.

Per felt extremely ill at ease with the ceremonial nature of this leave-taking. He had firmly believed that he would be spared such a torture. He held back for as long as possible; but in the end he had no choice but to walk towards the bed, and when he felt the already grave-cold hand of his father and heard his mother call out his name with (as it seemed to him) an emphasis in her voice, an ice cold terror came into his heart, and it was only his awareness that he was being closely watched by all his siblings (who were now all standing round the bed) that gave him the will to control his facial reactions. For a moment he had the completely crushing feeling of having been called forth by some omnipotent judge.

By now the time was between three and four o'clock in the morning. The night watchman could be heard just at that moment walking along the quiet street moving nearer to houses then fading again. Because of all the strewn tree bark out there, his steps could barely be heard. All that could be heard was his monotonous chant, penetrating the room like a ghostly proclamation announcing the arrival of the grim reaper.

> Now black night slinks away
> and a new day dawns.
> God preserve us sinners
> from all those who wish us ill.
> O Holy Father up above
> soften our hearts with your love.
> And in your mercy set us free!

Once the house servants had been presented to the dying patriarch, he signaled by a small nod of his head that he wished to say something.

In a whisper that only his wife could understand, he asked them to sing a psalm. The children went into the sitting room and gathered around the piano. Then, while Signe played, they sang with subdued voices some verses from the psalm "The Lord is my Shepherd there is nothing I shall want."

The only person, besides their mother, who remained in the bedroom was Per. Following his last ever handshake with his father, he had sat down in a dark corner, where he might feel less captive to the will of others. As the quiet singing of his brothers and sisters washed over him, carried by the soft but indomitable strength of their convictions, and they filled with pride as they saw the gates of heaven open above their heads and the gleaming aura of the Lord revealed to them, His outstretched arms ready to receive their father's transfigured soul, Per sat by himself fighting the urge to be swept up in their rapture. Nothing had turned out as he had imagined it would. His mouth quivering and his eyes dilating, he stared over at his father's shriveled head, which lay there in such peaceful repose on the pillow, enveloped by a glow of white hair, like the halo of some holy saint. And with Senior Boatswain Olufsen's gruesome demise still fresh in his mind, he said to himself: And that is how a God fearing Christian meets his death!

When the psalm singing was over, all Per's siblings gradually returned to the death bed scene. By this time, their father's mouth had begun to open slightly and his eyes had collapsed even further into his head. Not long afterwards, the final death throes began.

Fru Sidenius held his right hand and wiped the perspiration from his brow with a cloth. Eberhard and Signe were standing at the other side of the bed, ready to lend a hand if needed.

An hour was passed in this way. Awaiting the final moment, the rest of the children were scattered around the room, in any place where they could find a seat, though the youngest remained standing at the foot of the bed, from whence they gazed down on their father with large sympathetic eyes.

For the second time, they all heard the night watchman's monotone singing out in the quiet street.

All ye heavenly hosts
sing praise to God eternal
who seeks to guide us
on our earthly journey.
Now arise to the new dawn!
For gentle night has
yielded to God's might.
Seize the time while ye can!

Almost nothing stirred in their father's room. The only sound was the steadily weakening gasps of his troubled breathing and the occasional suppressed sob from one of the children.

It was now approaching five o'clock in the morning. Fru Sidenius's upper body was now almost prostrate on the bed and her forehead was pressed against her dying husband's lifeless hand, her tears dropping through his fingers. Eberhard was holding his father's left wrist in a perfunctory fashion. As he counted his father's slowly declining pulse, Signe watched his face intently for any change in its expression. The clock in the sitting room was just about to strike the hour. At that same moment, Eberhard turned towards her—as if listening intently to something. Shortly afterwards, he walked softly around the end of the bed to his mother and placed his hand gingerly on her shoulder: "Mother dearest. Father has passed on."

In an instant, everybody in the room stood up and moved to form a circle around the bed. Only Fru Sidenius remained seated. At first, she looked up at Eberhard with a pleading expression of helplessness. Then she buried her face into her dead husband's hand—it was as if she could not bear to look at his face and its voided stare. But now she raised her head and looked at him for some time in silence. Then she said: "Well my dear children. Your father has left us. But—thanks be to God and all praise to Him!—it is not goodbye for ever. He has just gone before us to our heavenly home, where at some point, with God's grace and help, we will be brought together again."

In a gripping valediction, she then thanked him for all the things he had been and meant for them all, praised his faithfulness to her and their home, thanked him for the great love he had shown and the sacrifices he had made—and in a very moving way, the feelings from the days of their youthful romance were resurrected in the tenderness with which she stroked his white hair and kissed his forehead.

The children remained, for some considerable time, standing around the bed in silent prayer and reflection. But at the first visible signs of rigid death, Eberhard and Thomas spread a sheet very gingerly over the corpse and led their mother away.

Shortly afterwards, Per went up to his room. The lamp on his table was still lit. The window shutters were still open and the first ribbons of daylight were beginning to illuminate the room. For a long time, he simply stood at the window, staring out across the town as it woke to a new dawn. Even though the sound of carts and wagons was beginning to rise in the morning air, to accompany the clatter of work-bound clogs in nearby streets, some pale stars were still clinging to the heavenly vault.

A conviction arose in Per's heart that the things he had experienced that night represented a watershed in his life. But beyond that, he could not arrange his feelings into any kind of clear, overall idea. He was still too taken up with the momentous occasion that he had just witnessed to be able to think clearly.

At last he sat down at the table and got out his travel stationery. He felt the need to communicate with someone and decided to write to Jakobe. The previous day he had sent her a fairly terse note declaring his presence back in Denmark. Now he wrote: "I thought I should inform you right away that my aging father passed away just a few minutes ago. Nor will I hide from you the fact that I am glad I took the decision to come here. Regardless of the differences that arose between myself and father, it has to be said that he only ever acted in accordance with his convictions and conscience. He died a beautiful death. He was conscious almost right to the end and faced death with an admirable mental and spiritual fortitude."

His hand stopped at that point. And as he cast his eye over what he had written, Per's cheeks colored. He then sat still with a self-conscious look in his eyes and biting at the end of his pen. Then he suddenly tore the letter up and began again.

"My dearest Jakobe! I have the unfortunate duty to inform you that my father died in the night. In other words, I got here with enough time to pay my last respects, as was my intention. He was fully conscious and completely at ease until the very end. But that, of course, goes without saying! His whole life has been one long, so to speak, preparation for death. I send these few lines in all haste. You will hear from me again soon."

After having signed the letter, he sat back and pondered things uneasily for some time. Then, as a PS, he added: "I may stay on for the burial."

Pastor Sidenius was buried five days later. From the crack of dawn onwards, flags were flown at half mast all about the town and, in keeping with the tradition of honoring the dead, sand and spruce twigs had been strewn along the lengthy route from the church to the graveyard. Even the church had been adorned the day before by young schoolgirls who had put up plants and foliage. Wreaths and memorial garlands also hung from the altar and the intricately carved baptismal font. Both of the twelve-armed polished brass chandeliers were fully lit and the organ issued subdued, mournful tones as the congregation filed in just after the church clock had signaled noon.

Proof that it was not just curiosity that had brought so many people there was given by the hushed atmosphere that reigned across the pews, and the many contemplative faces. In life, and now in death, Pastor Sidenius had experienced the usual run of things where strong taskmasters are concerned: once resistance to his strict regime had been broken, it was very quickly replaced by idolization. And (as is also usually the case), the very characteristics that had originally caused so much resentment—his assumed imperious authority; his contempt for accepted conventions in the town; his strictly frugal lifestyle and conservative mode of dress—were now praised as bearing witness to his truly apostolic fervor and piety. Yet, it was also true that he had changed somewhat over the years. Gradually, after the people had yielded to the Church's fiat, the more rounded and endearing side of his nature had come to the fore. But that did not mean a change in his essential quiet aloofness, nor his steadfast refusal to engage with the very active social circuit in the town. His own door he kept firmly shut, except for those who were in spiritual crisis. And in this regard, he never forgot a single soul who had come to him regarding matters of faith and conscience. A true supplicant never left him without feeling spiritually strengthened and enriched. Moreover, and in spite of Pastor Sidenius's alleged spiritually restricted horizons, he had proved to be a highly gifted man—meditative, eloquent and always highly engaged with the latest theological conflicts. He would even sometimes lift his own pen and make a personal intervention in such discussions. The little town's population had always felt honored whenever they saw that he had been mentioned in such religious journals and pamphlets that were to be found in most homes, and this, of course, had also contributed to the sea change in attitudes towards their pastor, so much so that he enjoyed a different standing within the priest class as a whole to that of the finely dressed rural deans and provosts who had previously been the main source of pride in the town.

All this goodwill was now augmented by dint of his lengthy bedridden sickness and the extraordinary equanimity he had shown, not only in the face of his obvious suffering, but also when it became clear that he was going to die. The good pastor had been confined to bed for more than half a year with the full knowledge that he was marked for death. And not only had he never complained about his fate, he refused all others the right to sympathize on his behalf. "We will have none of that talk here," he had commanded a certain person one day, who had tried to console him by expressing the hope that Pastor Sidenius might yet recover: "Are we God's children, yet cannot show our gratitude when our Father calls us home?"

The black coffin had been placed up in the church choir and, in accordance with the wishes of the deceased, bore no decoration other than a simple cross made of spruce on top of the lid. Pastor Sidenius had always spoken out against what he called people's cringing need to prettify death and "place garlands around something that was nothing more than a useful pit for hungry worms," as he would often say. However, around fifty ornately dressed clergymen sat around the coffin as a kind of honor guard and the town's most eminent personages were to be seen in the coveted pews at the top of the aisle: state functionaries in uniform, members of the town council; indeed, even officers from the army garrison were there in their spanking bandoliers and gleaming dragoon helmets in their laps.

Per looked about the church with a rising sense of astonishment. It was true that he had already gained an insight into the hegemony which the church hierarchy had gained in this town, a town that formerly had only worshipped at the altar of Mammon and paid no more than lip service to God. Yet with each moment that now passed, his preconceptions about his father and his personal significance were being turned upside down. One minister after another rose from behind the coffin to speak and the church echoed to words and songs of praise to God for his departed servant and the great works and labors he had performed while on earth. Finally, once all the speeches had at last come to an end, eight young men of the cloth lifted the coffin down from the bier, the congregation rose as one and formed up behind the horse-drawn hearse that was waiting outside. The procession then made its way through the streets of the town in the long walk to the cemetery.

Per did not understand it. That it really was his own father—the same man of whom he had felt so ashamed, given that he had formerly been the butt of ridicule and mockery right across the town—that this funeral cortege was like that of a prince being followed to his grave by a grieving populace! He found it difficult to take it all in. For here was one of his proudest childhood dreams writ large but in an unexpected and mortifying way—his dream from that time when he imagined that he had been switched as a baby, that he was really the son of a king snatched by gypsies, who would one day return home and bask in his father's reflected glory.

On the way home from the funeral, Per ended up walking with

his brother Thomas, who had officiated at the graveside and was still clad in his vestments. Of all the Sidenius siblings, and despite the difference in age, Thomas had been the one who had shown most understanding and patience towards Per, perhaps because he himself had, during his own youth, sometimes felt a similar sense of oppression under their father's absolute authority. In his student years, Thomas had been enamored with certain, less prescriptive movements within the Christian congregation than their father felt was appropriate and there had been an element of compulsion in his reluctant donning of the official garb of the Lutheran Danish State Church— that long, funereal coverlet, which, apart from anything else, was ill suited to his red cheeks and light baby blue eyes.

Per had noticed that, during his time at home and in a situation where they had been together quite often, Thomas had made several attempts at breaking down the barrier that stood between them. But Per was not interested in any kind of reconciliation. His warning antennae had been raised by the rather sanctimonious niceness that was second nature to his brother Thomas, and via which he had occasionally won Per's confidence in the old days. Thus, on this occasion as well, Per denied his brother any chance of initiating a real conversation. A great unease had come over him and he felt an instinctive fear at the idea of confiding his thoughts, even to his possibly well-meaning brother.

In the end, Thomas abandoned his attempts at making an approach to Per and the two brothers walked side by side in silence for the remainder of the journey back to the rectory.

When everybody had returned home, they all went in to their mother, who was lying in bed and had been too weak to attend the burial service. Now that the unending tension she had lived through had vanished following her husband's death, she suffered an immediate collapse, and the doctor had ordered complete rest and the least possible agitation. Per had, therefore, hardly seen her during this period. He was only called in to her once and he had sat for a couple of minutes by her bedside, but she was able to do little more than ask a few simple questions as to his general wellbeing.

Nor on this occasion was there anything other than a single word and a handshake and Per went up to his room straight afterwards in order to pack his things. He burned with impatience to get away and had resolved to leave that very evening.

This was not because he had, in any way, grounds for complaint regarding his stay at the rectory. Not only Thomas, but all his other brothers and sisters had, as if by silent oath, made it their business to attend to his needs as much as they possibly could, or at least as far as their conscience would allow. It was also true that he spent most of his time in his room or in taking long walking tours around the area. In fact, on one particular day, he had been away from the house a full twenty-four hours, as he had taken the opportunity to travel up to a new cement factory on the banks of the Limfjord, which he had been wanting to inspect for some time.

Neither his mother nor any of his brothers and sisters had so much as breathed a word about his engagement; and as he could not imagine that Eberhard had refrained from announcing this huge news, Per felt somewhat stung by their silence. At the same time, there were reasons to be satisfied that Jakobe's name had never been mentioned, even if he was no longer thinking of breaking from her. The things he had experienced over the preceding days had already persuaded him of that—had got him in fact to think again, caused him to draw in his horns. The champagne-fueled fervor that had driven his desire to claim a place at the top table of the European money elite had been destroyed during that fateful night he had spent in his father's dark vault of death. Now he could not even bare to think such thoughts. But precisely because he felt such real shame over the disloyalty his sudden pompous whim had betrayed towards Jakobe, his preference was to avoid having to speak about her at all.

In the gathering gloom of early evening, Per went in to his mother to take leave of her, safe in the knowledge that his siblings had all gone to the cemetery in order to inspect and tend to their father's grave and thus he could be sure to be left alone with her.

"Sit down there next to me son," she said. Once more her voice had reverted to that dispiriting, plaintive tone he knew so well from his childhood days. "We've barely had a chance to get talking to each other. And now you're heading off again your brothers and sisters tell me."

"Yes mother, I've to get back to my work."

His mother lay for a while, waiting for him to continue. But when no further explanation was forthcoming, she said: "Your work? Aye well, I know so little about what you get up to Peter Andreas, or where you come and go to. You were in Germany now. Isn't that right . . . Berlin, I believe."

"Yes."

Again his mother gave a pause. Then she continued: "Well now, your father, may God have mercy on him, and myself came to understand that you must have gained some sort of wealthy benefactor, seeing that you can go rushing round Europe the way you are doing. For you've no real work as far as we can see."

Per's ears pricked up at this. He now understood that his mother knew nothing about his engagement. His brothers and sisters had obviously kept the news from her, presumably so as to protect her from yet another cause for sorrow. Or perhaps Eberhard had actually refrained from even mentioning it to anyone, be that his parents or his siblings. That would be just like him. And if that was the case, it was hardly done simply out of concern for his parents.

While Per was preoccupied with this question, his mother had turned to a little table beside the bed's headboard and had taken something from its draw compartment.

"Now, Peter Andreas, you are going to leave us again, without finding out what your father would have liked to say to you before he closed his eyes for the last time. But I can tell you as your mother, that he had an unshakable belief that you would one day find yourself again and seek out the path of humility, and there was never a day went by where he didn't speak of this and include you in his prayers. A while ago, when he heard that you had gone to live abroad, and therefore believed that he had to give up any hope of seeing you again, he asked me to send this keepsake to you after he died."

She handed him the little object she had taken from the draw. It was his father's old silver watch, which Pastor Sidenius had always held in great esteem and had worn until the very end. He was wont to describe it as the only earthly treasure he had ever possessed.

"This watch," his mother continued, "has a history to it and your father would have told the whole thing if he could have just spoken to you one more time. But I can do it in his stead, and when you have heard it, you yourself will understand why it was just this gift that he felt was right for you."

She reclined slightly and, for the rest of the time she spoke, kept her eyes closed, just as Per's father had done throughout his own lengthy sickness.

"When your father was just a half-grown boy, he was once at home at the rectory up on the heath for the Christmas holidays and was due to go back to grammar school. Then your grandfather asked him for the key to his travel bag so that, as he put it, he could check whether everything had been packed properly and nothing overlooked before it was put into the carriage. Now your father was highly offended at this—just as right throughout his youth he was very quick to take offense—and he left the house without even saying a proper farewell to his father. When he got to school that evening and opened up his suitcase he saw that his clothes were just as he had packed them and had not been disturbed in any way. But in one of the corners was a small paper parcel. It was that watch you are now holding in your hand. It was a gift from your grandfather to his own son and, of course, your father now understood that the whole carry-on with the key had been a ruse so that he could leave it in the suitcase, without your father seeing it. That way it would be a lovely surprise for him, something to cherish from home now that he was back in that strange place. When your father understood this, he cried sore and when he was cried out and repented his hastiness, he put on his overcoat and hat and walked that very same night the twenty miles back home, and could not settle his heart until he had put his arms around his father's neck and begged his forgiveness. See my boy. That's the reason your father kept that watch throughout his whole blessed life as a sort of holy relic. I remember he once called it God's christening gift to him. Because that very same night, Peter Andreas, after your father had walked through the fires of penitence and humbled himself before his earthly father, he also found the way, the truth and the light and peace descended upon him—God the heavenly father had sent the Holy Ghost and he was anointed with the flame of salvation and was saved."

While she spoke, Per sat there with the watch and felt it becoming heavier and heavier, like a tomb in his hand. When she stopped speaking, he said nothing. The room was by now in complete darkness. His mother had opened her eyes but could not see her son's facial expressions. Not a word was said.

Per rose to leave shortly afterwards and as his mother kissed his brow, she whispered a prayer over his head: "May the Lord always watch over you and give you peace!"

Not long after that Per took a carriage to the station. His brothers and sisters had all returned from the graveyard, but he was determined to go to the station on his own and had very firmly rejected all offers of company.

When Signe went up to Per's room an hour later, she found her father's timepiece lying in the middle of the table. It had clearly been placed there in such a way that it could not be missed, or be construed as having been left behind by accident.

13

PER WAS back in Berlin but the city no longer held the same attraction for him. Fritjof had gone home in the meantime and the sheer size of the city simply served to reinforce his sense of loneliness. There was also the fact that autumn had well and truly set in. Many shops and cafés were lit up from the start of the day onwards, a mizzling rain fell from the heavens early and late, and then the more regular heavy belts of rain left inch-high puddles on the pavements. Most of the time, Per sat at home on his own and tried to study. His hope was that a concentrated bout of hard work would conquer the immense feeling of ennui, which he had brought back with him from the rectory, but even his own private rooms gave him no peace or sense of comfort. His landlady, Frau Kumminach—a slothful and unhygienic stump of a woman, who had a boil the size of a fist on one side of her neck—cooked sauerkraut all day and everyday; the stove in his main room leaked smoke and fumes and, from the floor above him, where there was a small garment factory came a constant and monotonous din from ten sewing machines—all of this would often leave him half-demented.

Always strongly impressionable, the more so as he got older, Per gradually came to perceive the hellish side of life in a modern, sprawling city. To add fuel to this fire, and very quickly after his return from Denmark, a series of small incidents gave him an even more intimate view of the living conditions that were typical for millions of Berlin's citizens—the kind of insight that had an unsettling effect upon him.

When he had originally rented his rooms, Per made sure to insist that no fellow lodgers would be imposed upon him, with all the

330 · HENRIK PONTOPPIDAN

330 · HENRIK PONTOPPIDAN

disruption of his work this would entail, and the landlady had sworn on her highest honor that this would be the case. In fact, she had even waved a police document around, which clearly stated that she was prohibited from renting out anything other than the two modest rooms he was now inhabiting. Besides which, the entire apartment consisted of nothing more than those small rooms and then a little dungeon-like space behind the kitchen, where an iron bed could just about fit, and where the proprietress herself seemed to have her abode. Nevertheless, he had not been there many days before it became clear to him that at least one more person was lodging in the environs of his apartment. He knew this because, on a couple of occasions, he had been woken in the night by the sound of a man's hollow coughing and Per had finally worked out that this noise was emanating from the hallway, or rather, from the space between the hallway ceiling and a closet-like enclosure out there, which served as a wardrobe. Per then began to interrogate the landlady but she, not without a certain edge to her voice, swore on all that was holy that Per was impugning her reputation. She continued to produce a string of explanations, even when he surprised a young bleach-faced fellow in the kitchen one Sunday morning, who sat in shirtsleeves, shaving himself in front of a stump of mirror. After this incident, Per gave up trying to get to the bottom of the whole affair, even though he could not be wholly certain that she did not have more night guests hidden away in other nooks and crannies in the apartment. For the fact was that, alongside the dry coughing, he had also one night heard the sonorous sound of deep and satisfied snoring, and such eruptions did not, as far as he could make out, come from the landlady's room. Then, by inquiring amongst others, Per found out that, in many places, the actual lodger often merely served as a decoy for an irregular mass of drifters, consisting of those nomadic souls who flock like moths to the bright lights of any big city—not con-merchants or professional idlers who might be pleased to admit that their night lodgings were not exactly "choice," but relatively well reared young men: shop assistants and clerks, factory workers and barbers apprentices, waiters and so on, people for whom having a home was a superfluous luxury. They spent their leisure hours roaming the streets, in shebeens, low-life dancehalls, and public houses, and then, somewhere or other, they would have recourse to a sleeping billet where they might spend what few hours of the night were remaining. Their only possessions were those they stood up in, and they moved from area to area at the drop of a hat. It was a way of life that was forced upon them by the struggle for survival that constantly raged in this kind of metropolis—a struggle that very quickly became second nature to them. The ones for whom living on their wits in the streets came most easily, and who were in general happy to move around, were also the ones who had least problems finding some kind of work. For nomads such as these, domestic bliss, peace, and contentedness were completely alien concepts and therefore were not found wanting in their lives. Overall, and despite his initial feelings, Per decided that it was pointless to indulge in too much sympathy for these people. What was there to cry over really? It was just a change in social conventions, that was all.

But then, one morning, he happened to overhear his landlady in conversation with a male voice out in the hallway. It was a police officer who was trying to verify some information given by a barber's apprentice. The night before this man had ended up in one of the city's hospitals and had given the landlady's address as his sleeping quarters—the place where he slept. This apprentice had suffered a violent hemorrhage while drinking in an alehouse and had died shortly after being admitted to hospital. When Frau Kumminach, who had otherwise remained silent, heard this last detail, she suddenly exploded into verbal eloquence. What utter nonsense! The police knew very well that she was not allowed to take on that kind of lodger. And nothing but a barber's apprentice! That anyone could imagine that she, a respectable woman with the noblest of guests, would be happy to entertain a vagabond like that, someone who was not only a stinking scoundrel but was also TB-ridden and had snuffed it in the street!

Per's very spine turned cold as he listened to this ghoulish description of his fellow "phantom" lodger. He was quite certain that the young man whose posthumous reputation was now being so badly traduced was the very same man whose nightly living quarters had been the wall space in the ceiling; nor had he heard his familiar, hollow cough for a few days now. Per could not help but reflect on what his own fate might be were he, for example, to fall sick in this place and require constant medical attention. Nor was this simply a figment of his momentarily fevered imagination, as he really did feel quite unwell. Some kind of influenza had descended upon him during his return trip from home and, in the damp weather that prevailed here in Berlin, he had been unable to shake it off.

This was another reason to refrain from going out, unless this was absolutely necessary. He had not even made attempts to keep alive his acquaintanceship with Fritjof's brotherhood of artists at the pub in Leipzigerstrasse, preferring instead to eat at a restaurant around the corner from where he lived. Not even the delights of the Commercial Consul's hospitality could tempt him anymore.

He wrote to Jakobe almost daily during this period of inner desolation and it was not to be helped that his letters bore the stamp of the angst he felt, regardless of the trouble he took to try and hide it from her. Of himself, and against his usual custom, he wrote nothing at all. On the other hand, he wrote expansively and at furious speed about the random incidents he had witnessed out in the streets of the city; or he would entertain her with rather shameless sketches depicting Frau Kumminach and the dead barber's apprentice, and that persistent stink of sauerkraut.

Thus, Per drove the time in this way until the end of November. Then, one day, he received a letter via Ivan from Blackbourn & Gries, the large English engineering company to whom Per's future father-in-law had written a letter of recommendation. There was no question of obtaining a position with the firm; all that was promised him was the facility, as a student intern, to follow daily work assignments on a large-scale realignment scheme and he would be told more about this at a later date. But Per saw that even this could be of great benefit to him and, on the spot, he resolved to leave Berlin immediately. He was hardly going to learn anything new by extending his stay and, besides, there was no doubt that a change of air would improve his feelings of hang-dog flu. He knew very little about the town of Dresack, where the work was being carried out, other than the fact that it was a small settlement up in the Austrian Alps. His plan now was to spend the winter there and, once the snows had begun to melt, to go across to Vienna. From there he would go on to Budapest where he could inspect the huge dredging operations that were taking place at the mouth of the Danube. After that he would go to Paris, London, and then New York.

On the journey down to Dresack, Per stopped at Linz because of the nine-hundred-foot-long railway bridge that was to be viewed there. He arrived there late in the afternoon, and it was from here that he first caught sight of the ethereal white peaks of the Alps edging the far horizon. As they reflected the distant glow of a fiery sunset, they seemed to hover in the evening haze like a vision from the beginnings of time. The next morning Per was traveling through the heart of these very same mountains and as the weather was magnificent, and the fact that he had been extremely irritated by oafish and over-familiar fellow travelers from Germany, he stepped off the train at a small rural station. Despite the time of year, he spent the rest of the day under open skies. There was something up there in that wasteland of snow and rocks that called out to him. He was drawn higher and higher along the upland meadows, as if by some secret charm that might carry him away from all earthly troubles and oppression.

Alone, and without a guide, he followed a mountain trail, which wound its way up a steep and barren cliff side. Down at the station, he had been warned against setting off without a guide, but Per's wish was to defy the anxiety that undoubtedly pressed upon him in these singular and mighty surroundings. He began to climb without further thought. So this was a mountain landscape! He breathed great drafts of the strong, snow-cold air and felt only elation, looked at the clouds sailing far below him in the valley, and felt a bond emerging with nature in these few hours that he had never known before.

As a boy growing up, the forests and meadows had been his play-ground—the refuge to which he would always yearn to escape, his secret place where he could just run riot and be cleansed of the oppressive atmosphere at home. Since that time, he had never had the chance to be so intimately engaged with nature and the great outdoors. Instead, he had sat there in his poky Nyboder backroom, studying the natural environment through the prism of ordinance survey maps, shamelessly viewing the natural world as nothing more than a vehicle for his creative urges. A simple question of some rocks and lumps of earth that were there to be exploited. At the sight of a field, his thoughts would immediately turn to level instruments and slide rules; and he had never been able to sit by a window in a railway carriage for very long before the powers of his imagination would begin to wrestle with the landscape through which he was traveling—the new roads that could be laid, marshland that could be reclaimed, bridges and channel excavations that could be put in place.

With these new horizons, it was not in fact the beauty of nature that struck him with such effect. It was still the case that he lacked all feeling for color and linear effect. No, it was the grandeur out here, the spirit, nature's abiding mystery. The unease in his mind had now made him receptive to these things. The sheer vastness of those massive peaks; the majestic forms that dominated nature's realm and the profound and eternal silence that prevailed there. All this provoked feelings and emotions that were new and remarkable to him.

More accurately still, it was not so much the landscape itself that had affected him, but rather the way in which it had combined with his sense of utter isolation to bring about such a reaction in him. He had now reached an altitude of several thousand feet and all that lay ahead of him was a vast snowfield, which at its upper reaches was broken by overhanging ridges of naked cliff. The rocks had taken on a russet-gray hue from the sun's rays. Out of breath from the exertions of his climb and the rarefied air, Per was frequently forced to stop in order to catch his breath. And as he stood there leaning on his walking stick, beholding the wild and silent scene that was all about him, he found that he could lose himself in long bouts of wonder at his own feelings. He asked himself how it was possible that there could be anything attractive, indeed mentally exhilarating, in walking hour after hour through a completely mute and lifeless desert of stone and rock. How was it that something as undesirable as the sheer silence that reigned here could have such a momentous and liberating effect on his mind? Or were there, in fact, things he could hear? Were those of a religious persuasion to some extent correct when they spoke of there being natural phenomena that were "beyond our ken"? Were there sound waves in the ether that could not be picked up by the human ear? And that which we called death, was it not, perhaps, just another form of life, which could only be divined by the awakened senses of the "Soul"?

He remembered how one of the ministers who spoke beside his father's coffin had described nature's stillness as "God's voice," and he had used this point to explain why the ancient prophets had always, in their moments of doubt and despair, sought refuge in the solitude that the desert could offer them. God's voice! Well, was the truth not more the fact that when one came face to face with the empty and silent void, the human mind became gripped by "horror vacui"—just as the ancients had described it all those eons ago. And that angst created hallucinations, and the hallucinations begat new fear, and so it had progressed down through the ages until God was created and Heaven and Hell populated.

He climbed another few hundred feet and stopped once more to regain his breath. Always, that same frozen wilderness, that same sense of mute calm! These snow-covered titans really did give a powerful sense of the forces that had been at play on that ur-night when mother earth was created. And as he surveyed their extreme heights, he was gripped by a dizzying sense that he had come close to the epicenter of that primeval moment. All notions of time shrank to nothing at the sight of these rigid masses of stone and their sheer indifference to all things. They were as bare and untouched as they had been millions of years ago when the almighty architect had been "pleased to create them by his own hand"—or at least that was what was written. Really? A divine architect? A glowing ur-mist? A still-nascent solar system! And behind it? Nothing! Absolutely nothing! Ice cold and dark! Deathly quiet.

Evening had descended by the time Per arrived back at the village railway station. Concerns had already been raised about his wellbeing down in the village, and at the inn where he had left his luggage there had been talk of sending out a rescue party to look for him. Dog-tired after the day's exertions, and his head buzzing from too much thinking, Per's only thought was to get to bed; but there was now a new situation to consider. As soon as he had arrived in the village earlier that day, he had noticed that preparations were being made for some kind of event in the town. The doorway leading into the guest house was garlanded with green ivy and the staff had been so busy that they barely had time to show him his room. It was clear now that a wedding was taking place. A large crowd was milling about in the reception area and he too was soon invited to the festivities. In the first instance he politely declined, but had barely had time to slip into his room before there was a knock at the door and two young girls presented themselves. They bowed, started to speak at the same time, giggled, and began shoving at each other with their elbows. They then gave some kind of long winded speech, the gist of which Per took to mean that the bride and groom requested the honor of his attendance at their wedding celebrations. With that his resistance collapsed and he was obliged to drink and dance the whole night, to the point where his senses became quite scrambled.

Although the invitation may have been an expected gesture to a stranger, he was overwhelmed by the generosity that was shown him. The men were nearly going so far as to offer their womenfolk to him, so keen were they that he should be made welcome and enjoy himself. Outside, by the exterior gateway, which was as high and wide as a barn door, a dance floor had been laid and a cither and harmonica provided the rhythm for the sturdy, studded dancing shoes worn by the locals. In the reception room, were two covered trestle tables, one of which groaned under the weight of a whole, roasted goat with gilded horns. The wine was poured from large tin jugs and, as the night progressed, the open pleasure in drinking and consorting with the opposite sex stood in marked contrast to the large number of crucifixes and religious symbols that adorned the house and indeed were to be seen on every roadway in the country.

Gradually, Per too embraced this rural Bacchanal. He recalled what Fritjof had always preached about such children of nature—that they were always the happiest of people. With a toss of their heads at those two pieces of wood that were nailed together to form a cross, they cocked a snook at all those life and death mysteries and simply allowed the music to banish their sorrows.

It had been his intention to move on the next morning; but one day went by, and then two, and yes it was nearly a week before he finally departed. At the wedding party, he had made the acquaintance of a young lady who had held him captive. She was a broad-shouldered farmer's girl with that tendency towards solidity and ungainliness for which the women of the Alps were renowned; but for all that she had a bold, upturned nose and the kind of cherry-blond hair which had always held an allure for him. Quite by chance, they had come to sit next to each other on a bench beside the gateway. Per had sat down simply to watch the dancing but the pair had soon fallen into conversation. He had not understood very much of what she said, and she had not understood him at all. For this reason, there was much laughter and gesticulation and they soon became more intimate. She was twenty-two years of age and lived just outside the village with her mother, who Per managed to temporarily blind by flashing a number of large gold florins on his first visit to her house.

He had thrown himself into this liaison with a lack of restraint that was not solely due to erotic attraction. As with most of his emotions, there was an element of deliberation there, and it was with genuine reluctance that he was unfaithful to Jakobe. However, he needed to get away from the ceaseless and futile brooding that had plagued him since the death of his father and which, he now realized, was sending him down the road to mental illness. He understood that he had to guard against isolation and, for this reason, when he was not with his young wench he would retire to the taproom at the guesthouse and enjoy the company of the proprietor and other towns-folk. The wine would flow and the exhalations from so many pipes left blue clouds of smoke hovering below the ceiling in the room. At the same time, the circle of conversation grew ever greater around him as the most fantastic rumors about why Per had landed amongst them and the size of his private fortune were bandied about by local people.

After a full week of this, he suddenly broke camp. A wine-fueled crowd of well-wishers followed him to the station, while the cherry-blond maid sat at home on the edge of her bed and cried sorely.

But his father's shadow followed him still.

Dresack lay in a narrow, half-mile-long ravine which was rarely touched by the sun. At the base of the ravine, a quick-flowing mountain stream developed into a river, which tumbled downwards and formed an unbroken series of minor waterfalls. The upper mountain reaches directly above Dresack were covered in forest, almost all the way to the top of the mountain peaks; but the view to the south was closed off by a vast, and completely bare, reddish-gray escarpment—"Hoher Göll," whose snow-covered ridges were hidden by clouds for most of the year. The village lay roughly at the bottom of this escarpment and consisted of two rows of wooden houses in a compact terrace arrangement. These houses formed an *S* shape on either side of a steeply climbing street, which was effectively the continuation of the main roadway that ran along the right side of the river. Just outside the village, at the top of a small protruding hill, around which the river flowed, lay the old remnants of a castle. The local populace used this as a public meeting place. On the other side of the road, the church rose above the village with its spear-sharp, blood-colored spire.

For up to almost a year before Per's arrival, fertile meadowlands had stretched along either side of the river, and by the largest of the cascades there had been two sawmills and a bone mill for animal feed. Now, however, the bottom of the valley was a riot of fallen trees, mountains of gravel, slices of huge rock and mounds of stone. Large expanses of forest lay in tangled heaps with tree stumps and roots projecting into the air and their crowns buried in pools of clay. Remnants of buildings protruded at certain points between the clumps of stone and tree roots; here there might be a shattered timber beam, there a set of rusting machine parts. The whole of the most low-lying part of the village, along with the railway station, had been washed away one night in early spring when Hoher Göll had shaken its long white snowy locks after eight days of uninterrupted rain. The resulting deluge of water had struck so suddenly that the people of Dresack were forced to flee their homes in nothing but their nightwear. Five people, along with around fifty head of cattle, were dragged away by the avalanche and crushed against nearby rocks.

Eight months after this, the clean-up work had got to the stage where the railway line was now usable again. Stretches of roadway leading into the village that had been washed away had been temporarily replaced with wooden bridges. Work had also started on changing the course of the stream by dynamiting. The idea was to create a kind of emergency flood plain behind the projecting hillock on which the old castle was situated. The presence of this large physical obstruction had been part of the reason for the subsequent flooding. A hundred workers were engaged full time at the site and three of Blackbourn & Gries's engineers had taken up residence in Dresack.

Per had rented some rooms from the widow of an old saddlemaker who lived in the middle of the village. The house was a brown, tarred log house with a tiled roof and a partially enclosed upper gallery that looked out across the valley. He had two spacious but dark rooms with low ceilings in the upper storey of this house and had organized his things with an almost military precision—something that was inimical to the creation of a cozy atmosphere. In spite of his almost obsessive attention to domestic detail and his abiding need for home comforts, Per was quite lacking in the ability to create a sense of homeliness around himself. It was as if his frequent mental turmoil immediately left its mark on the places he chose to inhabit. From his makeshift study, there was a door that led out to the ornate gallery that overhung the street, and here it was that he stood for the first time in the evening, wrapped in his traveling cape and looking out across the gloomy and foreboding mountain chasms up around Hoher Göll, whose vast snowfield was bathed in moonlight. Deep in the valley below, he could hear the river tumbling and gurgling. He could also just about hear its irregular passage through the debris of stone and rubble further down, which in places was illuminated by warning flares at the points where dynamiting had taken place that day.

The feeling of helplessness in the face of nature's omnipotence that had gripped him at his first sight of the colossal Alps, at once uplifting and yet somehow so discouraging, had not diminished since. In his manifesto he had preached that man, who was previously enslaved by the wild elements, would very soon be able to harness thunder and lightning itself to drive his triumphal chariot of progress—storms would be his riding whip. But now, when confronted with this monstrous act of natural destruction in the village, he was forced to acknowledge that mankind's existence in this world was still subject to Mother Nature's whim and caprice. After a few more weeks of staying in the village, Per wrote to Jakobe. She had been waiting impatiently for him to issue a public defense of his manifesto after a spiteful attack that had been made against it in a professional journal:

"You ask me whether or not I have received the copy of the *Industrial Times* and seem to be surprised that I have not responded to its negative pronouncements on my book. But why, tell me Jakobe, do I need to give any response? How important is that criticism really? You write that you were looking forward to seeing me destroy my opponent and rip up his doubtful calculations like old newspapers, but it seems to me that you are taking the whole thing far too seriously. For God's sake, Jakobe! It's only a book after all—and on top of that, a book that I'm no longer completely happy with. I have to admit that it contains elements of youthful naiveté here and there which should really have been left out. Unfortunately—humiliating as it undoubtedly is for us human beings—we have no choice but to admit that at the moment our mastery over nature has very weak foundations, and the explanation for this, we might reasonably conclude, lies in the fact that so many people, and I'm talking about relatively enlightened folk, still see the trace of an eternal guiding hand in the natural world—an immutable power and overarching will."

Jakobe never answered this letter and Per, for his part, never broached the subject of his book and its fate ever again. Per was not, in truth, unhappy with the silence, or even indifference, with which his book had been received in all other places outside of the heavily undersubscribed *Industrial Times*. Overall, his letters to Jakobe became shorter and more seldom as the winter progressed. He wrote mostly about the weather, the progress with the clean-up work and related issues; or he gave brief sketches of life in the village, often, once again, in a humorous tone. All this was meant to conceal the spiritual crisis he was suffering, the significance of which he finally came to understand.

In truth, he experienced very little more that he could write about, apart from those things he did not wish to speak of because of the shame he felt. He met the Blackbourn & Gries engineers on a daily basis at the works site but otherwise did not fraternize with them. They were three cold-blooded whisky drinkers, who had caroused and gallivanted in all four corners of the world and from the very first day had dealt with Per—or the "Greenlander" as they called him—with a wounding arrogance, partly because of his barbaric utterances when trying to speak English. However, their attitude was changed after they had invited Per to Christmas Eve at the local inn, "The Good Neighbor," which was their nightly drinking den. For Per proceeded to drink them all so severely under the table on this occasion that two of them were given emergency beds at the inn and the third was trundled home in a wheelbarrow. With this great feat, he took the view that his honor had been restored and this engineering triumvirate really did change their behavior towards him from that day forth. Be that as it may, Per never became a member of their drinking club and was rarely seen in the taproom.

He chose instead to spend the long evenings in his own company and occupied himself by reading. It was often well into the small hours before he extinguished his lamp. He had once again, and with all that stubborn determination for which Jutlanders are famous, thrown himself into the task of acquiring knowledge in a discipline far removed from his own profession. Nor was this, as had been the case the previous year, just in order to satisfy a vainglorious desire to keep abreast of the topics being discussed in high society, but rather

from a real, deeply felt urge to obtain a more fundamental understanding of life's deepest philosophical questions. He was absolutely
methodical in his reading schedule. Accustomed as he was from his
studies in mathematics and natural science, to search for evidence
via an unbroken chain of deductions, he went systematically from
one book and then on to another, to which reference had been made
in the previous book. In this way, he pursued the idea he was wrestling
with back to even older texts, attempting to find his way to the original
argument and, thus, arrive at the definitive truth of a proposition that
would remove all uncertainty. In order that Jakobe should not get wind
of it, he arranged for the books to be sent to him directly from a Copenhagen bookseller without—as he normally would—using Ivan as
the middle man. Gradually, a veritable library of philosophical, aesthetic,
and theological treatises were stacked up on his work table.

But the more he read, the more confused he became. Throughout
his steadfast search for the touchstone of that final and incontrovert-
ible phrase or word that for all time would banish every superstitious
belief in the existence of "the other side," he staggered around as if
in some mental game of blind man's bluff played in the dark of his
own confusion. Every time he felt that he had got close to the final
proof, he heard a cry of "here!" right at the other end of the echoing
halls of speculation; or he would feel that his head had suddenly
struck a brick wall in the form of an ancient and impenetrable work
by an old Greek or Latin philosopher. For all that, he never gave up
hope. With the implicit faith in books, which every autodidact de-
velops, he even stayed at home through the day so that he might get
that bit closer to squeezing out a result from his studies. For he was
in a hurry! Weeks, even months, had now passed and he had made
that promise to himself that he would not leave Dresack before he
had achieved full clarity, absolute assurance of what it actually meant
to exist.

One evening at the start of March, Per was walking homewards
from one of the works sites on the other side of the river. He was tired
after the day's exertions and dragged his feet as he walked along the
road in a pair of calf-length, hook-laced engineering boots. Spring

had suddenly arrived in the air over the last few days. The sound of avalanches high up in the mountains had been heard down in the valley with greater frequency and the floodwaters had risen by several feet. The first anniversary of the village's great catastrophe was approaching and Per, who had already been made anxious by his fruitless brooding and the sheer solitude of life here below the threatening banks of mountains and cliffs overhead, was slightly spooked by the overwrought sensibilities of the local populace. The local newspaper had already reported several substantial landslides in the higher reaches of the mountains.

The sun had just gone down behind the massive crest of mountains in the west. Hoher Goll's white peak was aglow and its snowfields were dressed like lava streams around its flanks.

On the temporary timber bridge that had been laid across the river, a group of men had taken up their by now usual positions, holding long fishing harpoons with which they impaled and hooked out the bits of wood that regularly flowed downstream. Per would usually stop for a moment and watch these fishers of river flotsam, whose long spikes regularly plumped into the water, with the accuracy of Zeus himself, to pluck out even the smallest stump of wood that was tumbling and swirling around in the foaming water below. But this evening he passed them by while lost in his own thoughts, and in his self-preoccupied state answered their German greeting "Gott zum Gruss" with a simple "good evening."

Per's thoughts were solely focused on Denmark and home. One of his main concerns was whether a letter might have arrived from Jakobe. He had not heard from her in over a week and could not fathom her sudden silence. It was true that he himself had not written for some time. The truth was that the obligation to compose these irrelevant jottings, and the constant dissembling they involved, had become a mental torture for him. But, as far as he was concerned, his own silence meant just one more reason why Jakobe ought to have written to him by now. For all she knew, he could have fallen seriously ill, or some other even worse mishap could have befallen him, something that would have made it impossible for him to write.

"Was there any mail for me today?" he asked his landlady, old Frau Babi, who had hurried to open the hall door for him after spying his approach through her window.

"No, sir," the little matron replied with a severely exaggerated bow.

Despite this, when he got up to his rooms, Per could not refrain from glancing over at his work table, from whence Jakobe's oblong envelopes, with her large and familiar slanted style of writing, would normally be there to greet him. Up until now, these had always been there every other day on his return from work. He gave a deliberate shrug of his shoulders and walked around the room for a while, a low whistle on his lips—all this representing a failed attempt to shake off the cloak of despondency that had settled over him. Then he sat down in an old armchair in front of the open stove in which two weighty pieces of wood burned brightly. Day turned to evening in an instant. Darkness spread from every nook and cranny in the grim and forbidding room, while Per sat in a prone position with his elbows on his knees staring into the flames.

Jakobe's silence had begun to worry him greatly. Had she fallen ill? No, if that was the case he would have definitely heard from Ivan. No. There was some other reason. But what?

He saw her in his mind's eye, just as she probably was right that minute, sitting at the sumptuous dinner table at home along with her parents, brothers, and sisters. He saw the expansive table, illuminated by the brilliant chandelier, the festive table decorations, the flower arrangements and the perennially bulging fruit bowl. There was Philip Salomon with pride of place in his high-backed, gilt-leather chair with his serviette under his chin. Ivan, Nanny, and all the other children scattered at random, without regard to age or gender—all chattering and talking across each other with such great buoyancy. Only Jakobe, as always, was sitting there quietly, somewhat aloof, pale and serious of countenance—"The Wise Old Owl" as her father had humorously dubbed her—while Nanny more venomously had preferred the moniker "House Matron Strict."

Then, out of the blue, another figure emerged in the tapestry—Eybert. Per was aware that Jakobe's former worshipper had once more begun frequenting the house. Jakobe herself had informed him of this. She had, he supposed, never really been able to completely rid herself of a certain fondness for this apostle of sobriety and restraint with his prim face and plastered-down strands of hair. And now he thought of it, there had been some element of reserve, something doubtful and secretive in her most recent letters. Was she perhaps considering breaking off their engagement? And was her silence the best way to prepare him for that fateful moment? What was going on?

One thing was certain, the mutual attraction they had discovered was not, either for him or for her, developed from any heightened or refined sensibilities; nor were they based on a harmonic meeting of minds and character. Particularly in this last while, it had become frighteningly clear to him how essentially different they were in every regard. He was convinced that, even if he were able to persuade himself to admit his innermost thoughts to her, and the kind of things he had been brooding over during the long winter months—well, she would never have understood what he was talking about. Various statements Jakobe had made came to his mind—where she had spoken in disparaging terms of those people who suffered "sudden attacks of religious scruples." Perhaps it really would be for the best, for both of them, if they parted now before things became more awkward still.

As he sat there engrossed in these twilight thoughts, the door leading onto the landing was opened and Frau Babi stole into the room. From the very first day there had been something about this small busybody woman, who in her quick, mouse-like, and timorous movements, indeed in her very essence, strongly reminded Per of the simple and equally timid Trine at the house in Nyboder. On occasions, he actually had difficulty shaking off the superstitious notion that she really was the reincarnation of his ever dutiful personal servant from those poverty-stricken years who now fussed over him like some old maid.

She had come in to light the lamp and set Per's table for his evening meal, but when the splay of light from the stove revealed to her that he was still sat in his muddied work boots, she went directly into his bedroom and fetched his slippers.

"Would sir not prefer to change his shoes?" she asked, placing the shoes down in front of him.

Per gave no answer. It was only when she began busying herself with lighting the lamp and closing the window shutters that he became conscious of her presence. Shortly afterwards, she left the room again.

Per remained sitting by the stove in a prone position. With his arms resting heavily on his knees, he stared at the dying light of the fire and quickly sank back into his dark musing. However, it was not Jakobe he was thinking of anymore. Constantly during this period, whenever he had time to think for himself, his thoughts would turn to his mother, wander uneasily around the rectory and end at his father's grave. Then he gave a sudden start—just as he had done every time, either in his dreams or fully awake, when he called his father's old timepiece to mind. Despite the fact that it had been just as much a case of fear as defiance or contempt that had motivated him to behave in that way towards his mother, he preferred to dismiss all thoughts of the incident and quickly turn to some other subject. He would not—could not—dwell on it.

He rose quickly from his chair. Frau Babi, who had been down in the kitchen, entered the room at the same moment with the evening's supper dish on a tray.

"And what do you have for me today?" he asked.

"A bit of ham, sir!"

"Ham, always ham!" he muttered in a low breath—he felt the urge to give voice to his bad mood. "Do you not think you could be a bit more imaginative?"

While his landlady laid the table, he went out on to the balcony to embrace the shock of the brisk evening air, which swooped down through the valley from the heights of Hoher Göll. Darkness now reigned over the village. Flames danced from braziers lit by night watchmen at some of the work places and a line of oil lamps outside the railway station blinked their drowsy light into the night air.

Everywhere was still. Only the river was to be heard and the muffled rumble of a train some distance away. There was one other rumble—the distant shuddering sound of an avalanche. Dark and threatening cloud banks hung over the mountain tops, but directly over Per's head the skies were clear and the constellations made their march across the heavens.

How many times in the last few months had he stood there in the evening, exhausted and dejected after yet more fruitless reading, and staring up at that writhing luminous mass of planets and stars? Then he had imagined that this celestial scripture perhaps held the key to the mysteries of life and death for the person who could interpret its symbolic code. And what mysterious symbols! Just like the most ancient of pictorial creations from the dawn of mankind, here were all kinds of animal shapes clearly depicted in flaming points of form: the Lion, the Great Bear, the Serpent, Taurus the Bull—the whole lost paradise writ large, man's first ABC. And at the center of all these wild animals: the Sign of the Cross, more clear and ablaze than any other constellation and crowned by the light of the Milky Way, like some regal aura.

For the second time that evening, he flinched involuntarily. A sharp and drawn-out whistle echoed across the valley. The express train coming down from the north was announcing its arrival. Per could already see the fiery eyes of the locomotive blazing through the dark plain; then came the hiss of brakes and, some minutes after that, the short train rattled into the station like an overridden horse being pulled up sharply in front of the station building. Its delay there was only momentary. A couple of carriage doors were opened and banged shut, a bell was sounded, a guard whistled, then the driver gave a short hoot to signal the train's onward journey.

Per kept following the train and its brightly illuminated carriages rolling through the night, right to the point where, with a sharp whistle, the long twist of white smoke from its funnel disappeared into the tunnel below Hoher Göll. And, as so often before, this whole scene of thundering energy reminded him that all that he needed was to will it to be so and, within a few hours, he could be hundreds of miles from this stone dungeon in which he had been incarcerated for almost three months. As quickly as the next day, he could be traveling through northern Italy with its bright and festive landscapes, the fragrance of flowers and good food all about him. Was he not his own Lord and Master? There were no duties or obligations that tied him to this place. But then how would that help? How would dashing off to somewhere else in that huge world out there help solve his problems, while he had still not vanquished that continual nightmare, which paralyzed his thoughts and sapped him of all blood, energy, and fortitude? No, it was here, where he had set his battle standard, that the fight would be fought to the end. Here in this dark mountain crypt, he would conquer those monsters and phantoms—or they would conquer him.

When he came into his sitting room again, the table had been laid. Frau Babi waited humbly by the side of his chair, so that she could slide it into place as he sat down.

"All right," he cried aloud, in a new attempt to cheer himself up. "Let me try and devour this ham."

"Please don't be annoyed," the little housewife stammered, full of remorse. "You know yourself, sir, that in these parts it is so difficult to get fresh food."

She even speaks like Trine! Per thought to himself.

"Now madam. Don't take it to heart," Per said, suddenly completely disarmed. "I'm well aware that I've been somewhat, shall we say, unreasonable this last while. But it's only fair to tell you that certain things have not been going too well."

"I nearly guessed that myself sir. And, sir, you have not looked the best in recent days, if you don't mind me saying."

"Ahh! Do you think so?" he asked, feeling immediately less well. He then tried to clear his throat but found that he was hoarse. It had to be the dose he had picked up in Berlin that was still lodged in his body. There was nothing else for it but to go to a doctor and have his lungs checked.

At that very moment there was a knock down below at the door leading out onto the street and Frau Babi went down to see who was there. Shortly afterwards she returned with highly flushed cheeks to say that there was a lady who wished to speak with him.

"A lady?" said Per as he lowered his fork. "There must be some mistake. I know no lady in this town."

"Oh she is not from Dresack. She must have come in on the train."

"On the train," Per said with no little surprise and looking doubtfully at his landlady.

Footsteps could now be heard coming up the staircase. Moments later, a dark lady in traveling apparel and with a smile on her face appeared in the doorway. An expensive fur stole was hanging loosely from her shoulders.

"I heard your voice Per," she said. "Good evening sir! Don't look so worried."

Per was now on his feet.

"My God … Jakobe! It's you?"

"Yes it really is me standing in front of you!" she said, with an apparently calm demeanor—with the strict self-control she was able to exert upon her delicate sensitivities whenever she was full of emotion, an agitated state exacerbated by a worry that her sudden appearance was not entirely welcome.

"But … what … I mean how—?"

"Yes, I know I should have sent a telegram, but for the whole journey there was barely a chance to do anything. And then I thought of the surprise you would get if I just turned up unannounced. Of course I was banking on the fact that you would actually be at home. But take off my coat man! At least make a pretense at gallantry!"

Only when Jakobe had been relieved of her traveling cape, had removed her hat and rearranged her hair, did she allow a quite disoriented Per to take her into his hesitant, outstretched arms. Even though she trembled with the urge to throw herself into a passionate embrace, she sufficed with taking his head between her hands and kissing his brow.

"Welcome—is what one would normally say. Or are you not glad to see me at all?"

Per had not immediately been clear as to what exactly it was—this feeling that had overwhelmed him on seeing her once again. His first thought—the one his guilty conscience had provoked in him—was that she had come to spy on him. But now that he held her in his arms and saw her large dark eyes, radiating nothing but love and self-sacrifice he understood everything. At that moment it was as if a huge lump of iron that had been crushing his chest had suddenly melted. For the first time since his initial romance, when he fell for the little saddlemaker's daughter from Kerteminde, he became gripped by such emotions that tears began to well in his eyes.

"So that's why you stopped writing!"

"And you never guessed why?"

At the sight of Per's moistened eyes, tears broke freely from her own; and when she heard Frau Babi close the door behind her, after the landlady had finally understood that her presence was superfluous to requirements, Jakobe could wait no longer. With a great shout of joy, she threw her arms around his shoulders and pressed herself into him.

"So you have missed me terribly, just like I've missed you. And now I'm here Per! It's really true! The moment I've dreamed of so often!" She closed her eyes and clung more closely to his chest—"No, it's not a dream anymore! I can hear your strong beating heart once again. Ah Per—my darling Per! My friend! My best friend and my very own man!"

They stood locked in this embrace, heedless of all time. Per stroked her hair in silence—he could still not find sufficient words, so overwhelmed was he, and so many questions tumbling around in his mind. At last, they composed themselves somewhat and were able to speak in whole sentences.

"Why I didn't write to say that I was on the way?" she asked rhetorically when they had sat down beside each other. They were on the wooden bench between the two windows, still holding hands and continually breaking off attempts to speak so as to steal yet more kisses. "No my darling man. It was better this way! Don't forget that I was not really sure about how things would go, until I could actually look into your eyes. Though it's true that I had thought about making the journey for quite some time. I mean, that I had to come down here before you took off to somewhere much further away... Per, I felt that you had drifted away from me over the course of this long winter; you wrote so little about yourself and what your thoughts were that in the end I felt I barely knew you anymore!... So the other day I told my mother and father that I wanted to pay Klara Hertz a visit down in Breslau—you know, she's one of my old friends from school and lives down there. Well, they saw nothing wrong in that and gave me their blessing but, at the same time, I didn't dare really—a hundred and one things could have gone wrong—you can imagine how I was Per. I was on pins!— then at the last moment, Ivan decides that he wants to travel with me. But, as you can imagine, that was soon knocked on the head. And so here I am!"

Several times during Jakobe's explanation, Per had looked at the ground. He understood only too well that she set great store by being truthful and honest (her slightly regretful tone had also revealed this), and the personal price she would have paid by embroiling herself in so much intrigue vis-à-vis her parents and siblings. And all this she had willingly offered up; all that worry and fretting, so many possible pitfalls, and then the prejudices she had defied, all because she had understood that he needed her!

He could barely look at her anymore due to his shame over what he had been thinking about only minutes before her arrival. "And now?" he asked hesitantly. "Now you are going to stay here?"

"Yes. For two days. I daren't stay any longer without sending a letter. Then I'll move on to Breslau. I take it there's some kind of inn or guesthouse where I can stay?"

"No, you won't be staying there, Jakobe, it's an awful place. You can stay here and I'll move down to the inn for the time that you're here. You saw my landlady earlier. She's not the worst of them. A kindly soul and she will look after you well."

"Yes of course dear. If that's what you want. But now darling," she said as she gave a maternal stroke of his hair and looked directly into his eyes. "Now you have to tell all. How are you really?... Not great, I think?... You seem anxious and strained to me."

Per became uneasy and looked away so as to avoid her gaze.

"Oh, I've been doing all right I suppose. Naturally, as you can imagine, things have not exactly been fun and games here, Jakobe.

But this part of the world has its own wonderful attractions...and the work has been really interesting and informative."

Jakobe had slowly removed her hand and a momentary silence emerged between them. But then she turned directly towards him again and softly placed her arms around his neck.

"Per," she said. "Why do you still not place your trust in me? Do you really believe that you would be able to hide things from me?... No, no—please don't start making excuses! Just be completely honest with me! And, anyway, is there any reason why the two of us shouldn't be able to speak frankly to each other about things like this? Even though I may not understand everything, I know enough to realize that people who have been brought up in a strict Christian tradition—regardless of whether they now believe or not—will be subject to sudden attacks of scruples and doubt, and from the start I have assumed that Per Sidenius would be no different. But I've also always been convinced that you would be able to overcome them."

"You are right, of course," Per said, his cheeks scarlet with mortification. He freed himself from her and stood up. "I really have been in a kind of mental turmoil." He now proceeded to pace the floor. "It is laughable really! Well almost laughable anyway. I suppose it's the sheer isolation of this place and...and then that damned priest blood running through my veins—that whole pack of pipe-collared ancestors who suddenly began to haunt me. But don't you worry, Jakobe. All that is behind me now! I can assure you of that...I'm back to my old self now! Oh yes..."

Jakobe remained sitting on the bench in silence for a moment, withdrawn and contemplative. Then she stood up and went over to Per. Instead of offering her views, she stroked him on the cheek and said: "Well there'll be no more talk of that tonight darling angel! And I'm so sorry, I forgot! I landed right in the middle of your evening meal. But that's perfect because I've just realized that I could eat a horse. I hardly ate at all on the journey down here. We'll have to eat together."

"Yes, of course, my love!" Per cried, delighted at the change of subject. "I'll call the landlady right now. I just hope she has something that you can actually eat."

"Per, at this point I'm past caring. When I'm this hungry, I'm like a pig, or blazing fire even—everything gets devoured! Go and talk to the lady of the house and I'll make myself a bit more respectable. Will you bring my small travel bag as well Per? I left it at the foot of the stairs."

While Per got the table rearranged and had poor Frau Babi quite demented with his torrent of requests, Jakobe retreated to her bedroom next door and, when she finally emerged from there, she had reset the small curls at her temples and decorated her dark gray travel dress with a broad, high collar, a profusion of black lacework and lilac silk ribbons. She took a small spray of violets from her belt and fastened them into the buttonhole of Per's jacket and, after once more taking his head between her hands and showering him with hot fervent kisses, they sat down to eat.

Despite Per's genuine happiness and gratitude that she had come to see him, some restraint and hesitation had still hampered his interaction with her. He had felt oppressed by the imbalance between her great, self-sacrificial, consciously reckless love for him and his own feelings for her. He had never attempted to kid himself with regard to the nature of his feelings for her. At every stage of their relationship, he had been very clear about exactly what, and how much, she meant to him. If it was the case that she had, on occasions, aroused intimations in him of the heavenly joys that love could offer, it was also true that her overdelicate, stick-like body, and the whole alien nature of her outward appearance, offered little attraction to his male sensuality. And the seismic fervor with which, for her part, she had embraced their relationship, had acted more like an ice-water bath than an aphrodisiac.

Now though, as they sat there at the table, which from precious little means had been transformed by way of a shining white tablecloth and a pair of old three-branched copper candleholders, she aroused for the first time the whole of his desire—even though the large collar arrangement over her dress did not entirely suit her. It had been such a long time since he had even been physically close to a young woman; he had lived like a cloistered monk in this dungeon of stone and rock—lost in the shadows of his own thoughts and tribulations. His lusts and desires were now fully alive in his blood, his courage and energy had returned, and he was in full spate.

Glass after glass of the strong mountain wine he drank. Jakobe's cheeks also became more and more flushed and, despite her hunger, she sometimes forgot to eat with all the clinking of glasses, salutations, kisses and embraces.

When they finally rose from the table, Per gave an excited cry: "But wait Jakobe, you haven't done the tour of my apartment yet. First of all, you have to see the view."

Per threw her cape around her shoulders and led her out onto the balcony. All about in the village, and down by the station building, most lights had already been extinguished. But the heavens were a vast canopy of twinkling stars and planets. The clouds had rolled down from the mountain ridges and settled in the ravines and crevices, where they would stay for the night. Only over Hoher Göll's snowfields was there a dark, brownish fog.

Per began to describe how night after night he had stood there and listened to Mother Nature speaking to him through the dark foaming river, feeling as if he were the very last person in a world that had actually ceased to be. But Jakobe was no longer listening to a word he said. She had pressed herself close into him and interrupted him every other minute by putting her lips to his. At last, he too stopped talking and they simply stood holding each other, their only form of enunciation being the gazes they exchanged and long long kisses.

All at once came the long rolling boom of an avalanche high up in Hoher Göll. Per lifted his head in order to listen, but Jakobe remained stock still. Even when he alerted her to the deep rumble and its import, which was repeated a few minutes later, she still gave no answer. The only thing she heard in the whole wide world was the mutual beating of their hearts.

When they had finally come into the sitting room again, Per mentioned the lateness of the hour and the fact that he would soon have to find a bed for himself. To this she gave no answer. Somewhat bewildered, he then went into his bedroom to collect his toiletry bag and other small things. When he returned, she was standing by the window with her back to him.

"Right then, Jakobe, I'll head down to the inn," he said, moving towards her so as to bid her good night. She did not turn around, and he kissed her twice on the cheek without obtaining any equivalent sign of affection from her. But when he made to go, she seized his hand and held him there—quiet but determined.

Per looked searchingly at her.

Then she nodded towards the wooden sofa and said: "Would it not be better if you slept on that. Then you would be near to me the whole night and I could take care of you. I don't like the thought of you being in a some rough tavern."

Per bent down towards her. Not being entirely sure if he had understood her correctly, he wanted to look into her eyes. She leaned into him and pressed her hand against his heart.

The next morning she was woken by the feel of sunlight, warm on her cheeks, as it fell in squares of light through the window frames. She raised herself on one elbow and looked around with surprised, wide open eyes. The door leading into the other room was ajar and when she heard someone tentatively pottering around in there, her face broadened into a smile.

"Per!" she called out with joy.

On hearing his footsteps, her cheeks colored for a moment. But even before he came through the door, her arms were stretched out to greet him.

He walked in quietly and knelt by the side of the bed. "Well, you had a good sleep my love!" he said, as he grabbed her hands.

"I know Per, can you believe it! Me, who in the last six months or so could not get a wink of sleep without my Amylen tablets. In fact, I've been living on my nerves and have hardly been able to string two words together from the moment you left me . . . But hold on? You're up and dressed and have obviously already been out. I can smell the morning freshness in your hair."

"No, I was just out on the balcony. I didn't want to be too far away from you."

"Ah—now I understand!—it was you all along that I heard moving around in my dreams. But then you must have been up and about for ages. Did you not sleep well yourself?... Not a wink?... Not even a snooze? My poor little Per! Then that bench in there was too hard for you after all. Now what did I say?"

"No it wasn't that at all. But, Jakobe, there is something!"

"What? What is it angel of my heart?" She now saw for the first time how upset, in fact distraught, he was and a fear came upon her. "What is it Per? Has something happened?"

"Jakobe—I'm going to tell you everything. I won't get peace until I own up to something... I have to tell you that—"

She placed her hand gently over his mouth.

"I already know everything that you are going to say... but I don't want to hear any of it. Per, whatever is in the past can stay in the past and is forgotten!"

"And you can forgive me... all that? Will you forget that I spoke to you about love and won your heart and returned your kisses before I even knew what love really meant? Because it's true—I have to say it right out—only after last night do I really understand what love is about. And I feel ashamed at how mean and low I've been, and how little I've understood of life really. Will you forgive me those things?"

"Per, my darling!" she said. She then gave a look, like a woman carrying a burden she was happy to bear, and pulled his head to her breast. "Do you not understand that I did that a long, long time ago."

Several days later, Jakobe and Per were to be found climbing a steep mountain pathway, which wound its way upwards between alternating terrain of bare rock and bush vegetation. The sun had reached its zenith and burned down on the russet gray rocks; spring pulsed in the air around them in strong scents of spruce and pine.

They were on the slopes of the Laugen range, on the southern side of the Alps. The very next day after Jakobe's appearance in Dresack, they had broken camp to go southwards and greet the approaching summer weather and this was now the eighth day of their wandering either side of the Etsch Valley, like two intrepid explorers. They had slept in Alpine lodges, bought bread and eggs in mountain villages, and slaked their thirst in forest streams. On the third day of their Alpine odyssey, Jakobe wrote home and informed her mother exactly where she was because, as she calmly explained, she simply could not resist the temptation of welcoming the arrival of spring and so she had done a detour on her way to Breslau via South Tyrol. Without expressly naming Per, she had also told her mother not to fret about her as she had "obtained the services of a perfect Alpine guide."

Now she staggered slowly and falteringly up the rocky pathway, an Alpine walking stick in her hand and the skirts of her dress raised clear of her shoes. Per marched resolutely in her wake. He carried a simple green rucksack on his back, which contained all their traveling baggage. Jakobe would often stop and turn around so as to take Per into her arms and give him a kiss. They had both become tanned by the spring sunshine, and the normally so correctly arranged locks at Jakobe's temple flowed wild and free, gypsy fashion, around her ears and neck. And how her eyes shone, and her lips blushed with the joys of love.

It has to be said that she would never make a mountaineer. Every half hour or so, she had been forced to take a rest and Per had carried her over streams and helped her along in places where the path was either too steep or fell away too abruptly. But he was far from unhappy at this. She was so light and seraphic that he loved to feel her in his arms. Moreover, these frequent rest stops as they traversed forests and mountain glens were a perfect pretext for idyllic, or more ardent, scenes of passion and romance, which both of them would best reflect on when a full day's hiking and exploring had come to an end.

For Per, these days really had meant the birth of something new, a new baptism. All at once, life took on a fullness and beauty he had never dreamed of. He had wandered the Alps in a daze of revelation and with a feeling that he had acquired a new set of senses. Everything that he had ever prayed for in terms of happiness and good fortune seemed to him now to be trivial and petty in comparison with the amount of pleasure that might lie hidden in one single kiss. Jakobe too had become transformed for him. He loved her now as that woman who had bestowed a new life upon him—who had expanded the world for him exponentially, and in whose zealous embrace he had found the charm that drove death's shadow from his door.

But now these halcyon days were over—at least temporarily. Out of deference to her parents, Jakobe could not postpone the dreaded moment of separation any longer. They had been determined to reach Botzen before evening time. From there, Jakobe was to take the night train northwards, while Per would go back to Dresack to put his things in order and then continue his journey out into the big wide world, just as had been planned and agreed.

Thus, on this day, they were more inwardly charged. When their eyes met, Jakobe would still smile; but even the most subtle of her caresses carried an underlying fervor, which signaled the pain in her heart. In the end, she refused to let go of him, preferring to walk slowly by his side with his arm about her waist and her head tucked into his shoulder; and when they stopped to kiss, she closed her eyes, so that she could embrace that joyous now and etch it into her memory forever.

They had once again reached a part of the trail which involved a steep, winding descent. Here stood a pair of small chestnut trees, which offered a measure of shade on the otherwise bare rock face, so they resolved to pause for a while. Per spread a travel blanket on the ground for Jakobe, who plumped gratefully to the ground. Then they suddenly recalled that they had quite forgotten about their lunch, which still lay uneaten in the rucksack. A bout of laughter ensued, which gave them momentary respite from the pain of their impending separation.

Per removed the canvas bag from his back and proceeded to lay out the food. At the same moment, he noticed a cross that had been raised between the rocks on the other side of the pathway. This was one of the wooden crosses that were common in the area. It bore a roughly painted image of Christ crucified.

"Ugh, would you look at that!" he cried. "We're not going to eat our lunch being watched by a ghost! Let's move somewhere else, Jakobe."

"Ah Per, can we not just stay where we are!" Jakobe pleaded. "If I don't eat something right now, I think I'm going to faint."

"All right, all right! We can always turn our backs to him. And look darling—look at the beauty of this place!"

With their attention turned firmly towards the valley below that was bathed in hazy sunshine, they enjoyed their modest repast—some dry bread, cheese, and eggs. Per had moved closer to Jakobe, and when they had finished eating, he lit a cigarette. Hand in hand, they sat on the bare rock, exchanging small talk and looking out over the golden valley.

Suddenly Per cocked his head to one side and began listening intently.

"Do you hear that, Jakobe?" he asked.

"Hear what?"

"Can you not hear them? Church bells again!"

"Where?"

"Somewhere down in the valley."

"No Per...Oh wait, yes I think I can now...Imagine that you could hear them so clearly!"

"It's a horrible sound isn't it?...To think that we are still persecuted by that morbid noise even up here in this land of adventure and enchantment!"

"Well Per, it has to be said that you are perhaps oversensitive to the sound of church bells," said Jakobe playfully.

But Per now explained to her more fully how, even when quite a young boy, he had hated and feared this sound, which had sought him out in all those places he had been forbidden from frequenting, a sound that had rung in his ears ever since, like some baleful mantra in his mind. Jakobe squeezed his hand and stroked it tenderly, explaining that for her too, the cacophony of church bells had always sounded like the triumphalist threats of a dark power. She could still remember that, as a young girl, she had hidden away on Sundays when the churches began to ring out their chimes, so that nobody would see her tears of indignation; and when she got older, she had often on her way home from school sent a defiant gaze up at the bell tower in Garnison Church, where the families of two of her classmates had their own pews in the church and had always boasted about this.

"Just imagine Per! Even back then we shared the same thoughts and feelings. Is it really so strange that we found our way to each other?"

He put his arm about her waist and they spoke at some length about their future together, speculated and fantasized on the new century that was to come—a century that would finally restore spiritual and intellectual freedom to mankind, rejuvenate imagination and initiative amongst the people and see the raising of new altars for the veneration of human strength and great deeds upon the ruins of extinct churches.

"Do you know, Jakobe," said Per, "in the last while, I have often thought of a tale I was once told by the one-eyed nanny there at home at the rectory. It was about a peasant boy who wanted to be a magic marksman—a real devil-may-care, sure-shot marksman. Maybe you know the story?"

"A magic marksman? What's that?"

"You've never heard the story, Jakobe! You see, this is a rifleman who makes a pact with the devil so that a certain number of bullets are charmed and hit everything they are aimed at, no matter how high the target is flying over his head. But in order to get this special shooting skill, he must, one clear and moonlit night, bring himself to a road or way that is watched over by a crucifix. Then he has to shoot a bullet at the image of Christ . . . straight through the heart."

"Ah—you mean a Freischütz!"

"But then, when it came to the moment of truth, the young man in the tale loses his nerve. Every time he lifted his rifle and aimed at the crucifix, his hand began to shake and as soon as he went to pull the trigger his whole arm went lame—and from that day on, he was nothing more than a Sunday morning duck shooter. I think that story captures the whole problem perfectly—man's impotence in the face of phantom superstitions. Nobody could ever find the nerve to just smash the idolatrous images right through the head. For whatever damned reason . . . at the crucial moment we always get attacks of nerves, guilt, or fear."

He turned quickly to face the image of Christ behind him and continued with rising agitation: "Look at that pale, pathetic image of a man hanging there! When will we ever work up the courage to spit right in his face? Take a good look at him, Jakobe! With all that fake humility! The deliberately crude display of his abjectness! Well all that rubbish will soon be a thing of the past! Make way for our army of deadly marksmen! And we shoot with magic bullets! Look!"

He leaped urgently to his feet and pulled a heavy caliber revolver out of a leather holster, which he had been carrying under his hiking jacket. Before Jakobe could even think of stopping him, he had cocked the trigger and taken aim. Crying: "Here's a shot to herald the dawn of a new century." He fired towards the crucifix with the result that shards and splinters of wood were thrown up in the air from one side of the cross.

That very same instant, the air all around them seemed to let out a great sigh. From the valley below came a hollow boom, which as it continually grew in strength cannonaded backwards and forwards across the mountain rock faces like long, rolling underground thunder.

Per had turned away from the cross again. He was now deathly pale. But when he realized what it was, he broke out in lusty bursts of laughter. Now he remembered that during their climb, there had been signs along the way in three languages saying: "Please note the echo!"

"Aye, rumble all ye want shades and spooks!" he roared with sheer elation, lifted the revolver once more and let off the remaining shots straight up into the air, so that new and stronger reverberations and rolling rumbles filled the valley, as if legions of mountain spirits had been let loose into the air.

"Per, I swear, you are half mad!" cried Jakobe, who was now on her feet and, partially fearful but also secretly thrilled, threw herself into his arms. "What has come over you?"

"Ah—I was just blasting some lingering shadows out of my way Jakobe! But never mind that. Come on! Let's move on! Our time is precious. We have to make the mail van within two hours. And in five hours, Jakobe, we'll no longer be in each other's arms!"

"Oh Per, we won't think or talk about that," she said, as she nestled her head into his shoulder and closed her eyes.

And on they went, slowly downwards, embracing the glorious sunshine that bathed the valley as they went, overwhelmed by the heady scents of spring.

14

FOR SOME time, life in Denmark's capital city had taken on a new and strongly vibrant tone. Folk from the provinces, or from abroad, who arrived in the city after several years of absence were hardly able to recognize it, given how much it had grown and transformed itself in every conceivable way. A wave of fresh cultural influences from the heart of Europe, with Dr. Nathan in particular riding at its crest, had swept over the country and not only provoked a long dormant intellectual ferment but also inspired a swathe of revolutionary poets and writers, scientists and politicians; even in purely technical areas, it had unleashed an explosion of raw and audacious social energy, which was seeking an outlet for all its pent-up vitality. Per Sidenius was just one amongst many fame-seeking and dynamic young men who had been so inflamed by the thundering zeal of the new age and the almost fairy-tale expansion of the giant industrial nations that they went round "as if a million bluebottles had been put in their heads"—or so the complaint went from peevish old begrudgers. At the same time as Per had been standing whistling over his drawing board in that dingy little back room in Nyboder, other intrepid dreamers had gathered around swivel stools in centers of commerce, fidgeted on leather-cushioned desks in the bowels of banks, doodled on the back benches of university lecture halls—they too secretly planning their grab for the reins of power in the country. Moreover, some of the brightest and most adroit of them had already succeeded in gaining prominence in areas of public life, places which hitherto had been the preserve of the reactionary government party and a nothing short of imbecilic Royal Court.

There was no doubt that Copenhagen was on the brink of embracing the spirit of the new age. Not only had the city's boundaries and rapidly burgeoning population pushed its ranking towards that of an international metropolis, but with each passing day, the bustle in its streets, the nature of its leisure time pursuits, the fresh approach in its newspapers, and the select ambience that prevailed in its social scene had made it more and more European in outlook.

Out in the provinces, on the other hand, and especially in the market towns, life meandered on in the tired old-fashioned ways of yore. Town hall bureaucrats were still in the ascendancy here by virtue of family ties and academic letters; here too a lyrically inclined student would still be a hero for a day on returning to the town in the summer holidays with his silk student's tammy hat billowing like a balloon around his curly head. That a captain of industry or giant in commerce, regardless of how powerful he were, might be afforded equivalent rank with a jumped-up and bemedalled town clerk was unthinkable in the provinces—with or without an alderman's title.

Nor was there anywhere out in the country where the farming community had embraced the future in a decisive way. Yes it's true that a smoke stack might be seen here and there rising above dairy and threshing machines, and harvesters were gradually replacing the flail and scythe, but despite these small technical improvements, and despite the rising awareness of modernization, the country people had actually slipped further and further into poverty and debt. Mortgage and interest payments on properties grew ever steeper. More broadly, the nation's foreign liabilities were growing by millions of crowns with each year that passed.

Nonetheless, the broad-beamed Danish farmer still looked upon himself as the soul of the nation, its powerhouse and hope for the future. This was an attitude which had, during the run of the century, been transformed into a national dogma, a shibboleth that was finally sanctified by venerable Pastor Grundtvig himself and his evangelizing Folk High School movement. From Skagen to Gedser, town and country was united in reverence and worship around the altar of ancient Denmark's butter and bacon production.

In the meantime, the country's rivers and fjord inlets became more and more choked and clogged. These former royal highways of aquatic trade and commerce, which even fifty years before had seen such lively shipping traffic that individual burghers could boast of a fleet of up to twenty ocean-going vessels, now carried nothing more than a scattering of decrepit fishing smacks. The enormous labor value that was latent in the ceaseless westerly winds that drove across the country was still only harnessed by windmills used for flour production. And along the extensive Danish seaboard, the perennial waves rose and fell, but their great power crashed down with a great roar onto a dead and empty shoreline. Thus, while other nations all round the world gave their life's blood and all they possessed for the sake of reclaiming even one single stretch of coastline, or say to erect a power station, the two-hundred mile coastal stretch from Skagen to Esbjerg—the expanse of an international class navigation channel—was left as a sandblown wasteland without a single harbor, never mind an actual town.

Worse, various places around the country had seen manmade efforts to actually encourage the damage that time and nature was already doing with the filling in of river inlets and draining of estuaries so as to acquire more grazing land for cattle. Where once fully loaded merchant ships approached from the sea, bringing a whiff of spice and distant lands with them, there were now green meadows and indolent cattle with fat udders, invoking a false impression of prosperity. Even where as an exception to the rule—as on the Jutland heath—efforts had been made to carry out real and comprehensive land clearance work, this was again with the intention of creating yet more plots of arable and pasture land, yet more smallholders and crofters, yet more oppressed people whose ignorance of their own true poverty was bliss, as Per had so scathingly described the situation in his polemical pamphlet.

In this way, and by contrast, Copenhagen rose to ever more majestic heights as the rest of the country fell back into the mire and became nothing more than commonage for the capital city. It was to the capital that the country's work-hungry laborers streamed, capital and revenue went in the same direction, tempted by the high percentages promised by money speculation.

Thus, the only thing that sparked public debate and interest was the capital city and its stellar development, and this was one of the reasons that Per's pamphlet, despite the fact that its express purpose was to stir up controversy and agitation, had been completely ignored both in Copenhagen and out in the provinces. In vain, his unwavering friend and prospective brother-in-law, Ivan Salomon, had stormed the editorial offices of every newspaper, urging them to let the trumpets of invention roar. In every instance he was met with indifference and a shrugging of shoulders. A canal system over in Jutland! Wind and wave motors at Blaavandshuk! There was nothing sensational about that they cried. Even Dyhring, who had certain grounds to be more accommodating, made his excuses by pointing out that he had already brought enough trouble on his head with the article he had, at Ivan's incitement, written on the issue.

Ivan's luck in trying to tempt money men and speculators with his friend's masterwork was equally bad. Nor was it for the want of leg work and persuasive speeches in personally trying to convince the leading lights in the world of finance—first and foremost his own father, who had, however, dismissed all talk of his participation in words and looks that left no room for doubt on the issue.

Philip Salomon still had no confidence in his daughter's fiancé and his wife shared his disquiet, just as she did with most of the other feelings and concerns that would knit his brow. Though neither of them had expressly stated this view, they had still not given up the hope that Jakobe would see sense and, before it was too late, break a connection that any reasonable human being could see was only going to bring her disappointment and sorrow.

Not long after these events, in the month of March, and after the evening meal at the Salomon household where Philip Salomon had been unusually taciturn, the family patriarch requested a conversation with Ivan. This was on the same day that Fru Salomon had received the letter from Jakobe, whom all had believed was safely ensconced with her friend in Breslau, but who was now found to be writing from a small Austrian border town. Not only that, Jakobe gave to understand, between the lines, that she had met up with her fiancé and that the pair of them had taken off on a trip into the mountains.

However, Philip Salomon said nothing to Ivan about Jakobe's apparent admission to her parents. Instead, and like the inveterate businessman he was, Salomon went straight to the heart of the financial matter, which was how Per and Ivan's efforts to form a venture partnership in order to develop his friend's alleged inventions were coming along. He had not, as he chose to put it, heard anything about it for some time.

Ivan pulled a face and gave a dismissive wave of his hand.

"Ach! . . . Let's talk about something else, father. . . . How are things going? How do you think things are going when the ones who are supposed to be the foremost visionaries and businessmen here are completely indifferent to the whole thing. I have told you before that the first thing that people always ask when I approach them is what your attitude is to the project. The whole of the Exchange, father, is by now well aware that Jakobe is engaged to Sidenius."

"Well Ivan, I've been giving the whole thing some thought," Philip Salomon said without changing his own gentle tone, despite his son's agitated, in fact recalcitrant, tone. "Tell me this Ivan—how much are we actually talking about here?"

"Why do you ask? You've read his book just like I have."

"Yes of course! That's true! But I told you at the time Ivan that I couldn't really make head or tail of it. All right, maybe I just flicked through it too quickly, or maybe the truth is that I just didn't understand a word of it. As you know, he has his own particular way of writing about those kinds of things. And that's why it occurred to me to ask you whether you could—very briefly—explain the main gist of the book . . . I mean, a concise explanation but with the beginning, middle and end of what your friend's ideas and plans are actually trying to achieve."

Now here was a subject that was close to Ivan's heart. In all haste, he pulled out the necessary maps and papers and, for over an hour, held his father captive in his chair with a torrent of explanations and demonstrations.

Per's project, as it had been sketched out in his book, was revealed in its essence to be the following: Just outside the Graadyb navigation channel, where it leads into Hjerting bay, is a deserted and as good as abandoned marsh island called Langli. As one navigates around Skallingen Head, Langli island reveals itself as a long, gray-green range of sand dunes. Here and there, old thatched fishermen's cottages peep out from low rises. Along the easterly side, an old navigation channel runs up to Hjerting—southwest Jutland's original marine landing stage, which was now nothing more than a tiny and half-collapsed fishing village, the only reminders of its former glory being a couple of large and desolate merchant transport depots and a forlorn customs station.

One of Per Sidenius's key assertions was that the pen pushers had committed a major blunder when, at the end of the 1860s, they had selected Esbjerg as the port facility for the region. He attacked this decision, partly on the basis of the actual harbor's exposed geographical position, but more especially because it could only be connected to the rest of the country by railway line.

Per's strongly argued proposal was to move the marine landing stage for South Jutland back to its former location, or rather, to a place a bit further north at Tarp, which lies at the mouth of the Varde river. From here, traffic could be conveyed by water further into the interior of the country. In its new deepened and regulated state, this water channel would, with the help of a two-tier lock system, be connected to Vejle river and, together with this river, comprise the southernmost element of the two canals which, according to his plan, would unite the North Sea with the Baltic.

Per wrote that only the introduction of, at the very least, one of these connection routes would provide an effective way of competing with the north German port facilities, and in particular Hamburg, whose growing trading supremacy could, in his opinion, even threaten Denmark's independence as a nation. In the war over trading markets, upon which—openly or secretly—international politics in the modern world was effectively based, a defeat for Denmark posed an ever greater threat, but a victory would herald a new and golden dawn. The might and cultural influence of Russia was growing relentlessly and here was an opportunity to move the center of political and financial power eastward.

In this context, it was easy to see the strategic importance of Langli island and its huge potential as a kind of maritime emporium. But over and above that, Per had a much wider vision as to how this tiny lump of sand dunes out at sea could be massively developed. He proposed the establishment of a free port and his book had described in vivid detail how, with this kind of freeport trading status, shipyards, docks, and monster warehouses would rise up out of the once barren sand and how, running parallel with this, a new metropolis would quickly develop in the river delta on the mainland side of the island—a Nordic Venice. In every instance, the necessary power supply would come by way of his new and improved wind motors, or be extracted from the surf rolling in from the North Sea and then be conveyed via cables over Skallingen by means of transformers that were Per Sidenius's very own invention.

For the moment, it was this industrial development side of Per's ambitious project for which Ivan had sought support from the Copenhagen business and finance world. Even he could see that the realization of the wider canal project was an issue of national importance and only the state had the wherewithal to push that element through. On the other hand, the factory facilities and the development of the small island, as well as the procurement of the required land area at the mouth of the river, would need to be managed by a private consortium with the inherent advantage that the actual extent of industrial plant and factory installations would then be governed by the amount of support that could be obtained. The clarification of the maritime trading facilities actually available would, in turn, push the project towards what was most profitable for its investors. Per himself had proposed a shipyard, a steel foundry, and a giant factory for the production of staves for butter casks, the raw materials for which being at that time brought in from great distances and then distributed via wagon to small factories around the country for assembly. The overall cost for this part of the project he estimated to be around five million.

While Ivan explained all this, his father's face took on an increasingly engaged and interested, indeed surprised, expression. But his son went on for too long and in the end the patriarch interrupted him, saying: "Yes Ivan, good man! We can go into more detail some other time. Just one more question. What's the lie of the land—being brutally honest—with these inventions that Sidenius says he has come up with? Did he actually ever get a patent for them?"

"Well, we've made applications both here and abroad. I'm expecting an answer any day now from the patents commission."

"It seems to me Ivan that you both should have made sure that the patents were in order before making a big song and dance about it all. Without the patents in your hand, the whole project has neither a foundation nor value on which to build. All the other things you have talked about can sound very appealing but it's all just castles in the air. An invention on the other hand, when it has the authority of a patent behind it, is something tangible—regardless of the significance one might otherwise attach to it."

Ivan threw himself back in his chair, placed both hands behind his neck and stared up at the ceiling with a look of utter despair.

"Father, you have not understood a word of what I have said!" he cried. And as he leaned forward towards the table with his arms stretched out, in an almost protective way, over Per's drawings, he went into something of rant: "It is precisely with the aim of asserting the significance of the inventions that the factories need to be established. And, of course, the factory element is no use without the other facilities—docks and wharves and accommodation for workers in the area around the estuary. The whole thing stands or falls together father. That is what is so ingenious about the plan!"

"That I understand very well son! But, nevertheless, it's always a good rule of thumb when building a house to start with the foundations and not with the roof and fancy turrets. And to argue that so many installations and facilities are absolutely necessary to test what, after all, is a simple mechanism . . . well, you'll never get anyone to buy that one. What matters at the moment is to inject some impetus into the whole thing. If it gets some sort of momentum, those grandiose developments you are talking about will evolve by themselves."

"Oh yes, I've heard it all before father! I know that business patter only too well! A great new idea with a big vision finally comes along, and, as ever, it has to be dragged about, pummeled, and then put through the mangler before it can be officially approved. Even talking about it is a waste of time. You don't believe in Sidenius. And that's that!"

"Believe?! Believe! Ivan, what do I know about canals and dock building? What do you know about windmills for heaven's sake? I say again: You two have grabbed the wrong end of the stick. The first mistake was to stir a lot of things together, which didn't necessarily belong together. Then you didn't even have the patents ready, which might have helped sort the mess. Even if your friend had been able to produce a few endorsements from the acknowledged experts in the field—people who had thoroughly examined his projects—at least then there would have been a minimal guarantee that the scheme was actually feasible. But the idea that seasoned businessmen and industrialists should just willy-nilly accept bread from some half-baked and unknown young Turk . . . that's called being naive my dear child!"

"Be honest father—is it not just as naive to expect an endorsement from the very same people for whom this project represents nothing more or less than a challenge to their hegemony? It is precisely that gang of old bureaucratic dilettantes here at home that Sidenius wants to overthrow—the same timeservers that his book denounces in such trenchant terms. And by the way, I can inform you that Per made an approach to our so called 'leading' experts a long time ago, both private individuals and public institutions, but it goes without saying that he was met with either downright scorn, or at best indifference. However, Colonel Bjerregrav—you know, Dyhring's uncle—did once promise to push the idea in the Engineering Association's journal, but when it came to the bit, his nerve failed him. Those kind of people are all the same, father. Sidenius has exposed their petty, narrow mindedness; so they have ganged together to knock him down. I know for a fact that they are all livid with him."

"Well there is nothing for it, Ivan, only to win over that resistance ... one way or another. I don't see why your friend cannot make another attempt at getting Colonel Bjerregrav on board. After all, he is a man with great influence."

"That would just be a waste of time. I know for another fact that this particular meeting led to a huge row between them, and that Sidenius more or less insulted the Colonel before he left."

"Well then he can just go and apologize. Colonel Bjerregrav is not a vengeful person from what I hear."

"Sidenius—apologize! That just shows how little you know him. You might as well ask the Russian Emperor."

"Well then—you two will just have to find some other way. Because, if you think you'll get anywhere without some sort of support from that quarter, well, you are both very much mistaken."

"Anyway papa dearest. What are you actually driving at with all these questions? There's no point in having this conversation if you won't give us your backing. I have already said that the reason for all this apathy is mainly down to your ambivalence."

"And that, Ivan, is precisely why I wanted to talk to you about it. But, before I go any further, I want to make it clear that my view of the whole affair has not changed and will not be changed. If you were a bit less bamboozled by your great hero, you would soon see that it is impossible for me to get our company mixed up in a completely speculative enterprise of this kind ... not as things stand at the moment at any rate. On the other hand, I want to make you a proposition. I have been thinking about putting a certain sum of money at your disposal ... you can then use it in whatever way you will and in your own name—bearing in mind that you have often expressed a desire to try your own luck in your own independent company. My thinking is that, for various reasons, now might be the right time for just such a venture."

Ivan's eyes narrowed and he looked at Philip Salomon with ill-disguised suspicion. While, in all other regards, father and son trusted each other implicitly as soon as their conversation shifted towards business matters, they were both suddenly on their guard.

"Is it some sort of loan we are talking about? Or is the idea that I will cover the costs for this 'company'?"

"You can make whatever arrangements you see fit. There are absolutely no strings attached Ivan. The only thing that matters to me is—as I have said—that things start moving in some shape or form. It seems to me that there has been an awful lot of talk for an awfully long time. Time to put up or shut up!"

"But you know that it will take more than the change in your pocket for that to happen don't you? Before we start, we're going to need at least a few hundred thousand just to get the ball rolling."

"Ah now Ivan, I don't think you will need that much. But that's enough talk for one day. You can sleep on my offer. Then we can discuss it further in the morning."

Some two weeks after this—in the beginning of April—Jakobe returned from her travels across Europe. After spending a week with her old school friend in Breslau, she was overcome by an irrepressible longing to be back at home. Copenhagen was in the grip of a blinding snowstorm on the evening her train pulled into the station and she remained in her room for almost all of the following morning so that she could write to Per.

"Well here I am back at home again and I can, at last, write you a proper letter. I presume you got the two hurried notes I dashed off to you from Breslau? I nearly wish that you hadn't, because I'm a bit ashamed of them now and I ask you to forgive both their confused presentation (but I had to sneak off and write them very late in the evening after I had returned half-dead from a party or the theater), and also their content, which I suppose was far more of a lamentation than a celebration. What I really wanted to write was my endless gratitude to you, love of my heart, for all those things we did and shared together. The whole of my seven-day stay in Breslau seems like some kind of misty imagining to me now—almost as if I was never there at all and I must admit to feeling pangs of guilt towards my friend and her husband who did their best to entertain me. They invited their friends over, took me to concerts, plays, even to an equestrian event, which I can't abide; but the truth is that my thoughts were ever and always with you. In my mind, I roamed around Dresack in Ausserhof again and again—I relived and experienced everything, as if in a lovely waking dream.

"I came straight home when I arrived last night and immediately got some news that put a bit of a damper on my spirits, even though it wasn't entirely unexpected. Nanny got engaged to Dyhring the day before yesterday. I'll say straight out that this particular match fills me with dread. I have never warmed to Dyhring, either as a journalist or even as a person. That said, Nanny seems to be thrilled. In fairness, he seems to be as besotted with my sister as it is possible to be—for the moment anyway. He was here last night when I got back and, as you can imagine, it was a bit strange for me to see them going into the side room, where we used to sit, and hear them whispering and canoodling. But don't worry, I'm not going to fall back into all that melancholic brooding again. Our day will come Per! I take comfort from the fact that nine days have now passed since we parted—nine whole days out of God knows how many hundred that still have to roll on day after night, until I once again hold you in my arms!

"I wonder where you are today? In Vienna? In Budapest? I can see you in front of me—all too clearly I'm afraid!—in your dark peacoat and your blessed red cheeks, which in my mind's eye I shower with kisses. Do you know that I had another dream about that big forest in the Laugen valley? Never will I forget one single minute of the wonderful day we spent there. Time seemed to stand still. Do you remember the little bird that settled in the branches over our heads and started to sing? And the time we stopped by the stream where you (as you put it) drank forgiveness for the sins of your youth out of my cupped hands? But we'll say no more about all that.

"As for me, I am actually glad to have returned home Per—sitting here in my own room surrounded by your small portraits and other little reminders of you—you the person whom I've missed and longed for so much. All these things, along with our books, will be my comfort and refuge in my loneliest moments. Can you guess which book I'm going to start with first? It's going to be Poulsen's little primer in hydrostatics. I'm sure you remember that during the winter, and at your recommendation I read his book on dynamics and was really surprised and thrilled by its form of creative clarity. There is much more of a poetical writer in him than anything else. In reality, he is the only proper, fully modern lyricist that we have here at home. Parts of his explanation of the rate of fall struck me really strongly as being redolent of the philosophical poems that Goethe wrote in his day. Yes really!

"I have a feeling by the way that something is afoot here where you are concerned. No sooner was I in the door yesterday evening when Ivan was whispering some furtive words to me about an 'emerging venture partnership,' and this morning when I slipped down quickly for tea, he rushed by me, making a big show of not saying a word about the spanking new folder he had tucked under his arm. As soon as I have found out more, I'll give you a full briefing.

"Other than that, there is not much other news from here. My mother and father are kind and gentle as always, even though I can sense that they were not exactly pleased with our meeting. But there's nothing you or I can do about that. Today the sun's rays have a real heat to them and the birds seem to feel that too in their chorus; but even yesterday, the weather was quite wintry, and I arrived here in one of those snowstorms in which the arrival of spring is announced across the Nordic countries. For a moment, I was actually worried that the train would get stuck in snowdrifts, and then I would have had to spend yet another night in a village inn—but this time on my own, without you!

"Don't worry Per darling, I won't bore you with a running commentary on the rest of my travel experiences. But this is just a little experience that I simply have to tell you about—I know very well that it means nothing in itself but now that I've admitted as much I know that you won't just laugh and put it down to the gossipy side of my nature. I once told you about a scene I came across quite by accident at one of Berlin's main railway stations, a scene that had a terrible effect on me, so much so that I believe I have never really recovered from it. I am referring of course to that pitiful column of Russian Jews—conscientious, law-abiding people, who for no other reason than their racial origins were driven from house and home, but not before they were robbed, manhandled and in some cases battered and broken. Just like a line of convicts, they had been led under police guard, and accompanied by the catcalls and scorn of the mob, all the way through the heartlands of civilized Europe, their only crime being the urge to seek a safe haven amongst some half-wild native tribes in America. I'm sure you remember me telling you about them, Per.

"Now it was my turn on this trip, and again in a Berlin railway station, to be reminded that I too belong to the same race as those wandering and persecuted souls. I was sitting in the train compartment along with another lady and the train was just about to depart when an older gentleman came in, accompanied by a young army officer. As soon as he set eyes on my ill-fated visage, he promptly turned round and left. The young lieutenant followed him and let out a roar of appreciative laughter. The guard was just about to close the door and the old man gave his explanation in such a loud voice that it was impossible for me not to have heard it: 'Christ almighty! It reeks of garlic in here.'

"Yes, that was about the height of it, and you are probably wondering why I am insisting on telling you about it. But it's not so much the little incident itself but the way it affected me that makes it important. Even now, right this minute, it arouses a particularly heightened sense of wonder in me when I think of it. You see—it actually didn't disturb me that much at all! At most, I was probably left with a slightly sad heart. When the lady I mentioned tried to be nice to me after the two gentlemen left the compartment—clearly to try and cheer me up after the deliberately wounding remark had been delivered—I did not throw her kindness back in her face as I would have done in previous times. No Per, I began to chat to her as if nothing had happened. Do you understand the significance now? I, Jakobe Salomon, who even in her early childhood years was described as completely stubborn and unforgiving—I can't even get angry anymore! That's what my newfound love, luck, and happiness has done to me! The feeling I have, which at this very moment fills my senses when I think of that great mass of blind and confused humanity, is one of enduring compassion—an all-encompassing forgiveness.

"Ah but Per ... I've already had to start on my third sheet of paper, and yet I feel I've hardly begun to tell you what's really in my heart. That's enough for today. I'm terrible taking up so much of your time like this when, God knows, you need time to yourself as well. But it's so difficult to leave you darling. Because I know how empty I'm going to feel when I've sealed this letter. Now just one last kiss—and another the very last for now—and then goodbye Per."

It took a few weeks after the conversation with his father before Ivan was able to arrange a meeting that brought together a group of the requisite money men. This was hosted by the well-known Senior Solicitor Max Bernhardt to whom Ivan had turned on previous occasions to lobby for Per's cause—all to no avail. Bernhardt had now agreed to convene a meeting with some of his business contacts at his office so as to give Ivan the chance to promote Per Sidenius's canal project—the idea being that serious consideration would be given as to how it might be put into action.

Max Bernhardt was, despite being only forty years old and a Jew by birth, already a man of no mean influence in Denmark's capital city. Amongst other things, he had gained fame as the central motivating force within that band of buccaneering speculators who within the last decade had knocked down much of old Copenhagen and transformed the city from a parochial backwater to a great city in the grand European style. He had also, and precisely because of his pioneering enterprise, gained many enemies; but even those who were most against him had to admit that he had an outstanding flair for business and a razor-sharp mind—someone who in terms of clarity of thinking and knowledge of jurisprudence and commercial transactions was unequalled. On the other hand, even his own supporters had to cede to the accusation that he was as empty as a worm-eaten walnut in that place where his conscience was supposed to be and that he would happily slit a competitor's throat if said competitor posed a threat to Bernhardt's personal ambitions.

It was for the above reasons that, during these turbulent years, every time the Danish middle classes rose up in new and threatening protests, alarmed as they were by the new and more aggressive form of capitalism, some great financial crash or the suicide of a speculator who had gambled all and lost the shirt off his back, the anger would invariably gather around the lightning conductor that was Max Bernhardt. As far as the general public was concerned, he was the epitome of the disease that had spread from Europe over the last generation or more and, according to common street lore, was carried by the Jew's inherent streak of selfishness and self-interest.

Now far be it from this man to make any attempt to change what people thought of him. Quite the contrary. He took immense pleasure from that particular form of curiosity mixed with fear—not least amongst women—which people displayed when watching him as he left his office to go home, always at the same stroke of the hour every day. Everyone recognized his small exotic figure, which had so often been caricatured in the illustrated pages of the satirical press. He was always very elegantly dressed when he appeared in the street, with a slight stoop and both hands pushed down inside his overcoat as if in fear of the cold wind. From behind his upturned collar and lowered hat, he would observe his fellow pedestrians with half-closed, expressionless eyes that gazed out from beneath his dark brow.

In reality, he was not exactly the epitome of the image he liked to present to the world. People who had known him since childhood remembered him as a quiet and withdrawn child who was forever poring over books, a boy who avoided the horseplay in which his friends indulged because of the constant persecution and rough excesses to which he was constantly subjected because of his Jewish origins and small stature. His father, a modest shopkeeper in a side street in the town, had been very unhappy with him because all that reading had provoked a strong aversion to commercial life in the boy.

At seventeen years of age, he sat the university entrance exam and passed it with distinction. He then opted to study law. At that time, his intention was to build a career in the civil service. Ultimately, he wanted to be a judge. The persecution to which he had been subjected as he grew up had created a passionate sense of justice in him. The wearing of the dark red velvet robes of a supreme court judge very quickly became this diminutive son of a shopkeeper's secret goal.

But one day it was pointed out to him that, as an unbaptized person, he had no prospect whatsoever of becoming an officer of the law. Yes it was true that there was no actual legal statute in this regard but it was simply not allowed. In spite of the constitution's guarantee of equality for all citizens before the law, no Jew had ever occupied a judge's chair in Denmark.

Once Bernhardt had graduated, he was forced to look on as, now this and then that blond meathead amongst his fellow students, was launched onto the legal and academic royal highway that leads to honor, power and social standing, while he was pushed out into that very world of commerce which he so despised. Thus, with the inherent self-esteem of the Israelite—that proud aversion to being the subject of pity—he had in the meantime armed himself with a disconcertingly rigid level of self-control. Even in these early days he displayed a cold, mocking man-of-the-world disguise as he moved amongst people, but beneath this, his heart secretly knocked as nervously as a young girl entering a society ball for the fist time.

His public image meant that nobody expressed the least surprise when, on gaining his license to practice as a solicitor, Bernhardt launched a series of bold business raids that were solely based on speculation and inside knowledge. His specialty soon became that of forming building consortia and founding limited companies and he had almost immediately provoked outrage amongst his legal peers by using methods which had previously been regarded as beyond the pale where judicial business practice was concerned. Amongst other things, and based on practices extant in foreign countries, Bernhardt had developed a close relationship with certain members of the press. By bribing a number of reporters and in particular by greasing the palms of editors and newspaper proprietors by offering lucrative regulatory posts or directorships in his various limited companies, he had gradually formed a secret society of sympathetic agents of influence. With this cabal behind him, Bernhardt was in a position to manipulate public opinion and pursue without mercy anyone who might offer the least resistance.

Now, after just ten years, he had become one of Copenhagen's wealthiest people and was acknowledged by all as a major power broker in the capital. Regardless of the persistent grumbling over the way he operated, in the business world, at least, people had finally bowed before his brilliance and the wonderful aura of providence that seemed to surround everything that he touched. With the exception of a couple of the oldest and most aristocratic trading establishments, and a single bank, which still showed a reluctance to engage with him, no one dared any longer to oppose his influence, which grew stronger with each passing day.

All this success notwithstanding, Bernhardt was far from satisfied and his burning ambition remained undimmed. He whose great hope it had been to attain the relatively modest esteem enjoyed by a supreme court judge had now set himself a quite different goal for his ceaseless scheming. For the early injustices visited upon him had created a drive to dominate all he encountered, a furious momentum, which constantly sought yet more areas of conquest.

However, he well understood that, because of his racial origins, he himself would never be able to attain any of the absolute elite positions in Danish society, the only things that were really worth fighting for. As recompense for this, amongst the small army of dependents he had gradually gathered around him and made obedient instruments of his will, there were already several generals in the field who had battled their way to strategic points of influence—in other words, Bernhardt's plan was to gather all the de facto reins of power in the country into his own hands.

Little wonder then that Ivan had been particularly eager to win this man for Per's cause, or that now, when he seemed to have achieved this aim, he should naturally feel that victory was almost at hand.

Amongst the seven gentlemen who had assembled to discuss the plan was a stock broker by the name of Herløv. He was a personal friend of Max Bernhardt's and his perennial accomplice. Herløv was a large, rotund man who gave the impression of being half-asleep and lethargic. The truth was, however, that his head for business was almost as brilliant as Bernhardt's, and he actually surpassed his partner where ingenuity and cunning were concerned. At the Exchange, it was said of him that he was Max Bernhardt's third eye. Herløv it invariably was that came up with the visionary ideas and, with calculating prudence, laid out a vision of how the joint ventures should proceed. Bernhardt, meanwhile, was the straight-talking male powerhouse who put those ideas into action.

In general, their personal interests in life could not have been more different, but it was for this very reason that their business cooperation was so unrivalled. This stock broker was brazenly open about his one true ambition. For in complete contrast to Max Bernhardt, who cared only for the wielding of power, Herløv had no other goal than to widen his profit margins—no great task other than the hoarding of shillings. He didn't even have a purpose for all the money he had amassed. He was not married and had only one relatively cheap passion, namely that after his day's work was done he would settle his considerable bulk into one of the plush chairs belonging to one or other of Copenhagen's more refined restaurants. Here he would take a private cabinet and in glorious solitude, apart from some newspapers, devour a dinner of some seven or eight courses. Water was his only liquid refreshment as he wanted to watch his health.

There Herløv stood now in Max Bernhardt's spacious and expensively furnished reception room, lurching forward like an ox, with his hands behind him and tucked under his coat tails. With that bovine gaze behind his spectacles, he looked for all the world as if he might just go off and lie down somewhere. He had fallen into conversation with one of the other hand-picked guests, a blond-haired and loudly dressed young man of fashion who was known all over Copenhagen from Østergade and on down to the theater area where he had been dubbed "The Gilded Lamb's Head." His real name was

Sivertsen, and he was the only child of a once well-known coffee wholesaler. On his father's death, and when he was just twenty-seven years old, he became heir to a vast fortune. He was one of the town's many theater peacocks whose sole choice of conversation revolved around who was starring where, the latest backstage gossip, and the chatter from the critics. He was a close friend of Dyhring's, whom Sivertsen said he "admired both as a gentleman and author." Dyhring it was who had initiated his contact with Max Bernhardt in the first place. And Bernhardt had not been slow to draw him in to his inner sanctum, after which he had marshalled Sivertsen's millions as he saw fit—though this was far from having damaged the young gadabout whose theater-mania would very quickly have ruined him, given that he was willing to pay an extortionate price for the honor of calling the latest thespian hero his dear friend or consort.

Also present was a certain Hr. Nørrehave, whose name one would, likewise, invariably see being listed under Max Bernhardt's share offers. His business card pronounced him a "former agriculturalist" and it was indeed true that he had once owned a farm in Jutland. But that was twenty years ago and his time since then had been spent wheeling and dealing in Copenhagen. Initially, he had put his money to beneficial use as a loan shark and secondhand goods merchant. He then moved into property letting and brokerage, which set him up nicely for his move into the stock market and share speculation—a true capitalist on a grand scale. His original name had been Madsen, but this he changed at the same time as he swapped his shop in a cellar for a plush set of offices. On the other hand, he had kept his sturdy and trust-inspiring title of "country estate holder," as well as the Jutland roll on the "r," which for Copenhagen ears signaled that here was a real man whose word was his bond. Max Bernhardt tended, in all confidence, to describe him as the wiliest fox that ever dug a lair in Denmark.

Once everyone was gathered around a table, upon which Per's drawings and calculations had been laid out, Ivan wasted no time in making his pitch, and the assembled gentlemen were more than willing to lend their ears to his carefully crafted lecture—at least for the first half hour. After that, the audience began to get restless and the former agriculturalist, in typical blunt country fashion, openly pulled his watch from his jacket several times.

When Ivan finally brought his speech to an end, a lengthy silence fell over the gathering. The guests shot glances at Max Bernhardt but he remained aloof and watchful.

In the end, it was stock broker Herløv who broke the silence and began to ask questions about the project and, gradually, a more general discussion ensued.

What then emerged was that these potential backers—just like Philip Salomon—saw the procurement of a meticulous assessment of the plan from a recognized technical expert as being absolutely essential. This professional adjudication would then be fed to the press in order to raise public awareness. Various names were then mentioned and the consensus was that the former colonel and renowned engineer Bjerregrav would be the man whose judgment on this matter would carry most weight around the country.

With no little vehemence, Ivan then repeated what he had already said to his father, namely that any kind of support for their venture was hardly likely to come from that particular quarter, given that Bjerregrav—not without good cause—saw Per's project as not only an attack on his profession in general but also on him personally. In fact he knew for a fact that where the colonel was concerned, and for purely personal reasons, Bjerregrav was extremely hostile to the plan and its originator.

The stockbroker's response to this was that the colonel would obviously be offered a seat on the company board, and as board positions no doubt would be salaried, that kind of personal ill will could be smoothed over fairly easily.

"If that were our biggest problem," he add drily, "the whole thing would be up and running in no time."

With regard to Per's energy-converting machines and other inventions, which Ivan had portrayed as epoch making, the assembled gentlemen showed no confidence in them whatsoever. On this point, and in contrast to Philip Salomon, they wished to concentrate on the harbor project and especially the acquisition of the small island and its designation as a freeport. Indeed, Max Bernhardt bluntly declared that, as far as he was concerned, only this element of the project was worth discussing. On the other hand, he spoke with great animation against some of the other gentlemen when they came up with further restrictions to Per's plan so as to make it more workable.

"Any further amputations would in fact be an execution," he said. "For my part, I want to insist that we seek to establish the freeport project to its full extent…as a national crusade, for which the public's support must be aroused, just as Hr. Salomon has quite rightly described it…otherwise we must decide that the whole thing is impossible to achieve and walk away from it right now."

Ivan's eyes widened at this. In view of Max Bernhardt's prior reluctance to engage with the plan, he could never have dared hope that he would get such unconditional support from him. It was clear that some of the others were also taken aback by the unusual enthusiasm with which Max Bernhardt jumped into the breach on behalf of a venture which, in their eyes, appeared highly dubious.

However, there was a hidden agenda to the sudden interest shown by Max Bernhardt and stockbroker Herløv in Per's work. For they had gotten wind of a freeport project that was being developed by one of Copenhagen's major banks—a bank moreover with which they were at loggerheads at that present time. This enemy freeport plan was of course to be established in Copenhagen. It was now their intention to ambush their opponents with this fully developed West Jutland project, about which they could begin to foment press coverage with just a day's notice. In reality, they had no great confidence that they would be able to whip up any kind of genuine support for it in the business world, their strategy was more to do with using Per's project as a kind of grenade that they could throw into the debate and thereby fragment the interest that clearly existed around the country into separate warring factions. For at that moment, their opponents were banking on having a free run when exploiting that freeport enthusiasm for their own Copenhagen project.

After further negotiations, the meeting was closed with a decision that an approach should be made to Colonel Bjerregrav in order to persuade him to accept a place on the provisional board of directors. As soon as his answer was obtained, a new meeting would be convened so that, in consultation with the colonel, certain decisions could be made about the specific steps that needed to be taken to finally make the plan concrete.

As events unfolded in Denmark, Per was to be found in Vienna. He had spent a couple of weeks in the marshland areas around the mouth of the Danube in order to study the large-scale river flow regulation systems and port facilities there. One moment riding a horse, the next in an open boat or a barge that was half submerged in the silt water, he had been in constant motion, and there had been times where it had been difficult to get a roof over his head for the night.

Exhausted after such travails, which were a new experience for him, he now sat outside a café in Vienna and considered his options. He felt an urgent need to have a conversation with another human being about something other than pile driving and mud clearance. Since he and Jakobe had gone their separate ways, his only form of human contact had been civil engineers ... engineers who were a different breed to the basic variety at home. These were technicians schooled in the cut and thrust of international competition—men with phenomenal professional expertise in their craft but often in very specific and restricted areas. Thus, outside of their chosen calling their world view could be astoundingly narrow and they would have scant interest in anything that was not directly related to the Holy Grail of engineering excellence and their personal prestige in that field.

Per felt the same way about these people as he did about the three cold-blooded English whisky drinkers with whom he had spent the winter in Dresack. There, too, it had been impossible to have a conversation about the main questions in life, which at that time had weighed heavily on his mind. He was, and would ever be, a stranger in that kind of company. Regardless of how much he admired their technical dexterity and discernment, and despite the fact that they exuded superiority to the point where he often wished he could be like them, the deepest feelings they aroused in him were ones of pity—pity for the kind of person who could not raise his thoughts any higher than the cigar smoke he blew into the air.

Now here he was, sitting outside a café with a newspaper in his hand. While his thoughts dwelled upon Jakobe, whom he missed ten times more in this huge city that was completely strange to him, he scanned the hotel lists out of old habit to see whether anyone else from Denmark was staying there. To his amazement, he saw the name of Baroness von Bernt-Adlersborg.

The hard winter had pushed this old lady far from his thoughts. The intervening time in his life and his own personal development had led him so far away from the superficial sheen of wealth and power that he could not remember anymore how he had even been tempted by "uncle Heinrich" into taking advantage of this poor woman's friendship so as to grab the title of baron.

However, in his longing to talk to another person in his own language, and about everyday things and events, he resolved to pay the baroness a visit. He found her in one of the town's most elegant hotels, where she was staying with her sister, Dame Prangen, wife of the Master of the Royal Hunt. The two ladies had arrived in Vienna a few days before and were using it as a staging post on their way to Italy.

The baroness did not seem to have benefited much from the almost full year she had spent at the German health spa. Yes it was true that her cheeks had lost some of that highly flushed and rare tone, her countenance was more settled and the hands shook less, but her speech was still just as confused and revealed her weakened mental state. For all that, her singular affection for Per remained undiminished. The baroness had all but dragged him to her bosom on his arrival and repeatedly during their ensuing conversation, she took his hands in hers to declare her delight and gratitude for his visit.

The old lady said nothing at all about her time at the health spa. Her only words were that her darling little sister had traveled down to fetch her and that they now intended to go on to Rome where—as she explained in confidential tones when Dame Prangen left the room—they would seek an audience with the Pope himself.

The baroness wasted no time in urging Per to accompany them on their trip south, and when she heard from him that he intended to leave Vienna the very next day so as to move on to Paris, her complaints at this suggestion were so vehement and heartfelt that in the end he had to yield and promised to stay in Vienna for as long as the baroness and Dame Prangen remained in the city.

That very same afternoon, Per played escort to the two ladies as they enjoyed a drive out to the Prater public park.

In his letter to Jakobe, in which he recounted these events, he described Dame Prangen in the following way:

"The baroness's sister is tall and very imposing—a lady in every respect. I would say she is heading towards six foot and has a stout figure to match her height. She's around fifty years old. Was obviously once very attractive. And even now her sparkling eyes give her a certain appeal. By nature she is more reserved than the baroness and in contrast to her sister does not say very much. Clearly very religious. Last night we jumped straight into a long and sometimes heated discussion about the Christian doctrine of immortality. I get the feeling that she has hopes of bringing me back to the fold. Well now, Jakobe, I'll enjoy renewing my struggle against the Dark Ages! At the very least, she appears to have lived an interesting life and thought deeply about things and funnily enough, despite all her piety, she is not by any means a killjoy. All in all a very interesting couple."

This letter made Jakobe somewhat uneasy. Without actually mentioning either Dame Prangen or her sister by name in her hastily composed reply, she said the following:

"There is one thing about our little trip together that upsets me a bit Per, and that is that we never really got talking about things that so occupied your mind in the winter, and following on from your father's death. But each day flew by and love will assert its claim above all else. You may perhaps now tell me that there was nothing further to discuss—that it was your loneliness and isolation that had made you so troubled—and I believe that myself. And anyway (and this is true isn't it my darling?), now we share all things without exception, and you will never try to hide the things that are troubling you from me ever again Per. You've promised me that!

"Here at home we are suffering yet another outbreak of theological scaremongering and persecution. As I think I wrote to you last time, Dr. Nathan has come back to Denmark and it is as if this one event has sent the whole church hierarchy into a blind panic. They use every and any opportunity at the moment to rail against the new times and its foremost leaders. Just this evening, in fact, the *Berlingske* newspaper devoted nearly a whole page to a funeral oration given by some archdeacon or other for a deceased privy counselor at Vor Frue Church. I should really send you the cutting. I don't think I've ever read anything that has annoyed me as much as this stupid and arrogant nonsense. Of course, this holy man of the cloth gushed on and on about the pity he felt for those 'miserable souls' who went through life without any hope of eternal salvation, those for whom death simply meant a terrifying gateway into a bottomless void. And there's the usual self-congratulatory joy in his own true faith without which 'life would simply be unbearable.' Now how can he be so sure tell me? Did he die and come back? My old half uncle Philip used to tell us that he had the same religious beliefs as his stove—namely that life was all bangs, flashes, flames, and smoke and 'there's nothing above the chimney.' But at the same time, and right into his old age, he was a very happy and cheerful man. When he was lying on his deathbed and the doctors couldn't work out what was wrong with him, he started joking with them and told them that he was raging with them because they weren't able to tell him what he was dying of. And that is by no means the only example of they way he was. Both in my own family and amongst people that I have known there have been lots of people who have had no religious convictions whatsoever, and they have all gone to their deaths as proud and undaunted as any holy archdeacon.

"I often wonder whether the exaggerated fear that Christians seem to have of death—no doubt originally coming from the doctrine of there being a judgment waiting for them on the other side—is not also linked to the fact that Christianity emerged and developed amongst peasants and fishermen who were also an oppressed people. That is not how the other major religions evolved. There is almost certainly a connection between a profound fear of death and the angst felt by slaves. I'll never forget how affected I was at a museum in Germany once when I saw some plaster-cast models of the finds made at the excavations in Pompeii. Amongst other fascinating things, there was a lord and his slave, both of whom had obviously been caught unawares by the torrent of ash falling from the skies and were suffocated in a matter of minutes. But Per my love, what a difference in the two faces! The slave's face showed the most abject terror—he had thrown himself onto his back, his eyebrows were almost up at his hairline and his blubbery mouth was wide open. You could almost hear him screaming like a stuck pig. The other figure, though, had retained his Caesar-like dignity in the face of death. The firmly closed eyes, the primly shut mouth; everything carried the bearing of the proudest and most beautiful resignation at his inevitable fate.

"For me this is precisely the most significant charge that may be leveled against Christianity with its promise of eternal life—that it robs life of its deep gravity in the here and now and therefore its inherent beauty. If we view our life here on earth as some kind of rehearsal for the real show that's going to take place upstairs, how can we celebrate our existence here properly?

"But even though I was never personally fully convinced that life's greatest philosophical goal is our own annihilation and that this belief is supposed to symbolize the highest intellect in man—that we can so easily reconcile ourselves to such a selfless principle as simply dying and returning to Mother Nature all those energies and forces that existed within us and view this as the most harmonious end to life possible, while all those Christian dreams of immortality and heavenly joy are nothing more than ancient, barbaric visions of the eternal hunt and Valhalla dressed up in new way—well, what was it I was going to say Per?

"You'll really have to forgive me darling, but I'll have to get back to this point some other time. Oh wait. Now I know what it was! I wanted to say that even though I do not see in death the final and absolute human sacrifice, the final letting go into that great universe and our indissoluble union with it, I do not wish to know anything about what is going to happen to me or those I love when I leave this mortal coil. After all, no human being wants the power to see into his worldly future. In fact, we all accept the wisdom of that view and allow it to draw a veil over what's in store for us in the coming days. If we knew with a fair degree of certainty how our lives were going to unfold, regardless of how fortunate that future would be, I am sure it would be just unbearable. And that's before we start talking about an eternal life in the hereafter!

"Is it not true Per? All this neverending theologizing! 'Handed down from our fathers before us'—that's the mantra the enemies of human enlightenment are using at the moment here at home and its all part of that same parochial edifice. Do you not find it terribly embarrassing and depressing—yes it would actually make you despair—that people are still raising different battle standards and wasting precious time and energy on the most basic questions that we all should have agreed on long ago? Who can any longer be in any doubt that it is precisely those 'inherited' traits we have that we all, both Christian and Jew, are duty bound to fight against—if not for any other reason than they are just based on sheer chance. We could just as easily have inherited a completely opposite set of values. How long do we have to wait, how much more misery do we have to inflict upon each other, before we understand and make it our new religion, the only permitted dogma, that our own lives and that of all nations should not be based on chance and coincidence but on the basic humanity that is in all of us!"

The meeting at Max Bernhardt's offices had delegated Ivan to make the approach to Colonel Bjerregrav and to seek to overcome his hostility to the new enterprise and its callow originator by way of an invitation to join the board of directors.

However, Ivan was not exactly thrilled to have been handed this diplomatic mission. In general, he would never shirk from a fight on Per's behalf (indeed there had been occasions when he had been forced to suffer ejection down metaphorical flights of stairs for his cause), but the old colonel induced a particularly large measure of awe in Ivan's mind. He was familiar with the colonel's ruddy face and bustling gait from having often seen him in the street and he had also heard many reports concerning his irascibility and impulsive disposition. Dyhring, the colonel's nephew, had once told him with glee in his voice that Bjerregrav would still go into fits of rage on hearing Per's name being mentioned.

In his hesitant state of mind, Ivan confided in his uncle Heinrich, who often acted as his advisor when he was in a fix and would usually, after grumbling and complaining about it, act to lift him out of his difficulties.

"I'll see what I can do. I know a bit about this Bjerregrav. Have done him a few small favors every now and again. I'll drop a few hints to make him more amenable. Can you both ask any more of me than that?"

There was some truth in his proud boast that he really did have a connection to the colonel. For despite the fact that he would not admit it openly, and his family for that very reason pretended they knew nothing about it, this sham wheeler dealer ran a small business obtaining commission on sales, and the returns from this formed a not insignificant part of his core income. Amongst other things, he acted as an agent for an English company that manufactured iron and steel girders and it was in this capacity that he would present himself twice a year at the colonel's offices with the current price list.

A few days after his conversation with Ivan, uncle Heinrich set off to pay his client a visit. After being forced to wait in the hall for half an hour, he was finally allowed to enter the inner sanctum and found the colonel to be in the best of form, his cheeks aglow after a hearty lunch.

The old military man made no attempt to hide his mirth at the sight of this diminutive and distasteful Jew, who entered his office wearing gray spats, a cylinder hat, and with a pair of gloves in his raised hand, like some third-rate actor playing an aristocrat in a provincial comedy review.

"Well no—are you back again!" he said as he sat down at his desk, without offering his visitor the other seat. "How are things my little desert wanderer?"

Hr. Delft placed his blue-tinted monocle in front of his eye and wheezed with pretend delight. He sensed that good business might be done here and was too crafty to wreck his chances by revealing his annoyance.

And sure enough, after a bout of negotiations he succeeded in getting a stock order from the colonel.

Uncle Heinrich already had his things gathered and stood once again with his hat and gloves in his hand as if to leave when he suddenly cocked his head to one side in the manner of a chimpanzee and said: "May I ask the good colonel a question in all confidence?"

"Which is?"

"Has Hr. Colonel heard anything about this big new national enterprise that has been ventilated in certain parts just recently?"

"Know nothing about it."

"Really, nothing at all?"

"I hold my own counsel ... stay clear of all that hot air and nonsense; that you know sir."

Hr. Delft looked away as his craftiest smile appeared on his face. Now, with his business done and dusted, was the time to reply in kind to the colonel's jibe about the wandering Jew.

"Ach—yes!" he cried and shook his curly head. "Times have changed so much. Everywhere one looks, colonel, it is the young that people look to for salvation. The old tried and tested specialists are just pushed aside, discarded ... ignored plain and simple. It is the youth that has taken the center of the stage!"

"What point exactly are you trying to make?" the colonel interjected, suddenly impatient and with a note of command in his voice.

"A major freeport project is in the pipeline. Started by a very young man—quite a fledgling altogether. Sidenius is his name."

"Ah—that big-mouthed baboon!" the colonel snorted. "As it happens, I know this person. It wasn't that long ago when he had us all tortured with this 'national crusade' of his. I'm well aware that nowadays there is a derangement abroad that makes people want to get rid of their money at the drop of a hat, but I doubt whether those schoolboy fantasies would seriously tempt anyone."

"The whole venture is fully subscribed . . . where finance is concerned Hr. Colonel. I know that for a fact."

"What?"

"The whole thing is in the bag, good sir. The only thing that is now required is the necessary statutory sanction. Yes, Hr. Colonel it is just as you say. Danish financial circles seem to have lottery fever at the moment. They've started dancing to the piper's tune and cannot stop again for as long as the music goes on. And besides, Hr. Sidenius seems to be well got in certain circles at the Exchange."

The colonel was suddenly deathly still. He had lowered his waxed eyebrows and the vigor imparted to his cheeks by his hearty lunch seemed to have been sucked into his eyes, which began to glower like a bull's.

"So it's actually true. This small pup is engaged to one of Philip Salomon's daughters? You of all people must know Hr. Delft. Is Philip Salomon not your brother-in-law?"

"Hr. Colonel, my lips are sealed! I am unfortunately not privy to the affairs of my nieces' hearts and their secret loves."

The colonel could not help but laugh.

"You are a born diplomat Delft! Well, what do I care. If people wish to throw their savings into some lake, canal or sea, good luck to them is what I say. It would be a pity to deny them their moment of pleasure. Prosit Mahlzeit, gentlemen! It would take a lot of gold bullion to fill up Hjerting bay."

"With God as my judge, you never said a truer word Hr. Colonel!"

"Yes, as I say, I'm keeping well away from the whole swindle. For my part, the less said the better. Adieu, Hr. Delft."

"My honored respects sir," said the little Israelite, as he retired with the most subservient of bows.

The colonel remained sitting there with his hand under his chin and his bottom teeth tugging animatedly at his moustache. Straight-forward rage was what gripped this choleric old man on hearing these kinds of stories. He who had once himself in his youthful arrogance thrown down a gauntlet to the national disease of slackness and obfuscation and had dreamed of being a champion and leader within his profession was now counted as one of the bitterest opponents of the new revolutionary age. Just like most other old liberals in the country, his hatred for these young triumphant heralds of progress was informed by a venomous envy, which where Per was concerned had almost taken on the character of a mania. The very thought that the dream he had never been able to realize might be achieved by this country bumpkin, who had had the audacity to come to his own office and singe his beard was the stuff of his worst nightmares—not least because he privately acknowledged Per's superior abilities and that he possessed the necessary recklessness that he had lacked. In Per's combined freeport and canal project, he saw a really ingenious, albeit incomplete, vision, which with the appropriate adjustments had the potential of being of huge significance for the country's future; and when he nonetheless had resorted to using all the influence he could bring to bear so as to oppose him, this was because he (just like all the other old liberals) wished to resist an intellectual movement that was destructive of Denmark's people and its customs. Or at least this was how the colonel justified his actions.

For all that, the colonel had not entirely lost his former reputation as an open-minded and independent person—it was for this reason that both Philip Salomon and Max Bernhardt had immediately thought of his name when seeking a respected expert who might be willing to stand up for Per's ideas in the public domain. They were also aware that he was a vain man who was very fond of money and they assumed that he had become embittered at having to witness the success of one large-scale enterprise after another, all carried out by the young prophets of the new age and from which they had gained fame and fortune, while he himself had slipped more and more into the Lethean shadows.

As early as the following day, Hr. Delft paid another visit. The colonel had requested some information regarding weight differentials on some steel rails and, as a pretext for having to come back, uncle Heinrich had let on that he did not have the relevant tables with him.

As expected, the colonel led the conversation toward Per's project and sought to find out the names of the shareholders and financiers who were backing him. At first, Hr. Delft feigned incomprehension. Then he shook his head and gave a rueful smile, saying: "Ach, this amphibian Sidenius keeps going on about—that's what Hr. Colonel is referring to? I wouldn't set much store by that story. It's dead in the water."

"What did you say? Good God man! It was you yourself who stood here only yesterday telling me that the whole thing was in the bag. You knew that for a fact you said."

"I would ask Hr. Colonel to bear in mind that I said it had been secured where finance was concerned. I expressly added that statutory approval of the plan was required. And that will never be obtained."

"And why not? If the money really is on the table, why would the state actually wish to oppose the idea?"

Hr. Delft stood with hunched shoulders and he squirmed slightly as if to rid himself of some feeling of shame that passed over him.

"I'm sure the good colonel understands what I am referring to without my having to say any more."

"What are you going on about now man? Trying to be all damned secretive? What are you getting at?"

Hr. Delft remained silent and continued to turn his head, as if in diffidence, from one side to the other. He really did at this moment look like an overdressed monkey.

"But speak can't you!" the colonel roared.

"I'm sorry colonel, the thing is ... the government's hands are tied ... that's the top and bottom of it."

"Tied? By whom? I don't understand a word of what you are saying."

"Well, I won't keep the good colonel any longer. Again, my respects sir."

"Not a chance! Now Delft about-face and present arms! No more shilly-shallying! Explain what the hell would keep the state from giving its approval if the finance was in place and the plan was otherwise deemed to be sound and realistic?"

"That's precisely it Hr. Colonel, the plan is actually sound and realistic."

"Grrrh! Now I warn you. I will go berserk! Say exactly what you mean. Go on. Spit it out man!"

"Well—to speak frankly—do you really believe, Hr. Colonel, that our neighbors to the south would simply accept the establishment of a dangerous competitor to Hamburg? I don't think they would. Not till hell freezes over they won't!"

The colonel threw himself back in his chair and his hands dropped by his side. The whole of his already boiling face became puce.

"Well that takes the biscuit. Never in all my born bloody days have I heard such claptrap! Where did you get that mad notion from man? Do you really believe that the Germans are going to declare war on us because of that—eh?...eh?"

"Good God—War? Never! But they wouldn't need to. Just a discreet, precisely worded note from Berlin to Copenhagen would suffice...You would admit, sir, that this was all that was needed in the past and in similar circumstances."

The colonel looked down at the floor. His thumb was under his chin and he began to bite the knuckle on his index finger.

Hr. Delft shrugged his shoulders.

"That's one of life's realities for us small nations! We have to bend the knee...even if that means suffering in silence at an injustice. It's sad, very sad, but that's the reality of life. David actually very rarely beats Goliath and Denmark is just another little David with his pathetic sling...you have to bend the knee and be careful...extremely careful." Uncle Heinrich kept on in this vein when he saw how well he, on the one hand, was exacting his private revenge with malicious glee and, on the other, stoking the lust for battle in this veteran defender of the realm who still carried the scars from German bullets.

The colonel was still quiet, and his interlocutor used the moment to take his leave.

Uncle Heinrich got out just in time. He had just reached the door leading to the street when the colonel exploded from his chair like a steer stung by a horsefly. And as always when there were no guests present and he could give full vent to his anger, he burst out of his office into the sitting room of the house in order to let his wife know how he felt. He did not even baulk at having to call her from the kitchen. Then, and without paying any heed to her tearful protestations that her soup was going to catch and be ruined, he let forth in a string of treasonable oaths aimed at the cowardly, lumpen, and spineless spirit that had governed the Danish people since the last war with Germany.

On the very same day, uncle Heinrich enjoyed his usual eventide repast at his brother-in-law's home. As the table was being cleared, he took Ivan to one side and with that faux air of exasperation that was natural to him when, for a change, he had troubled himself to do a favor for someone else, he said: "The colonel is now there for the taking young man! It wasn't easy but he has taken the bait."

So as not to arouse suspicion, Ivan waited several days before making his move. He then sent a note to the colonel requesting the honor of an interview and explaining, very briefly, the context.

Upon receiving the note, the colonel was plunged into a daylong crisis. There was immediately something in the missive that undermined his defenses. Ivan possessed that finely honed Jewish trait of ingratiating himself with people by stroking their vanity in all the right places—and the colonel was highly susceptible to flattery. Moreover, the very name Salomon had a gold-plated ring to it that was tempting in the extreme to this money-obsessed man's ears.

But above all it was completely against his nature to sit twiddling his thumbs while others acted. In spite of his seventy years, he still had too much fire in his belly to be put out to grass without a fight. Thus, he had never been simply a pawn for the most reactionary elements in the country. Despite all the currying of his favor by those who held real power, his rebellious spirit had not been entirely extinguished. Buried deep beneath his bitterness and envy towards the new times, and the righteous indignation he had so carefully cultivated, there lay an inherent sympathy for the trailblazers. Just as he had maintained, in his outward behavior, the image of the intemperate firebrand who never minced his words, any strong and bold statement of intent would still exert a powerful attraction over him. Where his feelings for Per were concerned, in reality, a substantial element of infatuation lay at the bottom of everything.

However, when Ivan finally paid him a visit some days later, the colonel was still of a mind to show no mercy. It was only when Ivan stated flatly that the whole enterprise stood or fell on his support that he finally decided to yield.

But he insisted upon a number of conditions, amongst others that Per should be called home immediately, because various changes were needed in his outline sketches before they could be used as a basis for detailed plans.

Furthermore, he demanded that, for there to be any possibility of a fruitful working relationship between himself and the young engineer, Sidenius would have to make a personal request for him to get involved in the project and also take the first steps in cementing a new understanding between them.

At this point, Ivan implored him not to make this a condition.

But the colonel was unbending on this point. He had not forgotten the words Per had used that day as he took his leave: "The next time we meet, it will be because you, sir, are looking for me!" This arrogant prophecy would not come to pass in the way Sidenius had assumed it would!

Ivan made several more attempts to persuade the colonel, but the old campaigner, who had in general been noticeably nervous during the discussions, now erupted with rage and said: "That issue will not be discussed any further here young man. I regard every point as having been debated to the full."

With that Ivan rose and went his crestfallen way.

15

BY THE middle of April, Per had arrived in Rome. He had, finally, given in to the baroness's entreaties that he should accompany the two aristocratic sisters during their "pilgrimage" to the Eternal City… or more accurately to the increasing pleasure he found in her sister's company.

Even Per himself was not exactly clear over the nature of the comfort that he found in spending time with Dame Prangen. On the face of it, she was little more than an admittedly distinguished but aging gray-haired and over-embellished lady. On age grounds alone, he decided that there could no be question of any kind of erotic attraction, even though he had to admit that her figure was still pleasing and her skin tone had retained a freshness that many a young girl would envy. From that point of view, therefore, he felt reassured and able to write openly to Jakobe about his impressions of her personal appearance and character, but he failed to notice that Jakobe never mentioned this acquaintanceship, nor his descriptions of it.

It was the motherly way in which Dame Prangen engaged with Per that made her so attractive to him. Moreover, her concern for his intellectual and spiritual wellbeing satisfied certain deep-running emotions in him that even he did not fully apprehend. On top of that came this strange disparity between her, without doubt completely genuine piety and then the elegance in her mode of dress and refined lifestyle—between the solemn biblical pronouncements she delighted in using against him and certain enigmatic and thoroughly worldly glints in her eye and the way she smiled. The intimations he would sometimes glimpse in the movement of her mouth and her still iridescent dark blue eyes. Her combination of devoutness and worldly sophistication was a provocative mystery to him.

There was no little gossip amongst Danish expatriates living in Rome regarding the two aristocratic ladies and their youthful consort. It was the nature of Per's liaison with the baroness that tickled their curiosity most. As they traveled together, this lady's feelings for Per had blossomed into a quiet form of swooning worship. Every time somebody gave her news or new information, her eyes would fill, she would clasp her hands together and declare: "Oh you really must tell Hr. Sidenius"—or: "Now wait till our dear friend hears that!" Indeed, one of the first things she did on her arrival in Rome was to arrange a sitting with a sculptor so that she could have a bust made of Per.

For his part, Per was well aware that the old lady had become putty in his hands. She had pressed him to tell her all his plans for the future and then immediately pledged her support. When she heard about the venture partnership, which was being set up at that very moment in order to bring his ideas to fruition, the baroness became so enthusiastic that she even spoke of selling one of her estates so as to secure the success of the undertaking.

However, Per could not bring himself to take any personal advantage whatsoever from his influence over this ailing and besotted old lady—not least as he began to realize, to his great horror, that the reason for her excessive affection was that she saw in him some kind of natural son and heir to her deceased brother—a delusion, of course, that he had not entirely discouraged in the past. Occasionally in her forgetfulness, she would address him as "my dear nephew," sometimes even "my own adopted son." The baroness's strong affinity disturbed Per greatly but, on the other hand, he just could not bring himself to muddy the waters of an albeit perverse but by now well-established narrative.

Furthermore, with each day that passed, he became more and more distracted by the exotic life and lifestyles he saw around him. He had been unprepared for a trip to Rome and arrived without any preconceived notions. For this reason, he was spared the sense of anti-climax that affects so many travelers in their first days there.

Like a sun-worshipping Viking, he simply enjoyed the clear skies and the balmy, gentle air. During his travels through the swamps and marshland that makes up the Danube delta he had once again caught a cold and, sensitive to any indications of ill health as he was, this had put something of a dampener on his stay in Vienna. But he found that the journey alone down through Italy had a rejuvenating effect upon him. Never had he felt so healthy and strong in both mind and body than he did now! Within the space of a few days, his face with its neat little goatee beard had taken on an almost bronze tone, which made his brilliant blue eyes twice as striking. When he strolled around Monte Pincio and its gardens accompanied by the baroness and Dame Prangen, clad in his new, bright gray summer suit, which dropped so easily and pleasingly around his powerful frame, it would often happen that some black-eyed beauty would send him a passionate stare from above the edge of her fan.

The long conversations, meanwhile, that he still had with Dame Prangen on religious affairs had a quite different effect upon him than the one she had intended. Per gained pleasure from them precisely because they held no power over him. The great mass of reading he had digested during his lonely winter evenings in Dresack now stood him in good stead, and it was a cause of great satisfaction to him that he could impress this lady at court with his philosophical learning and occasionally even gain a sense of superiority in their frequent debates.

But despite her completely failed attempt at proselytizing, Dame Prangen showed not the slightest sign of displeasure. She really was, as Per described her in his letters to Jakobe, an extraordinarily open-minded Christian and the friendship between them grew fonder with each day that passed.

Per was not staying at the same hotel as the two sisters; but he visited them every day and escorted them on their strolls through Rome, or he would go with them to the rooms of the Scandinavian Association where every afternoon they read the newspapers. Nor did he deny that he gained great pleasure from the aura of inherent refinement that the two aristocratic ladies bestowed upon him. For the fact was that he enjoyed (with a slightly guilty conscience it has to be said) the reverent titles the hotel servants used when addressing him. On the other hand, his basking in the reflected glory of the baroness no longer grated on his compatriots in Rome. It was true that his close association with Dame Prangen had smoothed some of the more awkward edges to his character, but his new man of the world image would never fully conceal his rough-hewn inner self. His fellow Scandinavians soon recognized that in any comedy, Per would always play the farmhand rather than the concealed prince. Moreover, if anybody meeting him for the first time were in any doubt about this, Per's own animated verbosity very quickly revealed his true outlook and aims in life, sometimes more than they cared to know.

He had not come to Rome as a pilgrim of any kind. In the same way that museums held no attraction for him, he would walk straight past the myriad church doors that were always open. Nevermind that his aristocratic companions, like so many foreign visitors, saw these thresholds as the gateway to authentic Rome. These four hundred dungeon-like rooms, stained by the smoke of oil lamps and candles, where the middle ages lived on in unadulterated intensity and power; a silent world in the midst of the tumult of the street; an antechamber to heaven where words could only be uttered in hushed tones and where benedictions, chants and songs of praise and never ceased. None of this held a spell over him.

Rather, it was Ancient Rome, the ruins from antiquity, that fired Per's mind in this city of cities—The Eternal City and its catacombs that housed the soul of the world. But even here it was far less the imposing architecture that affected him than the great mass carried by the walls, the overwhelming solidity of their binding elements, the inherent titanic power expressed in these two-thousand-year-old gigantic creations. Nothing, therefore, captivated him more than the baths built by Caracalla and Diocletian and then the astounding Coliseum. He was happy to sit for hours in the deserted expanse of the amphitheater's interior, glorying in the thought that he might rebuild it from the ground up, throw up a latticework of scaffolding around it for his giant workplace that would be strewn with blocks of stone, as if a Cyclops had thrown them about; there would be jostling oxcarts, clouds of dust, and the shouts of hundreds of sweating slaves. Brick by ancient brick, level by level, it would rise from its foundations to become a new Tower of Babel.

And such fantasies led him once again back to books and reading. These ancient massive walls aroused an urge in him to find out more about the people of Rome and their collective fate than the largely vague knowledge he had retained from his schooldays. Per loaned the German classical scholar Theodore Mommsen's *Römische Geschichte* from the library at the Scandinavian Association and with the stubborn powers of concentration he could sometimes muster, he rapidly plowed through its weighty volumes.

For the first time in his life he was in thrall to the grand sweep of human history. Prior to this, his gaze had always been directed expectantly towards the epoch-making time that was to come—the past had never entered his mind. Now, he could consciously indulge in sitting amongst the ruins of the Palatine Hill and, with his back leaning against the sun-warmed trunk of stone column, read about those men who had set out from this place to conquer the world. And in another first, these studies led him beyond the Christian period he so despised and into a culture that bore no stain of the spiritual and intellectual tyranny which for him was the curse of the present age. In the epic champions of the Roman Republic, Per found the heroic figures he hitherto had lacked. In this completely practically minded, daring, intelligent, and unsentimental race of pagans, he saw mankind in its pure elemental state—the race of Titans which had appeared fleetingly in his dreams and in whom he had felt such a close affinity.

In one of his letters to Jakobe, he wrote emotively:

"Never have I felt so strongly as I have down here the true extent of the atrocity Christianity has perpetrated against humanity. Never have I understood with such clarity, and a feeling of shame it must be said, how far we still have to go to even get near this great race of people whose human glory that anemic eunuch from Nazareth presumed to question. Do you know the story about the hunchback king? As the fates had deemed that his Majesty should be born with a crooked leg and a crick in his back, a decree was issued that turned all accepted norms in the country upside down. What was small was now to be called tall and what was crooked was now to be called straight. A straight back was described as hunched and a giant now termed a dwarf. That's a perfect description of the lunatic world in which we live today!"

After nearly two weeks in Rome, Dame Prangen received a telegram from her husband stating that he had fallen ill and wished her to return home. Thus the two sisters prepared to depart, with the baroness tearfully regretting that she was going to be leaving Rome without having been received by his holiness the Pope, which had become an obsession for her.

Their leave taking of Per was, for both ladies, an emotional affair. Dame Prangen secured a solemn promise from him that he would pay both herself and her husband a visit at Kærsholm, where her sister would also reside. Even as the train departed, the baroness, with tears in her eyes and waving her white lace handkerchief, continued calling out to him—"hope to see you soon Hr. Sidenius!"

Per had no choice but to remain in Rome due to the bust which his patron had commissioned and in which he himself had begun to take an interest. Besides, he was not exactly in a mad rush to get away. He still felt extremely comfortable there and the reports about the continuing cold and damp spring weather north of the Alps left him in no mood to break camp. A fear of loneliness would still grip his heart—for this reason, he always sought the company of others while in Rome.

There was also the fact that he had received word from Ivan that he should be prepared to leave at short notice as his presence at home might be required in order to advance his project. In fact, in the most recent missive, Ivan had boldly asked whether he might be able to leave with no more than a day's notice.

Per had declined to answer this letter. He had begun to weary of these almost daily messages from his brother-in-law with their incessant questions, recommendations and reminders. His attitude to what he called his life's work had, perhaps almost unknown to himself, undergone a sea change at the very moment the prospect of its implementation had become a reality. It was not so much that it had lost its value in his eyes; but the shine had been taken off it once his out-and-out revolutionary idea had fallen into the grubby hands of speculators and shareholders who discussed his dreams in the same way they might talk about opening a new bank account. Even the kind of commercialized babble which Ivan used when writing to him, this almost incomprehensible Jewish peddler jargon, left him with a sense of nausea at the whole business. Worse still, nearly every letter sent by Ivan contained new provisos, or proposals for scaling back, or further adjustments and amendments, so that in general and from sheer annoyance, he would leave them unanswered for several days.

The contrast between the despondency he felt at this turn of events and the inspiration he found in the aura of the Imperium that was all about him sharpened his indifference to such pettifogging matters that only left him downhearted and flat. In his most recent letter, Ivan had even had the temerity to suggest that he should hold out some kind of olive branch to Colonel Bjerregrav—to the very man who had once sought to coldly and calculatingly grind him into the dust. There we have it! In good time, this brother-in-law of his would get his reply!

All these aggravations from home gave his life as a carefree gadabout here in Rome a heightened attraction for him. He had made various acquaintances amongst his Scandinavian compatriots and this included the women, in whose company he gained rapid solace for having lost Dame Prangen's attentions. Per regularly spent the evenings in the company of this group at one or other of the rustic taverns on the outskirts of the city. Here these Nordic expatriates, following a long-established custom, would meet up and plunge into hedonistic festivities, like artists signaling their joy in life's passions. The wine would flow freely; there was song, dance and disputation (with arms bared on hot evenings) and Per took to this bohemian social set as a prince to ermine. He was always in top form. That springtime in which Jakobe had kindled his senses with her sun-kissed abandon now bore its fruit in Rome's sultry heat. The seeds of bright and festive sentiments that now blossomed captured all who were touched by them with their radiance and apparently undefiled freshness. Though he drank copious amounts of wine, Per never became truly intoxicated. On the other hand, he could sometimes be suddenly possessed by a childlike euphoria during which he held the company spellbound with his cascade of antics. And when shortly before dawn the party would break up and make its serenading way homewards, Per would usually be seen at the head of the procession, strewn with flowers, a crown of garlands on his head, and accompanied by a pair of adoring ladies—young or old—who had taken his arm as they strolled back into town.

One evening, while attending one of these gatherings, Per encountered one of the shaggy-haired German artists to whom Fritjof had introduced him during his stay in Berlin. At that moment, the man was one of the à la mode painters in Rome—a small dwarf-like man with an immense Victor Emanuel beard and two-inch heels on his shoes. They renewed acquaintances amidst the usual bacchanalian clamor of raised voices and glasses so the man of the moment invited Per to his studio for a more cultured chat.

There was a surprise in store for him. On an easel in the middle of the studio stood a recently completed full-length portrait of a young woman. She was a strawberry-blond Jewess, whose fine lines and timorous doe eyes he recognized straight away. For this was Jakobe's half cousin. The young daughter of the Commercial Consul in Berlin and sole heir to fifty million dollars.

"Is she in town?" he asked, unable to hide his astonishment.

"Was. She went home yesterday. You know her then?"

Per explained that he had visited her parents' mansion on a couple of occasions but he decided against revealing any further details of their acquaintanceship. He preferred not to dwell on his mad plan to conquer this wealthy heiress whose hand had already been sought by half of the German nobility.

"What's the lie of the land with her? Did she not get married recently?" he inquired, unable to take his eyes away from her seductive face, which looked at him with the same stolen glances she had sent his way on the evening of the concert.

"Yes, she is indeed married. She was down here with her paramour—lucky dog!"

"What was his name again?"

"Bieber—Dr. Bieber."

"Ah, of course! Now I remember. I saw him once in their home. He was not exactly Adonis incarnate it has to be said. In fact, between you and me, he was more Greek goat than Greek god."

"Ach—this glorified body rubbish!" the diminutive artist fulminated. It occurred to Per that he looked for all the world like a wombat as his hand pulled at his intemperate beard, a weighty amethyst ring dazzling in the light as he did so.

"I'd say he's loaded though?" Per ventured.

"Loaded? Not at all. He was as poor as a church mouse. You obviously don't know the full story! A steal of a story! Her meticulous parents filled their luxury pile with every eligible baron and officer in the land, regardless of their fiscal standing, to ensure that their daughter would marry into her own class. All commoners and bourgeois types were not allowed near. Except they forgot all about fat old Dr. Bieber. He was their doctor's assistant—and, of course, it had to be him!"

"Of course," Per mumbled, suddenly distracted—his gaze still fixed, as if spellbound, on the young woman's features.

"Given that you yourself Hr. Sidenius were a guest in her parents' palace in Tiergarten, I'm sure you are also aware that the place was nothing short of a resplendent torture chamber for that young lady. Her mother quite brazenly keeps a whole host of lovers and her father is nothing more than a scoundrel. The daughter just wanted out of that nightmare—at any price, that's the top and bottom of it! I do believe that she would have taken the first more or less presentable and half-decent man who had the gumption to lead her astray."

Per turned from the portrait and stared almost menacingly at this verbose little painter.

"He led her astray?"

"Well not quite literally. But he always kept a weather eye on the main chance. And despite being boot ugly and poverty stricken, not to mention his lowly station in life—his father works in the finer end of the second-hand goods market—he had the requisite fortitude . . . or perhaps self-confidence . . . indeed we might even say downright effrontery . . . to try his luck. Who knows? Maybe he did see himself as an Adonis. And on that self-deception was his victory built! . . . Now have you, young sir, grasped the perverse philosophy that resides in this whole story? Do you realize that, in reality, it's not so much what you are but what you can convince yourself you are that counts? Do you actually think that little lieutenant Napoleon would ever have become emperor of France if he had not had the insane idea that royal French blood flowed in his veins?"

At these words, the world-renowned dwarf artist lifted himself up on his high-heeled shoes and, as he rocked to and fro, began to twirl his martial moustache once again. But Per averted his eyes. He was suddenly reticent and sat for a long time without speaking—his mind being in another place entirely.

In the meantime, the main news coming from Copenhagen was that Nanny and Dyhring had exchanged wedding vows. Dyhring had resigned his position at *The Falcon* in order to take over as editor-in-chief of an older, more esteemed broadsheet, *The Citizen*, which had a particularly strong business constituency.

However, Dyhring's father-in-law Philip Salomon had not been the prime mover in this career elevation, which was solely down to the backstage influence of Max Bernhardt—Dyhring being one of Bernhardt's closest protégés. Indeed, because of his appealing countenance, his craftiness, and also the contempt he had developed at an early age for all man-made laws and statutes, Bernhardt had nurtured greater hopes for Dyhring than any other of his acolytes. It had been under the patronage of this hugely influential benefactor that Dyhring, as a twenty-year-old cub reporter, gained a prominent position at *The Falcon*, and while there had shown such absolute obedience to him that he had won not only Bernhardt's confidence but also his friendship.

Max Bernhardt had actually reacted angrily when Dyhring declared his engagement to Nanny. His bloodless face stiffened and two fierce lines emerged, running from the sides of his nose down to the bottom of his chin as he snapped at his favorite acolyte: "A Jewess of all things Dyhring! You disappoint me. Really, you do. I credited you with more sense than that. I have not been slow in directing your attention towards Royal Court Secretary Lindholm's daughter. She too is not only beautiful but very rich. And I'm sure you would have been just the man to make the required impression upon her."

But for the first time, Dyhring refused to be brought to heel. He really was in love with Nanny. The truth was that his inability to resist the charms of women like Nanny was the one chink in his armor.

Max Bernhardt recognized that, in this instance, he would have to yield. He himself was not entirely blind to the promise inherent in a pair of sensuously revealed lady's arms and the only moments of folly he would forgive in a man were those where a woman lay at the heart of the matter. The only thing he secured from Dyhring was a promise that he would keep the engagement secret until a more prestigious and independent position had been secured for him within the upper echelons of the press. And lo and behold, the very week afterwards, the way was cleared for Dyhring to rise to the throne of the very much sought after editor's position at *The Citizen*.

Here it was Max Bernhardt's intention to steal a march on Philip Salomon. His fear was great that he would lose some of his influence over Dyhring if he had his father-in-law to thank for the honor of being appointed a newspaper editor.

And so it came to pass that Dyhring and Nanny were married. There was neither pomp nor ceremony. One bright, sunny day, Nanny arrived home laughing and batting her eyelids at the newly baked newspaper editor. She curtsied before her parents and presented herself as Fru Dyhring. They had been joined in wedlock that morning at a dusty old registrar's office and had struggled awfully—as she breathlessly explained in a torrent of words—in trying to keep a straight face during the solemnities. Afterwards they had gone to a restaurant and had lunch with some friends of Dyhring's who just happened to be at the same place.

The Salomon household's main dining table was now prepared in all haste and as festively as possible. Philip Salomon then raised a wedding toast to his favorite daughter and her bridegroom. He did so with an ingrained solemnity that was in stark contrast to the almost frivolous poise displayed by the newly-weds. His wife too was highly emotional. Regardless of how much these aging parents had—after encouragement from their children—made efforts to keep up with the new times and its mores, on occasions such as this, their own natural inclinations would always prevail. Neither of them really looked to the future with any great feelings of hope. The stubbornly independent attitude of their daughters, in particular, fueled their hidden anxieties.

Be that as it may, they were gradually caught up in the revelry all around them and, in the end, the presence of the smallest children gave the joyous celebrations a tumultuous air. Only Jakobe sat quietly, as if excluding herself from it all. She was also the only one who had not dressed up for the occasion. She was so enraged at Nanny's flippant attitude and her besmirching of love's great ideal, which this wedding and the whole arrangement represented in her eyes, that it was only her mother's express instructions that had brought her to the table at all. She had at first made her excuses by claiming to be unwell. And, in reality, she actually did not feel well. Several times during the dinner she was overcome by dizzy spells and her whole body trembled with anxiety.

As dinner came to an end and people rose to leave, Jakobe made a quick exit, went up to her room, and was not seen again that day.

She sat herself down to write a furious missive to Per—she knew of no other way of dulling her longing for him and suppressing the wild, all-consuming jealousy that was on the brink of destroying her—body and soul.

It was not, for one moment, that she mistrusted Per. Any thought of betrayal on his part was so alien to her that even his all too brief messages, and the difficulty he quite clearly once more had in finding an intimate tone, did not really trouble her. Ever since their tender bond of love had been forged, she had felt him to be an inextricable part of her very being. With her proud and chaste nature, she refused to believe that Per could betray her. Nor would she ever forget the expression of happiness and gratitude that burned in his eyes the first time he lay in her arms. She stored this memory in her heart as a sacred vow. In those moments, she knew with absolute certainty— when she had otherwise doubted this truth—that she was a full-blooded woman and could be the object of her lover's undeniable desire.

But when she thought of all those people with whom Per was in contact on a daily basis—who had the privilege of being in his physical vicinity, to perhaps take his hand, hear his voice, bask in his smile . . . a form of hatred could then rise within her towards all these strangers who possessed, however fleetingly, all those precious things for which she longed. She envied the very pavement that carried his feet, the air that caressed his by now sun-kissed cheeks. Her jealous demons fired within her when she thought of the café waiters who brushed his arm when serving him coffee, the chamber maids in the hotels who made up his bed—that bed which still carried his body scent and the heat of his powerful limbs.

While down in the sitting room, Jakobe's mother sought to excuse her behavior to Dyhring and Nanny, the latter having made a cutting remark about her sister's abrupt exit.

"Jakobe has been so tense in the last while," Fru Salomon said. "I'm really worried about her."

Nanny smiled wanly but said nothing in reply. But when she was sitting beside Dyhring in the carriage that was to take them home to his bachelor apartment, where they were to spend the night, she snuggled into his arms and said: "You know what's wrong with Jakobe don't you? Because you must have noticed when we sat down for dinner. She is positively green with envy the poor thing! She is raging because it's not her that is rushing off to spend the night with her Per."

The following morning, the newly-weds took off abroad and intended to be away for several weeks. Their hope was that they could visit most of the countries in Europe within that timespan. Their travel ambitions even stretched as far as southern Spain, because Nanny absolutely had to see a bullfight.

Thus their honeymoon comprised for the most part of being either on a train or in a hotel. However this constantly shifting pattern where they met a myriad of people was precisely what they both wanted. Even in these very early days of love's first flowering, they felt no great urge to simply be alone together. Besides, there was no question of there being an overwhelming passion between them. Within a very short space of time, Dyhring's way of expressing his love for Nanny was via shameless shows of simpering affection and, in her relative innocence, Nanny obliged him in his penchant for provocative caresses, which gradually began to have a dubious effect on her far more wholesome sensibilities.

Overall, however, it must be said that they complemented each other because of the satisfaction they found in their mutual vanity. Dyhring enjoyed the stir that Nanny caused everywhere she went with her dusky, oriental beauty—not least because he was convinced that people assumed that she was more mistress than married. He knew very well that Nanny, both in her character and mode of dress, aroused in men the idea of an upper-class Demimonde—it was precisely this that made her such an object of his desires. He now piqued himself at seeing how even the debauched gentlemen of gay Paree shot furtive glances at him that were tinged with envy.

For her part, Nanny was proud of her husband, because of his elegant and precise features. His petite and refined figure, along with his gold-blond tresses, attracted comment and attention wherever they went. She herself would often say about him that he had the cut of a German prince. And furthermore, she was delighted that he was not a Jew. Though she had always insisted the opposite, she had sometimes felt great unease at her racial origins; and was now happy to admit that she was thrilled at having discarded the name of Salomon and become a solidly European Fru Dyhring.

Finally, she was proud of her new husband because, in his capacity as newspaper editor, he would often be able to procure access free of charge to attractions and events that others would either have to pay through the nose for, or in most cases never have a hope of gaining entry to. That sense for the value of money which, despite her indulgence in outward decor and splendors, had set her apart as a young girl was not going to be abandoned because of her new marital status. Thus, Dyhring's more expansive inclinations were a cause of a certain muted concern for her. She would regularly get an attack of nerves whenever their money was to be handed over. After staying in hotels, where he had rung for the maid incessantly for help with clothes or toiletry, she had no compunction in vacating their rooms without leaving a tip; or she might at most leave a half-franc piece on the washstand.

Cold spring weather and rain soon drove the honeymooners southwards. From Paris the itinerary was changed to go straight to Madrid. But on hearing rumors along the way that cholera had struck the Spanish capital, they beat a hasty retreat back across the Pyrenees. Now traveling along the Riviera, they decided to take a trip down through Italy.

Per was still in Rome at this point. Jakobe had written to him advising of their imminent arrival—something that had not actually been necessary. All the Danish newspapers had been carrying snippets of news and gossip about the glamorous young couple and their sojourn through Europe and Per had maintained his habit of reading these papers at the rooms of the Scandinavian Association.

Because of his role as a theater and variety show critic, Dyhring had always been something of a celebrity figure, though without commanding any real respect. But now, and at a stroke, he had become a man of real significance and influence at home. Hitherto, it was unheard of that the newspaper directors of a national institution like *The Citizen* would hand the editorial reins over to a man of such youth. A man, furthermore, who did not have the expected academic qualifications or equivalent background; in fact, it could not even be said that his reputation was unimpeachable. Nor had it been easy for

414 · HENRIK PONTOPPIDAN

Max Bernhardt to assert his will in this affair and he had been forced to play every card in his hand. However, while the Golden Boy himself meandered his way through Europe in velvet-lined carriages, allowing his beautiful wife to pamper and spoil him as they rolled on, a morality campaign had been launched against him in all the newspapers that had still not fallen under the influence of Max Bernhardt. The announcement of Dyhring's appointment proved to be the spark for a renewed flare-up in the constant conflict between young and old, radical and conservative. His name became the battleground in which a new thrusting dynamism and a fearful enervation, the crass arrogance of the innovators and the politely masked resentment of the old guard, was thrown together in turmoil. Newspapers at the lower end of the market ran long articles about him along with his portrait. The scandal sheets, meanwhile, served up colorful caricatures, which only encouraged the salacious gossip that spread like wildfire across the country about his debonair ways, his rooms adorned in satin, his orgies with gangs of loose women and the whole decadent lifestyle that would put the Borgias of Rome to shame.

It was, therefore, no surprise that the expected arrival of the man himself and his young bride in Rome provoked a wave of excitement amongst their compatriots in the city. The ladies, in particular, put all moral considerations to one side in their stir of excitement, which was not to Per's liking.

In general, he had never been one for begrudging another man's good luck. He had been too aware of his own elevated status as a chosen one—the exception to the rule who had been raised above the need to compete with others for a woman's favors. However, his travels over the last year or more had deepened his self-awareness in many areas of his life. Meeting such an array of different people, working in foreign lands and very often with complete strangers, had enabled him to make very thorough comparisons with his own personality. Then there was his recent visit to the dwarf painter and his story about the ugly and poverty-stricken Dr. Bieber and his fable-like triumph—all this had made him understand that there were weaknesses in his own character that had to be conquered. The feelings deep within him that had surfaced during his time in the artist's studio, and which were now rising again with even greater force in the face of Dyhring's growing fame, had, in reality, already been the dominant factor in his subconscious life for some considerable time. A hidden sense of essential impotence had followed him throughout his travels. Even during his bouts of greatest revelry and excess, it had lain in his mind like a trap ready to be sprung, a malaise of melancholy that simply awaited its moment.

When Per, while at the Association one day, discovered quite by chance that the newly-weds were expected in Rome on the afternoon train from Milan, he resolved after a moment's hesitation to greet their arrival at the station. He persuaded himself by saying that, given that he and Dyhring were now brothers-in-law, it would be in the interests of family harmony to hold out an olive branch to him. But more importantly, he was anxious that by shunning him, he would lay bare the envious feelings he bore in his breast—feelings that nagged at him and left him feeling unworthy.

Thus, he turned up at the station with a (hastily and cheaply bought) bouquet for Nanny and bid the couple a hearty welcome to Rome. The diminutive, ever-alert newspaper editor was, as usual, the height of studied politeness. He muttered some words of thanks and received Per's conciliatory outstretched hand with a subtle smirk—which fortunately only Nanny noticed.

She, on the other hand, showed an unrestrained joy at seeing him again, called Per her "brother-in-law" and brought greetings from Jakobe and everyone else at home. They made an arrangement to meet that evening for dinner at one of Rome's best French restaurants.

After the meal was eaten, Dyhring very quickly became unsociable and yawned quite openly behind his carefully manicured hand. Nanny on the other hand talked incessantly and her torrent of words and stories so engaged Per's attention that, fortunately for the success of the evening, he completely missed the insulting behavior of her husband.

They then sat down to drink coffee outside a café on the Piazza Colonna and here, just like everywhere else, Nanny's beauty, her appealing attire and free nature attracted much attention. From top to toe, she was dressed in white—from her lace hat down to the looping design on her shoes. In the sultry heat, this airy ensemble lifted and fell around her voluptuous body like a swan's mantel.

Per could not get over how brilliantly attractive Nanny was. He had almost forgotten the fact of her utter beauty. As they sat chatting and facing each other across the small, round coffee table, his glance drifted surreptitiously over her exposed throat and abundant bosom, and he came to recall something else he had half forgotten—how close he had once been to proposing to her, and that she had given the impression she might very well have said yes.

As the little threesome parted company later in the evening, it was agreed that Per should collect Nanny at the hotel the next morning and take her off somewhere, while Dyhring paid a courtesy call to the Danish Consulate so as to collect more material for a travelogue he intended to write for his new paper about trade conditions in Italy. It was Nanny herself that had suggested this arrangement and with his usual show of gallant indifference, Dyhring had agreed to it immediately.

It was also true that the only condition the newly-weds had set each other when they agreed to marry was that each party would be able to retain complete freedom in all matters. They had also agreed that the slightest attempt by the other party to introduce any kind of coercion into the relationship, especially where the opposite sex was concerned, would be deemed to be sufficient grounds for divorce.

When Per arrived at the hotel and went up to their rooms at the agreed time, Dyhring had already left. Nanny received him in full maquillage, which included yesterday's white dress. She was eager to start the day's adventure. She rose from her breakfast table (consisting only of chocolate and cakes) and without saying hello or greeting him in any way exclaimed: "Where are we off to then Hr. Sidenius? I really want to be properly entertained today!"

Per mentioned that there was a monthly flea market at a nearby piazza. He had actually just passed it on the way to the hotel and it sold all kinds of old bric-a-brac and scrap that had been brought in

from the four corners of Rome. When Nanny heard this, she was adamant that this would be their first port of call. The idea of wandering
around amongst huge piles of trash pricked her fancy greatly. Afterwards,
she said, they could take a carriage and go round the city to take in the
must-see "attractions."

As she passed Per when making a final inspection round of her
two rooms, she popped a macaroon into his mouth. Then they set off
to discover Rome.

As they approached the market, whose din and commotion could
be heard some streets away, she bade leave to take his arm. Nanny
was at once far less cocky on seeing the plethora of stalls, the tightly
packed mass of people and the narrow lanes through which they
thronged. With no little trepidation, she fired furtive glances at the
ragbag forms and shapes descending on the square from all directions.
Large gangs of men were already standing around mounds of old clothes,
clumps of scrap iron and copper wares that were green with verdigris—
all thrown down in heaps at the entrance to the piazza. Her head full
of the stories she had heard about the Roman mob and its filthy habits,
Nanny had gathered her skirts tightly about her, and as they pressed
further and further into the morass of people, she lifted them higher
and higher over her white shoes.

Per found her to be even more captivating than the day before. A
dizziness came upon him from walking with her arm linked to his
and feeling the soft shape of her body as she frequently pressed into
him for protection when a half-naked, or particularly ragged, individual pushed forward and tried to force his wares upon them. He
had hitherto been rather uncertain as to how he should handle her—
had felt a bit sheepish when confronted with the sheer boldness of
her sister-in-law's intimacies. Now he brusquely dismissed all thoughts
of Jakobe and threw himself with abandon into the thrill of the
moment.

Besides, any thoughts of preserving some sort of decorum were
hopeless in this mass of people. First with a stiff arm and next with
his whole body, he would have to guard her from being bumped and
banged. In the end he proposed that they retreat from the fray but

she would not hear of this. While struggling with her mortal fear of this ragbag army, which closed about them with increasing impudence, and in the midst of all this tumult, garlicky vapors, and the biting stink of sweat, she was also ecstatic and laughed constantly to the point of convulsions, like a woman being tickled for the first time.

"I'm really enjoying this Per!" she cried from within the tightest throng of the crowd. "Otto would never have brought me here for all the world!"

All at once a row broke out near a booth just along the passage. Two young men had begun a slanging match and a crowd of delighted onlookers had very quickly gathered round them to form an impromptu arena.

Per tried to lead Nanny away but she quietly, yet firmly, restrained him—in fact, pulled him towards the fracas and lifted herself onto the tips of her toes to get a better view.

In the customary manner of irate Italians, they stood toe to toe, eyeball to eyeball. They raised first the one and then the other clenched fist, while their black eyes threw sparks of anger and their red mouths spewed oaths and curses that carried across the electric crowd like the cries of wild animals.

Per was slightly disturbed by Nanny's enthusiasm. Her face was alternately flushed and pale, and her lips were quivering. Nor was there any doubt that she had now completely forgotten that it was not Otto Dyhring she was holding by the arm. This was clear by the way she clung in to him every time a fist was raised in the boxing arena.

"My God, do you think they are going to stab each other?" she whispered.

Per had to laugh. By now he was something of a veteran spectator at these street scenes, which gave the impression that desperate men were on the verge of a vicious life and death brawl—while in reality they were simply, and with an artist's discernment, intoxicating themselves in the throwing of belligerent poses. Once the show was over, the putative combatants would walk away from each other with no more than a mouthful of dirty insults having been exchanged.

This was exactly how this "battle" was played out. At the very moment when tempers seemed set to boil over into fisticuffs and worse, the hot air was becalmed and the two men moved away from each other like two actors, acknowledging the applause of the crowd as they went.

"What . . . is it over?" asked Nanny, turning to Per with a disappointed expression.

"Yes Nanny—after all that!—so all praise to our good old-fashioned Danish skull smashers, is what I say!" With that he took her firmly by the hand and pulled her away before the mass of onlookers began to break up.

With great difficulty, they managed to get to the edge of the square, where they could then move about freely and unmolested. But then Nanny pulled Per back and let out a cry that was almost a yelp: "But dear, we didn't buy a thing!"

Nanny then dragged him mercilessly back into the human melting pot.

Hooked to Per's arm, she burrowed her way through to a decrepit old wooden booth that announced a sale of what were claimed to be antique goods. An ancient ramshackle old man with a studied Barbary Pirate air, complete with a stubbly white beard down to his naked throat, greeted her with practiced Eastern-style humility. And without even bothering to haggle, Nanny bought a silver tumbler and a gilded hair clasp at an outrageous sum and then left Per to pay for everything.

She then declared herself ready to be escorted around the city. Per called to a passing jarvey and their carriage took off.

The road led them to Piazza del Popolo, which Nanny insisted that she absolutely had to see first, because she had once read a novel with that very title. They then drove up over Monte Pincio via the grounds of Gregoriana Park, on to Quirinal Hill and then further out—up hill and down dale—past Diocletian's Baths, the Capitoline Hill and then the Forum.

The jarvey had been ordered not to spare the horses. Nowhere did they stop and Nanny found great sport in trying to identify things with her opera glasses as they raced by. She did not fail to let out the obligatory cries of wonder, but in reality was solely concerned with herself and the impression she was making on her escort.

However, there was a residue of annoyance in her feelings for Per. She had never really forgiven him for the way he had once rejected her advances and had constantly watched for a chance to exact her revenge. This moment, she knew, had finally come. It was for this reason that she unleashed all her alluring powers as soon as they had met at the railway station.

She could not have cared less about her sister Jakobe. Spoiled as Nanny was, she had never been able to forgive her half sister's refusal to be bowled over by her charms. Indeed Jakobe had, on numerous occasions, openly admitted that Nanny's coquettish nature irritated her immensely. Nor did Nanny hold back when it came to satisfying a desire, passion or even the smallest notion that might occur to her. She, who her father in good faith had dubbed "my normal child," because she had bloomed forth as the very image of health and virtue, had in truth always gained an unnatural pleasure from inflicting heartbreak. Even while still at school, she had enjoyed causing mischief amongst her friends, and she was barely half grown when she started to use her more mature figure in the sport of coming between sworn lovers, igniting the flames of female jealousy and fury as she did so. And her schadenfreude was always potentially more damaging because, with her less than elastic intellect, she rarely grasped the scope of harm she was about to perpetrate. Like a child who in partial innocence sets fire to the neighbor's house, purely to see the flames jumping from the roof, Nanny was often deeply perplexed by the trail of destruction she had set in train.

But now and at the heel of the hunt, in the company of Per Sidenius, she reacted in the way she always did: her nerve failed her. The knowledge that he, of all men, was the one that had come closest to mastering her had the effect of undermining her self-confidence. She had become particularly wary given that Per seemed to become bolder as the day wore on and, if she was not mistaken, actually making advances towards her. As they bounced along in the carriage, it occurred to her that the way he had held on to her hand with such a firm grip, and longer than he should have done, as he helped her into the carriage was surely no accident. In fact, there had also been a couple of times when he edged so close to her that she had been forced to move to the edge of her seat to avoid their bodies banging together as their vehicle rocked and swayed. Regardless of the satisfaction she gained from Per's advances towards her, especially when she thought of Jakobe, she was disturbed by the way their roles had been reversed. She, who had initially been the chaser, was now being chased.

Be all that as it may, she still talked incessantly, waved her perfumed fan with its downy frill and laughed coquettishly. The Pantheon, the Trajan Column, the Arch of Titus—they all flashed past without her really seeing any of them.

Only when the Coliseum loomed into view did she become momentarily engaged with what was around her. After initial reluctance, she yielded to the proposal to leave the carriage for a while and enter the arena to have a look around.

"We were supposed to go to Madrid so that I could watch a bull-fight," she said in her refined Copenhagen accent. She took Per's arm and they disappeared into the gloomy, cool passageways that led into the heart of this vast and ethereal cauldron of stone. "But we couldn't go because of some rotten cholera outbreak. It was really annoying!"

While Per was involuntarily gripped by the historic atmosphere all about the place, Nanny blathered on. Not even when they came to stand in the mighty sacrificial bowl, which had been witness to so many blood-drenched ritual killings and hecatombs did she remain quiet for a moment. As she swept the vertiginous ranks of spectator benches with her opera glasses, her thoughts were solely concerned with the question of whether she would have worn the muslin shawl with the flower pattern with her red Spanish silk jacket. That particular arrangement had driven lieutenant Iversen to sheer distraction when she had worn it at the theater shortly before their departure.

Per began to explain the design and construction of the whole edifice, showed her the raised daises for Caesar and the Vestal Virgins, described how the arena could be artificially flooded, so that sea battles and clashes with river monsters could be enacted ... and gradually Nanny did in fact become interested. In particular, she was enthralled by the iron meshed gangways and portcullises via which the gladiators stepped out to kill or be killed for the enjoyment of the watching multitudes. She remembered a painting she had seen that depicted a Roman swordsman in a baying amphitheater ... a giant of a man with bulging muscles, and quite naked, apart from a metal helmet and a strip of cloth covering his loins. The painting was on display in a bookshop in Østergade during her last year at school and she had always made sure to take a little diversion on her way home so that she could look at it. She was struck by the thought that, on the very spot on which she stood, some naked, massively limbed giant of a man had stood there with his heel jammed down on his vanquished opponent's blood-smeared throat as he awaited, with a smile on his lips, Caesar's command and the acclaim of the crowd— and automatically her nostrils began to flare, as she felt the same ecstatic breath of cool air on her neck and back as the swan white Vestal Virgins sensed when they began to weigh the bloodlust all about them.

When, shortly afterwards, she took Per's arm in order to go back to the carriage, she threw an appraising look at his manly figure in one stolen glance. Then she retreated into silence.

Per proposed that they should forget the tourist "attractions" and drive up to the heights of Rome to enjoy some fresh air. After a moment's hesitation, Nanny agreed to this and the jarvey was told to go across the Tiber. Climbing the renowned, winding roadway, they reached the Janiculum summit with its wonderful view over Rome and the panorama it presents of Rome's Campagna and the still-bright Alban hills in the distance.

Enthused by the ambience, Per found new heights of verbal sophistication. For the most part, Nanny sat with her face partially turned away and pretended that she was actually listening to him as Per pointed out and explained the buildings, spires, and domes that were most prominent in the golden haze that rested over the city. Up there in this isolated place, the unease she had felt the whole time began to turn into a real fear. If Per so much as moved in his seat, she would give a nervous start. Without warning, she flatly declared that she was tired and wanted to go home.

And she was deaf to all Per's entreaties. She requested, no demanded, that the carriage be turned and they go home.

They parted company outside the entrance to the hotel.

Dyhring had returned from his visit to the consulate some hours before. He sat writing at a table in his shirtsleeves. As she walked through the door, all Nanny could see was the hairline on his neck and his narrow backbone. It struck her how old, in fact downright decrepit and emaciated, he looked when studied from behind.

"Ah you're back darling!" he said, giving just a slight turn of his face towards his shoulder.

His calm, even tone inflamed her. "Yes," she replied curtly, as she threw off her gloves and threw them onto the sofa.

"Had fun today?" he asked in a calm, measured tone.

"Oh Brilliant! A wonderful time! I nearly didn't come home again."

"Well. That's great. You'll excuse me for a moment while I get this finished."

"Oh, wouldn't dream of disturbing you!"

Dyhring continued quietly at his work, while Nanny, having got rid of her hat, dumped herself into an armchair at the other end of the room. She believed herself to be unobserved. She didn't realize that her husband, without having to alter his writing position, was able to watch her in a corner mirror, and that he divided his attentions more or less equally between her facial expressions and, belying his apparent distraction, a very well composed article. Here, in an expert and meticulously didactic tone, Dyhring gave the good readers of *The Citizen* an overview of trade conditions in Italy.

For about half an hour all was quiet in the room. Nanny's thoughts circled continuously around the defeat she had once again suffered at the hands of Per Sidenius. She just could not explain how her initial resolve had weakened and felt that the whole thing was an unbearable humiliation. At this moment in her life, she mused, there was definitely something wrong with her. Even while in Paris, she had not quite felt like her old self. But for the fact that she was absolutely sure that it was impossible, she would have sworn that she was pregnant. In the mornings, she would often wake with a desperate headache and feel faint right throughout the early part of the day. And all those mad notions and desires that would take hold of her! Not to mention the vivid dreams she was having that she dared not tell her husband about, so indecent and shocking were they!

In the four or five days the young couple still had left in Rome, Per met them on several occasions and on the surface at least his, admittedly very open, flirting with Nanny did not bother the husband in the least. Dyhring continued to treat him with the same practiced courteousness as before, but, already once bitten, Nanny made sure that she was never again left on her own with Per.

Only on the day of their departure, when they said their goodbyes at the railway station, did Nanny dare come out of her shell. Not only did she press Per's hand with unmistakeable affection, but when the train was about to depart, and she was standing at the window of their compartment, she allowed—with a brilliantly performed pose— her lovely eyes to rest upon him with passionate engagement, as if now at this moment of parting she was overwhelmed by all the feelings she had been struggling to suppress.

In her hands she held a beautiful and expensive arrangement of flowers—a goodbye bouquet from Per. And as the train began to move, she allowed one of them—a half-opened rose—to fall onto the platform. One could have viewed this occurrence as accidental; but it could also have been a sign, a mute admission, a symbolic covenant.

Per lifted the flower—unsure if he dared hope. When he looked up again at the window of the compartment, there was nobody there. He followed it with his eyes, but her carriage disappeared behind some large advertisement hoardings and she did not show herself again.

After wandering for hours in a long, distracted odyssey around the streets of Rome, he got back to his lodgings late in the evening. By then he had decided to break with Jakobe.

The idea had been smoldering within him for some time. During his stay in Rome, Jakobe had become more and more estranged to him. Each day that passed, with new signs of his flowering as an individual, had led him further away from her. He had realized how different, in essence, they really were. That Jakobe with her peculiar nature, for many an objectionable nature, was ill suited to the kind of daring and connoisseur lifestyle to which he aspired—the very thing that for him had represented the final goal of the new Renaissance, but whose significance he had only finally grasped while being in Rome. With festival torches and bonfires, accompanied by the sound of fanfares and clashing cymbals, would the trolls at home be trampled into the soil. But Jakobe was not the kind of woman who could help bring that kind of carnival atmosphere into his own life—only a woman of Nanny's scintillating disposition could do that.

Then there was the fact that Jakobe was not exactly young anymore. It had always been a bone of contention for him that she was older than he. And her frail constitution and sensibilities didn't make her look any younger either. Also her markedly Jewish facial features had begun to bother him once more. That time she had described in one of her letters how she had been insulted by two gentlemen—despite saying she was able to rise above it—had left him mortified.

However, it did not surprise him that he had once preferred her to Nanny. When he recalled his feelings at the time he had fallen for Jakobe—that winter's evening for example at the Salomon home, when Nanny returned all ablaze from a party and his gaze drifted involuntarily from her silk bedecked, gaily attired figure to the darkly austere Jakobe who sat there draped in black and serious of mien, a book nearby and her hand under her cheek as she pondered its contents—then he understood only too well that he once again had fallen victim to his hidden impulses, that dread of life which had been bequeathed to him, that anxious propensity to turn away from the world. Yes, these things had occasionally returned to haunt him in his adult life, like a ghostly hand seeking to direct his actions and the way he lived his life.

Of course, he knew that a break-up would cause great offense to Jakobe and wound her to the core. But he was not obliged to ruin his life because of a single moment's folly. Besides, there was more at stake here than just a woman's tears! With the great plans he nurtured for his life, he could simply not deny the destiny that lay before all men who aspired to greatness—to exert his will over mankind, and most of all over women. No. He would not be constrained anymore. That had been his problem up to that point: he had not been ruthless enough in bringing to bear the natural talents and forces he carried within him. This was the reason he had made so little progress thus far in his heroic odyssey.

But now the sails would be hoisted! Just recently he had received a new express mail from Ivan requesting with great urgency that he return home so that he could personally be involved in the negotiations regarding his project. As before, he had declined to answer the letter for a number of days. But now he immediately wired to announce his return home. That look of promise in Nanny's eyes pulled constantly at him. And he also recognized that now was the time for him to act. Per Sidenius would take command of the ship.

In plotting his new course, he would prepare Jakobe as gently as possible for the inevitable break. He would try and make her understand that, given the way his nature was, it was also for her own good if their relationship was ended before it was too late. But this could only be done gradually. He would slowly get her accustomed to the idea of a divorce, so that when they finally sat down to discuss it, they could bid each other farewell as friends, without bitterness or reproach.

Nor would it be a mere trifle on his part to utter the word farewell. He owed her an awful lot; but he could not sacrifice his own freedom for her sake. He was not going to put his whole future in jeopardy. He now had to show that the time he had spent amongst those mighty Caesars had not been in vain—that he could bravely cross the daunting bridge of man's High Will over the Rubicon's muddied and despairing waters, so that he could finally declare that the die of his life had been cast: *Jacta est alea!*

16

AT THE start of the business day, and shortly before Per was due to return from Rome, a group of men were to be seen entering the chambers of Senior Solicitor Max Bernhardt. It was the same small group of financiers that had met previously to discuss the possibility of getting Per's freeport initiative in West Jutland up and running.

Ivan was also present but his facial expression suggested that he would rather have been anywhere else but there. While the other gentlemen stood by the window and engaged in lively conversation, he remained aloof and paced about the room, only stopping to finger nervously at the books and newspapers that had been laid on the table.

He was devastated by his failure to bring about a truce in the conflict between Colonel Bjerregrav and Per. It was true that he himself had not expected that Per would simply hold his hands up straight away and accept that he would have to make an approach; but the way Per had spoken about the colonel in his reply meant that any hope of a reconciliation was a complete non-starter. In fact, with the flippancy that had been a feature of his letters from Italy, he had used up almost a page with his sarcastic invective against the colonel—recommending, for example, that the colonel be painted green and placed atop Vor Frelser church "to strike fear and trembling into the populace below."

But by this stage, Ivan had become tired of Per's witticisms, which very often appeared to be somewhat forced. He could not comprehend the indifference Per had shown in recent times about his own work and its fate. When he had wired him with the great news about Max Bernhardt offering his backing to the project, and then in another letter described his hopes that a consortium with real financial clout could soon be formed, Per sent back a terse reply: "A man once set off from the town of Jericho but fell amongst robbers and bandits . . ."

Once everybody was seated around the table, on which rolls of drawings, maps, calculations, etc., had already been placed, Max Bernhardt led off the discussion with the news that Hr. Salomon had unfortunately been unable to end the conflict between Colonel Bjerregrav and Hr. Sidenius and that this was causing a temporary blockage to the colonel's participation in the enterprise. This question would have to be addressed more specifically so that a final decision could be made on the composition of the proposed company's board of directors.

Ivan responded immediately to this and reminded everybody how, at their first meeting, he had raised doubts over the proposal that the brilliant young instigator of this project could work with a conservative technocrat who was very much of the old school. He made an earnest plea that, despite the negative result of his overtures to the colonel, the good gentlemen would not regard the venture as any less promising. He was convinced that the extreme importance of the project would strike home with the general public, even without the support of an archaic and envious ruling elite, once it had been announced with sufficient fanfare and, of course, widespread follow-up publicity. Ivan also pointed out that positive press coverage might be achieved in other ways as well.

Max Bernhardt's reply to this made the others laugh, as he pointed out that he had great confidence in the press's ability to influence events but far less confidence in the discerning powers of the general public. He then declared that he completely disagreed with Ivan as to the way things stood and the notion that forward movement was possible without Bjerregrav's involvement. It was clear that the colonel had signaled his willingness to get involved and the few conditions he had demanded were nothing more than was reasonable but were still to be fulfilled. Thus, he was now going to propose a new and more pointed request to Hr. Sidenius to bring his purely personal spat with the colonel to an end as quickly as possible.

Ivan opposed this suggestion repeatedly. He insisted that it was not just a case of smoothing over personal differences arising from a clash of opinions. The conflict had much deeper roots. It was a repetition of the immemorial conflict between old and new, the past and the future. As technical experts, and even in their different personalities, Colonel Bjerregrav and Hr. Sidenius were at completely opposite ends of their professional perspectives and never the twain would meet.

Finally, Max Bernhardt cut across Ivan in an almost brutal fashion and declared that he was sure the gentlemen present had no wish to have to sit and listen to a philosophy lecture. That was just a waste of time for everyone and time was pressing. Given that they had all agreed that Colonel Bjerregrav was absolutely the best technical expert who could give support and advice for the venture, which was now urgently required, and given that the colonel had declared himself a willing party in this regard, there was no sense in discussing what their position should be any longer.

The other gentlemen in attendance gave Max Bernhardt their full backing with a round of "hear! hear!" and "quite so!" And now that the issue was deemed to have been dealt with, they went on to discuss the prevailing currency rates and share fluctuations.

In the end, Max Bernhardt proposed that they should now regard the freeport company as having been finally established and that there should, therefore, be no delay in letting the press know about it. Notwithstanding the serious doubts expressed by some of those present about being so precipitate—with the exception of Bernhardt's confidante, stockbroker Herløv, and his perennial echo, young Sivertsen—some Copenhagen newspapers were already carrying the story the following morning with banner headlines such as "A New National Trade and Industry Initiative."

However Per's own name was nowhere to be found in the press coverage, which overall had a transitory feel to it and carried descriptions such as "according to rumors circling in finance circles." But the day after, those same newspapers could also report in more concrete language that "a range of influential businessmen and highly regarded financial institutions" stood behind the huge undertaking.

The reason why Max Bernhardt was in such a hurry to generate publicity about Per's project had very little do with his interest in it and much more to do with his hope that it could help strangle the rival Copenhagen freeport project at birth. Where the Sidenius project was concerned, he had little faith in the whole idea and, as far as he was concerned, it could be dropped as soon as it had served his ulterior purpose. And the reason he had declined to cite Per's name in the newspapers was to keep everybody guessing for as long as possible about exactly which project was being talked about. His reasons for completely dismissing the notion that Per Sidenius could be some kind of trailblazer was because, as far as he was concerned, anyone born and reared in a Danish vicarage was a lost cause. He had actually met Per once at a party in the Salomon household, where Ivan had been very keen to get them talking to each other, but he had very quickly realized that the vociferous young man who was so full of himself but bore the look of a country seminarian was not made of the kind of stuff he could use.

Moreover, Bernhardt was mulling over the idea of removing Per completely from the picture if necessary and replacing him with someone who could better serve his needs. He already had the potential replacement in his sights—a certain engineer by the name of Steiner who had just appeared in one of the provincial newspapers with another West Jutland harbor project, which it had to be said was obviously inspired (not to stay stolen) from Sidenius's own idea. However, certain parts of Steiner's proposals could be passed off as having been independently conceived, or at least they could certainly be put to work in Bernhardt's service.

The Salomon household had already moved out to Skovbakken by the start of May, even though the spring had been wet and stormy.

Worries about Jakobe's health had injected a certain haste in their move from the city and Jakobe herself had expressed a wish to get out to the countryside. It was not just the peace and quiet she longed for, but also the fresh air and the chance to go for long walks. This was the same Jakobe who, despite all her physical sufferings, had always neglected her health because she felt there was no prospect of ever getting better. But lately she had become extremely self-protective, almost to a fault. The fact that she now had so much to live for had inspired a belief that her poor frail body and constitution might obtain new energy and strength.

The mountain of books on a wide range of subjects that were a permanent feature on her writing desk, now also included works on medicinal subjects and health periodicals, which she studied religiously. During this period, and having first girded herself like some latter-day Spartan hero, she had plunged into a stringent health cure with ice-cold baths and punishing route marches. Even while still in Copenhagen, she had taken to walking out to Langelinje early in the morning, regardless of the weather and conditions underfoot—defying also the ridicule of friends of the family who lived in Bredgade and would watch her forced march and rain-battered umbrella from their windows as she returned at around nine o'clock.

But all this dogged persistence had given no tangible results. Everybody could see the way she was failing. Her sense of longing was simply too overwhelming. In the end, she could barely tolerate the sight of other people. And nights for her were like waiting for eternity to end. Even in her deepest sleep, the faint sound of a buzzing fly would rouse her.

But for all that, Jakobe was rarely in bad form. Just as her letters to Per never contained a single complaint, she herself—even at her lowest points—was full of hope. Ever since childhood, she was so used to bodily afflictions that they no longer affected her general mood or disposition. In fact, it might be said that she had befriended her pains down through the years. Thus, her hidden worries were the only thing that could really affect her.

She had become more and more convinced that she was pregnant. In contradiction to what, for discretion's sake, she had told her mother after the family matriarch had begun to press with more intimate questions than usual, Jakobe had seen and felt certain signs which strengthened her suspicions. She had said nothing to Per about it because she could not be absolutely sure. Her natural functions had always been characterized by a marked irregularity. The actual thought of being a mother only worried her insomuch as she sometimes dreaded that she may not have the physical strength to bring a child into the world. In fact, at certain moments her maternal portents could arouse a light but slightly somber joy in her heart, as if her soul had been momentarily bathed in pale sunshine. But overall, the question of her possible maternity occupied her mind far less than she would have previously believed possible. No. Each and every time her thoughts turned towards herself and her inner state, they would begin to circle a hundred times more around Per. Far more ferocious and debilitating was her insuperable and completely reckless jealousy.

She had lived in an increased state of angst and tension since the talk had started about calling Per home. Not one word, however, had she uttered in trying to influence his decision, even though Ivan had increasingly pressured her to do so. That said, she could not really understand his dallying in Rome, especially when it had not even been on his original itinerary, and where he could hardly learn more about hydraulics or river engineering. If it was simply about that bust (as he had stated in his missives to her) that was yet to be finished—well that was unforgivably selfish of him.

And now, in the last few days, he had sent a couple of strange and incoherent letters. To be sure, they could not be said to lack affection, quite the opposite, but they had unsettled her and gave her much to think about. But all her worries disappeared when a telegram came announcing that he would be in Copenhagen within the next few days. So that she could savor this news all to herself, she went out to the woods and, for the first time in her life, she felt the absence of a higher being for whom she could drop to her knees and offer all praise and thanksgiving.

On the day that Per was expected home, Jakobe was already up and about by daybreak. She then dressed herself with the studied calmness that was second nature to her whenever she became affected by an underlying sense of agitation. She was poised for departure several hours before the hansom cab was due to take her to the local station. Per was meant to be arriving in Copenhagen with the morning express train and she did not intend to miss it.

The weather had been beautiful in the last few days. This day too was bathed in sunshine as Jakobe boarded the morning school train as it made its way into the central railway station.

In the meantime, Per had seen native soil once more and his train was now steaming through Zealand. Now it was Per's turn to be ill at ease and feel torn. Even as his train had pulled away from the platform in Rome, he was still determined to break off the engagement. However, he had not written those fateful words while in the eternal city. He had found that all the packing and preparations for departure had left him with no time to reflect properly. Per had then resolved to stop off on the way home, either in Munich or Berlin, so that he could compose his final explanation.

But gradually, as he traveled northwards, and especially as his train approached the forest-clad alpine slopes, which only a few months before had formed the backdrop to their lovers' idyll, his gripping memory of it all began more and more to overpower him. That night, as the train traversed the Alps, he sat awake and stared out across the moonlit mountains from the window of his compartment. If he was not mistaken, he recognized the silhouette of a towering bluff, bedecked with trees, or a snow-glittering high peak, the very ones they had used as compass points in their passionate odyssey... and his heart sank at the thought.

So it was that Per began to ponder his brain. With a not fully conscious, but decidedly Pharisaic and Sidenius-like method of reasoning, he decided it would be best to begin looking at things from a purely practical point of view. Was it, he asked himself, all that clever of him to break a connection at precisely the moment when that connection could be of incalculable use to him, considering the battle he was now facing into? All things prudently considered, was he really going to turn his back on the support the Salomon household had, without a doubt, already given him in this whole affair? For the moment at least, this had to be his primary concern. The great battle that was going to mean death or glory was now at hand. And he longed to bestride the field of war. As he had traveled north through Germany's hammering and pulsating factory towns with their palatial railway buildings and forests of chimneys belching steam and smoke, an urge to act came upon him, a veritable work fever, which swept aside the lethargy that had seeped into him during his long, balmy Roman hiatus. Would he ever forgive himself if he placed his whole life's work and destiny in jeopardy, or even delay it for a moment, for the sake of some pleasing female figure or other and her alluring smile?

The three-day rail journey through Europe had given him plenty of time for contemplation and both Munich and Berlin passed by without any desire on his part to break his journey. In the end, his turmoil was resolved and his decision made. He would, for the moment, avoid anything that might hinder, not to say put a stop to, his progress or put his final vindication and victory into doubt. For the time being at least, everything had to be sacrificed at the altar of his legacy to the world—including the pleasures of love and the flesh. It might be that Jakobe was no longer the one that suited him best but wise counsel advised him to let the hare sit. As for domestic bliss, the two of them would just have to hope for the best. Those chosen few, whom the Fates had selected to answer a higher call, could not be bound by such common bourgeois concerns. Just like royal personages, where affairs of the heart were concerned, they had a duty to sacrifice their private feelings for the greater good.

However, when the train thundered into Copenhagen's main railway station, he was still apprehensive and in a nervous state of mind. But something unexpected awaited him.

As he spied Jakobe standing there on the platform as she studied each carriage window that passed, some logjam broke within him. On seeing her again, he was suddenly awash with emotion. Without thinking, he grabbed his travel hat and began waving through the open window.

He had to admit that Jakobe cut an extraordinary dash. She had bought a new, very broad-brimmed summer hat, which suited her face extremely well. Her obvious excitement and the fresh morning air had blushed her cheeks. She was wearing a light dress with an embroidered cape of ephemeral lace that exaggerated her figure somewhat to provide a certain fullness of form that she usually lacked. All this spoke directly and pleasingly to Per's greatest emotion where Jakobe was concerned—his own vanity.

He jumped out of the carriage without waiting for the train to stop. And though the platform was thronged with people, he put his arm through hers as if to cock a deliberate snook at anyone who might object that their engagement had still not been officially announced. With that, he bowled along with her, making an exit into the street through the first-class waiting room. Per could not get over his shock at finding her so much younger and more beautiful than he could ever have expected. Jakobe looked far less Jewish than the recent proximity and influence of Nanny's persona had led him to believe.

Jakobe's utter joy had left her mute. But her gaze was directed constantly upwards at Per's face and while they were still pushing through the mill of people in the main concourse, her heart hammered like a piston, so much so that Per could feel its drumbeat along his own arm. He smiled and looked down into her eyes—eyes whose depths were the gateway to their intimate and mutual memories. He squeezed her arm gently but urgently and whispered: "Darling Jakobe—"

They darted into a covered hackney carriage, and when Jakobe threw her arms about him and pressed her body close to his, Per abandoned all thoughts of gentlemanly reserve. The carriage took off at a brisk pace and, before either of them could regain their composure, it pulled up outside the hotel.

Jakobe remained sitting in the vehicle while Per went in, booked a room, and performed a quick wash and change of dress. They then went straight to Skovbakken without bothering to use the train. There was too much to tell each other in private for them to use a more public form of transport.

Once the carriage reached the coast road, they stopped to have the hood rolled back. By midday, the sun carried real heat and there was not a puff of wind.

Per let out a deep sigh. It was as if his very being was expanding with a joyous feeling of liberation after the endless torture of being constrained in a straitjacket of doubt, and his heart was filled with gratitude to Jakobe who, with her beauty and obvious delight at seeing him again, had vindicated his decision. In truth, he was also more than happy to once again have the course of his life mapped out for him. Nor was the effort involved in persuading his conscience as great as he had liked to believe. Then there was the simple feeling of comfort at being on home soil again and hearing his mother tongue all about him. Sitting in the carriage, hand in hand with Jakobe, and looking out over this familiar land and seascape—the just recently bloomed forest and the Øresund strait where so many white sails dotted the blue sea—he was momentarily overcome with an actual feeling of bourgeois contentment. So much so that when he saw the red and white of the Danish flag catching what little wind there was above one of the villa gardens, he was quite moved.

"My God, Jakobe—our good Dannebrog!" he cried.

But then Jakobe began to talk about Dyhring and Nanny.

"They got home just before you, last night," she said. "They did an unbelievable amount of traveling. But, of course, you met them in Rome. What did you make of the two of them—as a couple?"

"What did I 'make' of them? Well. I mean. I'm not sure..."

"Per, I swear. I think, it's over between them already. Nanny, at any rate, has obviously not changed the flirty flighty ways that she always had. I'm fairly sure she's joining us for dinner by the way. She told me that she was looking forward to recounting her Italian experiences with you."

Per, whose face was looking out to sea, attempted a smile but gave no reply. And at an opportune moment, he eased the conversation over to other subjects.

Nanny did indeed arrive for dinner. Or rather, she landed half an hour after everyone else had sat down and took off again before coffee was served because she was going to a party that evening. She seemed to be in flying form and looked fabulous in a yellow dress with a flowered pattern and a short, sharply cut Spanish jacket of red silk.

However, her overall deportment confirmed a criticism of Per's, with which he sought to steel himself against her charms. There was a flippancy in her character, and especially as it was expressed in her torrent of words in that urban Copenhagen accent that repelled him. Yes, he had been entertained by it and its clang of home while they were in Rome together, but here it was just embarrassing. To his own satisfaction, he found that she came across as being rather cheap.

For all that, he felt a great relief when she left. For as long as she was present, he found it difficult to act normally and keep the usual facial expressions—not least when Jakobe looked his way.

But even after Nanny's departure he could not really relax. For despite the fact that he had no grounds for complaint over the way he had been received at Skovbakken (Philip Salomon had even requested that champagne be served on account of the day), his first rush of joy at coming home had dissipated bit by bit, like runoff from a high tide, and he had been left with a tinge of melancholy—an emptiness, some kind of loss—he himself could not fully describe it.

But then it struck him that the same thing had happened before and he glimpsed an explanation. For as comfortable as he was in the sumptuous dwelling of his prospective in-laws, he had never felt truly at home there. There was, in the whole way the family lived and interacted with each other, so much that seemed alien to him. It was not even the fact that they were Jewish or Old Testament in their ways (this was not anyway a prominent feature of the home or the social set in which they moved); rather it was the new and changing winds from modern Europe that constantly blew through their culture, which would unsettle him and send shivers through his spine. Just as now after dinner when, as usual, friends and acquaintances would call in from the surrounding holiday villas—they would be primarily Jews—and he was struck by the distinct feeling that he was still in some foreign land.

Per and Jakobe then went down to the garden. Linking arms, they walked for some considerable time up and down along the path that ran close to the beach, where interruptions from family or guests would be far less likely.

It was obvious now that Jakobe no longer cared to hide the real nature of their relationship from public scrutiny. In the very near future, a large-scale social occasion was planned at Skovbakken to celebrate the marriage of Nanny and Dyhring, and Jakobe knew that it was her parents' wish to avail of this gathering to announce their own engagement. Jakobe's mother, in particular, had pushed this strongly and declared that it was about time their thoughts turned to getting married. It was for this very reason that Jakobe had guided Per down to the garden, so as to discuss this with him and, at the same time, confide something to him of which she was no longer in doubt—that she was with child.

At that precise moment, she chose to say very little, preferring to put her head against his shoulder and at every other turn lean her mouth up to his for a kiss. It was with a concealed reluctance that Per returned her increasingly more passionate caresses. He was forced to admit to himself that Nanny still held sway over his sensual emotions. Every time Jakobe's lips met his, the image of her sister's face would hover into view and confuse his responses.

Instinctively affected by his hesitancy, Jakobe felt suddenly wary of revealing her big secret; there was also the fact that she just didn't know how Per was going to react. In the end, she resolved to wait until the next occasion when they were on their own.

Once more she stopped, turned to Per and pressed his hand to her heart, as she told him to make sure and be at the hotel the following morning as she wanted to come and visit him.

At first, Per let on that he did not understand her point and then said: "Can't! I'm afraid it's impossible my love! Your very own Ivan has just warned me of a business meeting with Max Bernhardt tomorrow morning at ten. The time for gallivanting is over—work, work, work!"

"All right . . . later in the day then. Whenever suits you best."

"No, that's not on either sweetest! We have to be careful here."

She looked at him slightly shocked. There was something in that nervous little laugh he gave as he had begun to speak that wounded her.

She walked on and said no more on the subject.

By now they had left the lane and went out on to the beach. Here, close to the water's edge, was a bench with a semi-circular screen at its back. The sun had just left the skies and, looking across to Sweden, the sound lay like shiny beaten metal under russet skies. The gravel cliffs over on Ven island still pulsed in a vague haze of heat. From within the Royal Deer Park came the sound of that seething rustle which can hold in a forest long after all winds have died to nothing. Otherwise, all was still. Far out in the sound they could both hear the regular splash of oars from a rowboat.

In order to avoid any more questions, Per began to skim stones. As a boy he had been a champion at this, and he was amused to discover that after all those years he had still not lost his touch. Jakobe remained sitting on the bench, leaning forward and resting her head in one hand as she looked on. Every time Per turned to her for approval after a successful throw, she smiled and nodded, but when he turned away again her face became serious, her expression brooding and distant.

"See that! Eight skips!" Per exclaimed proudly.

Now he was fired up. With precise care, he sought out the stones that were most suitable. In the end, he even removed his jacket. The joy at being home again, which he had lost up at the Salomon villa, was now won back in that wide expanse of sea and shore. The soft wash of the waves falling along the strand, the hum emanating from the depths of the living forest behind him, those soft yet persistent thumps from the oars of the invisible boat far out in the Øresund—in all this, there was something that spoke to his inner self and raised his spirits. He said nothing to Jakobe about his real feelings, but it was as if, via these things, he heard that comfortable and comforting "welcome back" to his native land that he had been waiting for.

While still at Skovbakken, Per had agreed with Ivan that he should collect him at the hotel the following morning, from whence they could go together to the meeting that had been set up at Max Bernhardt's chambers. The same group of interested financiers and stock brokers had also been invited. Exhausted by the multitude of conflicting emotions and impressions he had experienced that day, not to speak of the travel weariness from the preceding days, Per left Skovbakken unusually early, went straight to bed and was dead to the world until the chime of a tram brought him around the next morning.

When he realized where he was and the weighty things that were ahead of him this day, he became wide awake and was on his feet in a thrice. Despite the utter distaste he felt at the thought of these shyster businessmen with whom he was now expected to make common cause and, in effect, offer up a precious part of himself as a hostage, he was eager to get going. And his hope was that his presence in person at this gathering would put some backbone into these lily-livered moneygrubbers who were obviously petrified at the thought that they might lose a cent or two from their vast pockets. What they needed was the great vision that lay at the heart of his work—something they had not had the benefit of thus far.

As he hung his shaving mirror up on the side window frame, his gaze fell on to the square below and he remained standing there for some time, his soap brush in his hand, watching people's progress as they moved up and down the street. This was the so-called Haymarket, a broad thoroughfare, which with its irregular shape and dilapidated condition stood as a symbol for the raggedness that was still a feature of much of the city. Like a patchwork amongst the small number of "exclusive buildings" in the modern European coffeehouse-style, remnants could be seen of the city's old ramparts that were embellished somewhat with a clump of broad crowned trees. These had once graced a centuries-old boulevard running atop the walls of the city, tatty symbols of a bygone rural age. Indeed, Per spied an old windmill at the far end of the square that might have been in a country parish, except that its blades almost touched the paving stones as it made its slow revolutions.

A garish slash of sunshine illuminated the large square at that moment, the light bouncing from dirty puddles and the wet pavement flags that had been doused in overnight rain. The morning rush hour was building up a head of steam and the hub of the city sucked in its people from the suburbs so as to populate its stores, offices, schools, and garment workshops, a human tide flowing in from Vesterbro across the two lines of uneven pavement, which offered the only route through the sooty surface water.

"The Danish People! My very own Sideniuses!" Per smiled as he observed the square, angular physiognomy of the people below. He felt as if he knew all of them and that they were all brothers and sisters.

He then fell to thinking.

It was really true! His great revolutionary project was about to get underway. It was a strange feeling. After so many years of head-wrecking deliberations, after all the countless preparations and false starts, today, finally, on this fourteenth day in the month of May, the foundation stone would be laid for the new empire that he, Per Sidenius, had designed bit by bit from the chaos of his thoughts and imaginings, really since he was just a boy of eleven years of age. And his countrymen walked in their thousands down there right now, oblivious to it all—the raw material for the future Denmark, the dead mass of mud and clay that he, like some God of the New Age, had dreamed of reshaping in his own likeness and then imparting life to it by means of a single soft breath from his free spirit.

He smiled again, and nearly winked, as he finally proceeded to soap his cheeks with shaving lather.

All right, there was a certain recklessness in the whole thing—he could see that now. But that didn't scare him one jot. Quite the contrary, it was a source of satisfaction and comfort to him that he possessed that element of madness which the world-weary painter in Rome had described as a prerequisite for any man who wished to perform incredible feats.

Once his ablutions were completed, Per rang for the maid to bring him his morning coffee and newspapers. He was hungry, and the table in his room, laid in that quintessentially Danish way, further sharpened his appetite. What heaven, after so many long months, to once more taste that dark rye bread of the North and butter lashed with salt! No feast he had consumed in recent times could come near it! He was soon done with the newspapers. He had no interest in the minutiae of domestic politics and, following an old habit, he jumped over the reams of articles covering the theater, literature, and art exhibitions.

Of a sudden, he sat bolt upright and the color drained from his face. By chance his eyes came to rest upon a notice in one of the advertisement columns that carried his sister Signe's name. "Teacher seeks beginner level music students" was the headline and below her name was a house address, a place not far from Vesterbro in one of the small side streets leading to the start of Gammel Kongevej.

During his time in Italy, his family had again been rubbed out of his life. Or more accurately, Rome had been the same as Dresack for him. It happened that he would be startled awake in the middle of the night because he had dreamed about something or other to do with the family rectory, but during his waking hours, and for many months at a time, his own family had not cost him a single thought. Just as in his younger days, and with iron deliberation, he had made himself impervious to all thoughts of his lineage. But this was no longer due to youthful spite, nor even any deep animosity towards them, but he had realized how important it had been to break free from all feelings of kinship in order to safeguard his sovereign integrity as a free individual. And he had justified this stance by pointing to the fact that he was, in his own way, simply following the example of Christ who had, without compunction, seen fit to leave his mother and father in order to answer an inner call for the fulfillment of his own destiny.

He could not drag his eyes away from the small notice. He could now clearly recall that at his father's funeral, the others had spoken of moving to Copenhagen on the statutory April "flitting day." This was because of his two younger brothers—the twins. One of them had just secured a place at a chemist's in the capital and the other at a bookshop. In other words, it was obvious that his mother and most of his brothers and sisters were now in Copenhagen!

Just then there was a knock at the door. Ivan tumbled in as if having been shot from a cannon. He carried two large document ledgers under each arm.

He had also brought flowers and good-luck wishes from Jakobe and even took the liberty of passing on greetings from his parents in order to contrive a way of telling Per that his in-laws had been extremely glad to see him back safely in Denmark again—a pronouncement which, by the by, was very close to the truth. Philip Salomon, in particular, had been taken aback at how much more sophisticated Per had become.

"All very good Ivan but let's cut to the chase!" Per interjected impatiently as he stood up. He then began to pace up and down in his room, still half-dressed in his shirtsleeves and morning slippers.

"Yes, ahm, indeed—to the chase!" Ivan replied weakly as he fidgeted uncomfortably in his chair; then he felt his throat, as if he were being strangled. He was at a loss to know how he was going to explain to Per just how perilous his position was at that moment, and how to prepare him for the abject capitulation that would be demanded of him at this imminent meeting.

Thus, in order to buy time, Ivan began to expand upon the minutes from the first meeting of the board of directors, which he had already given to Per in a précis in the letters he had sent to Rome. He then expanded further with the various statements and opinions that were expressed at that time about the project.

Per interjected here and there with grunted comments. He was now standing back at the mirror at the window and concentrating on getting his necktie just right. But it could not be said that Ivan had his undivided attention. Per's thoughts returned at every moment to his mother. He found the idea that she was living in Copenhagen unnerving, actually in the very same area; in fact she could be just around the corner!

"May I ask you a question?" Ivan ventured after a slight hesitation—his voice was more pleading than inquiring.

"Go ahead!"

"Tell me Per . . . could it . . . I mean would it . . . you know . . . be completely out of the question for you to patch things up with Colonel Bjerregrav?"

Per turned his head slowly towards him. He was unsure whether to laugh, or roar at Ivan. He chose the former.

"Now stop dribbling little Ivan, there's a good man!" he said, as he once more turned to the mirror. "I think that old scoundrel has you all spooked! If he has hoodwinked you all into thinking that we cannot do without his assistance, just send greetings from me and tell him that he can go and—you know the rest. Relax! The dog that barks loudest never bites."

"Of course Per, you are—in one way anyway—completely right," Ivan replied. "It is of course—in a certain sense—quite ridiculous to ascribe any great significance to his support—not in any decisive way at least. But, on the other hand, given that our dear fellow directors cannot be disabused of the idea that he is actually indispensable, and given that he has declared himself willing—under certain conditions—to lend his name to our venture, well—"

"And what if he has?"

"Well then ... I mean ... you see then ... ," Ivan replied, squirming as if from stomach cramps, "it would of course grease the wheels of everything if you could find it in yourself to make the kind of erm ... declaration he has ... has ... requested."

"Rubbish little friend! You haven't a clue what you're talking about. But listen. Now I'll get talking myself to these chaps you have been banging on about so much and if they have the intelligence I am assuming they have—well then, they'll soon understand that I neither can, nor will, put up with any kind of mentor or supervisor on this project."

"But that's not what they have in mind Per, dear friend! This is purely window dressing for the public. That's the only reason they want his name there. And I can personally guarantee the most effusive and friendly welcome for you from Bjerregrav's side. Ever since the newspapers began running with the story, he's been going around like a clucking, brooding hen. This I know from my own uncle."

"Well Ivan, that's neither here or there as far as I'm concerned. And I will not hear another word about it."

"May I just say one more small thing? As much as I am usually happy in all respects to bow to your superior expertise and convictions, in this one instance I believe—sorry may I finish!—that you have miscalculated here. In particular where Max Bernhardt is concerned—"

At the sound of this name, Per lost all patience. He rounded on Ivan and said: "Would you give over with your eternal and infernal Max Bernhardt! Listen. It's me who makes the damned decisions about my project. Nobody else! Don't you worry your little banker's head about it. Enough of this anyway! Let's get going."

All the other gentlemen were already assembled when Per and Ivan walked into Max Bernhardt's elegant, Parisian style reception room a half hour later. Only Herløv the stockbroker and Max Bernhardt himself were nowhere to be seen. The other members of the board stood in a group at one of the high windows and they received Per with that particular haughty and brutal disdain for which stockbrokers are particularly renowned.

For a moment Per was completely knocked off his stride. He had never expected such a reception. Rather, his greatest fear had been an embarrassing display of unctuousness from these men who were hoping to further enrich themselves on the back of his work. And now the reality was that they could barely deign to return his salutation. The "former estate owner" simply stared at him with a pair of tight pig eyes, which sat under a fringe of beetling white eyebrows. He did not even bother to take his hands from his trouser pockets when bidding Per a curt good day.

Per, his eyes ablaze, responded to this by looking the man up and down and then turning to Ivan who had made the introduction and saying: "I believe this gentleman forgot to give his name."

"Hr. Nørrehave," Ivan whispered as he stood there shuffling his feet and clearly mortified by Per's provocative demeanor towards these men who, very soon, were going to decide the fate of his life's work.

"I see," said Per slowly as he continued to stare at the fat, erstwhile farmer, whose whole head eventually reddened. Nørrehave then turned his back to Per with a haughty sniff but his hands were now out of his pockets and had moved to the rear of his broad coat where he now proceeded to flick his coattails up and down.

The fact was that these gentlemen were still very dubious about having allowed their names to be used in support of an undertaking in which they had little confidence. Indeed, they were all aware that only their collective, and hitherto unshakable, faith in Max Bernhardt had brought them there in the first place. Most of them were not far short of viewing Per as a crafty charlatan who, by some extraordinary stroke of luck, had managed to pull the wool over the eyes of Copenhagen's wiliest senior solicitor. In reality, they were all trying to work out a way in which they could extricate themselves from the whole business, but without making an enemy of Bernhardt at the same time.

Now the man himself appeared from a side room, along with the stockbroker Herløv. The directors sat down around a large table in the center of the room and, after some stops and starts, a discussion of sorts ensued. To begin with, the conversation mainly dealt with issues that were only very loosely connected, or had no connection whatsoever, to Per's project. References were made to previous points that had been raised, or questions were asked about other ventures in which the gentlemen had an interest that had no link to the matter in hand; then the latest gossip at the Exchange came up and what was being said on the streets; in fact young Hr. Sivertsen was turned in his seat entertaining the man beside him with an anecdote he had heard about one of the town's most popular actors.

Max Bernhardt was forced to bang on the table a couple of times with a ruler and firmly request that the assembled gentlemen concentrate on the day's agenda.

"Gentlemen, gentlemen! We must turn our full attention to Hjerting bay! Our aim is to turn our frequently lauded North Sea coast into one big floating share option!" he cried with that goading and ironic delivery he always used, even during the most high-wire negotiations.

Ivan looked as if he was sitting on hot coals. He stole a quick despairing glance across to his brother-in-law, who was leaning back in his chair and bore a facial expression that spoke of a looming tempest. For the moment Per responded well—albeit somewhat dismissively— to the questions that were occasionally put to him, but it was clear to Ivan that he was quivering with indignation. At first, Per tried to deal with the situation by adopting an air of superiority. He should never, he told himself, have expected anything different from these people, who did not even have the grace to conceal the fact that they only cared about one thing—making money. But as the meeting progressed, Per found that he could no longer rein in his anger. There was also the fact that a residue of distress still coursed around his body after his discovery that his family had moved to Copenhagen. Even though Per cared not to think about it in such terms, this awareness lay like a trap in his mind, making him cautious and prickly. He had an overwhelming urge to simply stand up and walk out. When he surveyed these Exchange bandits sitting there with their slapdash ways, haughtily denigrating and bowdlerizing a work that for many years had been his one and only concern, in fact was his life, he felt personally defiled and sullied by them.

What Per did not notice was that he himself was the subject of intense scrutiny from the other end of the table, where Max Bernhardt sat with one elbow perched on the arm of his chair, and resting his dark head on his white manicured hand. His large puffed up eyelids cowled in a dark blue shadow, were as usual half closed, so that it was impossible to see exactly where his gaze was directed—but it rested almost exclusively on Per.

It was Per's tightly pursed mouth and the bulging veins in his proudly chiseled and jutting forehead which captivated this connoisseur of men. Bernhardt was wont to boast that he would, on his deathbed, issue prizes for every even half noble head he had ever seen in his life as opposed to the majority of bovine meatheads he had observed in the Danish race. Privately, Bernhardt admitted to himself that he had been surprised by this Sidenius fellow's imposing man-of-the-world appearance. This was not how he remembered Per at all from that dinner party at Philip Salomon's house, where he had come across as a rather distasteful cross between a failed student and a pimp that plied his trade in brothels and gin palaces. Could he have been so wrong? Was it actually possible that a rural Danish vicarage could have lain a perfect egg of a man with a modicum of spunk in his body?

448 · HENRIK PONTOPPIDAN

Bernhardt suddenly saw Per's stubbornness where Colonel Bjerregrav was concerned in an entirely new light. In fact, he began to
wonder about the wisdom of ever having engaged with this young
man in any shape or form. Nothing could put fear into this man more
than people whom he could not bend and manipulate according to
his needs. In his position of public prominence, he saw an opponent
and competitor in any person who did not willingly cede to his patronage. The more he watched Per, the more convinced he became
that here was a man who could be a great danger to him and, therefore,
had to be neutralized and removed from the scene. Of course, he had
the long-fingered engineer Steiner to replace Sidenius, and given that
he had been careful enough not to link Per's name to the venture,
any change of personnel could be effected without the need to inform
the public thereof.

In the meantime, the question of favorable comments from the
press was raised. In fatherly and patronizing tones, stockbroker
Herløv told Per that he really should pay courtesy calls to the various
editorial offices, preferably both here in Copenhagen and in the
provinces and better today than tomorrow. He reeled off the names
of some of the more influential newspapers and added that it would
of course be best if he could get permission to guarantee the newspapers a dedicated sum for avertissements—"that kind of gesture is
always appreciated one finds," he concluded, in his dry wit, and turning to his fellow gentlemen to receive their appreciation.

Per let on that he had not heard a word of this and simply looked
away.

But now Max Bernhardt spoke up properly for the first time. In
signaling his approval of his august colleague's last remarks, he
wished to raise the matter of Colonel Bjerregrav. Turning to Per and
maintaining his apparently jocular tone he said: "It really is unfortunate, Hr. Sidenius, that you and the good colonel, according to
what we hear anyway, once went through a bout of scratching and
pulling each other's hair...well, perhaps not literally where the good
colonel is concerned because the last time I checked he was bald as
a coot."

A ripple of laughter spread around the table and the young Hr. Sivertsen began braying like an ass, a verbal eruption that made Per clench his teeth and go positively white about the mouth.

"I say unfortunate," Bernhardt continued, "because Colonel Bjerregrav is without doubt the man amongst the raft of experts who can be of greatest service to our cause ... not to mention the fact that he would otherwise prove a difficult and perhaps dangerous adversary. However, we have fortunately—as you know—managed to secure a promise of support from the colonel on condition that you, young sir, take the initial conciliatory steps to establish a mutual understanding—a perfectly reasonable demand, we all agree, given his vintage and superb social standing."

During this speech, all eyes were turned expectantly towards Per, whose demeanor had gradually aroused a certain bewilderment amongst the assembled gentlemen. Per was not long in providing a retort.

"I will oppose outright any attempt to force some kind of supervisory figure on my project," he said. "I have created this whole ambitious plan without extraneous assistance and I have no wish, nor need, to be placed in harness with a pointless and superfluous joint project leader."

Ivan visibly crumpled, as if he had been shot in the stomach. In fact everyone around the table reacted with shock and stupefaction, so unusual was it that anybody—never mind a young, completely unknown man—would dare to defy Max Bernhardt's express wishes.

The senior solicitor himself nearly let his smiling mask slip. However he regained his composure just in time and made an attempt at levity in offering Per a chance to make amends for his rash outburst: "Hr. Sidenius obviously got out of bed on the wrong side this morning." And then turning directly to Per he said: "How on earth can you be so hostile to an honorable man like Colonel Bjerregrav, a war veteran and invalid, a defender of the fatherland! I'm sure he's a very lovable person really!"

In dutiful expression of his admiration Hr. Sivertsen once again emitted his donkey laugh but stopped abruptly when he noticed the grave quiet that had descended upon the gathering. But then Per completely lost the run of himself. His face was ashen as he rose from his chair and slammed the table with the palm of his hand, saying: "May I remind you gentlemen that it was your good selves who came looking for me—not the other way about. So it obviously follows that I am the one—and not you gentlemen, nor indeed anybody else—who sets the conditions on this project."

He then sat down again and adopted an icy silence. Everybody else looked towards Max Bernhardt, whose elbow was now once again on the table and his head resting on his hand. His half-closed eyes gave the impression that he was looking down at the floor. His candle-wax face had adopted the ritually grim and stiffened expression it always showed whenever he prepared to don his black cap and pronounce sentence. Surreptitiously, he had exchanged a few glances with stock-broker Herløv. The latter sat with both arms resting on the table, his upper body and fatted red head lurching forward like a sitting som-nambulist, but in reality he was on high alert and had, with the slight-est of nods, sealed Per's fate.

"Are we then to take it sir," the apparently indifferent Max Bern-hardt now continued, "that you do not intend to facilitate Colonel Bjerregrav—and thereby us assembled directors—in the way that has been agreed?"

"Yes."

"And is that your final, irrevocable answer?"

"Categorically!"

"Well, gentlemen, that is the end of it! Our proposal has not been accepted and the project is deemed to be liquidated. Given that there was never much enthusiasm for it amongst my esteemed colleagues, it would be pointless to spend time mourning its passing."

With that Max Bernhardt stood up from the table. And one by one, the others also rose, most of them with a feeling of great relief at having been freed so unexpectedly quickly from this, in their eyes, stillborn project. However, some of them were somewhat unhappy with this violently executed about-face. This was especially true of gentleman farmer Nørrehave who had been mightily impressed with Per's refusal to back down and his narrow pig-like eyes now watched

Per very closely, who—after the briefest of goodbyes—stormed out of the room, with Ivan in tow.

As soon as the door was shut, Max Bernhardt spoke up again: "I presume that I don't have to tell any of you that this does not mean I have given up the idea of establishing a freeport. Indeed, I am already in a position to advise my fellow directors that in the very near future this whole thing will be relaunched, but on a much sounder basis. In other words, we are to meet on the first of next month as planned gentlemen!"

That same morning, out in the country at Skovbakken, Jakobe went around as if under a dark, oppressive cloud. Of course, the huge sense of expectation that had lain in her breast in the preceding days and nights, which she had counted one by one until Per's return, was all too charged for her not to experience some kind of anticlimax. She felt a little disappointed with him—more, in fact, than she was ready to admit to herself.

She could not deny the fact that he had changed. That extreme control, almost aloofness, that had now seemed to come over him, and which her parents had taken as a good sign, was decidedly not to her liking. It reminded her too much of the tone he had adopted in his last letters from Italy. If this was just a passing phase, a man-of-the-world affectation, she would soon put a stop to it—in her eyes, it didn't suit him one bit. She still loved him as the wild bear he was when she first got to know him, just like he had been even two months ago on their final day together in the Alpine forest of Laugen. She had become used to sitting there with her heart in her mouth as soon as they were in company, out of a dread that he would, in some way or other, start annoying people and cause offense—and she had no wish to be free of this little sacrifice for him. It was almost as if she sensed a danger of loving him less if he were no longer the subject of opprobrium and misunderstanding.

Just as she walked around and pondered these questions, Ivan landed at the house with his bombshell news from the meeting with

Max Bernhardt. She was in the summerhouse with her mother when her brother stormed in with his bulging briefcase.

Her first instinct on hearing the news was to laugh. This new turn in events came like some strange bolt-out-of-the-blue riposte to everything she had only seconds before been worrying about. Indeed, the welling tears in her brother's eyes and her mother's horrified reaction filled her with a momentary glee. Now there was her bear letting out his roar!

But Jakobe soon saw that there were serious grounds for concern over what had happened. In fact, after gathering her thoughts, and especially after grasping from Ivan's account how reckless and scattergun Per had been in his approach, she was even more vexed and embarrassed on his behalf than anybody else. Her worries were not so much about what he, and therefore she herself, were now facing into (though given the way things stood with her now, the prospect of living on a knife edge with regard to their future gave her a cold dread)—no, her anger was more to do with the disregard he had shown in behaving like that towards everything her father, and especially Ivan, had done both to promote his project and for him personally.

Per gave forewarning of his arrival via telegram that afternoon. Jakobe walked down to the station along the railway path through the forest, and even at some distance he began calling to her with a broad smile on his face: "I suppose you have heard the news? I followed Christ's example and drove the merchants from the Temple!"

This outburst caused Jakobe further pain, even though she understood that it was more a ploy to hide his own embarrassment. If he had simply gathered her into his arms and warded off her reproaches by closing her mouth with kisses, she would have forgiven him on the spot and all her worries would have disappeared as she collapsed into his manly embrace. But Per made no such gesture. Even from the platform, he had picked up the disapproval in her face; and in spite of the fact that he really did feel somewhat sheepish over the depressing outcome of discussions that he had anticipated so eagerly, he felt aggrieved and wounded by her censorious air. He had been so convinced that she at least would understand him and acknowledge

the importance of standing up to these glorified gamblers and speculators—she who had not only always spoken out with such passion
against just these kinds of ruthless freebooters, but had also condemned
the central role a man like Max Bernhardt had now come to play in
public life as one of the most prominent men of the New Age.

But on that score, Per mused bitterly, she was not one bit better
than the rest of them. The chandler's spirit was ingrained in her as
well and lay in wait to ambush her proud independence and steal it
away. Yes, indeed—the truth had to be faced!—the Jews had their
own ghosts to contend with! Even the most freeborn of them carried
superstitious reverence for the power of gold and it could reduce them
to slaves at the flash of a coin.

By now they had reached the edge of the forest, and Jakobe, who
felt tired but in no rush to get home, sat down on the first available
bench that lay under the shade of a tree. Even though the way she
pulled her dress into herself was a clear signal for Per to sit beside her,
he declined the invitation. With the tips of his fingers stuck in the
pockets of his waistcoat, he continued to pace up and down in front
of her, explaining and defending his motivations for acting the way
he had.

Saying nothing in reply, Jakobe leaned against the bench, her free
arm resting along the backrest. And as she watched his toing and
froing with a wary expression, she was struck by how much he had
changed. What had happened to him?—she wondered, and a flame
of mistrust flickered in her jet-brown searching eyes. Was something
lurking, unadmitted, behind this strange vacillation with her? Did
yesterday's reticence and today's irascibility have the same hidden
root cause? And his very final letter from Italy? His endless hesitation
about coming home?

She smoothed her hair back from her darkened brow with both
hands, as if she might squeeze all these demonic thoughts out of her
head—desperately wanting to trust him.

"It's Ivan I feel for most. He really has gone out on a limb in his
eagerness to fight your corner. In fact I don't think he could have
done any more, even if it were his own future that was on the line."

At first Per chose not to respond to this. It had really begun to stick in his craw that he had to listen to this constant talk about the sacrifices Ivan had made, whereas he didn't attach much significance to this.

"Yes, I know it's very unfortunate. Where your brother is concerned I do feel terrible . . . but what's done is done Jakobe. And Ivan, by the way, should have realized that putting me in amongst that kind of crowd was like putting a cat amongst pigeons."

"But you yourself accepted them Per."

"Jakobe, I didn't know them! And then that philistine pompousness they all had sitting around that table—as if it was them doing me the greatest favor in consenting to stuff their pockets through my work! If that's the kind of individual who is going to reign in these modern times—well, we've jumped from the frying pan into the fire."

"What are you going to do now?" Jakobe asked after a moment's pause.

"It's quite simple Jakobe—to continue the way I began. Agitate, write, ring the alarm bells, until the people finally listen. There must be people in this country other than sharks and moneygrubbers who are willing to hear me out. Imagine Jakobe. They actually had the audacity to demand that I should go cap in hand to the newspaper editors. Now what do you say to that? Having to request an audience with a press pimp like Dyhring!"

"Indeed, Per—God forbid that you should have to sink so low!"

He stopped his pacing and looked at her with renewed surprise.

"You mean you'd actually support that?"

"Per, if it was going to be of some use to your project—and no doubt things like that would—is there a reason not to do it?"

"I can't believe you are actually saying that? I have to say Jakobe that you have surprised me this day, really you have."

"What I'm saying Per is that if you are trying to gain influence—because you need it for whatever reason—surely it makes sense to simply accept that real power lies with those who are wielding it at the moment, instead of wasting time analyzing how they got that power."

"Well I'm sorry Jakobe but I happen to have a different view of what is required of a man. Why, tell me, is it any less shameful to humiliate yourself before Mammon and the Golden Calf than for the crucifix? And what I have gone through today has left me with such a disgust for that whole gang of swindlers that I will be a long time recovering."

Jakobe said nothing in response to this. She was pained by the fact that Per continued to be so defensive with her. She just wanted him to cease coming out with all his excuses and explanations, which in her eyes were nothing more than distractions and digressions, desperate attempts to assert himself by drowning everything else out with his constant monologue.

But Per kept on talking. Jakobe's sustained and open disapproval of his actions, her complete inability to understand what had spurred him on to his one-man rebellion—in the end, his own inadequate ability to be clear and honest with himself and Jakobe about the inner motivations which had driven him to that point—all this incensed him and repeatedly pricked at his battle lust.

"I must say that the admiration you have suddenly developed for Max Bernhardt and his entourage amuses me greatly. You've never talked that way before. It's as if you are saying it just to undermine me. Talk about kick a man when he's down!"

"I'm going to ignore that last remark Per," Jakobe replied. She was struggling to maintain her inner calm but was determined to make her point. "And, by the way, I don't remember ever expressing or using a word like admiration for any of them—including Max Bernhardt, though I suspect there is more to him than rumor suggests. I happen to know that he is said to be a very charitable person, behind the scenes, and supports a large number of poor Jewish families here in this very city."

"Aye madam. To salve his conscience because of all the misery he has caused to hundreds of families all over the country. I mean, did you also just 'happen to hear' that he is said to be responsible for a large number of ruined homes and broken families?"

"Well, I give you that he will fight to the death for his cause. 'War

456 · HENRIK PONTOPPIDAN

is my stock in trade,' he is once supposed to have said. He is ruthless and unrelenting. No doubt he can also be downright cruel as well. And for that reason I was, for a while, wary of his growing influence—again I will give you that Per. But it could be that I misunderstood him and on the whole underestimated the benefits a person like that can have. Maybe that's what we need Per—a man like that here in Denmark, where we seem to run scared from a man with a truly iron will."

"You speak as if he is some kind of role model for God's sake."

"Well at least we know where we stand with him Per—there's no doubt he is a conqueror. The hint of a Caesar about him."

"And tell me Jakobe. How many suicides does he have on his conscience, this Caesar of yours?"

"Ah, all that stupid talk!"

"But you can't deny—"

"And so what if it's true? That's my very point—the almighty fuss that is kicked up every time he wields his power to neutralize an opponent, or push his own man forward say, shows better than anything how slow people are in this country to accept that the end justifies the means—instead of all the procrastination, hand wringing and interminable discussions that go on here. Action Per. Not words."

Per looked at her for a moment in silence. Her words had hit home in a way that she had neither intended nor could have fully understood.

"My God Jakobe, all of a sudden you're sharp as a tack," he said. Some choice words burned on his lips. What he really wanted to say to her was that if he had actually taken her words seriously, and followed the philosophy she was now espousing, this would have been their last ever conversation. However, he made do with telling her that he found it comical that she should upbraid him, him of all people, on that point. He could assure her that, for his part, there had been many times when he had occasion to weigh up his goals and the means to achieve them and in a much more significant context than what was being discussed here. In general, he had nothing against the maxim she was invoking, but he was shocked to find that she was happy to go so far as to defend a fellow like Max Bernhardt, whose aspirations were of the meanest kind possible—slaking an arrogant thirst for power, or perhaps a straightforward avaricious taste for money—a man who in the whole way he went about his business had proved to be nothing more than a common little—he wanted to say "Jewboy on the make" but at the last second switched it to "Exchange hog."

"However, I admit," Per added with a shrug of his shoulders as he turned away from her, "you have certain inherent traits that I singularly lack in being able to admire a character like that."

Jakobe shot a lightning glance at him and then looked away again. Still she remained silent.

"But as I say," he continued, "this whole affair is not worth all this fuss. It seems to me Jakobe that you are taking all this far too seriously. Because you have to admit that you really have got up on your high heels about it."

"High horse, Per... high horse you mean!"

"Oh Jakobe stop being so pompous! You know what I mean."

"Well haven't we always agreed that language is sacrosanct? A word or phrase is either correct or it's not Per. It's called science and you going round like a bull in a china shop won't change that."

And so they went on. One bitter and wounding word being the catalyst for the next one—until Jakobe suddenly put her hand over her eyes and willed herself to calm down—no, no, she did not want to mistrust him. She would go deaf to those demons whispering sweet jealous nothings in her ears. She would refuse to believe that there was any danger.

She stood up very quickly, took Per's head in her hands and forced him to look into her eyes.

"Per," she said. "What are we like the pair of us? We should be ashamed of ourselves. Kiss me now and let's wipe away all those horrible things we have said to each other. You can tell me that I am to blame for everything as long as you come back to being the old Per I love with all my heart. And then we must each swear that nothing like this will ever happen between us again. Won't we? We have to promise each other that!"

Per came round an instant. In these traumatic days, he had no defense against a loving or affectionate word.

"You are right Jakobe . . . this is stupid. It's just that I was so convinced that you, at least, would approve of what I had done. And I feel that now, more than ever, I am going to need your support and understanding."

"Per. You won't find me wanting in that regard!" she cried.

And they sealed their reconciliation with a long kiss.

Per and Jakobe's rapprochement did little to ease the forced atmosphere around the dinner table at Skovbakken later that day. Philip Salomon, who had been informed of what had happened while still in town, uttered not a single word. Indeed, very little would have been said by anyone about anything but for the presence of the youngest children. Their carefree banter took at least some of the edge off the tension felt by the adults.

Per's demeanor was of someone ready to turn any required defense into an attack. After the way Ivan and Jakobe had taken the news, he was prepared for a demand from his parents-in-law that he explain himself, perhaps even seek to assert some kind of authority over him, given that he was, at that moment, living under their patronage. For this reason, he was very much on his guard—fully determined to reject any obvious attempt to influence his personal decisions.

However, on this occasion, a staunch defense of his position was not needed. Fortunately for the assembled diners, Philip Salomon, who had once and for all made his mind up about Per's plans for the future, successfully resisted his undoubted temptation to deliver a lecture to Per about manners and decorum in the world of business. Nor did the mother-in-law, for her part, make any reference to what had taken place.

When the table was cleared, Jakobe and Per went down to the garden. They walked arm in arm but their reconciliation did not lead to the restoration of old intimacies. Afraid to say anything that might reopen the freshly healed wounds from the earlier battle, they both chose to hide their real thoughts from each other and spoke instead about inconsequential things. Thus, Jakobe was in no position to touch on the public announcement of their engagement, never mind disclose her suspicions on the true nature of her physical condition. Per, meanwhile, could not bring himself to tell her about his family's move to Copenhagen, despite the fact that this occupied his mind just as much as the huge events of that morning. He was also on tenterhooks because he feared that Nanny might suddenly appear down in the garden. At dinner there had been talk of her staying overnight at Skovbakken because of a social gathering she was attending the following day. His ears were therefore pricked and turned towards the villa up above, but at the same time he had to be careful that Jakobe did not notice how distracted he was.

Eventually, they agreed to sit on the bench at the beach where there was good shelter from the rising wind. It was about the same time of day as when they had visited the beach the previous day, but now Mother Nature showed a different face entirely. Stretching out far to the north, the separate coastlines of Denmark and Sweden were sharply delineated. The island of Ven stood out so clearly on the Swedish side that the waves could clearly be seen breaking against its gravel cliffs, which flashed intermittently in the racing sun. The wind had switched to a westerly and in the lee of the Zealand coast, the water surface was almost quiet; indeed at some points where dunes and earth banks reared up above the edge of the shore it was almost shining and becalmed and could reflect the shape of jetties and villa gardens. However, out in the main channel, white horses rode the dark-blue waves. A number of yachts and sailboats with half-reefed sails tumbled about on the agitated waves. At the same time, a green-painted freight ship stove up the channel, warning the pleasure boats as it plowed on with hoarse blasts from its steam whistle. The thick coils of coal smoke that hung over it like a shawl captured the last rays of the dying sun and dragged a long, livid pall of smoke in its wake.

Lost in these new maritime images, Per was gripped by thoughts of Fritjof. He began to reminisce about Berlin and the lively evenings with that mad painter and his crazed brothers in art. The dimly lit and convivial pub in Leipzigerstrasse suddenly beckoned.

At heart, even he did not really understand what had attracted him to those people, to the extent that at a moment like this he could feel such a longing to be swallowed up by their company once again. In a way, he regarded Fritjof as nothing more than a fool, nor could he grasp the significance of his big canvases and stirring imagery. Then he remembered how annoyed he had been when Fritjof's friends had seen a certain likeness between them, had even assumed that they were related.

Through vague intimations he began to see, however, that it was Fritjof's infamous lack of social decorum that appealed to him, that there was something in the capricious volatility of the views he expressed and the way he acted that was so seductive. It was a counterweight to the stiff and predictable mindset shown by Jakobe and the whole Salomon household—the unbending conformity of their familial philosophy. While the denizens of Skovbakken always had their thoughts and pronouncements ready to hand in fixed and predefined symmetry, a perfect reflection of the household's bright and elaborate but for him sterile and anesthetized rooms, at every turnabout Fritjof could proclaim a suddenly different opinion on some issue than the one he had been ranting about the day before, but still with the same monstrous conviction and no less passion. Despite an inclination towards overindulgence and extravagance, the Salomon clan always cleaved to the same side of life, namely practical application and common sense, whereas, Fritjof's vagabond spirit had seemingly steered him through several different philosophical odysseys. During these life journeys, he had capsized on both its day and night sides before finally finding his fortune in that very fact of being a restless spirit.

Eventually, Per could not resist the urge to talk about him, and Jakobe then reported that she had seen him on Østergade a few days before.

"So he's in town the old brigand!" Per cried with some animation. "But that's strange, he told me last autumn that he wanted to move to Spain for good. Said he hated Denmark—"well...'hated the new Jew land' were his exact words."

"Oh no doubt Per that he has wanted to go to everywhere else on the planet in the meantime and settle in every other village, town and city—but the actual truth is that he rarely moves more than a day's journey from Copenhagen. You're probably not even aware that he has momentarily gone back to being a progressive—indeed a firebrand apostle of the New Age."

"I don't believe you Jakobe!"

"Oh yes. Since the Germans decided he was the best thing since pumpernickel, he is in vogue here at home as well. As for his rabid anti-Semitism, he seems to have abandoned that altogether. Just recently, Markus Levi bought a rake of Fritjof's paintings for his collection—word has it for twenty thousand crowns—and by all accounts Denmark's greatest bigot cannot now praise the Jews and the Jewish sense of enterprise highly enough, not to speak of the blessings that the new monster industries have brought to Danish life."

Per let out a roar of laughter.

"It wouldn't be like him Jakobe! I met him of course in Berlin last year, and I must say that for all his bluster and bravado, I got to really like him. But it is undoubtedly a bit difficult to work out where the real person in him begins and the comedian, bully and braggart, speculator and poseur actually ends."

"His 'real' personality probably doesn't start or end anywhere Per—he's an artist from top to toe."

"Yes, perhaps that's the explanation. One thing for sure is that he is an amazing phenomenon. I recall one evening, a good while ago now, in the good old days of the Cauldron—you might remember I've mentioned that place before. Fritjof had just that day sold a painting and in celebration went on a champagne binge to which he invited basically anyone who could be scraped together. He had already painted the rest of the town red the whole day beforehand and as night turned into a new day, the owner of the Cauldron refused to serve anymore for fear of losing his license. Fritjof went completely berserk. Jakobe, if you saw what happened next. It was so funny that

I'll never forget it! He thrust down into his trouser pocket and then launched a whole handful of gold coins across the floor of the bar. Well you can imagine the pandemonium. The money was gathered up again and we finally got him out of the door and into a cab. But here's the best bit Jakobe. I found out from the owner subsequently that the very next morning our man turned up, sober as a judge, and asked in all confidence whether a twenty-crown piece had been found by the cleaners. Some of his money was missing he said and he remembered that when he had thrown the gold coins about the room that one of them had rolled under a spittoon—and lo and behold that's where they found it. In other words: even though he had apparently been off his head with the drink and didn't know what he was doing, he had kept an eye on every penny and every finger that touched them during his moment of madness. Now what do you have to say to that? I mean, fine if the whole thing had been done to raise a laugh from his audience Jakobe, but it was absolutely not done in jest. It really was a spur of the moment thing. It's more like there are ten different people in the same Fritjof—all living their own separate lives. But maybe the same is true of everybody to some extent . . . at least where we Nordic tribes are concerned."

Jakobe declined to answer this. She had already, even while Per was staying in Berlin, been concerned by his obvious infatuation with Fritjof, a man who, in her eyes, was both an idiot and a bore, a tragicomic Falstaff type to whom bounteous Mother Nature, in a fleeting moment of perversity, had imparted a touch of artistic genius so as to mock the general order of mankind. Yes she acknowledged his virtuoso talents and the epic scale of his vision, but she could not allow talent to be used as an excuse for personal failings. Quite the opposite, her view was that with great gifts came great obligations and she believed that the way Fritjof's behavior and alleged lack of breeding was indulged by everybody represented an insult to other truly great artistic visions and also a contempt for art itself.

Just as he had done the day before, Per left Skovbakken early. He felt tired and because of this Jakobe did not press him to stay. Nanny had not appeared by the time he left. There was a chance she would come on the last train but that was all the more reason for Per to leave beforehand.

However, the evening was well progressed by the time he reached the town center. Haymarket square still carried a tinge of twilight but the surrounding streets lay in darkness. Brackets of light spilled from the long row of cafés on one side of the square and were reflected in the windows of one of the newly erected "exclusive buildings" that stood empty and forlorn. At the very far end of the other side of the square, the old windmill by the ruined ramparts hovered like a ghost against the deathly horizon. When seen from a distance, it looked like a big squat troll woman who with outstretched arms slung a torrent of invective over the modern city and its inhabitants.

Per didn't go home straight away. As tired as he was, he yielded to an impulse that he sensed had been waiting for this moment to ambush him throughout the gamut of thoughts and mood swings he had experienced that day. Slowly—and half reluctantly—he walked towards Vesterbro, whose rows of street lamps could be seen from a distance. The usual noise and evening traffic commotion of this major thoroughfare grew louder as Per approached it.

At Bagerstræde he turned away from the bridge that skirted the lake and slipped into the streets around Gammel Kongevej. In no time, he was standing at the street corner where his mother now lived. In order not to be recognized were he to meet any members of the family, he threw up the collar of his coat and tipped his hat well down over his forehead. At that moment, there was not a soul to be seen. He first went over to the side of the street where the house was meant to be, but when he had located it he moved back to the other side of the roadway and stood back from the footpath in a place that afforded some shadow.

What he looked back at from this vantage point was a normal four-storey building that was somewhat frayed at the edges and housed numerous small apartments, with perhaps three but no more than four rooms to each of them. Per's gaze had quickly scanned the windows on the second floor to the left of the entrance port but here there was nothing more to see than some painted-over window panes.

That meant that he must have misremembered the details in the newspaper. The apartment up there was obviously unoccupied and under repair. Then he realized that the way the staircase seemed to be arranged in the building, an apartment lying "to the left"—as it had said in his sister's advertisement—would actually be to the right of the entrance when one was looking up from the street.

There, where his eyes now alighted, he saw a weak light illuminating the interior room. In the adjoining room, the blind had not been pulled down and he could see a narrow strip of light being reflected on to the ceiling. Per deducted that the door of this unlit room which led into the illuminated room had been left ajar. But his attempts to discern any other sign of life were in vain. Besides, he could hardly believe that his mother actually did live in that completely alien building.

But then he took a step from the shadows and looked more closely at an object that stood between two flowerpots on the window sill—and suddenly his heart's blood was banging in his head. It was his mother's red wooden bowl that she used to store her balls of wool and thread. The vivid memory of it went so far back that Per could now feel the way he felt as a child when staring into its unfathomable depths.

The next moment, a shadow slipped across the window blind in the main room up there.

"Was that mother?" he asked himself and gave an involuntary shudder in the suddenly cold night air.

After a few more minutes, the shadow flickered again, but was so brief and unclear that he could not even say whether it was a man or a woman. And given that in the same moment he could hear approaching voices from a raucous group of night-time revelers, he moved away.

Slowly, and retracing his earlier steps, he made his way back to the center of town.

Per was lamed by an excruciating fatigue, but when he got to his hotel the reluctance he felt, indeed it was a terror, of having to face the loneliness of that strange room meant that he turned around at the hotel entrance and was pulled in the direction of the café on the other side of the square. He went inside and sat down in a quiet corner with a glass of beer and tried to gather his thoughts.

It was only at this point, when he could finally draw up a balance sheet of the day's events and the options now available to him, that he realized what great difficulties he had created for himself. All his pat phrases and posturing could not change that bald fact. He was forced to admit that Jakobe and the others had been right to view the matter as gravely as they had done. Here he was again at the bottom of the pile, once more feeling abandoned in a vast and oppressive space but unable to discern an escape route. Yes, of course there was one. Colonel Bjerregrav. In fact, if all else failed, there was yet another one. The mad baroness.

But his essential choices remained the same: like Dyhring and so many others he could eat crow, sacrifice his personal integrity, castrate himself and become a public eunuch, or he could take a leaf from Max Bernhardt's book and with cold-blooded care and deliberation identify potential victims and proceed to ransack them. In that sense, too, Jakobe had been right. It looked like there was no other way out of his dilemma. And after all, "the end justifies the means."

No—he had to admit it—he was not made of the stuff conquerors of the world were made of, as he had previously believed. He could not bring himself to pay the severe price that fame and fortune demanded. Or rather: he felt the same way about social esteem and power as he had with other highly coveted attractions in life—the closer he got to them, the more they lost their shine and value. He felt that the sacrifice demanded of him so as to reach those dizzy heights was ridiculously high.

One man came into his thoughts as he pondered all this ... good old Neergaard. What was it that he had said in that fateful valedictory speech on the night before his death?

In the same instant, the glass door of the café looking out onto the square was thrown open. A giant of a man strode in. He had a huge gray beard, was wearing a bright cloak and his hand held his cane in place on his right shoulder as if it were a two-handed battle sword—Fritjof!

466 · HENRIK PONTOPPIDAN

Per was on the brink of calling out his name out loud, so happy was he in his surprise. But just as he made to rise in order to reveal himself, Per began to think better of it and remained seated. He even went so far as to lift a newspaper and hide behind it as Fritjof bowled on into the adjacent room.

It was a certain sense of embarrassment that made Per want to hide. It had suddenly occurred to him that Fritjof, once he had trotted out his own recent triumphs, would reasonably enough want to know how his own big plans had progressed. Per did not want this conversation, because during their verbal jousts in Berlin he had occasionally used some rather incautious words to describe the acclaim his ideas had attracted and the huge expectations that had been expressed by leading experts with regards to the implementation of his project.

The whole moment crystallized a harsh fact for him—remaining in Copenhagen would be unbearable—a place where, at every turn, he would be faced with this kind of painful and embarrassing encounter. Sheer terror came to his mind when he thought of the pomp and ceremony that would be on display the following evening at Skovbakken, where the whole Salomon tribe and its acolytes would be in attendance. The way things stood now, daily contact with his parents-in-law would, to say the least, be awkward for him; besides which, he knew in his heart that it was time to move on. The evangelizing and agitation he had resolved to start anew, be that by way of a new polemical pamphlet or a series of newspaper articles, could just as well—in fact perhaps preferably—be published from abroad. And then there was the whole thing with Nanny . . . and the other thing . . . the fact that his mother should be in this very city, something he never could have predicted.

Yes, he would have to hit the road. And preferably as soon as possible. He would talk to Jakobe about it the very next day. Anyway, the plan had always been that his present stay in Copenhagen was going to be temporary.

He drained his glass and walked out.

As he left the noise and harsh light from the café behind him and was engulfed by the dark and desolate square, his eyes came to rest on the old windmill in the distance. Without being consciously aware that he was doing so, he stood stock still in the middle of the square. He was gripped by the melancholy atmosphere that this decrepit old relic from the past exerted over its environs.

Then he turned and walked slowly towards the hotel.

17

PHILIP Salomon was not a man for throwing truly lavish parties, but when these did occur, they were events of magnificent style and substance. On such occasions, Ivan—the family's permanently designated master of ceremonies—always worked out an order of events a long time in advance, which he then presented to his parents for approval. Moreover, he always ensured that there was a surprise element, which he used—as he put it—"to help cement the success of the occasion." This might be a particularly striking flower arrangement in each of the rooms or, say, a genius idea for the dessert—or for the cotillion if a ball was being arranged.

This time, Ivan had gone way beyond the call of duty. In the hope that this party—apart from celebrating the return of the newly-weds from their European tour—would also be the effective public unveiling of Per's *magnum opus*, he had proposed that the garden should be fully illuminated and a huge firework display performed. Philip Salomon rejected this idea out of hand. Ivan did, however, receive permission to hang some paper moons in the trees right down by the edge of the sea, which he hoped would have a similar grandiose effect. He also had another much bigger surprise up his sleeve. Privately, he called this the party's pièce de résistance.

Per had arrived even before the rooms had been fully decorated and while the various family members were still in their bedrooms and boudoirs putting the final touches to their party apparel and accoutrements. He had forgotten to ask the exact time that guests were meant to arrive and now found himself in the awkward situation of being an hour early.

This did not help his already foul mood. On arriving back at the hotel the night before, he found that a large roll of papers had been left on his table by the concierge. These had been sent from Max Bernhardt's office, who was now returning the drawings and calculation sheets he had once received from Ivan. Despite his utter weariness and despite the fact that night was quickly moving towards morning, Per opened up the package and—with a tentative curiosity—began to study his papers anew. It had been a long time since he had touched and navigated these pages and most of them were already yellowed with age. Somewhat to his own surprise, he became quite enthused by what he read. The work as a whole, which for several years had really only occupied his mind as a broad concept, he suddenly saw in a new light—all those half-forgotten detailed plans for carefully installed lock systems and sluice gates, pier heads and fascine embankments, all the meticulously calculated numbers in their columns and rows and the labyrinthine diagrams. Here in front of him was the pure essence of the heavenly aspirations he had nurtured during his youth.

The emotions that gripped him at this thought were ones of momentous shock. He was bowled over by what he had achieved. Such productivity! Such initiative and drive! With each new sheet that he lifted from the roll, his self-admiration grew apace, but also (niggling beneath this) a gut-churning sense of decline.

He remained sitting with the last drawing in front of him and dark thoughts began to crowd in on him. He saw his own self and the bare work cell in his tiny back room in Nyboder, where he had stood whistling cheerfully over his drawing board, even though he very often did not have the price of a loaf. A strange mixture of longing and reminiscence arose in him for those years, which might have been spent in penury, but resounded with his dauntless courage—a time when the night trolls could not plague his conscience and tear down those parts of his enchanted castle he had built during his waking hours, a time when any reverse in his life was just one more incitement to fight on, because of the increased and perverse satisfaction he felt at being a victim of misjudgment and injustice, a time in other words, when in defiance of hunger, chronic debt and threadbare trousers he would drift into sleep happy as a sovereign king and arise in the morning like some young god rising to a new dawn.

In the morning, Per had once again inspected his drawings, but the admiration he had felt in his enervated night-time rush of excitement began to fade as he looked at the papers more closely in the light of a new day. With the new expertise and insights he had gained during his travels, he very soon found certain points that were open to criticism. In fact, there were certain impossible propositions, the discovery of which made him more and more apprehensive. His self-confidence, which had received so many heavy blows recently, was now seriously undermined. Thus, for most of the day that was supposed to be a big build-up to the lavish party at Salomons that evening, he had remained in his hotel room, sitting at the table and more and more feverishly trying to alter and improve what he saw. Nothing could escape his criticism and, in this mood, the more he struggled to find the positives, the more he was eventually forced to conclude that there was actually not one single good idea in any of it. The myriad of insights and revelations, buzzing from his mind to the tips of his fingers, that he would always feel when sitting over his drawings and papers refused to appear this time. For the first time in his life, a laming sense of impotence took an unshakable hold on him, and to Per it was the first real and terrifying intimation of death, like a foul taste he could not rid from his throat or tongue.

Now here he was in the Salomon country villa, pacing up and down on the terrace adjoining the garden room. His brow was furrowed and he wished himself a thousand miles away from the place. Though it has to be said that he still cut quite a dash. He was wearing a highly fashionable dinner suit with a white satin vest and brocaded shirt front, upon which two gleaming diamond pins could be glimpsed (a gift from Jakobe). In accordance with the latest trend in Europe, his machine-clipped hair, that followed the curve of his head like dark velvet, was shaved along the neckline so as to accentuate his neck muscles. His small, tight moustaches were turned upwards at the ends in military officer style and his goatee, which had been gradually reduced in size during his travels around Europe, now consisted of nothing more than a V shape below his bottom lip.

Suddenly he heard a small commotion and the rustle of silk from a gown coming from inside the garden room. When he turned, he saw Nanny bent over in the door opening as if she were looking for something.

She was well aware that he had arrived early. From upstairs in her room, she had seen his carriage coming up the drive and hurried to get dressed so that she could be downstairs before the others. She had actually been in the room for some time and had stood behind one of the windows watching him as she tried to pick up the courage to reveal herself. She still found it difficult to be her usual bold and brazen self while in his presence.

Now she showed herself fleetingly in the doorway, sent him an apparently desultory nod and went inside the garden room again, still apparently searching for something important.

Per remained standing where he was, watching her. He too had been struck by a certain hesitancy on seeing her again. Up to this point, Nanny could not have been further from his thoughts that day.

After a moment of further vacillation, he went after her. It was time to settle things once and for all.

"If you are looking for something Frue?... two pairs of eyes are better than one."

"Ah thank you. It's nothing really," she said, but still letting on she had lost something. "It's just the buttons from my glove. I think they came off here somewhere. But really it's nothing. I went in to Jakobe and lent a pair of hers. It seems that we are early for a change Hr. Sidenius," she added after a short pause.

"Indeed, I'm here for almost an hour."

"Ah—you poor thing!" she cried, sending him a pouting look of sympathy from across her raised and bare shoulder.

Once again, Per wavered momentarily. But he then stepped resolutely up to her, gave a bow, and with a comic, exaggerated politeness, offered her his arm: "Well madam. I see that more guests have arrived and that the celebration is about to get underway, may I be so bold as to request the honor."

She shot a quick, shy glance up at him, as if seeking to construe the real intention in his words, whereupon she lamely threw out her fan, as if deciding that any hesitancy or reservations were simply a nuisance, took his arm and, in turning her head away from his face, declared: "You are completely right! We may as well at least pretend that we are enjoying ourselves."

"It seems that the good lady is not in the best of form today," he said, as they entered the adjoining room—a white-lacquered and gilded restroom in the Rococo style. "Has something happened to upset you?"

"Not in the least! I just wish this whole horrible day was done and over with."

"Why, tell me?"

"Ah, I hate these society functions!"

"Hmm. I must say you surprise me. You've turned a new leaf then Fru Dyhring?"

"Perhaps so. But then I'm supposedly a different person now anyway. I am now called madam. Before I know it they'll be calling me granny."

"Well there's no escaping the fact that society now demands certain wifely functions from you, which eventually lead to the esteemed title of grandmother. Shall we sit for a moment?"

He had stopped before a silk-covered sofa and gestured towards it with his hand.

"Or would you be worried that your gown might become creased before the festivities start in earnest?" he added, on seeing that she shrank back slightly from the idea of sitting.

Once again, she threw him off balance by stealing a quick and knowing glance up at him, as if she acknowledged at least the possibility of a bold and ulterior meaning behind his words. Without answering his question, she fanned out her dress and sat down in a corner of the sofa.

"Can you believe," he asked with a hint of forwardness as he sat down beside her. "I mean can you actually comprehend the idea that it is only eight days ago that we took leave of each other in Rome?"

"Well, yes—why shouldn't I?"

"Do you not somehow feel that an eternity has passed since that morning when we said goodbye to each other...you remember... down at the railway station?"

For a moment, Nanny stared straight ahead of her with a look of incomprehension and then shook her head decisively.

"No, I can't say that I've given it a single thought."

"Really—not once?"

"No...never. And Rome was just grim and hideous. Do you not think?"

"Do you think so? You didn't give that impression when you were down there."

"Really? Perhaps you're right."

"So, in other words, you are glad to be back home again?"

"Oh glad blad," Nanny gave a shrug of resignation and looked away from him. "I think everywhere is equally appalling. And worst of all here at home."

Per could not help but laugh.

"My my madam. You really are impossible today. Who or what on earth has made you so ahm—?"

"What I was actually going to say," she cut across him abruptly and with an exaggerated display of tentativeness, "was that you Hr. Sidenius obviously enjoyed Rome very much. In fact you seemed to be ecstatic about the place."

"Well, in a way yes, that's true. But if I'm to be brutally honest, the whole drama lost much of its shine after you—and your husband naturally—left the stage. You know, of course, that I left the place very soon after you."

In reaction to these words, Nanny sat quietly for a moment and looked down at her fan. A perfectly executed hint of a knowing smile then passed over her lips. She lifted her exquisite eyes and gave him one of her soft gazes, so full of hidden portents that he felt she was secretly caressing him.

Now it was Per's turn to be seriously unnerved. He was once again utterly captivated by her personal aura. Though it was also true that she had spared no effort in making sure that her beauty and charm would be displayed in all its glory on this day of days. She had dressed in her most appealing color—that glamorous golden yellow, which contrasted so alluringly with her Levantine skin tone and black hair. And, like a Geisha girl, she had put her hair up in a rigorous and dramatic fashion, keeping it in place with an ostentatious comb made of tortoiseshell, a perfect frame for her proud face. By her exposed breasts, two dark roses shook softly on her dress with each move she made.

Per had to literally bite his tongue and clench his hands to avoid making an unseemly grab for her. Nanny sensed this immediately and became instantly more cautious—not least with regard to her own behavior. She was well aware that the game they were playing was bordering on the reckless where she was concerned. But she no longer felt any shame in this—it simply heightened the elation she felt at such crackling tension. Besides which, she did not feel that she was in any immediate moral danger. If it was true that at certain moments she simply seethed with lust and a desire to throw her arms about his manly neck and taste the passion in his red lips, it was equally true that she would never dream of actually doing so. Her sheer delight in her superior social status was too great for her to take such a step. The thought, moreover, of committing some abject betrayal of Dyhring was very far from her mind. Yes, of course, there were times when her rage at his either affected or actually genuine indifference knew no bounds, and yes there were times when she did not shrink from telling him so. However, her pride in her husband and his prominent place in society was much too great for her to risk being cast off because of some passing fancy. Never a day would pass without her heart swelling with pride at the thought that the whole city, right from government ministers down to barroom chanteuses, curried his favor. Then there were the great expectations she could now nurture in her breast by dint of the simple fact that she was the willing wife of such a man.

However, there was still a cool method in the mad game she was playing with Per. In fact, she might even assert that there was a reasonable and common-sense argument behind it from her point of view. For Nanny was well aware from other times when a man had gained more purchase on her than she cared to admit or like, that if she could just manage to lead him on to the very precipice of desire and then stand suddenly back as erotic vertigo finally gripped him, then in that very instant, his hold on her would vanish. Her own lust and obsessions fully sated, she could calmly walk away as he was left to plummet to his fate.

Now they were disturbed by the older maid and one of the younger servant girls who came in to check the flower arrangement in the parlor, as they called it. Per had once again moved slightly away from her and they proceeded to hold a conversation on entirely trivial matters.

While the servants were still present in the room, Nanny suddenly cried out: "But where is Jakobe hiding? She must know by now that you have arrived Hr. Sidenius. And she was almost done when I called in to see her."

Per made no reply to this. His preference was to avoid the subject.

Nanny led on regardless: "But it will be worth the wait, when you finally see her. She looks simply magnificent in her new dress. For all I know Sidenius, you may have picked it for her yourself?"

"Me? Not at all!" Per mumbled moodily. His forehead had noticeably reddened.

"Ah yes. Now I think on it, Jakobe must have ordered it before you came home. But no doubt she picked it because she knows what her fiancé likes. She must have mentioned it to you?"

"'fraid not ... not that I remember."

"Well then it's supposed to be a surprise and perhaps my lips should have remained sealed."

Per said nothing. He had suddenly become distant, lost in his own thoughts, but his gaze, taking in the whole shape of the woman beside him, was far more revealing than mere words. Every ounce and remnant of mutiny and freebooting license in his character had been roused by

the effect her delightful body had exerted upon him. His foul humor—
that dissatisfaction he felt with himself and wished to avoid having
to think about—all these things egged him on in his decision to walk
out on to the narrow ledge of chance. He was drawn to her like an
addictive drug he now needed again so as to restore equilibrium to
his mind and emotions. Only Nanny, he decided, could bestow the
amnesiac libation of power and exhilaration that he craved. Thoughts
of Jakobe would have to yield to a greater aspiration: namely the
restoration of his powers as a warrior and artisan. Now that by choosing his official wife he had fulfilled his obligation—in the same way
that royal personages did—of paying due deference to the social
contract, he was also at liberty to claim that special right of being
somewhat less strict with regards to notions of complete faithfulness
in marriage. Besides, wasn't it Jakobe herself who had exhorted him
to do that very thing? The end justifies the means, she had said.

Once the servants had left, he again moved himself closer to Nanny.
As he once more began to talk about Rome and the moment they
took leave of each other there, he lay his hand on the back of the sofa
behind her. Now she experienced the same feelings as that day when
they had driven out to the top of Rome's Janiculum hill; this open
and audacious advance had once again taken her aback and made her
far less sure of herself as she flinched in her seat.

She could not deny that there was something in his gaze that
evoked disturbing memories of a dream she had on the night of leaving Italy—one of those strange, unpleasant yet salacious dreams,
which always left her with a banging headache the next morning.
A few days before, she had gone to Rome's zoological gardens and
was enthralled by a huge tiger and its flaming yellow fur. This animal now came surging across the floor of her bedroom, pushing
against the bed and stroking its shag of hair against her exposed
arm and shoulder. Then, with all its grace and power, it gave a short
spring and was on top of her, placing all its weight on her breasts
and upper body so that she was pinioned to the bed. Suddenly, in
those animal eyes, she recognized Per's bold stare.

"Do you remember the rose that fell from your bouquet as the train was pulling out of the station?" Per asked. "I picked it up and have kept it ever since."

"Lord above! I'm not sure it was that important."

"Well that all depends doesn't it? What can't be denied is that it fell from a pair of delightfully attractive hands."

Without quite realizing it, Per had said something she wanted to hear, perhaps more than anything else. Her hands were her most sensitive point. It could not be said that they were merely plain, but she had to quietly accept that her fingers would never be long enough to claim them as a classic lady's hand.

"I think you should save your compliments for Jakobe," she continued, once again adjusting her position so as to avoid his penetrating gaze.

"Why do you say that Nanny?" he asked.

It was now or never. Now was the time to chance his luck, come hell or high water. "Is it really such a sin to tell a beautiful woman that she is simply that—beautiful? Am I expected to lie to you, dear sister-in-law, and say that I do not find you the most absolutely stunning... in fact the most criminally attractive and dangerous woman I have ever met. And what difference would it make anyway? You are well aware of that! I did once, in the fervor of my youth, presume to harbor certain romantic aspirations... something you I'm sure did not fail to notice. But we'll not dwell on those old mischiefs! You didn't want me. And I had to quietly accept my fate. You presumably felt that you were too fine and beautiful for me!"

Nanny's cheeks had gradually become pale. She was also now almost completely pressed into the corner of the sofa, from whence she stared up at him, as if hypnotized.

But Per was already afraid that he had been too hasty in his approach. He felt—quite correctly—that he had caught a fleeting glimpse of hatred in her eyes, and his ears began to buzz at the thought of the likely consequences if his attack had been miscalculated.

Then, in a flash, his shoulders and neck were embraced by her two slender arms and her burning lips were on his mouth.

It was as quick as a thought. And before he could recover, she had got up and was standing by the window with her back to him. There she remained—in her bewilderment, holding a hand to her hot cheek as if she had been slapped.

In that same instant, Ivan's haranguing voice was heard out in the hall, and into the room he came, careering forward on his two busy pins in the manner of a wind-up doll. Like a tin-pot general arranging his army for battle, a small platoon of staff officers followed hard on his heels in the form of a pair of overdressed hired-in waiters and a blousy interior designer.

On discovering that these two, in complete contravention of the day's itinerary of events, had ensconced themselves in the downstairs restroom, he visibly baulked for a second.

"Excuse me! The reception will begin shortly in the drawing room!" he proclaimed, upon which he bombed forward, dragging his staff with him. The latter were all tittering and covering their mouths behind his back.

Neither Nanny nor Per had moved in the slightest. But Per now rose from his seat—still slightly baffled and disoriented.

On hearing the sound of his steps behind her, she turned sharply toward him and stopped him dead with a withering look. Unhappiness and shame were written in her face but also something decisive. Yes, she seemed bitterly to say, she forbade him to take a step closer. And when several voices were suddenly heard in the garden room, she went white with angst and pushed quickly past him with a bowed head.

But at the threshold to the door, she stopped, put her fan up to her face so that only her eyes were really visible and almost whispered a challenge: "If you so much as dare to think about revealing to anyone the liberties you have taken here, well—

"And what? What then Nanny?" Per asked. He burned with reckless fervor.

"Well then—" she continued with a suddenly mocking enchantment in her bewitching eyes, "then—we may very well have to stop being such good friends Per Sidenius."

She snapped her fan shut and disappeared.

*

The voices coming from the garden room belonged to Philip Salomon and his wife. They had entered the room arm in arm and this burly, veteran stockbroker seemed simply disarmed with delight in his wife Lea, who was wearing an expensive wine-red dress with dramatic lacework. But when he caught sight of Per, who was just emerging from the side room, his smile was instantly wiped away.

For Salomon had been reminded of the painful task that lay ahead of him—that of announcing his daughter's engagement to a fiancé who was, in his eyes, an utterly inadequate and useless specimen of a man. It had been his intention to brief Per as to the announcement the day before, but on hearing of his exploits at Max Bernhardt's offices, he could not bring himself to do it. He felt no different now. He could not even bring himself to shake the hand of his prospective son-in-law—though Per's demeanor hardly showed any eagerness in that regard.

Then Ivan appeared again like a metronome—this time to assure himself that all immediate family members were present and in order, a worry occasioned by the fact that the first carriage with guests had just rolled up to the front steps. The smallest children came bursting in at that moment dressed in their white sailor and little madam uniforms. Rosalie had also appeared. However, Jakobe was still nowhere to be seen. She had been delayed by a series of mishaps while dressing. Unaccustomed as she was to creating any kind of extra fuss in her manner of dress, her efforts to get her bodice to sit right had left her literally in knots. In the end she was forced to call one of the house girls for help.

Over half of the guests had already arrived by the time she felt ready to reveal herself downstairs.

Nanny, who had made sure to keep Per in her sights so that she could watch his face at the very moment when he saw Jakobe, gained a huge thrill from the detonation of her carefully planted landmine. Per was suddenly puce with rage.

For Jakobe had unfortunately got the notion in her head that her new dress should have an extremely low-cut frontage, something that her figure could never have carried off. Her erotic excitement at the thought of greeting her bridegroom to be—as well as certain joyous memories from their passionate rendezvous in the Alps—had combined to make her commit this terrible society faux pas. Worse, she had struck Per a savage blow in his most sacred of places because he could not help but notice that a few gentlemen had begun to smirk and nudge each other as soon as she appeared; so at first he would not even look towards that part of the room where he presumed she was.

In the meantime, guests continued to pour in from the large reception hall, where the house girls and hired-in waiters were busy relieving people of their overgarments and coats. Carriage after carriage rolled up in front of the red-carpeted stairway, while out along the coast road a long queue of liveried carriages and hired cabs carrying the rich and famous edged its way slowly towards the villa in stop-start gradations.

In the end, some hundred or so people were gathered in the garden room and the two adjoining side rooms.

It was only natural that the world of finance was well represented here. This was also obvious from the crushing style of the ladies' dresses and adornments, but university dons, doctors, artists, and writers were also to the fore. The whole ambience and tone of this gathering, as with the cut and dash of the gowns the ladies wore, showed the clear influence of the new European liberalities that were abroad. The greater part of the very young debutantes presented in full ball regalia, their excuse being that a dance would follow the dinner, but it was also clear that a good number of the older, especially Jewish, ladies had brazenly advised their seamstresses to allow as much of their fading beauty to be revealed as the occasion and prevailing mores allowed.

Almost all the members of Per's doomed freeport consortium had politely declined an invitation to attend and Ivan had expected nothing else after the events of the day before. Only the "former gentleman farmer," Hr. Nørrehave, had presented himself, and his rustic figure, along with the ostentatiously displayed heavy gold chain and sturdy, double-soled boots attracted no little attention in such an otherwise elegant gathering.

Ivan, who by chance had seen his hackney carriage as it arrived, noticed that he was accompanied by Hr. Hasselager, a Copenhagen barrister, and immediately began to speculate on the grounds for this double act, though he was well aware that Hr. Nørrehave was well got with most of the prominent barristers across the country. It then crossed Ivan's mind that they might have something up their sleeve with regards to Per's project. He recalled that, at the fateful meeting, Hr. Nørrehave had shown a certain displeasure at the way the negotiations had been terminated so abruptly, and as far as Barrister Hasselager, was concerned, he was viewed as one of the young Turks in business circles who had consciously modeled his approach on that of Max Bernhardt. Thus, it was not beyond the realms of possibility that the apprentice was tempted to realize a work in progress that the master had abandoned. Without, it must be said, possessing any other of the characteristics of his legal and financial mentor, apart from ruthlessness, Hr. Hasselager had—bolstered by an imposing exterior and pleasing high-society manners and tone—already made a name for himself in the capital as a smart fellow.

Amongst the Salmon family's usual so-called "Sunday visitors," Aron Israel and—towering above all others—the insatiable intellectual Hr. Balling were in attendance. The appearance of the latter and his various guises as a former student, literary historian, and master of ready quotes evoked comparisons with the Pharaoh's dream of the ugly cattle in the Book of Genesis—they devoured their more favored counterparts but never seemed to gain anything from it. The far more reticent figure of Aron Israel had planted his nervous figure in a quiet corner, but his many friends soon discovered his hiding place. Hr. Balling on the other hand made sure to place himself in the most conspicuous place possible by the side of a door, but despite his fabled length, the frequent rolling of his eyes and striking facial pallor—caused, he incessantly proclaimed, by an interesting "overactive liver" condition—he unfortunately remained as invisible as his literary profile. This sudden attack of blindness amongst the guests also affected Rosalie, who had once been somewhat amused at his advances, but who now went straight past him, a female friend linking her arm, without even acknowledging his presence in this world. This diminutive not yet sixteen-year-old girl, who already dressed as a complete lady, was otherwise known to have eyes as keen as a hawk!

Per Sidenius gradually became a focus of attention, more even than he cared to receive on this occasion. His robust, suntanned figure also stood in marked contrast to the pallid winter faces of the other guests, who were usually to be found in offices and sitting rooms. There was also the fact that most of the guests were now well aware of the nature of his relationship with the Salomon household, and many of them were seeing him here in the flesh for the first time. Those guests who knew about this Sidenius at all—for example by having heard of his book—were shocked by his sheer youth. They had also expected something more in the way of a pale and sensitive writer and were stunned to find that, in physical form at least, he appeared like a man who could literally move mountains and break new paths with his bear hands.

However, nobody at this esteemed gathering attracted anywhere near the attention that was bestowed upon Dr. Nathan. He was holding court outside on the terrace, where he stood surrounded by a large audience of admirers who all laughed when he spoke and were otherwise highly animated. Someone had challenged him to state his view on a newly published book, which had provoked much debate—a lengthy poem entitled "Jacob's struggle with God." The author of the poem was Povl Berger, the young lyricist with the blanched and strained face who had once been a frequent visitor to the Salomon abode, and who was yet another of Nanny's worshippers made miserable by that condition.

As a writer, Berger was previously counted amongst that circle of free spirits who had gathered most tightly around Dr. Nathan and sought shelter under the wings of his authority and influence. His poetry had revealed a fine linguistic nuance that brought Enevoldsen himself to mind, but it also carried the stamp of a disturbing and eerie discord in his character. At the feet of the master Enevoldsen, he had learned to patiently work at perfecting his rhymes and finessing his adjectives, and in a series of tiny pamphlets (which year by year by year became thinner) he had doggedly retold the sad story of his youth with a lyricism that—in common with most of the other creative artists of that time—was a strange mixture of deathly pale romanticism and the most full-blooded Teutonic naturalism, just as the tone of the lyric would swing arbitrarily between mawkishness and contrived defiance of earthly and spiritual powers. Then, about a year prior to this society gathering, Berger published a book of poems that not even his closest friends or admirers were able to praise and this was more than he could bear. He disappeared overnight from Copenhagen, and for a long time nothing was heard of him. But one day, a rumor surfaced that he had hidden himself away in a remote village in Jutland, where he lived like a hermit in a wretched cabin, his back to the world and preoccupied with introspection and the meaning of his life. It was from this rural redoubt that Berger had issued his new controversial book, the foreword of which wasted no time in publicly renouncing his rebellious past and declaring that he had, after a prolonged spiritual struggle, found happiness and peace in humbly raising the cross of Christ and following his path.

While, overall, his previous friends tended to doubt the integrity of this conversion, Dr. Nathan insisted that such sudden religious fervor, born as it was out of a wounded literary vanity, a thirst for vengeance, and an unvented spleen, was genuine enough. Indeed, in his opinion and historically speaking, these types of conversion were actually quite typical; this Nathan tried to demonstrate, much to the amusement of his audience, by recounting a list of the most celebrated public abnegations within the church, right down to the folk church hero N. F. S. Grundtvig.

Dr. Nathan also pointed out that the poem itself bore very clear witness to the value of the breakthrough its writer had experienced, not least in his stature as a poet. Each and every page of this ambitious book spoke of a mind moved by passion and the intensity of his newly formed emotions and feelings—all of which were expressed in a

484 · HENRIK PONTOPPIDAN

consciously crafted and authoritative art form. In the ten or so odes that made up the poem as a whole, Nathan argued, a series of images depicting the barren and somber Jutland landscape at twilight had been drawn. These had been heightened in significance by stark portrayals of the color-drained folk life that was this poet's daily lot. However, the pictures thereby painted, though they were executed in an extremely realist style, seemed pervaded by a light emanating from an invisible world that lay behind everything. And here was the most remarkable and surprising thing about the book—that this poet, who up to this point had fumbled about in the dark looking for the spark that would light his soul, had now not only regained the religious faith of his childhood but had also found his authentic inner voice. Moreover, this voice was so markedly virile. It held a barrel-chested bass tone, full of dark resonance and clang, a voice from the depths . . . from the underworld.

At that point a commotion was heard in the rooms of the house, gongs were rung and the head waiter moved from room to room with a hand bell. The doors to the dining room had been thrown open. All the male guests moved to collect their female dinner companion and take their appointed seats at the table.

Immediately before the guests took their seats, and using Ivan as his go-between, Philip Salomon advised Per that he deemed the occasion appropriate for the declaration of his daughter's engagement to same. Salomon had spoken to Jakobe in person about this just beforehand and, as she gave no reply on the matter, he took her silence to imply a tacit agreement. The reality was, however, that she had not been listening. Her thoughts revolved around one single issue: to find an explanation for Per's changed behavior towards her.

Nor was she long in picking up the scent of what she hunted. Though Per sought to mask his emotions by freely imbibing the wine that was on offer, this could not conceal his discomfiture. For right opposite him sat none other than Nanny, who was amusing herself no end with a gentleman sitting beside her. She was of course accompanied by her husband in the seat on the other side of her, but she had made sure that one of her long-term admirers, the former cavalry lieutenant, now assurance broker Hansen-Iversen, was placed next to her, and it was with this blade that she constantly entertained herself.

Yes, of course, she would occasionally place a fawning cheek on her husband's shoulder with the clear intention of pacifying him. Nor did Dyhring seem to take offense at her behavior, responding to her expressions of affection with an almost imperceptible nod and an indulgent blink of his eyelids.

It was not that Dyhring was as unsuspecting as Nanny assumed, but he was quite sure that she would not abuse the license he gave her by overstepping the boundary of what he considered acceptable. Once he had gained a finer appreciation of her nature and character, and especially after he had (as further reassurance for himself) adroitly fanned the flames of her ambition by depicting a future, not too far hence, where the Royal Court itself would become a fitting platform for her charms, he was convinced that she would shrink back from any hint of public scandal. Regardless of how much she might be tempted, Nanny would no doubt react in the same way she did in the boutiques of the city where she would, with starry eyes, continually circle and caress some thing or other she coveted. However, she would invariably drop it like a hot coal the moment she was informed that she herself would have to pay for it.

Not once did Nanny look in Per's direction. He sat in vain, waiting for a secretly thrown look of reassurance. He was, and would remain, invisible to her.

That her fixation with the dashing lieutenant could be a device, a conceit, had of course crossed Per's mind, but that was no compensation. Once and for all, Nanny destroyed the fantasy in which he had occasionally indulged since their leave-taking in Rome—that there might, from her side, be a more serious intent to the game they had been playing. This ice-cold reality chastened his lust to conquer her to the point of its extinction. Moreover, her gaiety did not in any way appear to be an artifice. Thus his male indignation knew no bounds.

Then came more fuel for his ire.

Very soon after Philip Salomon had raised a toast to the new man and wife, he again called guests to order to announce the engagement. He did this as quickly and briefly as possible, but nevertheless—and despite the fact that most people were prepared for it—the announcement provoked a lively reaction around the table.

As Per now rose, glass in hand, to receive and respond to the salutations of guests and family, and while the very air around him seemed to surge and crackle with his name, he could not help but reflect that this homage was not for his sake but solely for Jakobe's benefit, and then for him as Philip Salomon's putative son-in-law. And this thought caused great offense to his Sidenius self-esteem and did little to soften his attitude towards the gathering before him. Never more than at this moment had he been aware of the utter aversion he had inherited from his ancestors towards this comfortably cosmopolitan and openly epicurean social set which deemed itself to be esteemed among men. The wall of noise that deluged forth from the hundred or more voices around him, within which he could discern the sound of certain foreign tongues babbling away, brought the unbidden image of a cacophony of parrots to his mind. Enough. The time when he allowed himself to be blinded by the luster radiating from the rich man's groaning table was now over. Each thing he looked at stoked his anger still further. The extravagant flower arrangements on the table which (by his reckoning) must have cost an avalanche of Danish crowns; the massive serving stands of pure silver and other superfluously embellished tableware; the jumped-up waiters in their pantomime suits and the endless changing of plates for each new course—everything was, in his eyes, a huge show of the boastful ostentation so typical of the rich Jew.

Stung further by Nanny's laughter, whose increasingly high spirits and tones pullulated on his eardrums above the general noise, Per finally turned to Jakobe and told her straight out that he found the whole occasion stuck up and pathetic.

Jakobe gave no reply. From the moment her suspicions regarding her sister had been aroused, she had not broken breath to him.

Nanny's apparent fascination for the former cavalry lieutenant sitting beside her could not pull the wool over Jakobe's eyes. She knew her sister inside out and was well aware that, in the love game Nanny played, the greatest piquancy was to drive her worshipping victim insane with jealousy. She also knew that Nanny, due to a certain fickle fear of being swept away by genuine feelings of love, would always seek shelter in the undying admiration of yet more men.

For that very reason, she doubted whether things had gone quite that far between Nanny and Per. But, against that, Jakobe was under no illusions that Nanny would feel bound by any sense of loyalty towards her sister. In fact, she could imagine that Nanny would take particular pleasure from luring her fiancé above all others onto her siren rocks, and Jakobe now understood that it was exultant triumph that she had read in Nanny's eyes on that occasion when, immediately after her return home, she had begun to speak of her encounter with Per in Rome.

Never would Jakobe let the world see what she felt. With the almost superhuman self-control her natural frailty had instilled in her from childhood onwards, she bravely played the part of the happy bride. Even though she saw and heard everything as if through a swirling mist and had the constant feeling that she was on a wildly swinging ship, there was nothing to show it in her outward countenance, other than the fact that she was slightly paler than usual and appeared drained of energy. The only person with whom she could not pretend was Per Sidenius. Every time he spoke to her, she turned her head away. She could hardly bear to hear his voice. Should his arm even touch her own, every fiber in her being would turn to ice.

It was fortunate that, for the moment at least, she had little time to think too deeply. With each minute that passed, she was torn away from the onset of complete despair by the approach of friends and acquaintances wishing to drink a private toast with "the very soon to be bride and groom." Even Nanny saw fit to hail their marriage and also looked at Per for the first time. With an insouciance that stunned him to the spot, Jakobe's half sister laughed and nodded to both of them as she raised her glass.

"Skål, dear brother-in-law! . . . Skål, Jakobe!"

Now she's gone too far! Per said to himself. He had visibly reddened and could not bring himself to return her gaze.

Jakobe, on the other hand, put her glass to her mouth in an apparently cool and calm manner, but not a drop of wine passed her lips. She even confronted the fear of having to once again see the look of triumph in her sister's eyes by steadfastly returning Nanny's celebratory nod.

However, it was Per and his ideas for the future that became the most common topic of conversation up and down the long table, at least amongst those not sitting in his immediate vicinity. The ladies in particular spent much time studying the household's new son-in-law, and Per's severe and brooding demeanor, along with the cool deliberation he displayed when receiving even the most enthusiastic invitations to share a drink, increased his stature and the respect his observers already felt having seen his imposing masculine figure.

"Yes, indeed those Sideniuses seem to be characters all right," a voice was heard to say somewhere near where Philip Salomon was sitting. However, he seemed not to hear the remark, even though it had been specifically addressed to him.

But amongst the guests there was another gentleman at the other end of the table—an older, solid, and heavily stooped figure with an impressive gray beard—upon whom this observation did leave its mark. This was the well-known honorary State Counsel Hr. Erichsen, one of Copenhagen's richest men—indeed perhaps the richest of all, but at the same time a philanthropist on a national scale. Even before guests were called to the table, Senior Barrister Hasselager had whispered in his ear about Per and sought to interest him in his engineering project. Hr. Erichsen admitted at once that he was neither aware of these plans, nor had he even heard a word spoken about them. It was for this reason that he now sat and watched Per from behind his massive beard, just as he paid close attention to everything that was being said by the guests around him about this young man and his venerable forebears.

Just after dessert had been served, Philip Salomon tapped his glass sharply for a third time. This time, however, it was not—as much to the amusement of his audience he immediately explained—in order to give away yet another daughter. No, this time he wished to propose a toast to Dr. Nathan and bid him welcome back from his long state of exile in foreign lands, which of course, and fortunately for Denmark, had only further cemented his ties to the country and, in particular, its youth. The toast was drunk with great gusto. A good number of the guests—including the ladies—rose from their seats and surrounded the doctor in order to clink their glasses against his.

"He's not changed a bit," several voices were heard to say around the table.

"Well apart from the hair. He's starting to go gray."

"I suppose so. But it doesn't make him look any older!"

Indeed, what did he actually look like, this widely acclaimed man who was also the subject of sustained and ferocious attacks? A man who had, in a more conscious and dynamic way than any other figure, prepared the ground for the future Denmark and who, via his lectures and prodigious literary output, had raised a storm the like of which had not been seen in any intellectual or spiritual movement since the Reformation.

He was diminutive of stature and the general verdict amongst people was that his face bordered on the ugly. At the very least there was something irregular in his features, but it also has to be pointed out that this aspect of his appearance was hard to judge because its shape was forever in motion. This, no doubt, was mostly a reflection of Nathan's highly active inner thought processes, which were played out on his face as a series of convulsive facial tics and movements. However, his closest observers would accept that these idiosyncrasies had become somewhat purposely exaggerated over the years. His face was at its most appealing when he listened to others. For it was then that he adopted an expression that radiated the finest points in his nature: his thirst for knowledge, his insatiable delight in discovering new things . . . nay his insatiable lust for discovering new things. But such close attention to the words of others was rare for him where informal social gatherings were concerned. His overwhelming preference was to hold the floor. For even now, as his temples turned gray, and running side by side with his boundless receptiveness, Nathan still possessed an urgent need to pronounce his views on all things and at all times, rather in the way of a chattering schoolgirl. Likewise, his constant stream of speech was not always free of mere gossip and betimes a hint of malice.

More than Dr. Nathan himself understood, this reckless, almost feminine, exuberance had been the biggest factor in the wave of opposition and ill will that existed towards him in Denmark. Time after time, he had managed to drive away even close friends and natural allies by offending their sacrosanct beliefs in the concept of Nordic male dignity. Overall, his natural disposition was so alien, so irreconcilable with the Danish national character that it was inevitable he would step on people's toes, not least because he—in stark contrast to previous Jewish writers who had left their mark in Danish literature—neither sought to adjust his foreign foibles to suit local conditions, nor even to strike an enigmatic pose that would entertain people as he announced in self-righteous tones: "Why would I want to be part of your world anyway?" No, Dr. Nathan had never doubted for one second his right to speak out. In fact from very early in his career, he had felt himself called to play a role in Danish cultural life, precisely because of the non-national aspect of his racial origins, which enabled him to observe domestic life from a distance, as it were, and without any home-grown prejudices.

There was also the fact that his educational background was not of the usual Dano-German type. Nathan's intellectual background had its roots in Latin cultures and his predilection for French sophistication and taste—which he practiced as a young man by displaying a certain dandyish elegance—immediately made him a subject of suspicion amongst his compatriots, not least within the learned Academe. Indeed, his bitterest critics resided within the walls of the university itself. As far as the old professors of theology were concerned, Dr. Nathan was, with his thick and lustrous head of well-groomed hair, his dazzlingly white shirt front, indeed his whole pampered and cultivated exterior, the epitome of a charlatan.

Though all this was still not enough to explain the, without the slightest doubt, epoch-making effect of his eruption onto the cultural scene. Of course, Dr. Nathan was a man of outstanding abilities, but he was not, however, what is broadly understood to be a "genius." He was no *sui generis*, no primary innovator. He could even, when compared to homemade originals like Grundtvig or Kierkegaard, seem to lack a deeper-lying singularity. He had been too impatient to develop his own independent philosophy, too vivacious and engrossed in life to opt for such a tough, somber and dwarf-like existence, hammering away in the gloom of his own mind to find the bright gold of revelation. Lesser mortals than Dr. Nathan have gone down this route and, at best, have sometimes managed to find the occasional auric nugget, and only then by chance. With his restless striving, Nathan stood better comparison with a worker bee who, come rain or shine, seeks out the stamen of cultural intellect and steadfastly returns home to the hive with his weighty load of honey. With an unerring instinct and as if having a myriad of eyes, he traversed all national boundaries and the literature of all times to extract the sources of inspiration that could be carried back home. On his return, he would employ all his ingenuity and skill to produce the essence of his life stimulus and then feed his colony, which was the youth of Denmark—a honey that was at one moment bitter the next sweetly spiced. He could boil a whole historical epoch down to a few pages, so that it became infused with the sweep of drama and full-blooded life. Nathan's mind could illuminate the most obscure of philosophical labyrinths with just a few brief lightning strokes of inspiration, so that even the most dim-witted student could perceive some sense in what was being said.

This singular power to recreate and depict an art form carried with it the secret that explained the extraordinary hold he had established over the minds of the youth. Not only were they simply dazzled by its immediate brilliance, it was also warmly embraced by a characteristic of the Danish people as a whole, which to Danes has always had its advantages but was actually fiercely fought against by Dr. Nathan himself: Danish indolence.

Never before had the young student fraternity here at home been in a position to assimilate knowledge in such an easy and entertaining way. While said student lay stretched out on his sofa puffing contentedly on his long pipe, the giants of world literature strode vibrant and lifelike across the pages of his book. Moreover, the content of the works they had created was revealed and interpreted with such digestible lucidity by Dr. Nathan that the supine scholar afterwards felt that he had read and thought deeply about every one of them. Of course this meant, for the majority of students, that they need not bother reading the source documents themselves. They accepted Dr. Nathan's judgments and views without objection, because they were viewed as being their own. The purely personal emotions and sensibilities Nathan displayed in his life were emulated as lifestyle declarations. His essentially Levantine sympathies and antipathies were swallowed wholesale like some magic potion that promised eternal enrichment. In short, never before had upcoming scholars been so inflamed with audacious attitudes and a love of free thought. Even the most thick-blooded farm student reacted as if intoxicated by the urge to perform great deeds after several hours of reading Dr. Nathan's polemic and would leap up with utter conviction from his couch so as to tamp his pipe again.

Inevitably, it was rarely more than a passing spark, and it soon blew out. Then the ensuing backlash was very often far more powerful than the original impulse. The poet Povl Berger was far from being the only one whose decision to heed Dr. Nathan's clarion call, and submit to his baptism of intellectual fire, paved the way eventually towards a religious rebirth. In Denmark, it could never have been otherwise. In those instances where an intellectual seed had been sown and the germination thereby directed deep into the Danish earth, there was no other cultivated soil where it could take root except in theology. The only real expression of social culture amongst the people was expressed almost exclusively through the Church. Going any deeper than the surface brought the seeker of truth either to the Middle Ages or the great void.

In a way, the extent of Nathan's significance was therefore, at this time, best assessed by the nature and caliber of his opponents. Amongst a good number of these, he had managed to arouse the active indignation and passion, the fanatical fires, that he had, in vain, sought to inculcate amongst his own camp followers. The waves of the religious backwash against Nathan were yet to reach the capital, where minds were still occupied by the explosion of commercial activity. However, out in the provinces and more particularly in very rural areas, the agitated waters were quietly rising, swirling around rectories, congregations, and folk high school like a biblical deluge waiting only for the natural, inevitable moment to break over the country.

Once people rose from the dining table, Per and Jakobe performed a modest presentation in a corner of the garden room, where the large cut-glass chandelier had now been lit.

Amongst the first ones to approach them and offer congratulations was the former gentleman farmer Hr. Nørrehave. With a most emphatic country rolling of his r's, the permanently perspiring Jutlander expressed his heartfelt outrage at the events of the previous day at Max Bernhardt's chambers, and was at pains to stress that he personally totally rejected Bernhardt's "interpretation of the situation."

Per was only really half listening to what was being said. His attention was still drawn towards Nanny, who was standing at the opposite end of the room, basking in the attentions being lavished upon her a by circle of smirking would-be philanderers. Even though he had firmly decided to let her sail her own turbid waters, he just could not stop watching her. Now he saw how lieutenant Iversen, who had gone to the hall to fetch her ermine stole, placed this garment with lingering care about her shoulders, and how he absolutely had to be allowed to close the clasp beneath her raised chin, a permission that was obviously denied him as Nanny slapped him playfully across his fingers. But immediately after this, she boldly took his proffered arm and marched off with him through the room and into the garden, to which the more youthful element of this gathering had repaired in order to drink coffee in the Norwegian summer pavilion.

In the meantime, the country farmer Hr. Nørrehave had continued his conversation with Per, who now realized that it was this man's intention to get him talking about the events of yesterday so that he could then broach the subject of what he now intended to do to promote his freeport idea. In order to avoid revealing that he in fact had no new plans up his sleeve, Per resorted to reluctant speech and inscrutability, which tactic however only increased this Jutlander's curiosity and egged him further in his attempts to get Per to confide in him.

After what seemed to be an age, Hr. Nørrehave finally moved away. But this proved to be only a temporary respite. For now someone else approached him, skirting the congratulatory group that had formed around Jakobe as he did so. It was Aron Israel. As already noted, this small, timorous scholar had a naive admiration for anything that was not in his field of expertise, especially anything that was of a mechanical or practical nature. He was also permanently awkward in such large social gatherings and had been hovering around Per awaiting a chance to salute him but without wishing to interrupt other well-wishers. Now that he had finally gripped Per's hand, he was reluctant to let go and continued pressing it between his own two scholarly hands.

"And may I use the occasion, Hr. Sidenius, to offer you sincere thanks for your small but significant monograph of last winter. It was nothing less than a fizzing dynamite bomb . . . a kind of assassination in effect . . . but carried out for the good of mankind. I'm well aware that you will hardly be interested in what I—who completely lacks any knowledge in this area—have to say about your book but nonetheless I cannot refrain from letting you know that I, despite the vehement way that many of your points are made—which no doubt caused alarm in certain quarters—found the book truly inspiring."

Per looked at this diminutive man with some uncertainty. It was true that he was not the only guest who had talked to him about his pamphlet, using general words of praise. But while Per had viewed the acclaim of others as being no more than polite phraseology, he could hardly question Aron Israel's sincerity. He had heard too much about this reticent sage and the exalted integrity of his philosophical investigations and striving for truth to doubt him. Nor was it the first time that Israel had shown an interest in him and his plans for the future.

Per replied by saying that he was surprised that Hr. Israel had come across the book in the first place, which was true. It had received next to no publicity and was hardly a huge talking point. The newspapers had completely ignored it just after it was published, whereas in the same period, the Copenhagen papers had used up many column inches in discussing a proposal to move Tivoli gardens from its present location.

"I noticed that all right," Aron Israel said. "And it was for that very reason that I struggled with an urge to write to you. I felt that you should be aware that there are actually people here in Denmark who were inspired and edified by your proud and fearless belief in the human potential for progress and your great future vision as to how nature can be bent to man's will. And yes Hr. Sidenius ... I use that word 'edify' deliberately. In my opinion, your book deserves esteem as a genuinely edifying and enlightening literary work. The effect it had on me was like the first fresh winds of spring—a rather heady experience but as invigorating as a sea breeze. It is my fervent wish that your natural science gospel, young sir, will be taken to heart by our dear youth here at home. It would be about time, as they seem to regard technical knowledge with a certain superior disdain and it may be for this reason that they so depressingly quickly become disheartened with life."

By now Per had eased his hand out of Israel's grip and had visibly reddened.

This was always the way with him. For despite all his provocative self-confidence, all his surging hopes of glory and admiration, as soon as somebody praised him to the heavens, he became embarrassed and wanted to hide. Per also had his own reasons, at that moment, to avoid going deeply into this issue and so sought to lead the conversation elsewhere.

But Aron Israel was too eager to discuss the subject for this to happen. He started talking about Dr. Nathan, whose endeavors Per had referred to in one part of his book with something of that disdain he still held for all aesthetes during the period of the book's gestation. Aron Israel told Per that, ignoring for the moment the almost boundless admiration he felt for Nathan, he had to admit that his lack of scientific and technical insight was regrettable, and possibly fatal for that large element of Danish youth for whom Nathan had been a mentor and icon. Undoubtedly, things would have been far healthier if his huge output could have attracted more men of action and fewer intellectuals. Here, without doubt, was a lacuna that needed to be remedied, and in order to achieve this—perhaps the greatest challenge of the current epoch—it seemed that the author of *The Future State*— let it be said plainly and without a hint of flattery—was possessed of just the right qualities. The younger generation was clearly waiting for their own insurrectionist and future leader. The throne had been abandoned. Society marked time, anxious for news of the coming of the chosen one, the native king of a lost line.

But here Israel was forced to abruptly halt his speech. A hush had suddenly descended over the room. A man with a thick mane of black hair had sat down by the massive grand piano and began practicing some scales and chords while Ivan, his face beaming like a newly minted coin, led a tall and heavy-bosomed lady to a standing position by the side of the pianist.

This was the unveiling of the great surprise that Ivan had promised—his pièce de résistance. The imposing lady, a famous singer from the Royal Opera House, had done the family the honor of accepting an invitation to the gathering and (in return for a handsome sum of money by the by) would now sing two post-prandial songs and a da capo aria. Most of the gathering being opera aficionados, they were well aware that this huge privilege was only ever bestowed upon the most esteemed of families and the nobility.

Per, who was absolutely tone deaf where opera was concerned, quickly sought an escape route. He observed how other gentlemen, for whom the peace and tranquillity of one of the smoking rooms suddenly beckoned, were able to quietly filter their way out along the sidewalls. But he was worried that the nearest escape door was just too far away. Shortly before he reached said door, an operatic opening salvo rang throughout the room and soon after came a pianissimo very quickly fading to nothing, all of which resigned him to his fate.

But he barely heard the song being sung. It was Aron Israel's words that thrummed in his mind, made him giddy and unsteady on his feet. Was there not some kind of higher meaning in the fact that he should encounter this ardent affirmation just at the point when he himself had begun to doubt whether he really did number amongst those who had been called to perform great feats? His blood had run cold when that peculiar little man began, in his own inimitable and prophetic way, to speak of "the vacant royal throne." The proudest hope of his boyhood years—the aspiration he had effectively given up on—came with these words rushing back into his mind like an eagle finding its eyrie again after being disturbed by other predators.

He was jolted out of his thoughts when the singer stopped and her pianist delivered their last notes and the applause—led by Ivan—crashed through the room like a hailstorm. Then Nanny entered his thoughts. She had still not returned with her escort. "No doubt they have found lots to amuse themselves with, he said to himself. A bitter notion took hold of him to make a detour down to the garden to see what they were up to out there in the dark solitude of the falling evening.

Just at the door leading into the garden, he bumped into uncle Heinrich. On account of the occasion, the old stager had curled every hair in his head using hot irons and also proudly wore his large and very bright, but very false, diamond-crusted pin on his shirt front, as if it were a decoration from the king himself.

Per made to go past him. Since his return from Rome, he had wherever possible sought to avoid the Salomon household's very own demon, who had constantly posed as Per's champion, and whose loose and acerbic diatribes Per chose to put up with during his days as a suitor for fear of becoming the butt of his poisonous tongue.

But on this occasion uncle Heinrich stood directly in front of him and then with a conspiratorial wink pulled him to one side.

"A quick word in your ear my dear young friend! But of course, forgive me—first my heartfelt compliments! Everything seems to be going marvellously tonight?"

"What do you mean by that?" asked Per, without any attempt at hiding his irritation.

"What's this?...Ah it's like that is it?...You want to play your little comedy with me too. But there's no need for that with me Hr. Sidenius my sweet friend. By God we know each other far too well for that. No no—please don't be offended. Please keep up your role play—why it probably suits you best anyway. Your mask of—shall we call it severity?—has a very grandiose effect, I may tell your sir. Herr Gott von Mannheim, how I have enjoyed the whole show! All the guests speak of this veritable lion of a man. Now tell me. Is that not comical? But do carry on my friend! Lead them all by the nose—every one of them! Blind their eyes with a puff of snuff! Hammering gold out of base metal. Oh yes! Strike, strike, and strike again my friend. The more you strike the more I admire you!"

Per stared down at this hideous little man with a look of pure disgust. Heinrich was obviously inebriated and his half-ingrown iguana eyes positively glowed with malice. This sham "director" was never more venomous than on the occasions when his brother-in-law threw a party, precisely because he was forever shunned by all of the guests. The Exchange fraternity, in particular, openly displayed their aversion to him.

"What the devil are you wittering on about man?" said Per. "If you have something to say to me, spit it out and be done."

"Your humble servant sir! With the utmost respect!...Do you know what? You remind me of a piece I saw at the Royal Theater... an idiotic sort of piece naturally—a knights and maidens spectacle, full of verse and froth. There was a young man in it, a ne'er do well, a clodhopper and dolt. But the strange thing was that all who saw him became entranced by him when he appeared at the king's court. The ladies would gather round him and swoon, and the king himself lost the run of himself with admiration, so much so that he appointed this yokel as his special minister. All this was achieved you see by way of 'ein kleines Ding' that the dolt carried hidden about his person, a thing of course with troll powers—that made him so attractive in everyone's eyes. Tell me! This magic ring has been surely handed down to you sweet gentleman! Or what other explanation is there do you think? You come back from your travels and immediately contrive to make a scandal that would shame the devil himself. And yet here we are today and you are still the hero of the hour and hammering that gold. But you of course, good sir, find all this to be perfectly in order!"

The day will come, Per said to himself, when I'll get my chance to shut that gob of his once and for all. But in that instant, he was seized by a joyously inspired idea. No—dear old uncle Heinrich could keep his foul tongue and thoughts! He would be the fool in Per's royal court—a jester whose pure malice would divert him in the quieter hours of this absurd masquerade called life!

Per placed his hand patronizingly, but amicably enough, on one of uncle Heinrich's upholstered monkey shoulders and said: "All right dearest uncle! Enough of the playacting. If you really do have something to say to me then tell me what it is. I can't wait here all night my friend."

"Oh good, well then—wait till you hear this! Do you know that a new consortium is being set up in your name? You know him, of course, that waddling farmer who's here tonight stinking the place out with his sour-smelling dung boots—Nørrehave he's called. I saw him talking to you earlier. You didn't pick anything up Sidenius?"

"No—not particularly."

"Ha—no, of course you didn't! But what I'm saying is still true. Both he and that long bottle of wind Hasselager—a barrister, you know—have put their feelers out. I myself was watching the whole show. I saw them a while ago conspiring together and then they went over to him—that clown, the State Counsel Erichsen. You know him, the man with a face like a big ox who everybody makes such a big fuss of. He's supposed to be a paragon and patriot just because he can shout louder than anyone else about loving one's country, a national reawakening and a new spiritual and intellectual Dannevirke and I don't know what else … idiot. Ah it's Sidenius they're conflabbing about says uncle Heinrich to himself and I drew closer, discreetly you understand, the better to hear what they were saying. I do believe that Erichsen took the bait. The barrister was hooked on every word the two gentlemen came out with and looked very impressed. That's why I'm saying to you Sidenius: no more silly strokes young man. Strike while the iron's hot and hammer out that gold! Mark my words. Lady Fortune will not always be so kind again!"

Per stood quietly for a moment without saying anything. He placed no great trust in anything that uncle Heinrich said but, inspired as he was after his conversation with Aron Israel, he was not going to dismiss this intelligence entirely.

"So was that all you wanted to tell me?" he asked.

"No young sir. It isn't."

"You mean there's more?"

"Yes . . . but you'll never guess what it is," he said, looking sideways at Per and screwing his eyes up. Heinrich then said nothing for a while in order to pique Per's curiosity. Finally, he spoke.

"As I'm taking my morning constitutional today along Vimmel-skaftet, who of all people do I meet coming the opposite way . . . why yes Colonel Bjerregrav."

Per gave a start on hearing this name.

"And of course, you had to stop and have a chat," Per said.

"Naturally!"

"And I suppose you had no choice but to tell him what happened at Max Bernhardt's chambers?"

"Naturally!"

"Aha—and what did he say to that?"

"He already knew about it."

"Well well . . . from whom might I ask?"

"He wouldn't say. But I've worked it out since. He happened to mention this fellow Nørrehave and asked me—in all confidence he said—whether I knew anything about him and what class of a man he was. In other words that wily fox was quick to make his move and was already up seeing Bjerregrav yesterday. I'm telling you Sidenius. The colonel knew everything, to the finest detail, about what happened between you and Max. And—imagine this! You've gone up a thousandfold in his estimation young sir. May God strike me dead, he positively beamed with delight—that you had the nerve to give Max one in the eye. What? Of course he wants all these pushy Jews hanged—and God bless him for that . . . oh yes! His eyes were shining with delight. I take my hat off to that young buck says he . . . and of course I understood Bjerregrav's little game in telling me all this. He wanted me to pass this on to you and here I am—your humble servant. He's buttering up to you. Do you understand? He still has hopes of a reconciliation. That's a man after my own heart, he said. That's our own cocksure Danish youth with a sharp axe in his brawny hands, clearing all the deadwood, weeds, and dross that have been allowed to grow unchecked in this country. These were the man's very words . . . comical, or what? Wonderful. I love it!"

Again Per retreated into silence.

"Do you give me that I have a right to call you Fortune's Favored Son? The more foolish things you do, the more acclaim rises for your name."

Other guests standing nearby began to shush uncle Heinrich. The opera singer had lifted a new song sheet from the piano and the room became as quiet as a graveyard.

Per chose his moment to slip quietly through the door.

He then slowly made his way through the side room and carried on out into the hallway. From here he saw that the door leading into the library was open, as was a door at the back that led into the billiards room. Both rooms were being used as smoking rooms. A dense fog of Havana cigar smoke was already drifting out of the first room, where a group of voluble gentlemen were engaged in a lively debate. Very little of their faces could be seen from the hall, but their voices were beginning to drown out the music coming from the garden room.

A few steps short of the open doorway, Per stopped in his tracks. His name had been mentioned by someone in the room. His cheeks burning and his heart banging, he stayed where he was to listen. It was him they were arguing about. His project was the subject of a passionate dispute. There seemed to be two gentlemen in particular who were adamant that, precisely for the sake of the country as a whole, Copenhagen's interests could not under any circumstances be undermined, whereas another man—the owner of a booming voice— replied that the whole attraction and innovation that lay in Sidenius's approach was the decisive break it made with the current disastrous Copenhagen-centric policy—the very policy that had done untold damage to the country and shunted Denmark further away from the centers of trade and commerce than was necessary given its geographical position.

Per did not want to hear any more. He turned away, tucking his face shyly into his shoulder, and walked back to the empty side room. He stood there, deep in thought, by an open window that looked out towards the country road running away in the distance before disappearing into the forest. The evening sky still retained a hint of light.

So his time had actually come! It occurred to him (and he smiled ironically to himself at this)—when he had weighed the likely effect of what had happened here today—that this moment was fairly close to the calculations he had made a long time ago. With the public announcement of his engagement, his "fortune" had been officially sealed and stamped. Fame's gilded crown of thorns was now officially about to be placed on his head.

A new burst of applause rang out from the music performance and moments later people began to drift away—once again filtering through to the different rooms. Per, who by now was somewhat groggy from the heat and perfume-scented air that was saturating all the rooms, had no wish to be caught up once more in a crush of people. Making a quick decision, he went out to the hall once more, found his hat and coat on the bulging coat rack and left the house—heading for the country road that skirted the villa.

The evening was redolent of summer. On one side he had the forest, and on the other he could look out over the Øresund strait, over which a silken white mist now drifted. Per stopped a few times and exhaled deeply, the better to completely fill his lungs with the air that was so heavy with twilight dew. Like a cleansing and purifying sprit, he felt the draft coursing through every part of his body. His hat was still in his hand and, in his haste to get away, he had simply thrown his long-tailed overcoat around his shoulders, with the effect that it looked more like an artist's cape.

He was now very strongly aware that he was obliged to carry out a root and branch examination of his project. And he would, he knew, find the solutions to its flaws. The lack of clarity he had suffered that morning must have been due to the distractions he felt were crowding in on him. Now everything was clear and tomorrow was a new day.

At a swing in the road that brought him close to the water's edge, he stopped again. The sheer expanse of sea lay in all its glory before him at this point—the two opposing Danish and Swedish coastlines running away to infinity and an almost cloudless sky arching over them.

For several minutes, he stood stock still and listened to the soft clunk of the water along the shore. Just like the evening of his homecoming, when he had stood there below Skovbakken along with Jakobe, he was struck by the strange effect this simple sound had upon him— a sound that in its deep tranquillity seemed to echo the comfortable and intimate small talk of all eternity.

The stars, too, came so close to him that he felt the breath of their orbit. There was one small, brightly lit star in particular which beckoned to him from above the island of Ven just at that moment. It was as if it recognized him and wished to remind him of something. Do you not remember me?—it seemed to ask. Have you forgotten that time ... long long ago ... far away from here ... traversing across endless space and time ...

The jingle jangle from some carriages carrying forest picnic parties tore him back to reality. Then he saw—some way off, but just further down the strand—some kind of dancing light, which for a second took him aback, indeed made the hairs on the nape of his neck stand on end. But he quickly realized that it was only Ivan's paper moons reflecting in the still water that gave the impression of a row of burning columns. A bit higher up the slope from the strand, he could now see the fully illuminated villa through the clumps of trees in the garden. The quiet of the evening, along with the salt air, combined with the whole scene to create a fantastic effect on him—like a fairy palace floating in free space.

At the same moment, he recalled that he had planned to spy on Nanny and her cavalier out in that very garden. He also realized that he had not thought of her once, and was glad of this. "Let him keep her!" he said, and with these words turned his back irrevocably on Nanny and paltry paramour games of any kind. Out here, face to face with nature's serene infinity, the frenetic human search for sexual passion was distasteful to him. Yes, actually filled him with disgust.

Per strolled further down the coast road and soon came upon a lively scene. He had come to an area where a large number of summer residents had formed a colony of coastal dwellings and the fine weather had tempted many people out into their gardens and onto their verandas.

But this was the last thing Per wanted. He turned around and walked slowly back northwards into the darkness.

When he came to the next house, where strains of music were drifting across the night air, he halted his passage for a moment to look in over a tall, thorny hedge. This formed a significant bulwark against the road and its traffic. Inside was a thatched villa house set in an old garden, where a group of teenagers who had all just passed their university entrance exams ran amok in the garden.

Here too, in other words, there was revelry and excitement. But then he was struck by the difference between this party and the one he had left an hour before. The young ladies here were all brightly dressed, but bore no trace of the flamboyant liberality that was in vogue in Europe. Moreover, the game they were playing was just a good old red-blooded innocent child's game of Danish hide and seek. A student had, just at that moment, placed himself under a tree with his student cap covering his face, while the others fanned out over lawns and paths to find the best place to hide amongst the trees and bushes. Moving back slightly towards the garden gate, Per could see a half-cleared family dinner table out on the veranda, around which a couple of older men were sat, one of them wearing a round woolen smoking cap. All the men were tamping and sucking contentedly at their pipes and completed the impression of homely bourgeois comfort and equanimity. Again, there was that music that had stopped him in the first place—thin, almost plaintive piano tones from the very same kind of ancient instrument that his sister Signe used to play at home in the rectory, and which he could never hear without being moved by its timbre.

Two wisps of teenage girls appeared from the courtyard area behind the villa. They walked slowly and with their arms around each other's waist. Per moved away into the darkness of the road as they sat down on the steps leading up to the garden gate. The two girls sighed almost simultaneously and adopted a romantic pose as they looked up at the stars. Some other young ladies, out of breath after their game, joined the first two and gradually a clump of ethereal figures dressed in white were gathered together—all looking up at the heavens as they waved their handkerchiefs across their flushed faces.

"Ah, I'd love to see a shooting star!" one of them said.

"And what wish would you make?" asked another.

"I wouldn't say for all the world!"

"Would you not even tell me what it is Frøken Jensen?" a male student asked, who along with some other young fellows had thrown himself down on a strip of lawn opposite the girls.

"I don't know now—ah well what the heck—as long as you promise me that you won't breathe a word to anyone else—ever."

"Madam I swear on my honor!" the young man cried, placing his outspread hand over his heart. "So what wish would you make?"

"My dearest wish would be . . . that I don't burn the porridge again tomorrow morning."

Shrieks of delight and applause from the whole group. But then another youth asked: "Are we not going to sing?"

"What a lovely idea children," an older lady called out to them. She had emerged at the front door some moments before. "You can all entertain us while we put the dessert out."

However, without knowing it, Per had been observed by the only couple who were still walking around the grounds of the garden and, like Per, had sought the darkest corner. The next moment a man appeared in front of him on the other side of the hedge. He raised his hat and asked with a slightly mocking politeness whether he was perhaps waiting for someone?

Per muttered some excuse and stole away.

But when he had gone some fifty yards or so, he stopped again and cocked his ear. They had indeed begun to sing back there and, straight away, he recognized both the air and the words—it was one of those popular evensongs that his own brothers and sisters had also sung out of doors in the summer:

> Peace reigns over town and country,
> the world's commotion calmed.
> A happy moon lights the heavens
> and bright orbs salute their fellow stars.

Per listened with bated breath. Never, he felt, had he heard such wonderful voices. The calm of the evening also played its part in this regard. Despite the distance between them and him, each word of the song came to his ears with astonishing clarity. There was almost a supernatural quality to the sounds, as if the song had risen up from the earth around him, ringing out from the exposed, expectant soil like a subterranean choir of angels.

> And the sparkling ocean, smooth and tranquil
> cradles the heavens in her arms.
> While a guard patrols the distant ramparts
> praising God who keeps us from all harm.

Per had closed his eyes. A dull ache seared through him. It was as if these tones in the night air provoked a sobbing echo in the hidden depths of his soul.

> All is so peaceful and hushed
> between heaven and earth!
> Be also at peace in my breast
> oh restless soul residing there.

Back at Skovbakken, the dance had now begun. Though it was mainly the younger element that was brave enough to try any lively movements after the heavy dinner. Older family members and guests had dispersed to various rooms and corners, or sat watching the cavorting youths from seats running along the sidewalls.

The previously buoyant atmosphere, which in the period directly after the music recital had threatened to ebb away, had picked up again with the commencement of the ball and strong digestifs being served in the smoking rooms.

Dr. Nathan came storming through one of the side rooms with two of the evening's youngest and most beautiful women holding on to each arm—the dance being their destination. At no time was this remarkable man more worthy of admiration than when he was in the thick of a social gathering. Regardless of how long his working day, or night, had been—and the lamp in his study often burned until the break of day—his energy knew no bounds and he would throw himself into some new entertainment with the same youthful vim and vigor that he had always shown. Nathan had never felt the need of artificial sources of inspiration. It was true that the endless battles with his opponents had left him cynical in the extreme with regard to how stupid humans could be, but this had never conquered his zest for life. Festively decorated dining rooms and halls, alluring ladies, bright smiles and flowers, would always rejuvenate his spirit. Wherever and whenever he was seen, if he was not dancing, he was explaining, regaling, and convincing. Just as much as in his literary activities, in any social scene he was both conqueror and wizard, and yet for all his haughty provocations, he was always worried about not being liked. The view of him, held by even the most insignificant young student, was never entirely irrelevant to Nathan. Yes, he would often mock life and its illusory nature in his writings—but anywhere where he encountered those illusions, he would always succumb to their power. Even the least attractive aspects of life always held some kind of attraction for Nathan, precisely because he sensed the same overwhelming, invulnerable force of nature running through his own self. He was a man born and bred in the noise and tumult of the capital, but with the torrent of Mother Nature's eternal abundance coursing in his veins, as if Copenhagen's material fabric had produced this phenomenon. He was a rare Danish plant—like some exotic cactus born out of the heat and flame of the eastern deserts and standing alone on rocky slopes that were otherwise devoid of life.

It was this powder-keg response to every facet of life that had made Nathan such a curious being in an otherwise sedate and bucolic backwater like Denmark. In the literary concert of the times, where every kind of instrument from God's last trumpet blast, to the fanfares of the market, to pious organ playing could be heard, Nathan was, and would ever, denoting the rhythms of Nature itself—a sound that both compelled and repelled at one and the same time. Just as here, where he rushed towards the dance floor with the two young blushing females at his arms, though gray and bearded like an old billy goat and showing a slight limp as he went by, his physical form was a living embodiment of what he had meant for Denmark's youth: the Pied Piper, come from the Great Forest who, with his magic pipe had lured even the most reticent child down the path to the enchanted land—the same Pan figure who had even got the priest-ridden Danish people to forget their hymns and dances, at least for a while.

Jakobe was one of many spectators in the ballroom. She preferred to remain there because the music and the whole tumult of the dancing appealed to her, as it stopped her from having to think. The perennial intellectual Balling sat by her side talking about Povl Berger.

But Jakobe heard very little of what he was saying. For her worried eyes were too busy looking round the room for Per. She could not see him anywhere, whereas Nanny's yellow, butterfly-bright figure could be seen constantly moving between the other dancers. She assumed then that he had retired to one of the smoking rooms, and her only wish was that he would stay there. As she sat there, her biggest fear was that he would suddenly appear and ask her to dance. She did not believe she could be responsible for her actions any longer if he should attempt to make some kind of overture.

The beanpole literary pedant by her side never noticed Jakobe's distracted state. For as usual, his own powers of concentration were limited. Every other moment, he would stop talking and turn his donkey ears, now to that side, now to this, so as to pick up snatches of what was being said by those adjacent to him. In truth, Balling had once been one of those original, wide-eyed and good-natured Danish youths who had followed Dr. Nathan's lead and launched themselves like battle-hungry lions into the fray, but who also subsequently acknowledged their error without ever being able to publicly admit it, never mind—as Povl Berger had done—attracting the name of Judas by moving over to the enemy camp. Hr. Balling was one of the many faint-hearted auxiliaries who brought up the rear of the New Age army. They had only ever decided to follow Dr. Nathan's banners and flags for fear of being left behind, but in their Danish heart of hearts, they rejoiced in every defeat the army suffered along the way. In Balling's own eyes, the fact that he had, in a sense, sacrificed his honor to chase a dream, made him a tragic hero, and a vague red flush of embarrassment passed across his face when Dr. Nathan himself—The Conquering Hero—suddenly entered the room accompanied by his young and attractive escorts.

Nanny's yellow whirling dervish figure was once again in the thick of the dance. Nevertheless, she too was keeping a weather eye out for Per. She had been watching out for him everywhere she went and just could not understand where he had got to. In spite of her devil-may-care demeanor, she had been on tenterhooks the whole evening, wracked with worry about the scene in the side room parlor. Her whole behavior since had been calculated to throw Per off the scent and thereby push away her own thoughts about it, but now she began to worry that she had gone too far in cold shouldering Per and that he might, out of sheer spite, actually let the cat out of the bag.

Just at that point, Per had returned to the house. He was standing in the entrance hall, hanging his overgarments up on the coat rack when he looked across through the open door to the now jam-packed smoking rooms. By chance, he saw that the man sitting there surrounded by a circle of brokers was none other than Otto Dyhring.

Just as the astute Dyhring had built up his profile and reputation by scandalizing Danish opinion, he had now (with the same clever calculation) donned his new mask, which he would use to say and write precisely those things which bourgeois Denmark—and people at the Exchange especially—wished to hear at that moment. His dispatches from abroad on French and Italian trading conditions had, therefore, attracted widespread acclaim within the business community, which now credited him with a surprising level of business expertise. In these, he had continually emphasized Danish integrity and solidity in contrast to that of the more capricious sensibilities abroad, and those same businessmen now acknowledged that Dyhring was indeed an old head on young shoulders and worthy of his position as editor-in-chief of a venerable business newspaper. His articles had been found to display, they said, a gravitas and a sense of restraint that one hardly dare expect from the former variety critic at *The Falcon*. Moreover, they bore further witness to Max Bernhardt's unrivalled talent for selecting his people and placing them in the appropriate social arena, bearing in mind that Dyhring's appointment had initially provoked such howls of protest.

Per's first plan was to mingle with the other gentlemen as they enjoyed their cigars. His desire was to shake off the lonely thoughts that had come upon him with a glass of whisky and try to acclimatize once more to the more rarefied atmosphere that prevailed here. But the sight of the new king of the press holding court immediately dispelled all thoughts of reconciliation and he checked his stride abruptly and turned towards the other rooms.

In his features and whole demeanor, he still carried with him an afterglow of something that belonged to a more optimistic and happier world. But gradually as he now pushed his way through the throng in the crowded and overheated rooms, pressing past flushed cheeks and faces, the fluttering fans being worked so feverishly by the ladies, the darkly severe appearance he had displayed at the dinner table came over him again. He was also partially blinded by the needle-sharp light from the crystal chandeliers. The passage from the evening quiet of the country road to this boisterous and effervescent party crowd had a quite disorienting effect upon him. He felt that he had blundered into the core of a pounding machine that was being worked at abnormally high revolutions.

When he reached the ballroom, he remained standing at the door to watch the dancing. In the last while, it had become even more lively. A good number of the older guests had now decided to stretch their legs.

Almost at once his heart melted, as in the middle of this dancing pandemonium he spied Jakobe, who was sitting near the far wall—the exact place where he had left her well over an hour earlier. Yes, he thought, it was only, and ever would be, with her that he would feel at home. The emotions that had drawn him to her were not vestiges of craven instincts but actually the essential core of his will to live, even before he had been fully able to grasp their full import. He was also struck by how alien she herself looked in these surroundings. It was clear that she had taken no part in the dancing, both her fan and her gloves lay in her lap.

Seeing Jakobe again in this light was something of a revelation for him. Never had he felt so strongly that they were intrinsically wedded together. Yes, in fact, Jakobe's love for him was the only thing of real value he had won thus far in his search for fortune and luck in the land of fable and riches.

From now on, he swore, he would take better care of it! While this new dawn settled upon him, he continued to gaze at Jakobe's fine, pale, and perceptive face with its heavy eyelids and the pronounced but so decidedly feminine shape of her mouth. Even the unfortunate dress she had chosen now moved him, precisely because she had a martyred herself for him.

He moved to slip across the dance floor to get to Jakobe, but Nanny saw her chance to speak to him and was there in an instant, her gentleman in tow. She was flushed and animated by the dance.

"And where may I ask did you disappear to young man? Here we are, we ladies, waiting for the chance to dance with the new groom and you are—psst—gone, like that! Now that's hardly manners is it?"

Per looked coldly at her.

"I'm afraid I'll have to decline your offer Fru Dyhring. Jakobe is a bit tired, so I'm not dancing either."

With that he turned on his heels, while Nanny tried to laugh in an attempt to conceal the fact that Per's words and his harsh gaze had cut her to the quick.

Her lips quivering, and pulling quickly away from Per, she turned to her consort and said: "Let's go in and get something to cool us down. It's suddenly so clammy in here. That's an awful pig of a man my sister has landed. Do you not think?"

Jakobe had seen Per the moment he appeared at the door of the ballroom. She may have been giving the impression that she was, at all times, looking the other way, but she had observed the little scene between her fiancé and Nanny and when she now saw him turn in her direction, she sensed that a rupture of some sort had, however discreetly, taken place between them.

Per nodded warmly to her and sat down on the chair that had just been vacated by Hr. Balling.

Shortly afterwards, he moved a bit closer to her and placed his hand over hers, where she had left it exposed at the edge of her chair. She did not remove it, being simply unable to do so. She had already been won over by his mute plea for forgiveness. However, she could not bring herself to answer in kind when he squeezed her hand, not to speak of meeting his gaze, which he was quite clearly waiting for. No. Her pride still suffered too much from the fact that she simply could not resist his caresses.

"My God Jakobe, your hands are so cold," he said. "You must be freezing. Shall I fetch you a wrap or a shawl?"

"No. I'm fine."

"But are you not getting a draft from that door?"

"No. I can't feel a thing."

"Well even so, will you not just let me—?"

"No I said. No—please stop fussing!"

"As you will darling."

There was a hint of both anger and anguish in Jakobe's tone but Per had not picked this up. He stroked her hand and moved it up towards his chest, so that her arm came to rest in his. At the same time, he leaned a little more into her, so that their shoulders were also now in intimate contact. When she moved as if to pull her hand away, he moved his other hand across so that both of them held her limb captive. And now he whispered into her ear and her cheeks immediately flamed and flushed because she once again heard the tone of voice he had used in their night-time trysts in the mountains: "Dear Jakobe . . . my friend and dearest love!"

"Have you danced yet?" he asked a while later.

She shook her head.

"Would you like to now?"

"No. Not in the slightest. I am too tired," this last she added after a brief pause out of fear that he should misinterpret her reluctance.

"Then I have a suggestion to make. It's such a wonderful evening out there. And not in the least bit cold. It could almost be a high summer evening. What would you say to taking a little walk around the garden, Jakobe?"

When he saw that she hesitated with her reply, he pushed on: "I think that the fresh air will do you good, I really do. And besides . . . I have something to say to you, Jakobe."

Now, for the first time, she looked at him—purely instinctively it must be said, because her thoughts were decidedly elsewhere. Though, once again, she picked up the tone of his voice as he spoke. It was sincere and intimate. It was their tone.

Then she stood up. And once Per had fetched some overgarments for both of them, they went out via the garden room exit.

There was a lively atmosphere around some of the tables out on the terrace, which was being used by the dancers to cool off, and they made good use of the cool drinks and refreshments that had been left there for them. Here, under the starlit night, Nanny and her faithful escort were also to be found. She had just begun to devour a portion of iced fruit, when she saw Per and Jakobe walking across the terrace arm in arm and then disappear down the marble staircase.

Now he's going to blab the whole thing to her! The thought stabbed at her heart. Her mouth had become flecked with white spots of angst, hate, and downright lust.

She pushed the only half-consumed plate away from her and headed back to the ballroom. All right, she continued in her thoughts, as she began a new dance with her gentleman escort. Jakobe's gloating would not last for very long! She would see to that! If she wanted war she would get war!

Per and Jakobe went right down through the garden to the water's edge and sat on a bench in a recess that was surrounded by a hedge. This had become their favorite place when they did not want to be disturbed. Here in this quiet seclusion, Jakobe yielded completely. Per put his arm around her and she lay so closely into him that her head came to rest on his chest.

And they stayed like that, hardly moving. In front of their feet, the water from the sea slapped and glugged as if turning in its sleep, while the reflections from Ivan's paper moons shimmied in the water like shoals of goldfish.

"Are you sure you are not freezing to death Jakobe?" Per asked as he pulled the fur wrap tighter around her.

"No. I told you—not at all," she replied, again slightly irritated.

In support of the discussion they had had the previous day, Per said that, by observing the social soiree that evening, he had become even more convinced that the men of progress in Denmark's so-called New Age were on the verge of collapse and dissolution. The spell they had once held over him was forever broken now. He was forced, he said, to admit that she had been absolutely right in once saying, or writing to him, that a society where a person like Dyhring received such an exalted status had condemned itself by its own actions. He was now completely clear in his mind that, if there was to be any hope of a final victory for unfettered and visionary thinking in Denmark, well then other forces would have to step into the breach—men in the true meaning of that word, men who were serious and high-minded beings, men who raised life's aspirations well above the everyday senseless and avaricious pursuit of money, women, or purely personal acclaim.

Per now warmed to this theme and spoke with the increased eloquence he had attained following his travels around Europe. But Jakobe had not heard a word. His stream of earnest and genuinely felt arguments flew over her head like an empty rush of wind.

However, when Per finally requested the favor of a kiss as a symbol of their mutual concord she heard every syllable. In a flash, her head was raised and she was offering her mouth, like a flower scorched by frost, turning towards the rising sun to embrace its life-giving heat.

18

WHEN PER woke the next morning he felt decidedly unwell. Never being entirely restful in his sleep, he had thrown off his blankets during the night and had become chilled to the bone.

As he sat up in bed, a stinging pain shot through his chest and alarm bells of angst rang out in his heart and soul. He knew that pain for what it was. It was the very same sensation that had filled him with fear a couple of times during his travels in Europe—the last time being in Vienna after those grueling and very often drenching boat trips in the Danube delta. Up to that point, and due to his distrust of foreign doctors and also a certain fear of having to face the problem that might come to light, he had shied away from a medical examination. But now it just had to be done. He rang for the maid and asked for a note to be sent to one of the foremost consultants in Copenhagen.

It was several hours before the doctor arrived. This enforced solitude in his room gave him ample time to convince himself that these repeated spasms were increasingly more painful intimations of his earthly demise.

To die so young? At twenty-four years of age! With his life's work unfulfilled. In fact not even started! That would be quite ridiculous, completely illogical—as illogical as life could possibly be.

But yes, he had to admit, the time was long gone when he would storm forwards without the slightest concern for life or limb, happy to defy death in the conviction that life could not go on without him—that it was only his talents and abilities, to the exclusion of all others, that could restore Denmark to its former ancient glory and then launch the country into the modern age. Of course he knew better now. Greater minds and talents than his had gone to the grave without ever achieving the heroic deeds of which they had been capable. Nature was infinitely bounteous and all powerful, so a single life was neither here nor there. Did the Grim Reaper ever ask leave to enter a dwelling? No. Just as the sun shined on both the just and the unjust, the Angel of Death came with its dark gaping eyes and indiscriminately touched the brow of both genius and buffoon alike. He asked not who was worthy or unworthy.

However, Per also recognized with pleasant surprise that the terror he had previously felt when thinking of his own physical annihilation was no longer as strong as it once was. Lying there in his huge luxury bed that was covered by a dazzling silk mantle, and waiting for the announcement of his imminent death, he was relatively calm and collected. In fact, even when there was no pain in his body, there were moments when, in his utter fatigue, he would have almost welcomed the thought of passing away and being freed from life's pointless travails. The piercing racket from the carriages in the square outside, the eternal bell ringing from the trams, and then the thought that he was facing into yet more negotiations with idiotic and pompous finance speculators—all these things filled him, in moments like this, with an unspeakable disgust.

But then time passed in his room and it became increasingly difficult for him to face his inner terror. For a crushing feeling of being alone and abandoned gripped his heart, to the extent that waves of cold sweat shivered his body. Imagine if he actually was lying there about to die, and without a soul beside him to comfort him!

In order to distract himself, he decided to try and read. The previous day, he had unpacked the books he had brought back with him from Rome; these were mainly large and expensive technical works, but there was also a collection of more general arts-based educational material, which he had built up during the long winter months in Dresack and had subsequently augmented in Rome.

From this latter collection, he picked out a compendium volume of Greek and Latin philosophers in German translation, a book that had once before offered him some solace in similar circumstances.

However, he had not got very far in his reading when the doctor arrived. He was a diminutive man with a precise gray beard who sat down on a chair beside the bed without saying much more than a word or two. He then proceeded to fire quick staccato medical questions, after which he began to perform the actual physical examination. The doctor made no attempt to hide his doubts about Per's alleged illness. After prodding and knocking at Per's sides, back, and chest, the doctor said: "Is it your lungs you think have a problem with young man? If so, then think again. They are like two huge bellows in an iron foundry…Where do you say the pains are?"

Per pointed vaguely to a place on the right side of his chest near the lowest ribs.

"Oh here is it? But you said when I came in that they were on the left side."

"Yes, they seem to move around."

"Ah…move around—hmm. Is it very sore if I—sort of—press hard here?"

"No I can't say that it is."

"Do you feel anything particular?"

"No."

"Are we saying that the pains have disappeared?"

Per had to admit that the vicious, searing spasms in his chest and sides had disappeared. He could in fact breathe in deeply, without any pains stabbing through him.

The doctor said nothing but began to examine his abdomen and legs.

"Your lungs are in damned good shape Hr. Sidenius," he said when he was finished. "You'll never get a better pair. But your muscle groups are somewhat flabby and puffy. And it wouldn't harm if your heart were a bit more active. Tell me, young sir…what's your normal daily routine? Do you practice any serious kind of gymnastics? Do you take a cold shower every morning? You really should start doing that. And how about dumbbells? There is nothing as invigorating before breakfast as some rigorous arm swings with two hefty dumbbells. You also, in general, need to get your blessed blood moving a bit quicker.

Otherwise there is not much wrong with you, but at your tender age I wouldn't normally expect even these small things. Stay in bed for a few days and try and get your nervous system back in balance. In general, I would advise you to take better care of yourself. For despite the undeniable male physique that you can boast of good sir, you clearly have a disposition towards—how shall I describe it in layman's terms?—well, a sort of tendency for the collywobbles, such as you have experienced first thing this morning. It's all very understandable really. Look, you have just come off the back of a bone-shaking rail journey lasting some three or four days. So you've not slept properly, or enjoyed regular mealtimes. Then—as you yourself have explained Hr. Sidenius—you returned and were immediately plunged into high stakes business meetings, tension, friction, and late night soirees. All that is more than enough to tip the scales with the kind of sago-pudding constitution we Danes have, even though it's housed in an ox-like frame."

The doctor made this last remark with a malicious glint in his small, slightly squinting eyes, though Per failed to notice this. Indeed the truth was that Per had lost interest in the man. After having received the intelligence that he was not in reality walking around with the first sprouting tentacles of lung disease, he now felt absolutely fine and his only thought was how to be rid of this suddenly verbose and jumped-up medic.

He got up as soon as the doctor had left the room. Flush with a renewed sense of life's endless possibilities, he paced up and down his hotel room humming a tune. He then got dressed, ate a hearty breakfast, and sat down at his work table. The urge to plunge into his project once again was upon him. He pulled out his drawings, his calculation equipment, statistical tables, and other accoutrements. Now was the time to stoke the engine fires! Full steam ahead!

He had just finished arranging everything on his table when he spied the book he had begun to read just before the doctor arrived. He had thrown the book onto the table between the rolls of drawings and could not now resist the temptation to browse through it again before getting to work. There was a bookmark in a place in the compendium—this was Plato's account of the startlingly frank discussion about death that Socrates had with his followers shortly before he was due to be put to death by poisoning. Per stopped at the passage where Socrates describes the human body as a lump of heavy and glutinous dough within which the soul has been pummeled and kneaded, and that it was for this very reason that man could not reach the things to which he aspired, other than the most base of hopes and desires.

"For the body causes us a thousand troubles. It fills us with lust and avarice, with deep fear and many kinds of false impressions and vanity... All wars are caused by the love of money, but we only need money for the sake and in the service of the body and even when we have satisfied this need, and can begin to speculate on important matters, the body is always breaking in upon us in so many ways, causing turmoil and confusion in our inquiries and, because of it, we are unable to perceive life's deeper truths—thus, while we live on earth, we can only come close to spiritual revelation when we have the least possible intercourse or communion with it, and do not allow ourselves to become surfeit with its nature."

Per lowered the book and looked out into space with a puckered brow. Remarkable!—he thought to himself. These words, spoken four hundred years before Christ, could have been written for a Christian evangelist book!

He read the rest of the page and then the next page and then the one after that... he just could not stop turning the pages. These profound metaphysical mind games sparked his most intimate spiritual and intellectual feelings into dramatic life. The morning was nearly over before he once again looked to his measuring tools and statistical tables.

Per made no more progress with this day's work on his project than he had had on the previous day. Despite a momentous effort, he found that he simply could not marshal his thoughts. Normally, he could not even pass a scrap of paper with some kind of map on it without being gripped by work fever. His biggest problem up until then had been how to carefully regulate and make best use of the myriad thoughts and ideas that ran through him like waves of goose flesh as he worked at his desk. Now the lines and calculations in front of him provoked no such creative response and the slightest extraneous thing, every shout from the street, every bell rung in the hotel, disturbed his focus and distracted him.

Just as the day before, this too ended with him being awash with neurotic agitation and finding fault with the whole enterprise. At last, he just sat there with his head in his hands, gripped by dark pessimism and despair.

Then he came to think of Professor Pfefferkorn, who had shown so much interest in him and his work during his time in Berlin. At the professor's encouragement, he had once sent him a written account of his ideas and as an expression of thanks, the professor had sent him a fairly lengthy reply. Per now fished this out from his papers.

"First of all, with regard to your ideas about the hydraulic motor, I'll be careful in my own comments. You are, of course, going down a completely new path, and it is only reasonable to expect that the first steps will be tentative. I know that I have mentioned during one of our conversations that similar attempts have been made in America and that much work is being done in trying to solve this really mammoth and truly spell-binding problem: how the inexhaustible power of the oceans might be placed in the harness of man's genius. It can only be to your credit that you too have been inspired by this thought, but whether or not the procedure you have suggested will lead us to the ultimate goal, I would not like to say. On the other hand, and after carrying out an in-depth study of your new system for the regulation of wind motors, I believe that you have made a fortunate discovery. The proposed internal weight-bearing lever and the design to assist balancing really appeals to me. There can be no doubt that you are pointing towards a system that deserves investigation. Again, whether you have actually found the decisive and definitive solution to this large-scale and difficult problem, which is of the greatest significance for all countries not blessed with mountains and great flowing rivers—well, you yourself would, of course, not make that claim. There is possibly no other area of life like the technical sphere where ultimate perfection is gained through an unending series of tiny improvements, and I know that you, for one, would not be happy to simply rest on your laurels with the progress you have already made. In assuring you that I will always follow your career, wherever and whenever conditions allow me to, I look forward with particular interest to any sign that you have made yet more breakthroughs in your continued work in this dynamic area of research. Of course, you have no doubts about your own abundant abilities, and I am sure you will make great strides, especially if you can manage to combine your remarkable grasp of the overall shape of things and your global vision with an immersion in the finer details of your work—the small things that impetuous youth tends to deprecate, but the things in reality upon which large-scale and hugely imaginative ideas ultimately depend. I seem to recall that it was your intention to continue your study tour by visiting North America. I have no doubt that this would be highly beneficial. Over there, and far more than in any other country, you will get the chance to enrich your experience in purely practical matters—and I believe that this does not just apply to mechanical problems; there are many other areas where we have become apprentices to the New World. In particular, you will get to see, in this land of the big invention, how even the mightiest of results was often achieved by the apparently most insignificant of means."

This old, half-forgotten letter, which had meant very little to Per when he received it, because he felt that it had not acknowledged him sufficiently, now resurrected his self-esteem. It also confirmed his view that he had to get away from Copenhagen and continue his interrupted odyssey of edification. Thus, he would once again place the running of his affairs in Ivan's hands. In particular, he would hand over full responsibility for any possible new negotiations with finance speculators to his brother-in-law. In the meantime, he would simply disappear—and this time head straight for America. It was not worth exposing himself once again to the distractions and temptations that the Old World held out for him.

In the afternoon, he went out to Skovbakken in order to talk to

Jakobe about his new plans. She was in the garden when he arrived, sitting on a bench near the timbered summer house that was bathed in sunshine.

Though she had clearly heard Per's voice up on the terrace, she calmly remained seated; nor did she give any sign, by way of a call or wave, as to where she might be found. When he finally tracked her down, she showed her cheek for him to kiss, even though Per had clearly sought her mouth. Nor could Jakobe bring herself to thank him for the flowers he presented—particularly because she could clearly feel that he expected her praise.

For that whole day, she had gone round in an anxious and debilitating daze as she tried to forget what had happened. She, Jakobe Salomon, who otherwise worshipped at the altar of clarity in all things, had now in her relationship with Per begun to betray her own core principles; wherever possible, she had closed her eyes to the truth in any situation where she felt her happiness from being in love might be threatened. Like somebody who has been woken from a sweet dream and turns back into the covers in the hope of continuing that dream, she had even indulged and enjoyed her self-delusion.

For his part, Per found it suddenly awkward to tell her that he would soon be leaving her once again. His decision to leave Denmark had by no means been an easy one to take. In truth, he found traveling quite tiresome, and the fact that he always struggled to make himself understood in foreign languages, of which only German really came naturally to him, exacerbated his reluctance to take off once again. Then it was hard for him to leave Jakobe just at the very moment when they had found each other again and were united in an open and mutual understanding of each other. But it could not be helped—it had to be done.

At first, Per had been too self-obsessed to notice the change in Jakobe's attitude this day. But as he sat there by her side on the bench, trying in his head to compose the best formulation that would prepare her for his news, he saw that she quickly wiped something away from her cheek. Jakobe's quick movement tried to imply the swatting of a fly, but Per realized that it was in fact a tear.

He was shocked. He had never seen her cry before.

"My God—dearest Jakobe love!" he said. "What is the matter? Has something happened?"

"No, nothing's happened Per . . . it's just one of my anxiety moments," she replied, as she pushed his arm away when he tried to place it around her waist.

"I mean, are you sick or something?"

"Of course I'm not. As I say, it's nothing really . . . Shall we go for a walk? I'm a bit cold sitting here."

She stood up very quickly—his obvious concern pained her—and they went down to the beach. Per was then struck by how haggard and miserable she looked—and he soon started to second-guess his decision to leave.

Then a blindingly obvious solution cleansed his dejected state of mind. In the same way that a solitary sunbeam breaking through a mass of cloud can suddenly transform a drab landscape, his inspired thought completely changed his life's perspective. Of course! Jakobe could go with him! They could marry straight away and then travel together as a respectable couple in the eyes of God and man. Why had he not thought of that before! All the difficulties normally associated with a long trip—strange hotels, feelings of loneliness and isolation, in short everything that made him despondent was suddenly transformed into a thing of excitement and joy. Of course, he knew from experience what an excellent travel companion Jakobe was—game for anything, self-sufficient, so maternal in her dealings with him, and on top of that so pleasingly at her ease in a range of foreign languages.

"Jakobe! Jakobe!" Per stopped in the middle of the garden path and before she could prevent him from doing so, he had thrown his arms around her. And he now confessed to her all the things that he had experienced and gone through since the previous day, and the plans he now had for the both of them.

For a while, Jakobe walked quietly by his side, with her head leaning on his shoulder in a kind of joyous self-administered amnesia that drained the very blood from her jowls and lips. She was well aware that she neither would, nor could, go with him. It would be quite impossible for her, in her condition, to even contemplate such a long journey. Per was talking about being away for at least six months. A trip of any shorter length would be of little use in terms of what he might learn. Besides which, she would only be a burden and source of worry for him.

"So you've nothing to say," he said, when they had arrived at their favorite spot by the strand with its free view across the sound to the sun-kissed Swedish coastline on the opposite shore. "Do you not think it's a brilliant idea Jakobe?"

"I'm not sure what to say Per," Jakobe said. She sat almost bent over and partially turned away from him. Her elbow was on her knee and her chin rested on her free hand. Per would not let go of the other hand. "Of course I understand that you have to continue your travels. I've been saying to myself that you really need to keep going... but Per darling, to be clear, you won't get me to go with you across the Atlantic Ocean!"

"But why Jakobe? Why would you be worried? I'll be there with you the whole time. And I promise that I'll take really good care of you. Or is it the sea crossing that's putting you off?"

"Yes Per. That's another reason not to go. And so I'll be staying here at home... waiting for you. And don't worry my love. I'll be more than patient. But I think your suggestion about getting married is the right thing to do. It makes sense for a number of reasons."

"So you're telling me Jakobe that, at the very moment we become man and wife, we are going to go separate ways. You are not actually serious? Because that would be the worst kind of torture. Sometimes I wonder if I really know you at all Jakobe? Where do you get those kinds of notions from? Tell me. That's not really what you want. Is it?"

She nodded insistently, gravely.

"Do you know what? I don't believe you. You've been acting so strangely in the last while. Are you keeping something from me?"

"No, darling Per, I'm not!" she said, suddenly squeezing his hand fervently. Now more than ever, she could not bring herself to tell him the full truth. She dared not. No. She bore no illusions any longer with regard to the real nature of his personality, and she feared that he would end up using her condition as a pretext to delay—or even completely abandon—his travels. Under no circumstances did she want to have that on her conscience. She realized only too well how beneficial and significant a stay in America, above all other places, might be for him, and now more than ever she had resolved to drive him on. If, previously, she had imagined that every hurdle could be overcome by the simple fact of his love for her, she now instinctively moved to gain recompense in another way for what she had lost on that count.

"Per, wait!" she cried, finally interrupting his attempts to persuade her. "Now I have an idea. You've no choice but to go to England first off, and I can go with you at least that far. We can spend eight days in London, and eight days in the country, or by the sea. And then in, I think it's Liverpool, you can go on and I will come home. How's that for a plan?"

"Well obviously it's better than nothing. Then at least I have the hope that you will change your mind when we get to Liverpool."

"That would be pointless, Per. Not least from your own point of view darling! Remember also that we wont be able to live in a hotel room when you come back. We have to get our own home. And I'll have enough to occupy me, with decorating and furnishing that while you are away."

"That's true! You are right Jakobe—as usual. You actually do have a wise head on those shoulders. I'm already looking forward to coming back my love! . . . Just think! Our own home! . . . It won't need to be particularly grand and palatial—do you think? And it would preferably be somewhere just outside the city, in some big open space, and with great views of forests and coastline. What do you think Jakobe? Us two—me and you!"

In his euphoria, he had once again pulled her into him and, in a state of sudden and complete enervation, she now placed her head on his shoulder and closed her eyes.

"Ah yes, it's so true," he continued. "Everything else in life is basically so meaningless and trivial in comparison with those magical things that are, you could say, the same for everybody—rich and poor—and are found in all of existence, as naturally as fruit dropping from a tree. There is something back to front in our life priorities—and the same goes for this New Age society. And I'm just so glad that I managed to work this out before it was too late. Because I swear, Jakobe, I was very close to getting caught up in all that mess and slime!"

Once more Jakobe was disturbed by his words. For, in spite of the fact that Per was really only using her own words—yes, in fact the very words she had once dreamed that she might hear from his mouth—they now scared her to death. She had, of course, changed a great deal since then. In particular, these last few days had seen a great change in her attitude to life's so-called "true values."

"I think you are making a false assessment of the way things really are Per," she said, with a hardness in her voice that was usually foreign to her.

"Well just look about you Jakobe and tell me whether you don't think that selfishness, vainglory, brutality, and lust for power are not just as entrenched in this new society as they were in the old?"

"Yes, of course they are Per—and why shouldn't they be?"

"Why shouldn't they be?"

"Yes Per—those values you are talking about are actually the basic human traits that make us all tick and drive society forward. So they can't be as awful as some people make them out to be."

Per laughed. He assumed that she was joking.

"And I suppose you are going to tell me that those same values are actually admirable?"

"I'm not sure. Are they not, at the end of the day, the things that bring us comfort, wealth, and wellbeing?"

From the tone in her voice, Per now understood that Jakobe was deadly serious and he looked at her in surprise. But the last thing he wanted to do was to bicker with her, so he tried to make a joke of it all.

"Now, isn't that what I've been saying—at the moment you seem set on contradicting me, even if that means denying your own opinions."

Jakobe said nothing. She too was disinclined to reignite the row from the other day. With that, they began to make travel plans and discuss the best destinations and routes to use.

In this same period, a public stir had been roused after the attack Max Bernhardt had launched—powerfully supported by Dyhring's *The Citizen*—against the backers of the Copenhagen freeport project. In the end, Bernhardt had his former opponents running scared. The truth was that they had set themselves a huge task that would require a massive commitment of capital. In the meantime, and against all expectations, the standing of *The Citizen*, the business paper that had been a thorn in their side, had risen to great heights in the business community under its new editor. Other newspapers with which Max Bernhardt had obtained leverage were now declaring that they too had great doubts about the Copenhagen harbor project as a viable business proposition. In order to pre-empt a collapse at the forthcoming share offer, the scheme's overlords felt that they had no choice but to go crawling to this hated senior solicitor and offer him a seat on the board.

This was the very outcome of the affair that Bernhardt himself had hoped for and had been working towards. Thus, he showed little surprise when the position was offered to him. At a major celebration that took place the same day, the reconciliation between Bernhardt and his old adversary, the previously omnipotent bank director, was officially sealed as the director made a great show of requesting the honor of toasting Bernhardt's name—a remarkable event that was dutifully recorded in all of Copenhagen's newspapers the next morning. *The Citizen* even went so far as to use the following headline: A HISTORIC MOMENT.

This crushing victory was important to Max Bernhardt. He had now succeeded in hammering into the public conscience the fact that nothing of consequence could be initiated without his imprimatur. Even the most venerable knights of the stock exchange had to wait for his authorization before engaging in serious business combat. Ivan was almost speechless when he heard the news. He now felt that all hope for Per's project was irrevocably doomed, at least for the foreseeable future, and in a sudden eruption of hysterical rage, he roared out loud about the treachery and assassination that had been perpetrated.

Maintaining a superior air, Per simply shrugged his shoulders.

"What did I say?" he said, turning to Jakobe, who had also been alarmed by this turn of events. "Will you now accept, Jakobe, that Hr. Max has the whiff of a common bandit and poacher about him and that we are lucky I didn't fall for his well-laid trap. Otherwise I'd have been left standing here now like a perfect idiot! No, no. It's just like I've been saying all along—we need a new movement here at home that can rid public life of that kind of vermin once and for all. If we don't do that, all sense of honor and civic pride will just go down the drain for good."

Jakobe gave a start at this but she decided not to respond. She saw no benefit in continuing that discussion at the present moment. She now placed all her hopes on getting Per to America and broadening this outlook by seeing more of the world. Besides, she had resolved to rein herself in with regard to her newfound critique of his views. She had determined once more to love him as he was, not how she thought he should be.

Ivan's despairing view of Per's future prospects actually proved to be far too pessimistic. Max Bernhardt's new and outstanding triumph stung his detractors and secret opponents into renewed action. The gentleman farmer Nørrehave was well to the fore in this regard, as he regarded himself as having been personally betrayed in this affair. In tandem with Barrister Hr. Hasselager, he threw himself into the battle on behalf of Per's project. Joining these two men, and of his own volition and without any preconditions, came a third party— Colonel Bjerregrav.

A sense of justice denied and patriotic duty had finally combined to push any residual feelings of jealousy in the old man's heart to one side. Bjerregrav's anti-Semitism had burst forth with all its instinctive power in this old campaigner for whom patriotism had become a new religion. As far as he was concerned, every Jewish person in Denmark, even the most home-baked of the breed, was nothing more than a half-naturalized German who nurtured hidden sympathies for the arch enemy. He insisted—not without some justification—that the majority of Jewish merchants and entrepreneurs in Copenhagen were quite simply local agents for German companies—just as it was primarily money from Jewish-owned banks in Hamburg and Berlin that had underpinned the wholesale modernization of Denmark's capital city. This influence spread to the provinces—yes all the way out to the most secluded of debt-ridden farms where a multi-million German finance system held rural Denmark in hock, and in this way completed that conquest of the country, which began with the roar of cannons in 1864. The thing that had always particularly attracted him to Per Sidenius's freeport plan was that here at last, he felt, was an attempt to assert Denmark's financial independence vis-à-vis its huge neighbor to the south. The idea of establishing a freeport in Copenhagen, meanwhile, he saw as a complete folly. The city's geographical situation, as well as its narrow and low-lying navigation channel, would never attract large-scale world trade to Denmark's shores.

He had now taken the decision that he himself would take the first step towards a reconciliation with Per. He would turn a blind eye to the bad blood that had existed between them—indeed, it was the very arrogance Per had shown a few years back when leaving his office, on the day of their fateful clash, that now simply seemed like one more spur for him to make his move. Now that he was fully convinced that Per was the country's savior, there was a kind of religious fervor in his wish to see that prophecy realized in all its glory.

In the meantime, Per sat at the table in his hotel room arranging things for his imminent departure. However, he was still trying to work on his drawings. A hope lingered in his breast that he might yet complete the most necessary changes, at the very least where his plans for the harbor itself were concerned. And it has to be said that he applied himself diligently to the task. He was up and about by daybreak and remained locked in his room for almost the whole day. But, still, the flow of thoughts that once came so easily and naturally to him failed to materialize. He toiled rather than worked, and his thoughts would constantly drift towards the distractions of life in the street outside.

Indeed, a pattern began to emerge, effectively established on that first day back at his drawings and calculations, where he would regularly break off from his logarithm tables and turn at random to a history or, better still, a popular philosophical text from his small library. These books were now stacked between the other books on his work table. He just could not resist the temptation to begin leafing through their pages and he would then usually end up becoming utterly engrossed in some topic or disputation that was far removed from thoughts of freeports and navigation channels. Moreover, at such moments, no commotion in the street or hotel bell would ever disturb his concentration. Without noticing the time going by, Per could sit for hours reading this kind of literature, without ever once lifting his gaze from its pages.

At around nine o'clock on one of these mornings, a knock came at Per's door while he was sitting at the table. He recognized the particular rap of Ivan's knuckles and quickly sought to conceal the book he had been reading beneath a pile of his drawings and papers. As his brother-in-law burst into the room, Per sat quickly back in his chair, with a slightly flustered and sheepish look on his face, like someone who had been caught unawares while engaging in some secret vice.

"Well Ivan. What news?" Per cried in a blustering welcome.

"Yet another scandalous stroke. That's what news! A complete blackguarding swindle of the highest order! . . . Look at this!"

Ivan's documents folder had almost become a physical adjunct to his person by this stage, and he now pulled a newspaper from it and thrust it into Per's hands. The paper was that day's edition of one of the more insignificant business organs in the town.

"Read there!"

Under a headline that read A LAND REBORN, there was a lengthy, well-argued leader column about Denmark's maritime trading conditions. As the leader soon pointed out, it was more or less an abstract of various articles that had been previously printed in a provincial newspaper and written by a hydraulics engineer by the name of Steiner. These articles described a plan which the leader column continually referred to as the "Steiner Project," but was in reality Per's creation with a small number of insignificant changes.

"Now what do you have to say Per, eh?" asked Ivan, looking eagerly at Per, whose face while reading the leader column had blanched almost to white. "It's bloody theft. Pure and simple! . . . Do you know anything about this man?"

Per shook his head.

"He must be exposed. Today!" Ivan continued, "What are you going to do now?"

"Nothing," said Per, after some moments of mulling over it. He then handed the newspaper back to Ivan.

"You cannot be serious Per! This man must be taken out of the picture. You have to defend yourself. You have to assert your fundamental rights here!"

"Defend myself?" said Per in a flash of temper.

"Yes Per—I mean, sorry to be so blunt—but you can't just act as if nothing has happened. That could be dangerous for you. Bear in mind that you are not short of enemies, who would just love to see you shoved into the ditch to make way for some other person who then takes all the credit for your work. Your genius for God's sake."

"Oh Ivan, it's not that serious! They won't get rid of me that easily! And even if they could!" he added, still influenced by the state of mind which Ivan's arrival had so disrupted (and a deep shadow now flitted across over his brow). "I'm getting a little tired of fighting over this nonsense. If we really have to start stooping to their level, it gets to the stage where you seriously start asking yourself whether it's a game you want to be in, and is it really worth all that grief. And to speak of something else entirely: Are you aware that your sister and I are thinking of getting married sooner rather than later?"

"My mother and father have mentioned this."

"Well, to tell you the truth Ivan, that issue is of more concern to me at the moment than all that rubbish in the papers. Tell me Ivan— as I have you here right now—would you know exactly what papers are needed so that a man can be legally married in this country?"

"What? Have you not made those arrangements yet Per? I thought—"

"I know, I know. It's very remiss of me. It completely slipped my mind . . . or, to be absolutely honest, I just couldn't bear the thought of traipsing round all those public departments—the people in there drive me up the walls with their officiousness and superior airs. I always end up having a huge row and causing scandal. Would you not do me the favor of arranging all that for me my good man? I know, for example, that you're supposed to apply to the town hall— or some registration office anyway Ivan. I don't know. The whole thing is a damn circus with me cast as some sort of trapeze artist."

Ivan, who by now was well used to the fact that Per used him as his errand boy whenever and wherever he could, said yes without any further deliberation. Though he did, as quid pro quo, secure a promise from Per that he would watch out for this mysterious Hr. Steiner and intervene immediately should there be the slightest repeat of his being named as the originator of the West Jutland freeport project.

Ivan had already thrust his documents folder under his arm and was standing in the doorway ready to depart when he swung around and looked at Per who was still sitting at his writing table: "Oh by the way . . . Tell me this Per. Is there anyone in your family called Kirstine Margrete? A clergyman's widow living here in Copenhagen?"

Per gave a start in his seat. These were his mother's forenames.

"No!" he said, but unable to conceal his dumbfounded expression. "Why do you ask, by the way?"

Ivan started his reply with the kind of awkward mumble he always came out with on the rare occasions that he spoke to Per about the Sidenius family. "Ahm, I just happened to notice the name Sidenius in the deaths columns in the *Berlingske*. Well then, I'll be off! I suppose we'll see you some time after lunch?"

Per was still sitting in his chair motionless several minutes after Ivan had closed the door behind him. For a second or two, when he finally rose to go to the service bell, he staggered slightly and everything went black in front of him. But at the same time, on righting himself, certain feelings of almost downright annoyance went through his mind. Of all things to happen to him! Just at this very moment in his life! He really was cursed!

"Will you bring the *Berlingske* morning paper up to me please," he said to the maid when she came into the room.

Shortly afterwards, he stood in the middle of the room with the newspaper spread out between his hands. The color drained from his face when he saw his mother's name in bold as he looked down the columns in the death notices section. It said:

"On this day, the soul of our dear mother, Kirstine Margrete Sidenius, widow of Pastor Johannes Sidenius, departed from this life to join her beloved husband in eternal rest at God's right hand."

The notice was signed: "Her surviving children." And Per remained staring at these words until his eyes filled and the letters swam in a wash of emotion.

Only a few days previously, he had repeated his nocturnal visit to his mother's dwelling and he now felt shivers down his spine at the thought that she may, perhaps that very night, have been suffering her final death throes. Just like the previous time, the soft glow of a lamp could be seen through one of the windows, and he had seen shadows passing across the roller blinds.

But anyway—he told himself in a half-hearted attempt at self-reassurance—his presence there with them would not have helped in the slightest. The idea of even reaching some kind of mutual understanding, never mind the kind of complete capitulation that his mother would have accepted, was never going to happen. For that reason, it was probably just as well that she believed him to be on the other side of the world, just as it was better for him that he had not been aware of her true condition. He might otherwise have let himself be persuaded to make a hypocritical announcement about returning to the family fold so as to reassure her on her death bed. He would then have regretted it for the rest of his life. Poor mother! Her physical frailty, fears, and scruples had dominated her whole life. All those long years stuck inside that sick room with its permanently drawn curtains had whittled her down to a nervous wreck. There was no doubt that, for her, death was not a horror but a liberation.

Per had begun walking up and down the length of his room to try and calm his mind. He was not generally a man for great swings of emotion. In fact, he instinctively shrank away from them, fearing their power. And now he remembered Jakobe, who as usual would be expecting him out at Skovbakken, and at the usual time. What was he to do? He would hardly, he said to himself, be able to sit there calm as you like talking about their travel plans, or he knew not what, and anyway he felt guilty because he had still not told her that his family had moved to Copenhagen.

He sat down and dashed a few lines off to her. She should not expect him that day, he said, using his usual excuse of being just too busy. At the end of the note, he added a postscript to the effect that his mother according to a death notice in the *Berlingske* had passed away while residing in the city.

He rang for the maid once again and arranged for the note to be sent to Jakobe via a messenger. But, at once, he was gripped by a strange feeling of restlessness. Several times, he sat down and began to look at his drawings but rose from the table again almost immediately. He could not even sit still for a second, never mind gather enough thoughts together to start concentrating on curve differentials and number sequences. Even when he took to desperately squeezing his head in his hands and willing it to do some damn work, his thoughts continued to revolve around the same things. The image of his mother, his childhood memories, his grief at not knowing anything about her last days on this mortal coil, the need to speak to someone, anyone, that had known her—all these things overwhelmed him in the end.

Thus, he abandoned all thoughts of work, got dressed, and went out onto the street. He sat himself down at the first and best restaurant he came across and ate lunch. Then he went for a walk in one of the large public parks that grace Copenhagen in order to distract himself and watch human life going on around him. He then settled down on a bench to listen to a military orchestra that was playing there.

When, later in the afternoon, he returned to the hotel, the porter informed him that a lady had come to see him and was waiting in his room. His heart's blood banged in his chest. He immediately assumed that it was one of his sisters who, in some way or other, had discovered that he was actually in Copenhagen, had found his address, and was here to report his mother's death.

Not for a second did it occur to him that it might be Jakobe. At that moment, she was so far removed from his thoughts that he did not immediately recognize her when he walked into his room and she rose to meet him from a chair by one of the windows.

Surprise and disappointment was so starkly etched in his face that Jakobe could not fail to see it. But she had been prepared for a hostile reception. She knew him now. She had previously encountered this irritated gruffness, which he used as a shield when he was in torment.

Jakobe also understood how carefully, and along which secret paths, she had to proceed to gain admittance to his confidence, and how incredibly difficult it was, even for her, to get him to truly open up and speak from the heart on anything that touched on his family. Nevertheless, she walked towards him with full fortitude, took his head in her hands and kissed him, saying: "I'm sure you understand, Per, that I couldn't bear just sitting there at home after getting your note. I had to see you. Look you in the eye. Darling Per. I know the sadness in your heart! I cried and cried when I read your note. I couldn't stop myself. And why? Because I share your grief. We are both bereaved."

Per shot a quick glance at her from under his brow and mumbled something about his mother having been dead for him a long time ago. So really, nothing much had changed as far as he was concerned.

"Ah that's just something people say to try and console themselves. Isn't it, my love? Be honest, Per. I understand your loss. Why should we hide anything, anything at all, from each other? And to think that your poor mother was here amongst us! And that you never told me! Oh Per, when are you going to stop hiding away from me, at the very times when we need each other most? Unless you didn't know she was here?"

As he freed himself from her hands, Per told her that he had always meant to tell her but that every time they had been together some other issue suddenly came up and he had completely forgotten his intention.

"So let's talk about it right now then!" she cried aloud. "Come on, let's sit down! I feel like there's still so much you haven't told me."

Jakobe threw off her overcoat and set down her hat and gloves by the sofa.

"Did you know that your mother was sick?"

"I knew nothing about it Jakobe. But I've already told you that she was bedridden for years."

"And you never tried to visit her...or even your brothers and sisters?" she asked, looking inquiringly at him from her corner of the sofa.

"No," Per answered, his hands shaking slightly as he hung her coat up on the rack at the front door.

"So how did you find out that she was here in town?"

"Quite by chance I saw a newspaper article where my Sister Signe was offering piano lessons. But I should say that a move to Copenhagen was being discussed as far back as my father's funeral. They wanted to move over here because two of my younger brothers got positions here."

He sat down on a chair, some distance away from her. Jakobe sat for a while looking into the distance with her chin resting delicately on the tips of her hand.

"Do you know what?" she said after a period of silence. "I think that if I had known that your mother was so close to me, I could never have avoided going to see her. Especially Per, as you will understand, when I had just got back from the Alps and felt so terribly lonely and would have desperately loved to talk to somebody about you. Do you think that she would have agreed to see me?"

"I don't know."

"Ah Per... I'm sure she would have. I am convinced that she would have...and that, in the end, she would have understood...well, us I suppose. Me and you."

"Do you remember the time when you thought the exact same thing about Eberhard and took off to visit him? And the only thing you got was disappointment."

It took a while for Jakobe to answer this. It was not because she could not recall her encounter with Per's brother. Her memory of the strange scene in Eberhard's cold, grim, and forbidding office, so bare of adornment and personality, had been very much on her mind in this very period; indeed it had aroused a concealed worry on her part, as she had come to realize that Per was more like his brother than he cared to admit.

"Ah well, it's slightly different with brothers and sisters I suppose," she said, stroking a lock of hair away from her forehead, as if at the same time trying to push away a painful thought. "I know that from my own crowd. But everybody always likes their mother, even if it's only the smallest of soft spots—regardless of how far you physically leave her behind. So I find it hard to believe that your mother and I would not, at the very least Per, have been able to hold a conversation, even though I'm sure we really are as different as two people can possibly be."

"You most certainly were, Jakobe."

"Yes but I refuse to believe that we would not, eventually, have come to understand each other. From what little you've told me about her, I've formed a picture of someone that I've actually became fond of. I seem to see her in front of me so clearly. She was small in stature wasn't she? And had different eyes to that of you and your brother... they were darker. The children obviously leaned towards their father where looks were concerned. Then she had to use a stick any time she was out of bed. My grandmother was the same. Perhaps that's why I see your mother so clearly. And likewise, for all her physical frailty, she must have been strong willed—indomitable! I think she deserves so much praise and admiration, and it is so moving that for years she ran the whole of that big house from the confines of her bed. And in the middle of her own terrible afflictions, she watched over all of you and could even make sure that nothing the family had went to waste. Just imagine—what a terrible fate for a mother to have to lie chained to a bed for eight years. And then your father, as you have said, was a bone-hard and unbending man. And I'm sure you are right. Nor was the family living in the lap of luxury in that house. And yet not one word of complaint! I remember you once telling me what your mother said to someone who expressed sympathy for her position: 'Please do not feel sorry for me. Pray for my husband and children!' I think that it is a beautiful story and shows what a great heart she had."

As Jakobe spoke, Per had remained sitting but his posture had grown more and more bowed with his elbows finally resting on his knees. The free fingers of his right hand rubbed the knuckles of his left hand at an increasing tempo. Now he rose, as if in impatience, and strode quickly across the floor, interrupting her as he did so.

"Right then, Jakobe. Let that be the end of it. What's gone is gone. And there's no use talking anymore about what might have been or could have been or would have been."

He positioned himself by one of the windows and looked out across the square, where the shadows thrown by the houses had already lengthened towards night. Fully lit by the setting sun, the old windmill stood by the ruins of the city ramparts at the end of the square. As if welcoming the sun's demise with open arms.

"You are right," said Jakobe after a short silence. "What's gone is gone! But tell me love, would you object if, at some point, I was to read some of the old letters your mother sent to you? I know that we rarely talk about your family anyway, but I do feel some kind of loss at the fact that I do not know more than I do, particularly about your parents."

At first Per let on that he had simply not heard Jakobe's question and follow-up remark. When repeated it, he gave a terse reply: "I possess no letters, Jakobe."

"No, I know very well that in the past few years you have not been in correspondence with your family, but I'm thinking about your first years in Copenhagen. Your mother at least sometimes wrote to you, I remember you saying. It's those letters, Per, that I would really love to read with you."

"I'm afraid that's impossible . . . because I don't have them anymore."

"Where are they then?"

"Where are they? I burned them after reading them."

"Oh Per, how could you—"

She was abruptly cut off. Per had taken out his handkerchief and mopped his brow as if he had suddenly become too warm. But Jakobe noticed his eyelashes glistening and realized that he had started to cry and was trying to hide this from her.

It was the first time ever that she had witnessed Per being overcome with emotion and her first instinct was to rush over to him and throw her arms around his neck. But, just in time, her intuition and knowledge of him told her to stop and pretend that she hadn't seen it. Besides, there was something in these emotional throes that aroused a sense of fear in her and, at the same time, fleetingly provoked her jealousy.

She chose to sit quite still, until Per moved away from the window. She then went across to him and took his arm. And for some time, they walked up and down in the room.

Ah now! She knew very well that, in her state, she was not best suited to bring comfort to others. She herself was so insecure and despondent. Her renowned steadfastness just crumbled when her thoughts turned to the lengthy separation that was ahead of her. If she could only tell Per everything! Every day she fought a desperate struggle with herself so as not to reveal the truth to him—had to keep her eye on the high stakes that would come into play if she were to confide her big secret to him before he disappeared over the Atlantic Ocean.

Nor was it just the physical fact of the approaching birth of their child that made her fretful and ill at ease. She had also begun to worry about the gossip that would ensue when people worked out that her child was conceived before their marriage. Thus, a change had taken place in her since the time Per had returned home. Previously, she had been far too proud of her love for her man to worry too much about whether her willful abandon could be subsequently concealed. Now, as she looked with a much more dispassionate eye on her future husband, it was that same pride that suffered at the thought that their love might become the subject of lewd chitchat.

However, it was less for her own sake and more out of regard for her parents that she had decided that she would not now return to Denmark once she had taken leave of Per in England. No, she would go to some place or other in Germany, perhaps to her friend in Breslau, and have her child there. But then the thought of having to wait another half year before the big event drove her to the brink of despair with impatience. She also had to admit that she would have borne all these things without the slightest grumble, if only she had the same trust in Per as she had had some three months before when they said their passionate goodbyes in Tyrol. The whole episode with Nanny had shaken her to the core and she saw danger everywhere. And yet she was even less inclined to lose him now than ever. All the things she now saw in him, including all his weaknesses and fragility, made her not one bit less fond of him than the time when her critical eye had been asleep. Sometimes her longing for him could be so strong that she believed it to be on the verge of unhealthy. For this reason she now tended to conceal the true fire of her passions. She had chosen to suppress her inner self, even when alone with him. This gave the effect of making her appear more moody, capricious, even distant. But at the same time, he dominated her being so completely, with such sovereign power, that it often seemed to her that there was no longer a thing in the world she would not forgive him.

Per stopped their stroll in mid-stride and looked at his watch.

"What about your train, Jakobe? I mean, it's not that I'm chasing you away or anything, really I'm not. I am really glad and grateful that you came. But I know you. You don't like getting home at all hours. And it's eight o'clock already."

She looked up at his face, that was still pale and drawn.

"And what will you do when I'm gone?"

"Me? Well I'll just get back to my work . . . as you can see, there are a hundred and one things on that table that have to be fixed, corrected and cataloged. I may as well use this time to some advantage."

"No, no, no," said Jakobe, placing her arms, almost in protection, around his waist. "You're not going to sit here all on your own. Because tonight the work will just have to wait. And how would it help anyway? You'd still be weighed down by those sad and depressing thoughts sitting here all by yourself."

"What then, Jakobe ... are you going to stay here with me?"

"No—not tonight, and not here," she said, visibly reddening as she did so. "It's so depressing in here. So you are coming home with me and that's that—do you hear? And you're staying with us overnight. The guestrooms are always kept ready anyway, as you know. You won't be disturbing or upsetting anyone, and my mother and father would actually appreciate it if they get the news of your mother's death from you personally. And I think that you owe them that at least. Come on! Come on Per. Home with me! Tomorrow we'll go for a long walk in the forest and leave all our troubles behind us for a while!"

Marvelous spring sunshine greeted Jakobe and Per when they woke the next morning at Skovbakken. The sun had firmly established itself in the skies by the time they met at the tea table in the dining room and, after a hasty repast, they disappeared arm in arm down to the garden. Neither of them had been able to sleep the previous evening. The knowledge that they were so near to each other kept both of them wide awake in the auspicious spring night. At last, they found each other while the rest of the house slept. Long into the small hours, they lay by each other's side seeking the solace they coveted for their troubles.

Now they walked in the depths of the verdant garden, where the dripping dew still lingered on leaves and twigs. In these late morning hours, when the whole family except Fru Lea were at their offices in town or at school, an idyllic tranquillity and peace reigned over the house. It was the same in the forest, to which Per and Jakobe walked from the garden. A completely different atmosphere prevailed to that which would come later in the day when dust hung over the pathways from busy carriage wheels and all the rest benches were occupied. There was no sound except that of birdsong. For the whole duration of their walk, the only other souls they encountered were an old man being pushed in a wheelchair by his help. He nodded to them in the manner of a grandfather as they passed each other.

However, as their tour progressed, Per's agitation began to grow. Even while they had been strolling around the garden, he had moments where his thoughts were elsewhere, and he mentioned in passing that he would have to be in town again by two o'clock. His pretext was that he needed to get to certain public offices for information pertaining to his work and they all closed at three.

Once lunch was over, Per left immediately. When he got to the city center, he hailed a cab that took him to the administrative offices where his brother Eberhard worked. He told the jarvey to wait for him and disappeared through the gateway of the dirty gray building that lay by a murky canal.

In the year that had passed since Jakobe had walked through that same gateway, Eberhard's diligence and strict observance of his duties had been rewarded with yet another tiny elevation on the thousand-step civil service career ladder. His previous desk in the most prominent chambers was now occupied by another young and hopeful carrier of the flame of continuity in the pompous state machine. Eberhard himself had now been granted his own little side office with a proper writing table and a chair with armrests. However, Eberhard saw no grounds in this promotion for ridding himself of the remarkably narrow-sleeved, funereal black coat that had served him through many years of honorable toil. He being entirely indifferent to its shine at the elbows and lower back. Nor had his choice of tie and shoes become more imaginative, despite his new position.

At that very moment, Eberhard was sitting at his desk sharpening a pencil with the kind of precise care and commitment that a civil servant of his ilk is expected to show for such tasks. But as he heard his name being mentioned in the reception area, the door to which being ajar, he quickly stowed away his knife and grabbed hold of a large document.

Presenting now an appropriate image of authority to the world, he reclined in his seat awaiting the visitor's entrance.

"Enter!" Eberhard said in a stentorian voice as the knock came at the door. Simultaneously, he raised his eyes just enough to ensure that his stare looked over the edge of the document. However, his shock at seeing his brother Per was so great that he made no pretense at hiding it. With the expression of someone who had just seen a ghost, Eberhard rose slowly from his chair and, for what seemed an age, the two brothers looked at each other without uttering a word.

Per was forcibly struck by how much Eberhard, as he stood there at his desk, resembled their father—shaking slightly with suppressed emotion and holding on to his chair, as if to stop himself from falling forward. He had the same lines around his mouth as his father, the same old-fashioned, pared-back sideburns, as well as the red-rimmed eyes. This affect was compounded by Eberhard's deathly still gaze and ramrod posture—in all this, Per saw his father's shape and countenance, in exactly the same way that it had been burned into his memory from his childhood years onwards.

Of his own volition, Per made sure to close the office door, in order that they might speak without fear of interruption. He then seated himself on a small sofa that faced the door. Eberhard sat down at the same moment.

"I'm sure you realize why I'm here," was Per's opening gambit. "I saw an announcement in the newspaper that mother has left us."

"Indeed," Eberhard replied, with clear signs of having to keep his emotions in check. "I should say that we believed you to be out of the country."

"I came back about a fortnight ago."

"A fortnight! A fortnight in Copenhagen. But you were not, perhaps, aware that mother had moved up to the city?"

"Yes . . . actually I was aware of it," said Per, looking away at some far point in the distance.

He then asked whether his mother had been very ill for a long period.

Eberhard chose to let Per wait before deigning to reply. Finally he spoke up, with the kind of deliberation that seemed to indicate a serious weighing of the consequences thereof, saying that his mother had died quite suddenly and to the surprise, indeed shock, of all the family.

"Mother was spared, thanks be to God on high, the usual physical suffering. Apart from her residual frailty, there was little to suggest her imminent death. Yes, it is true that she had begun to speak of having more difficulty breathing and then we noticed that she was more restless at night, but we just assumed that this was part of her overall condition—she had after all been like this for many years. One morning, as Signe was combing her hair, mother asked her rather sharply to hurry up. She was so desperately tired she said and wanted to sleep for a while. When Signe looked into her some twenty minutes later, mother could no longer speak. She opened her eyes perhaps once or twice after that as if to say farewell and then just fell quietly asleep."

Eberhard allowed these last words to trail off to nothing. Having recovered from the initial shock of seeing Per walk into his chambers, he had adopted his usual trait of surreptitiously surveying his brother's apparel. With quick, sidelong glances Eberhard studied Per's silk-lined coat, his gloves, his Parisian shoes with the elongated toes and the diamond buttons in his shirt front.

"Of course," he continued, "we were no more completely unprepared for mother's possible departure than she herself was. She had been weak for too long for that. It seems in fact that she had experienced a premonition of her death. She did not just leave strict and detailed instructions regarding her burial service. On the allocation of the rectory's death estate, she also wrote separate valedictory letters to all her children who were not in daily contact with her. There is also a letter for you, Peter Andreas. And a small sealed casket."

He had given a little dramatic pause before this last sentence. At the same time, Eberhard watched his brother closely to see the effect this might have on him.

"For the moment, at least, Signe has kept both things," he continued. "We believed you to be overseas and therefore saw no point in trying to pass them on to you. I don't know whether you want to collect them yourself, Peter Andreas. Right at this minute, you will find all the family gathered here. Ingrid and Thomas have also arrived to help lay mother into the coffin. Other than that, mother shall, of course, be buried beside father at home in Jutland. The plan is to convey her remains by a ship that is leaving tomorrow afternoon. Prior to her burial at home, the family intends to hold a ceremony around the coffin. Now that we know you are here in Copenhagen, we would be most upset if you were to be absent from this service. I can say that, I am sure, on behalf of the whole family. So, this very evening, we are all traveling to Jutland by the overland route with the train—mother specifically requested this, given that neither Signe nor Ingrid can stomach sea travel, and also to ensure that we all traveled together. This means of course that, God willing, we will arrive over there long before the coffin arrives, and we can then make all the necessary arrangements for the burial service. The coffin will be transported directly from the ship to the chapel, where she will lie overnight until the removal and modest service the next day. All this is what mother expressly requested."

Per made no reply. Nor did he, in his countenance or disposition, reveal at this moment the emotions that were bestirred within him. When, a few minutes later, he gave signs of his imminent departure, Eberhard's question to him was almost conciliatory in nature:

"And how are things with you? Do you intend to stay in Denmark?"

"No. I'm going to America very shortly. I have things to do over there. I am also, by the way, getting married before I leave. I am sure that you are aware of my engagement to one of Philip Salomon's daughters."

Now it was Eberhard's turn to decline an answer. He quickly averted his gaze after once again allowing it to instinctively stray towards the diamond buttons in Per's shirt front.

Per stood up.

"I omitted to mention to you," said Eberhard with renewed self-control, "that we agreed to hold the small memorial service at half past three tomorrow afternoon. So if you are of a mind to attend you will—"

Per shook his head decisively.

"No. For a number of reasons, I think it best if I keep away," he said. "Quite apart from the other issues, I would not wish to be there without my fiancée. But she, on the other hand, would hardly fit in there—indeed would not even be made welcome, I would wager, at such a ceremony."

Again Eberhard declined to say anything in response. His face had once again become as stiff as a mask and betrayed none of the horror he felt at the slightest suggestion that an international sophisticate, and a Jewess to boot, would be present at their songs of praise around their mother's coffin.

Per bade his brother a brief farewell and left.

On his way out, just by the gatehouse, he bumped into a pair of youths who were marching in almost soldierly tandem as they entered the building. Deep in thought, Per only looked up because of the way they obediently moved to one side to let him pass. They were two half-grown lads of sixteen or seventeen years of age with a decidedly provincial appearance. In fact they looked like two young farmhands with their mass of unruly hair bursting out from beneath wide-brimmed woolen Grundtvig hats.

Per knew them at once. For these were his younger brothers—the twins—on their way up to see Eberhard. That they had recognized him, they revealed very clearly. They looked in terror at each other and their faces became red beetroots.

Per raised his arm gently to stop their onward movement. There had been something in the shy way that they had moved aside for him that struck at his heart—or more accurately made him feel ashamed. He was still in a conciliatory frame of mind and had not, while up with Eberhard, been able to fulfill his need to make some sort of overture to his brothers and sisters so as to atone for the guilt he felt with regard to his mother.

"Good day good sirs," he said, holding out his hand, which they took reluctantly and with shy downcast eyes. "You are on the way up to Eberhard I take it?"

"Aye," they replied as one.

"I was just up with him there now to find out more about mother passing away."

At these words, the two brothers looked down again and one of them began to explore a crack in the pavement with the point of his boot.

Per understood the indictment being laid against him in this embarrassed silence. He frowned deeply but felt no anger towards them. Whatever remnant of contrariness and animosity he had retained during his conversation with Eberhard now melted away when faced with his two young twin brothers, who now appeared before him as the still-artless expression of innocence and contented simplicity from their childhood home. Despite their half-yokel appearance—indeed precisely because of it—he had to grapple with a huge urge within him to take both their heads between his hands and kiss them.

But for all his need to be familiar with them, he could find no more words to say. They stood there helplessly estranged from him and obviously feeling oppressed in his company.

All he could do was take their hand again. With a half-nod to the carriage waiting outside the gate, he mumbled some remark about how busy he was and a long journey that was ahead of him. Then he said goodbye.

But once he was inside the confines of the carriage, his emotions simply overwhelmed him. Rather than immediately going to the station so that he could be back at Skovbakken in time for dinner, as he had promised Jakobe, he asked the jarvey to take him back to the hotel. He had been thrown completely out of his stride and, where this was concerned, Jakobe could not help him.

Back at the hotel, the porter brought him a visitor's card. Per read: C.F. Bjerregrav, former engineer and retired colonel.

"Has this gentleman been here?"

"Yes sir. About an hour ago. I believe he wrote something on the back."

Per turned the card over. It said: "An old veteran called to wish you the best of luck and every success in your patriotic battle against the enemy."

Per's eyes glazed over for a second. He steadied himself on his feet, looked at the card again, and a vague smile appeared on his lips. Even though he himself had long forgotten the haughty prophecy he had once slung at the colonel, he felt this greeting, that came right in the middle of his mental turmoil, to be nothing more or less than a supernatural helping hand, a reaffirmation of his demonic pact with Lady Fortune.

He looked at his watch. He could just make the train and be at Skovbakken for dinner.

"Do you remember, Jakobe," Per said as soon as they were alone together, "that both yourself and Ivan scolded me for my behavior with Max Bernhardt, especially with regard to Colonel Bjerregrav, and you both went so far as to—"

"Per, we're not going back to that subject again," she interrupted him with anxiety in her voice.

"Oh yes we are, Jakobe! . . . Look at this!"

He handed the colonel's visiting card to her.

"My word. Did he visit you at the hotel?"

"Yes. And read what it says on the back! Well? Now what do you have to say to me darling?"

Jakobe really was lost for words. Her astonishment left her dumbfounded. Her smile, as she laid her hands on his shoulders, was almost awestruck, crying out: "My God, Per Sidenius. You are nothing short of a magician!"

The next morning, Per went down to the harbor and found the ship, which by his reckoning, would be taking his mother back to her native Jutland. By speaking to the first mate, he learned that a coffin actually had been listed in the ship's manifest, as well as the time it was due to arrive on the quay.

In a building just facing the ship, there was a rudimentary café. Per made a note of this café, which was in a raised position looking over the quay. In the early afternoon just before the appointed time, he placed himself at a table that looked out onto the quay. He ordered a glass of beer and, hiding behind a newspaper, his heart booming in his throat, awaited the arrival of the hearse.

Out on the quay, a summer rain fell in a steady, even pattern. However, the rain had no effect on the busy scene being played out along the broad quayside loading area, which was packed with stacks of barrels, grain sacks, tea chests, and boxes. There were only a few hours left before the ship was due to sail. Heavily laden wagons poured in from every angle, all thronging around the lading stage so as to be first to be unloaded. The steam winch clanked and hissed as large wooden boxes, iron girders, sacks of meal and barrels of petroleum were ripped out from the bottom of the flatbed parts of the wagons, were held hovering in space for a moment above the cargo hold and then dropped down into the voracious bowels of the ship. A large pig was also to be brought on board and this caused no little commotion. Two men were to be seen pulling it by the ears, while a third man energetically twisted the curls of its tail with great gusto as if it were a barrel organ. Yet the pig would not budge. The steady rain and mad bustle at the quay heightened people's spirits and there was much banter and ribaldry concerning the recalcitrant pig, which squealed so loudly that it seemed to be calling on all the spirits between heaven and earth for protection. At last, the pig was persuaded to run up the gangway, and with a short gallop disappeared into the maw of the foredeck. Then an altercation erupted between two drivers who had crashed their wagons into each other, careering into the stacks of cargo as they did so. They could maneuver neither forwards nor backwards and neutrals settled down to enjoy the inevitable bout of fisticuffs, but a constable came along and got the obstructing barrels moved so that traffic could flow again and order be restored.

The rain had slackened off, but the air still lay heavy and dark over the town. It was just about possible to glimpse the red roofs of the warehouses over on the Christianshavn side of the docks.

Suddenly Per spied a one-horse carriage of the type that is used to ferry the caskets of the dead from people's homes to church or chapel. A man dressed in working clothes could be seen on the trestle beside the driver as the carriage approached the quay. It drew up a good distance from the ship itself. Bringing up the rear was a closed carriage, from which four people now stepped out—his brothers. First came Eberhard, his silk top hat bedecked with flowers and his trousers turned up at the bottom. He put up his umbrella the moment he was outside the cab, even though it was not raining at that moment. The ruddy features of Thomas, the curate, were next to appear, and then finally the two younger brothers.

Over at the steam winch, the stevedores were just loading the last cargo bale from a supply wagon. When this vehicle was driven away, the driver of the hearse nudged his horse forward so as get into position. But a shout from the first mate, who was commanding the loading operations from up on the bridge, stopped him in his tracks. He was told to rein the horse in and stand by. A young and extremely skittish horse had to be brought on board and it became clear that this would take longer than expected. Just as with the rowdy pig, the first attempts involved leading the horse up the gangway and this looked at first to be successful. Though the beast shivered and snorted with anxiety to the extent that blood spurted from its nostrils, the stevedores had at least managed to get its forelegs on to the boards of the gangway, but as bad luck would have it, just at that moment one of the small tugboats that ceaselessly ply the harbor issued a couple of loud blasts from its horn. The horse went berserk. In the end, there was nothing else for it but to hoist the animal on board like a lump of dead freight. The ship's derrick was swung out across the loading area, where the animal had been pushed into a high-sided pen—a box made of strong wooden planking. There was just enough room for it to stand, but not to move. Two substantial iron cleats projecting out from the top of the horse box served as fastening points for the crane's hook and chain. Once everything was in place and the strain taken on the load, the steam winch was gunned into gear and the animal—which stiffened as if from a heart attack as it rose from the earth—was conveyed in a slow arc over the heads of the assembled dock workers and deposited on the ship's foredeck.

As all this took place, Per's eyes had never strayed from the hearse carrying his mother's coffin. In fact he had not even been conscious of the whole equine drama, which had attracted a small crowd of interested onlookers. But now an urgent sign was given to the driver of the hearse to get himself into position. Eberhard and the other brothers followed behind on foot.

The man dressed in a workman's overalls who had been seated on the trestle of the carriage had gone to the hatchway area in front of the cargo hold beforehand. Along with two other men, he now began to maneuver, with some difficulty, a six-foot-long timber box with a hinged lid that carried freightage instructions in red paint. In all haste, the hearse was opened from the back and a low casket, devoid of all decoration, became visible. Two of the dock workers stepped forward to lend a hand, but Thomas held them back as he and the other brothers then proceeded to carefully lay the coffin down into the timber box, which it almost filled completely. Once it was firmly packed in with hay, the box lid was closed and screwed down tightly.

As the box made of rough, unfinished timber lay there on the gray stone slabs with its precious contents, there was nothing to distinguish it from the rest of the cargo that lined the wet cobbles of the wharf as far as the eye could see. Especially after the departure of the hearse, very few people would guess that behind those planks of timber carrying the painted shipping legend, lay a human being, a mother, a world whose light had been extinguished, a being whose life, moreover, had been richer and more deeply inspired than most people's would ever be. The stevedores now placed an iron chain around the box, just as they had done with the sacks of meal and barrels of petroleum, and on a signal to the winch operator, it was hoisted away from solid ground. Directly over the ship's hold, it hovered in the air for a moment, until a shout came from below. With a great clanging and hissing from the steam engine driving the winch, this venerable pastor's wife from rural Jutland was lowered down between the beer barrels, the tubs of Danish schnapps and casks of sugar.

In behind the window panes of the café, Per's face steadily drained of color. The main waiter, who had been observing him the whole time because he had been so motionless and had not even touched his beer, jumped towards him at this point saying: "Are you feeling all right, sir?"

Per directed his disturbed gaze towards him. He had completely forgotten where he was and now felt the floor rising beneath him and the walls around him imploding into the room.

"Give me a cognac," he said.

He drank two glasses straight off and, directly after the second one, some color returned to his cheeks. In that moment when he saw his own mother hanging there, swaying in the breeze like some paltry dispatch item, dark night fell all about him. And in that blackness he caught a glimpse, like a flash of lightning, of the bare truth of existence itself. For he was staring at that same freezing void, cold and mute and eternally indifferent to the cares of man, that he had seen on his first trip through the Alps.

When he could finally look over at the ship again, work was continuing in the ship's hold with barrels and sacks being stowed away ready for departure.

On the quayside, his brothers were standing around the man in overalls as Eberhard conscientiously counted out the required sum of money and placed it into his outstretched hand. Having received the money, the workman remained standing there for a moment in the clear expectation of receiving a tip, but his wait was in vain. At this, the brothers peeled away in order of seniority and walked away from the quay in almost military rank and file.

Per remained sitting where he was. Despite the fact that he had become the subject of close inspection and gossip amongst the other patrons in the café, he found he was unable to tear himself away. His only concern was to remain close by his mother until the final possible moment. He could not bear the idea of leaving her remains just lying there with no one to watch over her. Then, all at once, a thought struck him—a solution to the problem. There was no need for him to leave her at this point at all. He could follow his mother on her journey, without anyone needing to know about it. He would be her secret guard of honor on her night crossing over the Kattegat. He could then hop ashore at one of the landing bays at the mouth of the fjord before the ship arrived at his home town in the early hours of the morning. From there he could get to a rail station on the East Jutland line some time before noon and be back in Copenhagen that same evening.

He looked at his watch. There was only two hours before the ship's departure, so there was of course no chance of getting out to Jakobe, who was the only person who really needed to be told about his hastily conceived journey. He would just have to make do with getting a note out to her.

But on arriving back at the hotel and dipping his pen into the inkwell, he realized that he could hardly explain his actions in a brief letter. Thus he lifted one of the telegram sheets made available to hotel guests and wrote out a short missive that gave the most important information.

He then began to pack his things into his small suitcase. But suddenly he stood stock still with a pair of travel boots in his hand—Colonel Bjerregrav loomed large in his mind.

There could be almost no doubt that the colonel expected the courtesy of a return visit from Per this very day. Putting the meeting off for even a couple of days would appear like a deliberate slight and might easily destroy a relationship that would be of incalculable help to him right at that very moment. What was he going to do? Damn it, he too would have to make do with a brief note. "Dear Colonel Bjerregrav, due to an unavoidable journey I am obliged to undertake at once—" he wrote.

Shortly afterwards, he was sitting in a carriage on the way to the steam packet.

As the boat steamed through the Øresund, it occurred to him that, given he was going to be in Jutland, he might as well make that visit to Kærsholm he had promised his old friends from his days in Rome—Dame Prangen and her sister the baroness. An undeniable longing came over him to see these two almost maternal friends once more, but besides that he had an ulterior motive for visiting them at that precise moment. Since returning from Rome, he had felt increasingly oppressed by his financial dependence on his parents-in-law, who were, and would always remain, strangers to him. For while it was true that Philip Salomon had never raised the question of their mutual financial affairs, it had always been a thorn in Per's flesh to be financially beholden to this man. However, he realized that he would be obliged to raise another loan if he were serious about going to America, and his purpose now was to seek out the good baroness, who had already, and completely of her own volition, offered, indeed implored him, to accept her offers of support.

Jakobe was up in her room when Per's telegram reached Skovbakken. Without knowing what on earth had kept him all day, she had gone into town after lunch to do some shopping and had then called into the hotel to see him. But when the porter informed her that he was not in the hotel, she became embarrassed and left neither a note nor even her card. After that she wandered around the streets for a while in the hope that she might meet him, but at the same time was rather anxious in doing this because she knew that Per did not appreciate such accidental encounters. In the end the rain drove her home.

But she found no peace in being at home. In the last few days, a restlessness had come over her and pricked her to perform all kinds of useless and ill-timed actions. And these could all be traced back to the preparations for her trip with Per to England, which had become an obsession for her. As far as was humanly possible, she dismissed from her thoughts everything that might lie on the other side of this "their second honeymoon" as she secretly called it. None of her usual anxieties, fears, or worries were going to be allowed to cast a shadow over their renewed vows of love for each other. In their all too brief fortnight together, they would live and breathe for their love only. Deep, and deeper still, would she slake her burning thirst for life before the long days of sackcloth and ashes descended upon her.

She blanched when she read the telegram—instinctively gripped by fearful portents, for which in the next moment she had no explanation. Was there really anything so strange or startling in what Per had done? His gesture was, she told herself, quite natural and actually rather sweet that he should wish to pay his dear mother his final respects in that way. In a few days time he would be back in her arms.

But then—when she read the telegram a second time—a great angst gripped her by the throat yet again. And for each time that she read his terse comments once more, she felt she could read more into them. Those twenty or so words raised more questions for her than answers. At what point exactly did Per make his decision? Because the day before he had said nothing to her about perhaps following his mother home. Had he spoken to someone in his family about it? And why did he wait until the last minute to send a telegram? And then taking off like that without saying a proper goodbye?

She remained sitting there with the telegram in her lap. Light was beginning to leave the skies and the deepening shadows that emerged from the many nooks and crannies of her small room took on a heavier and more menacing aspect and exacerbated her sense of foreboding.

Jakobe dwelled on the fact that, despite all her entreaties to Per on being more open with her and the importance of trusting each other, he still hid so many things from her—how little she actually knew about where he was during the day, what he did, and what his thoughts were—and she began to doubt whether she would ever defeat this furtive, closed, and disloyal side to his nature that caused her so much anguish.

Down in the garden room, meanwhile, a lively atmosphere prevailed. The family had received a visit from some of the other summer residents living nearby, and Nanny was at her entertaining best with her constant stream of anecdotes and gossip from life in town. She laughed nonstop but this laughter was somewhat forced and its tone signaled her disappointment that Per had not turned up.

Where Per was concerned, her timing was to say the least unfortunate. His trips to Skovbakken in the last while had become increasingly irregular. So despite the precise calculations she made so as to ensure that she would catch him there, she always seemed to arrive just after he had left, or she had been obliged to leave just when he was expected any minute. For this reason, she was almost beside herself with impatience to see him. However, her aspirations were no longer motivated by revenge. She knew from Jakobe's manner with her that Per had not revealed anything of what had transpired between them and, once she understood this, she admitted quite openly to herself that she was in love with him. With this secret complicity, which Nanny ascribed to his wishing to protect her and therefore indicated deep feelings of affection, he had won her melting heart entirely.

The idea that she might place her marriage, and the society ambitions she nurtured on the strength of it, in jeopardy for Per's sake, was no longer an absurdity to her. Nor would she shrink back from serious conflict with her sister over him. The fact that she had now heard about their wedding preparations simply made her even more fiercely disposed to take him from under her nose. Jakobe did not deserve to have this gorgeous bull of a man with his red mouth. The memory of his full, vibrant lips on hers sometimes drove her wild with longing.

And once again today, he had not shown up!

Nanny was not the only person who was waiting impatiently for a sign of Per. Only minutes before, Ivan had been pacing up and down the terrace, consulting his watch at every other turn.

He had an extremely important message for him. For he had received a letter from Barrister Hr. Hasselager, who had requested details of Per's address, as both he and the landed estate owner Hr. Nørrehave, as well as other businessmen, wished to arrange a meeting with him as early as the next day if possible. Ivan had been sure that he would find Per at Skovbakken by this point in the day, but when he discovered that Sidenius had sent a telegram to Jakobe he knew straight away that this meant Per was sending his apologies. Thus, he raced back to the railway station to see if it was possible to track him down somewhere in Copenhagen.

In the meantime, daylight had all but disappeared from the living room. The housemaid came in to shut the door leading to the garden, after which lamps were lit around the tables and desks.

Jakobe did not show herself. Even when tea was served, she declined to appear, despite being called several times. Nanny, who had also heard about the telegram, took this to be a good sign. So the marriage would come to nothing after all! And of course her parents hardly ever mentioned it, so they obviously had little faith in it.

Music was now played for an hour or so and when the clock struck eleven the visitors made ready to leave. Nanny, on the other hand, made so bold as to defy Dyhring's specific prohibition on her staying there overnight, her hope being that Per would come the following morning.

Then Ivan arrived back from town. He had on him his most perturbed face. Once the guests had left, he turned to his parents and Nanny saying: "Has Jakobe been down at all this evening?"

"No...why?"

"Sidenius has gone."

"Gone? Gone where?"

"I'd say to Jutland. At the hotel, they said that he will be away for a few days."

"Ah yes. He's probably gone over for the burial service," Ivan's mother said. "So that's why he sent the telegram to Jakobe."

"Yes but it's still very strange behavior...just taking off like that without saying anything. And now of all times!" said Ivan, as he proceeded to tell them about the letter he had received from Hasselager, and also about the colonel's visit, which magnanimous gesture still had not been reciprocated from Sidenius's side.

Fru Salomon looked probingly at her husband. But he said nothing. He had made it a rule not to express his opinion on matters concerning his prospective son-in-law. Finally, he shook his head and said: "Well, good children! I think it's time for bed!"

The ship upon which Per found himself now sailed in open sea.

Like some huge floating sarcophagus in the misty, crepuscular night, the huge black hull of the ship coasted over the tranquil surface of the sea. The smoke billowing from the ship's funnel flowed across it and into the water in the manner of bereavement flowers being continually cast astern. The heavens were covered in cloud, which lay heavy and dark along the horizon. But occasional rifts in the clouds offered glimpses of pale stars that were like the eyes of angels following the progression of this somber funeral cortege as it moved on through the waves.

Per sat alone on the upper middle deck, wrapped up in his greatcoat and looking out over the waves. He chose a place that would keep him as close as possible to the spot beneath which his mother's coffin was stowed.

All of the other passengers on the ship had gradually drifted away to take their rest in the covered accommodation. In the still night, no conversations could be heard anymore from either the compartments on the foredeck, or in the cabins below the decks.

The first mate was keeping watch up on the bridge and could be seen striding backwards and forwards with each soft roll of the ship. From the afterdeck came the clink, at regular intervals, of the ship's speed log. Otherwise, right across the whole of the ship, there was no other sound than the steady thump of the engine and the plash of the propeller. Now and then Per thought he could hear the scrape of shovels being lifted by the stokers down in the bowels of the ship.

Down in the southwest, the lighthouse on the island of Hesselø had come into view.

Up on the bridge, the watch was changed and a new sailor took over the wheel and the second mate replaced the first mate. Per noticed that these officers were discussing some topic that made them lower their voices.

Very soon afterwards, peace and stillness reigned once again all around him.

He entertained no thoughts of sleep. He wanted to be as close to his mother as possible, and besides, he knew that it would be impossible for him to sleep.

As he sat there and stared out across the luminescent surface of the sea, so many images from his childhood home came unbidden to him out of the dark night. Never before had he formed such a comprehensive tapestry of thoughts and emotions about his mother. Just as in her life she had been overshadowed by that dominating father figure, he realized that his memories of her had, in turn, been darkened by the utter distaste which invaded his mind whenever he thought of his father. He remembered her best from the days of her long confinement to her sickbed. When in his thoughts—awake or when dreaming—he had contemplated his mother (and this he realized had happened more than he was aware), he always thought of her bedridden in the half light of that room. The dark green blinds were always rolled down and either he or one of his brothers or sisters would sit at the end of her bed and rub her sickly legs. But in the last few days, more and more memories had risen to the surface of his mind from the time when she was still up and about at home in the rectory. There she was, in the early morning or evening, doing the washing and dressing of the youngest children, patching and sewing for the older ones, reading lessons and writing essays for the very eldest children; and when, every night, she did the rounds of the nursery and children's bedrooms in her long, white night-clothes, putting a pillow to rights here, puffing up a quilt there, with her remarkably soft hands, she would stroke their hair, when they opened their drowsy eyes for a second and turned contentedly in their beds.

Most clearly of all, he now remembered the war years, whose ca-lamities he was too young to understand, and whose disorder and agitation had therefore amused him. Their town was occupied by German troops for months. With a drum major leading their columns, the soldiers would march through the streets every day playing mil-itary music and present themselves for review in the main square, or at the horse track. The rectory itself was always full of soldiers—very often around twenty of them, as well as seven to eight horses that were stabled in the turf house. Every morning they were led out into the garden so as to be groomed and brushed under the watchful eye of an officer. A few small rooms were all that had been left for them as a family, and the great number of children had to be stuffed together in whatever way that could be worked. At the time he thought this was great fun. And they had been given syrup with their food, because they had no butter! But thinking about it now, he worked out that his mother must have been with child at the time, carrying her twelfth baby, preparing for the twelfth agonizing battle with death. And as if that was not enough, some of the children became very sick, and one of them, a little girl of three years of age, died after suffering great pain. As it was later told to him, just as a Hannover regiment was pulling out of the town and another was expected, the child issued her last breath while lying in her mother's arms.

Was it, then, really that surprising that his mother's natural disposition finally became so fraught and anxious? And was it not because of ignorance that the younger generation, which had grown up in an apparently much more peaceful and relaxed period, often displayed contempt for the feelings of insecurity and despondency shown by their parents, and in particular by those who had gone through the war with all its suffering and national humiliation? The biggest surprise was that mother had not suffered a complete collapse. Jakobe, who had suffered her own troubles, had of course wondered out loud the other day where his mother, despite her physical weakness, had obtained the almost superhuman inner strength to withstand all the blows that life had landed upon her.

Yes, where had she gained that strength from? And more generally, what internal force had carried the older generation more or less intact through the disasters of that time—the terrible anxiety that came with the war years and the deathlike national impotence that followed afterwards, in fact through the whole bloody collapse, for which his mother's individual martyrdom could serve as a fitting and heart-rending metaphor?

Of course, as far as his mother was concerned, there could be no doubt about the answer to this question. He remembered the words she would often quote:

It is not, oh Lord Jesus Christ, my honor that saves, but your sacrifice! He rose quickly and shivered heftily, as if someone had just walked over his own grave, and began to walk up and down a coarse hessian mat that ran along the side of the deck. But his legs were as heavy as sandbags, and his head felt so ponderous after the emotions and trauma of the last few days that he was forced to sit down again.

562 · HENRIK PONTOPPIDAN

Shortly afterwards, the first mate came down from the bridge and stood close to where Per was sitting. It was clear that he wanted to engage Per in conversation. He pointed out a group of small fishing boats that lay rocking on the waves with slack sails. He explained that they were flounder fishers that were drifting homewards on the southerly current from the banks around Anholt.

Per answered with a terse: "Is that so?"

Thoughts of the letter his mother had left him came to his mind, and also the package, which presumably contained his father's time-piece. He did not know how he was going to pluck up the courage to read that letter. His fervent hope was that his mother would not be too hard on him, but there had been something in the look his brother Eberhard had given him that did not bode well.

Per got up. He was gripped once again by a sudden and chilling sense of distress, and could not sit still.

"You'd be better off going below and getting a few hours rest, there's a good sir," said the first mate, moving much closer to Per, jutting his chin out and placing his hands in his coat pockets. "It's too bloody cold to be trying to walk your troubles off out here on deck."

The man's whole demeanor and his impudent tone brought Per up short. A commanding rebuke had just formed on Per's lips when he realized that the mate may have suspected that he had been sitting there considering suicide and that this was what the furtive conversa-tion had been about up on the bridge.

He bluntly asked the man whether he thought he was going to jump overboard.

"Well now that you mention it yourself, sir, I won't deny that we were thinking along those lines. These things happen and we, of course, would rather avoid anything like that, not least because of the mess we are left with afterwards, what with maritime inquiries and the whole circus. We actually got unlucky as recently as last autumn—there was a man who jumped overboard, and it was right here in this stretch of water as well."

"What kind of man was this?"

"He was a deck passenger, too. From Horsens he was. Something went twisted in his life, so they say. We saw nothing of him afterwards except his hat, and he was never found since. So he's mackerel meat now, no doubt."

Per instinctively looked away from the waves, said goodnight, and hurried below decks.

For a couple of hours he remained down in the oppressive passenger salon, squeezed up against the other snorting and groaning passengers, but he was unable to sleep. His thoughts raced as if with the tide. He sensed that a new spiritual and intellectual force was awakening in him this night—the fulfillment of a long gestating rebirth. It was as if in the gloom and mist of night a new world was opening out before him, but he could still not discern the path he was to take. The world his ship was leaving behind disappeared into a dark void. The figure of an old and palsied priest's widow had revealed a force to him, against which even great Caesar's empire seemed impoverished and trivial—a power and magnificence in suffering, in renunciation, in sacrifice.

He lay with his hands behind his head and looked out, his eyes wide open in the half light all around him. He was full of fearful premonitions of the inner struggles that were now ahead of him. But he was by no means downhearted. To his own great surprise, he felt no envy for the people nearby, who breathed heavily or snored under the influence of that sleeping potion that a settled conscience always produces. There was in his burgeoning remorse and pain something akin to the mysterious stirring of emotions provoked by the suffering of a woman in labor—a pronouncement that a new life is dawning, with new hopes and promises.

In the early morning light, Per left the ship at its first landing stage at the mouth of the fjord. From the top of a grass banking where a vast expanse of meadowland spread out before him, he followed the ship's slow progress as it wended its way round the many bends in the fjord—the same route he had taken eight years earlier as he had steamed out into the world, so full of youthful courage and bright hopes. Eight years ago! And "Fortune" really had kissed his brow. He had even won that very kingdom he had wished to conquer and the crown which he believed he was born to wear!

While the dew settled on his eyelashes like a rainbow of tears, he continued to stare after the gliding sarcophagus as it vanished into the meadows that swayed with bright flowers, until in the end it disappeared from his sight in the golden mist of morning, like a vision being accepted into the kingdom of heaven.

19

IN ONE of east Jutland's most fertile valleys lay a country estate, which with its majestic, russet-hued walls and crenelated gables was redolent of an abbey. This was Kærsholm. The estate lay at the edge of low-lying meadowlands, which wound their way through the surrounding countryside like a verdant watercourse guarded by a rise of fields and forest-clad heights to either side.

A lazy river flowed right through the center of these meadows—the modest remnant of a once majestic estuary that had covered the bottom of the valley for miles around. If one walked along through the meadows, but was not abreast of the river itself, its water and banks would be invisible to the eye. All one saw was the unending sward of gleaming green that was only patched, here and there, by a ditch or pool of still water.

It was hard to imagine that a mass of rolling seas had washed through the valley of this tranquil range of hills in times gone by—that here, where timid little brown and gray songbirds looped along the rushes, huge ocean-going seabirds had once crested the waves, the sun glinting on their wings. Here, where local trench diggers and muck spreaders now sat and gummed devoutly on their bread and dripping, battle-drunk pirates had swept inland aboard their blood-stained ships, glorying in the booty and treasures they were bringing home to their seaboard redoubts.

Up on the hills meanwhile, where now bright and welcoming tree groves swayed over the cornfields, dark masses of wild forest once loomed and wolves howled at the moon in the frost-bitten night. Even long after the landscape had risen up to more commanding heights, and the once vigorous seabed had become subject to the sedate rhythm of the farmer's plow, the interior forest remained a haven for audacious beings and their daring exploits. From this secluded bastion would come the sharp report of the hunting horn, blasted by those proud freeborn lords as they galloped towards the fray. A mocking death's head was their outrider as they burst through brush and thicket leaving a bloody trail in their wake. It was here also, in this primordial forest, that the winter storms gained their full voice—a wild choir of rushing voices like some phantom echo from the roar of the ocean deep of long ago, arousing the folk memory of a time when the pirate reign of terror was at its height.

But gradually the forest was encroached by dark, fertile soil. A weaponless army of strangers arrived and built dwellings there and cultivated the soil in order to live in peace and enjoy the fruits of the earth in its glorious seclusion. These strangers had come in their hordes from the south, raising holy images and the cross of Christ along the way. They wore cassocks and were shod in nothing other than sandals, and soon the first bells calling people to prayer rang out, proclaiming "peace on earth and good will to all men" across this ancient Viking land. And the years went by. From all sides, the farmer's axe, which had never tasted man's blood, ate into the darkest parts of the forest and the screeching of crows was now heard from the nests abandoned by eagles.

Years, then centuries, passed. From blooming fields and meadows, Mother Earth's bounties gushed forth and across the thresholds of the chosen few in this society. This rich produce was stored in barns and outhouses, filled monastery cellars to bulging and festooned the pantries of country estates with slaughtered animal joints and offal, not to speak of the honey-sweetened beers that were stored there. All this abundance ending up as the blubber and thick blood that bolstered the human forms that were to be found behind a monk's habit and a medieval knight's shining armor. And see how the pious friar who fattens his arteries in this way becomes gripped by the passions of the flesh. He gets notions about taking a wife, feeling that it is nothing more than his Christian duty to become a pater familias and, without pomp or ceremony you can be assured, share life's riches with his fellow descendants of Adam and Eve. In this way, the once penitent and pilgrim church mixed blood and bone with settled society. And from that fierce beginning in penitential sackcloth and rough-hemp belts emerged as if from a new chrysalis, the first Pastor Sidenius with his magnificently white clerical ruff and the huge train of children following behind him.

In tandem with this, the previously boisterous and belligerent high lords and masters became more and more pleased with social etiquette. With their inherited riches and social standing guaranteed by generous heredity laws and practice, these once proud eagles more and more preferred their feathered nest to hunting for quarry and a perilous life on the wing. The Viking bloodline fattened out into cattle dealers and haughty country squires with velvet breeches and ostentatious feather arrangements in their cocked hats. Broad of beam and meat heavy, bursting with energy unspent, they would ride round on their flatulent shire horses—the very image of pastoral contentment.

These were men such as Hr. Lave Eskesen Brok, who was locked in conflicts and legal disputes with the half of Jutland, or take Oluf Pedersen Gyldenstjerne, a paragon of the Order of Knights, whose very own sisters, Fru Elsebe and the spinster Lene, became so exasperated that they hauled him before Viborg assizes on account of "that great harm and injustice he has visited upon us with his predilection for striking and battering his own sisters and their household staff with all manner of potentially lethal implements, even his drawn sword, with the result that our houses are destroyed and have been robbed of their goods and chattel by his constant threats, or actual use, of great violence against our persons." In other words, they were men in whom the sea hawk blood that once ran in their veins and impelled them to great feats of daring and proud independence had shriveled to bullheadedness and a delight in persecuting others. Or take somebody like Jørgen Arnfeld, whose former savageries broke out anew in the form of a bloody religious fanaticism—a profession of faith mired in joyous sadism. Arnfeld it was who ordered that pipes be secreted down in the dungeons of his castle and routed up to his private chambers so that he might gloat in the shrieks and lamentations arising from the mouths of old hags condemned as witches and other spawn of Satan whom he was pleased, in the sacred name of Christ Jesus our Lord, to torture unto death down there in those grave-dark holes spattered with mud and other detritus.

The wide expanse of meadowland, meanwhile, now filled the valley between the surrounding hills like some green garden of the gods, leaving no room for roadways or paths and there was not a dwelling or tree to be seen. Except when the bulging wheat and hay fields were ready to be harvested, one could follow the winding riverbank without meeting a soul or sinner, nor could any sound be heard other than the babbling chatter of the river channel accompanied, now and then, by the dampened thunder of a steam train passing over a bridge in the far distance.

Remnants of a maritime past had been all but strangled—even the old tradition of navigating the bigger streams leading to the estuary with flat-bottomed barges was all but dead. Several weeks could go by without sight of a single one of these long, broad-bowed vessels which, when fully loaded, lay so deeply in the water that the crew—using enormous poles to push the boat against the current—could just about keep their feet dry when walking along the deck by the boat's railing.

It was more often the case that one would come across folk sitting along the banks who, in time-honored Danish fashion, nonchalantly held fishing rods as they smoked tobacco and contemplated their homespun philosophies. Occasionally there would also be eel catchers—men or women, who stood out in the middle of the river with water up to their waist, one holding a net on a pole and another driving the eels up from the glutinous slime of the river bed.

Then, as the greatest exception, the wanderer might come face to face with a hunter, whom the local people preferred not to encounter here—a tall, terse man, somber in appearance with high shoulders and long legs housed in knee-length riding boots. The man was similarly reticent and rarely responded to greetings. His facial coloring was pallid, the nose flat. A rough hewn, dark beard covered his jaws and mouth.

This was the Master of the Royal Hunt Prangen. The lord of Kærsholm himself.

While his two mottled hunting dogs yelped and scrambled about in the meadows and would occasionally disappear into the rushes with a splash, the lord of the manor would stride purposefully forward at his own deliberate pace. His rifle was normally slung over his shoulder and his hands deeply buried into the diagonal pockets of his coarse woolen hunting tunic. It was clear for all to see: this man ranged across these meadows and hills, not so much to hunt game, but to be alone with his dark thoughts.

People in the area would often speculate as to what it was exactly that the master of the royal hunt went and brooded over. He had never been an easy man to fathom. It was as if there were two people living in the same body. For it was also true that this dour man with the glowering gaze could suddenly be transformed into an exuberant table companion, a veritable Baron von Münchhausen, bursting with the most ridiculous vainglory. There was a time when people asserted that it was his wife's comportment and state of mind that had dragged him down to such a fretful, enervated state. But now the common opinion was that the legal wrangling and lawsuits in which he was permanently embroiled, invariably resulting in a bloody nose for him, were the explanation for it all. However, there were also rumors of serious stomach troubles, and there was no doubt that the messenger boy was often to be seen running down to the local village to fetch the master's "drops" from the pharmacist.

Not even Lord Prangen himself was able to put his finger on what it was that could suddenly make him so dispirited. Just as he sat in his own quarters, enjoying his pipe and watching the smoke clouds drift towards the window where the sun's rays would tinge them with rainbows, a powerful melancholy would descend on him, like a dark palsy of the mind, and suddenly extinguish all the light in his life. Lord Prangen would then begin to ponder the reasons for this malady and his vain search would simply lead him deeper into the mire of despair.

All around the stables, barns and threshing floors at Kærsholm, the word would quickly spread when the master was seized by a mood—and his staff would make quick exits or be on tenterhooks wherever they glimpsed his gangling frame moving about the house. Nor was he a pretty sight to behold in these moods, with his darkly hollowed blue eyes and the loping neck that gave him the demeanor of a sickly bullock with a white board on its head.

However, his wife Dame Prangen was too wise, and also too proud, to yield to his wild swings of temper, and she always carried on as if unaware of any change. She knew rightly that any attempt to cheer him up would simply make things worse. The Devil would insist on an appearance and would then vanish just as mysteriously as he had appeared. During their private meals, where Lord Prangen never once opened his mouth except when consuming what was on the table in front of him, she attended to his every whim and eased his troubles by ensuring that he got his favorite dishes. The lord of the house, it has to be said, was a big eater and even the blackest mood never affected his appetite. There were fat rounds of belly pork with stewed apples, spiced meat sausage with stewed cabbage, massive portions of rice pudding that had to be made with boiled milk and flavored with cinnamon and a dash of nutmeg and served with cool sweetened beer—all this he would gorge into him like some gluttonous abbot, black mood or not.

After his meals, Lord Prangen would retire to his own chambers, which were separated from the sitting room by a day room that led out onto the garden veranda. But Dame Prangen was always quick to ensure that the interconnecting doors were never closed, just as in the house as a whole she never allowed too great a physical distance between husband and wife. One wouldn't want the servants gossiping unduly. She was well aware that there was a good deal of loose talk regarding her somewhat colorful past and about the state of their marriage. In fact, there were several good reasons for her to make it clear to all that they were still intimate with each other.

Dame Prangen was over thirty years of age when she married her husband who, at that time, had been a common squire. The liaison had provoked no little jocularity and surprise within her own her social set, for whom Hr. Prangen, if he was known at all by them, enjoyed a reputation as a dolt and spinner of ridiculous yarns. Even at that early stage, local gossip in the area was busy dissecting her past. It was put about that, even when quite young, her beauty had aroused the passions of a high-ranking, married nobleman, but not even the best of the gossipmongers could place reliable flesh on the bones of the story. Nonetheless, a ripple of suppressed mirth would arise amongst the populace when the then local squire was heard boasting of his future wife's "connections at court."

Even long after they were married, Dame Prangen's rather free lifestyle had given cause for constant tittle tattle. Because of her frequent trips to Copenhagen and her long-term residences at foreign health spas, her name had been linked to, if not one famous aristocrat, then another gallant blue blood. But nobody really knew if there was any truth behind the persistent rumors, while Dame Prangen herself had always cleverly contrived to draw a veil in front of any prying eyes that looked too closely into her private life. Her husband, therefore, had never borne the slightest suspicion towards her, or, at least, any doubts on his part were momentary. But then he was often too distracted by his barrage of legal processes and frequent stomach complaints to care.

For her own part, at least in her younger days, Dame Prangen viewed these extramarital sins as a mere trifle. She had married Lord Prangen precisely because he was a perfect foil for her youthful passions. Besides, she justified her occasional excesses with the fact that her husband had received generous compensation by way of the title her birth right had enabled him to acquire—a title that his own breeding, financial standing, education and upbringing would otherwise have denied him.

But now, as her blood had cooled and she had advanced in years, a guilty conscience had begun to demand what was owing to it, and with the retrospective punitive interest it always applied. Thus, in recent times, Dame Prangen had been seized by a fervent interest in religion. In this regard, a certain Pastor Blomberg, who was a minister in a neighboring parish, had exerted a great influence upon her. Pastor Blomberg was not the type of blood and thunder preacher who in other areas of the country were busy dragging the Middle Ages up from the crypt of history. On the contrary, he was a steady and particularly humane priest who abhorred all overblown speech, all emotional eruptions. He was, in other words, a cheerful, reassuring champion of God's workaday Good News. The good pastor never made demands of impossible sacrifices where life's comforts and pleasures were concerned. For this reason, perhaps, he had attracted a large following in the district.

For her part, Dame Prangen was infinitely grateful for the fact that she had been able to assuage her guilt at having sinned with such a relatively easy and pain-free form of penitence. She fell completely in love with this kind of Christianity that was so movingly undemanding of one. And if, every now and again, she might have difficulty remembering her daily devotions, and if she also sometimes struggled to find just the right childlike tone in her personal invocations of the Almighty, she, on the other hand, followed all the more dramatic and disputed aspects of church life with her heart and soul. Her rooms were inundated with religious books and journals and in private prayer circles she might even speak up in the debates as she gradually stepped into the light as a missionary for Pastor Blomberg's religious philosophy.

Dame Prangen also sought to influence her husband in the same direction. For despite her apparent equanimity in the face of his capriciousness, in reality this caused her no little pain. Whenever his wife raised the question of religion, Lord Prangen became quite obdurate, but it was his wife's hope that she might gradually be able to overcome his indifference and make their joint participation in all the joys and solace that religious life offered a kind of atonement to him for her previous desecration of their marriage vows.

It was to this house, and to these people, that Per turned for refuge after his secret nocturnal crossing of the Kattegat with his mother's corpse. Foundered in both body and spirit, he reached Kærsholm in the early evening of the same day as he had left the fjord estuary with the dawn breaking at his back.

He got the best welcome imaginable, not just from Dame Prangen and her older sister the baroness, who was still there on a visit, but also from the master of the royal hunt himself. This may have been helped by the fact that he had just received word that he had won a court case over a roadside ditch. For Lord Prangen to actually win one of his lawsuits was a rare event and, on such occasions, he always became gripped by a most reckless state of mind.

In order to explain to Per the complex background to his latest lawsuit, he guided him into his chambers, where he also took advantage of having a captive audience to explain the other three victorious cases in his life. He impressed upon Per the fact that the legal points at issue in one of these cases were so extraordinary, unprecedented, and finely nuanced that in the end it had to go to the Supreme Court, where the greatest judges in the land had to weigh its consequences over three whole days before making their ruling.

Per was just glad for the chance to sit quietly with his own thoughts, which still followed his mother's coffin on its journey.

Lord Prangen, who was not used to having such a patient listener, confided to his wife afterwards that he found her young friend most appealing. At the dinner table, when Per raised the question of not outstaying his welcome and leaving fairly soon, the lord of the house was, if anything, more animated than anybody else in urging Per to take his ease for a while at Kærsholm now that summer had finally arrived.

Per did not take much persuading. He felt absolutely no longings for Copenhagen. Moreover, he said to himself, where would he get a better place in which to battle through the spiritual and intellectual crisis that he sensed was about to break over him? He had been given a quiet and beautifully appointed room that was in a side wing of the main building. It looked out over the woods and parkland whose bright daylight scene was softened by a row of tall chestnut trees with dense canopies of leaves. The flooring in the room was of scoured white timber and at its center was a solid oak table with heavy bulbous legs and four high-backed chairs. The bed was located behind a tasteful screen, and was guarded by an imposing iron stove, newly blacked and gleaming in the corner like a battle-ready knight of old. At the wall in between the windows was a bookshelf laden with books.

He was immediately taken with this room, which presented such a pleasing difference to the uniform and numbered hotel rooms in which he had been doomed to live for what, at this stage, had been a quite lengthy period. The moment's verdant light, with hints of the dusk to come, also harmonized with a note that rang within his own sense of anticipation—this was precisely the kind of hideaway, redolent of a monk's hermitage, that he now so desperately needed in his life. He was particularly glad of the small library, some of whose titles he had already ascertained from the titles on the spine of the books. They included spiritual and edifying texts and other theological works. Per remembered some of the titles, as Dame Prangen had warmly recommended them to him during their debates in Rome.

He sent a telegram to the hotel in Copenhagen with a request for some of his clothing to be sent on to him. He then wrote an explicatory letter to Jakobe in which he described the sudden notion that drove him to stand watch over his mother's remains, and that he was now taking advantage of the situation, given that he was on Jutland soil, to fulfill a promise he had made to visit his traveling companions from his time in Italy. On the reasons for his decision to remain at Kærsholm, he sufficed to say that he needed time to recuperate after the experience of accompanying his mother's corpse, and gather his energies for the impending journey to the new world. Per then sought his own private reassurance by asserting to himself that Jakobe lacked the necessary prerequisites to understand any more thoroughgoing explanation that he might write in a letter. That would have to wait. It had to be admitted, he said to himself, that the permanent fault line in their relationship lay in the fact that they were not born of the same spiritual and intellectual soil. Regardless of how much good will existed between them, the natural dichotomy in their respective characters precluded any truly profound intimacy.

Later in the evening, after he had posted the letter, a great sense of peace came over him. In the long glory of a Scandinavian sunset, while ensconced with the ladies in the sitting room, Per actually felt a sense of domestic bliss in these surroundings that were otherwise so new to him. He made no attempt at a deep analysis of why this was so, but in these spacious rooms with their slightly low ceilings, indomitable walls, and darkened tone, and in the way the last rays of the sun warmed the deep window ledges, in fact in the very snugness of the air that carried a vague hint of the turf being burned in the range in the kitchen—in all of this there was something quite other-worldly, lifting and enveloping him like a motherly embrace.

Lord Prangen, who had called in to see them, suddenly shot up noisily from his seat and then walked through the day room to his own quarters. As was the norm, the interconnecting doors were all open and he could be heard humming a tune. Shortly afterwards came the noise of a rummaging through things that made clinking and rattling noises. Next came the clear sound of a window being thrown open. Then all at once the tones of a French horn were blasted across the woods and onwards towards the hills.

Amongst the many ridiculous conceits which Lord Prangen used to bolster his mercurial self-esteem was a conviction that he was a virtuoso where brass wind instruments were concerned. First off, he sounded a few quick hunting signals and an echo over in the woods replied in kind with the hint of a fading horn from those distant times when his forefathers had cut their bloody path through the trees and undergrowth. Then came a few patriotic airs, which more and more collapsed into maudlin sentimentality—the poetic refuge of all simple-minded souls. It was an awful racket. To finish off, he played the melody to Grundtvig's song "Oh What Delight in Sharing the Road," and in order to add a gushing intensity to this traditional paean of praise to Danish hearth and home, he allowed his finale to tremble and die away in such a stop-start fashion that Per had to summon all his powers of concentration and stare firmly at a spot on the floor so as not to burst out laughing. Dame Prangen, meanwhile, sat with her hand under chin, looking out through the window with the kind of tender, wistful, and innocent smile that only women can conjure.

In the days that followed, Per shared the life of these country-estate aristocrats in a cozy and decidedly convivial manner. Lord Prangen remained in top form and showed him around the large expanse of his estate. In the company of the two ladies, Per also engaged in a number of jaunts by carriage around the picturesque district. Moreover, he made a few of his own exploratory trips, sometimes accompanied by the estate overseer, a young man of his own age.

Nor was it long before Per was physically restored to his former self, as his face took on that sun-kissed hue he had brought back with him from Italy and suited him so well. He rarely mentioned his connection to the Salomon household, a fact that was very quickly picked up by Dame Prangen, who never raised the issue subsequently. Similarly, where his mother was concerned, and with regards to the real reason that he had first arrived in Jutland, he kept his own counsel, or at least for as long as he believed that the two ladies were still under the illusion that his origins were shrouded in secrecy. However, he soon realized that Dame Prangen, at least, had become aware of the truth behind his family background, and took this to mean that she had found out through Pastor Blomberg. She had mentioned the pastor on several occasions in the most respectful of tones and Per assumed that said pastor would without doubt have known his father.

He actually felt a great sense of relief that this whole embarrassing issue was now out in the open, and he was extremely grateful to Dame Prangen for having the tact to avoid embarrassing him by raising the issue. His only wish now was that he had got just as far with the other painful boil in his life that required a swift lancing—obtaining a loan.

More than anything else, this was the issue that had brought him here in the first place, but he had been forced to abandon the idea of immediately approaching the old baroness about it. Despite the fact that she had, as early as the first day, repeated her offer of providing him with whatever support he needed, even going as far as to making him her legal heir if he wished, Per was left with exactly the same feeling as in Rome: he could not descend to the level of asking this poor addled creature to honor her words. He was actually somewhat afraid of being left alone with her, because her tone and whole demeanor would be so disturbingly intimate. Supporting her small and shriveled lace-bedecked head at the tips of two fingers, she would plunge in straight away with her florid language, talking once again about her dearly deceased brother and invariably ending up by reciting reams of poetry and verse. Thus, he would be subject to lengthy declamations of the works of Hertz, Carl Bagger, and in particular of Paludan-Muller whose *The Dancer* she knew by heart, right down to the errata that had been listed at the back of the book.

Under these impossible circumstances, his hopes turned towards the master of the royal hunt and his good wife Dame Prangen. Especially with the latter, he felt that he had more room to maneuver after the young overseer had revealed her life story, such as it was known. After this, he understood much better the particular attraction she had exerted upon him during their time together down south. He now saw that her indulgence of him, her considerate and gentle reaction to his ideas and demeanor, possibly revealed a provocative shared appreciation of human frailty in matters of the flesh.

However, Per did not for a moment doubt the sincerity of her religious beliefs. For this reason, he was happy to grant her the other attributes of a good heart, and it was now his hope that via her influence, he might be able to interest Lord Prangen and perhaps other members of the social elite in the area in his great project. Gaining the support of these people would not leave him feeling anywhere near as beholden and oppressed, a fact which reinforced his determination never to request a loan from his father-in-law ever again. What Hr. Salomon should bestow upon Jakobe as a dowry after their marriage was up to her to decide for herself. He did not want it to be said of him that he had always lived from the crumbs from Philip Salomon's table.

However, he had still not been presented with an opportune moment to raise the question of his project in a natural way. Kærsholm as a place occupied him with lots of other things. Nor did these things just pertain to his own inner world, but rather what was outside of him—above all, the great outdoors. So much so, in fact, that after almost a week, he had just about managed to mention to Dame Prangen that he planned to leave soon and commence his study trip to America.

The weather still held its summer glow and this particular time of year was when the area came into its very own. The fields, woods, and forests were at their freshest green, and the meadows were just one huge carpet of flowers. By then, Per had become somewhat of a bosom pal of the farm overseer. He would often spend the lazy rest period after lunch up in the overseer's room, which was a separate apartment in one of the wings of the storehouse. One side of the room offered a view of the dairy, where a constant traffic of milkmaids, their skirts hitched up above their ankles, went in and out all day bearing clinking pails; on the other side of the room, a window looked out across an enclosure behind the dungheap, where Kærsholm's massive prize-winning bull conducted its assignations with cows in heat. Stretched out on the sofa with a cigar in his mouth, Per was regally entertained here with all kinds of bucolic gossip and slander, or he might play with the overseer's dog—a black poodle that had pups. The farm overseer himself was an undemonstrative Jutlander of the type that, for all their apparent innocence, can prove to be so contemptuous of all those things which others set such great store by. He would have a mischievous story to tell about whomsoever or whatever the conversation threw up. Nor did he speak out of malicious intent but simply for the fun of it. Per really enjoyed his company, and overall these gossip sessions, as the estate farm's prolific bustle went on all around them, played a great part in banishing the feeling of dread that had hung like a cloud over him when he had first arrived there.

The river also held its own mystical attraction for him. Here was the very same gently flowing water that—only some twenty-five miles or so from here—gurgled along the moldering quay of his childhood, and which with its magical banks of rushes and hidden mudflats had been the great love of his boyhood life. When, one day, he caught sight of a boat in a boathouse along the riverbank, he became gripped by his old passion for fishing. With help from the overseer, he assembled the necessary equipment and, from then on, would sit for hours out on the river with his lines out and only the current and the play of the water for company.

Thus the days passed and the spiritual crisis he had anticipated with such nervousness and dread did not materialize. The explosive charge of spiritual dynamite that had built up in him that night on the steamship had evaporated in the summery outdoor life he had led at Kærsholm since that point. Dame Prangen's religious edifying texts had remained almost untouched on their shelf. The fact was that he was busy outside the whole livelong day, so much so that when he finally got back to his room and lit his lamp in order to settle down with a book, he would not complete many lines before a wonderful drowsiness came over him, like some blessing from nature drawing him into the simple delight of his bed.

For all that, bit by bit, a longing for Jakobe began to grow in him. When he was sitting in his boat, being happily baked by the sun, or when he stretched in the shade of his favorite spot at the edge of the woods, he would sometimes wish that he could share this summer idyll with her. There was no doubt that the country would do her a service by ridding her lungs of that coast road dust that hung around Skovbakken. Before he had left, she had begun to look so strained and overwrought. But then he told himself that she would probably decline the opportunity. The almost vegetative life that he led here was definitely not to her liking. Just lying there, for example, quite still with your hands behind your neck and letting your thoughts drift, with the clouds scudding across the bottomless blue overhead, feeling your own being rise up and meld with infinity—that kind of pleasure she would never understand. He recalled that once in a love letter she had described her mind as being "as restless as the sea." How true that was.

Another thing that contributed to his happiness at Kærsholm was the complete lack of formality—the dress code included. Lord Prangen himself would stalk the rooms of his mansion in his long boots and rarely bothered to change for dinner. Even Dame Prangen, while at home at least, was not particularly fussy about what she wore. There was no doubt that this rural informality appealed to Per enormously. The strict house etiquette applied by his parents-in-law, with its constant demands for a change in clothing for each event and time of day, something modern travel also demanded, was a torture to him.

One warm and sunny afternoon, as Per was returning from the river with his fishing rods bouncing on his shoulder, he bumped into Dame Prangen. She was in the company of a young lady who was blond of hue and dressed in a blue-striped dress. The two ladies were strolling along a lane lined by poplars, which led from the park in front of the main building down to the meadows. They walked with their arms about each other's waist; and there was something in the scene, particularly in the young woman, that made Per think of two lovers.

"This is Hr. Sidenius, an engineer from Copenhagen, Frøken Blomberg," Dame Prangen said by way of a quick introduction to both. She also mentioned, as they moved on, that Pastor Blomberg was sitting inside with her husband and would no doubt be delighted to meet Per in person.

Per cursed his luck as he walked on through the park and up to his room. He was convinced that the peace and wonderful tranquillity he had enjoyed was now over. He had already set his mind against this cleric, who was obviously highly esteemed in this house. Besides which, Per had gradually worked out who he was. For he now recalled that he had seen Pastor Blomberg's name occasionally mentioned in the newspapers as a gifted spokesperson for one of the many tendencies within the church, and he now vaguely recalled that his activities had been the subject of debate at home in the rectory, because his brother Thomas—the curate—had been more enamored of Blomberg's ideas than his father thought appropriate.

His preference would have been to simply remain in his room for the duration of Blomberg's visit, but Dame Prangen's request that he should present himself to their pastor was made, despite its winning charm, in such a way that refusal was not an option.

Per did indeed find the guest in Lord Prangen's quarters where, under a cloud of tobacco smoke, the two gentlemen sat on either side of a table that was replete with a full coffee set and sweet morsels. As he knocked and showed himself in the doorway, their conversation quickly died away, leaving the distinct impression that Per Sidenius had been the very thing they sat discussing.

Pastor Blomberg's physical appearance gave Per an immediate surprise. After everything he had heard during his time at Kærsholm about this latter-day Luther and his struggle for what had been called a more humane view of spiritual issues, Per had imagined some sort of giant, wild-bearded Nordic apostle figure, a Christian Viking. What he now saw in front of him was a tubby little fellow with wobbly jowls. In other words, Pastor Blomberg did not distinguish himself in any noticeable way from the typical image of an affable Danish cleric. From a large head, ringed by a froth of blue-blond hair and beard, a pair of clear, animated eyes shone out—they resembled two large teardrops within which heaven's arch was reflected. Both in his mode of dress (he wore a shortened summer jacket of black Italian cloth) and the way he reclined in his chair and puffed on the well-chewed cigar, there was a hint of a wish to occlude his unmistakeable stamp of class privilege—to cast off that "reverence" which he frequently denounced and ridiculed, much to the chagrin of his fellow preachers. However, one could never be in doubt for a moment that this was a man of the cloth that stood before you. No, Pastor Blomberg's whole shape and demeanor was all too obviously animated by that particular form of religious self-righteousness which Per knew only too well. He positively oozed the patriarchal air of presumed authority, which clings stubbornly to clerics like the moldy damp that emanates from old Church grounds, despite all the new-fangled types of heating and ventilation systems.

Pastor Blomberg rose, a bit arthritically, from his chair and pressed Per's hand with a heartfelt, country sincerity.

"Well now there we have him—yes indeed!" he said, as he scrutinized Per closely and without the slightest pretense at doing otherwise. "Welcome to our own humble little patch, Hr. Engineer!"

Behind his warm and welcoming tone there was something paternal and overly sympathetic, which put Per on his guard.

"Of course, I am not unfamiliar with the name Sidenius," the pastor continued. "Not least because your own father was a greatly esteemed person within our clerical ranks. To my sorrow, I never met him personally, even though we were in neighboring dioceses. Yes, his view and my view of the Church's role were without doubt very different, and in so many ways, but his name is blessed and his great work speaks to us, even from the grave! He was an extremely diligent shepherd of his flock!"

When Per gave no answer, Pastor Blomberg sat down again and there was a moment's silence. The minister then turned back to Lord Prangen and began discussing local issues that had recently arisen.

Per took a chair over by the window and lit a cigarette. Half-turned away from the room, he looked out over the wide lawn directly in front of the main building, where a sundial in the middle of the green expanse was glinting in the sun's rays.

He noticed that Dame Prangen and the young woman were coming back along the laneway and had just sat down on a bench that lay in the shade of a large beech tree at the far corner of the lawn. Dame Prangen collapsed her parasol and her young female escort placed her wide-brimmed summer hat beside her on the bench and then stroked a lock of hair away from her forehead.

Per now began to study this priest's daughter a bit more closely. She was around nineteen years of age by the look of her and bore no resemblance to her father apart from being blond. She was tall, almost gangly, but her figure was refined with shapely flanks. Because of the distance between them, he could not properly discern her facial characteristics, but the overall impression she gave was very captivating. Sitting there in the tree's dark shadow, her legs crossed and bending forward slightly as she twirled a flower she had plucked, nosing it every now and again for its scent, she cut a dreamlike figure in the shade of the bower. Indeed, when viewed next to the large bulk of Dame Prangen, whose amplitude was made even more prominent by the gray silk jerkin that spanned her broad bosom like an armored breastplate, the young maiden's diaphanous costume was possessed of an ethereal quality.

It occurred to Per that she reminded him very strongly of someone else. Even when he had seen her fleetingly in the laneway, he had felt the same thing. That fine sapling figure, her blond, almost silvery, and full-bodied hair, as well as the long slope of her fine shoulders—there was something in all of this that was intimately familiar and known to him of old, something in fact that gave him a feeling of melancholy.

In the meantime, Pastor Blomberg had risen from the table and was about to leave.

He explained that he was obliged to call out to a sick man who lived nearby and who had opted for his ministry in favor of another congregation. The poor man had been severely injured while handling a temperamental bull. On his way back, he would call in again to collect his daughter.

When he said goodbye to Per, he held his hand for a moment longer and, once again looking penetratingly and without pretense at him, told him that if his travels should ever take him past Bøstrup rectory, he would be only delighted to see him there.

"Of course I am well aware," he said teasingly, "that the youth of Copenhagen regard the church as nothing more than the temple of superstition and ignorance with the rectory as its main entrance. But perhaps we are not quite as bad as your newspaper and literary elite in Copenhagen wish to portray us. Anyway, I'm quite sure you can make up your own mind!"

Despite the patronizing tone in the pastor's address, Per shook his hand firmly this time and issued a politely murmured thank you. The affect his daughter had worked upon him had made him more well disposed to this self-satisfied little man.

Lord Prangen followed the pastor out of his room. However, Per lifted the large straw hat he had brought back with him from Italy, and went out through the day room. Once on the outside terrace, he began to study the skies, using his hat as a shade, and letting on that he was completely unaware of the ladies in the garden.

Dame Prangen called out to him.

"Hr. Sidenius, Hr. Sidenius . . . can you guess what Frøken Blomberg thinks you look like?" she asked.

The young girl, whose hand was being held in Dame Prangen's lap, went immediately scarlet and made attempts to cover the dame's mouth with her free hand.

"But dearest, why am I not allowed to tell him what you said? I think it's a priceless description. Frøken Blomberg believes that you resemble a young nabob. And she is completely right. There is something very exotic about you today."

"A nabob?" Per inquired, as he looked down at his yellow suit made of light cotton. The suit, just like the hat, had been bought in Italy, and he was wearing it for the first time today because of the heat and strong sunshine. "I am of course flattered. All I need now are the millions to go with the title."

"Ah but you'll get them soon enough no doubt," Dame Prangen cried, an almost regretful tone entering her voice at the last, as if the words fell from her mouth half against her will. She regretted them immediately and began to speak of other things, while at the same time using all of her graces to get Per to come down and sit with them—a folded garden chair was leaning against the bench as if for that very purpose.

However, Per had caught the significance of her previous words only too well—and was immediately dejected. In other words, they had been sitting there talking about his engagement, and of course his father-in-law's great wealth had been mentioned. As far as everybody was concerned, the two things had become entwined in their imaginations. Per also now realized that Miss Blomberg's nabob comparison might not exactly pass as a compliment.

He sat down to the side of them and ran a proper rule over this young lady. Now that he had her at much closer quarters, he could carry out a sober assessment of her figure and form and come to a judgment, as befitted a connoisseur. He had to admit that there was very little there to criticize. Despite his sense of despondency at their topic of conversation, he was amazed that he hadn't noticed how beautiful she was when they had first met along the path. What a pair of crystal clear and innocent eyes! And that gorgeous mouth, strawberry soft, still a bit immature perhaps and thus lacking in fullness but, on the other hand, completely unspoiled and chaste as an innocent wild rose.

The two ladies had begun talking about the same farm accident that Pastor Blomberg had just referred to in Lord Prangen's rooms. In terms and expressions that sounded suspiciously like her father's, the young lady described how that "poor unfortunate soul" had had his whole innards torn out and that the doctor very much doubted whether he would survive. But Per had suddenly lost interest in what was being said. He now realized who it was that the delectable Frøken reminded him of. It was Francesca. His Nyboder sweetheart!—My God! he mused, his heart softening as he did so—how long it now was since she had been in his thoughts!

While the ladies continued to chat, Per drifted off to indulge in his memories. Though he still kept an eye on the pastor's daughter, who did not look at him once, and gave the impression, at least, that she was unaware of Per's attentions.

Yes, Per said to himself, the resemblance was clear. Her height and whole demeanor were very similar. And undeniable! Frøken Blomberg was more distinguished in stature, slimmer along her lines—a more refined version of Francesca. There was also something about the play of her mouth that reminded him of her. Every time she smiled, the tip of her tongue would habitually run across her upper lip in a de-lightful little movement that seemed to laughingly lick her smile away.

"Oh dear. It's starting to get chilly you know. Would you not cover up your neck and shoulders little darling?"

Dame Prangen was suddenly all concern. The sun had sunk behind the trees in the park and the damp from the shaded soil on their side of the garden was soon noticed here beneath the leaves.

"I'm not in the least bit cold. I couldn't be better sitting here," she said, clearly happy that Dame Prangen had once again taken her hand and was busy patting it.

"Well dear, I still think you should put your wrap on. I think you left it in the sitting room."

Per stood up.

"I'll get it," he said.

But at the same moment, the young lady had shot up from the bench. "No, Hr. Sidenius, you'll never find it," she hurried to say. And as she was afraid that he might follow her, she raced off across the lawn.

"Isn't she just so sweet?" Asked Dame Prangen, when she had gone and Per had sat down again.

"Yes, she is quite pretty," he answered somewhat tersely.

"Well yes, she's that too, and with such a good nature, so open and sincere. Unfortunately, her health is not the best."

"Is Frøken Blomberg sick?"

"My dear Sidenius, she spent the whole winter laid up in bed with typhoid fever, poor girl. As she says herself, she was more dead than alive for over three months. Can you not see it in her?"

"Well, I suppose she does leave a rather ethereal impression. But to say that she looked weak, I don't know Dame Prangen—"

"Yes—and thanks be to God—she is over the worst now, and this glorious summer will hopefully do the rest. That dear child, who is the light and joy of so many of us here, and who herself is so grateful just to be alive, as only they can be that came close to death while still very young—indeed, who know that the gift of life comes by God's grace Hr. Sidenius!"

Per looked away. Just recently he had begun to feel slightly embarrassed whenever Dame Prangen began to speak of religious matters.

"Frøken Blomberg obviously thinks the world of you Dame Prangen," he said, in order to lead the conversation onto a different track.

"Ah, she loves to come here, the dear angel. She tells me all the time that she gets such enjoyment from coming to Kærsholm. I would say that life at her parents' house is perhaps a bit monotonous for such a lively young girl. But now it has to be said that Pastor Blomberg's rectory is perfectly lovely. You really should make a point of paying the pastor a visit. I've no doubt that he would be delighted to speak to you."

Over at the entrance to the garden, the gardener himself appeared and stood at a respectful distance.

"What is it Petersen?" Dame Prangen asked.

The gardener took a few steps forward with his cap in his hand. He wished to ask her grace if she would be so kind as to come down to the kitchen garden for a moment when her grace found it convenient.

"I'll be there shortly," said Dame Prangen, whose idea of Christian fraternity had still not managed to embrace her own underlings.

Shortly afterwards, she got up and headed off towards the vegetable garden. In the meantime, the young lady had returned and looked the height of discomfort on finding that she had been left alone with Per. She sat with both hands at her sides and gripping the front edge of the bench seat. Her face visibly colored a number of times. And then suddenly she called out to Dame Prangen, who could still be seen in the distance, asking whether she might go with her.

Almost before she received an answer, she was up from the bench and rushed off.

"Oh, dear, remember . . . you're not supposed to run!" Dame Prangen called out in alarm.

Per looked sidelong at the girl as she moved away—and a shadow passed over his face.

There was something about her reticence that provoked troubling memories for him. His brothers and sisters had fled from his presence in exactly the same way during their childhood years, especially after morning or evening prayers when his father had pronounced the wrath of God upon him. And of course he'd had the same experience with his twin brothers just recently. He saw them before him now, standing sheepishly outside Eberhard's offices and unsure whether they even dared look at him.

A nabob! That was meant disparagingly of course. This slip of a girl had run away from him as if he were the devil personified. Well— so what? Was he really going to fret over what a little pastor's girl thought about him? Since when had he sunk so low that he would begin worrying about the opinion of every Tom, Dick, and Harry on Per Sidenius? Or was there something else that lay behind it all? Was the truth not rather that he himself was beginning to feel that his rampaging hunt for Lady Fortune was actually nothing more than a sham?

But there was no use in wallowing in that kind of useless speculation. He had to fight down and defeat that exaggerated sensitivity of his, which lately had left him at the complete mercy of his dangerously shifting moods. It was about time he pulled himself together, put an end to his idleness and got back to work. Whatever offenses he had committed, either against his better self or other people—in the battles he had fought, in his honest endeavor in trying to create something positive and useful in this world—all this he would, from now on, hold to account and seek to justify, even though, in the final reckoning, they might not lead to the great victory he had envisaged.

A window was thrown open up in the main building. It was the baroness who had risen from her long afternoon nap. Shortly afterwards, she appeared on the veranda. Her raiments were an attempt at coquettishness, with a dramatic white shawl of Spanish lace draped about her head and pinned to the back of her hair, her face strongly rouged and powdered, as was her wont in the afternoon, so as to conceal the angry blotches that would flare up as the day progressed.

Per was gone in a flash. In order not to be left alone with this poor, confused creature, he made a discreet exit from the park and then decided to take a stroll along the adjoining roadway that ran by the side of the meadows and into the woods.

It was one of those extremely bright and tranquil summer evenings, which are so hushed that they can feel dead and oppressive. Mute and empty, the shadowless landscape stretched into the distance under heavens that seemed extinguished, devoid of sun, moon or stars. The sun had indeed disappeared without ceremony, leaving only a faint red haze on the horizon as evidence that it had been there at all. Not one cloud was there in the sky, one cloud that might capture the last of the sun's rays and reflect them across the contours of the land as a remembrance of the delight the day had carried. Just here and there on the hills, a window pane showed a small reflected red glow—otherwise nothing.

But down near the river, different life forces began to stir as soon as the sun had disappeared. The meadows began to weave a misty web of silver gray about them and very quickly the bottom of the extensive valley was submerged in a cloak of undulating white vapor. As evening descended, it was as if the fjord of old was returning in ghostly form to reclaim its lost dominion. Like furious surf in a phantom sea, the pale mist tumbled and fell about the base of the hills.

Then of a sudden, other signs of life stirred themselves in the near beyond. A horned head appeared out of the mist and bellowed. Close by the upper half of a human body could now be discerned, a man, whose rear parts seemed to consist of a dark animal shape with a raised tail. Soon after that a throng of horned heads now emerged around Per as he walked, their snouts raised and steam coming from their nostrils. The man swung something over his head and gave a roar—the whole scene was redolent of a centaur in combat with a pack of sea monsters.

It was Kærsholm's three hundred head of cattle being driven homeward by a herdsman who brandished a rasping whip. Seen from the roadway, the animals looked as though they were sleepwalking. The only thing that could be seen of them was their heads and dark backs, which had their own rocking or swaying movement. The swirl of mist would then drive over them and rub out every outline.

Per decided to rest for a while on a bench that was under a tree on the other side of the roadway ditch. With his head cocked to one side and resting on his hand, he followed the progress of the homeward-bound cattle as it moved into a patch of brighter light and was then swallowed up into the low mist again. Small flocks of crows now came pulling across the sky above his head and he could hear how they screeched with joy when reaching their nests in the woods behind him. Somewhere nearby, he thought he recognized the sound of a frog, gurgling in self-satisfaction at its own particular pond. Then stillness again for miles around him.

In these moments, a withering sense of rootlessness snuck its way into his soul. He thought of those words from the bible: Foxes have holes and birds have nests, but the Son of Man has no place to rest. He himself did not know of one spot to which he was emotionally attached by way of happy or striking memories. His forthcoming long journey in mind, Per told himself that, in reality, it was irrelevant what part of the world he happened to be in. He would not be any more homeless in the middle of the Atlantic Ocean, or the American prairies, than he would be here in the heart of his own native home.

Out of the blue he was struck by another phrase from scripture and his veins turned to ice. It was the biblical curse that his father had pronounced upon him: "Thou shalt be banished and without peace wherever in the world thou art." His father's words had now been fulfilled. The fate of Cain stamped on his son's forehead.

One more enticing images of Francesca arose from his memory, all framed by those small, yellow-washed houses in Nyboder with their narrow green strips of garden, enclosed by tarred timber fences. How he really really liked her! It was by no means easy for him to turn his back on her spring-fresh love. Of course—he knew very well—he had not lost out in the exchange. Jakobe was a far more well-rounded person, whose importance for his development he would never deny. But at the same time he had to ask himself whether they had ever really belonged to each other, apart from their physical attraction. When, by contrast, he thought back to his and Francesca's leisurely promenades in the Copenhagen twilight, innocent of all overheated lust, as they skirted the sunset-tinged waters of Sortedamsø, and then the bittersweet parting in the shade of the ancient trees up on the remains of the Østervold ramparts—now those times radiated forth in his memory as oases of beauty and calm in an otherwise depressing, wildly turbulent period of his young life.

Did she ever get married? he wondered. If any woman deserved a good man, it was her. Perhaps she was somewhere in the provinces that very minute, a happy conventional wife and mother with a child suckling at her breast. It occurred to him that he could, without doubt, find out from his old Nyboder connections whether she still lived with her parents in Kerteminde, or what had become of her since. His old home in Hjertensfrydgade was broken up for good now. Madam Olufsen, he knew, had that very same autumn followed her Senior Boatswain in "Charon's black barge" to the dark beyond.

But he was sure there were still others in the area who would have news of Francesca.

Another flock of crows flew above him and disappeared into the woods with screeches of delight. At the same moment, he became aware of horses' hooves on the roadway and the racket of a moving carriage coming from Kærsholm. Soon afterwards, a four-wheeled barouche carriage appeared with a pair of large roan horses in harness. It was moving at walking pace as it began ascending the incline, which was quite steep in the place where Per sat.

When Per realized that it was Pastor Blomberg's carriage, he got up straight away and began walking in the same direction as the carriage, in the hope that he would not be recognized from behind.

But in this he miscalculated. When the vehicle ran alongside him, the minister called out a greeting and threw out his hand in a cheerful wave, calling the carriage to a halt as he did so.

"Well there we have you again, Hr. Sidenius! Dreaming no doubt about your great plans for the future in the quiet evening air! And yes—you have to agree!—it's so lovely here isn't it? I was just saying that very thing to my daughter. It's no wonder that our old folk poetry—where in a way it is Nature itself that is singing—is so full of supernatural creatures. There really is something fantastically magical about an evening like this. And it seems we mere mortals still have a feel for the great mysteries of Nature, given that a modern go-ahead engineer like yourself can still be captivated by its powers, even in these progressive, naturalistic times, eh?"

The pastor said this last with a roguishness that softened the challenge that lay in the words themselves. Turning now to his daughter (who, sitting by her father's side, seemed much cockier towards Per, even perhaps looking at him with a certain superiority) the pastor continued:

"Listen dearest . . . our guest in the district here, engineer Sidenius, really does appeal to me. I've a mind to stretch my legs a little. Go you on to the grocers and get the goods we need, there's a good girl, and I'll be with you shortly. That's of course if Hr. Sidenius has no objection to my joining him for part of the way?"

Per managed to mumble a "not at all" and the pastor got down from the carriage, not without some difficulty.

"Ah yes, Hr. Sidenius, the body doesn't get enough physical circulation in this breathless steam age of ours." The pastor stamped on the roadway as he spoke, as if to invoke the long-deceased powers of his youth. "Our railways, which I otherwise praise from my heart, are leading us astray from Nature . . . making us violate her motherly ways. Whenever I watch one of those long black railway monsters go steaming and whistling across God's green earth, I always come to think of the serpent in Paradise. In the old days, when I had errands to do, say at the market town, I often took Shanks's pony so as to spare the real horse belonging to my tenant—it was ten miles there and ten miles back. But still, time never dragged for me the way it does now when I can roll in to town on the train within about half an hour. If the train's late, or there is some other kind of delay, I am beside myself with impatience, be the delay no more than five minutes. In the old days, we rarely took our watch from our pockets and we judged the time by the sun instead, and the sun has no seconds hand! And then when you had tramped a couple of miles or so . . . well, the little picnic you had by some haystack or grass verge was heaven! Young people today will never understand how wonderful—in fact spiritual—the experience can be of simply sitting on the bare earth and tucking into a cheese sandwich as the larks, starlings, and lapwings fly about you and provide the table music. As old, decrepit, and portly as I've become, Hr. Sidenius, I can still be gripped with an actual longing to feel the King's highway under my feet once again. When a body has been stuck sitting at home day after day twiddling its thumbs, or getting its head bombarded with all these new notions in books and newspapers, how lovely it is to just hit the road and put one foot after another mile after mile! You can almost feel how the soul stretches out in pleasure—like someone who has awoken from a horrible dream and now sees the sun shining through his window and hears the birds singing in the treetops outside. Wait, listen to that!" the pastor cried, as he stopped in his tracks and placed his hand on Per's arm. "Do you hear the lark up there! It's still singing for the sun!" Pastor Blomberg stood there for a whole minute, listening to the birdsong and with an ecstatic look on his face. "Isn't that just a gift to the spirit! It puts me in mind of a woman who, after her love has departed, has to start humming a tune to stop herself from crying. And have you, by the way, Hr. Engineer, noticed the deep life wisdom that little natural melody-maker can express? Never will you listen in vain when it sings of its sadness or joys. I'll admit, between you and me, that I have gained more spiritual sustenance from its clear little chirruping than I have from the whole collection of sermons on my bookshelves. But promise me, good sir, that you'll never tell anyone what I've just said!" he added, laughing suddenly, and shaking Per's arm. "My fellow clerics in Christ would never forgive such outrageous blasphemy!"

He laughed out loud at his own words and took to walking once again.

Per, who was already touched by the pastor's confiding in him, began to be taken with this man in another way. For he had to accept Dame Prangen's assertion that Pastor Blomberg was not your usual fire and brimstone man, but a different kind altogether.

After a couple of yards, the pastor stopped once again and threw his arm out as if to bless the whole landscape. The evening was already well advanced. The weak outline of a few stars could even be discerned here and there in the green-blue heavens.

"Will you tell me one thing in all honesty, Hr. Engineer?" When, on an evening like this, you look out over our lovely green and fertile land, would you really be happy to destroy all this with chimneys, coal smoke, and ashes? Yes, I admit that I know a little about your attack on our romantic national and, dare I say it, pastoral preconceptions. Though I should point out that I have not actually read your pamphlet, but Dame Prangen has explained your ideas to me, and of course I find them characteristic of the times in which we live. So I will ask you straight out young man…do you basically think that it would be more appealing to see a lot of smoke-belching monsters or steamships plying our river and see its flower-bedecked banks transformed into slag heaps for factories that spew fumes out all day? Naturally, I'm not just thinking about the aesthetic effect. My head's not completely in the clouds. I understand that aesthetic considerations are still subject to life's practical demands. But, that said, are there not other and more important life values at risk here? Look at that little house over there on the hill with the wisps of turf smoke coming out of the chimney. There's a family in that house that I know personally. They are modest smallholders of the type that number around a quarter of a million in this country. They make just about enough to feed and clothe themselves, but if you knew them, you would envy their joyfulness and pleasure in what they see as their good fortune. Husband and wife work in the fields, while their gaggle of children tumble around in the fresh air. They have an old horse and one cow and actually view themselves as being blessed with riches. Would you really, in all conscience, wish to commit that man to a life of drudge inside a stinking dark factory, where he would slave at a machine, while his wife and children are condemned to live in the sixth or seventh floor in a workman's barracks? Tell me truthfully!"

Per's ire was inflamed somewhat by the aggressive nature of the question. For that reason—and because he had in the last while become less sure of himself on the points of this argument—there was a note of marked defiance in his reply.

"I don't see what difference my or anyone else's opinion makes to the kind of scenario you are describing Pastor Blomberg. Social progress moves on regardless and does not ask for our blessing. And irrespective of whether we welcome it or hate it, we have no choice but to adjust our lives, customs and habits to the demands it makes upon us. Trying to fight against it is like trying to turn the tide. It's just a waste of time and energy."

"Yes, you say that so categorically Sidenius. But even though you might be speaking sense, we old-fashioned rustics could still form part of that 'progress' of which you speak."

"I totally disagree! In fact, I think this is our last chance, if it's not too late already. All the statistical tables show very clearly that the standard of living in rural areas is decreasing year by year. Whatever about the idyllic happiness to which Hr. Pastor referred, it must now rest on a very shaky surface—which of course makes it increasingly less idyllic."

"Hmm, I don't know Sidenius," the pastor muttered in a somewhat dismissive way as he began walking again. "It is perhaps true that, just at this moment, things are a bit bleak for Danish agriculture—I know that myself. But that doesn't mean—"

"Hr. Pastor, the brutal truth is that things are as good as they possibly can be, not just for our peasants and smallholders but for farmers across Europe as a whole. It is the practice itself that no longer fits the gears of modern times in a civilized society. The whole notion of a farmer will very soon be an outdated concept in Europe."

"Dear Lord above, how can you even say such a thing Hr. Sidenius! To my ears that's the talk of a madman! Why, the reputation of our agricultural industry is the subject of the highest interest and admiration all over the world. We read that every day in our newspapers."

Per answered this immediately as the hint of a patronizing smile passed his lips: "Well if it is admiration, it certainly isn't driven by envy. It is a well-known fact that we, the people of this land—this lovely green and fertile land, as Hr. Pastor has just described it—with all its multitudes of cattle and miles and miles of buildings, do not actually own much more than the half of it. The rest of it has been sequestered, over the last twenty years or so, through speculation capital from the major industrial countries, especially Germany. It is a fact, Hr. Pastor, that should you walk the whole country, you will find very few farms or production outlets that are not owned, at least to a substantial degree, by a foreign speculator. Via our own banks and credit institutions, our country has, piece by piece, been mortgaged to foreign capitalists and in a way which—as I pointed out in my book—calls our utter humiliation under Christopher the Second to mind."

"Oh come on now. Bits of land and bits of cattle here and there!" the priest cried, issuing a rather forced laugh as he did so. "Sidenius, your animus in all of this is really making you go too far now, my good man!"

"Not in the least Hr. Pastor! All one needs to do is browse through one of the bigger German finance papers and look through the shares list to discover how much German capital there actually is in this country, and also the close attention they pay to Danish affairs. The enormity of the situation really struck me in all its horror when I was recently down in the far south of Germany and saw a newspaper that carried daily share postings from even the tiniest limited companies and savings banks in Jutland. It is that kind of thing that makes you sit up and take notice."

"Imagine that things should really have got that bad," said the pastor after a moment's silence, which was a backhanded admission that this was an issue which undoubtedly deserved the most serious consideration on the part of whoever was responsible for these affairs. "You are effectively saying, Hr. Engineer, that not only in spiritual terms but also in purely worldly terms the people of Denmark are living their lives on false dogmas and aspirations, which of course undermines their vigor and sense of purpose. It may well be true! Perhaps there should really be a campaign for our economic liberation running alongside the battle for spiritual enlightenment here at home. It's actually a very pleasant thought, come to think of it. And if that's the case, it's no use just going halfway. I for one am not afraid of making a clean sweep of everything. That which no longer serves the greater good has to be sacrificed, regardless of how important it has become for us. And of course we do have God's gift to us, which is that no revolution, no matter how tempestuous it might appear, could actually change the basic values of life. I barely need to mention that, of course, even under this present tyranny of steam power, we remain Our Lord's children—whether we wish to acknowledge that paternity or not, but, furthermore, all our other deep-seated feelings as human souls remain untouched by exterior ups and downs. It is thanks to God that life can bloom and grow, even in the most lowly abode. Wherever man is to be found, happiness in love and domestic pleasures will follow, even unto the darkest back hovels and regardless of how rough and ready they are. All that is really happening, beyond the human drama itself, is a change of scenery for the next act in the theater of life. Otherwise we remain what and who we are throughout all time and eternity."

The reassuring tone that the pastor had used brought a sympathetic smile to Per's lips once again. He knew only too well that this man of the cloth was completely wrong. He had immersed himself sufficiently in modern cultural developments to understand how a drastic change in material conditions, such as the advent of the "whirring steel wheel" that had been created for the benefit of people, gradually transformed the lives and culture of those people. He began to describe his travel experiences to the pastor, in particular his stay in Berlin and his impression of the fight for survival in which the inhabitants of a huge industrial metropolis are engaged. He described the hordes of itinerant workers—both men and women—for whom words such as home, family, security and comfort had already pretty much lost their meaning—people whose only abode in this huge human zoo was some small cubicle or other, just big enough to fit their bodies into—people who actually lived their lives on the street, in the ale houses, or other public places, and who finally left this world quite simply as a number on a hospital tag.

But Pastor Blomberg was no longer listening. He soon realized that the conversation had gone down a dubious track and, as was his wont when a discussion strayed into an area of expertise he could not cope with, he simply turned a deaf ear.

The pastor stopped now and apologized, saying it had not been his intention to lead Per over hill and dale. They stood, he explained, right at the parish boundary, so this was a good place to take leave of each other.

On departing, Pastor Blomberg repeated his invitation to Per to visit his rectory one day. "We can perhaps continue this conversation. But dear sir, you may have to hurry somewhat to get back in time for supper. It has probably not escaped your attention that Lord Prangen is a stickler for punctuality where meals are concerned. Ha ha!"

20

IN THE whole fortnight or so that Per had been at Kærsholm, he had not received a single word from Jakobe. Even though he himself wrote to her every other day, and at some length, describing his surroundings and experiences, there was just silence from her side.

There were a number of reasons for her stance. Right from the moment that she got his first letter from over there, she became convinced that she would never see him again. Moreover, she now asked herself whether it wouldn't be best for both of them if they were to make a decisive break with each other. She was exhausted from the endless struggle with this hidden and alien power that time and again robbed him from her, just when she felt that he was most embraced by her love. She was not even sure that she would be able to win him back this time. As for his own steadfastness, she doubted this less and less. For the first time, she saw him as he actually was. That part of his nature, at least, that she was actually in a position to observe and assess over time, she now knew inside out. No longer did she allow herself to be deceived by love's urgent need to beautify and exalt. For all his primeval power, Per Sidenius, in her eyes, was a man without genuine passion, without an instinct for what was really best for him in life. Or rather, he possessed only the negative attributes of passion, its cold night side: defiance, selfishness, willfulness—not its storming desire, not its all-consuming longing, not its annealing and purging fervor and flame.

And thus, was it not hopeless to continue struggling against the inevitable? In these days, she had often had cause to remember how Per, half jokingly, had compared himself with one of those mountain

598

trolls from folk myths who crawled up through a mole hill because he wanted to live with human children but could not tolerate the glare of the sun, and in his terror of the light would always retreat back down his grubby little bolthole before dawn broke. She saw now that there was a greater element of self-awareness in what he had said than she realized at the time, or even wished to attribute to him.

Yes, it was true. In his heart of hearts, Per belonged to a different world that was suffused with a different light. Regardless of how different he appeared, and claimed to feel, from his contemporaries, he was in his very essence a true son of the Cimbrian soil, a natural-born child of the bloodless Danish race with its cold-eyed stare and ultimately cautious mindset . . . the mountain trolls who could not face the sun without sneezing, the shadow beings that only really came alive as twilight descended and they could sit on their little hillock playing their fiddle or dainty little glockenspiel. Then were they in their element, sawing at their instruments and conjuring fantastical visions across the misty meadows and evening sky—the only way they had of raising their spirits and comforting their timid hearts . . . a race of Rumpelstiltskins with large pondering heads and a child's feeble limbs—a twilight folk that could hear the grass grow and the sighs of flowers, but disappeared into their warrens as soon as the cock crowed to greet the new day.

In the end, Per became uneasy in the face of Jakobe's silence. Even he had to admit that she had grounds for complaint over his prolonged absence—the more so because he no longer had any excuse for staying away. If pushed, he would say that he still hadn't brought his maneuvering over his financial affairs to a successful conclusion. Every morning, he resolved to raise the issue with Dame Prangen or her husband, but when it came to the bit, he just could not bring himself to do it. It's true that he spoke to them about his plans for the future, and they both seemed to take a keen interest in what he was saying, but a direct request for a loan he could not drag past the threshold of his lips. He had also begun to wonder whether a request for a loan might not arouse their suspicions, because the Prangens could never understand the feelings that made it so unpleasant for him to receive any kind of monetary support from his father-in-law. Thus he decided to let the question slide until just shortly before his departure; the problem was that this too was postponed every day. In purely physical terms, he felt so extraordinarily well at Kærsholm, and the thought of his forthcoming travails in a strange and very distant part of the world made it doubly hard to tear himself away from the comforts of the moment.

He spent most of his time out under Nature's open skies. There was so much he still wanted to do out here, so much that provoked his enthusiasm, and so much that was second nature to him from his youth but that he was now seeing in a new light.

He had of course rekindled his abiding love of being out on the river with his fishing rods—not so much for the sake of the fishing, but for the sheer pleasure he gained from being in the middle of that vast expanse of tranquillity. As the water glugged about the boat and he stared down into the broad-leaved, greeny-brown plants in the riverbed, it was as if they frolicked and cavorted in a leisurely dance with the onward-rushing whirlpools—a somnambulant world, a hypnotized existence that also seemed to be plagued by uneasy slumbers. He had already had frequent occasion thus far to reflect on Pastor Blomberg's praise of the life wisdom that was to be found in Nature, even if it was only to listen to the lark in the clear air. One really did, at such moments and in some mystic manner, feel that the soul was united with all living things. Some kind of joyous spiritual immersion took place with that complete abandonment into Mother Nature's embrace. The imagination rose up in wave after wave of images and ideas just flooded in. It was as if the ur-force of life itself was slowly and steadily attuning mind and body to finally produce a myriad of golden chords in the imagination.

No doubt, Per thought, such existential sounds brought tidings from the eternal essence of life itself. Whole peoples could die out and great cities disappear without trace; but just as the water gurgled here under his boat, so had it also glugged and eddied around the first person in the first canoe that ever was, and this sound would run on until the end of all days, not just here on earth but in all the heavenly planets where there was water giving life and an ear to listen. With those kinds of sounds, man's spirit was led to life's primordial source—to the "Immortal."

For Per, all of these meditations brought the sense of his having made an important intellectual and spiritual discovery. He recalled very well that he had once before experienced a somewhat vague but similar reaction to the natural world. This was when he had traveled through Switzerland for the first time and saw the high Alps and their massive range of snow-capped peaks looming over the horizon. It had been like a vision from the early dawn of time. But in the Alps its effect had been to leave him anxious and uneasy. In those earlier times, he had not developed any of that "sixth sense," which greets the infinite like an intimate friend. Now, however, as he sat quite still in the thwart of his boat and watched the bobbing, red-tinged angling float, a feeling of weightlessness buoying him and completely lost in the moment, he could actually begin to grasp the meaning of words such as "heaven" or "elation." He was able to feel a sense of being released from the constraints of the purely physical and embraced by a pure, inviolable, perfect soul.

And in such moments, how petty and demeaning all purely human aspirations and struggles appeared! How empty and meaningless everything felt in comparison with this feeling of ascending into omnipotent Mother Nature's arms! The whole farce of material life—this breathless hunt for so-called "Fortune"; how paltry it all was. In fact, worse than that. So strangely unreal, so ephemeral—a shadow play, pure and simple!

One day, Per received a letter from Ivan, who had discovered his whereabouts via Jakobe. His brother-in-law wrote to inform him that he awaited Per's return to Copenhagen with no little impatience, given that he—in spite of everything—still retained hopes of a positive outcome in the matter of his project. Barrister Hasselager and Commissioner Nørrehave were still in negotiations with others, Ivan wrote, and the antipathy towards the Copenhagen project was spreading rapidly, particularly in the provinces. Ivan urged Per to seize the moment by holding a series of public lectures about his own crusade in some of the larger towns in Jutland. This, Ivan continued, had become a pressing issue for another reason, as he had found out that the mysterious engineer Steiner was traveling around Jutland "as we speak" and engaging in discussions with Chambers of Commerce, industrial bodies and so on.

For Per, this correspondence had the effect of lancing a long festering boil. It became quite clear to him that, as far as the practical implementation of an idea was concerned, he would never be the controlling maestro. All those ructions with Max Bernhardt had not happened by accident. Nor did his clashes with Colonel Bjerregrav tell a lie. For the fact was that the day-to-day business end of engineering work had essentially never been his forte. He was a pioneer, a technician—not a finance shark or wheeler dealer.

In a letter to Jakobe that same evening, he went to great lengths to explain his decision in this regard. At the same time he informed her that, with the way things stood just at that moment, he felt it best to keep away from Copenhagen until the statutory confirmation of their forthcoming marriage was enacted in a couple of weeks time, at which point they could marry.

"Where my combined canal and harbor project is concerned," he wrote, "I regard the venture as over; at least from my perspective. I hereby bequeath my ideas to the nation for its delectation and practical implementation, whereas I will now push on to my next project, which is the further development of my wind and wave machine. This, of course, is precisely what Professor Pfefferkorn in Berlin recommended and, to that end, I expect to gain great insights into this problem during my time in America. You may object, Jakobe, not for the first time, that such a lack of respect for the centers of financial power will ultimately damage me. If true, so be it. I admit that it may well be that I do not possess the requisite vanity or ambition to be able to defy my essential nature on this point. This may be said to be a fault on my part, but I won't listen to those whose own behavior is far more suspect than mine. Otherwise I will write to your brother first thing tomorrow and formally transfer the handling of my interests during my absence over to him. There is no doubt, anyway, that these matters are best dealt with by him rather than me."

This time, Per got an immediate answer. Without saying anything about the reason for her long silence, nor a single word on the preparations for their marriage and proposed trip to England, she rebuked him in mocking tones for the conclusion he had reached via his "personal development."

"You speak of your lack of vanity," she wrote finally. "Yet you beat your breast and give thanks to God that you are nothing like all those other poor sinners. Good God man, shall this last sorry remnant of pride in ourselves also now be the subject of suspicion and doubt? Yes, it is true that I once burned with fiery radicalism on this point, but with the passing years, I have been able to look at things with a more perceptive eye. Overall, my view of mankind is becoming more old-fashioned. Even with silly things like honors and titles, I'm starting to at least understand why people feel reassured by them. It is sometimes very instructive to observe the spirit of industry and adventure that can be aroused, even in the greatest idiot of a man, when he believes the path may have been opened for some royal gong or other. In particular, it seems that Danish people in general do not have the natural wherewithal to generate their own internal 'Hothouse Development' systems—a phrase that would very often be on your lips in the old days and which I myself have to come to cherish. No, the encouragement has to come from without.

"I'll give you an example from here at Skovbakken. We had a drunken gardener who, when the prospect of becoming chairman of the local temperance group arose, suddenly gained the strength to resurrect himself in utter sobriety, a condition that no amount of exhortations or threats had previously been able to impose upon the fellow. The moral of the story being that vanity's loudly decried vices may well turn out to actually be morally correct! If I were a poet and writer, I would compose paeans of praise to it. And if I were a priest (with or without a Lutheran pastor's ruff and collar), I would strike it from the list of sins, which is far too long even as things stand."

Per was obliged to read Jakobe's letter a number of times before

604 · HENRIK PONTOPPIDAN

he could take it all in. This was not the Jakobe he knew and loved. And the tone she used! He was the more put out because he had felt such joyous relief in finally achieving personal clarity over an issue that was such a bone of contention for everybody.

In his first moments of extreme indignation, he considered writing back immediately and putting her in her place in no uncertain terms. But he thought better of it. Regardless of the fact that his spiritual stirrings had receded somewhat in his immediate thinking, subconsciously their influence continued to work, rounding his irascible edges and provoking a need to test his newfound resolve against increasingly challenging circumstances. This was particularly so in relation to Jakobe. For this reason, he now told himself that he should make allowances for her. After all, he had so much ground to recover in terms of the injustices he had visited upon her that he should nearly welcome this chance to debase himself before her in sacrificial atonement.

A few days after Pastor Blomberg and his daughter had been to Kærsholm, Dame Prangen suggested that their usual afternoon excursion should take a detour in the direction of Bøstrup in order to call in to the pastor and his family. Per had no great urge to take part in this visit but made no objections. She announced that Lord Prangen would also accompany them, but by the time the carriage had rolled up to the main doors, he had changed his mind. Once again he had been struck by one of his attacks of thick-blooded melancholia, and Dame Prangen had to summon all her wifely adroitness to deal with his sudden malicious volatility.

The farm overseer's lunchtime yarns and tales had already alerted Per to these sudden mood swings on the part of his host. Nevertheless, he was uncertain as to what way he should interpret Lord Prangen's baleful gaze. He began to worry that he had overstayed his welcome at Kærsholm and he now used their afternoon drive to sound out Dame Prangen on the matter. But she declared immediately that if he was contemplating some sort of sudden departure, both she and her husband would view this as a declaration that he had not enjoyed his time with them and that they would then be forced to regret ever having urged him to stay at Kærsholm in the first place.

Per was highly delighted with this firm reassurance—not least because it seemed to affirm his thinking in relation to Jakobe and staying away from Copenhagen.

The distance from Kærsholm to Bøstrup rectory was some five to six kilometers. After a steep incline, the road brought the traveler level with, and then across, the surrounding hills before descending again, following the contours of the meadows very closely as it did so. The weather was quiet but the skies were overcast, so the sun was not too harsh. On one side was the prospect across the green valley with its winding river, and on the other was the sight of tree groves on the crest of hills, where crows executed their endless patterns of grouping and circling.

Enthralled by this sight, the baroness began to declaim one of her favorite poems:

> Behold the bird soaring high
> its wings so dark against the sky.
> From the blue beyond it looks far and wide
> and all things great and wondrous below,
> it praises in glorious tones.

Not far from Kærsholm, they drove through a village, Borup, whose church was the country estate's official parish church. Here too there was a rich variety of bird life, a fact which bore witness to the abundance of crops in the surrounding fields. Squadrons of sparrows cavorted and squabbled in dust pockets on the road. Starlings in their thousands gathered in the treetops.

Also along the roadside was a row of poorly thatched huts, which shamelessly displayed their poverty. The nearby farmsteads, however, were more secluded from the main road, had stork nests in their roofs and were surrounded by orchards. Per already knew almost every house and every person in this little village. He had walked through this place on almost a daily basis during his long rambles. He also often stopped to chat to some of the locals. It was the first time in his life that he had come face to face with real farmers and he was fascinated to hear them talk about their own lives and then life in general. It struck him force-fully that the high interest they were paying on their farms did not seem to bother them unduly. They showed him around their properties with a bright, comfortable and smiling demeanor, as if the fact that the whole horse and pony show was enmired in hock never cost them a thought. Per was also aware that these people were descendants of forebears who were worth their weight in gold, but in these changed modern times, the only financial talk there was revolved around how much, or how little, a man was in debt.

In the hollow that ran down towards the meadows lay a ramshackle parsonage. Its three soot-blackened chimneys and the treetops from its garden could be seen from the main road. An older, religious man lived here—Pastor Fjaltring by name—a man who had been mentioned several times at Kærsholm in very disparaging tones. Dame Prangen had even gone so far as to declare that the most charitable way one could explain this man's behavior and whole way of life was that he was soft in the head. Following their example, most of the parishio-ners in the area had renounced their local parish affiliation to join Pastor Blomberg in the neighboring parish.

Per began to talk about this Pastor Fjaltring and expressed surprise that he had not encountered him during his walks through the vil-lage. But Dame Prangen replied that there was nothing strange in that. Pastor Fjaltring rarely emerged from his hovel—at least not until darkness had descended. He was like a dark owl, a creature that shunned the light—in truth, a spirit of the night who brought noth-ing but shame and scandal on the name of the district.

"But he is one of the faithful is he not?" Per asked cautiously. "In fact I think I'm right in saying that locals described him to me as very, ehm, orthodox?"

"Oh yes—that's what he pretends up in the pulpit. But in his black heart he is a blasphemer and a heretic. That's from his own mouth—as he said to a man here one day: 'I believe with all my heart and all my soul in both God above and the Devil below. The problem is that

I am not always quite sure which of the two I am most against?' Now Hr. Sidenius . . . have you ever heard the like?"

"But how can someone like that remain a serving minister?"

"Exactly—and it is a complete scandal. But he is crafty enough to save his real profanities until he gets people on their own—no witnesses you understand. In his sermons now, as you yourself have heard, he plays it strictly by the book but that doesn't stop them being horribly trivial and boring."

At that moment, two women, who were near a water standpipe, waved a friendly greeting to the passing carriage. Dame Prangen, who thought it important to show a common touch, called the vehicle to a halt for a moment and exchanged pleasantries about the weather and children. Then they drove on.

Outside the village, the road slipped downwards again, and after twenty minutes of working the horses at a fast clip, they saw Bøstrup village ahead of them. Per observed that it was in a picturesque setting at the foot of forest-clad hills.

They found Pastor Blomberg and his whole family gathered in a small field beyond the garden, where a sports area had been set up for the children. Three flaxen-haired boys, in just their shirtsleeves and ranging from ten to sixteen years of age, were playing a game of rounders. The priest himself saw fit to simply conduct proceedings but shouted more loudly than anyone else when a player had to get to a base before the ball was thrown. His wife watched nearby along with a little girl who was holding her hand. Frøken Inger, the eldest of the pastor's children, was sitting alone on the raised boundary at the edge of garden. She was reading a book, which she held in her lap.

No one had heard the visitors approach, who, for their part, had gone straight from the carriage and through to the garden so as to cause their hosts the greatest surprise.

The first one to see them was Frøken Inger. In a flash, she jumped to her feet and threw her arms around Dame Prangen's neck. Then general greetings were exchanged all around, interspersed with shouts of joy and surprise.

Pastor Blomberg gave Per a hearty slap on the shoulder and bade him welcome.

"Do you keep yourself fit, Hr. Engineer?" he asked, as he removed his large straw hat and mopped his brow with his handkerchief. "Ahh, it's a wonderful thing! We didn't really have these kinds of games in my day. And now I'm too old to get started. I'm afraid I have to make do with being a mere spectator on this battlefield. But even that does you the world of good. It's as if one's own physique is being toned just by watching these youngsters leaping around. Besides, it's great to have someone to do the running for you. It's the best exercise I've ever done!"

Still chuckling, the rotund little man led the whole party back through the garden, as he strode before them in all his pomp like some heavenly umpire dressed in a white linen coat and flannels that were raised above his ankles.

The pastor elected a place in the shade just outside the garden room. Before long, the outside table was laid for afternoon coffee in generous rustic fashion. The mood was heightened by the aroma coming from the coffeepot made of gleaming copper and the enticing smell of warm fresh bread and pastries. Frøken Inger acted as an impromptu chef and waitress and was a joy to watch. In his quiet meditation on the scene, Per allowed himself the private objection that she was a bit too aware of her own brilliant performance.

As is the custom in the country when ladies are sitting around a coffee table, the conversation gradually turned towards matters of house and home. Even Pastor Blomberg gave his pennyworth with a couple of humorous observations regarding baking and pickling until he was suddenly called away when a man arrived to speak to him.

When it was revealed that the cakes on the table were all Frøken Inger's own work, the baroness and Dame Prangen began competing to see who could praise them most highly and the pastor's wife affirmed these commendations by stroking her daughter's cheek and saying that she was such a good girl.

The young lady herself barely acknowledged these ringing endorsements. In fact, she even began to pout and pull away slightly when her mother caressed her. Per watched all this and decided that he was observing a very spoiled lady. But it could not be denied that she was gorgeous. He found that she was even more captivating than the first time he had seen her in the park at Kærsholm as twilight fell. As she moved around the table, it was as if she had only now become real to him. Her figure was bathed in the full light of day and her little white apron emphasized her athletic yet delicate arms as she poured coffee into the cups. However, he had to admit to himself that he no longer saw Francesca's likeness in her.

In deference to Per, Dame Prangen made several attempts to divert the subject away from baking and cooking by talking about Copenhagen, but Per had chosen to remain aloof regardless and the pastor's wife very quickly—and almost pointedly—steered the conversation back to domestic affairs. The house's first lady was tall and slim with something of a regal bearing about her. It was not difficult to see that it was from her side that the daughter had inherited her exterior charms. In contrast to her husband, Fru Blomberg showed a decided reserve towards Per. Without actually being impolite, she had still not addressed him directly or inquired of his opinion and it was precisely to make amends for this that Dame Prangen had constantly tried to draw him into the conversation. But now the guests rose at the behest of the hostess and it was proposed that they should make an excursion around the extensive and beautifully maintained garden. Per's preference was to remain seated. He was not comfortable in this gathering and was impatient to escape from the whole thing.

The three older ladies went in front and chattered away to each other. Per followed behind with Frøken Inger but was at a loss to know what to say to her. He, who otherwise never wanted for eloquence, could not find the approach that would suit a girl from a country village.

However, Inger was on home soil and was much more expansive with him than the last time at Kærsholm. It struck Per that she seemed more grown up, more womanly. She clearly understood that certain duties befell her as the daughter of the house and she performed those functions with no little dignity.

"I believe you are a frequent visitor to Kærsholm Miss Blomberg," said Per, who felt he had to say something.

"Not as often as I'd like Hr. Sidenius. But it's quite a distance from here and I can't always get use of the carriage."

"You seem to be very fond of Dame Prangen, if I may say so."

"Indeed," she replied—this time rather tersely, as if this subject was far too elevated to be discussed between relative strangers. "Of course, you already knew Dame Prangen and the baroness from having met them in Italy," she added, by way of diversion.

"That is correct, yes."

"Oh, it must be wonderful to go to faraway places like that," she said, and then explained to Per that her parents had long talked about traveling to Switzerland and bringing her with them. But her father had never been able to get time away. People in the congregation simply would not let him go for such a long period. He could barely get a week in Copenhagen without people beginning to complain.

Per noticed that she seemed to raise herself higher in her shoes whenever she mentioned her father. In this, she reminded him of his own sister Signe, and without really knowing why this made him smile.

At the same moment, Per caught sight of an iron hook. This had been painted red and driven into a tree trunk that stood beside the pathway. The hook had been rammed into the tree at around his own head height.

"Is that for people who want to hang themselves?" he asked, as he stopped in order to look at it.

Despite her Christian principles, Frøken Inger could not help laughing. She then pointed across the path to a small iron ring that hung down from a long rope on a tree that was directly opposite the tree with the hook. The whole arrangement was a brilliant game—the trick, she explained, was in being able to throw the ring from the tree on one side onto the hook on the other side.

Per immediately wanted to try. A good way of killing time, at least, he said to himself.

His efforts were not a great success.

"There's obviously a knack to it," he said after trying several times. In the end he asked her to show him how it was done. "Because I assume, Frøken, that you are a wizard at it!"

Inger hesitated a bit, clearly in two minds. However, she was unable to resist the urge to show off her skill in this game. The ring and its line snaked out of her hand, described a magnificent arc across the divide from tree to tree, and as the line became taut dropped perfectly over the hook with the kind of flourish that might be shown by a young woman who discovers that she has fallen into the arms of her own dearest darling in a game of blind man's bluff.

Per was impressed. There was nothing for it, he said, but to try harder. But still his luck was out.

"No, it's much more difficult than it looks! Do try again Miss Blomberg, you must!" he said, as he handed her the ring.

Inger once again allowed herself to be persuaded, even though she had already looked around a few times to check the progress of the other ladies, who by now were at the bottom end of the garden. And whether the fault lay with this distraction, or some other cause, her assuredness deserted her on this attempt. The next one too was a disaster. Inger's face and forehead reddened to scarlet. She now took very careful aim and threw out the ring once again. But still it was hopeless.

Per, who could see that her failed attempts were a source of great embarrassment to her, did not have the heart to rib her about it. Even when the fifth and sixth throw proved as bad as the rest, he maintained a diplomatic silence.

Though Inger felt that even his considerateness was a kind of humiliation, Per conquered a part of her heart with that moment of kindliness. When, in her eagerness, she continued to throw wide or short of the target, she finally laughed out loud, declared herself to be a clumsy oaf and then began to throw with even greater passion.

The ladies returned and walked right into the middle of this scene. Neither Per nor Inger had heard them approaching or stopping behind them.

"Inger," the pastor's wife called out rather sharply. "Run along and see after your brothers and sister, my child." And turning to the other ladies, she said: "I think perhaps we should go inside now ladies."

Pastor Blomberg emerged at the door to the garden, puffing on his pipe and welcoming the returning company.

"At last! I thought I might have to arrange a rescue party for you, Hr. Engineer. I'd say you are dying for a smoke after all that! Come on. We'll retire to my inner sanctum. Then the ladies won't have to worry their heads about all our grown-up men's talk," he said, with a twinkle in his eye as he turned back into the house, laughing out loud as he went.

In order to get to the pastor's private chambers, they were obliged to navigate their way through most of the house. Thus Per was able to gain a vivid impression of the solid comfort and wellbeing that prevailed in the Blombergian home. It was a vintage Danish parson's rectory—the epitome of time-honored tradition. The massive, dark and immovable mahogany furnishings lent their own weighty character to the rooms, as if God's carpenter himself had built them with eternity in mind. Fru Blomberg came from an old civil service family that had been very well to do. Indeed, one family member had been a State Prefect and a Lord Chamberlain and visitors to the house were often reminded of this fact. Pastor Blomberg's own forebears, on the other hand, were not mentioned quite as often, least of all by the pastor himself. Most people were simply aware that he was the son of a teacher from a provincial town, and there was something in the way he spoke that revealed his provenance to be one of Denmark's islands rather than the Jutland peninsula.

Pastor Blomberg's quarters were in a separate part of the house that lay on the other side of the main entrance hall. Here was a genuine sanctorum, boasting huge book collections that were held in a phalanx of shelves—the kind of library that does so much to maintain the social standing of the Church amongst its flock, even though these are often nothing more than a screen to conceal literary ignorance. However, this was not the case here. For while it is true that Pastor Blomberg was far from being a learned man, he was diligent in his reading and was more receptive to learning through books than even he himself sometimes realized. His constant urge was to be part of everything new that emerged in the commotion of the times; but he would only take these new things to his bosom in so far as they could nourish his spirit and not impact upon his Christian faith. Thus with this approach he was something of a Jesuit. In common with the tendency within the Church that he followed, he privately digested the delights of modern science at the same time as he saw fit to cast doubt on its findings in the eyes of his congregation. But to be fair, a logical progression from thought to deed had never been the pastor's forte. He was an instinctive person, and given that his overall life had always progressed in an uncommonly harmonious way, he had never had cause to subject himself to any stern self-examination of his conscience. In his youth, it must be said, he had not been free of worries concerning the procurement of his daily bread, while in later life, he had sustained a number of defeats with regard to positions in the civil service that he coveted. In other words, despite the fact that he was idolized by his flock and his name known across the country, he retained certain feelings of thwarted ambition. However, life had not visited any really serious setbacks upon him and those that he had encountered in the tribulations of other people were simply absorbed by his own innate, broad-beamed satisfaction with things.

In fact, it was precisely Pastor Blomberg's irrepressible cheerfulness that had raised his stature within the Danish Church, which was undoubtedly going through one of its periods of crisis at that time. That storm, that veritable hurricane, which the New Society's critique of the Bible had unleashed in the heart and soul of many believers just passed him by. Indeed, he could so little understand the angst and agitation which led his fellow Christians to take up the cudgels against science and scientists that he viewed it as a kind of sickness, or perhaps a deliberate, and therefore sinful, form of posturing. His own Evangelium was a practical Christianity that could both roll with the tide of history, yet remain wedded to the rock of the Danish people's ancient profession of faith. Thus, his preaching laid poetic stress on the popular empathy that had always carried the Church through—leavened with as much new thinking as would leave the congregation feeling that some sort of way, at least, was being made through open seas.

When Per was finally seated in the pastor's sofa and had begun to puff on a cigar, Pastor Blomberg plumped down in an armchair over by a windowed alcove. Once his pipe was lit, he launched into a stream of words. He told a couple of entertaining stories from the area, and just as in their first conversation near the woods outside Kærsholm, Per felt no little gratification in the way the pastor addressed him in such a straightforward way, exactly as if he were speaking to a person of equal standing and merit.

Per Sidenius would have been much less impressed had he known that the whole thing was an act, prearranged by the priest and Dame Prangen—the latter having, in her missionary zeal, recommended Per as someone who would perhaps "not be unreceptive to religious ideas." Nor was it long before Pastor Blomberg resurrected the conversation from a few days before, and precisely at the place where he had been forced into something of a retreat because of a lack of preparation. But he was now in much better fettle and led off by asking Per how it was that he, still a young man, had cast himself headlong into eminently bourgeois and sensible issues such as improving the country's economic standing. Per's reply was straight from the heart. He felt, he said, that he could trace his interest in these matters back to the vivid impressions he had gained from the time after the war—especially from events in his own home. But it was true also, he continued, that very early in his studies he had become aware of developments abroad with regard to industrial and social innovations, and asking why the same could not be achieved in Denmark was the obvious next step.

"Yes—of course it was," the pastor said. "And those types of comparisons between little provincial Denmark and the great world outside with all its splendors—well, it can often have a disheartening effect on a young mind, one feels. I get the impression, furthermore, that Dr. Nathan's writings have had a certain influence upon you, Hr. Engineer, where the question of progress is concerned; just as he has on so many other of today's young and dynamic men. Would I be right?"

Per objected immediately to this. Nathan was an aesthete, he said, nothing more and nothing less. "He bookended a cultural period and it was only in that sense that he could be seen as one of the figures who paved the way for the New Age." Per then rammed his point home by asserting that, in reality, Nathan did not understand the actual dynamics of the coming times at all.

"Hm, I see—interesting!" Pastor Blomberg puffed vigorously on his pipe and said nothing for a moment. That Dr. Nathan might be regarded as old hat by Denmark's youth came as a great surprise to him and momentarily threw him off balance. And even though he really would have liked to explore this issue further, he chose to avoid doing so, for fear of once again being led down a conversational path that was new to him. "But you do at least accept Hr. Sidenius that Nathan's influence on the spiritual and intellectual development of today's youth has been significant," he continued. This line brought the pastor back into the prearranged plan for the conversation with Per. "Of course, as you would expect, Hr. Engineer, I'm looking at it from a mostly religious and spiritual perspective. I think, for example, that I am right in saying that you yourself—though being the son of a priest—have made a firm decision to turn your back on the Church, and it was my assumption that Dr. Nathan's influence may have been the cause of that decision."

Per admitted the pastor's point but insisted that Dr. Nathan's books and writings had simply confirmed and underpinned a life philosophy he had already acquired in a rudimentary form while growing up in his own father's rectory.

"Imagine! At such a young age you had already become a stranger amongst God's people!"

"Yes," Per replied flatly and with a clear note of defiance.

Pastor Blomberg shook his head in a show of empathy.

"Ah dear, Sidenius! That happens all too often unfortunately! As I believe I mentioned the last time we spoke, I never knew your dear departed father personally; but I am well aware that he had that rather narrow old-time Lutheran view of life—a strangely one-eyed perspective, if I may say so and without speaking ill of the dead. Oh yes, that unfortunate and rigidly orthodox mindset! It still hangs over church and home in many areas like a bad dream and drives away many of our best and brightest young spirits. And then a clearly brilliant and eloquent advocate like Dr. Nathan comes along and reaffirms the suspicions of our young people that God's church is in fact a derelict house—and, of course, it ends with a complete rejection of the beliefs in which they were reared. I understand it only too well!"

Per said nothing. He had become slightly uneasy at the direction the conversation was taking. But now the pastor began talking about Dr. Nathan in glowing terms. His only complaint, he continued, was that such a gifted and talented man had taken such a decidedly hostile attitude to Christianity. Pastor Blomberg then expressed the opinion that the excesses of Lutheran orthodoxy both here at home and abroad had, of course, added fuel to his fire.

"But, of course, Nathan shares some of the blame for the spread of false doctrine about what is still the mightiest spiritual power the world has ever known. In truth, Nathan is no different from all the others who claim to use science to attack Christianity—they themselves simply become just as dogmatic in their negativity; they become just as 'one-eyed' if you like. Their error is not so much that they avail of cool reason but that they do not follow their arguments through to the logical conclusion. When, for example, our modern scientists say that they are simply recording natural laws, and thereby assert that nature only exists in things that can be broken down into atoms and that have certain mechanical or chemical properties—well, this is a very unsatisfactory interpretation and it comes straight out of research faculties and laboratories. At the end of the day, it explains nothing. We who actually live in Nature could never accept such a meager way of looking at things. Because we know, of course, and have time without number experienced that Mother Nature is imbued with a spirit—likewise that behind all visible things and the mechanically driven forces that affect our senses, there also resides a spirit, a spirit that speaks directly to our hearts. And once we have become attuned to the resonance of this spirit in the air around us, then in the end we only hear its timbre above all else—sense it both at the height of the storm and in the slightest zephyr dancing about a blade of grass. And not only do we sense it, we intuitively understand its message to us. It is nothing other than the same immortal spirit that resides and inspires our own internal human essence. If we ramble through a forest any day we choose and hear the canopy of leaves rustling and sighing above our heads, or if we stop, say, in a sudden moment of loneliness and listen to the purl of a small stream— yes, of course, a modern physicist can explain to us that these sounds come from the mass of leaves in movement or the friction of water against a riverbank; but if the scientist thereby believes that he has explained everything, we say to him: Oh now stop there a moment my good man! You have left something out there sir. Actually, you have left out the most important element of all. With all your calcu- lations, you can tell us nothing about that curious intimacy—that almost sisterly passion—with which a little watercourse like that can converse with us in our loneliness. Because—and this is so true!—the fact that an apparently spiritually dead thing like that can acquire a voice holds absolutely no fears for us, and we take no offense at the fact that this same little stream speaks in an immediately familiar tone to us!

"No, quite the opposite, we feel instantly comforted and at home when Mother Nature embraces us and gives us that sense of belong- ing. But really, it is all very simple, Hr. Engineer. All it means is that behind the visible world's infinite variety, an essential unity is woven through everything via the common origin of all living things. That strange feeling of being in a dream that moves in us at such moments is a longing to return home. And should that learned physicist now seek to persuade us that this feeling is the product of some internal mechanical or chemical function of ours, an affinity or attraction to primordial elements—well I would recommend to him that he leave all his books and his laboratory experiments and seek true wisdom out there in living breathing nature. Let him seek out that little stream in the forest! Let him linger there of an evening time when his heart is full of troubles and then, unless his spiritual sensitivities have been totally crippled, he will discover how its humble song actually leads into the depths of eternity—is a stairway to heaven that connects mortal time with infinity, dust and ashes with the immortal spirit, death to eternal life. He will perceive that the umbilical cord which binds us to our supernatural origins was never and will never be cut, and that it is still through this link—in worship and moments of prayer—that the soul is uplifted with a new living vitality from the eternal stream of life that we Christians call our God and Strength, our ever merciful Father."

Per remained silent while the pastor spoke. He had become irritated by the pastor's tone, which had gradually become more hectoring as he warmed to his theme; but he could find nothing objectionable in what he had said. In fact, at certain points, Pastor Blomberg was merely expressing ideas that he himself had vaguely perceived in this period where he was once again in more intimate contact with Nature.

The pastor continued: "But it is important not to forget that what applies to the spirit resonating through Nature, and its revelation of the divine, also applies to the spirit resonating through the history of man—the other rich source of edification for mankind. For the science of history, too, reaffirms Christian faith, belief and hope—especially when one avoids, unlike so many of those allegedly clever bookworms, getting bogged down in minute historical details, so that the overall view and profundity of events can be grasped. Even the much vaunted historical and linguistic critique of the Church's ancient articles of faith, which initially might seem to pose a risk to our basic tenets, has simply strengthened the arm of those who in religion find life's truth behind our creed, the spirit behind the written word. Besides, letting more light and air into the Church can only be a good thing—light and air are after all ancient symbols of spring. At the end of the day, all our dogmas and creeds are nothing more than outward signs, the husk, whose rupturing in springtime reveals the true kernel of faith. As it is in heaven, so it is on earth and in all things. Far from viewing science with trepidation, we Christians should embrace it, as we can safely assume that it is precisely from that quarter we will gain the most critical help in the search for truth. How could it be otherwise?

"Take any scientific issue . . . for example the newly proven law of physics that absolutely nothing in Mother Nature's housekeeping goes to waste; not one atom is lost—even if it doesn't always appear that way—but is simply transformed into a different existential state. Let us take just one example of that. Crop stubble and debris is being burned in a field. Looking at the burning pyre, one would think that everything is being burned to nothing, leaving just a small residue of ash behind. But the reality is different. By dint of the fire's combustion, this vegetable matter takes on a different existential form, except that now, in this new form, it is invisible to the human eye. Now is this not, in a remarkable way, very similar to the Christian belief in immortality? Or consider, for example, modern theories of heredity and related medical experts' demonstration of the way a particular disease is passed on from one generation to the next. There is a direct comparison here with the Bible's words that the sins of the father will be visited upon his children to the third and fourth generation. Or take modern economic or political science. In fact, take the slogan used by all the social democratic parties: liberty, equality and fraternity—this basically sums up tenets of the first Christians communities, whose idealism now receives its scientific stamp of approval in the modern world. We can see that where the most thoroughgoing research and experiments are being carried out, relating to all spheres of our lives, the basic truths upon which the people of God have with confidence and faith based their lives for thousands of years have been rediscovered. May we not speak of this as being nothing short of a revelation? Is it really an exaggeration to say that Christ's followers have lived as a chosen people under God's merciful gaze and, in an almost childish way, intuitively grasped what the world's most brilliant minds only gradually came to learn after centuries of often disastrous trial and error."

Pastor Blomberg puffed vigorously on his pipe and was just about to continue when footsteps were heard in the corridor outside; then

Inger popped her head in to say that Dame Prangen and the baroness wished to depart.

"Ah well, we'll have to call a halt to our conversation then, for today at least," the pastor said as he rose from his chair. And as he, quite naturally, placed his hand on Per's shoulder, he added: "It really has been a pleasure to sit down and have a chat with you Hr. Sidenius. Hopefully we'll get a chance very soon to continue our debate. I suspect that, in essence, we are not so far apart from each other that we would not eventually come to a shared view of things."

Just as they entered the sitting room, where the ladies were waiting, a carriage rolled in to the forecourt.

"That's the magistrate's coach father," Inger reported as she looked out of the window. "And Gerda and Lise have come too."

Lay Magistrate Clausen, who was also the estate manager on a huge demesne belonging to a local count, was one of the area's most enthusiastic Blomberg supporters. As such, he was also one of Dame Prangen's closest associates, and when it now transpired that magistrate Clausen and family intended to spend the evening at the rectory, both she and her sister yielded to entreaties that they should remain there as well. Per was also asked, but he was hardly in a position to object, even though his wish was to leave forthwith. The conversation with Pastor Blomberg had left him in a contemplative mood. For while there really was nothing new in what the pastor had said, the sparkle and passion the priest had shown in his arguments, the things, in fact, which characterized the man's whole personality, had moved and disturbed him somewhat.

Magistrate Clausen was a small, wiry man with white sideburns and gold-rimmed spectacles. His wife, on the other hand, was a mountain of flesh, who was still gasping for breath after the exertions of alighting from the carriage. The daughters were a pair of young women who were around the same age as Inger.

A table for the evening meal was laid out in the garden and the conversation soon became very lively. Amongst other subjects, Pastor Fjaltring's name was mentioned more than once. Lay Magistrate Clausen had just recently heard a new and shocking story about this religious cynic and heretic who, he asserted, lived a depraved life with a drunk and decrepit hag and who himself—as it was said of him— was of a weak and dubious character, the very reason why he could not decide where, or even if, he spiritually "belonged." One of the most esteemed young farmers in the area, who inclined towards the Blomberg school of thought had, the magistrate continued, recently approached Pastor Fjaltring with regard to some bureaucratic parish matter and, during this conversation, Fjaltring had actually encouraged him to engage in debauchery and excess. "You are not sinning enough, young man, go forth and sin some more" is what he apparently said. "With the kind of life you are living at the moment, you will never become a proper Christian" is how this infamous preacher had finished his conversation.

While the ladies present issued howls of protest and disgust at this, Pastor Blomberg shook his head in a tolerant fashion, raised one hand and said: "No, no, no—please remember that poor Pastor Fjaltring is a very unhappy soul!"

Just then the bells began to ring in the adjacent white church tower. This structure soared towards the heavens from behind the tree canopy in the garden and was tinged with red from the setting sun. The sudden cacophony caused the visitors to visibly jump, unused as they were to this sound falling right on top of them. Pastor Blomberg, who clearly wished to get away from the subject of Pastor Fjaltring, began to laugh and said the din from those bells really was indefensible. The Public Health Board should ban them altogether.

But Dame Prangen bristled at this and said that the bells of evensong were beautiful when heard from a distance—so beautiful in fact that they actually served to inspire people, a reminder perhaps to gather one's thoughts after the day's travails. But Pastor Blomberg never took kindly to being contradicted, least of all by his own acolytes. Though his comment about the bells had been a throwaway remark—one of those slightly daring jokes with which, in the spirit of Martin Luther himself was wont to spice up his sermons—he now took up this question in all seriousness.

He did not, he averred, appreciate that kind of regularly timed call to prayer. And he would prefer to avoid, thank you very much, having to stand to spiritual attention at the command of some overarching worldly power. There was something very Roman Catholic in that idea, which went completely against his beliefs. God did not see people by appointment like a doctor or town hall bureaucrat. If they wanted a metaphor—well, it was a bit infantile to see the sun as being Our Lord's pocket watch. The whole idea was almost blasphemous.

The pastor's comments gradually developed into a complete sermon in which he raised the issue to a point of the highest religious principle as to mankind's ability to have a fruitful and honest relationship with God.

By now, both the guests and their hosts had finished eating. The young ladies had asked to be excused from the table and went off to a quiet corner of the garden. The two Clausen ladies were both pretty, fresh-faced brunettes; the eldest in particular. Gerda was a curvaceous mother earth-type figure with eyes that shone with a lust for life.

When the table was cleared, Pastor Blomberg wondered whether they might sing an evening benediction. The girls were called back and the pastor's wife went into the garden room where the piano was housed.

"Peace reigns over town and country, the world's commotion calmed—"

The light had begun to fall in the garden. From the branches of a hazelnut tree a blackbird began to accompany the somewhat irregular tones of the party with its effortless song of praise to nature.

A happy moon sits in the night sky
and stars salute their fellow stars.

They girls had settled down by the steps leading up to the door of the garden room. There they sat in their bright dresses singing confidently and with luster, as the pastor and magistrate provided a bass harmony. These latter choirists had placed their arms across their chests and brummed their lines with a puckered brow and flapping lips. The three female guests, who were still at the table, took part by providing a somewhat unhelpful falsetto hum; the pastor's wife meanwhile, who boasted a voluminous and well trained voice, gradually began to dominate the song altogether.

> And the sparkling ocean, smooth and tranquil
> cradles the heavens in her arms—

Per was the only one who declined to sing. And yet nobody had been moved more by this moment as deeply as he had been. He recalled with great clarity the circumstances in which he had last heard this song. The time he had stood outside a tall garden hedge on the Copenhagen coast road and had longed to join the company on the other side of that divide. Now here he was actually in a garden filled with evensong but still superfluous, an intruder. It seemed that this was to be his fate. He was, and would ever be, banished and without peace wherever in the world the spirit of his childhood home reigned.

When the song was concluded, the pastor folded his hands and said an Our Father. A few more psalms were then sung, by which time the carriages were brought around to the front door.

When the guests had departed, Pastor Blomberg sat down in the garden room, along with his wife, to enjoy his evening pipe. He then began to comment on the events of the day and the individual guests. Inger was also present. She had already bade her parents goodnight and was on her way out of the room when she heard her father mention Per's name and suddenly found something that needed rearranging in the music cabinet.

Pastor Blomberg spoke of Per Sidenius in admiring tones and praised his exceptional qualities. He also extolled his handsome physical appearance as a "man's man" and a "true son of Jutland." But then his wife suddenly became uneasy when she realized that her daughter was still in the room.

"What on earth are you footering with, my girl?...Off to bed with you at once."

Per was still and reticent during the trip back to Kærsholm and Dame Prangen—who had her suspicions as to the reasons for his introspection—chose not to disturb him and began speaking with her sister about domestic issues.

When the carriage had come to the other side of Borup village, a tall man passed in the opposite direction as he walked at the edge of the road. Per didn't see him but Dame Prangen grabbed her sister's arm, saying: "Dear God, that was Pastor Fjaltring!"

Per turned round and stuck his head out of the carriage. He spied a tall, slim figure just before the shape was enveloped by the surrounding dark and disappeared.

"Was that the mad priest?" he asked.

"Indeed it was—this is the hour when he roams about. Locals say that he sometimes goes up and down the roads around here the whole night through."

Per sank back into his seat and resumed his silent passage. His thoughts remained with this restless nightwalker and a cold shiver ran through his very soul. That biblical curse again: "Thou shalt be banished and without peace wherever in the world thou art"—cannoned once more in his mind from the commanding tones of his father's voice. For him, the sight of the deranged priest on the road had been a portent of his own destiny.

The following day, Per finally made a serious effort to explore the small library of religious books that Dame Prangen had provided for his room. He took down one of Pastor Blomberg's collections of sermons, *The Way to God*. Even though it was a windy day, he preferred to be outdoors and took the book with him as he made for the woods. Once there, he lay down in his favorite spot just under a substantial hedge. In this way, he had the woods behind him as a windbreak, while before him lay the rolling meadows and the winding river, all the way up to the slopes on the other side of the valley.

This vista, he felt, was just perfect for the type of book he was about to read. Pastor Blomberg's discourses were immediately redolent of precisely this kind of Danish meadow landscape in cool summer weather: a high pressure belt, blue skies, white clouds glinting in the sun, a chorus of birdsong, here and there a calf bellowing, lush, verdant land softly undulating in an unobstructed landscape that was mostly flat, up to an horizon of low hills. As a preacher, Pastor Blomberg was a virtuoso of the poetic language inherent in Danish folk culture. In this regard, he was a true prophet of that tendency within the Danish Lutheran church that was born of Grundtvig's book of psalms and which had never lost the stamp of its poetic and literary origins.

However, what captured Per's imagination most was the pastor's clear way of explaining things. His background in mathematics and the natural sciences had made him particularly intolerant of conjuring metaphors. Again and again, it was concrete evidence he looked for behind the flowery words. It was the thought itself that he pursued relentlessly to try and reach some kind of clarity over life's great mysteries, whose truths had now become so indistinct to him that he had begun to despair.

His two conversations with Pastor Blomberg had already given him an idea of the type of Christianity he professed, which was so different to the one in which he had been raised. It was only now that Per really grasped how far religious life had moved on from the gloomy orthodoxy of yore, with its scourging of the flesh, its crucifixion of any attempt at reason—the whole medieval theory of base humanity and tortured souls whose only hope was a vague dream of eventual salvation in the afterlife and the delights of Paradise. With Blomberg, there was nothing that sought to strangle clear thinking or inflame the passions; nothing that was carried aloft in a cloud of metaphysical speculation; nothing that was dragged down into the realm of dark emotions. More than anything, there were no huge contradictions to contend with. The essential mystery of life was laid out in all its simple clarity. All the issues raised in the pastor's discourse seemed, in a natural way, to follow on from each other in a pleasing symmetry. Moreover, they were clearly directed towards people's lives in terms of their practical needs and requirements. The Devil, and not without some humor, was stowed away in a box room for outdated artifacts, like an effigy that had been fashioned by some spooked medieval monk. The belief in eternal damnation, meanwhile, was bluntly denounced as barbaric and loathsome and something that was in direct contravention of the Christian belief in a God of mercy and love. The afterlife was barely mentioned. In essence, what this Blombergian worldview stressed was that the Christian should, cheerfully and with confidence, walk along his chosen path of life, placing his trust in the heavenly Father's merciful and all-embracing love.

In all this, there was a joyous message for Per and he had to admit the truth of what Dame Prangen had always said about Pastor Blomberg's teachings—that they always seemed so wonderfully reassuring. The crushing weight that had dragged down his mind since the previous evening, and which had clung to him in his dreams, had been lifted in these last few hours.

Finally, he closed the book and lay for a while with his hands beneath his head, looking at the ever-changing sky, or out across the meadows. He felt like someone who had worried about a long and distressing night crossing over the sea to an unknown country, only to wake in the morning and discover that the passage had been completed, the storms survived, and the strange country greeting him warmly with sunshine rising over green forests. He also admitted to himself that the reasons why he had in the last while resisted the outbreak of a spiritual crisis was not just due to his fear of the strictures he would suffer from his guilty conscience, but also a certain dread of the new and unfamiliar way of life into which he might be thrown by such a mental and spiritual upheaval. But all this was now behind him and he was becalmed. He was clear that what was required of him was really only the same regime of focused and sincere self-development that he had been practicing of his own volition for some weeks now anyway.

At lunch, Dame Prangen told him about a festival that was to take place that same afternoon. The venue was in a nearby forest and Pastor Blomberg was one of the speakers. She had, she said, made so bold as to make an arrangement with lay magistrate Clausen, Pastor Blomberg and their respective families that they would meet together down there. The baroness would also doubtless attend. Did he feel the urge to accompany them?

Per replied with the exact truth—that he would very much like to finally hear Pastor Blomberg give a public speech. Per made no reference, however, to the fact that the prospect of being in the company of the young women of the two families was another tempting factor, though he only really realized this in the same moment as he agreed to attend. The girls had not entered his thoughts since the previous evening and even then, as far as he was aware, they had not really occupied his mind. And yet they had never left his thoughts. Just as his eyes had the whole time followed their brightly clad feminine form as they walked arm in arm around the garden, without the need for any specific concentration on his part, he had in a quiet corner of his soul, and in spite of his self-obsession, been receptive to the impression they created. He had also retained a very vivid picture of the three of them.

At around four o'clock, the Landau rolled up to the main entrance and after a period of waiting around—the baroness never being able to be ready on time—they drove off. At the last moment, Lord Prangen decided that he would, after all, go with them and during the journey went out of his way to atone for the breaches in social etiquette he had committed in the preceding days.

After an hour's driving, they reached the site of the festival: a wide green space that lay at the bottom of a deep forest basin. This offered a perfect shelter from the wind. Several hundred farmers and country people—men and women—were standing in front of a speaker's podium which had been decorated with flags. Hymns and psalms were already being sung. The arrival of the lord and lady of the manor attracted no little attention within the gathered crowd but there was no suggestion of anybody being awestruck—indeed the long-legged squire figure of Lord Prangen with his short, tight overcoat pleated at the back and pheasant feathers in his hat provoked a ripple of mirth here and there as he led his female entourage up to a seating area directly in front of the speaker's podium. This space had been specially reserved for the more elite members of the local populace.

Per remained by himself at the back of the gathering. He had been rather overwhelmed at the sight of such a mass of people and therefore preferred to avoid having to press through the crowd. He saw that, up at the front, the magistrate's family had risen to greet the arrival of Lord Prangen and his party. He now espied Pastor Blomberg's brown velvet hat and his wife's lofty head rising from the seated area. But he scanned the crowd for some time, and in vain, for a sign of Frøken Inger and her friends. Then he saw Dame Prangen turn slightly to one side and wave briefly in the direction of the slope leading to the forest. Now he saw the three young female figures in their summer dresses who had taken their place up there like a divine chorus.

The singing died away now as Pastor Blomberg moved to the speaker's podium.

He began by speaking about the Danish language—about its importance as the language of Danish hearts, in contrast to foreign languages that could, at best, only be used to discuss intellectual matters. Our native language, he said, was the divine breast milk from which the Danes imbibed their national soul. The language possessed by a people was like a receptacle for the entire spiritual and intellectual riches possessed by the people of a nation—an inheritance through which one's ancestors spoke intimately to us over a hundred generations and shaped us anew in their likeness. For that reason, we were obliged to honor our language and pronounce it sacred. Just as we guarded and protected those sources from which our body drank its daily needs so that it would not be polluted, so was it even more important to protect the spiritual source of nourishment that was the word as expressed in the Danish tongue. But if one listened to the people's everyday discourse, one would unfortunately find much that was unclean, in fact rotten, and country people were not much better than city folk in that regard. Yes, it had to be admitted that there were many who could not speak without their words having a double meaning and foul language spewing from their mouths like toads from the mouth of the princess in the well-known fairy tale. Here was a mammoth task for the people—

perhaps the most important of our times. He wished especially to appeal to young people, in whom lewd and indecent manners of speech were still not ingrained. Nothing less than a national movement was required to develop awareness of the purity of the soul, which was of course just as important in people's lives as bodily cleanliness. All the positive power of the spirit that moved within the people had to be brought to bear in order to defend our young people against the base language to which they were now exposed on a daily basis.

Initially, Per listened intently to the pastor's words, but gradually, as he began to sermonize on moral issues, his attention began to drift. The presence of the young ladies was a contributory factor in this, but it was also because the whole scene was so new to him. This was the first time he had ever taken part in an open-air religious folk gathering and the audience, therefore, attracted his attention just as much as the speaker. He looked across this tightly packed mass of people in their rough-spun clothes, their fiercely attentive, open and eager faces; and at that moment he understood for the first time the kind of spiritual movement into which he had been led.

He had often heard people speak of the Grundtvig revivalist movement and its promotion of a strong cultural folk movement as opposed to reliance on scientific and technological advances, but given that for him the whole concept of "farmer" was outdated, he had never thought it worth the effort to discover more about this popular crusade, despite its undeniable widespread support. In the Copenhagen circles in which he moved, Grundtvig and his many followers were usually dismissed with an imperious contempt.

Per could not help but draw a comparison between this gathering of Danish farmers and country people and the Austrian and Italian farmers he had got to know on his travels, and he realized that his countrymen by no means were shamed in that comparison. He was forcibly struck by the difference between the alertness and vivacity shown by the gathered assembly and the dozy herd of Tyrolean mountain dwellers which the priests drove in procession through Dresack like so many bleating sheep on a Sunday morning. But even when compared to the local farmers of this area in days gone by, at least as he remembered them from his childhood and at a distance when they came into town on market day, this assembly was evidence of more remarkable progress. Here was clear and undeniable evidence that major advances had in fact taken place. The region had become a place of liberation, which had happened during the same period when he himself had been carried forward by other social changes—and it was also clear that these developments had brought a general feeling of happiness amongst the people.

Suddenly, Per understood the startling equanimity displayed by these farmers and smallholders, despite their having been dragged down into a spiral of land and property debt. As recompense for the material wealth they had lost, they had discovered a far richer spiritual and intellectual life—a more noble way of conducting their lives. And in their efforts to dispute the prevailing zeitgeist and steadfastly assert that they were still the fulcrum point of Danish society, it was clear that they had found a common bond, a feeling of comradeship, which made them strong and proud.

When Pastor Blomberg had completed his speech and a few more hymns were sung, the main organizer of the festival, a smiling young farmer with a mop of blond hair, stepped forward to announce that there would be a short intermission for refreshments, after which the principal of the folk high school, Hr. Broager, would give an address.

The assembly fanned out, moving slowly away from the speech platform and across the field, with most of them choosing a place to sit down on the grass.

Per walked over to Inger and her friends. The girls had just got up to go over to their parents, but Per suggested they use the intermission to explore the beautiful forest. Magistrate Clausen's daughters agreed immediately to this. However, Inger was not so sure. She stole a quick and uncertain glance over towards the speaker's podium, where her mother stood in conversation with Dame Prangen. Inger took after her mother, and indeed the whole of her local patrician family on the maternal side, in being very careful to observe good form. But the eldest Clausen girl, the full-bosomed and willful Gerda, took Inger resolutely under her arm, grabbed her sister with the other arm and dragged them both under the tree canopy.

The same Frøken Gerda had found it difficult to keep her vivacious brown eyes off Per. However, her rather forward, almost masculine, deportment was really only a masquerade with which to conceal her decidedly female attraction toward Hr. Engineer Sidenius. Her sister, meanwhile, who was still really nothing more than a child, allowed herself to be smitten by Gerda's tone like an overexcited school girl.

But Per's thoughts solely concerned Inger. Close up like this, he found the two sisters quite pathetic, and he wondered whether poor Frøken Inger was not a little embarrassed on her friend's behalf. At any rate, he duly noted that the more idiotically they clowned around, the more subdued Inger became.

Even the previous evening, Per had been impressed by how stately Inger's bearing was in comparison with the other two young women— how confident and proud she was of her status as a latter-day Maid of Honor; her head held regally aloft, as if she would look beyond all of life's tat, dirt, and inconsequence. Now it struck him that it was more her fresh virginal appeal, rather than any particular exterior feature, that put him in mind of Francesca. She too had also possessed that same aura of chaste reserve, which was so redolent of the fragrance of wild roses. He could still recall that the smallest reference to the mysteries of sexual attraction could fire the blood into Francesca's pale cheeks, whereas Jakobe, well, it had to be said, that her outlook was completely different; nor could he deny that his fiancée's lack of modesty had sometimes offended him, that overall, he had found the unbridled and lustful passion with which she had plunged into a sexual relationship with him to be somewhat distasteful.

They had now emerged on the other side of the forest. Impressive gravel slopes towered directly above them, covered only by sparse grass and dark patches of heather. This was the mighty Rolhøj, the highest point in the area, whose summit offered views of a vast part of Jutland.

Even though the two Clausen girls gradually came to realize that they were superfluous to requirements, they gave no sign of this, at least not with signs of annoyance. Quite the opposite. As the doughty Jutland girls they were, they exacted revenge for a lack of appreciation by being even more outrageously unrestrained.

"First one to the top is king of the castle!" Frøken Gerda roared as she suddenly rushed the slope, immediately followed by her sister. In the mad haste, the younger sister lost her hat and a wild hunt across the hill then ensued to retrieve it from the grip of a tricky wind.

Inger was about to join the fray, but Per, who was mindful of Dame Prangen's earlier warnings to her about running, earnestly entreated her to desist: "Please bear in mind, Frøken, that you were quite sick not so long ago! I happen to be aware that you are supposed to avoid too much physical exertion."

Once again without realizing it, Per had won another piece of Inger's otherwise stoutly defended heart. She was still enough of a convalescent to find pleasure in being told that she was weaker than she actually was. But now, she announced with a slight toss of her head, she was going up there anyway, and when Per proposed that she at least should take his arm, Inger dismissed even the thought of it. There was nothing wrong with her now, not in the slightest, she said. There was nothing to fret about.

Nevertheless, Per kept very close to her as they climbed, so that he could catch her if she should stumble. At one point, which was particularly steep, she actually did take the hand he proffered. This was not done without a certain deliberation, but she could not see how this might be seen as improper—not least because Hr. Sidenius was already engaged. And, privately, she acknowledged that it was not in the least bit unpleasant to be led, almost floating, up the steep incline.

Per felt a constant urge to tell her that he had spent the whole morning reading one of her father's books, and that he had gained great benefit from it. But he was afraid that she would just take his words as fawning blandishments and chose not to mention the book. He sufficed with saying that he had really enjoyed his visit to the rectory the previous day—something she clearly took as only natural.

Inger's exertions had brought her out in a sweat and she paused for a moment to draw her breath. She removed her hat, holding it low in her hand, while the disturbed strands of her fine, golden hair were illuminated in a glorious halo by the late afternoon sun. She was once more at this moment, Per thought, the image of Francesca. Indeed, a more perfect form of Francesca.

The two Clausen girls had reached the summit by now. There they stood, their hands pressing their hats down onto their heads, as the wind tugged at their skirts like invisible hands trying to flay their clothes from them. When Inger and Per finally appeared further down, the younger sister cried out: "Would you just look at the way those two are dawdling!"

"Inger is so annoying like that," Frøken Gerda replied. "The minute anyone shows her the slightest interest, she starts playing the simpering kitten."

"Aye, but it has to be said that he is some buck, him—a fine thing," the younger girl said.

"Fine thing! He's a complete ugh!"

"Ah now Gerda, you don't really think that. Just yesterday evening you said—"

"Me? You are off your rocker Lise!" Have you had a proper look at his peepers? Lord above, what a pair of milk buckets!"

Inger and Per finally arrived at the top and began to look about from this renowned viewpoint. The two sisters began to count church steeples and towers. On a clear day like this, it was said that thirty-five churches could be picked out. The Clausen sisters knew the names of all of them, but Per was only interested in those that Inger was able to point out. "Oh look, is that not Tebberup?" he cried. "What? Oh Ramlev, is it?" as if these place names awoke sacred memories for him—and the two sisters nudged each other with their elbows.

By now the wind had really picked up and even made it difficult for one person to hear what the other was saying, as skirts and hats flapped. Thus it wasn't long before they decided to go back down.

When they were once again surrounded by forest, they stopped for a moment to make themselves more presentable. The wind had ravaged much of the artistry in the young ladies' coiffures. Inger was particularly disheveled. In the end, she had to remove both her gloves so as to handle her hair properly and get it into shape, and just as she stood for a second with her hatpin in her mouth and the two sisters busy with their own grooming, she asked Per to hold the gloves for her. This simple request had not cost her a thought but the two sisters immediately fired glances at each other; and on more than one occasion on the way back through the forest, they found some cause or other to nudge and giggle.

When they reached the festival area again, the public meeting had resumed. Up on the speaker's podium was a tall man. He was serious of countenance, his face framed by dark hair and an imposing beard. This was school principal Broager, the head of a nearby folk high school and Pastor Blomberg's rival in the struggle for popular acclaim, particularly from the youth of the area.

As unobtrusively as possible, the girls reoccupied their previous position at the edge of the trees. Inger gave a quick look down to the place where her mother was sitting—she had suddenly reconsidered the wisdom of disappearing like that, especially when the whole thing had taken far longer than she had expected. As luck would have it, it appeared that her mother had not missed her in the least, because she sat there quite calmly listening to the speech being made by the school principal and seemingly giving it her full attention.

And this was actually true. The pastor's wife was a jealous watchdog of her husband's reputation as a public speaker. And though this would never be obvious to anyone, she became a bag of nerves every time some other person, and especially the folk high school principal, rose to speak; and it was for this reason that, despite Per's presence, she had not in fact looked for her daughter in the intervening period.

Pastor Blomberg himself actually suffered from a similar affliction to his wife's. Now it was quite true that he would always be the one who applauded other speakers more loudly than anyone else, and laughed loudest at their witticisms, but a close observer would detect the blood flushing into his cheeks to betray his displeasure as soon as he felt that someone other than himself had won the crowd's approval.

When the festival was brought to an end with a few more hymns, and while people waited for their carriages and vehicles, which had been parked in the shelter of the forest, Dame Prangen and Inger walked arm in arm a short distance away from the crowd. Dame Prangen spoke first:

"You ladies went for a walk with Hr. Sidenius, I noticed."

"Indeed—we went for a quick walk up to Rolhøj. You don't think, Dame Prangen, that there was something improper in doing that?" Inger asked, as she looked rather worriedly at her inquisitor.

Dame Prangen began to laugh.

"No, not at all my dear."

"No, especially when he is already engaged to be married."

"Yes, of course."

"Though I must say, Dame Prangen, that it is strange how he doesn't seem to show it—that he is promised I mean."

"Yes, well my child—I would say that this supposed 'promise' doesn't count for very much."

Inger stopped dead in her tracks with a terrified look on her face.

"What are you saying, Dame Prangen?"

"Well, of course, I know nothing really. But I have a feeling that that particular association is no source of pleasure for Hr. Sidenius. You know of course that she's a Jewess."

Inger said nothing else. She should have known! She now felt a hot rush of shame at the thought that she had behaved so freely with him.

At the same moment she heard her parents calling from the carriage, which had now been driven forward. Pastor Blomberg and his wife were already sat well packed into their half-calash and Inger's father was showing signs of impatience, so there was no time for proper leave-taking.

When Inger was ensconced in the carriage and went to put on her gloves she found that they were missing and, in a new attack of alarm, she realized that, in all likelihood, Hr. Sidenius still had them about his person.

There was still time to retrieve them—Lord Prangen's carriage had still not left—but she was so mortified that she dared not say a thing that might betray her behavior to her mother. Indeed, the pastor's daughter was at such sixes and sevens that she would not even look back as they left for home, and all through the journey, she kept her exposed hands firmly concealed under one of the carriage blankets.

When they had gone a little distance, Fru Blomberg turned to her husband, saying: "I think the school principal let us down today dearest."

"Oh absolutely. So boring!" Blomberg answered, shaking his head. "Not one of his better days. Really not one of his better days, dear," he said again after a couple of minutes, even though by this time they had moved on to a different subject altogether.

Per, for his part, spoke animatedly during his own journey home about everything he had experienced that day—everything, that is, except Inger of whom he said not a word. Dame Prangen, who picked this up straight away, kept her own counsel on the matter. She leaned back into the plush folds of her seat and sank into a tender reverie.

The sun had gone down and it was almost dark by the time they reached home.

Per immediately recognized the hollow rumble of the wheels on the driveway as they passed through the gate at Kærsholm, and when he saw the spill of warm lights in the big house welcoming their return, he became gripped by a new and strange feeling of elation. For the first time in his life, he sensed that he had found a place to which he felt an emotional bond. As if to confirm this very thought, the farm overseer's dog came bounding towards him, whining and whimpering and madly wagging its tail as it licked his hand in utter joy at seeing him again. The poor creature, whose pups had been taken from her, had transferred all her motherly affection to Per. Quite moved, Per dropped down to his knees, patting the dog's flanks and tugging softly at its ears and muzzle.

But as he looked up at the house, all his private anxiety and dejection at the thought of his imminent departure from Kærsholm came back to haunt him. He just could not fathom how he would actually tear himself away from the place. But it had to happen. And very soon. He had been there now for the best part of a month.

When he entered his room, a shudder ran through him at the sight of a letter that had been left on his table. His gaze took on a guilt-ridden aspect—a letter from Jakobe no doubt, he thought to himself. He baulked at even lifting it. Then when he recognized Ivan's scrawl on the envelope, he breathed a sigh of relief. But a strong underlying feeling of apprehension stayed with him. His brother-in-law's hand-writing was a stark and uncomfortable reminder that his money conundrum remained unresolved, a conundrum which every evening made him squirm in anguish before he could finally fall asleep.

Per put the letter to one side—business matters could wait until the morning. As he made to return to the sitting room, he put his hand in his coat pocket and pulled out a soft, light gray lump of something. It was a pair of velvety, but coarse-textured, gloves—also known as Randers gloves. Inger's gloves.

Per admitted to himself that holding on to them out in the forest was not entirely an accident. The truth was that he had felt a peculiar thrill in carrying something that belonged to her. During the mad rush of the departure from the meeting, he had forgotten to hand them back.

As he now straightened and then folded them with great care, he spent a long time simply looking at them. He put them up to his face and plunged into their fragrance with great gusto—smiling, deep in thought as he did so. He now had the perfect excuse to pay another visit to the rectory; the next day even, he mused ... or ...

Or was it perhaps best for him to avoid that? Was he not in danger of truly falling in love with Inger if he kept on seeing her? His basic instincts, ancient Adam's sinful ways, stirred within him once again. But then what was the point? He had no right to expect that a new love might blossom in his life. After all, he had cut himself off for ever from life's pleasures ... if he had ever known them in the first place.

21

THAT TIME had now arrived in Copenhagen when the villas and summer houses dotted along the Øresund coast were revealed day by day in ever brighter and more festive colors. The deepening sense of languor that sunshine and summer stillness brings to "real" country areas was absent here. The great throbbing pulse of the big city was thrummed along its railway tracks—running mile after mile and ever outwards into the enervated landscape. Huge steamships, bulging with passengers, lurched into landing stages and unloaded their human cargo. Railway carriages, a quarter of a kilometer in length, pulled into coastal stations and discharged a flood of humanity, which then conveyed the mighty agitation of the metropolis deep into the heart of North Zealand's forest areas.

As all this unfolded, a pressured atmosphere prevailed at Skovbakken. Philip Salomon and his wife Fru Lea were engaged in long and tense conversations with each other about their children.

Nor was it only Jakobe whose future filled them with anxiety; Nanny's personal affairs had also become a source of the most serious concern. As a palliative for the swingeing defeat Nanny's vanity had suffered at the hands of Per Sidenius, she had sought redress in the form of her old worshipper—the young ex-soldier Hansen-Iversen; and because this time she really did need a significant distraction, she had thrown herself into a knife-edge game of teasing and flirting with him. But it transpired that the former cavalry lieutenant with the dashing moustache was not quite the dauntless warrior he had let on to be. One day he went home and fired a bullet through his head. That was not all. For he also left behind a letter, which proclaimed to the world his disturbed state and cursed Nanny Salomon for all eternity.

Thanks to her husband's pivotal role in the press, the whole affair was successfully hushed up, and in order to further protect his wife's reputation, Otto Dyhring made sure that the happy couple were regularly seen together at public occasions in the ensuing days, with Nanny holding on to his arm as the loyal wife. Dyhring also tried to make light of the issue by quipping to fellow journalists and scribes that it truly was dangerous to have a wife whose eyes not only sometimes looked like, but also functioned like, the barrel of a gun. Privately, however, he had given Nanny a severe tongue lashing during a third-degree interrogation, which she received without complaint. She reasoned that she had got off lightly, given what had happened and her terror at the possible consequences. Indeed, after the anger and passion he had shown, she actually became seriously attracted to her husband for the first time and was for a period afterwards his humble slave who willingly—and with increased understanding—facilitated his own sexual excesses.

However, it was inevitable that something would leak out regarding the reasons for the young lieutenant's suicide. The Copenhagen gossip circuit, which in the summer months also extended far out into the countryside, got wind of the despairing note that was left behind, and when Philip Salomon and his wife took their customary evening ride along the coast road, greeting and being greeted by friends and detractors as they went, a lively round of muttering and whispering ensued in the summer houses and villas once they had passed by. Of course, there were those who could never forgive Nanny her beauty, and for that reason alone the question of her virtue was always a hotly disputed topic in the rich and incestuous enclave surrounding the Salomon mansion in Bredgade—an area of Copenhagen that was more like a small provincial town where everybody knew each other's business down to the color of their underwear.

Nanny's parents were the harshest critics of her behavior. In fact, Philip Salomon felt impelled to make a frank and open apology to Dyhring on his own behalf as head of the immediate family and then on behalf of the whole extended Salomon clan. Strangely enough, the only person amongst Nanny's relatives who offered at least some support to her was Jakobe—that same Jakobe who had otherwise always been so scathing in her criticism of her sister, but who now just shrugged her shoulders at the whole affair. She could not fathom why people were treating it as such a grave matter. Life demanded its regular supply of human blood if it was to be lived to the full, she said. If you wanted to be part of it, you had to be ready for the moment when it was your own blood that was being shed!

But then Jakobe had changed so much in the last while. Not only was she disconcertingly failed in her appearance, in her whole demeanor the same tired and unnatural indifference to everything, that had been a feature of her past, had now returned to possess her once again. Should anyone inquire as to her wellbeing, she would automatically reply that she was well. Of her fiancé, she spoke less and less; though she made no objections when her parents raised the issue of her forthcoming wedding. But at the same time, she would mention that she was thinking of paying her friend in Breslau another visit—nobody could really work out her true intentions.

Except perhaps that Rosalie had some understanding of Jakobe's state of mind. Her own room lay next door to Jakobe's, and one night she was woken by the sound of crying from her big sister's room. Believing that she might be sick, Rosalie got up straight away, but she found the door was locked and Jakobe would not let her into the room. Jakobe's explanation the next morning was that she had suddenly got an awful toothache. But Rosalie was no longer the kid sister. She herself had begun her first hunting expeditions in love's secret forest, following Nanny's footsteps as she went. In fact, she had already bagged her first "game." For the self-proclaimed intellectual Balling had now openly declared his undying love for her, and Rosalie took great pleasure in feigning incomprehension and watching this elongated bookworm wriggle and writhe in fear and uncertainty.

More than anything, the thing that twisted Jakobe's mind into such despair and dejection that she, too, sometimes thought of suicide was that she could not bring herself to make a final break with Per. Even though she had realized for a long time where things were leading, and even though she suspected that another woman had come into the picture, she put off the ultimate decision day after day. Only glorious love could bring such humiliation! How low and shameless she could be for something that she had held up as life's highest reward!

During all this pain, however, she found comfort, indeed some small sense of revenge, in the fact that she had not revealed her true physical condition to Per. She had not handed her most intimate secret to him. She was determined that her motherhood would remain unsullied. She would be spared the worst humiliation possible: to become the subject of his pity.

For some time now, she had readopted the policy of leaving his letters unanswered. In fact, it was a struggle for her to read them at all. His obsession with that "reforming pastor" actually led her to feel sorry for him. In one of his most recent letters, he had actually recommended that she obtain this man's writings (something she had already done), and given the fact that he had mentioned this collection of sermons in the clear hope that they would persuade her to adopt Christian beliefs, she became irate enough to send a reply. Here was an opportunity for her to give full vent to her feelings but without having to humiliate herself. And though, just as in her previous letter, she did not touch on their personal relationship with so much as a word, she sensed that she was preparing herself for their final break as she wrote.

"Up until now, I have not felt any need to heed the request you made in your last letter to consider an issue that has now clearly come to animate your thinking once more—I'm referring to your Christian beliefs. You may have worked out for yourself that my silence does not imply a lack of overall interest; but it has become more and more obvious to me that there are certain issues where attempts at a discussion would be pointless. In particular, where religious beliefs are concerned, we do not as a rule allow rational argument to influence our judgment. We get the faith that circumstance creates for us. Our religious sensibilities develop in the same naturally ordained way as the heart and lungs, and all artificial attempts to alter, for example, inherited traits will probably only have one outcome and that is to weaken the whole organism as a result.

"However, in the last letter I got from you I can see that there is a direct question hidden between the lines, and it demands an answer—if not for any other reason than the fact that you might see my silence as some sort of tacit acceptance.

"My own attitude towards Christianity is naturally no less conditioned by the circumstances of my birth and how I was brought up than your own. From being a very young girl, the persecution that Christians have traditionally perpetrated against my people has always aroused a desire for revenge in me. And yet I believe that I might almost be able to ignore all that if I could see the good deeds the Church was carrying out in wider society. But regardless of where and what I read about its two thousand-year-old history, I discover that underneath its mask of piety lies the same devious and vicious drive to tyrannize, the same cold-blooded indifference to what measures are used in order to satisfy its lust for power. Never has a religious movement, surely, adopted the basest of human characteristics in this way in order to suit its purpose? And it is because of this policy—solely because of it—that Christianity has spread across the globe so widely.

"But for me, what is completely incomprehensible—yes the most incomprehensible thing of all—is that otherwise fine and honorable people, who are able to read and think, are not disgusted by the actions and history of this religious conspiracy under whose patronage the most hideous oppression, the darkest ignorance, the most bestial outrages, have found a home, or at least have been tolerated. And at the same time, all those values emerging in society that stressed healthy, proud, and courageous efforts to lead mankind forward towards the light—to greater justice, more prosperity and happiness—have been opposed by this envious and uncompromising enemy. It's true that the Reformation did, perhaps, bring about certain improvements in what I'm talking about, but it didn't make that much of a difference to the underlying problem. Moreover, these new modern-day tendencies, which seem to want to establish a more benign attitude to 'dissenters,' do not give me any reassurance whatsoever. Quite the opposite. Protestantism, too, has its Jesuits, who in tough times for the Church show an apparently open and liberal face, which functions as a mask to smooth over the concessions it has to make because of changes in society. It is a phenomenon that is as old as Christianity itself. Just as from the very start the Church was clever in establishing footholds in various countries by initially adopting heathen customs and ideas that proved difficult to eradicate, the New Age Christians are well aware that in a situation where outright defeat becomes a possibility, they need to adapt in a sophisticated way to the challenges posed by new scientific developments or huge changes in society. The fact that the Church, all the above notwithstanding, asserts that it is the repository of the one, true, eternally abiding and God-given truth is an astounding piece of hypocrisy the like of which the world has never seen before or since.

"And yet, after all I've said, I am not the Church's implacable enemy. I would even accept that some kind of rapprochement with Christian beliefs might be possible, as its creed does contain elements of truth that are of significance for the wellbeing of mankind and society. There is only one condition I would make before holding my hand out to the church—that it repented its sins and finally showed an honest face to the world. And one more thing: that the Church, as proof of the sincerity of its transformation, would accept the same penance as it demands from its own adherents. Let the old sinner bow his head, as it is written, and admit his guilt before all the people. That is the beginning we need! The Church on its knees before the people—those very people whose innocence it abused for its own ends. The Church must beg forgiveness for its sins. On its knees willing to suffer for the truth—the truth it has suppressed—for justice, which it has blinded. It must kneel, in other words, in abject remorse and beg forgiveness for its past! Only then—and not a moment before then—can it expect to gain the trust of those who really are the guardians of life and the light that never dies."

*

At Kærsholm, the days slipped by in the kind of rustic invariability that makes time so transient and life so short. Sunday had already come around once again and Lord Prangen and his entourage traveled down to Bøstrup church in time-honored fashion to hear Pastor Blomberg's sermon.

After what Per had said following the folk festival, Dame Prangen felt justified in her assumption that he would join them. In a way, Per was not averse to attending church—not least because he would presumably see Inger once again. But, at the same time, taking part in a formal Sunday service with all its psalms, Our Fathers, blessings, standing and sitting was a step too far for him. He had received Jakobe's letter the previous evening and its impassioned tone, he had to admit, had affected him and made him unsure once again.

When the carriage had driven off, he suddenly felt very alone at Kærsholm. He went out into the garden and walked up a landscaped embankment at the edge of the park, which offered a view of the surrounding countryside. He sat down on a bench and looked out over the area.

All around—near and far—church bells were calling the people to prayer. In the still morning air, the tones carried for miles across the forests, hills and meadows. He could even distinguish the church bells at Bøstrup from the rest. Nor did they call in vain. Out on the main roadway, which arched around the estate, a stream of carriages and vehicles carrying farmers and their families, all dressed in their Sunday best, could be seen heading towards Bøstrup church. Per followed their progress until they disappeared beyond the steep slope of Borup hill. When the last carriage disappeared over the horizon, he felt that all of life had been extinguished right across the land— as if the people had been wiped out and he was the only man left alive.

He remembered this Sunday morning alienation so well from his younger days—a feeling he had not had since the day he walked into the Salomon household—a world where no church bell rang. But he felt no sense of longing whatsoever for Skovbakken. His thoughts quickly returned without any pang of grief to that procession of happy and brightly dressed country people. The salt of the earth who were decorating their day with gladness.

One after the other, the bells subsided. Still, and ever more strongly, he was gripped by an awful feeling of desolation. The faint sound of a carriage dying away on some road he could not see magnified the eerie feeling he had of being on the other side of an invisible veil. He felt like a dead soul, who in the realm of shades could hear life's hurly burly passing over his grave.

Once again his thoughts returned to Jakobe's letter. He now knew what reply he would give to her. This solemn and tranquil morning; all these farmers and rustic types in their best clothes and spruced-up carriages; the thousands upon thousands of homes all over the world from which a stream of humanity poured on this day—all heading with utter conviction to church in order to gain renewed fortitude and strength in the struggle that was their daily lives. Here was life's own resounding protest against her words. It might well be, he would write, that the Church had terrible sins on its conscience—and he too thought this was so—but these were strongly counterbalanced by the good it had bestowed upon mankind. At any rate—as Pastor Blomberg had correctly explained the other day at the folk festival—the Nordic peoples, in fact the Germanic race as a whole, had particular reasons for showing Christianity, at the very least, a modicum of respect. After all, it was those missionaries for Christ that had liberated them from barbarism. They had, so to speak, formed the spirit of the tribe from day one. Christianity was the North's spiritual and intellectual breast milk, which could never be completely weaned from it blood.

But what need was there anyway of historical proof? It was precisely that point that had struck him so forcefully on that fateful night crossing across the Kattegat sea—that Christianity must have provided a new source of human willpower, since it had given his poor old, crippled mother such mighty reserves of self-sacrifice. While it was true that the Christian belief in a fatherly, all-loving God was nothing more than a sweet dream, it had in his mother's case, and in millions of other scenarios, proven its worth for mankind's wellbeing. But why should he doubt this anyway? Did he not personally feel more strongly, with each passing day, the impossibility of keeping up his spirits without help from a higher power? And did not each passing day provide new testimony from those who had fallen by the wayside in this New Age of the need for a God—a heavenly shield and comforter?

Amongst those books and weekly periodicals that Dame Prangen had regularly passed on to him, Per also found a copy of Povl Berger's *Jacob's Struggle*, the pamphlet he had heard so much about while he was in Copenhagen. Now he had read it from start to finish. This extensive confessional tract, which had been written in a consciously stylish and Old Testament way, had moved him greatly. In one of the strophes, Povl Berger took direct aim at the intellectual spirit that had come from abroad and had gained dominance in the country— not least via Dr. Nathan's influence. He compared this spirit to spring showers that not only brought nature alive but also encouraged weeds and sterile corn to proliferate across the land, giving the barren soil a deceitful appearance of abundance and fertility.

"But when the heat of summer comes and then the autumn rains swell the harvest—whither are ye then oh rootless intruders who flounced along every roadside and cast a thousand colors across the land, like some harbinger of the delights of Paradise? Alas and alack— your withered and barren stalks pronounce their own judgment. That same sun, which bestowed the light so that you could bloom, also dried you out and before the harvest came the storms did blast you hence—because the wages of sin is death. All praise to those who prefer to humbly sink their roots in the ancient and fertile hallowed soil during spring's season of growth. From here doth our eternal life source ever spring!"

It was these words in particular that had taken root in him, to the extent that he knew them off by heart. The first time he read them he felt that he was reading his own gravestone inscription. Because it was precisely that kind of intellectual and spiritual atrophy, that barren produce, he felt he had suffered in recent years—a gradual, inevitable dissipation of his power and abilities. He had just never been able to admit it to himself.

"So farewell, oh bleak and desolate times! My wandering in the desert is over. The portals of Paradise have opened for me and, blinded by their light, I kneel at their glorious threshold in repentance and supplication."

Per bowed his head and placed it in the cup of his hands. He sat still for he knew not how long and asked himself whether by this stage it was nothing more than false pride that stopped him from becoming reconciled with the God of his ancestors. Was the truth not rather that he could not bear admitting his pig-headedness and acknowledging a higher power, whose existence he had previously denied? Humility! Here again was one of those weighty Bible words, whose life and death significance he was only now beginning to understand. To be humble was the last and biggest hurdle he had to face. It was heaven's reward for the peace that was bestowed upon the soul when he first came into the world.

Per lifted his head. The faint sound of bells could still be heard from the church at Borup, which was the nearest church to Kærsholm. The distance was no more than two kilometers—he could still make it down there he thought.

He remained sitting another few minutes. But then he stood up resolutely. In haste now he began to make his way through the garden and surrounding park.

He succeeded in reaching the church, before the pastor had ascended the pulpit. Standing just at the door of the arched entrance, the strains of the psalm being sung drifted out to him and he stood to listen.

He found that his inner agitation was not due to the need to worship, or even to prostrate himself. Even as his hand closed around the weighty door latch so as to lift it and walk in, Per thought again. Standing on the brink, the need to will himself to enter came over him. It was as if he had to question his conversion in order to see it through.

He sought a space on the bench nearest to the door; and when he was finally seated and the people scattered sparsely around the church had satisfied their initial curiosity by turning occasionally and looking at him, he soon regained his composure.

Nor was this a gathering that was suited to maintain Per's sense of a momentous occasion having taken place. The pastor was standing at the altar wiping his nose with some diligence. His back was turned to the congregation, which in all consisted of a dozen or so people—primarily older people who did not display any great signs of inspiration. The male side of the house was particularly depleted. Nor was the psalm singing any help in whipping up devotional fervor. Apart from the parish clerk's voice, only a pair of wailing old wives' voices were to be heard. The interior of the church was a low structure that put one in mind of a cellar. There were large damp patches and streaks of green mold on the walls, which lent a sour smell to the whitewash paint. A layer of chalky dust covered the pew in front of him.

But now the pastor ascended the pulpit, and it was only at this moment that Per realized that he would be hearing the words of the infamous Pastor Fjaltring for the first time. There he stood, up under the blue-painted and carved vault—a handsome, pale man with regular features and silver gray hair that had been water-combed back and away from his forehead. There was nothing of the diabolical in him that Per had assumed he would find. His face was smooth shaven, his mouth broad with finely sculptured lines—and his eyes were dark and imposing. His body movements were measured and calm and his bearing refined except that every now and then—or so it appeared—a stab of pain seemed to pass from his shoulders and across his face.

After a short introductory prayer, Pastor Fjaltring picked up the altar book in order to read the day's text. But when he discovered Per's presence in the church at that same moment, he stopped and looked at him in clear surprise . . . until he finally realized that he had become distracted and began the day's reading.

Pastor Fjaltring's sermon lasted for nearly an hour. His address was delivered in the usual preacher's tone and contained nothing beyond conventional church rhetoric about sin and God's mercy and redemption, before returning once again to sin and the eternal fires and anguish of hell. Per became more and more impatient. His heightened disposition was irrevocably shattered. He realized now that if he had declined to go to Bøstrup with the others, he should have just stayed at home.

His relief was immense when the service was finally brought to an end and he got the chance to slip out quietly. Embarrassed with himself and highly disgruntled, he took off in the direction of Kærsholm. He felt shamed to the core at this unexpected and disastrous outcome to his first church attendance as an adult and vowed never to reveal this to anyone.

Feeling the need to kill time before the return of Lord Prangen, he went up to the farm overseer's room for some distracting gossip while he smoked his pipe. One of the rustic habits he had developed here at Kærsholm was a taste for long pipes with large bowls that could be smoked for an hour or more without having to be refilled. He had just such a "smoke machine" hanging on a wall in the farm overseer's room, which was still his preferred place of lunchtime retreat.

"Tell me sir—what do you have against Pastor Blomberg?" Per asked in an attempt at treating the subject lightly, and only after they had spoken of other things.

"Me?"

"Yes, you—I seem to mind that you once made a quite cutting remark about him."

A broad grin broke out from the farm overseer's blond curly beard.

"Far be it from me to say anything disparaging about His Reverency! I am not that daft."

"But you did say something as I recall."

"Well, I suppose I might have just been wondering out loud how he could abandon his poor old father to rack and ruin."

"Is Pastor Blomberg's father still alive?"

"He is surely. Over on Zealand somewhere. And he is in rag order by all accounts. Both mangy and lousy. I really think now that Blomberg could do the decent thing and start looking after his father in his old age."

"Well is there something wrong with his father which makes that impossible?" Per asked. "Maybe he's a hopeless drunk? Or maybe Pastor Blomberg just doesn't have the money to look after him."

"Blomberg doesn't have to watch his damn pennies. He knows

very well where to go should the need arise. Because he knows that people in this parish hang on to him like a baby at its mother's breast."

"How do you mean . . . he knows where to go if he needs to?"

"Well, just like last year when he needed two new carriage horses. He leaves a few words here and there saying that on account of his children he simply could not justify staying in the area any longer and would have to obtain a ministry in a more affluent parish. So, of course, his parishioners were horrified and there were collections and donations and before ye know it, he not only has two new horses but a Landau to boot. And he barely thanked them for it afterwards. He seems to think that folk owed it to him. Have you heard what Pastor Fjaltring calls him?"

"No, what?"

"The merchant priest of Bøstrup."

"What's that supposed to mean?"

"Well, I'm not sure, Sidenius. But—strangely enough—I think it suits Blomberg down to the ground."

Per sat in silence for a while and watched his pipe smoke drift to the ceiling.

"What do you think of his daughter?" Per inquired at last.

The farm overseer grinned once more.

"What I think of her is that she is obviously a pretty girl."

"Nothing more?"

"All right then my man. Let's say she's a very pretty girl."

"Would she be of premium value? Isn't that the expression you always use?"

"Well, since you ask—I would say that Frøken Blomberg is a bit too stuck up for her own good."

Per frowned darkly at this. He found the farm overseer's sarcastic tone extremely annoying today. The man was obviously more spiteful than he had first understood. His description of Pastor Blomberg was no doubt pure character assassination without any basis in fact.

At that same moment, Lord Prangen's carriage could be heard swinging into the courtyard. Per got up and went out without saying goodbye.

Dame Prangen received him in the sitting room with a cry of joy.

"Hr. Sidenius, you've no idea what you missed today! Pastor Blomberg's sermon was simply wonderful."

But Per was not listening. For by her side stood none other than Inger. And his surprise and joy at seeing her again was so great that he was overcome with shyness.

"And now, the dining table awaits us!" Dame Prangen said as she slipped her arm around Inger's waist—shooting a look at Per, as if to purposely inflame his jealousy. "My husband has already gone in."

Unusually, it had taken some persuasion to get Inger to come to Kærsholm. After the return from the folk festival in the forest, her mother had spoken to her about Per in a way that was clearly designed to warn her off. Thus, in order to reassure her mother, Inger insisted to Dame Prangen that she be brought back home before evening set in. The pastor and his wife also ruled that they would personally come to pick her up in the run of the afternoon.

The only reason that she could bring herself to visit Kærsholm at all while Per was still there was to retrieve the gloves she had forgotten. She had not been able to summon the courage to send a message for them, but absolutely had to get them back. The thought that she shared a secret with a man she hardly knew—that something belonging to her was in his possession, lay perhaps on his table, or had been kept in his pocket as some sort of secret sign of a shared intimacy had tormented her.

Nor had she been left alone with him for more than a couple of seconds, after lunch was finished, when she blurted out her request.

Per looked at her for a moment. The truth was that he had thought about asking her permission to retain the goods that had been entrusted to his care as a keepsake, but now it would be impossible to make such a request. Her face was set and determined and, as he had noted before, there was something in her disposition that put a kink in the smooth-tongued gallantries he was wont to come out with.

So he bowed gravely and went to fetch the gloves from his room.

When Per got back and found that Inger was still on her own—as soon as lunch was over, Dame Prangen had made herself invisible—he made so bold as to suggest a stroll in the garden. Inger hesitated for a moment, but decided that a refusal would be impolite. However, she made sure that the arc of their walk never went so far from the veranda that Dame Prangen could not see them when she returned.

It could not be said that they held a conversation as they walked; they were both far too occupied with their own thoughts for that to happen. The moment Per had seen Inger, he realized that he had fallen in love with her, and this made him cautious, and withdrawn, almost severe in his demeanor. For her part, Inger was thinking of something Dame Prangen had said during their carriage ride back to Kærsholm about Hr. Sidenius being in such bad form this last while. There was no doubt, she had said, that his depressed state was related to his ill-starred engagement. On a couple of occasions during lunch, Inger had looked over to him and it did indeed seem to her that he looked in bad spirits. This left her feeling really sorry for him. She could not think of anything more terrible than being tied to somebody you didn't like, perhaps didn't even respect.

"Do you not think, Frøken Inger, that the air would be a bit fresher out in the field there?" Per asked as he stopped by a gate in the garden fence that led out into open countryside. "The air is so oppressive here under the trees today. I can see that the flies are annoying you as well."

This last point was very true and Inger made no objections. Dame Prangen had faded into the background; indeed Inger thought no more about her. Besides, there was something in the sophisticated "man of the world" deportment and the cool politeness with which Per opened the gate and stepped aside for her that she found irresistible.

They came out on to a small field of grass that sloped gently down towards the meadows. The wind had begun to pick up somewhat. In the distance, a swirl of dust could be seen flitting backwards and forwards on the main roadway. The clouds had dispersed but the air was still heavy with heat.

"This heat's very draining isn't it," said Per. "Would you not like to sit for a while? The grass is very dry here. And this spot catches the breeze nicely."

Inger, who remarked to herself that she actually was a bit tired, reacted warily to the suggestion but in the end chose a spot at the edge of the field. She sat down, tucking her dress beneath her and ensuring that it covered her ankles as she did so.

This delicate and chaste movement affected Per's burgeoning love for her like the soft puff of breath that brings a smoldering fire ablaze. It was only at this moment that Per realized how strong and deep his feelings for her had already become—how forcefully her bright, pristine maiden figure had gripped his imagination.

She sat quietly with a straw in her mouth, looking out across the meadows. She had tied her large soft straw hat down around her ears, so that it encircled her head more like a bonnet. She had done this because of the rising breeze, but was, of course, not unaware that it suited the shape of her face. Her own father had once said half-jokingly that with her hat arranged that way, she only needed a stave bedecked with flowers and a little white lamb on a lead and she would be the perfect princess disguised as a shepherd girl—and Inger was not one to forget those kinds of recommendation.

Per had sat down at a slight distance from her. He forced himself to look beyond Inger to what he was doing with his life.

I have to leave, and preferably immediately, he said to himself. I'm not going to make an idiot of myself by falling victim to a hopeless infatuation.

After they had seated themselves, their conversation had come to a complete halt. For Inger's part, this had not happened because she was worried about being alone with him; she was no longer affected by a guilty conscience—in fact she felt that her mother had done Per a dishonor in warning her about him: his behavior was the height of gentlemanliness. But at the same time, the whole situation was so daring and new for her that she had the feeling of floating above it all.

Per began to entertain her with stories from his travels, a thing he would do when he was lost for any other kinds of words. But Inger was not really listening. She had again begun to think about something Dame Prangen had said about him. And that was that he was no doubt a ladies' man and it was this passion of his that had led him astray. She took these words to mean that, quite apart from being extremely rich, his betrothed was also glamorous and beautiful—and that was how she had always imagined her. She did not know why, but she could not believe that Hr. Sidenius would have courted her just for her great wealth.

Per had once again sent stolen glances at the woman beside him. She was still sitting with a grass straw in her mouth and looking out across the meadows and their carpet of flowers. She had bent forward slightly and lifted one of her knees a touch so that she could rest her arm upon it. Her eyes were half closed and peering somewhat against the sun.

"Am I boring you, Frøken?" Per asked after a period of silence.

She gave a start, as if his voice had called her back from somewhere. She also reddened visibly.

Then they heard a carriage moving along the driveway to the castle.

"That can't be your parents already?" Per cried with some alarm.

"Indeed it is," she said and got up. "I'd better get back."

However, Inger showed no particular haste as she walked back through the garden. She even stopped at the gate when she spotted some lovely daisies and plucked a few to keep.

There was a hint of deliberate disobedience against her mother in this action. But first and foremost it was an expression of her deeply felt integrity. As far as she was concerned, there had been nothing improper in their walking together and she was therefore not of a mind to conceal from her parents the identity of the person that had escorted her.

Per did not follow her inside. Right then he had no wish to be obliged to exchange pleasantries with anyone. They parted at the steps of the veranda and he went straight to his room, which could be accessed through a separate entrance at the gable end of the house.

He paced backwards and forwards across the floor of his room to try and think more clearly. Now he really had to get away from Kærsholm. But where to? Could he go back to Jakobe after this? Was it not his duty to openly admit that he had fallen for someone else? And then what?

Did he really have the option of breaking with Jakobe and her family? He was in dire need of more money. He had to have money! Horrible, stupid, dirty money! He had abandoned his plans to raise a sum of money from Lord Prangen. There had been one occasion where he had not exactly directly requested a loan; but he had referred to his money problems in such a way that Lord Prangen was bound to understand his hidden purpose.

Per stopped his walking for a moment and looked out from one of the windows. His clasped hands lay heavily behind his back as he stared at the halo of light adorning the dark mass of leaves in the chestnut tree.

At the very least, there was no doubt that he had to go back to Copenhagen. And here another thought struck him—his relationship with Jakobe was threatened from a different quarter in that very city. For he would, of course, meet Nanny once more. And then what? It was true that Nanny had not occupied his thoughts much while he had been at Kærsholm, but subconsciously she was still there. On more than one occasion he had woken in the night, his head weighed down with sensual dreams; and to his shame he had to admit to himself that it was Nanny's pale arms that were snaked around his.

The kiss she had flung at his lips in such a wanton manner that day still coursed in his mind and blood and he had no good grounds to think that his powers of resistance would be more reliable the next time around. When he thought of her and the way that she would come to greet him with her too obvious wiggle, her cloying, lascivious she-cat coquettishness—full of promise and smiling, her gaze looking slightly askance like a shameless caress—it was as if he could already hear her silk underwear whispering to him with bold intimacy, that with her he would find succor for the anguish of the love he dare not name.

He placed his hand over his eyes as if reacting to a crushing blow. Like a series of dark waves, he saw the coming days rolling towards him and in the end closing over his head in a great wash of noise.

He turned away from the window and once again began to pace the floor with an unsteady gait. His hands had again come to rest on his lower back. His head lurched forward slightly—there was something tired, feeble, and defeatist over his whole demeanor.

Over on the table lay an opened book. It was Povl Berger's poem— it was this book to which he was continually drawn, because it seemed to interpret his own spiritual and intellectual crisis at that moment in a way that astonished him.

He lifted the book, threw himself down into one of the large armchairs and then opened it where a page marker had been left. He began to read aloud:

"I am like the hungry man who refuses sustenance—the sick man who will not accept the cure for his malady. Behold, it is evening and the winds have eased and yet my heart is full of foreboding. I sit on the crest of a hill and watch the sun as it slowly sinks into the sea. Like a great golden bell it fills the air with a clanging sound as it hangs over the mirror of darkening blue. Hark, it rings a heavenly tone! It heralds a choir of angels! Why do I not bow my head? Why do I not clasp my hands in prayer? What stops me from falling to my knees and crying: Father? This is still beyond me. And yet I think; indeed I know it, because my soul has told me this—that in God alone there is salvation. Truly, I say to you, if you feel your life is a withered vine, joyless and barren, he will bestow great bounty and abundance upon you. If your heart is tortured with the burdens of each passing day, he will transform the world's ponderous yoke upon your shoulders to wings that will lift you from all sorrow."

Pastor Blomberg and his wife had only intended to pay a flying visit, but Dame Prangen was able to persuade them to stay for dinner without much trouble. Prior to dinner, it was decided that they should take a walk in the fields to look at the corn and general crop situation.

Inger went along as well—unusually for her, she stayed by her mother's side, even taking her arm for most of the tour.

Per had still not appeared and neither Pastor Blomberg nor his wife had made any reference to him. Though this was by no means because he was not in their thoughts. In fact, Per's continued residence at Kærsholm had become something of a talking point in the district as a whole. The local gossip was that this young man had attained a position of great influence at the country estate, not just with Dame Prangen and the baroness, but also with the squire himself.

This was increasingly proving to be the case and there was a particular reason that this was so: for several years, Lord Prangen had pondered the idea of reclaiming a substantial area of marshland that lay hidden between the hills on his land. On one occasion, during an after-dinner coffee chat, he had raised this issue with Per and had told him that it was now his intention to get the local surveyor out to the area in order to measure and mark out the terrain and its contours. Eager to seize the opportunity to do some work and also to offer recompense for the hospitality he had been shown at Kærsholm, Per had offered to carry out this work himself, and Lord Prangen (who was enough of a farmer to see where he might save a few shillings) was delighted to accept his offer.

The necessary measuring equipment was already to be found on the estate and, in the run of a few mornings, the extensive mapping and surveying work was completed.

But during this work, Per had got the idea for a more general reclamation and watercourse realignment project—not just for Kærsholm's land but for the surrounding meadowlands, which would encompass several thousand acres. Half-jokingly—but also with the idea of getting support for the venture by way of the loan that was effectively refused—Per had sketched out a proposal for Lord Prangen who, despite often being somewhat slow on the uptake of things, quickly saw the advantage in such a plan. With the abundant inventiveness Per had developed from his own natural abilities, and which in fortuitous moments gave him the spark of genius, he had seen that with a few dexterous adjustments to the course of the river he could create the conditions whereby the area's groundwater level could be lowered by several inches. This would result in the transformation of large stretches of putrid and swampy marshland, at a relatively modest cost, to fertile arable and pasture land.

But with a slyness that was a trademark of the Prangen line, Lord Prangen was, on the face of it, completely dismissive of the whole idea, even though he was in fact so gripped by the proposal that he could barely sleep at night. The more the squire of Kærsholm thought about the idea, the better he understood what it might mean, not just for his own estate but for the whole district. And the thing that particularly attracted him to the idea was that, now he came to think on it, he himself had come up with a very similar idea not that long ago. Thus, if the project became a reality, and proved a success, he could claim all the credit.

At the precise stroke of six o'clock, people were called to the table by the drone of a loud gong. But in general, this dinner occasion followed the same informal approach that was a feature of life at Kærsholm. In spite of the fact that Pastor Blomberg and family were visiting, and that it was a Sunday, Lord Prangen sat at the table with his usual tight-fitting, short overcoat with pleats at the back and a high-necked shirt and collar. And while it is true that his wife came to the table wearing a silk dress with many puffed elements and tassels, it was all too obvious that it was an old dress, no good for anything else. Not even the table decor could be said to be particularly ceremonial, as it was not quite proper. There was not so much as one flower on the table, and the glasses and porcelain dishes could only be described as humble.

Lord Prangen spoke very little at the start of the meal but this simply meant that he was wolfing the food into him. He also drank a large quantity of wine. What was more, he entertained himself by secretly filling Pastor Blomberg's glass every time the pastor turned away or was distracted. The inevitable consequence of all this was that the faces of the two elder statesmen at the table became quite flushed, and as the baroness, who was otherwise abstemious in the extreme, had already displayed a suspicious glow through her makeup as she sat down to dinner and had "allowed herself to be persuaded" to down a couple of sherries, the volume levels around the table began to rise noticeably.

Sitting in the backwash of all this liveliness, Per was allowed to sit quietly with his own thoughts. Only Inger could not fail to notice his peculiar state of distraction. She had (much against her will it must be said) been placed alongside Per at the table. Given that her father was on the other side of her, she was, so to speak, responsible for his entertainment. Right opposite them sat Inger's mother, who surreptitiously followed their every word and move, at least until her husband's increasingly high spirits diverted her hawk eyes to her new target.

Per's preoccupied air aroused an involuntary mirth in Inger. She had no idea as to the reasons for his altered state and she could not help but gain an almost childlike amusement over his clear difficulty in doing even the simplest thing like passing her the salt cellar or receiving the preserves from her. For the whole of the first part of the meal, Inger was highly animated and the tip of her tongue was frequently engaged in that little movement of hers where she graced her upper lip just before smiling.

But then it occurred to her that, since they had last met, he may have received some kind of unpleasant news in the post—perhaps even from his fiancée. From that point on, the tip of her tongue was not revealed anymore.

Right near the end of the meal, and to the general shock of those around the table, Per stood up and called people to order by tapping his glass. He then requested a moment of their attention as there was something he wanted to say. He wished, he continued, to use the occasion to express his extreme gratitude for the outstanding hospitality he had been shown at Kærsholm, even though this went far above and beyond what could be reasonably expected and also that he had abused this largesse by staying far too long.

"Good God, you are not leaving, Sidenius?" Dame Prangen interrupted, with a look of horror and with a fleeting glance at Inger.

"Unfortunately Dame Prangen, I must! I dare no longer ignore the call of duty, which comes from the other side of the Atlantic

Ocean! Besides which, my fear is great that I have used up what currency I had to the good here in terms of the patience of my hosts."

"Oh rubbish! How can you even say that! You're staying and that's that!" Dame Prangen cried with no little animation. Her outburst received a hoarse echo of support from her husband whose reactions by this stage were somewhat slurred.

Per showed his thanks with a bow of his head, but then continued: "As excruciatingly difficult as it is for me to leave this place, which has become so dear and like home to me, I have no choice but to insist on my departure. It is, I am afraid, unavoidable. But I could not, in all conscience, take my leave of you all without making clear that I will always treasure the memories from my stay at Kærsholm—and if I may say so, my gratitude and affection is no less for those at Bøstrup rectory. In particular, I would like to express to Hr. Pastor Blomberg my sincerest thanks for the enriching and edifying conversations we have had, whose effect on me I will not describe in detail here, but please rest assured that they will never be forgotten."

This last reassurance notwithstanding, Dame Prangen was devastated. This was not the ending she had either planned or imagined. His departure would, of course, have to be stopped. She would speak to him in private about this later on. She was not going to simply admit defeat in her battle to win this soul for the Blombergian creed—a triumph she had worked night and day for, and for so long. Only the achievement of a Pauline conversion here at Kærsholm would fulfill her role as Pastor Blomberg's apostle. And she had in her possession the very thing that would make that happen, she thought to herself, as she cast a new and loving gaze towards Inger.

Per's speech had made a good impression on Inger's parents. Fru Blomberg even softened towards him somewhat. Instinctively, she became less hard on him now that she had the reassurance of his imminent departure.

When Per had stood up to speak, Inger almost collapsed with nerves. What now? she had thought to herself. His dark introspection at the table had gradually made her more nervous—she had become gripped by the kind of fear one feels when standing next to a loaded cannon. However, when she realized that he was going to make a short speech, she was immediately reassured, because at least this explained his severe distraction. But then, of course, she became the victim of a new bout of anxiety. Her heart was in her mouth during the first part of his speech in case he should dry up or get a fit of nerves—and a wave of sweet release ran through her when she found that he was the height of diplomacy and chose his words well and with taste.

Per's actual declaration did not surprise her in the least. She had long understood that he could leave at a moment's notice. But she was sure that it was some kind of letter from his fiancée that had provoked his sudden decision to leave. Perhaps he had even been summoned back to Copenhagen. This Jewish lady obviously had him at her mercy. Poor man! His face showed no great urge to go back to the capital and see her again. Inger's heart went out to him. But at the same time, she found it hard to understand how he had just launched himself into a situation that could never be anything other than torture for him. The explanation could only be that his betrothed, quite apart from being stunningly beautiful and very rich, was also a sly fox—just as that class of society lady always was. She remembered how Dame Prangen had once hinted that Hr. Sidenius had blundered quite innocently into that relationship. No doubt, he was a bit naive in that regard.

Dame Prangen now bade her guests *Velbekomme* after their thanks and praise for the food, and all rose from the table.

Per bowed ceremonially to Inger, who responded with an apparently casual nod of the head. But she then turned quickly about towards her father—quite against her usual cautious grain—threw her arms about his throat and kissed him.

In the midst of the general post-prandial contentment, nobody really noticed this highly unusual outbreak of affection. Her father patted her head gently and he too let out a hearty "Velbekomme, Inger, my pet!" Only Per was stunned by this exchange that made his heart stop for he knew not how long, and for a couple of seconds the room began to turn around him.

Never ever had he really entertained the idea that his love for her might be reciprocated. But this fleeting scene aroused an intimation in him that both showed him the way to Paradise and led him to the gates of hell.

Coffee was served out in the garden, where shortly afterwards something occurred that led the Blombergs to depart with no little haste. Lord Prangen had ordered that cognac and liqueurs be brought to the table and though the pastor ruefully admitted that he had already partaken more than was good for him and firmly refused any other refreshments of that sort, Lord Prangen blithely continued pouring into his glass and furtively pushed the tray towards him. When he then noticed shortly afterwards that the pastor's glass was once again empty, Lord Prangen chuckled inwardly—in his own tipsy state, he was not aware that in the course of the conversation he himself had knocked back both glasses. In the end, his mischievous delight was so enormous that he let out a number of very badly suppressed sniggers and laughs while his blurred and hooded eyes sought out Per so as to find a colluding witness to his triumph. But Per—who had also abstained—neither saw nor heard, what was going on around him.

The Blombergs requested that their carriage be prepared and Dame Prangen, who was mortified because of her husband's carry on and knew exactly how it might all end, made no attempt to hold them back. The pastor was incandescent with rage. The only reason he chose not to say anything was because he had once, many moons ago, sworn that he would at all times overlook Lord Prangen's inadequacies and moral defects. He had made this decision first and foremost out of deference to Dame Prangen. However, as the practical man he was, the importance the people of the area placed on his role as a kind of prophet for the Prangen estate was not lost on him either.

The servant announced that the pastor's carriage awaited at the main entrance.

Dame Prangen and the baroness had already gone into the house. Inger had stayed away from the coffee table altogether. She had gone for a walk, deep down to the bottom of the garden, under the pretext of searching for four-leaf clovers but in reality because she could not bear the thought of having to talk to anyone. She now reappeared and was obviously in great haste to be away.

Though Per helped her into the carriage, she gave him no acknowledgment in either word or deed. Nor did she give him her hand to bid him farewell, even when her mother and especially her father had wished him a genial Godspeed.

As the visitors disappeared into the night, Lord Prangen stood, balanced somewhat precariously on his long, spindly legs, and watched them leave from the top steps of the veranda. Completely elated, he waved a large white handkerchief after them and beamed with satisfaction, because he was convinced that he had seen the priest staggering as he tried to get into his carriage.

Per went straight to his own room. His mind was reeling with agitation and he had to sit down the second he was inside. The room was quite black. Only a blood red hint of light was left in the sky. It seeped through the chestnut trees into the room, leaving its somber reflection on ceiling and wall.

Per collapsed into one of the large armchairs by the table and put his head in his hands. Never had he known such a tumult in his mind. At first he tried to kid himself that he had got the whole thing wrong. He willed himself to think that it was just a ridiculous fancy on his part. But his emotions won out over his attempts at reasoned argument. The very thought that his love for Inger might be returned in kind made him wild with anticipation. It was as if he saw a glimpse of the delights of paradise at the very moment when he was to be plunged into darkness for all eternity.

He pressed his hands against his temples and pushed them towards his eyes. He fought down the lump in his throat and the well of tears that threatened to burst forth. Truly, the hour of his scourging was upon him! God's judgment had been handed down! Cain's banishment to the desert—his mental torture was the hell that had been prophesied for him! But he could have no complaints. With full complicity, he had sold his soul to mammon and idolatrous gods. That pact he had made in his search for fame and fortune was the Devil's own charter. And the Dark One had paid him in abundance just as agreed. Gold and riches, great acclaim and the pleasures of the flesh—all manner of worldly delights spread before his feet. All he had to do was reach out and they would magically appear!

He jumped up, tearing at his hair and shaking his head. No, no, no! God could not be so pitiless. So far into the maelstrom of sin and debasement he had not plunged. He acknowledged that he had gone badly astray—and was ready to take his punishment for this. With cold and determined deliberation, he had sold the price of serenity in his heart and soul, sold his mother's love, his father's blessings and approval, the very birthright of his being. In truth, he had sacrificed his whole spiritual and intellectual bond with his own land and people on the blood-spattered altar of avarice and puerile vanity. And not only that! His reckless hunt for this perverse illusion had cast a blight upon other people's lives—he was a direct cause of grief to his parents and consternation to his brothers and sisters, a disappointment and embarrassment to his friends and those who wished him well. Jakobe, too, he had deceived!

He could no longer ignore or defy these excruciating pangs of conscience. He sank to his knees at the edge of the bed and hid his sobbing face in his hands: "God! Oh, God! Yes, yes, I know! I deserve all this torture! All of it! Every last bit!"

Over the rest of that evening and long night, Per broke decisively with his past and prostrated himself before the God of his ancestors. He was awake the whole night while he examined his life, what he had done, what he had failed to do, and increasingly accepted the deep remorse he felt. The profound awareness of his sinfulness engendered the humility he had refused as recently as that previous morning after he had left the church service. And from this, finally, came the release of heartfelt prayer.

It was only as the dawn appeared that he found a semblance of peace. Thus, when the servant came in with tea, he had finally fallen asleep.

His first thought on awakening was for Jakobe and the letter he now had to write to her. For this too had become abundantly clear to him during the night—it was now his absolute duty to break a liaison that could never produce anything other than heartache and constant uncertainty for both parties. There was no need for any kind of long-winded explanation. Jakobe's last letter indicated clearly enough that she anticipated the final end to it all—in fact probably desired such an outcome in her heart of hearts.

As soon as Per was dressed, he sat down at the table and gathered his writing materials around him. However, the act of putting his confession down on paper proved far more difficult than he had imagined. With regard to the presence of God in his life, and when it came to put pen to paper, he could not give any sort of comprehensive explanation; it was all still too new for him and had to remain his sacred secret. He sufficed with general statements on their lack of an agreed life philosophy, without which no contented life together was possible. Moreover, he wished her to truly believe that it was only after a long inner struggle, and with a heavy heart, that he was now tearing asunder a bond that had been so precious to him.

Per rewrote the letter several times before finding it acceptable. Wishing to avoid the risk of causing Jakobe any further and unnecessary offense, he chose his words with the greatest care and accepted complete blame for the aberrational behavior that had brought them together in the first place.

Later on that morning, once the letter had been dispatched, he went to join Dame Prangen, who was sitting with her embroidery in one of the summer houses. She immediately gave him a length of yarn she wished to reel into a ball, and after they had spoken in a somewhat desultory manner for a while, Per could no longer suppress his urge to announce the bald truth that he had broken off his engagement.

Dame Prangen congratulated him on this and said that it was only what she had expected.

"And what are you going to do now Hr. Sidenius?" she asked after a brief silence. "You thereby walk away from an enormous dowry, do you not?"

Per answered that his new circumstances would of course affect his standing drastically and alter the course of his life. Amongst other things, there was now no question of his going to America, at least in the foreseeable future.

"Well, that is a sensible decision if I may say so. The very idea of that trip never appealed to me. You've done enough gallivanting in the last year or so. Do you know what occurs to me as a good idea, Sidenius? I know you have discussed this proposal for draining part of the land around here . . . an adjustment to the river, or whatever the proper term is. As I understand things, my husband is very taken with your proposal and there is therefore every chance that it can be realized. Would the idea, therefore, of carrying out this work not appeal to you? I mean, settling down here and working on that, at least until some larger project came along? After all, young man, you like the area . . . and you have friends here who would be only too delighted that they were going to keep you here."

Per's eyes widened at Dame Prangen's choice of words. They could only be a frank admission of Inger's feelings for him. Dame Prangen was her confidante and she would hardly propose such an arrangement if she thought that Inger would rather never see him again.

In purely practical terms, the proposal suited him very well. The kind of reclusive lifestyle that was in prospect was precisely the thing he needed if he was going to find the inner peace for which he searched. The income earned from his work would also be very welcome. It was, of course, a point of principle for him that he would repay his debt to Philip Salomon as quickly as possible.

"So, Hr. Sidenius, assuming I have your permission," Dame Prangen continued, "I shall speak with my husband about all this. And as it is probably best that you do not become involved in things, before the various interested parties have come to a final agreement, you have my blessings, young man, to leave us for a short while. As I say, I have no reason to doubt that things will go swimmingly and that your return will be sooner rather than later."

Per then resolved to leave the following morning.

However, he would not go directly to Copenhagen. He felt a great urge to divert his journey via his hometown, so as to inaugurate his new life with a visit to his parents' grave, as if to convince his own self of the sincerity and seriousness of his change of heart and mind. Simultaneously, he made another decision with regard to something that had occupied his thoughts for some time. The thought that he was not in possession of a professional qualification had begun to seriously prey on his mind. He knew that probably the greatest charge his parents had laid against him was that he had not completed his course at the National College of Engineering. Invariably, the first thing anyone would ask him once they heard he was an engineer was whether he was, in fact, a graduate of the college in Copenhagen. He now saw very clearly that without an official declaration on paper, which confirmed his professional expertise, he would never be able to secure the kind of fixed and secure position that he now required so that he could work on his inventions and theories with full peace of mind. It was particularly the case now, when he was no longer dazzled by the Salomon family's millions, that he should have the kind of prestige a professional certificate would give him.

Thus, in order to, as far as possible, make amends for his past frivolity and irresponsibility, he resolved to sit the chartered surveyor's exam, or, rather, sit the supplementary examination which he was allowed to do because he had already completed half the course at the college. This exam would qualify him as a highways inspector and statutory land surveyor. With an almighty effort in the period to come, Per reckoned that he could sit this exam within six months, and payment for this, and his daily upkeep, he would try and secure via a loan or advance from Barrister Hasselager, or one of the other businessmen who were happy to back his plans.

In the afternoon, he went for a long walk in the surrounding countryside, so as to take his leave of the area. The weather had been stifling for the last few days and the predictions were that it was to break. The skies were leaden and in the northwest the sun was a ball of bulging red fire in amongst the black clouds, like a vast candle that had burned down to its stump.

A heavy downpour ambushed him while he was standing at the brow of a hill, from which he had a clear view of Bøstrup church and its rectory. The first thing he felt was some heavy drops smacking onto the crown of his hat. He looked up and, at that moment, a cracking, rattling sound rent the air and the clouds were split by a blue flash of light that seemed to rock the ground beneath his feet. Moments later a deluge of water began to fall, as if a great sluice gate had been opened in the heavens. Trying to run to escape the storm was pointless—the distance back to Kærsholm was too great. Thus he sought shelter in one of the half-open barns that were dotted around the meadows and were used for hay saving. With the pulses of rain hard on his heels, he ran across the field and just managed to find shelter before the next peal of thunder clapped him about the ears.

It transpired that he was not the only man to have sought refuge in this place. Deep within the shadowed recesses of the barn, he discerned a tall, thin man, who wore a gray coat and whose head was covered by a soft, broad-brimmed and old-fashioned hat with a high crown. It was Pastor Fjaltring.

Per greeted him with no little surprise in his voice and some words were then exchanged about the weather. The priest was clearly put out by this encounter. He stood the whole time partly turned away from Per with his broad hand constantly passing across and rubbing his chin—that instinctive movement men have when they seem to regret not having shaved. Gradually as Per's eyes became accustomed to the dark of the place, he did indeed notice that Pastor Fjaltring's chin and cheeks were covered with several days of festering beard growth. All told, this man of the cloth looked slovenly and decidedly scruffy. With particular astonishment, Per studied the pastor's head; it was completely wrapped in some kind of black silk scarf, which could be seen peeping out from beneath his hat at the back—something that obviously caused the pastor severe embarrassment. At any rate, he had only made the slightest pretense at lifting his hat in response to Per's greeting, even though he was otherwise the height of courteousness.

Out in the west, the clouds were electrified by a new lightning bolt, and a few seconds afterwards, the earth was shaken by another mighty thunderclap.

"I think that struck over in the direction of Bøstrup," Per cried, somewhat anxiously.

"The young man is not exactly a stranger to this area—I can hear," the pastor said.

"Well I've been here a few weeks, Hr. Pastor."

"Am I also not wrong in saying that I saw you in our church at Borup?"

Per now formally presented himself and explained that he was a guest of Lord Prangen and family at Kærsholm.

"Yes, I think I heard that. You are an engineer, Hr. Sidenius. Isn't that right?"

Per confirmed that this was so.

"Indeed. We live, of course, in an age where the technician reigns supreme. The truth is, however, that this so called 'technician' is nothing more than a Jack of All Trades, to use the everyday speech of our folk," the pastor continued after a short pause. "It comes as a shock that railways and steamships have already done much to shrink the planet on which we live; even our own sense of wonder is diminished. The distance between countries is reduced by the day, and will presumably be completely negligible in the end."

"Presumably, Hr. Pastor."

"Perhaps we will even be able to reach both the moon and the stars with our machines... this is no longer a physical impossibility, and then the universe will be as familiar to us as our trouser pocket. But the distance between our nose and mouth will never be changed by all this," he added after another short pause.

Though he tried not to, Per could not help but smile at this. He also pitied the man, who gave the impression that he was slightly disturbed.

They then switched to talking about the weather again; the suddenness with which it had blown up, the barometer gauge that morning and so on. But when all this had run dry and the rain continued to batter down, the pastor turned once again to the hegemony of the technician in modern times.

"There was talk around these parts not so long ago of pushing a railway through the parish. In this day and age, it seems that there has to be a rail track running past every home. And I don't think they've completely abandoned the idea."

Per answered tersely that time-saving innovations in public transport were a vital necessity in any modern society.

The pastor considered this statement for a while. He was still standing with his body half turned away from Per as he looked out at the rain.

"A vital necessity," he said with a peculiar smile that blanched his lips. "Well, what hasn't become a vital necessity in our day, Hr. Engineer? Doctors and engineers, teachers and soldiers—take your pick. I pray that we do not go the way of certain apoplectics who die from a surfeit of blood, though we Danes are hardly first in line where that danger is concerned. We are obviously still trying to get back what we lost in '64."

"Get back," the pastor said again slowly as he continued to stare straight ahead with a gaze that offered fleeting reflections of the lightning flashes that still plumed in the clouds to the west. "I believe that we are still in the throes of, and kept sane by, the powerful spirit that was called forth in the people in those days of trauma. There really was at that time a moment when we almost realized that there are no other vital necessities than the mercy that only Our Lord can grant to us."

With some reticence, Per replied with the old phrase from the Bible: "The Lord helps those who help themselves." But the pastor shook his head.

"God's help—that is actually no help at all."

"But, pastor, we survived the crisis at that time."

"Who told us that this was with God's help? If we were to draw conclusions from what has come to pass in this country since those days, one would rather think that it was the Devil who came to our aid."

Per found it pointless to engage this half-mad creature in deep discussion. But there was something in his condemnation of the New Age that pricked at his newly restored conscience and he once again felt the urge to express his convictions.

Per said that the unwavering trust in God amongst the Danish people had fortified them in their darkest hour and had created heroes from the lowest and weakest ranks in society (here Per almost wept at the thought of his mother's sacrifice). That rock solid piety had not left them when peace was restored but had actually proved to be the primary force behind the country's rebirth, outside the capital at least.

But the pastor broke him off with a scathing rejoinder that a word like piety could never be used to describe today's Christians who peddled the lie that one might take Our Lord by the arm, engage him in market day chit chat, and pat him on the head when done with him; or when passions were roused high enough with hallelujahs, throw one's arms around his neck like a hysterical child. In a clear reference to Pastor Blomberg, he poured scorn on "our folk school and kindergarten Christianity" that was fast becoming Denmark's national religion, whose nursery-room language and poetic mawkishness was, of course, tailor made for a people such as the Danes who even in their religion preferred to be spoonfed with fairy stories and overblown verbiage rather than face the spiritual realities of suffering and passion.

"You mentioned the war earlier, Hr. Engineer. Aye well, you are probably too young to remember those days. Otherwise you would, like me, think back every now and again with a touch of longing on those momentous times and the pale anxious faces of our people. Anyone who has experienced those days ... anyone who witnessed that courage born of faith, that willingness to sacrifice all, that euphoric acceptance of possible martyrdom, which the Ragnarok fear that was abroad at that time engendered in even the feeblest mind ... well, they would understand ... or at least would have a sense of what our folk spirit might have developed into. It can only be a cause of regret that the threat which was made at that time to exterminate us from the roll call of nations was not acted upon. Now we can only wait until God in his infinite mercy wipes out the whole Germanic race into which we Danes will no doubt soon be swallowed up. Because the soul of a nation has exactly the same properties as that of an individual human being—its final liberation only comes with death.

In the distant past, it was the spirit of the ancient Greeks that prevailed in the minds of men as God's chosen herald. Then came the tribe of Israel with its sheep, lamb, and shepherd wisdom and we were obliged to listen to that as if it were a direct message from God himself. And then it fell to the Germanic peoples and their Nordic cousins, with our Lutheran barbarisms, to supposedly lift a corner of the holy veil and reveal the eternal truth that lies beyond."

Per was taken aback by the words of the pastor, who, when realizing this, stopped speaking—almost as if he was worried or regretted that he had allowed himself to stray too far into the territory of unguarded comment. He also left the barn very shortly afterwards. Despite the fact that it was still raining heavily, he bade a terse good day and hurried off into the deluge.

Even at the dinner table that evening, Per was still preoccupied with this meeting and he quizzed Dame Prangen at length about Pastor Fjaltring. Amongst other things, he wanted to know about the strange headcloth the pastor wore under his hat.

"Apparently, he suffers from neck pains," Dame Prangen explained. "And he is convinced that he has a large growth in his brain. All in all, he is a pathetic wretch of man."

22

JAKOBE had locked herself in her room. She was sitting by her small writing bureau with her head resting on her hand and looking out through the window at the trees in the garden whose crowns were swaying in the strong wind. Her eyes were wide and glistening, her chest heaving. In front of her on the bureau lay Per's letter, which she had just received in the late morning post—a four-page missive in fluid and stylish handwriting that was devoid of mistakes. In purely calligraphic terms, it was a minor masterpiece. She had only read the letter twice but already knew it off by heart.

She did not know what she should pity him most for—the stress it would have caused him to compose all those carefully constructed words and turns of phrase, or the complete hypocrisy he used to conceal, both from himself and from her, the real cause of their schism—that he could, right to the very end, show such a lack of backbone and ability to look the truth in the eye! She would have given the world and the stars just to see him, for once, stand up and admit honestly and openly that he had fallen for someone else. But no! His troll spirit was too deeply ingrained in his flesh and blood to be shaken off. He could never quite conquer his fear of the light. That was the true "Sidenius" part of him—that his natural feelings had to be sugar-coated so as to hide the bitter darkness within. Just as the supposed national significance of his project was used to mask his vanity and selfishness, religion would now serve as a cover for his essential timidity.

Enough! She stood up, put her hands to her head, and pressed her hair down resolutely until her hands reached her cheeks. Why should she wrestle any longer with all that nonsense? She would now accept that her thoughts and desires would no longer dwell on him. They need no longer traverse those gloomy and sinister places where his spirit thrived. She was free. The line was drawn over her blundering forays into affairs of the heart. Her pathetic attempts at romance were over.

All that was now left was to inform her parents. And then away from this place! The ground now burned beneath her in her urge to be gone. In all probability, Per would come back to Copenhagen to organize his affairs, and the last thing she wanted was to bump into him in the street. It was also the case that she could no longer hide her condition. She had a feeling that her mother had once again begun to suspect something and she was not ready for that conversation—at least not right then. For that reason she resolved to leave the very next day. She had already prepared her "flight," and there was no reason to wait.

Then it occurred to her that she would catch her mother alone right at that very moment. Rosalie had gone off swimming with the smaller children and her father and Ivan had gone into town a good while since.

Her mother was down in the sitting room working at her sewing machine and surrounded by a mountain of linen sheets that needed sewing or repaired.

"Always busy, little mother," said Jakobe as she kissed her brow. "If it's not the accounts, then you are stuck into some other huge task."

Her tone immediately made Fru Salomon suspicious. But without revealing anything to her daughter, Fru Lea stroked Jakobe on her cheek and said: "Yes indeed my girl, work was my generation's way of coping with life. And I still think, by the way, that it is really the only thing we have."

Fru Lea then returned her foot to the treadle and the machine began to whirr again.

She had taken to wearing spectacles while working—overall, she had aged considerably in the last year or so.

Jakobe wandered about the room for a while, browsed through a newspaper, put it down again, and then plumped down into an armchair not far from her mother.

"Mamma," she said, "remember I mentioned the other day that I'd love to go down to see Rebekka again in Breslau? I really think I'd like to do that now. But I've used up most of my allowance for this year already. Would you mind asking daddy for a top up."

"Oh, I'm sure I could," her mother answered rather hesitantly. "When are you thinking of going?"

"As soon as possible. Tomorrow perhaps."

Fru Lea stopped her machine dead and looked directly at her daughter.

"So you'd be traveling on your own?"

"Yes."

"What about your wedding?"

Jakobe had bent her head forward. She could not bear to look into her mother's eyes, which had grown so terribly large and black behind the clear glass of her spectacles.

"Well mother—the thing is," Jakobe said, as she repeatedly clenched, then opened her hands. "I may as well say it straight out right now— the engagement is off."

There was a lengthy silence.

"So that's why you've been behaving like a hermit this last while?"

"Was I? Then you'll all have to forgive me."

Her mother got up. She went over to Jakobe, took her head between her hands and lifted it so that they looked at each other.

"Is there anything else you are hiding from me, my child?"

"Now mother, you've no right to ask that," Jakobe said with tears in her eyes. "Anything to do with affairs of the heart should not be spoken of—you yourself taught me that."

Jakobe's mother stood for a moment, unsure what to do or say. She then put her hands down, moved away to the other end of the room and then turned to Jakobe.

"How much money do you need?" she asked as she fussed at things on tables and chairs. It was as if she could no longer find enough peace within her to sit down.

Jakobe mentioned a substantial sum.

Fru Lea looked at her again: "So you intend to be away for some time?"

"That's the plan mother. You can imagine that it won't be exactly pleasant for me here at home after what has happened. A broken engagement is a wonderful opportunity for gossips and scandalmongers. It cuts me to the quick that I have left you and father exposed to all that unpleasantness—but I know you will forgive me."

"Jakobe, you also know deep down that we were never exactly overjoyed with the relationship. But at the same time we thought that—" Her words trailed off when she saw the flash of impatience in her daughter's eyes. They now began to discuss practical things regarding Jakobe's imminent departure and the things that she would need.

As soon as Jakobe got back to her room, she began organizing the last of her things that needed packing and put aside those things that were to be left behind. Much of this had, in fact, already been done. Sometime beforehand, and without arousing attention, she had prepared herself for this new departure from the family home, which was more than likely the last of its kind. Amongst other things, she had carefully organized all the letters from her girlfriends, written the name of each individual sender on the top and then packed and sealed them, so that they should not fall into the wrong hands in the event that she never returned. She now did the same with her letters from Per. And when she wrote the name Sidenius on the top of the package, she managed a smile in spite of her doleful mood. At least now she would be spared having to bear that awful barbaric name!

Shortly before dinner, she was called downstairs by her father, who awaited her behind closed doors in his study. He kissed her in silence on her forehead then immediately started to talk money. The words Per Sidenius were never uttered.

"How much do you think you will need?" he asked as he pulled his diary towards him at his desk.

Jakobe mentioned a sum that was a good bit less than the amount she had quoted to her mother. She could not face more questions about how long she intended to be away.

Her father said nothing and immediately entered an amount into his diary that was double what his daughter had requested.

"I'll provide you with a credit note tomorrow morning."

At the dinner table, Jakobe made great efforts to be cheerful and, in truth, she was also happier and more optimistic than she had been for a long time. That strangulating fog which her doubts and suspicions had thrown around her spirits was now disappearing. If she could only rid herself of the feeling that in leaving she was moving towards the end of her life, she would otherwise have felt almost happy.

But intimations of death had imposed a daunting grip on her sensibilities. Like a freezing fever, her death fears sent stabbing ice pains through her soul every hour of the day. It was also for this reason that she could not reveal anything to her mother. The last thing she wanted was that she too would be laden with worry. Jakobe's hope was that her outward cheerfulness would allay any suspicions.

Both her father and mother also gave the impression of being quite calm. Ivan, however, made no such pretenses and was clearly devastated. The same Ivan, who normally was to be found speaking of twenty things at a time in between mouthfuls, did not say a single thing during the meal.

When the table was finally cleared, he went into his father's study and found him at his desk, already busy writing something.

"Am I disturbing you?"

"No, you've come just at the right time son. I was just about to send for you. Was there something you wanted to say, Ivan?"

"Ah, the same perhaps as you. I have received a letter from Sidenius—a few lines just—relating to his and your pecuniary relationship. He requests that I inform you that it is naturally his intention to pay back the money he owes you. All he asks, he says is, ahem, a period of grace."

Philip Salomon said nothing in reply. He simply could not bring himself to allow the name Per to cross his lips.

"I actually wanted to talk to you about something else Ivan," he said, as he took hold of the note he had just finished writing. "Will you do me the service of taking this into town straight away. And make sure that it is printed while you wait and as quickly as possible. As you will see, it is a formal announcement to our family, friends and business associates—you yourself can work out how many copies will be needed on your way in. But the whole thing must be done and dusted, Ivan, so that they are received by everybody no later than tomorrow morning."

The note carried nothing but the following words: "Philip Salomon and his wife Lea hereby announce that their daughter Jakobe's engagement to Hr. Engineer P. Sidenius has been annulled."

On the same evening as this news spread at breakneck speed around the Salomon household's circle of friends and associates, Per was sailing back to Copenhagen after spending a full day and night in the town of his childhood—a town still surrounded by large expanses of quiet meadowland.

Recognized by nobody and without himself seeking to find any of his old friends, he had spent the whole time there in the company of nothing but his memories. And this time around, he reacted in a much different way to when he had been there after the death of his father. No longer did he find its provincial modesty, crooked streets, and dingy shop fronts in any way comical or a source of pity. During the intervening period, his eyes had been opened to his unbreakable attachment to his place of birth. Indeed, as he had gradually moved to the point where it was his childhood memories that informed and developed his adult sensibilities, he now had to admit that the town had taken on an almost spiritual aspect in his life. From Berlin and the Tyrol mountains, from Rome and Copenhagen, his thoughts had often made a pilgrimage to this tiny corner of the world, to which all the strands of fate in his life came together and melded into eternity. Per came to realize that, for him, this little town with its rolling meadows and high riverbanks was both his gateway to the world and the terminus via which everything was returned to it origins.

That said, it was with no little hesitancy that he began to walk the town and seek out the places he remembered so well. In particular, it took him a long time to conquer his reluctance to enter the side street in which the rectory lay. His clear willingness to humble himself notwithstanding, the demons that hovered over his past still held too much sway over him. He could not get beyond that running tapestry of dark memories that came to his mind unbidden whenever he thought of that looming, decrepit building with its strange entrance like a prison gate. Not even in the church cemetery at his parents' grave would the expected sense of filial gratitude come upon him. In fact, the sight of the memorial stone, which the church congregation had raised at his father's grave, aroused the last remnants of old defiance in him.

It was not that he once again wished to wallow in the shadows that had plagued his life from childhood; but he could not help but reflect on how things could have been so very different if his father and mother had not been so rigid in following the prejudices that prevailed at that time—including their religious preconceptions. For there was no doubt that he could well have avoided many of the pitfalls and shameful blunders if, as a child, he had been cherished by the kind of gentle and humane concept of God that had now opened his heart to life's essential emotions. Moreover—and this was the hardest thing to bear—nothing could now be done to alleviate the loss he felt so keenly. Those feelings of loneliness and neglect he felt at that very moment would stay with him for the rest of his life. Regardless of the direction his future would now take—yes, even if that quiet hope of a love reciprocated he had felt as he took leave of Bøstrup rectory was fulfilled—there would always be an undeniable void in that place where most people held their most treasured memories. For no man was in essence poor, except he who did not have rich and happy childhood memories to sustain him.

When, in the evening, Per returned to his hotel and sat in the café eating a selection of *smørrebrød*, something of great moment occurred. Along with his evening meal, the waiter had brought him a selection of newspapers, including one of the town's own newspapers whose name and shape he remembered from his days at the rectory. For this reason, he looked at this first and on the front page was an extensive "Letter from the Capital" column that brought the latest news and controversy from Copenhagen. In amongst the news of the Royal Family and theatre gossip, reviews from entertainments at Tivoli Gardens and circus acts, he read a strange report on a "notorious suicide" in high society. According to reports, a young and ambitious man, a dashing former cavalry officer, had killed himself on the grounds of an ill-starred and fateful romance. He had—the article continued— loved, and believed himself to be loved in turn, by a young, newly wedded lady who came from the capital's Jewish finance aristocracy. However, on returning home with his hopes and expectations dashed after a lovers tryst with this lady, he shot a bullet through his head.

Per's face, while reading this, went first hot red and then ghastly white. The fact that no names were given in this report and the fact that he had not heard of lieutenant Iversen's death was irrelevant. It was obvious that he and Nanny were the people being described here—Nanny, whose naked arms had been wrapped around his own neck not so many weeks ago! With a feeling that a snake was slither- ing down his back, he read the rest of the article. In keeping with modern custom in reporting, the bloody details of the suicide were painstakingly described. The conscientious reporter left nothing to the reader's imagination when describing the blood-drenched floor where the corpse had been found, nor in his description of the sofa from whence the gore had dripped; the white table cloth that had become a butcher's apron because of the scattered mass of brain de- posited there; then the suicide note itself, which was reported in such a way that, while meticulously observing privacy laws, managed to satisfy the general public's demand for lascivious scandal.

Having suddenly lost his appetite, Per retreated upstairs to his room. As was his wont when agitated, he walked up and down for some time but could not shake off his astonishment. He was ready to faint at the thought of how near he himself had come to falling into this wretched woman's snare—that it could just as easily have been him who was the victim of some salacious journalist's pen, if he had not, just in time—yes—just in time!

He stopped dead in his tracks. It was as if all this opened a gateway into the depths of his soul and, as the light flooded in, hundreds of half-forgotten images from his former life flashed up before him like animated shades. He saw himself that night in the long ago when he had fled from Fru Engelhardt's boudoir gripped by a feeling of disgust at the pleasures that whoredom and licentiousness can bestow upon a man. Another image came—even further back in time, when as a young boy he had been tempted by that black-eyed tiger of a gypsy girl from Riisager's yard, but had been saved at the last moment by the fierce shame he had felt upon hearing the corrupted child's brazen words and gestures. And many other occasions came to him, where he would have become the victim of his own ruination if not for—well, if not for the fact that in his heart of hearts he had borne an instinctual aversion to sin and perversion—and, it had to be said, if not for his parents—and particularly from his father and standing behind him the centuries old line of priests—who had remained quietly but steadfastly true to those life-affirming forces he had, in his youthful arrogance, presumed to defy. The "Sidenius" legacy, which he had denounced as his life's curse, had actually proven to be the protective amulet, the blessed talisman, he had at all times secretly carried with him—the thing he had to thank for not having gone as far astray as he might have.

But this innate liberating power—this drive for self-preservation in the soul, that obviously worked quite independently of all the different creeds and dogmas—what was it other than God's own spirit working in man—the "holy spirit" of the Bible, each Christian's guiding light and guardian angel, which step by step had guarded his passage through life and delivered him safe from all anxiety and evil?

He had sat down by the window in his room, which looked out over a deserted laneway. He was a few storeys up and could see a maze of red-tiled roofs and white chimneys, beyond which the sun was just beginning to set.

It was as if it was only now he could really take in what had happened to him over the last few days. Yes, of course, he had become open to Christ's message once more while staying at Kærsholm, but that had not been due, in truth, to much more than the call of his worried conscience rather than an undeniable message from his head and heart. Only now in these moments did his faith come to him as a blinding light of revelation that cut through all the distracting fogs of mood, feeling and time. As he sat there with the side of his head resting on his cheek, looking out across the amber evening sky, the great wonder in his soul, the birth of a new man that had been so long in gestation, finally became manifest.

So it transpired that he was after all of royal blood! Life's Crown and Scepter, the filial concord with the eternal and immutable God, had been bestowed upon him from the cradle onward; and all true riches—the heart's contentment, peace of mind, happiness in life and fearlessness in death was the inheritance that had been left to man!

When, the next morning, he went to visit his parents' grave, the dark shadows from his past had been driven out. From that tabernacle in his heart, which he had always believed to be irrevocably barren, empty and dark, the resplendent treasure trove of his noble lineage now shone forth, the golden fleece of faith, jealously guarded by his forefathers from generation to generation, consecrated in the fires of self rigor and fortitude.

He took a seat on the little bench opposite the stone monument, where his father's name—Johannes Sidenius—was engraved in large gold letters. It was a lovely, utterly becalmed August morning that was full of sunshine, and he was completely alone. There was not another soul to be seen, or heard, in the whole of the wall-enclosed cemetery. The morning was shimmering with the myriad of rainbow-colored threads that summer can weave in the air. Hedges and bushes were dressed as if overladen with silver tissue and each flower cup and blade of grass was heavy with golden drops. A slight breeze was to be heard in the highest reaches of the old, towering poplar trees, which formed a broad avenue through the graveyard, but down there amongst the graves themselves not a thing stirred, and the quiet was so deep that it seemed to flow from eternity itself.

For over an hour, Per was able to sit there, quite undisturbed, in a euphoric and ceremonial mood, completely engrossed in the, for him, strange, yet wonderful feeling of being completely relaxed and at peace. Not even thoughts of Inger managed to find their way into his mind at that moment. On the other hand, he did sometimes think of Jakobe. When he himself had found the way to salvation, he was obliged to think of those who knew no counsel for their sorrows. For Jakobe there was hardly any hope. She belonged, of course, to a people that had made disloyalty and willful denial into a whole way of life. But for the youth of Denmark who had been led astray, the time was surely near when they would allow themselves to be gripped by the feeling of a new dawn rising, just as it now radiated and glowed through him. Some prophetic words from Povl Berger's major confessional tract came to his mind: "Dark night has retreated; God's day begins anew with peace and joy for all those who pray. Just as the flock of wild geese that looks and strains searchingly in its long trek over the desolate mountains suddenly sees the blue sea in the distance; just as the exhausted soldiers who, after a daylong march, burned by the sun and white from the dust in the road, throw themselves down at the stream to drink their fill—thus, oh wandering man, shall your thirst be slaked by the refound spring that is God's mercy!"

The break between Jakobe and her fiancé was a huge talking point in the Salomon household's social circle. Even hard-nosed businessmen at the Exchange discussed it at some length. Thus, for the second time in his career, Per became a subject of widespread conversation in Copenhagen, and again because of his connection with the Salomon family. Many asked what transgression this young man could have committed for such an abrupt break to become necessary. For a week or so at least, he won the sort of public profile that he once burned to attain.

Nanny, who had now begun to get over her shock at lieutenant Iversen's suicide, made it her business to be available for widespread consultation on the issue. She had very quickly worked out the truth of the matter and derived genuine pleasure from being able to report that, actually, it was her sister, Jakobe, that poor creature, who had been shamefully deceived. Dressed in a heavenly summer costume, with long, virginal white sleeves, and hanging floral trimmings and a hat that boasted small angel wings, she raced in and out of the homes of friends and acquaintances, revealing the secret, that they must under no circumstances pass on to others—her sister's betrothed, that scum of the earth!, had, instead of traveling to America, fallen in love with a farmer's girl. Imagine! A common milkmaid! With her eyes pointing skyward in mock piety, she quoted a ditty that was well known in Copenhagen:

> He soothed his heart and found his solace
> in her fat arms and sago pudding.

Amongst those who heard the rumor second hand was Colonel Bjerregrav. The old warrior had really been determined to help Per in his battle to push his big project through. In fact, he had decided that, if he were needed, he would personally and publicly enter the fray, so animated was he against the Copenhagen project. But gradually, as the days went by and Per failed to show, he had once again become hesitant. In fact, he was highly vexed that Per had withdrawn from the frontline at the very moment when his presence was absolutely vital. At first, he had regarded Per's behavior as just another youthful outburst of arrogance; but he soon came to realize that something much more serious was afoot, and on receiving this latest intelligence regarding the broken engagement, he became thoroughly disheartened.

In the meantime, Jakobe had quietly slipped away. Even before Per reached Copenhagen from Jutland, she was on her way to Berlin. After her long, prison-like solitude out in the country, even the boring railway journey was a liberation for her; and when in the evening she was driven from Stettiner Bahnhof to the Central Hotel, she actually felt the first rush of elation as the great metropolis took her into its arms like a foaming wall of surf. The wall of people in Friedrichsstrasse illuminated by the fairy-tale lights, the long queues of hackney carriages and their garrulous jarveys, the clip clop of horses' hooves on the asphalt, the brightly lit shop fronts and squares, the stadtbahn train thundering over her head as it left the station—even her huge hotel, where people flew in and out like bees in a hive, while every language under the sun could be heard on the stairs and corridors—all this made her tortured heart burst with an excruciating need to live life to the full once again.

She felt like someone who had come home to her own kingdom. In this seething and brilliantly lit sea of humanity, she felt safe. Of course, she knew very well how much evil lay in that great dark mass, how many poor shipwrecked souls it overwhelmed and buried every day in its slimy depths. She had met at close quarters the lost bands of the poor in the great cities of the world—the pale gray and hollow-eyed destitutes, who made the poverty of their ruddy-complexioned country cousins look like prosperity in comparison. But still! Even the life of such a dispossessed and foundered big city wretch seemed to her at this moment to be a hundred times richer than a farmer's self-satisfied mole existence, and she could well understand why, despite the hunger and misery they suffered, the poor of the metropolis preferred to cling desperately to the concrete pavement until death finally came to sweep them away. A huge city containing millions like this possessed something of the magic of the ocean. There was something of the siren call of the rolling waves in this murderous existence, in this wild tumult, this incessant ascending and descending, which right to the moment of extinction continued to hold out the promise of new and limitless opportunities.

As always at this time, her thoughts returned to the child she was to bring into the world. Her hope was that, were it to take after its Nordic forefathers, it would not be one of those moldy earth types—those hometown fixated peasants, for whom the world, or even just their happiness, ceased to exist once they moved beyond sight of the smoke from their mother's chimney. She would hope that her child, if a Nordic child it be, would be a scion of the wild seas, a Viking character, possessed of the urge to roam and who had inherited the restlessness in her own Jewish blood—instilled with the migratory urge and the kind of ceaseless but purposeful drive that had made the people of her own tribe leaders of men the world over.

Her definitive life philosophy had increasingly become the idea that joy could only be found in struggle—if not for any other reason than that this offered the highest form of oblivion. Life in that sense was exactly like all-out war: those who found themselves in the thick of the action thought least about their own safety and the blood and gore spilling all about them. It was always the milksops and vacillators whose stomachs turned. It was always the pale and insipid face of the scoundrel on which the terror of battle was etched.

23

IMMEDIATELY after his arrival in Copenhagen, Per started to look for an apartment to rent and settle his financial affairs, so that he could recommence his project. His plan was to approach Barrister Hasselager for a loan of some few thousand crowns; that would make his position secure for at least a year. As mortifying as it was to have to go cap in hand to these types, whose profiteering and whole way of life he now despised more than ever, he could think of no other way forward right at that moment. And the problem needed to be dealt with as soon as possible—he was eager to get working again.

As security for the loan, he intended to offer the two patents he had finally secured on his wind and wave motors—one Danish and one foreign. Yes, it was true that no likely investor had signaled an interest in them; nor did he intend to hide the fact that he himself set no great store by them. He regarded his invention as only halfway completed, but he assumed that Hasselager, who had the reputation of being a sly businessman and who also understood to some extent the possible significance of his concept, would immediately see the long-term benefits in providing him with an advance.

Hr. Hasselager, it has to be said, also received him with unimpeach-able politeness, but he had been informed the day before that Per's engagement had been called off and was, therefore, already on his guard. For a while, they discussed Per's plans and ambitions for the future, especially the further development of his inventions, and Per felt the need to push their cause with added enthusiasm. But when he finally came to raise the question of a loan, Hr. Hasselager became even more reticent. Deploying the most polished kind of courtesy that is a byword for the Copenhagen finance elite, he regretfully pointed out that he felt unable to facilitate Per in this regard—as a point of principle, he never entered into loan arrangements for which there was no proper security from a reputable financial institution. This was a point of finance honor which every broker was duty bound to follow, so as to avoid the slightest suspicion of being involved in business transactions that did not bear scrutiny.

Per then asked him whether he thought it might be possible to raise the loan he needed from one or other of the parties who had expressed a strong interest in his project but who were not as restricted by such considerations. To this, Hr. Hasselager, after a short deliberation and in complete bad faith, replied that he believed that possibility did actually exist. This fair-haired, corpulent and blood-rich Dane, who otherwise liked to emulate Max Bernhardt's wild audacity as a speculator and not without some success, possessed nothing of this pale buccaneer's ruthlessness when it came to the spilling of blood; his preference, in other words, was to allow others to administer the coup de grâce. In this instance, he referred Per to gentleman farmer Nørrehave, whom Per had actually thought of himself. Thus, the very next day, Per sought out this arch swindler masquerading as an agriculturist at his villa in the fittingly exclusive Frederiksberg area of Copenhagen.

The portly Jutlander, who had heard the rumors about the broken engagement but tried hard not to believe them, greeted Per's arrival with his most provincial smile and a warm, not to say sweaty, handshake. But Per had not spoken for very long before the man retreated into silence and his small albino-fringed pig eyes began to scrutinize the ring finger on Per's right hand more diligently. The longer Per went on, the wider this oafish farmer's bulk expanded as he slumped further and further back into his gold-studded armchair. In the end, he sighed, folded his arms across his chest and declared that he wanted nothing to do with the matter.

Per's anger was lit by this statement. He reminded the man that it was he who in the spring months, and along with Barrister Hasselager, had proposed a joint venture and in such a form that made his—Per's—approach to him perfectly natural. But the gentleman farmer shook his head dismissively and repeated his statement now in the full glory of his market town dialect: "Tha can be assured, young man, that a' wouldn't touch it wi' a bargepole!"

Per, however, was not of a mind to be just brushed off with that kind of answer and demanded an explanation. To which the country farmer replied with precisely the kind of bucolic bluntness that his partner Hasselager had reckoned with. The "situation" (his favorite word), he said, had completely changed since Per—from what he now understood—was no longer Philip Salomon's prospective son-in-law. In the same breath, he expressed his complete shock over the breaking of his important link with this patrician merchant's family and its business circle; in fact, he felt obliged to ask how this disaster could have possibly happened. But Per stood up from his chair, in a manner that caused the farmer to cease any further inquiry, and said: "Cards on the table, sir. You are actually serious when you say that you will not offer me the loan I have requested?"

Hr. Nørrehave became slightly unsure again after this. For a moment, the young man's belligerent tone reignited the timorous respect Per had aroused in him on the day that he openly defied Max Bernhardt in his chambers. He dropped his fat arms down to the armrests and placed his hands on his belly, which his pudgy thumbs then proceeded to tap. Then he raised his small white-fringed eyes and looked at Per with a calculating stare as he once again weighed the options and risks against each other.

"No," came his reply finally like a hobnail boot. "Not wi' a bargepole would a' touch thon project. A'm havin' nowt to do wi' it."

Almost before these words had left Hr. Nørrehave's mouth, Per grabbed his hat and was making for the door.

Once outside, however, his ire was cooled. He told himself that he really didn't have grounds for much complaint. He too had once joined in that cannibalistic orgy of sacrifice around the Golden Calf. He could hardly be surprised if the beast now bared its fangs because he refused to pay due homage!

But what now? Money he had to have. His cash reserve stood at no more than one hundred crowns.

In his musings, he had wandered into Frederiksberg Park. There he sat on a bench and wracked his brain for a solution to his problem. And as on many other difficult occasions, the inventiveness that was his strength as a technician did not fail him this time either. When he got up from the park bench and made his way home, he had his plan worked out. He would turn to Colonel Bjerregrav, on whom he was due to pay a courtesy call anyway. Though Per had no intention of asking him for money, all the good colonel had to do was be his middle man and then his champion when approaching State Counsel Erichsen, the well-known patron of the arts who, Per clearly recalled, had attended the gathering at the Salomon mansion on the night Nanny and her husband had been welcomed back from their tour of Europe and his engagement to Jakobe had been announced. Uncle Heinrich and others had described Hr. Erichsen as someone who was always keen to support technicians and scientists, even if only to bolster his own reputation. But precisely because he had met this State Counsel in the home of his former in-laws, Per was not in a position to make a personal approach himself. In any case, he could never simply walk up to a stranger with that kind of request.

That very same afternoon, Per was to be found sitting in Colonel Bjerregrav's study—in fact, in that same little easy chair in which he had sat some three years before while explaining his plans for the future with such enthusiasm to the colonel. Sitting at his desk, the veteran officer leaned back in his chair and observed Per from behind his lowered pince-nez spectacles. His gaze expressed a mixture of pity and curiosity. He had already been informed by his nephew, Otto Dyhring, that differences over religious beliefs had led Per to break off the engagement; and while—with God as his judge!—he would be the first to acknowledge the correctness of the underlying motive here, he still looked at Per as if observing someone who had suffered an accident and had lost the use of his brain.

Per began by offering an apology for his failure to reciprocate the colonel's highly appreciated visit and the calling card he had left; but he had—as Per described it—"for personal reasons" been obliged to stay away from Copenhagen for a while.

The colonel received this admission with a poised silence.

Without further ado, Per described his financial problems and explained how he thought he might overcome them. He had good grounds to believe, he said, that if he could count on the wholehearted support of the colonel, he would thereby get the backing of State Counsel Erichsen, as he knew from other sources that representations had been made to Hr. Erichsen in favor of his project.

Even though privately the colonel very quickly made up his mind to avoid Per like the plague, he made promising noises and pledged to consider the matter further and get back to him. He had come to the conclusion that this young Jutlander was probably slightly disturbed and that the best tactic was to humor him before sending him on his way again. And it could not be denied that, just at that moment, Per bore the aura of a man possessed as he spouted such a barrage of words that he barely knew himself the half of what he was saying. The inner struggles he had gone through and the joy he now felt at finally having vanquished his former self had produced a rather naive urge to reveal this new situation to others. He had changed significantly in other ways as well. His skin was sallow and he had lost weight. Deep, dark shadows had also appeared under his eyes. Compounding this effect was the fact that, during his time at Kærsholm, he had allowed his normally immaculately groomed hair to grow out and his beard to flourish, while both in his mode of dress and method of speech and expression, the first attempts to lend a more evangelical air in his demeanor were not hard to detect.

When Per had left, the colonel remained for some time in his chair and fell victim to melancholy reflections. Poor, poor man! he thought—he was clearly heading for some sort of collapse! A young man like him, who had shown such rare ability—yes, it had to be said, even flashes of genius! But if he were honest, he had to admit that he took a certain satisfaction from the fact that, just as with his own youthful ideas of revolutionary nation building, Per had proven not to be the Messiah for the New Age. However, as a patriot and true Dane, he saw that there was really no grounds for rejoicing. At the end of the day, he had actually nurtured great hopes for Per Sidenius and his project. In Per, he had seen portents of a reawakening of Denmark's agrarian and naval dynamism that would at last free the country from the yoke forced upon it by that brood of Jews and other closet Germans which had exploited the nation at its weakest hour in order to seize power by stealth.

The colonel's thoughts finally turned to his sister's son, who had just pulled off a new coup that very day. In order to secure backing from his newspaper, Otto Dyhring had just been voted onto the board of directors in one of the country's biggest quoted companies, a post that would bring him a huge source of extra income without him having to lift a finger to earn it. Soon he would be a member of parliament, no doubt. That Lady Fortune seemed to smile so readily upon this knave and charlatan almost made the colonel doubt the existence of a righteous divine providence. Bereft of physical prowess, completely without moral or religious beliefs, or feelings of patriotism, his nephew seemed able to rise without trace into positions that incrementally increased his prestige, social standing and authority, while the real chosen one, a born leader, who possessed both manly strength and robust health, and was not found wanting in terms of a love for his country, buckled under at the first real test. But it was ever thus in Denmark. Generation after generation had grown up— ruddy cheeked, clear eyed and strongly built. And generation after generation went to early graves bent and broken—a defeated people. It was as if some latent malady usurped the nation's potency, emasculated the best of its youth and left the country wide open to marauding invaders.

Per had rented a room in the home of an old widow in a modest villa that lay in one of the narrow side roads adjacent to the otherwise affluent Frederiksberg Park area. He had chosen this far end of town, not just to be in the vicinity of the Royal Veterinary and Agricultural College, where he was to attend lectures, but also to be as far away as possible from the Bredgade quarter and the many other places where lurking reminders of his past might spring out at him at any moment. His room was a frugal, humbly furnished attic space and, as was his wont, he did nothing to create a sense of coziness or comfort around himself. His only thought was to complete his exam as quickly as possible so that he could get away from Copenhagen.

Trusting completely in Colonel Bjerregrav's promises and therefore convinced that his money problems would soon be resolved, he arranged the collection of his books, drawings and other possessions from the hotel, where these had been stored during his absence. However, for the time being at least, those books and drawings would have to remain unopened in a corner of the attic, as he could not concentrate on anything other than his preparations for the surveyor's course at the college, which began on the first of September. But as soon as the examination was successfully completed and he had regained his equanimity while engaged in that small land reclamation job at Kærsholm, which he fervently hoped would be approved, he intended to get back to his study material and recommence work on his master project. He already had various good ideas for improving his wind and wave motors, and the big advantage he saw in this was that, in contrast to things like his canal project, they could be implemented by him alone and under his own steam. This meant that he was not forced into any form of unwelcome dependency on the likes of Max Bernhardt and Nørrehave, or any sort of partnership with people of that caliber. Once he was back out in the countryside again and adjacent to the coast, he would also have the wherewithal to carry out a range of practical tests, which in the long run could not be avoided. Presumably, he would also have to build a few trial engines, but all these thoughts would have to be shelved in the interim. One of the professors at his new college, whom he had immediately consulted so as to plan for his forthcoming studies, had told him that he would need to put aside a year and a half if he wanted to complete the course successfully. He himself believed that he could do it in half the time. And to rubber stamp this conviction, he invoked the bold war cry of his youth: I will. Therefore it is done!

Thus, Per found himself sitting once more in a poky little room, engaged in a life and death struggle for his future happiness and wellbeing. Just as with his time in Nyboder, he got up in the morning with the factories' morning chorus of horns and sirens, and his little window was invariably the last one behind which a light still burned come late evening in the quiet almost rural laneway on which the widow's villa stood. Even though his goals no longer bore the golden aura of his former fairy-tale aspirations, he plunged into his work with an energy and persistence which far surpassed his previous efforts. Nor was he plagued by the kind of sudden and punishing attacks of despondency that had often ambushed him in the past. In the long term, he did not envisage any huge material gains from his inventions; in fact this had nothing to do with his core motivation. It would be reward enough to know that his endeavors had contributed to the lot of mankind. For him personally, he hoped that his work could secure for him the right to live a normal, happy, and industrious life that ran in harmony with the hopes and desires that reigned in his heart.

However, with regard to his love for Inger, he still could not truly dare to dream of a future together. As often as his thoughts flew to Bøstrup rectory, it was as if they were stopped in mid-flight by a sword-wielding angel. In this matter, patience was the watchword. For that paradise, he was still not worthy—indeed now that he had come to truly appreciate his fall from grace, he wondered if he actually had the right to have such fortune in life. When faced with such innocence and a pure heart, he was obliged to lower his head and look away—that was his penance. He had no choice but to move through life with his hopes concealed about him like a thief with his torch and dared only think of that joyous moment when they would see each other again. Just before his departure from Kærsholm, Dame Prangen had asked him whether he might like to spend Christmas with them. And with a smile that seemed to want to raise his spirits, she added that there was also somebody in the rectory who would be delighted to see him again.

On the first Sunday after his return to Copenhagen, Per decided to attend church service at the Grundtvigian Vartov Church. It was a gorgeous day of sunshine and bright air, and he left his abode in good time so that he could walk the whole way into town and thus save the omnibus fare. But when he came out into the avenue and then encountered the gaily dressed mass of people in the main thoroughfare, all full of high spirits and set on spending Sunday in the nearby park, he jumped quickly into a tram.

He reached the modest prayer house in Løngangsstræde a quarter of an hour before the service was to commence. The church was already full; in fact it was full to overflowing. While many of the ministers in Copenhagen's large Lutheran churches preached in front of half-empty pews, there was always a crush of people at the modest meeting house that was Grundtvig's church in Copenhagen. Of course, a long time had passed since the founder of the church's own voice had rung across this congregation, but his spirit still reigned there, and people from all parts of the country flocked to this hallowed ground, where God had once more revealed himself to his people like the burning bush of yore.

With some difficulty, Per managed to push his way to a standing place by one of the walls. Broad rays of sunshine streamed in through a series of windows on the opposite side and bestowed haloes upon the heads of those standing near the church's center aisle. In amongst this throng of anointed heads, there was one which, unbeknownst to him, regularly turned towards him during the first part of the service. It was only when the second psalm was being sung that Per caught this person's glance. He saw a bright pair of eyes beneath thick conjoined eyebrows, and a shock ran through him as he realized that this was his sister Signe. By her side sat his younger brothers—the twins. The two boys were sat shoulder to shoulder and were following the same psalm book. It was clear that they were still unaware of his presence.

He felt the blood rushing to his cheeks and could barely bring himself to return his sister's almost imperceptible nod. Never for a moment had it occurred to him that he might meet some of his own family here. He had not even considered that by going there he ran the risk of being recognized by anyone he knew. Signe, on the other hand, did not seem remotely taken aback. She nodded calmly once more without interrupting her singing—it was as if, Sunday after Sunday, she had sat there awaiting his arrival.

Immediately after his return to Copenhagen, he had looked up his brothers and sisters at his mother's old apartment besides Gammel Kongevej, but inwardly admitted a feeling of great relief when he found that nobody was at home. He was at a loss as how to tell them that he was no longer engaged and what, overall, had happened to him in his life since then. He dreaded the effect their victory celebrations, no matter how muted, would have on him, and it was this emotion he had first looked for in his sister's face.

The singing ended and the minister appeared at the pulpit over the altar. But Per was no longer able to concentrate on what was being said. This unfortunate attendance at church went no better than his first attempt at Pastor Fjaltring's church at Borup. No matter how much he struggled to gather his thoughts, he once again felt desperately alienated from the whole event.

Even physically, he felt unwell. He had not felt quite himself in recent days. The memories of the stomach pains he had suffered before returned vividly and his sleep had been uneasy and full of disturbed dreams. The oppressive air in the packed church, the sun shining right in his eyes, the stress involved in having to stand for such a long period, and then the stress provoked by his imminent reunion with Signe and his brothers—all this made his head spin. There was a moment during the prayers immediately after the minister's long sermon when he felt he was going to collapse.

The culmination of all this was that when he met with his siblings outside the church at the end of the service, he felt extremely sick. Signe noticed this straight away and asked him what the matter was. In that same instant, the world began to turn in front of his eyes. He instinctively managed to stagger into the porter's lobby where he lost consciousness altogether and slumped to the ground.

When Per came round, his twin brothers led him out to a hackney carriage. He heard Signe tell the driver that they were all going back to the family home and he made no attempt to object. He felt so utterly weak and exhausted that he thought he was going to die. As soon as he was put to bed, he fell asleep.

Some hours later when he opened his eyes he found himself peering into a half-dark, low-slung room with a single window, which had its blind rolled down. It took a moment for him to orient himself as to exactly where he was and he then looked about him very self-consciously. There was his mother's mahogany bureau with its round, bone-white handle and key fittings. They stared at him with wide-shocked eyes. There was the wicker chair he remembered from his father's death room. And the puff stool with its hand-embroidered seat that his mother had always been so fond of. And over there on the mirror cabinet, just as in his boyhood days, lay the big African conch, whose blood-red interior seascape intoned the wild song of the oceans—that spellbinding cascade of noise to which he listened as a child, and which perhaps first aroused his dreams of escape into a magical world of adventures in strange and faraway worlds.

Per breathed in deeply and felt a joyous sense of liberation. Truly, he was at home now! The wild Icarus flight of his dreams was over. He had been returned safely to reality. Now he felt Mother Earth firmly beneath his feet.

The door to the adjoining room was ajar and he could hear his brothers and sisters chatting to each other in there. It all sounded so homely and familiar, so cozy. And then came the sound of a mantel clock striking the hour in the other room—three clear, ethereal clangs of silver metal. How he knew that sound so well! It was as if his whole childhood was revealed before him by some trick of time. He remembered how, as a very young lad, he had listened with reverence to this clock, which dutifully rang out each completed hour, just as the church clock tolled for the dead. As an older boy, he had speculated as to whether it was the soul of the dying hour that was being released to heaven by its clear silver tones. Even after his imagination had moved on from the otherworldly to secular mental gymnastics, these regular, almost somber, invocations of the hour had been able to raise a certain gravity in his mood. In essence, he had never really completely freed himself from this reverence for the march of time. Even when he had matured into manhood, he could not hear a clock strike without feeling that a secret oracle was being brought to him from the depths of eternity.

He began to think of the letter his mother had left behind for him. The whole summer through, it had loomed in his conscience like a huge, fearful mountain that had to be climbed. He had not had the nerve to write to them for it, but had longed to read it nonetheless. Now he felt that he was composed enough to ask his sister for it. He had begun to understand that the fear of his mother's final judgment upon him had acted as a hidden incitement for him in his final battle with the forces of darkness. As if from the other side of the grave, his mother had offered him a helping hand when he took those first agonizing steps on the road to salvation.

He decided to call for Signe to come in to him. But just then he heard the front door bell ring. Shortly afterwards, he heard his brother Eberhard's voice in the room next door.

Per lay for a while listening to this voice that was so reminiscent of his father's. Even Eberhard's footfall, as he paced up and down while speaking, was so like his father that Per got gooseflesh just listening to it. He heard Signe telling him what had happened; and though they both fell to speaking in low voices, he could roughly make out what they said to each other. Eberhard scolded Signe in no uncertain terms for what she had done. The correct thing to do, he said, would have been to convey him to the hospital. It was the only correct procedure when one could not be sure what was wrong with a person. Apart from that, perhaps some kind of infectious disease was involved. At the very least, a doctor should have been sent for.

Per turned his face to the wall. He did not wish to hear any more. For a moment, he struggled with an urge to forget all thoughts of reconciliation. But he forced himself to accept that Eberhard was right. Or at least: now, he said, he should and would complete his act of contrition—the moment when he had to show in deed that he was sincere in his wish to walk the path of penitence.

"Eberhard!" he called.

His brother entered the room and Signe came in shortly afterwards, placing herself at the end of the bed.

"I don't believe any of you need to be unduly alarmed." Per spoke rapidly, as if it was an effort of will to get his words out. "I doubt that there's much wrong with me, Eberhard. I have just been a bit over-wrought this last while. I can feel my spirits returning already."

"Well I must say Per that you don't look too bad considering—" said Eberhard as he offered Per his hand. His tone was completely friendly and engaging. "However, collapsing in the street is always a serious matter."

"Ah, honestly Eberhard, I was just out of sorts—nothing more than that. And I had been stood for a long time with the sun blazing right into my eyes; I've never been able to tolerate that. I feel fine now."

"Well I'm glad to hear it, but I must insist on sending for the doctor. Assuming that he is at home, we can have him here in a matter of minutes."

"Well I suppose if it reassures you all—of course, by all means. But as I say, I don't believe that my little turn has anything to do with an actual disease or sickness. It was just the sun Eberhard . . . and then perhaps the stifling air."

"Hmm indeed, I won't comment on what the real reasons might be," said Eberhard rather dismissively. "But even there, the doctor will be the best judge."

Despite all his good intentions, Per could not help searching for signs of triumph in his brother's demeanor that he feared most of all. But Eberhard was backlit against the light and, far more even than his sister, his prominent under lip was an unchanging leather mask whose sole point of animation resided in his gaze.

Per repeated that, of course, he was happy to comply with their wishes; all he requested was that a message be sent to a Professor Larsen whom he had once consulted after a similar incident.

But this request was met with open hostility, both by Eberhard and Signe as well. They looked at each other, and Per's brother then said: "Per, we have our own family doctor. He may not carry the title of professor, but he has our full confidence."

"Mother would not hear of anyone else," Per's sister added.

Per did not immediately understand their ire. He told them that he would feel uncomfortable being examined by a doctor other than the one who had already treated him and who, therefore, would best be able to judge his condition.

But Eberhard was unyielding.

"I can't comment on what's between you and this Professor Larsen," he said. "But as far as the family is concerned, we simply cannot be seen to demote, as it were, our own doctor, particularly when we are more than happy with him. And anyway, Professor Larsen would presumably not be doing his rounds at this hour of the day, at least not to people outside of his fixed clientele. So even from that point of view, Per, I really feel that—"

But Per now understood that they had interpreted his request as inappropriate vainglory, an attempt to show how much more sophisticated he was, and this cut him to the quick. Now he told them that if they took such exception to Professor Larsen's presence amongst them, he would rather just get up and go to his own home.

When Eberhard understood that Per was adamant in this, he left the room with a dark mien to give the girl orders to call the doctor.

Signe made to follow him, but Per called her back.

"Signe," he said. "You still have that letter mother left me, don't you?"

"I do. Do you want it now?"

"Yes please. It is strange, but I find that I can face reading it in the place where it was written."

Signe produced a bunch of keys from the pocket of her dress. She moved solemnly to the bureau and opened a drawer and then went to Per's side holding a sealed letter and a small package containing their father's timepiece.

Only when Per was alone did he dare look at the letter. His eyes then began to mist when he saw the writing in his mother's own palsied hand: "To my son Peter Andreas—to be read in a quiet hour." After that he broke the seal and read:

"In the name of our blessed Lord Jesus Christ! My dear son. I write as my last act for you before my eyes close forever. My hope is that I can reach your heart. The heart that you have closed. Not just to your dearly departed father, who sleeps in the peace of the Lord, and all others who hold you dear, but also to God the almighty Father and his mercy given through Jesus Christ. I am writing this, even though I have no idea where in the world you are. Unceasingly, you hide your face from us, and I suppose you have your reasons for doing that. Your brothers and sisters seem to think that you are far away from us. Perhaps in France or America. But whatever road you travel, Peter Andreas, you are not on God's road. You have chosen to enslave yourself under the yoke of worldly pleasures and desires. Yet it is written—Woe to him who hardens his heart in the hellfires of spite and sin—for the gospel will be hidden from that soul until the end of time.

"In one of his sermons, your father once said that the life of a Godless man is like that of a prisoner in a dungeon. There is not the smallest speck of light by which heaven's light can break in and offer solace. Nor does it have any other exit, other than a false floor that cunningly hides a bottomless abyss. Oh my poor wretched son! May the truth of this parable be revealed in all its horror to you. May you grasp the truth of scripture—he who lives according to the flesh will certainly die by it. But if by means of the Spirit you vanquish the deeds of the body, you will surely live for ever. May you learn, Peter Andreas, the meaning of dread at what eternity holds for you; so that I may yet have hope that my lost lamb will find its way back to Salvation. That you may turn away from the Dark One and humbly fall on your knees to pray for forgiveness and the cleansing of your sins— so that Jesus did not shed his blood and die in vain.

"There is much that I want to say to you, my dear son; but my hand is weary and my eyes fail me. So let these be your mother's last words to you in all your shame and degradation: Bow your head for the Lord thy God and open your sorry heart so the Holy Sprit can be set free in you by the power of the sacrifice made by our precious Lord Jesus Christ. May the merciful God turn his gaze upon you. So that on the final day of reckoning you are not roused from your sleep of the dead to hear the most terrible words of all: Get thee gone from me, oh unhappy wretch! I know thee not."

Per was still lying there with his mother's letter in his hand when Eberhard came in a half hour later to bring Professor Larsen's reply. At the unexpected appearance of his brother, Per hastily buried the letter beneath his bed cover.

Eberhard remained standing at the door. He was in a hurry and had to leave straight away.

"It was just as I predicted," he announced, with no little satisfaction. "Josephine brings word that the professor sees no need to call out to you, given that he has finished his rounds for today and there seemed to be no imminent danger. However, he's happy to call out here in the run of tomorrow morning, if he is still required."

Per just gave a nod in reply. In fact, he was not even sure, at first, what message Eberhard was talking about. He had not even immediately grasped that implicit in Eberhard's last words was a demand that he should abandon his request for his own doctor. Only when his brother turned around and closed the door more firmly than was necessary did Per become fully alert to the here and now.

He himself could not fathom the grim and oppressive feelings the reading of his mother's letter had provoked in him. He had been prepared for heavily censorious, yes even relentless words, but the overall affect of the letter was to leave him completely cold. His first deliberate thought, after he had read it a second time, was a wish that these valedictory words had never come into his hands.

However, he placed the blame for this disappointment squarely on his own shoulders. He scolded himself for not following his mother's exhortation on the outside of the letter more conscientiously. He should not have read it at a moment when his mind was still in uproar over that spat with Eberhard and Signe. He would now hide it away and then read it again in a "quiet hour," when he was alone and in his own home. For he had also been disheartened by the fact that, first Signe then one of the twins, had found some pretext to come into the room, clearly just to assess how his mother's letter had affected him.

The clock in the sitting room now struck four, and he was already anxious as to how the rest of the day would unfold. Though both Signe and the twins did their best to look after and humor him throughout the afternoon, the truth was that he already longed to get back to the peace and contentment of his own little room.

In the evening, Eberhard came to visit once again. He had still not completed a planned move to accommodation nearer the rest of the family and would otherwise only ever join them for dinner, which was eaten at three o'clock in their household. This had also been his habit when his mother was still alive. Thus, Per was somewhat touched that, despite their quarrel, he had come all the way from Christianshavn just to inquire as to his wellbeing.

For all that, he had still not managed to have a more intimate conversation, either with Eberhard or Signe. He was not even sure whether they were actually aware of his break with Jakobe. A number of times during the afternoon, he had made efforts to steer his conversation with Signe towards this subject; but she had reacted with great unease at every attempt and had quickly begun to speak about other things. Eberhard seemed similarly reluctant to touch the subject. Per got the sense that, their empathy and concern notwithstanding, they were still on their guard with him, and especially disposed to ascribe even the most innocent remark he might make as an attempt to boast about his past life and his eminent connections.

In this regard at least, he was not far wrong. At that moment, neither Eberhard nor Signe had any great confidence in the sincerity of his transformation—to them, Per did not seem anywhere near contrite or humbled enough. They had heard from other sources that his engagement to the daughter of the rich Jewish merchant had been broken off and this had given them great hope; but they knew nothing about the exact details and Signe, for her part, did not want to know anything more, because she wished to know absolutely nothing about Per's life other than that which bound them as a family and as believers.

The following morning, Professor Larsen called to examine Per. This little man with the strangely humble, indeed scruffy, appearance and the barrack-room tongue was peevish in the extreme when he first came in. He would barely admit to ever having seen Per before, and he started off by saying that he himself was unwell and really should not have been making any visits that day. And it has to be said that the doctor's gaunt and washed-out facial color, along with the large dark bags under his eyes, served to confirm his self-diagnosis.

After completing his examination, he became more amenable. He sat himself down by the side of Per's bed and said: "Young man, what is that you really want to know? Your bread basket is taking up too much room in your body and your circulation is sluggish—but I told you all this last time."

Per responded by saying that these sudden attacks of nerves had to have a more definite cause. In general, he never felt sick and he had—it was safe to say—an extraordinarily good and powerful body structure.

"Good and powerful body structure is it sir? A true son of Danish soil—eh? Well I suppose if it makes you happy! However, I would advise you not to put too much strain on that same apparently solid Danish soil. Because it will collapse. I'm sure I told you this last time, good sir. We Danish men with our bloated porridge and mother's soup bellies, we're no good for all this New Age dashing about. We're just like those shire horses used by the farmers—they look fine and they can be very useful for good old-fashioned plodding and pulling, very useful; but put them in a race and they will keel over, poor creatures. My dear man, it's not the width of the shoulders that makes the difference anymore! Or even a pair of well-formed thighs. No, it's the iron in the blood and the phosphorous in the brain, that wins the race in this day and age. And of course a sound arterial and nervous system that's not buried beneath tons of Danish butter, young sir! As I say, don't put too much faith in that constitution of yours. It's more sensitive than you think."

"Just at the very moment when I need all my strength and powers of concentration for my work," said Per, who then asked the professor what would be best for him to reinvigorate his body and system.

But the doctor gave a wry shake of his head.

"Reinvigoration? I know of nothing that can help you."

"But the last time we spoke doctor," Per continued, "you prescribed cold showers, gymnastics, and overall a body-hardening regime."

"Well we have to say something, young man. And that kind of approach can never do any harm. But it would have been better for you if I could have prescribed that kind of regime to your honorable forefathers, may God bless them. For we are now paying the price for all those thick layers of bed quilts, sweaty woolen jumpers, fatty pork, and milk puddings they've handed down to us. And that's before we start talking about how they buried themselves under mountains of books in their study chambers, while they smoked their stinking tobacco. Of course, I'm aware that you are the son of a priest, are you not? I drew that conclusion from your surname, as you would expect. And I know from my own personal experience what the daily fare is like in our idyllic vicarages. These establishments are usually teeming with children and family prayers are stretched out to cover the absence of a four square meal. By the way, did you ever actually take a cold shower on a regular basis as I prescribed?"

Per replied that the conditions under which he had been living in the last while had precluded any regular shock treatment to toughen himself up.

"Oh come on, sir—admit it! You don't much care for the thought of a cold plunge in the morning. And that is quite understandable. It is far from pleasant, when one has not been reared with the practice from childhood. Would you allow me to look in your gob once more?"

Per opened his mouth.

"Ah, thought as much. Nearly all your molars are destroyed! That tells me that you were probably a full-grown man before you were introduced to that devil's instrument that goes by the name of a toothbrush. I myself was over twenty before I met one. Up until then I made do with our ancient custom, handed down from father to son, to rinse the mouth out with nothing more than an Our Father. Well sir, enough of all these old trials and tribulations!" Here the doctor broke off suddenly with a gasp of pain and pressed his hand into his side.

Per would have been seriously outraged by being addressed in this way if he had not understood that he was confronted here with an ailing and pain-wracked man who in his discomfort was not really aware of what he was saying. For the very same reason, he was not unduly perturbed by his pessimistic statements. He saw clearly that the doctor was more concerned with his own condition than that of his patient.

He did, however, ask him one more question. Life in town did not seem to suit him, he said. Did the professor think he would be better off if he moved to the countryside, if this proved possible?

"Why, by all means young man! Put yourself out to grass! That's where we feel most at home. These concrete pavements don't suit our clogs at all. Not in this generation anyway. And probably not in the next either. But do rest up in bed for a few days and try and get your blessed nerves back in balance. I'll also prescribe a spoonful of potassium bromide, a sedative you know, to take in the evening. And then my fellow sufferant, let us allow our bloated intestines a bit more forbearance! We shall hopefully not be needing them in the next life."

Per managed to stay in bed until the next morning, and after one more day in the family home, he went back to his own modest redoubt. Shortly after that, his lectures and practical work began at the Royal Veterinary and Agricultural College, and from then on he disappeared completely into his coursework for the surveyors exam he had vowed to attain.

However, he was not deaf to the warning he had received about overreaching himself. Just as before, his working day stretched to seventeen-eighteen hours; but his work schedule was planned more sensibly. He took regular walks and, in his bachelor-like seclusion, he sought moments of diversion by making observations on the life around him and jotting them down in a notebook. However, he rarely strayed beyond Frederiksberg Park and its gardens, apart from on Sunday, when he went into town to go to church. He still shied away from the eastern end of town and tried to avoid any contact with his former fellow students from the Engineering College, or even anyone he had known in his previous life. On one occasion, while traveling in a tram, he had come to sit opposite someone who had been at the institute at the same time as him. The shocked countenance and nervous smile of recognition offered by this fellow had made Per so worried that he might start a conversation and begin interrogating him that he jumped off the tram at the next stop.

Nor did he strike up friendships with any of his new fellow students at the agricultural college. Now and again he would call out to his brothers and sisters. Eberhard had even come to visit him on one occasion; but no real intimacy developed between them and this was also now Per's own preference. Paying due deference to his nervous sensibilities, he never attended Grundtvig's Vartov prayer house again; rather, he sought out the less popular services where he was sure of being able to get a seat. Besides which, he did not really regard himself as a Grundtvig man. In fact, he was not even sure what this appellation meant in terms of Danish church theology. Where theology was concerned he remained a solitary seeker of truth; and his mother's letter, which he had now read while subject to various states of mind and moods, had only increased his uncertainty and given him yet more food for thought. He had still not got over the consternation he had felt when first reading it. In the end, he had been obliged to force himself not to dwell on it, so as to avoid falling victim to the doubt and anxiety it spread within him.

Autumn had now arrived. The hanging vines had proliferated all over the walls of the villas and large houses, and in Frederiksberg Park, russet and yellow leaves sailed in droves in the canals that were deep in shadow. Per had very quickly come to love this park, which offered him a place of peace and serenity within a hundred paces of his own home. In particular, he liked to go there early in the morning, when the paths and grounds were almost exclusively his own. It was still early enough to catch the freshness of the autumn night that lingered in the air and came to meet him from the large open lawns; the dew lay in a latticework of silver over the grass and mute swans slipped by him across the dark water of the canals. They carried the somber air of fairy-tale princesses that had been metamorphosed by some strange enchantment.

At other times, the park could be very lively, and the passage of people and folk scenes that unfolded throughout the day was particularly vibrant in the avenue running past Per's home. It was as if a visual tapestry depicting all of human life in all its capricious diversity ran before his eyes and aroused his imaginings. First thing in the morning, individual gentlemen and women would appear— mostly older types who, judging by their demeanor, were not there for enjoyment's sake. This was the hour for pensive reflection, when bullnecked society dinner aficionados paid the price for their excess of champagne and cigars the night before, or the overwrought lady vowed, after a sleepless night, to finally end her illicit love affair, for which her unsuspecting doctor had prescribed a rigorous cure in the springs at Karlsbad. But then, of a sudden, a commotion would blow up from beneath the trees. It was the schoolchildren pouring forth from the surrounding houses and filling the side avenues as they made for the park. And from then on the picture would change almost with each hour that was struck. Once breakfast time was over, elderly citizens began to come out onto the streets—evidence of the large number of pensioners who lived in the area, the oldest or weakest of them being pushed in wheelchairs. At the same time, women pushing prams or walking with small children came into view and the park and its environs became a forum where the aged and very young encountered each other and smiles and laughter were usually exchanged to confirm the often idyllic nature of this daylong tapestry of life. A small crowd would also sometimes gather around the little church in the neighborhood—it could have been anything from a christening to a funeral that attracted curious onlookers. Later in the afternoon, it was weddings that caused a stir. When the bridal carriage came up through the avenue with its white horses, even the old and infirm would quicken their pace so as not to miss the arrival at church. But as the last nuptial revelers departed into town, they would often cross the paths of a new procession of carriages going the other way, but this time carrying passengers with waxen faces and utterly somber in their demeanor. These were the low, black, and completely enclosed horse-drawn coaches which, as darkness fell across Copenhagen, ferried the corpses to the chapels of rest in the graveyards west of the city. One after another, carriage after carriage, they came jolting along from hospitals and private homes, either without any cortege whatsoever, or followed by a solitary coach. But at the same time as these bleak conveyances arrived at their final destination, the lights came on in a series of petite bourgeois garden hostelries that ran alongside the white walls of the church cemetery. Cellar bars with locally recruited chanteuses opened their doors; small orchestras with horn sections began to tune up for the expected crowds; fairground carousels threw bright shapes into the evening air; and as yet another life was committed to the immemorial soil, the vibrant and lusty youth of Copenhagen flocked out here by tram and omnibus to chase their hopes and dreams. It was long after midnight before the air became still again. Lights in the avenues around the park were extinguished; and when the last hackney carriage had rolled back into town with the last pair of lovers, reluctant to part, the only sound to be heard was the church bell striking on the rusty keys of the church clock and the occasional plaintive roar of a lion that dreamed of savannah grasslands in its cage at the Zoological Gardens.

These were the observations and mental jottings with which Per entertained himself on his walking tours around the area. In his self-willed seclusion, he had become receptive to impressions of life that he had never known before. Many of the, to him, previously inconsequential aspects of life now held his imagination captive and provoked further thinking.

In the meantime, the days went by and he had still not heard anything from Colonel Bjerregrav. This began to worry him. What little money he had left was all but spent; in fact he had been forced to pawn some items of clothing so that he could pay Professor Larsen. In the end, he wrote to the colonel to remind him of their conversation, and he actually received a reply the very next day, in which the colonel briefly informed him that, after considering the issue more thoroughly, he did not feel in a position to involve himself in the matter that was raised at their meeting.

Per stayed sitting there with the letter in his hand. Gradually, he worked out that he had been hoodwinked. Then he calmly put the letter to one side. He had no real right to be angry with the colonel. Lord Echo always answers in exactly the way he is spoken to! He only blamed himself for trying to get someone else to do his dirty work in looking for a loan. Of course, it was in no way pleasant to have to approach a complete stranger and ask him for money. Indeed, for Per Sidenius in particular, who had always dreamed of being a sovereign leader of his people, it was quite simply a torture to be forced to beg for his very sustenance. But he knew that he had called all this upon his own head. God will not be mocked! He had decreed that Per Sidenius must atone for his sinful pride by walking the streets with his begging bowl. A full penance was to be exacted for this and all the sin and debauchery of his past life.

State Counsel Erichsen had first floor offices at Højbro Plads, in a corner building of the square, looking out towards Slotsholmen canal. Per spent some time walking backwards and forwards on the pavement outside the entrance port. He needed time to compose himself and work out once again exactly what he wanted to say. Again on the stairway he paused before pressing on. Inside a large but poorly lit room, where one corner was cut off by a counter, some twenty people sat writing at big double desks. A young man approached him and inquired what his business was. Per requested an interview with State Counsel Erichsen.

The clerk looked surprised and ran the rule over Per.

Hr. State Counsel was not available at present, he said. He was abroad on business and would not be back for at least two months. Was there anything he could help him with?

Per had already turned towards the exit door. In order not to have to give his name, he rushed off without giving an explanation.

Once he reached the entrance gate, he stood still and looked out across the square. What now? Right in front of him was the gay pageant that was the fruit and flower market, vibrant in the September sunshine. Big-elbowed market women from Amager called out special offers to passers-by as they spread themselves amongst their tables and baskets. The wagons owned by market gardeners stood in a long queue waiting to unload their wares and the air was alive with the toing and froing, verbal altercations, and ribaldry of their drivers. In the midst of all this autumnal abundance, Per was ambushed by a type of terror that had never before been able to threaten him—a terror, not of the degradation of the soul but of the physical body, the affliction caused by demons that stalk the real life world: hunger, cold, filth. He thought about that twenty or so crowns he could still get by selling the rest of his wardrobe. How much time would that buy him? A week, maybe two. And then what?

By sheer strength of will, he shook off his mounting sense of dread and began his long walk home. The harsh inescapable fact was that he had to find another escape route, and he vowed not to fall prey to pessimism. Whatever woes and travails he now faced into, whatever new humiliations that lay in wait for him, he had no regrets and felt no temptation to face about and cast himself once more under the spell of mammon and its secular lords and masters. That the way to God was strewn with tests and trials was nothing new to him; rather, it was something he had learned at the foot of his mother's bed. That he had, nonetheless, been so shocked and terrified by the imminent reality of actually having to suffer for his convictions had to be because he, hitherto, had regarded these words as just rather high-blown rhetoric. Per learned something even more fundamental than this. For he now realized that Pastor Blomberg, who in his sermons and preaching was able to find such sensitive and incisive expressions for the joy and benefits of a life lived with God, completely lacked any persuasive effect when it came to the unavoidable sacrifices and suffering that this also involved. But it was perhaps the case that he needed a reminder, Per grimly accepted, that the words about paths strewn with thorns and bloody feet were to be taken literally. Nor did this strike fear in him, because he already knew that this type of physical suffering would only bring him nearer to God and bring clarity over much of that which now seemed hidden from him. It was the uncertainty that unnerved him and made him falter.

However, sustenance had to be gotten from somewhere, and his thoughts turned once again to Lord Prangen. But no! Anything other than that! Discretion was not a better part of the Prangens' valor, and there could be no doubt that his predicament would come to the ears of Inger and her parents. And what kind of impression would it create in their minds when they heard that his way of thanking the people at Kærsholm for all the hospitality they had shown him was to ask for a big loan? Besides, the result of the strong hints he had already dropped with Lord Prangen were evidence enough that such a request would be pointless, at least until his proposals for a land-reclamation initiative over there were finally approved and a position created for him. So what really were his options? A written appeal to State Counsel Erichsen would almost certainly be a waste of time and he had already tried to get the city works departments to buy his two patents from him without success.

Thus, he decided to bide his time and get through by seeing what he could make by selling, or pawning, the rest of his absolutely non-essential clothing and other valuables that could be jettisoned. He was still confident that the land-drainage work around Kærsholm would soon get the go ahead and, as soon as it did, he would simply ask for an advance on his salary. It was true that in a letter Dame Prangen had sent to him, as a reply to his own thank you note, she had done no more than mention the issue in passing. However, she did say that her hopes were still high that it would go ahead. In the same letter, she had also repeated her invitation to him to spend Christmas with them at Kærsholm.

A few more weeks went by. October came, and still there was no sign of help arriving. But Per refused to give up hope that he would soon see a silver lining in the sky. He almost refused to believe that the good Lord wished to tread him further into the mire. In the end, so that he could stretch his final resources as far as possible, he cut back drastically on his food intake. The key thing was simply to en-dure—at least until his surveyor's certificate had been successfully obtained. Presumably, then, he could get some sort of position and settle down in a quiet backwater as a private highways inspector and wait for things to improve. But without his examination certificate, without money or connections, his only prospect was either to starve or survive by getting unreliable jobs as a day laborer.

The days—now dark and sleety autumn days—passed slowly by and with each one that was survived his anxiety grew. Every morning he was to be found peering through his window, looking out for the red-coated post boy at the time when mail from Jutland might be expected. For it had to be from Kærsholm that salvation would come. He was by now in regular correspondence with Dame Prangen, who was clearly delighted with her role as go-between for Per and Bøstrup vicarage. Not that she ever passed on a direct greeting from Inger, but she did give him clearly to understand that he had not been forgotten by her young friend, and that they often spoke to each other about him. She did also once again mention the proposed land-drainage work, though with increasing reserve in each letter that arrived. She confirmed that a couple of meetings had been held involving the relevant site owners and that her husband had pushed the idea eagerly. "But unfortunately there was lots of disagreement about it," she wrote, "so at the moment things are not looking good."

As if to add insult to injury, in these same traumatic days a registered letter found its way to him; it had arrived via a circuitous route that had taken in Kærsholm amongst other places. The letter was from Rome and had been sent by the young artist who had been commissioned by the baroness to sculpt a bust of Per's head. The sculptor wished to inform him that the marble effigy was now ready and could be sent whenever it was convenient. He also went on to explain that he had already sent a note to the baroness advising her of this, along with a polite request that the agreed fee be sent to him without undue delay. However, to his shock and outrage, he had received a letter back from her Swedish estate administrator stating that her Grace had no recollection of ever having made any such commission, and that, more pertinently, she was not entitled to take such a step without first obtaining the permission of her estate trustees. In the light of this, the sculptor now bade Per, who was the person most acquainted with the background to the affair, to act as his spokesperson vis-à-vis the relevant person and help him recoup the badly needed money he was owed for this artwork.

Per found the reading of this letter painful in the extreme; not so much because of the request itself, but because of the memories it provoked from a time that now seemed to him to represent his deepest ignominy. He reddened with shame when he thought of this bust with its cocky and contrived emperor demeanor; and he wished he could send the man the money he was owed, if only so that he could then order him to smash up this "artwork" and throw the pieces into some place where roadworks were being carried out, as road aggregate was the only thing it was good for. But, for now, he saw no other option than to leave this polite letter unanswered, because an approach to either Dame Prangen or her husband about this problem might jeopardize his own aspirations, upon which his entire wellbeing now depended. The Prangens could very well take an extremely dim view of his meddling in the baroness's affairs; the more so because Dame Prangen herself had never openly admitted to him that her sister was mentally unbalanced.

Another few weeks went by, which brought Per to the end of November and face to face with the final catastrophe. Bit by bit, the remnants of his wardrobe had disappeared; most of his precious books were also sold—even the two diamond pins he had once been given as a special gift by Jakobe (when it had been his express intention to send these back as soon as he could), he had been forced to sell for a pittance. In a few days, his rent was due and he had also built up a sizable debt with the head waiter of a nearby hostelry where he took his evening meal.

Any thought of work was now impossible because he was at his wit's end. It was also the case that his lack of basic sustenance had left him emaciated and weak. For the first time in his life, the inherent rosy glow in his cheeks had disappeared completely. Throughout this whole period he never showed his face at the family home. He was well aware of how terrible he looked and he dreaded their inevitable questions as to why.

In desperation, he had plucked up the courage from somewhere to try State Counsel Erichsen again but with exactly the same result as the last time: Hr. State Counsel had taken ill while on his travels and would not now be home until Christmas at the earliest, he was told. There was now nothing else for it but to take the worst option of all and approach a moneylender—a loan shark. He spent a whole day poring over all the newspapers and scrutinizing the hackneyed announcements in the "small ads" section with which they posted their daily reminders as to where they might be found. In the end, he found a man by the name of Søndergaard—a name which in his ears had something trustworthy about it, mostly because there had been a respectable old pastry woman in his hometown with the same appellation. As he was already aware that one best met this kind of person outside of the normal working day, he waited until the church bell had struck six before starting his walk into town.

Hr. Søndergaard, who preferred the title of "property broker," had his abode in one of the quiet, tight streets near Copenhagen's magisterial courthouse, which people rushing home would take as a shortcut, but without ever registering a street name. Per, too, was forced to ask the way and read the plaques on the street corners before finding the correct street. This proved to be no more than a narrow ginnel, devoid of activity or people and boasting nothing more than a single street lamp, which actually stood in front of the very house he was seeking. Once at the house, Per stepped back onto the roadway so as to look up to the second floor, where Hr. Søndergaard was meant to live. There were only three windows and a light shone in each one of them. It appeared that the man was at home.

A little girl with curly red locks, who was six or seven years of age opened the door. Or rather, she held the door slightly ajar and looked at him from a pair of large blue doll eyes; and when she did not understand what he said asked in her childish way whether the gentleman would like to speak to her father. She then reached up on her tiptoes and released the safety chain before showing him in to a room that was indistinguishable from any other lower middle-class sitting room in Copenhagen. There was a carpet under the table, popular pictures on the wall and then some cheap books and albums and various bric-a-brac on a wall stand.

Per was pleasantly surprised—this was nothing like the cold, austere chamber he had expected. Over by a writing table at the window was a lamp with a shade made of red silk. There was even a picture of an ornately dressed priest and a village church amongst the portraits on a dresser near the sofa. And now in came Hr. Søndergaard himself through the living room—a tall, stocky figure with a reddish-gray full beard. He seemed somewhat uncertain in his demeanor at first. It was clear that he found it difficult to assess this stranger who had remained standing in the half light of the door to the apartment. Indeed Per himself could feel that, with his large dark beard and his raincoat that was buttoned all the way to his chin, he created an alien impression in this otherwise conventional environment. At last, with an attempt at a bow and scrape, Hr. Søndergaard bade Per be seated and inquired as to how he might be of service.

They sat.

Hr. Søndergaard had just risen from his evening meal. He had still not completely finished masticating and there was an unmistakeable reek of pungent cheese and dark rye bread about him. Per went straight to the point, stated the sum he was looking to loan and described his future prospects. As for the security he could provide for the loan, given that this was limited to his two patents, he was willing to offer a life assurance policy that he would take out for the value of the loan and its interest element. Hr. Søndergaard said nothing. He was sitting in an armchair by his writing table, and now that Per could see him properly, illuminated as he now was by his table lamp, this moneylender no longer offered such a favorable impression. From a large face, blotched with heat and the workings of his bulbous jowls, a pair of yellowish eyes issued an unpleasant and belligerent stare. On top of this, he had clearly eaten far more than his sufficiency that evening. His round expansive stomach gave regular hops and provoked occasional belches that he made no attempt to conceal.

However, Per took his reticence as a good sign and proceeded to inquire about the conditions for the agreed loan. But instead of answering this, Hr. Søndergaard asked Per to name his guarantors.

"Guarantors? Would guarantors be demanded?"

Hr. Søndergaard met Per's surprised outburst with an incredulous smile.

"Ah I see . . . you had not thought of that perhaps? But, of course, some type of real security comes in handy, you will understand, sir. And when you have such good prospects as you suggest, I wouldn't imagine that you would struggle to come up with a name or two. How much was it again you were looking to loan good sir?"

"A thousand crowns."

"And over what period of time?"

"Well I reckon that I need a year, Hr. Søndergaard. By then, I would hope to be almost certainly in a position to pay back both the amount loaned and the interest that has accrued."

"Well the interest now is paid in advance," Hr. Søndergaard remarked casually as he turned to the desk and lifted a large book. It was the street, name, and address directory for Copenhagen.

Meanwhile, the little girl who had opened the door for Per had come into the room. She nursed a doll in her arms. For a moment she had stood leaning against her father, who had proudly rubbed his corpulent hand on her red mop of curls. Now when he was obliged to let her go in order to browse through the book, she crept up into his lap and proceeded to observe Per with the type of conceited and bold impertinence that only a spoiled child can muster.

"I don't see your name listed as a resident anywhere here," Hr. Søndergaard said after searching for some time.

"I was abroad last year," Per explained.

"Ah—you were abroad."

His yellow eyes once again slipped upwards as he gave Per a wary, scrutinizing look from just over the edge of the book. Then they plunged downwards again.

"There's a B. Sidenius here, a former dean in the country. Are you related to him?"

"No."

"I see...well here's an F. Sidenius, accountant. Is he—?"

"No."

"E. Sidenius, a state lawyer and head clerk. I suppose you are not related to him either?"

Per hesitated before replying.

"Actually I am," he said finally.

"He might even be a close relative?"

"That is my brother."

"Well dear sir, there we have it. He would be an excellent guarantor. So perhaps now we can do business."

"No, I'm afraid that's not an option," Per said decisively but feeling more and more flustered.

"Ah, not an option." The eyes once more appeared over the rim of the book. "You are perhaps not on the best of terms with the gentleman listed here?"

"All I can say is that I would not approach him about providing such a service."

"No?—Well, that seems to be the end of that then," Hr. Søndergaard said in a more strident tone as he slammed the book shut.

A short pause ensued. Per remained sitting where he was. He was fearful of leaving with all hope lost. The dark and gloomy streets in the long walk home that was in prospect, and then the solitude of his cold chamber, opened before him like a yawning abyss. But approaching Eberhard on this matter—no, no, that was impossible! He just could not do it.

He then told Hr. Søndergaard that he would be happy to make do with five hundred crowns; in fact even less, and then throw in what he still owned in the way of evening wear and sought-after books as extra security. But the "property broker" had now adopted a superior attitude. He interrupted Per with a cutting observation about people who imagined they could get money on the strength of an appealing face. Good prospects! Of course, why not! That way every lunatic could come running in off the street and milk the golden cow. Because they all had damn good prospects—each and every one of them. No, no, no, cast-iron guarantees or collateral based on real and valuable assets was the bottom line—otherwise don't come to him.

With that, Per got up and left as quickly as he could.

He could not go home. His thoughts flashed wildly around his brain. What could he do? A mortal conflict arose in his psyche. Every fiber of his self esteem wanted to assert itself in a protest against God; but at the same time a commanding voice within called stop and said: In your heart of hearts, you see the righteousness of your punishment. There is a price that must be paid for every sin. Thus, you must face up to your penance! Here you stand before your most severe trial. Here is the eye of the needle through which you must pass if your soul is to find everlasting peace.

Without understanding exactly how, he had emerged via the small backstreets onto Kongens Nytorv, where Copenhagen's nightlife was in full festive swing, as if to deliberately spite the mist and the wet-soiled streets. Carriages crisscrossed the imposing square going in all directions. Chandeliers shone out from the grand entrances to theaters. The hotel on the far side of the square was also brilliantly illuminated and the light spilling from shop windows and street lamps bestrewed the damp pavements with a golden sheen. In his overwrought state, and unaccustomed as he now was to the hurly burly of city life, he stood for some time completely stunned by it all. The racket from carriage wheels felt like rifle volleys in his ears. The ground shook beneath his feet. Finally, a loud shout of "make way there!" roused him. A hackney carriage rushed past him so closely that the huge wheels brushed against his arm and flung street detritus all over him. From the glare of a street lamp that shone into the passing carriage, he caught a glimpse of a couple dressed in formal evening wear. The lady was clad in light blue silk, and her diamond-encrusted earrings flashed as she turned to look at him. The gentleman was in uniform and his chest boasted a row of medals. Then another carriage went past going in the opposite direction. This one contained a young couple that flirted and chattered like canaries in a cage.

Per moved on, slowly putting more distance between himself and his home. Unable to resist, he was led, as if by the hand of the arch Tempter himself, towards Store Kongensgade, on the way to the home of his former parents-in-law. A voice in his head spoke to him once more and said: Turn again! Turn before it's too late! You walk to your doom! But still he walked on.

He turned a corner and was now in the small side street where merchant Salomon's "palace" lay. Per then took up a position on the other side of the street that was mostly in shadow. He saw that some kind of soiree was taking place at the house. He could just make out the lights of the chandeliers through the heavy silk drapes in front of the windows.

Terrified that his presence there would attract attention, he moved along the street in the direction of Bredgade but immediately changed his mind and went back to his original vantage point. And once more his soul raised a protest against God and said: All this I sacrificed for you Lord! Like an abandoned dog, I stand here in distress, foundered and covered in filth from the street . . . and yet still you will not show me pity!

Very quickly, he pulled back further into the shadow offered by a gable wall. He had seen that the entrance gate over there was being opened. A small man carrying an umbrella was let out. Who was that? Ivan's rapid footsteps they were certainly not. Was it Eybert? Jakobe's old admirer? A ridiculous pang of jealousy flashed like a strange conceit through his mind. Then, with the aid of the light from a street lamp, he saw the hook-nosed profile, a black goatee shot through with gray, a pair of large turned-in feet. Aron Israel.

A flash of lightning went through him: here was salvation! Aron Israel would help him! Why had he not thought of him before! "Generosity personified." Per was sure that Aron Israel would not care in the slightest that he was no longer Philip Salomon's son-in-law. Even before his engagement to Jakobe, the venerated academic had shown great sympathy towards him and demonstrated an implicit confidence in his future plans. Any subject under the sun or stars could be freely discussed with him.

Per began to follow him as he walked into Store Kongensgade. But a voice rose from the depths of his soul and, once again in commanding tones, said: Go home! What good will all his generosity do you? You know the demands God has placed upon you. See them through! There is no hiding place. Wherever you may be, the call will grow louder in your ears and you will be without peace until you fulfill your task. Otherwise you will harden your heart and turn from God again. Woe to you if you prevaricate! For the sake of your own dignity, which means so much to you, do not try to haggle anew over the destiny that awaits you now! To work man! God awaits you.

Per had slowed his pace. At the corner of Kongens Nytorv he abruptly stopped his surveillance. With the look of a condemned man, Per watched the diminutive academic disappear beneath the lamp under the clock and turn into the direction of the Grønnegade quarter.

He then turned and began the long walk back to Frederiksberg. It was past ten o'clock before he reached the house. He declined to light a lamp. Nor would he go to bed. He simply sat there at his table with his head in his hands, and he remained sitting in darkness for most of the night without moving.

The next morning, he went straight to Eberhard's office. His older brother made no effort to ameliorate a full confession that Per felt was like tearing strips from his skin. Eberhard sat quietly with a face that betrayed no emotion as he demanded every last scrap of information. However, he did not refuse to help. He would not hear of any talk of guarantees or security; he also wished to consider the matter more fully and then consult the rest of the family, given that—as he put it himself—it would be more natural and more in the spirit of their parents if the loan was given to him by all of them acting as one.

Per made no attempt to object. He had suddenly become so indifferent to it all. That sense of peace, and joyous resurrection in his soul, that he had expected to feel once he had debased himself to the utmost degree simply did not come. Quite the opposite. He had never felt so depressingly empty, never more abandoned by all the forces for good in the world, than right at that very moment.

24

WHEN THE inhabitants of Bøstrup rectory received the news that Per Sidenius had broken off his engagement with the daughter of a Copenhagen finance magnate, Pastor Blomberg's wife became seriously alarmed. And when she now heard that Per was expected back at Kærsholm for the Christmas holidays, she waited one evening until she and her husband were in bed and then spoke openly about her serious concerns and proposed that they send Inger away for the duration of his stay. Pastor Blomberg, however, was having none of this. For while he admitted that he too was not exactly enthralled by the prospect of giving his daughter away to a man with Per's history, one should be careful, he said, of questioning divine providence. Moreover, the young man had owned up to having strayed from the flock and had shown that his spiritual conversion actually was sincere. This was vouchsafed by the huge material benefits and prestige he had sacrificed for the good of his soul.

"We should be wary of being overly dogmatic where God's guiding hand in faith is concerned. And true love is faith by another name. But you are right to be concerned, my love, and I will speak frankly with Inger about this issue. She needs to be told that it is not us who would shackle her heart. That way she will understand the great responsibility that rests on her shoulders."

Right from the start, Inger had never made any connection between herself and the fact that Per had separated from the lady in Copenhagen. It was not that she doubted for a moment her own self-worth, but she attributed Per's conversion as being solely a result of his debates and growing friendship with her father. It was her girlfriends, the two Clausen sisters, that steered her thoughts down the right track and since then she had gone round in a pleasant daze—simply from hearing how many millions the man had apparently renounced for her sake.

Beyond that, she was not entirely sure how she felt about the whole thing. She was fairly sure that Per's personality had not exactly left her spellbound. When she thought of him, she really only remembered his eyes, perhaps because on that first night after Per had visited the rectory, her father had compared his gaze to a wide ocean bay, where flocks of sun-kissed seabirds circled over half-buried shipwrecks in the golden sand—"reminders of the long dark winters and the chaos wrought by equinox storms." Back then, she had been puzzled by this description, whose allusions and metaphors she had not understood. But now that she appreciated what her father had said more fully, those pale, melancholy merman's eyes of his had captured her imagination and flooded her memory of him to the exclusion of all else. At the same time, Hr. Sidenius's antecedents, which they had also mentioned that night, felt like a millstone around her neck whenever she tried to raise her feelings about him. To yield to someone who had already publicly declared for another woman seemed an impossibility to her. But then, the fact that she knew absolutely nothing about this lady undoubtedly lightened her load, and she had also seen with her own eyes how unhappy and tortured he was at the way things had stood in that relationship.

Inger also believed that she actually liked him; but she didn't know whether she would ever be able to have him in her heart, to love him— because she was still unsure what true love actually felt like. Right enough, her two girlfriends had been keen to help her in understanding what it was all about. In particular, the lusty Gerda was forever pulling her to one side and wanting to reveal what her own experiences were, or what new secrets she had extricated from others about the mysteries of love. But Inger had never paid her any heed. Up to now at least, she had never been interested in delving into that completely uncharted territory.

Imagine her alarm, therefore, when one afternoon a few weeks before Christmas and just when she and her father had been left alone in the sitting room together, he started to talk about Per and his likely reappearance in the area.

"As I think you are aware Inger, Hr. Sidenius is no longer engaged to be married. Now, my dear child, because of the conclusions people might draw from the step he has taken, would you rather avoid seeing him here at the rectory? Speak from the heart darling!"

Inger took this question to be a veiled declaration that a proposal had been made. Her mind raced with the possibility that Per had written to her parents and she, to her hot shame, became so agitated that she was left dumb.

But Pastor Blomberg took her silence, and the rush of blood to her pale cheeks, as a sufficient answer to his question. That evening, when the house had retired to bed, he spoke to his wife about the conversation with Inger and repeated that forcing her into a corner over the issue was the wrong tactic—that Our Lord would give his blessing to the true feelings in her heart and, once that happened, grace and fortune would smile upon her. To the objection that Per had no social standing whatsoever and not even the prospect of employment, and so would be in no position to support a family, the pastor was gently reassuring and ventured that, here too, God's mysterious ways would no doubt prevail. What the pastor had in mind here was the river realignment that was being seriously discussed at that very moment in time. He was sure that God might also move him to intervene if this should prove necessary.

It was true that divine intervention was possibly required for this project, because its chances looked anything but bright. Throughout the autumn, and under the auspices of Lord Prangen, a number of public meetings had been held about the land-reclamation project. However, it had proved impossible to achieve a consensus amongst the two or three hundred site owners who owned plots of land of variable acreage in the relevant area. Without common agreement between these people, nothing could move forward. For despite the fact that each individual was convinced that the proposed land and watercourse realignment could be of benefit to him, he declared against it—or at least expressed grave doubts—due to a grave worry that a neighbor, a brother-in-law, or even a brother, might profit even more from it, or gain a cheaper advantage. There was also a general unwillingness to allow Lord Prangen to claim the honor of having initiated such a historically significant development for the area. In the end, the big farmers stayed away from the meetings altogether, and with that it was assumed that the plan was a lost cause.

But then Pastor Blomberg suddenly became involved in the affair. With the fortunate ability he possessed to, at all times, conflate his small private interests with that of wider society and his congregation, he decided—as he put it to his wife—"to grasp this stinging briar of nettles" that seemed to him to be a depressing example of how begrudgery and suspicion could still regularly proliferate like weeds and ragwort, even amongst a people that had been cleansed and liberated by the Holy Spirit. The pastor's first attempts were behind the scenes and sought to influence those site owners whose agreement was most crucial to the implementation of the plan, but when he met resistance, he became angry and went on open attack. At a major spiritual gathering, at which his whole congregation stood before him, he brought up the land project in the middle of his oration and issued strident admonishments to his parishioners not to obstruct progressive measures for reasons of narrow self-interest and vanity. For God's people understood very well, he declared, that the promotion of commerce and a thriving local economy would, in turn, promote the development of a healthy and happy, not to say honest, Christian way of life.

His words aroused great consternation amongst many of those present. There were even those who were seriously vexed with the pastor—firstly, because he had used the occasion of a spiritual gathering to lecture them on this subject and, secondly, because there were already rumors about a possibly imminent association between his daughter Inger and the young man that had first proposed the river plan. But Blomberg brazened out the storm. Nor was it the first time that he had aroused immediate outrage amongst his congregation with an audacious pronouncement. He was sure of the power he wielded and was happy to let people grumble and gripe. For the moment, he had achieved what he wanted: to inject new life into a cause that, in his eyes, was now nothing more or less than a matter of life and death for the area. Gradually, discussions began to break out amongst farmers and smallholders regarding the pastor's words at the meeting. In effect, what this meant was that negotiations about Per's project were taken up anew.

The day before Christmas Eve, Per traveled over to Kærsholm and found that everything was just as it always had been, except that the baroness had now departed and Lord Prangen's face had become even more like a withered maple leaf. All was immediately familiar to him and, in particular, the smell of turf smoke from the kitchen, which he picked up straight away, was like an intimate embrace to welcome him home.

On the other hand, Dame Prangen was not long in establishing that Per had changed dramatically, and it was not just a question of his appearance. She could sense that he had undergone some sort of stressful experience; but despite all her attempts to coax him into confiding with her by clucking around him like a motherly hen, she could not get him to talk about it. In the end, she felt rather affronted by his reticence.

On Christmas Day, Per accompanied her to morning service at Bøstrup church. Lord Prangen did not feel well and stayed at home. The first psalm had just begun when they entered the church. With one hand in the vent of his cassock, Pastor Blomberg was walking backwards and forwards in the middle aisle of the church, nodding to friends and parish stalwarts, while at the same time continuing to sing in a powerful voice. Every now and again, he would stop in front of the steps leading to the chancel and look out over the packed nave of the church, his face beaming in evangelical joy.

Per immediately looked for Inger, who was sitting beside her mother in the pews on the opposite side of the aisle. She was clad all in black—something that lent a fine, soft graciousness to her light blond features. Not once did she lift her eyes from her psalm book.

Even when the distinctive sound of a rustling silk dress announced the arrival of Dame Prangen and had made her mother turn round so as to greet her, Inger still looked down at her hymn book. But, at the same time, her cheeks quite clearly reddened, and Per who had prior reason to believe that she would not be completely unaware of his prospective attendance at church, took this as a victory sign and his heart began to thump against his chest in excitement and anticipation.

Following the service, both he and Dame Prangen, along with a number of other selected churchgoers, were invited to the rectory for coffee. These much sought-after invitations to a post-service repast, always made by the priest himself, were Pastor Blomberg's way of sowing dragons teeth in the soil of his congregation from which new warriors for his various causes could spring. All the parishioners kept a careful watch on who received invites and a complicated popularity tally was maintained to see who exactly was in the Pastor's good books at any given time. Per met four farmers with accompanying wives, upon whose faces it was clearly written—albeit in different script— that they were men of some substance and influence in the area. That Pastor Blomberg might have a particular purpose in including him in a gathering of these people never occurred to Per, not even when the pastor showed unusual eagerness in introducing him to each one of them in turn. Nor was the land-reclamation scheme raised by anyone as a subject of discussion; besides which, the gathering lasted no more than half an hour anyway. The pastor soon let it be known that he still had to give the final afternoon service in his subsidiary church and gave a strong hint to all that it was time to go. The farmers left first and then Dame Prangen and Per departed shortly afterwards—and Inger could breathe again.

Her heart had been constantly in her throat with the thought that she might be left alone with Per. She was still under the impression that he had written to her parents and had therefore already secured their agreement to a possible union, but she had still not made up her mind whether she actually liked him or not. Or more accurately: in her innocent state, she could not be clear whether the feelings she had for him were really feelings of love. However, she did feel that there was something out of the ordinary about him, which for her was an absolute must before she would consider giving her hand. Yes, she also felt that he would be good to her and take care of her; nor could she hide from herself that the prospect of seeing him again had made her skittish and kept her awake until long into the night over the last few days. Indeed, this very morning just before church, she had, to put it bluntly, suffered an attack of butterflies and stomach pains. But was that love?

For as long as Per was present in the house, she was fairly convinced that she did not much care for him. The severe change in his appearance contributed to her feeling that he was alien to her somehow, even though she had to admit that the look actually suited him. But now that he was gone she felt a light had gone out at the rectory and everything was strangely empty. The rest of the day just dawdled along for her without her being able to settle anywhere. She flitted from chair to chair, room to room, and began to curse the day that she had ever met him. This unease in her soul and general sense of indecorum, which was so alien to her nature, shamed her and wracked her emotions. In the end, she sat by the window in her own little room looking despairingly out across the garden, where the setting sun ran in streams of red behind the trees that were already white with frost.

Her thoughts were full of a character from an adventure story—a hero from a Viking saga, like the one Per had conjured up in her mind during his visit. It was an image that had possessed her since his departure. With his taciturn and aloof nature, his pale face and dark and imposing beard, and then with those disturbing merman eyes, he had put her in mind of the "The Flying Dutchman," at least the way she had seen the story presented in an opera she had been to in Copenhagen. In particular, she saw a recurring image of that momentous moment, when the poor, storm-tossed sailor, cursed by his maritime exile, put in for shelter amongst the Norwegian skerries and, with the slow and dampened blows of the kettledrum in the orchestra accompanying him, he steps into the coastal farmer's cottage, where the daughter of the house sits alone singing a song as she works her spinning wheel. And Inger suddenly laid her head on her arm and admitted that it probably was love that she felt for him, even if it didn't make her happy.

It was her decided view that the next day would bring with it a final decision. Along with her parents, she had been invited to dinner at Kærsholm, and as far as she knew they were to be the only guests. However, early the next morning the messenger boy from the estate galloped into the rectory courtyard and announced that the occasion had been called off—during the night, Lord Prangen had taken ill with severe stomach cramps.

That afternoon, Dame Prangen herself, accompanied by Per, then paid a visit to the rectory to offer her apologies. During their conversation, she made a passing reference to the four farmers who had attended the rectory the previous day and then said that there had, of course, already been strong talk in the area of the need to reconvene a meeting to discuss the river realignment project, and how glad she was that things finally seemed to be moving again where that was concerned.

"It does seem that everything will be fine now," she said. "And, of course, we then get to keep Hr. Sidenius here for the foreseeable future."

Pastor Blomberg, who had been pacing up and down the floor with his hands behind his back, stopped dead in his tracks at these words and his face took on a portentous expression.

"Yes, indeed," he said. "I too would hope that the spirit of charity and forbearance will win through in the end on this issue."

The pastor's wife said nothing. Dame Prangen, on the other hand, waxed lyrical in her enthusiasm for the subject and it soon became apparent that she already had a comprehensive plan in her head regarding Per's future.

"Now, I'm sure you are all familiar with that little white villa down by the station. It's available now after Pastor Petersen's widow died, and I cannot think of a more suitable home for Hr. Sidenius than that one. It's beautifully appointed, just off the road there, has been really well kept, has a wonderful garden, but is very handy to the village and all the amenities. As I say, I really cannot think of a more delightful location."

Inger rose from her chair. She was seized by indignation and highly embarrassed over this kind of talk, whose purpose she understood only too well. On the whole, she had lost much of her respect for Dame Prangen in recent times. Not only did she now understand that this lady had, in an underhand way, schemed to get her married to Per, but she also began to see that Dame Prangen's ardor concealed a highly inappropriate fixation with Per as a man. For Inger now recalled that she had even gone so far sometimes as to praise him and extol his virtues in a highly distasteful manner.

After coffee, the assembled party went for a stroll through the garden and out into the surrounding low hills, but Per and Inger never found the right moment to speak in private on this occasion either. Fru Blomberg kept a keen weather eye on them and Dame Prangen's carriage drove up to the door as soon as they got back. Dame Prangen wanted to get home to tend to her sick husband, and there was absolutely no suggestion that Per would be asked to stay on.

At the point of their departure, Dame Prangen made to embrace Inger and kiss her on the mouth, but Inger turned her sullen face away and offered her ear instead. Dame Prangen's caresses, which she had once appreciated so much, she now found almost repulsive.

Several days now passed without any contact between the two budding paramours. Dame Prangen was stuck at home minding her ailing husband and this meant that Per too was effectively quarantined and forced to miss the many Christmas celebrations that were always held in the area. However, his only complaint in that regard was that it robbed him of the chance of seeing Inger. He knew only too well that both because of her rare beauty and as Pastor Blomberg's daughter, she would be the glorified center of attraction amongst the youth, and the obvious choice for Fairy Queen or fabled princess in the processions and folk dances, the revival of which had been talked about amongst the parishioners as early as the previous summer. Even though he was fairly sure that there were no young and eligible men in the area, other than a few bumpkin sons of country gentlemen, and perhaps a few wet-behind-the-ear students, he found no reassurance in this and time dragged monumentally for him at Kærsholm during this whole period. The young farm overseer appeared every day, with his curly, blond beard and grinning face, to invite him out hunting, but he had quite lost his appetite for such pastimes. His preference was to stay indoors—partly because he hoped against hope that Inger might come to visit. Not even Dame Prangen's machinations for his future, or even the negotiations about his project, could retain his interest, because the significance of all these things for him rested solely on his doubtful hopes that Inger might return his love for her.

The bookshelf in his room was still just as replete with books and journals as it had been during his last stay, and he now turned to this for distraction and entertainment. But against his usual custom, he now sought to disappear into lighthearted literature and browsed through popular novels, plays, and short stories. This, he found, went some way to killing time and soothing his impatience. It was also a fact that he had developed something of an aversion to religious and spiritual works since the time when he had been obliged to humble himself in front of his brothers and sisters as penance for his sinful past. He found it hard to reconcile that God he had encountered during his emotional and spiritual trauma of the autumn months just past with the image of a loving and ever merciful comforter of wayward souls that had beckoned so welcomingly from Pastor Blomberg's spiritual and edifying texts. He had skimmed through these a couple of times but had felt the same disappointment that he had already felt with Pastor Blomberg's Christmas sermon. His thoughts were in no way captivated by these flowery and well-crafted, but ultimately banal, reflections on life and death, sin and forgiveness. In his confessional convictions, he had grown out of the stage where one's thoughts were satisfied by moving, but essentially shallow, rhetoric that does nothing to elevate religious clarity. His soul cried out for genuine spiritual nourishment, so that his yearning for essential truths could be sated, but he was being offered pretty flowers rather than life-giving bread. However, he had also resolved to grant a temporary period of soothing calm to his troubled thoughts. He was tired of all the fruitless searching that tortured his mind. For now, at least, he would close the gates to that impenetrable other-worldly kingdom and gather himself for the imminent roll of the dice that would determine his future life, fortune, and happiness in this mortal world.

Previously, he had discounted the idea of proposing to Inger before his surveyor examination results came through and he had obtained a secure position, or, at least, the definite prospect of a secure future. But in these days, before the turn of the year, where he impatiently awaited her arrival at any moment and was full of jealous thoughts, some of the reckless daring he once possessed was born anew in him. With a firm resolve, he decided that the matter would be settled, one way or the other, as soon as he could get speaking to her in private.

On the day before New Year's Eve, the pretext finally came for another visit to the rectory. For he was informed that several messages had been sent from there to inquire as to the health of Lord Prangen; and given that, on that very morning, the squire had shown marked signs of improved health, Per asked at the breakfast table whether he ought not to pay a visit to Bøstrup and bring the good news to the pastor and his family.

Dame Prangen could not suppress a short burst of laughter.

"Dear dear Hr. Sidenius, you took your time figuring that one out," she said with that undertone of innuendo in her voice that had startled Per on previous occasions.

Per left once the morning meal was over. He knew they ate dinner at the rectory at three o'clock and by his reckoning, the time between one and two was the optimum moment where he might find Inger alone in the sitting room. In all likelihood, her mother would be busy supervising the kitchen; her father would be in his study and, if practice followed custom, Inger would be in the middle of her music hour— Dame Prangen had once told him that, with her strict sense of duty, Inger never missed her music drills, day after day, the whole year round, with the exception of holy days.

So that he could make his approach as unobtrusively as possible, he had declined the offer of a carriage. Besides, the weather was glorious, the ground underfoot was good, and also, he just needed to get moving again after such a long time being stuck indoors. The low-slung winter sunshine threw long strips of hard shadow across the fields, where here and there a couple of pregnant ewes tugged at the sparse patches of grass. Per was in good heart and so calm that he even surprised himself. With a curious, almost religious, sense of elation, he listened to the steady tack and tandem of his own Sidenius footsteps on the frost-hardened ground. It was as if something in this sound joined him to a far-distant world, from whence, in some mysterious way, he was infused with a heightened bodily power, self-assurance and peace of mind.

Of course, things went completely differently to the way he had planned. The first thing he saw on walking through the gate leading to the rectory was Fru Blomberg, who was standing in the middle of the courtyard feeding corn to her hens. With a carefully measured show of cordiality, she thanked him for the message and greetings he brought from Kærsholm and invited him into the house. And, just as he had envisaged, Inger was sitting at the piano. But her mother made no sign of leaving the room and the level of conversation did not get much beyond Lord Prangen and his illness. In the end, Pastor Blomberg came into the room clad in his short black Italian cotton jacket and immediately took over the conversation. By this point, Per had accepted that he would have to leave with his mission unaccomplished.

Then, the clatter of horses' hooves was heard outside and, from the sitting room window, an old-fashioned calash carriage was seen swinging into the courtyard. This turned out to be an aging fellow priest from a neighboring parish who was making his annual Christmas visit along with his wife. Wine and cakes had already been brought into the room and the arrival of the visitors meant that chocolate and coffee was now also called for. Inger busied herself with serving the new guests. Per got up to go; but when Pastor Blomberg asked him to stay on for dinner, he took very little persuading.

An hour or so later, the old priest and his wife announced their intention to leave, and in those few minutes where Pastor Blomberg and his wife followed them out to their carriage, Inger and Per became pledged to each other.

When Fru Blomberg returned to the sitting room, she realized immediately that something had happened. Inger was standing by the flower arrangement at one of the windows with her back to the room. Per stood beside her.

"What's going on here?" she asked almost rudely.

Per turned, took a short step towards her, bowed his head slightly and almost apologetically said: "I have proposed to your daughter, Frue!"

Now the Pastor blundered in, still clad in his short house jacket, but stopped when he heard what had happened and was suddenly grave of countenance. In the very first moments, he expressed certain concerns natural to any parent; but—easily persuaded as he always was where his emotions were concerned—his face soon broke into a broad smile. Then, moving towards Inger, he spread his arms and embraced her, called Per his son and with tears in his eyes gave them both his blessing.

Per hardly knew himself exactly how the proposal was made. He had to get Inger to tell him afterwards and her description was not without a slightly comical tone. She told him that she went to follow her parents as they escorted the elderly priest and his wife to their carriage, but that he had suddenly grabbed her hand and held her back.

"I nearly shrieked, you gripped my hand so hard! It was actually very sore, just so that you know it."

She said this with no suggestion of jocularity. It was a serious complaint. On the whole, and for the moment at least, Inger was more enthused by the obvious joy she had bestowed upon Per than by the man himself. Nor was their any suggestion of her wanting to be in any way intimate with him. It was obvious to Per that she actually wished to avoid being left alone with him again. On his departure from the rectory, therefore, and out of fear of an embarrassing rejection, he declined to ask for a parting kiss when they had momentarily been left alone together in the hall. Nor did her shyness offend him.

It was precisely her haughty chasteness that from the very start, and more than anything else, had made her so alluring for him, and he made a private vow that he would be patient with her and careful not to offend this virtue.

In a conference that was convened in Pastor Blomberg's study, it had been decided that news of the engagement should be withheld until Per had been awarded his surveyor qualification. It was Fru Blomberg that was adamant about this and Per was happy to yield on this point. Not even Dame Prangen was to be told anything before anyone else. It was Inger who had insisted on this. But when Per got back to Kærsholm, this last promise came to immediate grief—his face betrayed everything.

"Hr. Sidenius! You've gone and got engaged!" Dame Prangen cried as soon as she saw him.

He then had no choice but to admit the truth and even allowed himself to be swayed into revealing more about the day's events than he subsequently would have wished.

Per was once again able to verify one of the golden rules of life—that just as an accident seldom happens on its own, good fortune was also usually accompanied by other triumphs. A few days later, he received an unexpected visit at Kærsholm. Two of the wealthy farmers he had met on Christmas Day at Pastor Blomberg's rectory, arrived one morning and requested a chat with him. They were two tall and very stout men, dressed in well-cut, homespun jackets and carrying an inherent dignity in their demeanor. Per bade them be seated and, though he was quite unprepared for this interview, and also unused to long conversations with farmers, the subsequent negotiations lasted several hours. The two men began by stating very clearly that they were not acting as emissaries for anybody else; they had simply wished to speak to him because they "had heard rumors" that he wished to carry out a realignment of the river and reclamation of the land in and around the meadows by lowering the water table. As far as they were both concerned, they said, if this rumor had substance to it, they wanted some time to give the matter much more detailed consideration. Overall, their utterances were marked by a calculating caution and a somewhat narrow-minded suspicion. This was in strange contrast to the robustness of their physique and their natural self-esteem. Even though it was very clear from the questions they put to Per that they had scrutinized the technical and legal aspects of the project very thoroughly, they still wished to give the impression they only knew the broad outlines of the scheme. In fact, when one of them let slip the idea of possibly reconvening the meetings between the interested parties, his confederate hurried to add that it was still very doubtful whether this would prove possible, at which point the first man completely switched tack and declared that he himself did not believe that the proposal would ever gain acceptance in the area.

Once they had gone, Per was more or less convinced that they had come to prepare him for the final rejection. But Dame Prangen, who asked Per to tell her exactly what they had said and who was far more practiced in the parleying skills of the farming fraternity, offered him her warmest congratulations and with that slightly suggestive laugh of hers told him that he could now start measuring his wedding shirt. Best wishes also came from the rectory, and it was not long before local gossip spoke of the same two men having traveled to Copenhagen to speak with the MP for the area about procuring a public grant for the setting up and implementation of the project.

Per gradually came to spend most of his day at Pastor Blomberg's rectory, and for each one of his visits, Inger yielded more and more to her feelings for him. True, she never changed her balanced and calm demeanor, and was still rather brusque with him when he kissed her on the cheek, but on the other hand she could now be quite touching in her concern for him. If he came to the rectory in bad weather, she always made sure to get him a warm drink, which she would then prevail on him to drink while it was still almost boiling; and in the evening when he set off walking, or took the carriage home, she would invariably lift her silk shawl as they took leave of each other in the hall and tie it around his neck herself to make sure he didn't catch a cold. In other words, her feelings of love had still not progressed beyond the stage of maternal embrace, and Per saw fit to endure being treated like a child, a stubborn youngster whose bad habits Inger would humor, without making a fuss about it.

With regard to the general familial situation at the rectory, Per became very quickly conversant with how things stood. Amongst other things, he wasn't long in noticing that only one force ruled in that house and that was the pastor's. Though it was not a question of Pastor Blomberg ever acting like a despot in his role of paterfamilias— rather, he ruled by dint of his natural superiority, with which he seemed to disempower his surroundings, without at any stage needing to bully or cajole. There was in all of this something that often made Per think of his own father and his relationship with his mother and siblings. There were other times when he would sometimes be reminded of his own childhood, as different as the two rectories otherwise were in lifestyle and tone. Thus, on one occasion, when he walked into the sitting room at the rectory, he immediately noticed a strange mood of dejection on the part of all present. His father-in-law was in his study and did not come out to greet him as was the norm. Inger and her mother were sitting down and occupied with their sewing and needlework but were muted and solemn, while two of the younger children had obviously worried faces as they played a quiet game in the dining room next door. When Per was finally alone with Inger, she told him that one of her brothers, the twelve-year-old Niels, had been caught lying, and even though her father had cast-iron proof of it, the boy would not own up and continued his denials. Her father had then summoned all the children and threatened to interrogate each one in turn, at which point the little sinner burst into tears and admitted his offense. He had now been ordered to stay in one of the guest rooms and would not be allowed out of the rectory for the rest of the holidays.

Per listened slightly ruefully to this account of what had happened, because it provoked memories of an event in his own childhood— namely, that scene at the dinner table after his thieving from the orchard had been discovered. That horrible scene which, for him, had been the defining experience of his upbringing, and which he still could not think about without feelings of defiance and revenge surging through him once more, like a phantasm of a former self. His preference, therefore, was to avoid the subject and he was glad to see Inger's mother returning, so that the conversation could slip naturally to other things.

In the meantime, Per's relationship with his mother-in-law had undergone a very favorable change. Out of regard for Inger, he had gone out of his way to soften Fru Blomberg's resentment towards him and this approach now seemed to be bearing fruit. He had observed that she always appreciated being entertained while sewing—preferably something that could be read aloud from some book or other from the reading and periodicals basket. So each afternoon he read some chapters from one of the so-called schoolmaster novels, which were highly popular in the rectory. And though these books were hardly to his liking, Per gradually discovered a certain pleasure in these hours, where his own voice melded with the sound of Inger's and his mother-in-law's diligent needlework. Even the occasional rumbles coming from the stove added to the sense of homely conviviality.

The day after the feast of the Epiphany, Per traveled back to Copenhagen. He dared not stay away from his studies any longer and, besides that, Lord Prangen's health had taken another turn for the worse and by all accounts he was quite poorly. He spent the whole of the last day at the rectory and, for the first time, saw a truly emotional Inger as he made to leave. She had tears in her eyes and held his hand as if she might fall were she to let go of it. As Per's carriage took off, Inger stood on the steps leading to the house along with his new in-laws—both parents and all his little brothers- and sisters-in-law. She waved an immaculately white handkerchief and then ran out to the garden and perched herself on the fence so as to wave a very last final farewell.

Despite all that, he still felt a tinge of disappointment. Until the very last moment, he had hoped that Inger would ask permission from her parents to accompany him to the station so that they could enjoy that little window of time on their own. It was true that the weather was cold and there was a stiff wind, but still, he was surprised that she had not even thought of it. As he sat there in the carriage, with the empty coach seat by his side, his thoughts instinctively turned to Jakobe. An expression she had once used in a letter to describe her longing for him leapt into his mind. She wrote that she would gladly travel the world thrice over to be with him for just one single minute. At the time, he found the remark bordering on hysterical. Now that he himself was truly in love, he fully understood it.

After half an hour or so of driving, the railway station came into view and then he passed the small house, which Dame Prangen had picked out as their love nest. The building lay a good bit off the main road at the foot of a hill. It was built in the style of a villa with impressive grounds and a lovely garden, which even in its winter bareness lent a cozy and inviting appearance to the place. He felt a surge of elation as he looked over the property. Was it actually possible that this unfamiliar building would become his home—that this small, snug haven stood there just waiting to facilitate his happiness and good fortune? Would he, Per Sidenius, a man who had contrived to offend all of life's divine spirits with his covetousness and avarice, some time soon be sitting behind those, for now, blank windows with Inger by his side and cosseted by the same gods that he had so foolishly defied? Indeed, would the laughter and wails of his children ring out some day from that pathway leading to that garden, which lay so quiet and still just then? And there at the top of the slope behind the house—yes, in fact, that would be the perfect place to set up his trial windmill. And who knew? Perhaps one day his great technological victory would be announced to the world from up there.

Per smiled to himself as he gazed ahead of him in deep rapture. He was forced to admit to himself that if God was a strict taskmaster who severely punished any breach of his commandments, well, he was also a forgiving and munificent sovereign who rewarded his subjects with regal bounty!

When he moved into his train compartment, and the train rumbled and jolted out of the station, Per found that he was in the company of a small, white-haired man, whom he soon realized was the priest that had visited his in-laws along with his wife on the very day he had become engaged to Inger. The pastor, a cheerful and talkative fellow, also recognized Per and they soon fell into animated conversation.

"I believe, young sir, that you are the son of the late Pastor Johannes Sidenius, may God rest his soul. Would I be right? Your father I only knew vaguely I'm afraid. Of course, he was not a man for socializing with his fellow priests. He preferred to work quietly and conscientiously, with the minimum of fuss. Your mother, on the other hand, Hr. Sidenius . . . I actually knew your mother very well in my much younger days. We were from the same town—both from Vejle—and about the same age. I can see a very strong resemblance. As soon as I saw you when we met at dear Pastor Blomberg's house, it struck me that your face reminded me of someone. Just at that moment, I could not recall your mother's maiden name. But of course, as soon as I got home, I realized that it was the features of the Thorsen family I had been looking at. It is quite remarkable. As I sit here now, it's as if I have your maternal grandfather right in front of me. I suppose you had never met him, Hr. Sidenius. He was a lovely man—a cheerful soul, always interested in what was going on around him, and full of the joys of life until his dying day. Hr. Thorsen's open hospitality was known all over that small town and your mother was the heart and soul of all the innocent games and entertainments we had to hand. Oh yes! Those happy days of long ago! I remember, for example, one Christmas that a masked ball was organized at a country estate about a mile out of town. All we youngsters had received invitations and, as you can imagine, we were like cats on hot bricks with excitement. But then, of all times, on the very afternoon of the dance, Jutland was hit by an almighty snowstorm. You can believe, young sir, that there came such a blizzard and huge drifts that nobody dared venture out and all of us young folk were in utter distress. But just as we are all sitting there cooped up at home and feeling sorry for ourselves, we hear sleigh bells and the crack of a whip out in the street, and who do we see when we run to our windows? . . . only Kirstine Thorsen and she on the way to the ball! Ha ha . . . ah dear dear! For your mother, there could be no talk of staying at home. In the end, she declared that if nobody would drive the sleigh there, she would walk in her white stockings so as to save her shoes. Well after that, the rest of us found a bit of backbone and our rather daring adventure got underway. The whole occasion went perfectly and we had mighty entertainment. All thanks to your mother, Hr. Sidenius!"

"I'm sorry Hr. Pastor," Per interrupted, rather sheepishly. "But with respect, I believe you are mistaken sir. That young lady you have described cannot be my mother."

"But sir, are you not the son of the late Johannes Sidenius?"

"Indeed I am."

"And was your mother's Christian name not Kirstine? And was she not one of the daughters of Eberhard Thorsen—one of the local doctors in Vejle?"

"She was indeed."

"Well then, there ye have it. I cannot be wrong!"

"My mother had a sister I think?"

"Ah yes poor Signe! But she was always weak and sickly and died very young. Your mother, on the other hand, was always a picture of rude health—never of any great height as you know yourself, but very fine featured and graceful. I remember another time one summer when we young folk organized what we called a 'pitch-in picnic' out in the forest. Off we went in three big, overloaded Holstein carriages to a forest almost ten miles outside Vejle. The owner of the forest was a baron who for some reason was on permanent war footing with the local populace. Now it's true that large placards had been up at all the entrances announcing that access to the forest was strictly forbidden, even though this forest stretched over thousands of acres of land and the baron himself lived a substantial distance away. Vehicles were not allowed to leave the appointed roads. Loud voices or games were banned so as not to upset the wildlife and the consumption of any kind of food in there was expressly forbidden under any circumstances. No doubt this long list of rules and regulations was what created so much bad feeling against the man and, of course, as young people are wont to do, particularly in our giddy state, we decided we would break them. So, without further ado, we set up camp in a lovely open meadow, out come the picnic baskets and the flasks of coffee and the world is just perfect. But the next minute we all get a very rude awakening. Like a punch in the stomach it was. For who do we see coming straight towards us, only the baron himself and his head gamekeeper. Now this baron was well known to be nothing short of a lout and his face alone was enough to scare us all witless. He was a huge man, had clubs for hands and an angry face with red and blue lines like a turkey. We didn't know what to do, Hr. Sidenius, and we were all, frankly, terrified. The next thing is your mother gets up, pours out a cup of coffee at great speed, and then proceeds to walk over the grass towards the baron with it. Ha ha ... I can still see her now so clearly in front of me. She was wearing a light mauve, very fine summer frock and a big straw hat with a floral band that framed her pretty face. She had such a charming figure and, added to that, a posture and step so light and floating that she was a revelation to watch. So she curtsies to Hr. Baron of the Forest, and with no little devilment in her voice, bids him do us that great honor of being our guest on the green. Of course—the invitation was irresistible. And I believe that, in essence, he was a good-hearted man. So he invites all of us to call in to his castle and sample his champagne on our way back to Vejle. Never would any of us forget that day. Has your mother never told you about it, may I ask Hr. Sidenius?"

"No. She never did Hr. Pastor."

The train stopped at the provincial town, where this effusive ancient was to disembark. Per was glad to be left alone. The stories the priest had told him had disturbed him and left him despondent.

As the train pulled away from the station, he pondered the fact that he actually knew very little about the maternal side of his family, or his mother's life when young. While his father had always gained so much satisfaction, and was so proud, when recalling his youth and life at his father's poverty-stricken rectory, his mother always seemed to shy away from telling her children about her own childhood home and her family. Her only brother had been a doctor somewhere on the island of Funen, and he had never even met him. He had never come to the Sidenius rectory, and his name was very rarely mentioned there.

Per stayed sitting by the window with the side of his face resting against his hand as he looked out at the passing fields. The shadow of dusk was already upon them. And he began to understand the reasons for the instinctive shudder that had gone through his soul that day as he read the letter his mother had left behind for him.

25

On the night between the ninth and tenth of January, a serious emergency suddenly erupted in the small Silesian town of Hirschberg near Breslau, to which Jakobe had fled. She had been there for over two months, seeking some sort of seclusion and tranquillity as she prepared for the arrival of her child. In the dead of night, she had been forced to send an urgent telegram to her close friend Rebekka in Breslau—the only person to whom she had divulged her secret. As the morning unfolded, a second telegram was sent to Breslau calling for a doctor to come to Jakobe's abode as soon as possible. As she then waited for assistance to arrive, Jakobe endured a day of such terror and suffering that she, who was already well acquainted with affliction, was subsequently forced to shut it from her mind forever. The child was alive as it tried to enter this world, but died during the frantic efforts to extricate it from the womb. Jakobe was not even allowed to see the child because the doctor had been forced to break the child's limbs in order to save its mother's life.

She was confined to bed for six weeks, and spring was almost over before she gained enough strength to sit out in her landlady's little garden, albeit well wrapped up in blankets, and look up at Schneekoppe and the other white-topped peaks which loomed over the burgeoning green landscape. But the natural beauty that was all around her meant nothing to her anyway. Worse, she was so heartbroken over the loss of her baby that she felt empty and worthless, and, on top of that, so helplessly weak that the only physical thing she was able, or wanted, to do was to cry. In the few brief months they had shared, she had become so intimate with her baby that it had come to dominate her waking thoughts. And as it grew inside her, it had filled her whole being, so that she was all baby and little else. Now, she was nothing more than an empty and torn shell. The fact that a great burden had been taken from her never crossed her mind. The shame, the humiliation, her wounded parents, the sympathy of the wider family circle—everything that had previously nagged at her conscience and weighed her down with worry had suddenly become pathetic and meaningless in comparison to the joy that had filled her life as she waited. With this child, she had thought, her hopes would be restored and her new life could begin again.

Both her mother and father, who still believed her to be in Breslau, wrote regularly to her with news from home. Thus, she discovered that Eybert had married a young seventeen-year-old girl, that her brother-in-law Otto Dyhring had been elected to parliament, and that Nanny had been to a ball at the royal palace and had been presented to one of the princes of the realm. But she didn't give a fig about all that. She sat there in her little garden, with a pillow behind her neck and her feet on a footstool, and with her grave, contemplative gaze, watched the children who would regularly pass along the footpath that was beside the garden fence.

They were mostly poor children—pallid and emaciated wretches, of the type that infested every factory town and even these small and apparently rustic towns, where the footpaths bloomed with grass and flowers in springtime. Twice a day, they would storm past Jakobe's lookout point, on the way to, or coming from, the alms house and school that lay nearby. In particular, she noticed a little waif of no more than ten years of age. His facial coloring was bluish and hollow and there were angry lesions at the sides of his nose and on his pockmarked cheeks. He always dragged behind the others carrying his slate under his arm and wearing rough wooden clogs that scraped the ground as he walked. When she had recovered enough of her strength to be able to venture short distances away from the garden, she stopped the boy one day and spoke to him gently, asking him whether he liked his school. With dull, cavernous eyes of pallid blue, the boy stared blankly up at her. His only concern was whether he was in trouble and when this proved not to be the case, he simply turned without a word and continued his leaden walk. When he had made safe distance away from Jakobe, he stole a nervous glance back at her, and when he saw that she was still standing there watching him, hunched his shoulders as if expecting a blow. "The poor little fellow!" she said out loud and made her way back to the garden—there was something about this abandoned child and his already heightened fear of adults that made her mother's heart thump against her breast.

One day sometime after, she followed him at a distance to see where he lived, and watched him as he disappeared into a long and ramshackle set of huts that had a door directly onto the street at every two or three windows. By way of discreet inquires in the area, she managed to find out the name of his parents and their living conditions. It was the all too common tragedy of a family slaved to factory work. Both the man and his wife had to work at machines from sunrise to sunset and leave the children in the care of an often cruel fate. They starved at home, were beaten at school, and on the streets were constantly watched and threatened by the police. In such circumstances, they either toughened up very quickly or slunk into dark corners and became dull, rough villains or layabouts and ne'er-do-wells.

Jakobe had never seen poverty at such close quarters, and the conditions she witnessed left her in shock. She made it her business to find out what the daily pay rate was for factory workers; the length of their working day; the furnishing and fittings, or lack of same, in their dormitories; the standards of hygiene in the factories; the type of support they could rely on in their old age and so on—everything she subsequently discovered caused her huge distress and outrage. The expression "capitalism's modern day barbarism," that she had so often come across in radical newspapers and believed to be hyperbole, she now saw afresh, as if it were printed in the very blood of the lower classes.

Nor was she satisfied any longer with simply feeling sorry for the oppressed. Just as every strongly felt idea provoked a need within her to act upon it, these new insights unleashed decisive action. With the blessing and support of her landlady, an upright widow of a junior army officer, Jakobe set up a rudimentary soup kitchen in a corner of the garden, where these emaciated urchins could enjoy a hot meal and a warm drink. She was in no doubts about the correctness of what she was doing and made sure the children could partake of this free service both on the way to and from school. That flood of tenderness and desire for self-sacrifice she had held in reserve for her own child now poured forth as a cleansing tide for these rejects of civil society. It washed over and rejuvenated some fifty scurvy heads and the number grew each week. At first, the children refused to come anywhere near the place and Jakobe became a laughing stock of Hirschberg. But then the aroma of real soup wafting across the picket fence, not to mention the sight of the permanently laid tables, gradually banished any worries or shyness they might feel. Even the little waif with the pale gray and scabrous face came to sit one wonderful day and eat his fill in the garden.

For Jakobe, this whole exercise prompted her to consider even more ambitious ideas. For gradually, as her physical strength returned, the tumult of life and all its challenges began to exert its old spell on her. She wrote about this very phenomenon to Rebekka in Breslau:

"Have you ever really considered what a terrible fate our times—our great, wonderful, industrious times!—have inflicted upon the children of the poor, and how outrageously little has been done by society to secure a humane existence for them, or just a basic and natural life? From bare, squalid rooms that are laughably called homes, where they rarely see their mother or father, these poor wretches are sent to schools that for most of them serve the function of glorified penal institutions. In some cases, they actually are prison buildings or workhouses. That same society, which they are told to regard with confidence and assurance as their unfailing guardian and protector, confronts them everywhere with the opposite of that. In fact, day after day they see only the most horrible aspects of the world in which we all live—such as a horrible schoolmaster, a brutal police force, an intrusive and arrogant Public Relief Board, a clergy that preaches only hellfire and damnation.

"In these circumstances, how will a spirit of social responsibility ever be kindled in these children, from which, in the run of time, an actual idea of shared citizenship can emerge? A reassertion of utterly destroyed family values is not even worth discussing. There seems to be little doubt that the parental home, which was previously the fulcrum around which all of social life revolved, has been made redundant by social and technical developments. But what do we put in its place? This question has occupied my mind so much in the last while that if I'm not lying awake at night thinking about it, then I fall asleep and dream about it.

"Adults are well catered for in public life. They have churches and variety shows, beer halls, theaters, and prayer houses. But what about the children? Where, tell me, can those poor little things turn in their fear and despair? I can't see any way around it other than that schools must gradually step in and take over what was once the role of the traditional home. But—of course!—the schools will have to be slowly changed. Bit by bit they have to go back to their original ethos and become more like the monasteries of old—asylums and precious sanctuaries to which fugitives could always turn. But they have to become far more beside that. Even in its outward appearance, the actual decoration and appointment of the physical building, as well as by the way things are taught, this new type of school would always represent something warm, welcoming and happy in the mind of each child. Because it is in this very place that children must receive those essential, bright and aspirational impressions of the world which will sustain them in later life and make them more durable in life's struggles. In all likelihood, make them even more adaptable than children raised in the old-fashioned (and even present-day) cloister-type academies who lose their faith in life at the first setback, decide that luck and happiness has deserted them and, like toddlers who bump their legs, go running to the breasts of their old and barren wet nurse—the church.

"But I can see the exclamation mark on your face. Why is Jakobe telling me all this, my friend asks. And your surprise is understandable. But, my dear friend, I'm going to be absolutely honest with you. During my lengthy time of isolation, a new world has been revealed to me, and I am no doubt in a bit of a spin about it all. This may surprise you but I'm deadly serious about it, Rebekka—I want to put the above thoughts into action out there in the real world. You might describe what I'm going to say as pure crazy, but I'm considering setting up a school for disadvantaged children in Copenhagen. It would be based on the kind of ethos I've outlined here. I know it will basically devour all of my savings, but what matter when I have nobody to pass them on to anyway? Is there any better way I could use that money?

"Oh, I know that its not going to happen either today or tomorrow, Rebekka. To start with, I have to research all previous attempts at this kind of thing very thoroughly. Really, I have to become an expert in the concept of schools for the poor and schooling generally. I vaguely recall that I either read or heard somewhere about a place in America where a similar initiative was set up; so don't be too alarmed if you one day get word that I'm heading off across the Atlantic—despite my fear of boats and water! But for the moment, I'll be staying here with my adopted children. Besides, I couldn't leave that little grave in the cemetery just yet. So I'll not be up to see you in Breslau any time soon."

When spring came, Per passed his final surveyor's examination with honors, but his joy was tainted by the fact that he walked almost directly from the examination table into an army barracks where he donned a soldiers uniform for the first time. This was yet another transgression from his past for which he now had to pay. Year after year, he had contrived to avoid his statutory conscription into the military, in the impudent hope that Philip Salomon would somehow use his influence and help him avoid it altogether. He had been drafted into the Engineering Corps and was forced to spend the whole summer digging trenches, lay and weave gabions for defense works, and then march endlessly up and down the flat grass plains just outside Copenhagen. He did this in the company of several hundred other young men who, in his eyes, were no more than half-grown boys. What pained him most about this constant drilling was not the physical exertion it demanded, as unaccustomed as he was to it, but rather the intellectual torpor that barrack life as a whole inflicted upon him. Per had brought some books with him, hoping that he might get a chance in his off-duty hours to do some decent reading. But he soon found that he had enough to be doing in simply satisfying his bodily requirements—food, rest, and sleep took over his life. There was also the fact that he soon fell into the army rhythm of doing everything as per command. So much so that, in the end, doing anything of his own volition seemed alien to him.

However, as early as the autumn of that year, he was suddenly released from this spiritual and intellectual doghouse. With Lady Fortune once more guiding his hand when lots were drawn for exemption from winter service, the name Per Sidenius came out amongst one of the very few tickets to be drawn that year. Indeed, he was not just excused from any further immediate service but was also informed that he was now exempt from all future recalls. Thus, in the last days of September, fresh and invigorated in mind and body, Per traveled to Jutland, where his engagement to Inger could now be made public in all ceremony and celebration. In the meantime, Lord Prangen had passed away, but this was more of a spur to the negotiations surrounding the river realignment than a hindrance, and preparations were now so well advanced that Per, to his utter joy, was able to start work with immediate effect.

Per's very first act was to set about installing himself in some of the rooms of the little villa, not far from the railway station in the local village—the home that Dame Prangen had picked out for him the previous Christmas and which was still unoccupied. There were five small rooms, and also a kitchen with attendant dining room and pantry. Up in the roof space, there were two attic rooms. For the present, he sufficed with purchasing furniture for just two of the rooms and overall established rather sparse living conditions for himself. That basic lack of either a need, or desire, in his character to create his own comfortable space around himself—a feature of all his forms of accommodation both in Denmark and abroad—was once again starkly exhibited here. At an auction of the effects of a lately deceased village shop owner, he bought two painted tables, a sofa of waxed fabric, some wooden chairs and similar items. Nor was making do with this mishmash of basic items simply a sign, as Per himself liked to believe, of financial circumstances, by which he could pay back his debts to his siblings and Philip Salomon as quickly as possible. For, as the genuine Sidenius he in essence was, with the attendant medieval and monk-like sensibilities, he found the idea of an astringent lifestyle under rigorous conditions secretly appealing. In the meantime, his mother-in-law had arranged a housekeeper for him. This was an old domestic servant that had once worked at the rectory. And thus, one day in the month of October, while the last remnants of summer still carried in the breeze, Per ate his first meal at his own table in his new home.

The little village itself—Rimalt by name—was one of the typical new settlements that quickly grow up around a railway station in a populous district—always carrying a hint of happenstance. There was an inn-cum-guest house, a secondary school, a chemist, a small number of shops and stores and some tradesmen, but neither a church nor rectory. A distance from the station, the railway track crossed the river by way of an impressive bridge and it had been the hollow rumble of the trains rolling over it that Per had heard right across the meadows and all the way to Kærsholm during his time there. For a radius of several miles around the bridge, people set their watches by this sound.

Per's land project covered the area lying on both sides of this bridge. It followed the river for five miles on one side and for three miles along the opposite bank, taking in parcels of meadow in Rimalt itself, then Bøstrup and Borup parishes. Every morning he drove out in his own little gig in order to draw maps, mark out drainage lines, adjust rough markings, and so on. Another advantage with this work was that he soon came to meet most of the farmers in the area. His love for this species was not increased by these encounters. Face to face, as individuals, they left a much different and far less favorable impression upon him than had been the case, that fine summer's day, when he first saw them as a solid mass at the large open-air meeting in the forest. But it was also the case that, as he lacked the prerequisites for being able to assess them as individuals, they all appeared much the same to him. Overall, the only thing he saw were the peculiarities that he found particular to their social group: an obsession with money, a pettifogging mulishness and shameless parochialism—in fact, all the ignoble characteristics that tend to proliferate in remote areas, full of narrow roads and narrow-minded people.

All of this served to strengthen an observation he had made while doing his military service. In his own company, there had been a mixture of tradesmen from provincial towns and then farmers, particularly from West Jutland. What had struck him very forcibly was the way a refreshing and very active sense of solidarity was often made manifest amongst the first group, even though most of these young men now represented the dregs of Copenhagen. The farmers, on the other hand, were quite devoid of any sense of fellowship; in fact, they gave no indication that they were even aware that such a thing existed. It was not that they were ever in conflict with anyone and they were happy to generally muck in with everybody else; but it would never have occurred to them to do someone else a good turn or favor, without first ensuring they would be repaid in kind; never would they themselves dare to request a favor without simultaneously offering something in return.

There were times when Per returned home from his surveying work completely dejected—his working day having been ruined by neighboring farmers, who were otherwise good friends, even coreligionists and political bedfellows, but who had crossed swords over the ownership of a ditch that was no wider than a kitchen mat and could have been dug up and carted away in a wheel barrow. In other words, despite the massive effort made by the Christian revivalist movement in the last generation or so, the idea of a Christian fellowship was nothing more than an outer garment that was worn at festive public gatherings, and every Sunday, but was forgotten when the working clogs and overalls came on again and was never allowed to impinge upon the hegemony of the farmer's wallet.

Nor did he find any great relief or entertainment amongst his social peers at home in Rimalt. Every evening, after the mailbag had been thrown from the train, the school principal, the village chemist, its stationmaster, and a couple of shop owners would settle in the lounge of the inn. It was a kind of unofficial gentleman's club to which Per had been invited. Here they would sit around a large table that was doused in a lazy light from a low overhanging lamp. Out would come the pipes and the air would very soon be thick with blue smoke as they read the newspapers and partook of a toddy or two. Occasionally, a conversation would erupt because of something in one of the newspapers, and nowhere on earth were world events discussed with a greater air of superiority than at this evening conflab in this little village in Jutland.

The secondary school headmaster was the club's guiding spirit. He was a man of around fifty years of age with a bright mind and broad general knowledge, which he knew how to use in the cut and thrust of debate and repartee. He was a former student with a degree in philosophy and had also made a disastrous attempt at becoming a political leader before being washed up in this quiet backwater as the head of a school with forty pupils. Thus, he found greatest satisfaction in belittling the importance of anything that was fortunate enough to cause a stir out there in the great world beyond Rimalt. The intricacies of war, polar expeditions, important developments in the arts world or scientific innovations, trade unions and the forward march of the proletariat—all these things aroused nothing more than a condescending pity in him. Even the huge technological strides that were being made in this New Age, and which local farmers followed with a childlike wonder, did not impress him in the least.

"Yes, well," he said one evening, when all the newspapers were carrying news of the newly invented telephone, whose more detailed function and form Per had been obliged to explain to them. "It really is beyond belief that an invention like that was not made years ago. I mean, it's actually ridiculous that as I can't just sit here and have a perfectly normal conversation with a man in China—in fact not just speak to him but see him, feel his presence, smell him. And that's the way it is in every area of our lives. It takes seven whole days to get from

Europe to America. It's a disgrace really! It shouldn't take any more than seven hours. After all, we are only hopping across a pond. In other words, we should be able to have breakfast in Copenhagen in the morning and then dine in New York in the evening. Only when we get to that stage will I take my hat off to science and scientists."

The chemist was another man who liked the sound of his own voice, though he would often stop midway through a sentence because he had forgotten what he was going to say. The stationmaster, meanwhile, who was a retired military officer, found more entertainment in the contents of his wineglass, while the two merchant store proprietors were happy to remain as a willing audience worshipping at the feet of these far more sophisticated gentlemen.

Per found no pleasure in these gatherings and went there less and less. He could not go to Bøstrup rectory every evening—it was just too far to go. After being worked all day, his horse had to be rested and, besides, he himself was tired after tramping the fields and byways from the morning onwards. Then, the three or four miles back again, and in all kinds of weather and road conditions, was not to be taken lightly. But the fact was that his own home felt lonely and lifeless. Yes, it was true that he had his books to keep him company, and he retreated into their world more and more frequently as the nights became so long that they were nearly as long as the day. But, for now at least, he could not find the inner calm that would help him recommence his work on his inventions. His thoughts were too preoccupied with the road leading to the rectory for that to happen. Only when his home was truly settled, and he could hear Inger humming a tune as she moved about the place, would he find the peace of mind he needed to begin serious work and research at home.

For this reason, he began to raise the issue of their wedding plans as early as that same Christmas. At first, his in-laws refused to even discuss this possibility because, they said, Inger was so young. They also pointed out that his future prospects were still not sufficiently secure. Even Inger only accepted the idea reluctantly, but after several rounds of lengthy negotiations, which for Per were often quite demeaning, he this time succeeded in asserting his own wishes and it was determined that the wedding would take place in May of the following year.

Quite apart from the loneliness that oppressed him, and the lack he felt in not having a real home of his own, there was a third (but secret) reason why he wished to expedite the marriage. He was no longer getting on very well with his father-in-law. His own thoughts and ideas had gradually led him so far away from Pastor Blomberg's philosophy that Per was not far off viewing him as an opponent. For the very idea that some kind of bourgeois Father Almighty ruled the world, with the general approval of mankind, in accordance with the pleasantest and most widely held humanitarian principles now seemed almost comical to Per.

In the storm of conflicting beliefs that had raged through his heart, mind, and soul in the last year, he believed that he had caught a glimpse of a world spirit that was far more awesome in nature and had a far more daunting purpose. His daily tours around the district, and the broader insight into human nature this gave him, had also helped to move him further and further away from the Blombergian faith in the Father Almighty. The rank poverty in the hovels where the small-holders lived; the devastation wrought by sickness and ignorance; the whole desperate injustice in the distribution of life's untold bounty when seen from a human perspective—all this lashed him to delve ever deeper into his religious conscience, ever deeper into the mysterious logic that seemed to underpin existence itself.

Of course, his father-in-law was not long in noticing this change of attitude and the arguments grew greater as the atmosphere soured. Pastor Blomberg, who so liberally gave people free reign to believe what they liked about God and the way of the world was, on the other hand, very meticulous about the way he himself was regarded, and he was so used to hearing the influence of his own voice in all the people around him that he took any and every contradiction of his views as a symptom of willful contrariness and evil intent. This same pastor, in other words, who rarely showed much respect for the opinions of others—indeed, who would not shy away from mocking, in a rather juvenile way, alternative religious convictions to his own—

immediately began to invoke the clerical might and authority of his station if he himself should come under attack—a policy of which any trueborn Sidenius would have been proud. When pondering this, Per had often found cause to recall words that Jakobe had either once said or written to him regarding the self-delusional zeal with which the Church had, from time immemorial, secretly gratified an unwholesome urge to despotism under a cloak of piety and virtue.

Moreover, he had also discovered other sources of inspiration during the seclusion of an interminably long winter. These presented other types of people altogether and provided nourishment for his mind and soul, further broadening his appreciation of life's profound tapestry.

There was no doubt that he had become something of a book fiend as the years had progressed. His eyes would always be instinctively drawn to any new volume that appeared before him. On entering the home of the farmers he was obliged to visit, almost the first thing he looked for was the small bookshelf they would invariably possess. Seldom did he leave again without having browsed through its contents.

It must be said that these shelves usually consisted of much the same thing: the Holy Bible, some historical novels by Ingemann, Holberg's comedies, a volume of popular science books, two or three farming manuals, a selection of the so-called schoolteacher literature written by schoolmasters, or its more highbrow cousin—curate and high school poetry—then usually a range of spiritual and edifying texts. Naturally enough in this district, these were of the Blombergian variety. However, in certain homes, examples could also be found of older religious tracts. These had survived purely by chance and were small, thick books with the most peculiar titles. One was called *The Oil of Salvation*, another *A Little Golden Treasure Trove of Faith*.

In one home, Per found a volume called *Four Books on the Imitation of Christ*. And he was particularly struck by *The Bleeding Wounds and Inflictions of Jesus as the Surest Refuge for all Sinners Beset by Distress*. These farmer folk became almost embarrassed when they were found to be in possession of such pietistic writings from a dark and benighted period in the country's past, and when, in reality, no one ever read them anymore, it was not difficult for Per to acquire some of them for his own library. It was the curiosity value of the books that had first attracted him; but when, one evening, he sat down and browsed through one of them, looking out in particular for sections carrying the most vivid stamp of former reading customs and the mindset they reflected, he realized that the florid and then alternatively naive and crude tone of these old popular tracts which should really have offended his sensibilities, were strangely appealing to him. And this brought him further down this path.

With his relentlessly growing need to get to the bottom of who and what he was, to understand the essence of his being even in its most transient sensations, he began a historical study of religious life in the period from which the greater part of these writings originated. By way of these investigations, he was led all the way back to the 1700s and the pietistic movement during the reign of King Christian the Sixth, and then forward again as the Age of Enlightenment arrived in Denmark, but also Moravian separatism, and finally the remarkable movement of lay preachers at the beginning of the 1800s. It was from this lay movement that the present-day folk-religious revival had developed. The portrayals of those farmers sons from Funen and Jutland, as well as the village tradesmen and their unwavering and stubborn fight against the rationalist orthodoxy of those times, gripped his imagination strongly. In the manner of latter-day apostles, these solitary figures moved from town to town professing their faith. And for this very reason, they were jeered and mocked by the rabble, hounded by clerics and imprisoned by the authorities. Then there were small congregations dotted here and there with their austere evangelical lives, their backs turned to the outside world—the whole movement was The New Testament re-enacted on Danish soil.

Per discovered that one of these dramatic stories from Denmark's history actually came from his father-in-law's own parish. In a small whitewashed and well-kept house by Bøstrup's general tillage land, there lived a clog maker and his family. These people kept themselves to themselves and never sought to engage with the local populace. The man drove into the local market town once a year with his clogs and other wooden items and sold them to marketgoers; otherwise he stayed at home—a home where above the door leading into the house, the following words had been painted onto a board: "I and this household wish only to serve the Lord." Per had inadvertently landed in this house on one occasion while doing a tour of the district looking for experienced fascine layers for the summer work in the fields. On entering the living room, he encountered a young mother standing by a baby's cot, and a couple of small children who played a game quietly. A door leading into an adjacent workshop was open and Per saw a man sitting over a cobbler's bench cutting leather. On seeing Per, the man got up and came into the main room with a somewhat reticent manner. He was a middle-aged man, tall, but slightly stooping. Per took immediate exception to his beardless and somewhat pale face and his sunken eyes. The man's young wife was no different. She stole quick, almost hostile, glances at Per as she rocked the cradle. Yes, the man bade him sit down, but there was no warmth in the request. He rejected out of hand Per's proposal that he might take employment in the summer months on the river realignment works. It was as if, in so doing, the idea was removed from his consciousness forever.

Despite this, Per remained sitting there for a while. For all the hostility that was shown towards him, there was something about this domestic scene that appealed to him. The cleanliness and order in the room was quite a rare phenomenon in houses of such modest means. It was as if the arrival of some eminent visitor was expected at any moment. The house, it seemed, should always be ready to receive a high-born guest. It was clear that veneration for God, which reigned in this house, was not just an affectation to be displayed during festive occasions. Rather, it was an undeniable expression of a faith that had transformed the inner essence of these people's lives. Even in the way the man took one of the children onto his lap during their conversation and gently wiped his nose with his finger did not seem worthy of ridicule. Rather, there was a somber gentleness in the act—a sign that their concerns were not of this world and its affectations.

Back at Pastor Blomberg's rectory, Per was told that this family belonged to a sect whose members called themselves "The Anointed," and that they had gained in popularity across the country in recent times. His father-in-law bluntly declared them to be a pack of sanctimonious hypocrites and that their presence in his area brought shame upon the congregation.

Every time Per subsequently read about, say, the apprentice cobbler Ole Henrik Svane, about Kristen Madsen on the island of Funen, or the other lay preachers from the time of the religious revival, he once again saw the small room with its air of anticipation out there by Bøstrup's tillage fields. There was also the fact that the names of the preachers he most frequently came across during his reading were already familiar to him from his father having mentioned them. He was even distantly related to some of them. Overall, it was these factors that made the accounts given in the books so vivid for him—the characters so believable, so close to him.

But at the same time, this process led him to a depressing realization. By comparing the innate belief in divine providence amongst these people with his own, he felt that he neither was, nor ever had been, a true believing Christian. In fact, he no longer felt the urge to become one of them.

It was not so much the strict asceticism that put him off. He understood more than anyone else the satisfaction that could be gained from such an inward-looking, self-abnegating approach to life. It was the blind fervor in their prayers, the nature of their dreams, that appalled him. He had prayed a lot himself in the last year. But prayers and acts of worship had for him mostly served as a fortification and purging of the soul, a flight from earthly impurities and desires. And though he also understood those who believed that prayer could truly provide protection from harm—that prayer would bring help in our hour of greatest danger and need—he also sensed a sigh of actual longing for troubles and afflictions within the prayers of those same pious Christians. In their rejection of all worldly values, in their terror of temptation, and in their conviction as true Christians that they were condemned to a life of ceaseless pilgrimage, they seemed to gladly call disaster and persecution upon their own heads.

"Feed me, O Lord, with the bread of tears and give me drink of tears in equal measure. To Thee I commend myself, and all that I have, for correction. Better is it to be punished here than hereafter. Thy discipline over me, and Thy rod itself, shall teach me. For this is Thy favor to Thy friend, that he should suffer and be troubled in the world for Thy love's sake. Lord I thank Thee, because Thou hast not excused my sins, but beaten me with terrible blows."

Upon encountering these words and this language, an involuntarily shiver ran through his very soul—just as it had on reading the letter his mother had left for him. For the core of his human sensibilities instinctively recoiled from this kind of voracious faith, which consumed the lifeblood of all existence.

"Verily, living upon this earth is a misery," wrote Thomas à Kempis in his book *The Imitation of Christ.* "To eat and drink, to keep watch and sleep, to rest, to labor, and to be bound by those other necessities of nature is truly a great woe and affliction to any devout man. Oh if there were nothing else to do but praise the Lord our God; then would you be far happier than you are now, where your every necessity makes you nothing more than a servant of the flesh."

What particularly disturbed Per as he delved into these texts was something that he had actually realized some years previously during his somewhat haphazard study of a translation of Plato's *Phaedo.* This was an increasing awareness that Christian values were actually older than Christ himself, in whom they had simply found their most complete expression—at least up to the present. In other words, he could not even console himself with the idea that these Christian thoughts and urges would simply have been a passing human fancy had state powers and emperors not chosen to bestow upon them the status of a spiritual imperium. These values seemed to have their roots in the very essence of man's primeval disposition and drew sustenance from an instinct that lay beyond Nature, and which, wherever they manifested themselves, could vanquish what appeared to be more natural motivations.

"For the body causes us a thousand troubles. Thus, while we live on earth, we can only come close to spiritual revelation when we have the least possible intercourse or communion with it, and do not allow ourselves to become surfeit with its nature."

The words of Socrates rang once again in his ears. And what about the Buddha's wisdom? A snatch of a Buddhist treatise he once read had burned into his mind and blazed like phosphorous scripture every time his inner conscience grew dark: "He who loves nothing in this world and carries neither hate nor desire in his heart—only he has no chains and is without fear."

From all the four corners of the world the same answer! Right down through the history of mankind the same command: the denial of the self, the expunging of the I—because happiness lay in a renunciation of this world. But the world cried out against this: self-assertion, vanity, and selfishness, the power of physical force and the triumph of the will—because happiness was appropriation and aggrandizement. There was no bridge to be found across the void between the two. Scourge the flesh or scourge the spirit—they were the only two options! There was no way around this stark choice if one didn't, as in the case of his father-in-law and many of his bedfellows, possess that happy faculty of self-delusion by which one's personal horizons could be occluded in an intellectual fog of rhapsodic platitudes. There seemed to be no way out other than nailing one's colors to a particular mast—either pledge oneself to the way of the cross or the champagne glass—and there could be no hesitation or misgivings; supreme confidence in one's convictions, in fact euphoria, was the name of the game that everybody played.

So in the end it came back to faith as the mainstay and vindicating force in life. The problem was that he, Per Sidenius, had no such reassuring belief anymore, either in heaven or in worldly affairs. He had no wish to be reconciled with the great mass of the world's offspring, and the Christian abode was a cold house for him. And, above all, there was no going back to that state of blind innocence professed by Pastor Blomberg and like a child—in ignorant equanimity—pluck flowers at the very edge of the abyss, blissfully unaware of the irresistible drag from the swirling demonic forces in the chasm below.

*

On a gray, dank morning in the beginning of March, Per's gig was to be seen waiting outside his door. Given that he was still without a stall of his own, he was forced to keep his horse and carriage at the inn. It was the stable lad from the inn who now stood there by the side of the horse. The lad cursed quietly to himself as he beat his arms across his chest in an effort to keep warm. He had already been waiting for nearly half an hour.

At last Per tumbled out of the front door. He was drunk with sleep and wearing his winter greatcoat. He got in, took the reins from the stable boy and jolted off. As usual, he had sat up half the night reading, and when he had finally gone to bed, his myriad thoughts and speculations had kept him awake until dawn. But now the fresh breeze out on the road quickly blew the night-time trance from his eyes. Besides, his trap was not exactly made for somnambulant travel. It was an old, worn-out puddle jumper, so dilapidated in its works that the slightest disproportion in the road provoked a violent jolting and clanging of its springs. On the other hand, his horse was a doughty Norwegian pony, whose only fault perhaps was that, from sheer caution, it had the habit of zigzagging from one side to the other if the road ever sloped too far from the norm. The beast's keen eyes were so discerning that it surpassed any level measurement he possessed and could detect the slightest deviation from the horizontal plane ahead of it. To begin with, and to preserve his reputation as an equestrian, Per made efforts to straighten out these bad habits by way of the whip and loud instructions, but he had soon grown so fond of this devoted and surefooted animal, who day after day hauled him around the district in all kinds of weather, that the horse was allowed to follow its nose more often than not.

Whenever possible, he arranged his day so that his route could pass by Bøstrup, so that he could bring a morning greeting to Inger. He knew that she always looked out for him at this time of day and, for that reason, these morning sojourns took on a particularly grand and festive air. But the drive itself at this time of day was a joy to him—

especially on mornings such as this when the fresh weather drove the morning mist and low cloud across the fields towards the horizon and flocks of crows shrieked as they hung in the gales that ran over the land. Here and now, there were no romantic notions in his head about his spirit melding with Mother Nature. No longer—unlike the time he was out fishing on the river at Kærsholm—did he feel any sense of experiencing some mystical revelation. No, it was once more like the days of his early youth—a purely physical sense of contentment and wellbeing that he felt when he observed the racing clouds up above and the swaying treetops that lined the road he traveled. His muscles bulged in his limbs and his blood pumped through his body. It was as if nature bestowed its power directly upon his physical frame.

When he now thought back to the things that had kept him awake at night and how he had once believed that he would never find peace in his soul until he had worked out all the mysteries of life, he almost smiled. In these precious moments, racing along in his gig, while his reflective self still slumbered and before the many minor annoyances of the day had managed to disturb his mental harmony, he once more embraced the world and its natural attractions with utter confidence. On such mornings, all of life's obscure and dubious issues became so meaningless to him, in comparison with the undeniable physical fact that he sat there, a young man in his own carriage, on the way to see the woman he loved, so that he could inaugurate the day with a kiss on her sweet mouth. He offered up praise to that God in whom he barely believed anymore, praised life with all its joys, sorrows, and hardships; all of it, he felt, was worthy of his gratitude, regardless of where it eventually led. What, therefore, was the point in endlessly deliberating things? Self-inflicted scruples were the devil's work. In essence, a refusal to accept that life would sometimes throw up problems and obstacles was just hypocritical arrogance. In two and a half months' time, his wedding was to take place. On the twentieth of May, Inger's birthday, he would bring her home as his flower-bestrewn bride and his doleful years of loneliness would be over forever!

On this particular day, Per intended to go somewhere that had been in the back of his mind for some time. Some of the meadow boundaries that would be affected by his river realignment work lay in the area covered by Borup rectory and this gave him a good pretext to head for that area. It was also the case that he had not spoken with Pastor Fjaltring since that chance meeting in the hay shed during the thunder storm a good one and a half years ago. There had been a couple of occasions where he had actually driven past this peculiar man around sunset as he took one of his notorious evening strolls down remote roads and byways; and of course he had always called out a greeting, but the pastor had not recognized him. Or at least that was the impression that was given. But in his travels across the district, Per had heard lots of people talking about Pastor Fjaltring and his unhappy family life. In particular, the most unbelievable rumors were being put about regarding his wife—not only was she supposed to be ruined with the drink, but in her younger days had committed sexual excesses of the most base kind. Furthermore, there was no doubt that her slovenliness and sloth were the main reasons that the pastor had repeatedly suffered the severest financial problems imaginable. All this had aroused Per's concern for the man. But the other reason why he had not acted sooner in visiting Pastor Fjaltring was that he imagined, as Pastor Blomberg's son-in-law, that he would hardly be welcomed with open arms. After all, his father-in-law had not only taken the greatest part of Fjaltring's congregation away from him but had also, thereby, robbed him of desperately required funds in tithe income.

The road dropped in a wide arc down to Bøstrup village and Per's face suddenly brightened. There behind the garden gate of the rectory he had caught sight of Inger, who was standing with a scarf covering her head and was obviously keeping watch for him.

"You big lazybones!" she cried in greeting. "Where have you been all morning?"

"Ah, sorry Inger. Have you been waiting long?"

"Per, I'm frozen stiff standing here this long."

"Ah—my poor darling Inger!"

He had now come quite close to the garden and steered the gig so near to her that their mouths—concealed from the house by a rose-hip bush—could meet across the low fence.

"Good morning my own sweet angel!"

"Good morning yourself! And what expedition are you going on today, my only dearest man?"

"Ah, Inger, I've a million things to do. In fact, I'd better get going."

"Per, darling. You are impossible. How am I going to keep up with you? Always busy and no time for poor Inger. Well, off with you then! Are you coming to see me this evening?"

"How could I stay away, sweet thing!"

There was another kiss, and then another. And then another, "just for the hell of it"—as Per put it.

"Ah, you bold boy! Well, off with you then, before I chain you!"

"Bye my darling!"

"Bye bye . . . and come back to me as quick as you can!"

"I will of course!"

"Goodbye then darling. You go first!"

"Bye bye."

"See you this evening, Per."

The light brown horse had already begun to pull away with a toss of its head, but they continued holding hands until they were almost literally torn apart. And there were more and goodbyes and "see you soon sweetheart" and then more waving, until the carriage disappeared behind the building of a neighboring farm.

Towards dinner time, and after having spent several hours out in the meadows with his theodolite and tripod, Per drove down to Borup rectory.

Pastor Fjaltring was at home and received him in his study. This was a large room, almost of hall proportions. It was also set in half darkness—partly because the only source of daylight came from two small windows. The size of the room also made what furnishing there was appear even more miserable and forlorn. The first thing Per saw was an open book that lay on a desk situated between the two windows. It was from here that this strange lair dweller had emerged and stepped towards him as soon as he had walked through the door.

There was in this priest's demeanor that same unsettling mixture of shyness, curiosity and arrogance which had struck Per on the day

766 · HENRIK PONTOPPIDAN

he had seen him in church. Pastor Fjaltring pulled up a few steps from him and greeted him with undoubted graciousness, but in almost complete silence, and with his hands behind his back. Per could not ascertain whether the pastor recognized him or not. Once Per had introduced himself, Pastor Fjaltring indicated towards the sofa with his hand and then sat down in an armchair a distance away. He then asked Per how he might be of service.

Per began by asking questions regarding the proposed excavation of some ditches in parcels of meadowland adjacent to the rectory. Pastor Fjaltring answered that, by rights, he had no authority to make personal decisions regarding glebe land, but given that the proposed work was minimal, it was probably safe to give his blessing. The only thing he would ask is that a short written presentation of the required land alterations be provided for possible future consultation and Per gladly assented to this.

The whole interview lasted no more than a few minutes and was followed by a lengthy silence. Pastor Fjaltring sat, bent forward slightly, over his clasped hands and was obviously waiting for Per to leave. But when Per gave sign that he actually was about to depart, his host seemed to become anxious at having been impolite. Pastor Fjaltring quickly asked Per what he thought of the area and when he heard that he had set up a home near the railway station, the priest remarked that "Hr. Engineer would not want for company." He went on to state that a minor market town had been established down there by Rimalt. Then he mentioned Per's neighbors—the school principal, the chemist, and a number of other people in the area. On the other hand, neither Per's father-in-law, nor his home at Bøstrup rectory, were mentioned at all.

Per, who had retained quite a strong impression of Pastor Fjaltring's personality and character from their encounter in the lightning storm, was slightly disappointed by his bland platitudes. He was also offended by the fact that the priest lumped him in with the so-called Toddy Club down at the inn by the station—especially as it was clear that Pastor Fjaltring—judging by his tone—had very little respect for these people. Thus, Per said, with some emphasis, that he did not make it his business to look for "company" in Rimalt. In fact, quite the opposite—he preferred to live alone and spend his time reading.

Pastor Fjaltring raised his head slightly. He still refrained from looking directly at Per, but an attentive almost listening expression appeared in his small, pale yellow face.

"Well, yes," the pastor said. "The reclusive life in the world of pure thought can have certain attractions. And, indeed, also has its comforts. One might almost say blessings."

His face then broadened into a smile as he added that it could sometimes even offer companionship. For it was often the case, he continued, that inward speculation led to the disturbing feeling that a stranger had taken up residence in one's own personality.

Per, who now felt slighted by this remark, sought to return the comparison by averring that such strangers unfortunately often proved to be very difficult guests who provoked distress, anxiety, and strange behavior.

Once again, that startled and almost attentive expression flickered across Pastor Fjaltring's face. However, he did not pursue the subject, only adding by way of a final comment that it was also true that one turned to the thoughts of others in order to chase away one's own. Books could be a great diversion. But the views people published in books were rarely meant to frighten or provoke real thought.

Once again a silence ensued. It was clear that Pastor Fjaltring had touched on something that he did not wish to investigate further. Per understood that the pastor was on his guard against him and there was no prospect of a real conversation. Thus he rose from his seat and, this time, Pastor Fjaltring made no attempt to delay his departure. But again he was the height of good manners. In fact, at the point of departure, the pastor even held out his hand—a strangely dry and hot hand—and courteously requested Per's forbearance in not following him to his carriage, for fear of the draft in the hallway.

As short and seemingly insignificant as this meeting had been, enough interest had been stirred in Per's mind for him to raise the matter at Bøstrup rectory during their evening meal. His in-laws were clearly not happy with the way he spoke so animatedly on the issue. He stopped talking as soon as he picked this up, at which point his father-in-law sought to smooth things over by resorting to a statement he often used when his neighboring priest came up in conversation: "That poor unfortunate man! I really do feel so sorry for him. If only he had never become a priest!"

As early as the very next day, Per set about preparing the report that Pastor Fjaltring had requested. He took great care over its several drafts and then carefully transcribed the final version onto a large sheet of paper. As a final flourish, he drew up an addendum that comprised a very precise ground plan of all the meadowlands that adjoined Pastor Fjaltring's rectory.

A week later, when Per's work in the district led him in the direction of Borup once again, he drove into the rectory in order to deliver the document. Pastor Fjaltring, who was so unused to anyone showing him a kindness, became embarrassed on seeing Per's finely crafted work and thanked him sincerely; and when Per then made immediate moves to leave, he became quite agitated and begged Per's forgiveness if on the previous occasion he had been somewhat out of sorts. In order to get Per to stay, Pastor Fjaltring almost dragged him to the sofa and before long a conversation ensued that was quite open and frank in nature.

It was the document Per had brought with him that paved the way for what was to come. For Per informed the pastor that he had found a layer of peat bog in the rectory meadow, and that it was a substantial deposit. It lay quite deeply in the soil, and there would possibly be some difficulty in getting to it, but, for that very reason, it was likely to be of high quality for turf burning. Thus, Per continued, he was convinced that investment in a modest pumping unit that would keep the excavation dry was worthwhile so that the beds could be dug out for fuel processing.

Pastor Fjaltring, who had remained standing directly in front of Per on a narrow carpet runner in the middle of an otherwise bare floor, shook his head and gave a somber smile that smacked of defeat. That kind of thing would have to be left in the hands of his successor, he said. His health and general constitution was not such that he could make any real plans for the future.

"Besides, Hr. Engineer, even if the grim reaper spares me for a while yet, I'm not sure how much longer the church authorities and my diligent clerical brothers in Christ will allow me to preach to empty pews."

Per reddened at this and made a polite attempt at an objection; but the pastor cut him off.

"Oh please, I'm under no illusions. Our so-called New Age has turned religion into a commodity, and it's quite understandable that people will seek out those market booths where they believe they can procure their redemption at the cheapest price."

Per looked away. It was not that he found the accusation unjust but, for Inger's sake, he felt duty bound to defend his father-in-law. He pointed out that, regardless of how banal and superficial modern religious movements seemed to be, they at least performed the function of raising awareness of spiritual matters and, therefore, were preparing a new cultural period in history. Where spiritual life and the receptiveness to same was concerned, Per continued, the conclusion he had drawn on his travels abroad was that Danish farmers and smallholders were far superior to their rural equals, particularly in Catholic countries. But Pastor Fjaltring's immediate reply to this was that a well-meaning or a religion "just in case" attitude, or even just a curious interest in life's great mysteries, was, in his eyes, far worse than having no interest whatsoever. Faith was a passion, and where this was absent, the "believer" was mocking God himself. Trying to raise spiritual consciousness amongst the people by planting artificial roots was so far removed from preparing the ground for a truly sincere and serious faith—or even sincere doubt—that, on the contrary, it actually strangled the genuine empathy with God that every human soul possessed innately.

Pastor Fjaltring had begun walking up and down the carpet as he spoke; but now he suddenly stopped at the other end of the room. It was as if he was trying to remind himself not to venture too far in his oration. But it was too late. The urge to profess had been aroused in his breast. All the thoughts he had wrestled with in all those long lonely hours now burst forth in an unstoppable torrent of words.

He told Per that modern technicians and engineers had to share some of the blame for the lack of reflection and superficiality—the twin curse afflicting the people of today. The ceaseless agitation of the machine age had infected religious and spiritual life. As could be seen in all areas of life, people had become accustomed to acquiring the necessities of life via as little personal endeavor as possible. Now this attitude had spread to religious belief, where it was hoped that faith could be obtained without much need for commitment in terms of time and energy. And as far as the Church's evangelists were concerned—be they men of the cloth or lay folk—they made every effort to satisfy this demand. We pointed with no little pride here in this country, the pastor said, at our folk high schools, which as you know have developed into a whole establishment in their own right—an establishment, moreover, where a modeled and guaranteed life philosophy is stamped onto its students in the run of three or four months. It looked like a miracle, but was actually one huge swindle. For in order to achieve that same simplification and reduced cost—why they found it more expedient to simply replace religion with poetry, give the travails of existence a more poetic gloss. Of course, the whole thing is a depressing and false veneer.

With this harsh critique of the Church in mind, the pastor then went on to assert that this was precisely why the alleged benefits of the so-called religious folk revival here at home had been nothing more than a well-glossed form of materialism.

The provocative tone in Pastor Fjaltring's address to Per left him with a feeling of quiet dejection—not least because this priest was only saying things that he actually agreed with. But still there was no stopping the man.

Yes—he continued—it was true that, with regards to the soul of man and the best conditions for its nurturing and development, very little was unfortunately known about it. However, it seemed fairly certain from the evidence of history, and also the testimony of many individuals, that, just like everything else of worth in the world, the soul required time and a certain element of resistance in order to grow. It was also widely admitted that a surfeit of happiness and good fortune in worldly affairs left a man empty and gelded.

The soul's natural sphere was sorrow, suffering, sacrifice. Joy was an animal remnant that had been left within us—and it was no doubt for this reason that, in prosperous and successful times, people were able to commit all kinds of idiocies and carry on like strutting peacocks; while in harsher times, when they reached deep inside themselves and found the divine source of their essential humanity, they would suddenly take on a completely blissful and transfigured demeanor. Yes it was true that Christianity came into the world proclaiming the Good News, but if this phrase was to be taken literally one became stuck in an irreconcilable contradiction. And this was that a creed professing tranquillity, peace of mind, and joy clogged up the very sources of nourishment required by the soul—extinguished all spiritual and intellectual life, in fact, healed the sick by actually killing the patient.

"Even the actual idea of a paradise on the other side of death, as a place of utter perfection, is difficult to reconcile with our present religious insights. It seems to me that the term 'Abandon hope, all ye who enter here,' which Dante told us was inscribed on the gateway to hell, could just as appropriately—and with far more terrible significance—be emblazoned above the gateway to the kind of heaven where things were supposedly so perfect that further personal development would not be an option. Indeed, for our limited human sensibilities, it would seem that, in the long run, it is the unredeemed amongst us—those who are either permanently or temporarily damned—that one will find the truly purged and purified souls and genuine blessedness. For is it not these souls that profess a genuine religious conviction and confession?

"But it is possible, Hr. Engineer, that we have completely misunderstood what God's Evangelium is all about. And if that is the case, this might explain the bald fact that after two thousand years, and despite all the high-minded words and promises, Christianity has still not managed to achieve much progress with regard to mankind's moral standing. Certain theologians even deny that Christ's birth was a divine act, and it has to be said that it is difficult to detect a family resemblance between him and the God of the Old Testament. Do we wildly exaggerate if we say that the one is the complete contradiction of the other—yes, actually a travesty of the other? Of course, Christ was also an abomination to the Jews. But if the man called Jesus was not the son of God, who then can guarantee that Our Lord did not in fact place him amongst us, and allow him to be tortured and suffer an ignominious death, so as to serve as a terrifying example of what true faith requires?"

Pastor Fjaltring once more stopped abruptly in his progress up and down the carpet—as if he himself was shocked by his own words. As his speech had progressed, his forehead had become enflamed with a red aura. A subtle but clearly visible nervous twitch also ran incessantly from his shoulder and across his face.

"Well, I trust that Hr. Sidenius understands that it is not my intention to mock the Lord with what I am discussing. All I am saying is that if the figure of Christ and its mission here in this world is to really become the subject of critical debate—and there is no doubt that we have now reached that point—well, let us have that debate to the very core of the issue and without fear or favor. Even if our very salvation is placed in jeopardy by so doing!"

Per was at a loss to know how to respond to this torrent of thoughts; and it was clear that Pastor Fjaltring was not conscious of how far he had traveled from their initial talking point. Nor did the pastor notice that the door behind him had been opened and his wife had come into the room. Only when Per stood up and gave a short bow of his head did he turn towards his wife. He then fell silent.

Privately, Per admitted that the gossip amongst the local populace was not exaggerated where her looks were concerned. She was enormously fat and her face boasted the florid copper tones of a lifelong sot. Her livid face gave her torpid eyes a blind whiteness against the color of her skin. Her slovenliness was all the more noticeable because she had obviously made efforts to beautify herself. She had flattened the front of her hair down with water and had put on a quite presentable dress; but under her skewed bonnet, the rest of her hair was making efforts to burst out like the filling in a ripped pillow. A glance at her footwear below her long dress, meanwhile, revealed a pair of worn-out and filthy shoes.

When her husband had introduced Per to her, she gave a most expansive smile.

"Would Hr. Sidenius do us the honor of sharing some lunch with us? The food is on the table."

For the second time, Per was stuck for words. His pity for poor Pastor Fjaltring crushed his heart. His preference would have been to say no, but he dreaded the offense he might cause, and so accepted the invitation.

However Per was surprised to discover that Pastor Fjaltring's attitude towards his wife showed no sign of gloom or desperation. True, he was a bit guarded throughout the whole meal and appeared distracted; but in his behavior towards his wife he was the epitome of the considerate husband—indeed there was the odd flash of gallantry. For her part, she obviously did not have the least idea of her personal degradation. She even led the conversation at the table, as she—in a confused and somewhat rambling way—described her younger days in Copenhagen and then memories of her childhood in North Zealand, where her father had been a priest. She also clearly had the habit of never paying attention to what anyone else said, which in the end meant that she was the only one who spoke.

When the two men returned to the pastor's study, Per sensed immediately that their interrupted conversation could not be continued. Nor did Pastor Fjaltring insist that he should stay. However, this time he followed Per out into the hallway and thanked him once again for the consideration he had shown him with regard to the fine ground plan. Moreover, he told Per that he would be glad to see him anytime his journey took him past the rectory.

Per was delighted by this request and made it his business, thereafter, to make frequent visits to the rectory whenever his work with trench and ditch excavations facilitated such visits. In the end, he visited Pastor Fjaltring without any excuse whatsoever and always felt very welcome. However, he never again set foot in Borup church, and it was not just due deference to his father-in-law that kept him away. The impression Pastor Fjaltring's sermon had made upon him, from the only time he had heard him preach, left him with no desire to repeat the experience. For up on the pulpit, Pastor Fjaltring produced the unfortunate effect of a Punch and Judy character.

The man was a truth seeker and never a lightning rod for collective emotions; nor was he a tub-thumping preacher. No. One had to seek this priest in his hermitage. And even there, if one appeared unannounced, he might sometimes flap around like a timid and panicking moth that had suddenly been exposed to a bright light. If he was not crushed with embarrassment at the thought of his clothing, which was rarely arranged for viewing by strangers, he was oppressed by his imagined ailments and would flit from one chair to the other never finding peace; or he might sit, almost bent over, with his hand pressed against his bandaged head. In Per's presence, this shyness abated quite quickly, and once it had been overcome, he could then speak for hours without seeming to flag.

Per never mentioned his continued contact with the heretic priest in Bøstrup rectory. Nor did he confide this information to Inger. He was well aware that, on behalf of her father, she would take grave offense at this and, in the interim, he would not be in a position to explain why this new relationship appealed so much to him. For the truth was that his prospective wife still retained a quite childlike belief in her father's infallibility. No, that conversation would have to wait until they could discuss things in private as man and wife. On those few occasions where a little verbal spat had broken out between himself and his father-in-law on matters spiritual, she had been extremely cross with him in the aftermath and gave Per to understand that his presumption in contradicting her father was viewed as nothing more than immature arrogance.

Thus, that clandestine and furtive air that came to rest over his visits to Pastor Fjaltring served to color the impressions he took away with him from them and added a mysterious glow to their encounters.

But Pastor Fjaltring's remarkably wide and esoteric knowledge added to this effect. For the first time in his life, Per was introduced to the concept and life view of medieval theology. Pastor Fjaltring led him into the byzantine meditative temples of the Scholastics; he was initiated into the fantastic Gothic dreamscapes of the pre-Reformation visionaries; heard about men like Meister Eckhart, Johannes Tauler, Blessed John of Ruysbroeck, and Gerard Groote—all of whom had clearly inspired Pastor Fjaltring to undertake extensive studies in their lives and personalities. Moreover, the pastor seemed not to take much offense at any school of thought or particular faith system, past or present. He even proved to be highly informed regarding certain grim and inverted religious visions such as Satan worship, the Rosicrucian Order and black mass rituals. Indeed, he was able to quote verbatim from long tracts written by authors that were members of these secret societies.

But what really grabbed Per's attention more than anything else during these visits was Pastor Fjaltring's own character and that stamp of personal experience he revealed and emphasized in all he said and spoke about. For just as he seemed to be familiar with every philosophy under the sun, he also seemed to know every aspect of human desire and affliction through intimate personal experience. Even when he spoke about Hell, he did so in a way and with such a baleful gaze that it was as if he had been there and, by speaking of it, was reliving its many terrors and torments. But in his brighter moments, he could also reflect Heaven in his refined, animated, and ever-changing features. Fleetingly, a distant look would come over his pale face that seemed to encapsulate the rare music of the planetary spheres that was otherwise beyond the human ear.

When Per subsequently found himself sitting in Bøstrup rectory listening to his ruddy-faced father-in-law, he felt more keenly than ever how little value could be imputed to such cheaply bought insouciance in comparison with a belief, yes even serious doubt, that had caused the believer endless internal discord and the price of his heart's blood.

This contradiction was particularly stark for him at one of the so-called private clerical conventions that were held at the rectory a couple of times each year. Here, the allegedly liberally minded clergy of the region would gather, under his father-in-law's watchful patronage, to debate the more controversial topics that were dominating church life at that time. Even in Pastor Fjaltring's most blasphemous fulminations, there seemed to Per to be more true holiness than all the Lutheran waffling and "hail fellow well met" games that were played with Our Lord by these fakers and chancers. When he looked at them sitting there—jovial, indifferent, or marked by the type of thespian self-obsession which the folk revivalist meetings had encouraged—and then saw how they prattled on with billowing pipes in their gobs about the forgiveness of sins, or exactly how God granted the prayers of the faithful; when he heard them trying to outdo each other in their false professions of equality and fairness; how they were happy to accommodate modern-day demands that religious experience be available at a discount, then did he truly understood both the term "merchant men" that Pastor Fjaltring had bestowed upon them, and the pastor's description of such an effete and lisping tendency as "exalted materialism."

In short, Per had grown much more critical of certain aspects of his father-in-law's character. In particular, his disapproval was increased when, by sheer accident, he discovered the true story behind Blomberg's strange treatment of his old father, whom the farm overseer at Kærsholm had already mentioned to him. Just as the rumors had suggested, the old man lived in wretched conditions some place or other on the island of Funen, and the reason his son, Pastor Blomberg, had turned his back on this already aging man was that he had transgressed the Sixth Commandment by committing adultery and making a servant girl pregnant. Pastor Blomberg, who loved to give the impression of being a free thinker where questions of theological beliefs were concerned, was not in any way pliant when it came to moral standards. In common with the vast majority of his fellow clerics, where matters of morality were concerned, he had planted his standard on the highest traditional ground so as to compensate for the territory the Church had been forced to cede to modern-day rational argument in the valley below.

Per also suspected that his father-in-law was actually quite glad to have an excuse to keep this difficult and apparently almost blind old man from his door. It seemed clear that there had never been any kind of wholehearted bond between father and son, and self-sacrifice did not form part of Pastor Blomberg's Christian armory. For while he himself kept a large house and had, without compunction, frequently demanded that his congregation show their appreciation of him in the form of a cascade of coins, he was always slow to offer a helping hand to others. On more than one occasion, Per had been witness to how his father-in-law dealt with the poor and destitute in the area who came to him for help, with the pastor sufficing with a promise that he would "enfold them in the warmth of his prayers."

All that considered, Per did not doubt the basic integrity of his father-in-law's religious convictions. But the thing he felt was out of kilter, and the thing that at the end of the day decided his position with regard to Christianity, was that where it did not, as was the practice with those deemed to be "holy," dismiss ordinary people outright, it seemed unable to have an ennobling and refining influence on human discourse and ideals. Rather, it was self-doubt and unbelief that seemed to possess the capacity for rebirth and resurrection.

When Per sought to understand why getting to know Pastor Fjaltring was of importance to him, he discovered that it was precisely because, through him, he had found comfort and solace for his divided self—that inability to be reconciled to a specifically defined life philosophy, an inability that in the past had brought him to the brink of despair. In his discourse, Pastor Fjaltring always returned to the point that doubt was the necessary prerequisite for faith—its "wonderful and eternally liberating catalyst." As sure as day followed night, and then night came again; and just as all life on earth was born out of this dialectic between the dark and the light, so too was religious life conditioned by this inexorable paradox that, with its conflicting forces, ensured that the soul was in constant flux. A Christian faith that was not continually renewed by doubt was a lifeless thing—nothing more than a broom handle, a crutch which might help a soul to forget its lameness for a while, but could never be a life-affirming construct.

In one of more humorous moments, Pastor Fjaltring had said: "If it is true that the road to Hell is paved with good intentions; why, surely the road to heaven must be paved with our bad ones?" Per subsequently worked out that there was more truth in this somewhat throwaway remark than was at first apparent, because—he told himself—just as the physical trajectory of the human body was a constant, if occasionally interrupted, downwards spiral, so was our spiritual progress towards perfection actually an unstoppable fall from grace, from which we were rescued by an instinctive urge to self-preservation that could only be of divine origin.

As Per looked back at his own spiritual and intellectual development, it seemed to him that it was an almost perfect illustration of this concept. And, as he now looked towards the future, he was full of confidence and hope.

Bøstrup rectory was alive with preparations for the forthcoming wedding. The sewing machine hummed and thrummed the whole day, and Fru Blomberg continually fed its supply line from her weekly trips to the market town where most of the nuptial paraphernalia had been ordered. Terms such as drill weave, coarse linen, insertions, reps, bolsters, grenadine, hair curlers, hickory wood finish, battered Per about the ears from the moment he walked through the door. To Per, Inger seemed more animated about carpenters and saddle-makers than the fact that an initiation into the delights of love and married life was supposed to be taking place. It was not long before he felt completely superfluous to requirements at the rectory.

Thus, he spent more and more time at his own home, quietly preparing for her arrival. By this time, he had managed to secure a sizable source of income. For quite apart from the land reclamation and river realignment work, he had taken on various smaller jobs about the district, which regularly provided him with handsome earnings. This meant that he had already been able to repay his debt to Eberhard and his other siblings; he had even managed to put aside the first repayment of his debt to Philip Salomon and Ivan.

So now he could turn to the task of knocking his own rather dilapidated home into shape—inside and out. He put up new wallpaper in all the rooms and replaced the cold and ancient flagstone floor in the kitchen with a timbered surface. Nor was his inventiveness found wanting in these more mundane, domestic requirements, but manifested itself in a number of small but practical design and installation ideas. The air draft for the chimney was improved; the water run-off for outside drains and funnels was aligned correctly, and so on. He knew that nothing would gladden Inger's heart more than a well-stocked and fitted kitchen, a bright, cool, and well-aired pantry, a freshly whitewashed cellar, and a bulging fuel room. She had inherited her mother's fondness for order and cleanliness and could become ecstatic over a shining plate, or newly polished copper implements, in a way that others might view a work of art.

Now things went as they normally do, when improving one thing revealed deficiencies in others. For when Per stood back and looked at the finished kitchen and pantry, he realized that the sitting room would have to have a new floor. In other words, without really noticing it himself, he had gradually become smitten by the fever of preparation that was abroad at the rectory. There was no longer time for visits to Pastor Fjaltring. In fact, in sheer terror that he would run of out of time, he finally—just like Inger—came to wish that the wedding could be delayed for a few weeks.

Other sources of grief arrived when the new furniture was delivered from town and had to be put in place. A wardrobe proved to be too big for the wall against which it was to be placed. A curtain rail, on the other hand, had been made too short and—to Inger's momentary despair—the new wallpaper in the sitting room did not go quite as well with the carpet and furniture covers as she had hoped. Every time Per arrived at the rectory, she flew at him with worried questions about, say, a wall panel between windows, or the dimensions of a floor; and on his departure, she often completely forgot to return his kiss because her mouth was full of reminders of things that still needed to be done.

The anxiety hanging over the house-moving arrangements lasted right up to the glorious day itself. Worse, a week before the actual wedding, this anxiety became formal panic because of what, in calmer times, might have been considered a humorous affair. All the furniture that had been ordered eventually arrived at Per's home; the only things missing were the beds. These were meant to have been delivered many weeks before. Repeated messages had been sent to a carpenter in the town about these beds and repeated replies had been received to say that they were on the way. In the end, Inger and her mother spoke of nothing other than the beds, which still refused to arrive. Per felt slightly insulted by this. He just could not understand how Inger, who was otherwise normally the height of social decorum, could give such free rein to her consternation and fault finding—not just in his presence, but in front of anyone else who happened to be in the rectory at the time. The high tension even spread outwards to embrace the whole town. The case of the missing beds became the talk of market, shop, and tavern and it was, therefore, not just Per and Inger who felt a sense of relief when they were finally put in place on the day before the wedding.

The sun shone with all its best summer brightness on the day of celebration itself. Flags were displayed in the village and people came out onto the street to watch the wedding procession as it made its way to church. Inger sat in an open-top carriage, accompanied by a handsome older gentleman with a rose in the buttonhole of his jacket and sporting a goatee beard that was as white as cotton wool. This was her mother's brother. The bride was as pretty as a picture, but more than one onlooker remarked that she was perhaps a bit too aware of this herself. Her aunties had dressed and decorated her and her longstanding female friends had placed the veil and wreath of blossoms on her head. All the wives and girls at the rectory had followed her to the carriage and they all declared to her that never had a more beautiful bride rode to Bøstrup church to be married.

Amongst the guests were also two of Per's siblings—Eberhard and Signe. In addition, all the district's local dignitaries were in attendance—Alderman Clausens, Dame Prangen, the school principal, the parish ombudsmen, and also other selected guests from Rimalt. In all, there were over fifty guests.

This figure could be said to have been augmented, however, by curious onlookers from the street who migrated to the open windows to view the style on display and listen to the speeches. Subsequently, a table was laid in the shade of the trees for all those outside. Every spectator, it was decreed, should receive refreshments and, as the crowd grew, the wedding celebration took on the nature of a folk festival.

Visiting guests from outside the area made their departure the very next morning—including Eberhard and Signe and then Inger's uncle. This man was a rather colorful character and something of an adventurer. He had tumbled about the world a good deal, before finally ending up as a very effective and skilled manager of a renowned shipyard in Fiume, an Austro-Hungarian port, where he still lived. After many years away, he had used the occasion of his niece's wedding to revisit his homeland and had stayed in Bøstrup for a week.

With his outlandish demeanor and exotic customs, he had found it somewhat difficult to get on with the inhabitants of the rectory. This was particularly so with Pastor Blomberg, who bluntly described Inger's uncle as a ridiculous old fop and a dandy. On the other hand, the uncle had greatly enjoyed being in the company of Per. His new nephew-in-law had taken him on several guided tours in order to show him the recently commenced excavations in the meadows; and though he was not an engineer by profession, he knew enough to be able to assess the value of the work involved. Back at the rectory, he expressed his admiration of Per to his sister and brother-in-law in words that—judiciously as he could—reflected his opinion that their son-in-law was far too talented to be stuck out here in the countryside digging ditches for farmers.

Fru Blomberg, who had carried a very distracted air all morning, could not settle to anything once the guests had begun to depart. She now followed her brother to the railway station, so that she could call in to the newlyweds on her way back.

She found them at the dining table partaking of a belated luncheon. She realized straight away that the atmosphere was anything but convivial. Per was flustered, Inger pale, muted, and indignant. Fru

Blomberg pretended not to notice anything. She knew precisely what had happened and had to suppress the smile that was on her lips. For it was as if she was reliving her own post-wedding morning twenty-two years earlier. She took coffee with the young couple and talked generally about the wedding reception and the recently departed guests. Afterwards, she and Inger went out to the kitchen and pantry in order to arrange the cutlery and utensils. Per went into his own room and stayed there for the remainder of his mother-in-law's visit.

He sat down by the window, his head resting on his hand and looking out over the fields. He knew of course that no great harm had been done. Nor was he in any doubt that Inger's shyness would gradually ease. But for all that, he felt a grave disappointment and could not help being dejected. What was supposed to have been the greatest moment of his life, and his most abiding memory, had become a scene that his thoughts would always return to with nothing other than mortification and distaste.

Unbidden, his thoughts edged their way back to another first night of union—the one with Jakobe—and he could not refrain from comparing the two. But suddenly something horrible stirred in the depths of his mind. It was as if a poisonous snake pricked his heart.

Could it be that the blame lay with him? Was he once again here being forced to pay for his past?

26

IN THE beginning, Per was not entirely happy in his marriage. His hope that he might inspire Inger to develop a more independent intellectual and spiritual outlook was not realized. Her level-headed, eminently practical, nature and her conviction that her father was Christendom's thirteenth Apostle meant that she could not even begin to understand his intentions in trying to persuade her otherwise. And, just like her father, she viewed her husband's "obsession" with Pastor Fjaltring as an expression of an immature urge to flout authority and make himself interesting.

Now it could not be denied that the double life Per was leading, and the unstable influences to which he was exposed, gradually left him so bewildered that he began to exude a distinctly disturbed air. He himself noticed this in the end and anxiously looked for some sort of firm ground on which to stand.

He found it in the place he had sought refuge before—in Mother Nature's hold on his sensibilities. The difference this time was that it was Inger who led him there. She was now heavily pregnant and, like most young mothers, her only thoughts were about the forthcoming birth and her preparations for it. Nonetheless, she was fully composed and, for all her inexperience, it was this sense of calm and inner fortitude radiating from her as she waited for her time that filled Per with admiration and gave him much to ponder.

Then came the night of the labor itself, Inger's recuperation and worries over both her and the child, then the proud father syndrome and the increased feelings of responsibility which this aroused—all these things acted to plant him in reality's solid ground.

However, even these events could not completely break his ties with Borup rectory and Pastor Fjaltring. The cavernous study, bathed in semidarkness, with its narrow carpet runner and the desk between the two low windows, still held a spell over him; but he stole there now with a guilty conscience, like a drunkard slipping furtively to his favorite hostelry but vowing never to go back. Per's visits did become less and less frequent, but one day the decision over whether to go or not to go was abruptly taken from him by a terrible event— an event that would be talked about forevermore in the district.

On a day at the beginning of autumn, alarm spread amongst the people with the rumor that Pastor Fjaltring had disappeared. Six months before this he had lost his wife; but instead of feeling a liberation in this, he shunned the daylight hours even more and avoided all contact with people. His parishioners suspected some sort of serious mishap the moment they realized he had gone missing. Per acted immediately to organize a search party. He sent one group to look through the forests where the pastor would walk at night and another to drag the river and all the ditches and bog holes thereabouts. In the end, they found the pastor up in his own attic, where he had used the rail in a large empty wardrobe to hang himself.

In the last year of his life, Per had been the only visitor Pastor Fjaltring had been glad to see. The only person, moreover, in whom he had confided quite openly. Just a few days before his disappearance, Per had sat with him for several hours and had actually been full of admiration for the apparent serenity and self-composure that he displayed while talking about himself and his sense of loneliness. The pastor had even made a joke about his physical afflictions. One should, he said, always be grateful for pain, because it kept the mind fresh and alert. This had led him to make a humorous remark about how he had once almost come to serious grief by becoming so weighed down with pondering the mysteries of Original Sin that he had teetered on the brink of losing his mind.

"But then the Lord sent a merciful draft through the house that started up my toothache—a serious back tooth martyrdom—and to Hell with all thoughts of Original Sin and other such fiendish self-indulgences. I would have given my very priestly vows for a blessed tooth tincture."

Now that he was gone, and where his horrible death itself had borne witness to the frailty of Pastor Fjaltring's life philosophy, Per had the same feeling of having escaped a mortal danger as when he first read about Lieutenant Iversen's suicide. Through this priest's feverish hand, he had been led into a dark, barren wilderness of the spirit, whose ultimately disappointing desert mirages and illusory heights had so tempted him from a distance. And yet! He would always remember this unhappy and solitary man with gratitude and genuine affection. Even in the death he had chosen, he had proven to be his teacher—indeed his savior.

For this reason, Per was outraged when witnessing the crowing and false sympathy displayed by local people who prattled on about his "desperate fate"; they who were cosseted by their own blithe indifference and utter lack of passion for life; they who had never felt the urge to engage in a titanic battle with their beliefs and with the gods. In particular, his father-in-law's condescending sighs and shakes of the head made his blood boil.

"Ah dear, yes . . . it was bound to end like that! I mean, I hate to say I told you so Per. He should never ever have become a priest. What else can you expect, if one cannot be reconciled to oneself? As you know, I have always felt so sorry for that man!"

A scathing riposte burned on Per's tongue; but as had so often been the case before, he kept his counsel for Inger's sake and declined the chance to reveal his true feelings.

Then one year went by, and then another, and then three more came and went very quickly after that—all disappearing with that curious, indiscernible speed that time possesses in the countryside, where a single day can crawl to its lazy conclusion but the years fly like an arrow. In that well-appointed, little villa house there were now three children who tumbled and cavorted by Rimalt's green riverbanks— one five-year-old boy and two small girls—quintessential Sideniuses, with pale blue eyes and a mass of brown curly hair. Per's large-scale river and land-reclamation work had long since finished and he had sometimes raised the idea with Inger of moving somewhere else to seek similar work. However, Inger was loath to move away from the area in which she had grown up; she also loved her new home in exactly the same way she had loved her old home at the rectory, and it was a matter of principle and pride for her to make their married home a model of order and comfort.

It was also the case that Per did not exactly burn with a desire to disrupt the life to which they had become accustomed. The days slipped by so peacefully here; the children were thriving, and Inger was overjoyed and grateful for the fact that she was able to remain in the vicinity of her parents and old friends. Yes, he still felt that, outside his own home, he was like a fish living outside his own water. But on the other hand, he had his own little patch of earth that he could call his own and the house and garden had become very dear to his heart. Thus, he took very little persuading to stay where he was and give up any thoughts of uprooting himself and his family. Per also had—up until the most recent time at any rate—enough to be doing around about in the district where his surveying work was concerned, and there were always smaller road and bridge assignments to keep him occupied. He had even finally managed to clear all his outstanding debts.

But with regard to his invention and the broader vision of his wind and wave scheme, he was completely becalmed. His desire to occupy himself with it had become more and more seldom as the years had gone by and his ability seemed to have gone the same way as his inspiration. At any rate, his previously so fertile mind had been gelded— to the point where he one day took a firm decision to abandon the idea for ever. Up on the hillock behind his house, where he once imagined a trial windmill might be raised, there was now nothing more than a bench put there so that he and Inger could gaze out across the valley at sunset and engage in small talk about the events of the day, while the children gambolled on the grass around them.

It was usually Inger who led the conversation. Per Sidenius, the once mighty raconteur, had become taciturn as the years had progressed, though there was still the odd moment, particularly when animated by the children, when he became almost ebullient. Overall, his moods would switch so frequently, and unpredictably, that Inger would sometimes become truly concerned. At the very moment when they sat and conversed in deepest intimacy, he could suddenly go quiet, as if his thoughts had become gripped by something or other that he preferred not to divulge. For hours—in fact for days—he could maintain this withdrawn state, and it was found that the best approach was to just leave him to his own devices and avoid pestering him about the why and the wherefore.

In the very first year of their marriage Inger had—just like her parents—viewed Per's mercurial mental state as a natural consequence of his acquaintanceship with Pastor Fjaltring. As another year passed with no change, Inger then blamed that "unfortunate invention" as the thing that plagued him. At that time, when he was still working on it, and had been in a state of constant annoyance, he complained that he could never get enough peace to work and allowed himself to be disturbed by the slightest noise in the house—all that blacking, cleaning, and window polishing, which always—he insisted—drove him from his room just when some great insight was on the verge of coming to him. Inger had therefore also made it her business to encourage him in his decision to finally abandon all thoughts of the project. After several more years, she was most disposed to ascribe his volatile mood swings to his bodily afflictions, which would break out in sudden attacks in exactly the same way, and which again made him touchy and quick to whimper and moan. And Per himself never offered any other kind of explanation.

Autumn had arrived once again and the garden drooped with berries of all sorts. Inger, as was now her tradition, was busy cooking the fruits and making preserves from them.

And in the same ritual, she was to be found one day in the middle of September sitting on her bench beneath the large walnut tree in the garden. She loved to sit here in the afternoon, while the children played in the field outside, under the careful watch of their nanny.

788 · HENRIK PONTOPPIDAN

With her love of order and preciseness, she maintained whenever possible a clear division in the day's labors, and her time under the walnut tree was dedicated to the planning that befalls a housewife, to inner reflection, and conclusions about how she viewed certain family matters. She was wearing a large apron and in her lap was an earthenware bowl, full to the brim with dark cherries. An empty bowl lay beside her on the bench and she placed berry after berry into this receptacle after first carefully picking the stone from each one with a needle. As in everything else she undertook, there was a blithe grace in the way she performed this task with her neat, quick movements, while the sumptuous red juice dripped from her white fingers. The slightly swaying leaves above her head displayed the first signs of autumn. A pale, dead leaf grinned out, here and there, from the mass of otherwise green foliage. Inger herself still carried the kiss of high summer—ample, luxuriant, almost matronly in spite of her still youthful twenty-seven years. The physical frailty that had restricted her flowering as a young women had disappeared with marriage and motherhood. She felt herself to be vigorously strong in root and branch, a joy partly derived from the fact that she had been able to breastfeed all of her children.

In principle, she was also happy in her marriage, albeit in a different way to what she had expected. Despite his volatile disposition, Per was both a loving and caring partner; but the gallant knight of which she had so often dreamed he was not and would never be. Sometimes she wondered why she was as fond of him as she actually was. But if she put up so well with his mood swings, it was because they appealed to her maternal nature. During his stubbornly recurrent attacks of deep depression—which had also become more frequent and drawn out as the years passed—she regarded him as an afflicted man who should not be scolded but humored. Thus, she understood that no one suffered more under these attacks than Per himself.

He was going through one of his difficult times at that very moment. The day before it had been their son Hagbarth's birthday, and Per had still been in the best of form all through the morning. He got up very early and had gone out to pluck flowers from the field so that the house could be decorated, and, when the children had got up, he went to the garden with them and played tag and hide and seek. The children had squealed with delight and Inger herself was tickled as she watched him crawling on all fours to hide behind the bushes. Then the mail arrived and that was the end of that. When she went into his study an hour later, she saw straight away that he was not the same. He was sitting over by the window with the newspaper in his lap and those deep shadows, that she knew only too well, had appeared across his brow and beneath his eyes. To the clear shock and disappointment of the children, their father hardly spoke a word at the festively garlanded midday dinner table; and when their grandparents' carriage rumbled into the drive in time for afternoon coffee and to offer birthday congratulations, Per mentioned a pressing business matter as a pretext to leave the house at once. He was not seen again until supper time.

There was something in the suddenness and vehemence with which these doleful moods came upon him that had recently, and in a worrying way, put Inger in mind of the late Lord Prangen. There seemed no doubt that his sickly mental condition was influenced by his bodily afflictions, perhaps from the cancer that led to his death. She had also made a promise to herself that she would mention her concerns to the family doctor when the next opportunity presented itself.

Then she was stirred from her ponderings by a shout of delight up above on the hillock. It was her little Hagbarth and his eldest sister Ingeborg. They had battled their way up there to keep a look out for their father and had now spied him out on the road with his fjord horse.

Inger got up and went into the house with her bowls to give orders to the house girl to put Per's dinner out on the table. In order not to cause disruption to the good running of the home, Per himself had made clear that they should not wait for him on any occasion when he could not get back for the usual meal times. Inger had personally arranged the portions for him. There was a pleasing broth of milk and groats and a homebrewed beer, then smoked eel with potatoes in white sauce—and she had not skimped on the servings. Per had been away since the early morning and had only taken a small selection of *smørrebrød* with him in his coat pocket. Thus, Inger was well aware that he would return with the hunger of a wolf after such a long day out of doors. Once again, this was the same disposition as Lord Prangen, whose frequent lurches into dejection never affected his appetite. On the contrary, she remembered how, even in his darkest humor, he would be almost insatiable.

By now Per and the fjord horse had reached the yard and both he and the gig were surrounded by children and hens with the nanny bringing up the rear; the yard help then came out to lend a hand. "Stub" reached her hands up from the nanny's arms for a kiss from her father; the two older children had already climbed up each of the two wheels and were sat either side of Per. Very soon they were fighting over who should hold the whip. Inger was standing by the side of the kitchen window, watching the whole scene unfold with maternal pride.

In the end, and not without a certain roughness, Per wrested himself free from the forest of eager arms and proceeded to give orders to the yard help with regard to the horse.

Just like Inger, Per too had filled out as the years had gone by. But he did not carry Inger's healthy freshness of face, and his large rather unruly beard made him look older than he actually was.

"Were there any visitors today, Inger?" he asked, when he had taken his seat in the dining room and had—without even thinking what it was he was eating—devoured the first shovelful.

"No Per, it's been very quiet all day," Inger replied as she took her knitting to the table to keep him company.

"Anything in the post?"

"No dear, just the newspaper."

"Is there anything strange or startling in it?"

"I really don't know. I have not read it."

A short pause now ensued.

"And did you not read the paper yesterday either?" Per asked somewhat hesitantly.

"Yesterday? I don't think so. Should I have done...was there something interesting in it?"

"Aye—well—just another report from the talks those engineers are having in Aarhus."

"Per darling, you really should have gone to that conference. You are so interested in it."

"Why should I go to it, Inger? I don't know any of those people ... and besides, I'm not even an engineer."

"Are there no surveyors going to it?"

"I don't think so."

"What I mean, Per, is that you are obviously very absorbed in what they are talking about. You've mentioned it a few times."

"Well, yes—it sometimes crosses my mind."

"You really should have gone, dear. To keep your hand in and keep your enthusiasm. What did yesterday's report say?"

"Ah it was just something about the talks they are having about a West Jutland canal and freeport project with Hjerting Bay as the basis for it. A lot of the papers have taken to calling it the Steiner Project, after that engineer chap, who's actually from Jutland. You might remember that I had the same idea myself once."

"The same idea? Per did you not write a whole book about it?"

"Yes Inger—I wrote a whole book about it."

"And are they saying now that the plan is going to go ahead?"

"No, I don't think so. The Copenhagen freeport project has been given the go-ahead. The Jutland project was being proposed as an alternative."

"Well it's funny that they still keep talking about it then."

"Ah that's just the usual local patriotism here in Jutland, Inger. They need to puff their chests out every now and again. And of course it suits Hr. Steiner to keep the drum banging for as long as possible. He's certainly doing all he can to keep the tom toms going. Judging by the reports, he got a prolonged standing ovation at the conference. They had a large dinner the other night—where the champagne was presumably flowing freely—and Steiner was hailed as Denmark's answer to Ferdinand de Lesseps—who built the Suez Canal! Is there more broth by the way Inger?"

"Oh Per, I'm sorry there's not—did you want more? But there is lots of the other food—the eel and potatoes and there's dessert."

"Ah right—thanks—that's fine then."

"But Per, remember not to eat too much. We're invited over to the chemist and his wife's for supper tonight, don't forget."

Per shook his and pulled a choleric face.

"Oh for God's sake! Completely slipped my mind! Listen Inger… is it not about time we started turning down some of these invitations? Neither you, nor I, enjoy what they so laughingly call a social circuit around here."

"Per darling, I'll give you that it's not much fun. And God knows I would much rather stay at home. But we can't start insulting people by turning our backs on them. We have to think of my father as well, Per. Anything we do reflects on him, good or bad. And he wouldn't be happy if we started refusing people. People are already saying that we don't mix as much as we should do. That we are a bit standoffish."

She received no reply to this. Per simply continued to eat in silence. Once he had finished, they took coffee together, which had been brought to his room. This lay on the other side of the hallway and was a rather constricted and dark construction that had a gable window looking out onto the fields; a concealed door led into a small bedroom. As the family had expanded, Per had been obliged to abandon his original large and sun-kissed study-cum-workroom for the sake of the children. But, generally speaking, this new and far more modest room was quite to his liking. Its quiet, secluded atmosphere was a place to which he could retreat and its simplicity also reminded him of his more youthful days when he lived as a closet hermit in Frederiksberg or in Nyboder. Indeed, he did not always appreciate Inger's occasional efforts to liven up his "quarters" with fresh flowers or perhaps some potted plants. His tolerance for flower fragrances was extremely low. And nature's bright saturations of color only very rarely harmonized with the kind of atmosphere in which his soul found most comfort and peace.

Only one work of art was to be seen in the room. This was a large marble bust, which had been placed up on one of his shelves and almost bumped the ceiling of this low chamber. This was a representation of a young handsome man, with vibrant curly hair, a broad and powerful forehead and a full, vigorous mouth, which—just like in genuine antique busts—had been left slightly open in order to make the figure more lifelike. The head was turned with a quite rigorous movement to the side, via which the action of muscles and tendons was revealed to full effect on a neck that would have been the envy of any ancient bareknuckle pugilist. From the center of this figure's forehead, a deep furrow of iron will and concentration ran all the way down to his thick conjoined brow; the gaze flashing from his eyes was belligerent—the smile brilliant, as if to stress the sheer abundance of valor and youthful vitality radiating from his being.

This was, of course, the idealized portrait of Per as a youth that had been commissioned by the late baroness and which he had modeled for during his stay in Rome. Dame Prangen, who had eventually accepted that she would have to pay for the commission on behalf of her dead sister, had sent it to Inger as a wedding present. But Inger found the bust completely loathsome and wanted to consign it to the loft space forever. In the interim, it had been stored on top of a corner press in the dining room, where it was not immediately obvious, until Per one day decided to take it into his room. And despite Inger's insistence that it really was not the done thing to have one's own image in one's own room, Per could not be parted with it.

As darkness now fell across fields and homes, the couple remained in their respective ends of Per's room discussing housekeeping issues and the children. Per had lit a cigar and moved over to the window seat with his coffee cup. It was still Inger who talked the most, at the same time as she flawlessly maintained the rhythm of her knitting. Amongst other things, she described how little Hagbarth, completely by his own devices, had worked out how to make a doll's pram for his sister out of an old clog. He was always inventing new contraptions and ways of doing things. And then there were those shovel-like hands of his that would pull and push at things and help him never to give up.

Per was brought back to the conversation by this.

"Yes, there's no doubt that he's every chance of becoming a great boy," Per said, more to himself than to his wife. He then retreated into his own thoughts again.

Inger twirled the yarn around her pins and went into the bedroom to dress for the party later that evening. Moments after she had disappeared through the door, Per reached over to his desk to lift a folded newspaper that lay hidden under some books and rolls of drawings, but in that same instant, he heard Inger coming back in and quickly pulled his hand away. When she came back in, she found Per gazing up from his chair at the sunset-tinged clouds.

Hr. Møller the village chemist was Rimalt's wealthiest citizen. It was also clear that he reveled in the fact that he was publicly listed as the highest taxpayer in the district. Thus, when arranging social gatherings, like that evening's extravaganza, he saw it as his duty to show he understood the obligations such an event carried for a man of substance like himself vis-à-vis his less well-heeled fellow burghers. When his guests were all assembled at around seven o'clock, they were led into a dining room where a large and immaculately laid table awaited them. Small, freshly baked rolls lay ensconced in pristine white serviettes and each dining place had three glasses in front of it. The host also had the pleasure of hearing his name being praised to the heavens for, without the slightest doubt, always laying on the most impressive feast in the whole area! The fact that the food had clearly not been made by any master cook, and that the actual contents of the wine bottles were not the vintage wonders proclaimed on the bottle labels, did not spoil the enjoyment for a single guest. For these were people whose palates had no time for fussiness. They judged their meals on the question of mass and volume; they took a deep breath when gazing at the abundance that was set before them and then launched themselves headlong into the task of bringing home as much from the banquet as they could possibly stuff into themselves.

On this evening also, Hr. Pharmicist augmented his reputation as a capital host in his personal handling of this Rimalt soiree as he moved amongst the guests, seeking to fan the flames of their gustation. Incessantly, high above the din of cutlery and crosstalk, his voice was to be heard.

"My ladies and gentlemen! You all really must do justice to these stuffed pigeons! Hr. Stationmaster! I hope this Château Beychevelle is to your liking. My dear lady! Sauternes is a feminine drink! Please imbibe at your leisure! Hr. Sidenius! Has your glass insulted you, sir? You've barely touched a drop. Ah yes, here. May I have the honor to present—Gentlemen!—this London Club 1879, which I have carefully decanted and that may only be consumed with reverence. May I kindly request, kind sirs, that you take a tipple and give me your judgment."

The gentlemen emptied their glasses, licked and smacked their lips, and then erupted in a clamor of sincerely meant panegyrics.

"What I would call a perfect mid-dinner bracer," the vet declared.

"A veritable tongue seductress no less," the stationmaster remarked, attempting the air of a connoisseur.

"Nectar of the Gods!" cried none other than Hr. Balling who was the new principal at the school for slightly less gifted children who struggled somewhat to gain their passage into higher education. He it was who now rose to call a toast for their host.

Yes this was the very same lanky strip of a man with the highbrow mane of hair whom Per had met on several occasions in the home of Philip Salomon. Balling had exceeded himself in the last few years. After things had gone horribly wrong for him in Copenhagen, he had decided to try his luck out in the provinces and here very quickly attained the esteem he so craved. He was now counted as a man of importance, not just here in Rimalt, where the locals were very proud of having a real writer in their midst, but also in the surrounding districts where Balling held lectures and projected himself as a latter-day apostle for a new movement in literature. This new crusade of scribes had, in the spirit of the rural high school movement, declared the inherent wit, wisdom and genius of the Danish people to be their guiding literary light. Inger's friend, the eldest daughter of the lay magistrate Hr. Clausen—the bawdy and buxom Gerda of the warm eyes and enticing smile—had immediately fallen for Balling's glorified charms and, in fact, they had married only a fortnight before this evening's soiree.

Rimalt had gained another participant in its social set in recent times. Several miles from the railway station was Budderuplund country estate and manor house. This lay on the opposite side of the road that led to the area around Kærsholm and Bøstrup. The owner of the large manor and farmland, Hr. State Counsel Brück, was an older man who came from renowned landed gentry stock in Schleswig-Holstein. He was extremely prosperous but had produced only one son and heir, who had lived in foreign climes for years because of the superior educational and career-advancement opportunities that were to be found abroad. However, this son had now returned to the Rimalt area to take over the running of his father's huge estate.

Hr Brück the younger was a handsome, powerfully built man who was at the start of his thirties. However, he was somewhat reserved in nature, possibly due to a slight stammer that affected his conversation. Per had immediately felt drawn to him and, despite their differing circumstances and interests—Hr. Brück loved nothing more than to ride to hounds and his preferred social set was the gentry and rural aristocracy—held hopes that a genuine friendship might quickly develop between them. It was therefore a great disappointment for him to discover that his immediate empathy was not reciprocated. At the same time, Per realized that Hr. Brück nurtured a warm interest in Inger and that she was probably the only reason he had attended the party. They had known each other since childhood; but Inger had said that she could not stand him and revealed this aversion, Per felt, in a sometimes wounding fashion. She seemed unable to give more specific reasons for her animosity toward Hr. Brück. The only thing she would say in response to Per's repeated questions on the matter was that she had found him distasteful even as a boy. Per also noticed that Hr. Brück, who had been given a seat directly opposite Inger, had tried to engage her in conversation on a number of occasions during the meal—all to no avail. Inger answered any remarks he made to her with some platitude or other and then simply turned to speak to someone else.

Once the dinner was over, and in time-honored provincial manner, the assembled revelers divided into two groups, with the ladies moving to the sitting room and the gentlemen retiring to the spacious study. Here they could slack off their cinches, light cigars, blow smoke rings, and talk more freely without the hindrance of female propriety. It was understood by all here that the social niceties of a party could be forgotten and free rein given to immodest and lewd storytelling; belches and flatulence could also be indulged in, and a man had a right to doze off for a while if he so wished.

Per had come to sit at such a vantage point that he could engage in conversation while still keeping an eye, via the partially open door, on proceedings amongst the women in the sitting room. A hanging lamp with a dark red shade shone its soft light over the divan table around which the ladies were gathered, their faces partially illuminated as from the flames of a ruddy fire. In this room, too, the chat flowed freely and it was not hard to discern the subject matter of their conversation. Only house management and the latest gossip and scandal relating to maids and servant lads could generate such gusto and animation. Even Inger's face, for all her apparent serenity, had taken on a decided glow, her cheeks red with ardor.

Per, who had already fallen victim to a wave of dejection, bit his lip at this sight. More often than not, he felt nothing but pride for his wife. This was not just because of her natural beauty, but also because of her inherent tact and refinement, which raised her head and shoulders above her female peers. But he always became deeply despondent whenever he saw how comfortable she was in the midst of such company. Despite the fact that she liked to protest otherwise, the reality was that she felt completely at home amongst this kind of people. Only when the gossip went beyond the limits of decency did she remove herself from the fray. And it had to be said that she had not allowed herself to be smitten by the unrestrained tone that sometimes affected the other ladies of Rimalt. With that sense of rectitude that was a part of her very being, something that had marked her out even in her early schooldays, she still as a married woman turned her eyes and ears away from anything that might offend her highly attuned feminine sensitivities. But Per increasingly felt that this was simply more of the same sanctimonious Blomberg hypocrisy. What she did not wish to know, she didn't hear. What it didn't suit her to believe, no matter how true it was, she refused to believe. For this reason, she could remain friends with the wife of both the chemist and the stationmaster, even though it was an open secret that the former was having an affair with the latter's husband, and that both wives were, at the same time, besotted with Rimalt's new literary sensation, and newlywed, Hr. Balling. It was for this same reason that she was able to speak, using one of her father's favorite expressions, of "the licentious and immoral life in the capital," in spite of the fact that life all around her was a pathetic and shrunken mirror image of that same sort of life; be it in the home of the most idyllically appointed farm and mansion, or the worst kind of smallholder's hovel, the most appalling things took place there, and often without even pretense or concealment.

The time dragged on to ten o'clock when the dessert was brought in. Pale and red eyed with fatigue, the good housewives of Rimalt were sat around the divan table and in the end made not even a pretense at merrymaking or fitting deportment. Some of them yawned openly before covering their mouths up with work-scoured hands. Even Inger's eyelids had begun to droop and became dreamy. The party's hostess and the stationmaster's wife, however, were still in a state of high excitement. For the object of their mutual admiration, the literary aesthete Hr. Balling, had retired to the empty parlor room with his young wife where all was dark within, save for a weakly burning lamp. There had been at least four attempts to call them in for dessert, and when the pair did eventually emerge, Gerda's hot-cheeked visage and ruffled hair revealed exactly what had been going on; not that she made any effort to hide the bare facts.

Not long after this, the assembled revelers began to leave for home. They left in small groups and walked through the little moonlit hamlet. These groups then coalesced outside the respective garden gates so that a lengthy and verbose leave-taking could be performed.

Inger was walking alongside the local doctor, a middle-aged and eminently sensible man, whom she had known since childhood. They had dallied somewhat behind the main group and chose the moment to have a serious conversation about Per.

"Doctor, may I ask whether you noticed how remarkably quiet and withdrawn my husband was this evening?"

"Well, yes—now that you mention it Fru Sidenius. Is something bothering him unduly?"

"I don't think it's one particular thing doctor. But—I will speak frankly if I may—you are aware of course that my husband very often suffers from bouts of despondency. I must say that I've become more and more worried about it just recently. Do you think he could be suffering some kind of hidden ailment?"

The doctor slowed his walk and pondered this for a moment before saying: "I am glad you have approached me about this. Because just lately I said to myself that I probably ought to speak to you in private about it."

Inger was immediately terrified by the doctor's solemn tone and stopped dead in her tracks.

"Dear Doctor!" she almost shrieked as she grabbed his arm.

"Now, now—no need to be afraid Fru Inger. It's nothing like that. There is no doubt that your husband has what is commonly called 'nerves.' And it should be stressed that these attacks of dizziness and the stinging sensations he sometimes complains about seem real to him and can be unpleasant enough . . . perhaps. But is there a case for serious concern? I really don't think so."

"But what is it then? If you don't mind me saying, Doctor, you are muttering something into your beard."

"What? Oh yes, I suppose I am . . . I mean . . . well I suppose I think . . . do you not think your husband is a bit, ahm, underworked?"

"My God, he's on his feet and on the go almost from first thing and then right through to evening time. You know that yourself, Doctor."

"Yes but is he busy with the kind of work that really engages him? My view, after thinking about it, is that he may well need a bigger, more challenging mission in his life that left him with far less time for dark introspection."

"Do you know Doctor, I have sometimes thought the same thing" said Inger after a short pause. "But there will never be any job of the size you are talking about around here."

"No—I'm afraid there never will."

"So that means we would have to move away—to a town maybe, even go to Copenhagen—"

"There's no doubt about it, yes. And, of course Fru Sidenius, that would be a great loss to our community here. But I would hope that my advice is seen as coming from a longstanding friend of the family."

"Yes Doctor, I understand. As I say, I have been thinking about this very thing myself. But I am convinced that my husband is actually better off living here in the peace and quiet of the countryside. He has said that himself. With all the worries he has about his health, I really doubt whether his constitution could tolerate any kind of long-term and stressful employment."

"Hmm . . . I'm not sure that you have the complete measure of your husband in this regard, Fru Inger. Because for all his minor foibles and frailties, he is also a physical powerhouse who, there is no doubt, actively thrives when he has to battle with some major project. And yes, now that I have raised the issue, I may as well say it straight out. I am aware that your uncle in Fiume has sent messages to your husband, inviting him to take up employment at his shipyard down there. Would you not consider moving down there Fru Inger—down to the highly celebrated Adriatic coast?"

"Dear God, and be murdered in our beds by robbers?"

"Well it's true all right, that the area is rather volatile. But the climate would work wonders for your husband. He'll get all the sun and heat that he needs down there to kindle his soul afresh and he'll be as brown as a berry. No . . . I'm afraid I really am certain that a few years in warm foreign climes will work wonders for him."

Inger made no further comment to the doctor. She had instinctively shrunk away from him and avoided eye contact. Shortly afterwards, they stopped at the doctor's own residence, where the larger party was already stood waiting in order to bid him goodnight.

Per and Inger had furthest to go home and were thus obliged to participate in every extended leave-taking ceremony at every house. Inger had quietly linked her arm through Per's, and when they were finally alone, they pressed together with that vehement longing that sometimes fired up between them on evenings such as this, when they were forced to sit amongst people who were no more than occasional friends. Inger placed a loving cheek on his shoulder. They then walked in this fashion until they finally stopped in the middle of a lane to exchange a kiss that carried with it the lustrous promise of the moonlit night sky.

A shame then that Inger felt the need to do some quick household chore out in the kitchen when they got home. She had come to think of some cucumbers that she had told the kitchen girl to place in brine for pickling and her strict sense of a housewife's inalienable duties would not let her retire to the marital bed until she was sure that her orders had been followed. Then she looked into the nursery to ask the girl whether everything had been quiet.

"Ingeborg has had more stomach pains, darling," she said when she eventually came back to Per who by now had gone to his room and had lit the lamp. He was sitting at his desk with a book in front of him and letting on that he was engrossed in his reading.

"Ah again," he replied tersely as he turned a page.

Inger was familiar with this tone. She also understood the message in his having lit a new cigar.

"You're not coming to bed then?" she asked.

"No Inger. I'm not at all tired."

She made no attempt at talking him around. She knew that it was pointless to try and change his moods. Completely calm—too proud and pristine to even contemplate revealing her disappointment—she went over to him, stroked the hair from his brow and kissed his forehead.

"Goodnight, darling Per."

"Night Inger," he said without moving.

Shortly after she had left the room, Per pushed the book away from him and simply sat there resting his head in his hands and looking into the seething flame of the lamp. When he heard that she was safely ensconced in bed, he picked up the folded newspaper he had hidden under his books and rolls of drawings and spread it out across the surface of his desk. It was yesterday's edition of one of Jutland's larger provincial newspapers and contained a report from the conference of engineers and technicians in Aarhus. His eyes quickly searched the page until he came to a place in the second column, where it said:

"The main subject of the afternoon session of the conference concentrated on the 'Steiner Harbor and Freeport Project.' This ambitious and technically daring plan will already be familiar to our readers via the various reports this newspaper has carried on the project. There was a special attraction for delegates in that the discussion was introduced by none other than the brilliant creator of the plan himself—Hr. Anton Steiner, a native son of Jutland. Hr. Steiner not only received a hearty reception on taking to the podium but, after his highly elucidating and inspiring lecture, the conference rose as one to provide him with a prolonged standing ovation."

The veins around Per's temple had started to bulge as he read the article through. "The neck of him . . . he has no shame that bastard!" he mouthed through gritted teeth. In the last two years or so, it had been almost impossible to pick up a provincial newspaper without coming across Steiner's name somewhere in its pages. In other words, Anton Steiner was well on the way to becoming a national hero—at least in Jutland. He was everywhere: holding lectures, available at all times to journalists, overall presenting a clearly pre-planned glorification of himself and his "crusade."

A tree branch, its leaves heavy with night-time dew, tapped its twigs softly against the window as if in time with the clock in the sitting room striking the hour—twelve.

Per pressed his fingers against the balls of his closed eyes and sat like that for a long time. This "Sidenius" legacy—it had proved to be his life's curse after all! Was it really that much better, or less ignominious, to sit there like an enfeebled fool, being slowly devoured by endless soul-searching and dissatisfaction, than just to a put a gun to your head so that, in a flash, all the weariness and ennui was gone? Could it be that Lieutenant Iversen and Neergaard, even Pastor

Fjaltring with that awful noose, had actually done the right, the honorable, thing? His life was over; his life energy and willpower spent! He was like a clock which day by day hour by hour had played out its momentum down to a final stop.

Slowly and half-reluctantly, he raised his eyes towards his bookcase, where the white luminance of his marble bust glowed in the surrounding murk below the ceiling. Just recently, his gaze had increasingly turned, in an almost worshipful way, to this effigy of his former self—an image he at one time had wanted to smash. He was starting to become infatuated with his own youth. He no longer cared to dwell on what a raw-boned, impudent, and arrogant rascal he had been in those days—a fool very often and then other times nothing more than a lout, yes all right, even sometimes a bully, with no sense or feeling other than to grab what he wanted. But at least it had been life's very own musical opus that had sung through his veins and had infused his dreams of conquest! Now his anima was deathly still. Only the faintest panpipe note could now sometimes be discerned from the raucous, madcap, exuberant opera that had once sung in his soul.

He who was lonely and felt abandoned; he who was stranded in the cold wastes of life's shadow side—yes it was true that people like that often suffered terribly. But then the awareness on the part of that person that he was the victim of an injustice and had been frozen out; this could be his greatest motivation and burning solace in even his darkest moments. He always had the fire of his ambition and vow of vengeance to keep him warm. And never was that man who burned to gain his retribution as pitiable as he who, amidst all the glorious sunshine of life, allowed the cold pall of death to course through his veins; as he who had the great fortune to sit at royal life's bounteous table and yet was consumed by hunger and want; as he who every day saw his longings and dreams fulfilled all around him and yet felt nothing but the urge to flee! Yet this was precisely his fate.

A modest home and hearth, along with domestic tranquillity, that was all he could now claim as his legacy. A dream of a windmill and a potato patch were the only things over which he ruled in this world

804 · HENRIK PONTOPPIDAN

that he had set out to conquer in all his youthful exuberance and cockiness. Inger's love, the sheer exultation of his children, the comfort and coziness of the home they had built—all these things had been bestowed upon him as a recompense for his great loss.

And in a way this meant that he could no longer claim that a wrong had been done to him. In fact, that was the very reason he could never share his sense of loss with Inger. For in all this she was a completely innocent party. Besides, she would just be bewildered and understand nothing. And wasn't that the strangest thing about it? He, Per Sidenius, did not himself understand the overwhelming feelings of impotence and meaninglessness that he constantly suffered. The fact that he had grown to love his home—that Inger was very reluctant to leave the area where she grew up; and also that he had become something of a creature of habit as the years had passed—none of this explained the hypnotic spell that this insignificant patch of ground held over him, despite his often excruciating sense of loneliness. Certainly, the fear that he might not be able to provide for his family was not the thing that held him in stasis there. Quite apart from the invitation made by Inger's uncle, which had never tempted him, he had also rejected many other quite enticing offers; moreover, he had also gained a potential patron in the form of the county governor himself. This august personage had been very impressed by his river and land realignment and, quite unsolicited, had announced that he had personally recommended him to the minister of home affairs and the director of the state's hydraulic engineering department, both of whom were also close friends of his.

Least of all was it concerns over his health that provoked such anxiety in him—his grumbles about aches and pains notwithstanding. If he thought about his health at all, it was mainly out of concern for Inger and their children. That terror he had suffered in early adulthood about his imminent earthly demise whenever he felt the slightest twinge— a terror that had sucked the very marrow from his bones—had long since been overcome. Rather, it was a feeling almost of envy, just as at the funerals he attended, when he watched a coffin being lowered into the depths of the earth; and there were times when no sound seemed more enchanting to him than the hollow report arising from the open grave as the three shovelfuls of soil fell onto the casket—the sacred echo from the Kingdom of the Dead, the promise and reassurance of final annihilation. Let it all just end.

He had sometimes asked himself whether it would not be for the better all round, even for Inger, if he were gone from this mortal coil. She was still young and beautiful to behold. Presumably she would marry again and he had no doubt that she would find real happiness the next time around. Lately, he had begun to wonder whether her extreme aversion to the young land proprietor, Hr. Brück, did not rather conceal an instinctive, unconscious fear of the attraction that lay in his manly handsomeness and powerful physique. There was still so very much in Inger that lay dormant, slumbering, and now as he was being brutally honest with himself, he accepted that he had neither the patience, nor perhaps even the ability, to arouse those things in her.

A couple of days after this, they were again sitting taking afternoon coffee in Per's room—Inger in the sofa corner with her sewing, Per over by the window enjoying a cigar. After a silence had arisen between them for some time Inger raised her head and asked: "Do you want me to go?"

"No—why?"

"You look like you would rather be alone Per."

"Not at all darling. I was actually just sitting here thinking that it's nice to have you in the room doing your mending and sewing."

"Ah good; because there's something I wanted to talk to you about—something very important."

"And what's that dearest?"

"Well, you see Per—I have been wondering seriously whether it wouldn't be better after all if we just moved from Rimalt altogether, before we are forced to do it anyway. You yourself have said just recently that the income is all but drying up. And the truth is Per that, long term, it's going to be impossible for you to secure enough work if we stay around here."

Per looked at Inger with clear shock.

"What's brought this on all of a sudden?"

"Oh Per, we've discussed this so many times."

"Yes that's true. But why are you making an issue of it right now?"

His wary gaze rested on his wife's head. She sat bent over her sewing and would not look up. Had something happened? Now he came to think of it, she had been strangely quiet in the last few days; in fact, since the party at the chemist's home. Had her inner fears about Hr. Brück spooked her?

"And where do you think we should move then?"

"I don't know. But the county governor is your great supporter. He has told you a number of times that he can get you a position."

"Inger, the county governor is almost certainly talking about some post or other in the civil service in Copenhagen. He knows the minister of home affairs. But you've already said you don't want to go to Copenhagen."

"Want? Per, it's not a question of what I want. It's about what you think is for the best and the right thing to do. That's precisely what I've been scolding myself over—that I have possibly been selfish, that I've been holding your career back. Of course, I've been thinking mostly about the children. The thought of living in some third-floor apartment after all the space and freedom we have had here...well, it would be like living in a cage for them and I suppose I felt sorry for their sakes. But now I think it might work anyway. For part of the summer at least, they will be over here with my mother and father. They'll get all the fresh air and sunshine they need and go nice and brown. Then with God's help they'll always have that to look forward to during the rest of the year when they have to put up with city air, the fog and the smoke."

"And what about yourself, Inger?"

"Me?" She now looked up at him with a gaze so open and innocent that a huge strangling weight of emotion was lifted from his breast. "Oh never worry about me, dear. I'm strong now; and even though at first our standard of living over there will, I'm sure, be a bit restricted—because there's no doubt that a four-room apartment is all we'll be able to afford in the beginning—we'll just have to get used to it. I've also been thinking that we will have to let Laura go. City life is not really for her and she's so slow anyway. So from now on—temporarily anyway—we'll have make do with one house girl. I can take the children for walks and entertain them myself anyway."

Per was hardly listening. He had put his cigar down and blood banged in his head, heart—all over his body. He felt lamed by the stabs of angst that had lanced him.

"There is only one other thing that is worrying me greatly, Per," Inger continued in her matter-of-fact way.

"What is it Inger? Tell me."

There was a pause before she continued.

"Well Per, I've wanted to talk to you about this for some time. But you've been so distant recently."

"Have I? Are you sure you're not mixing the two of us up," he said jokingly and in an attempt to dispel the tension he felt. "It's actually you, Inger, who has been moping around so suspiciously in the last few days. So get it off your chest. Tell me."

"Well . . . I wanted to ask you Per whether you don't think you could make a bit more of an effort with the children. Of course I know that you are fond of them—but I can definitely sense from them, especially from Hagbarth—that they are sad you don't spend more time with them."

"What are you talking about? Are you saying I don't spend any time with the children? Of course I do."

"I know what you mean when you say that. And when the mood takes you darling, it's obvious that you really enjoy playing with them. And of course they love those times. But on a lot of other occasions, too many occasions Per, you push them away—and that makes them unsure and hesitant towards you. So now my fear is great that, if we go to Copenhagen, where you will almost certainly be spending even less time at home, the children will become complete strangers to you—and you for them."

"But Inger—I just don't understand what you're on about. I mean, I think that I am always—"

"Per, you're obviously not aware yourself of how much you cut

808 · HENRIK PONTOPPIDAN

yourself off from us," Inger interrupted with a sad sigh and a slight shake of her head. "And of course you don't do it on purpose, or even notice it, when you all too clearly let the children know that they are irritating you. But trust me darling—children have a very finely tuned awareness of things like that. I think therefore, and also for your own sake, you should be a bit more sensitive to these things. And since we are talking about it, I have to tell you what Hagbarth said to me on the night of his birthday when you disappeared for so long that he didn't get saying good night to you. He had tears in his eyes and he was really upset: 'Daddy doesn't like me—I know it Mammy.' Now don't take offense, or be annoyed with the children, because I've told you this Per. I'm not trying to hurt you. I just want to make sure that, if we are indeed going to Copenhagen—or wherever in the world it might be—that you are more considerate of little Hagbarth . . . just taking him for walks every now and again, talking to him and discussing the things you see along the way. He adores you so much and is so proud of you as his dad. Ah Per, he is such a darling boy and so clever. He's so aware of what's going on around him. Now I know it's precisely those endless, childish questions that plague you. But, at the end of the day, they are our flesh and blood and we have to make sacrifices for them."

Per sat still for a while without saying anything. Then he got up and proceeded to walk up and down the floor, as he always did when he was animated about something. Inger's words had wounded and scared him. Her quiet, dignified reproach had struck him far deeper than even she could know because it touched on his own boyhood memories, of which he never spoke anymore.

"I'm going to Copenhagen tomorrow," Per said finally. "I'm also going to write to the county governor this very evening. Are my travel clothes all ready? Tell Laura to hang everything out to air and to brush everything up. The suit probably needs to be knocked back into shape and pressed. And my dress coat—I'll need that if I end up going to see the minister. Oh yes my boots. Were they cleaned and polished after the party?"

Inger was completely bewildered. Such spur of the moment outbursts were anathema to her. Quietly, she asked her husband to think things through properly before dashing off hither and thither. There was no immediate rush and, besides, they still had to sit down and discuss the idea with her parents. But Per was having none of that. Right this minute was the best time because he had no real work commitments. Anyway, they had talked about this very idea so many times, both between themselves and with her parents.

"No more shilly-shallying, Inger. Let's just get on with it right now. If we just continue to talk about it, we'll end up doing what we've done all the other times the issue has come up—precisely nothing. Ah, Inger! It's so exciting. We are actually going to take life by the throat and see where it leads us! Do you know, in the last while I've actually been thinking along the same lines as yourself. Now I can tell you everything. Do you remember that fellow I've talked about, the engineer Hr. Steiner, you remember I've talked about him? A total bluffer he is, Inger, and, yes I will admit, that it cuts me to the quick that this fellow has appropriated, in fact stolen, my ideas and proposals and has gained huge public recognition for them. Can you believe he is supposed to have declared at that conference in Aarhus that he is going to conquer Copenhagen now that he has the provinces at his command? That pup! That's what it said in yesterday's newspaper anyway. It also said that he has already been invited to a meeting in the capital next week or the week after that. Do you know what? I've half a mind to use the occasion to take the wind right out of that man's sails. I'll stand up and calmly explain to the assembled gentlemen exactly why the so called Steiner Project is actually the Sidenius Project! And I've good reasons for believing that my pleas will not fall on deaf ears amongst the people of Copenhagen. There's no doubt that his bad reputation has gone ahead of him and they know him for the charlatan he is. And don't forget, Inger, there will be engineers and technicians, not to mention journalists, at a meeting like that who will still remember Per Sidenius and his crusading pamphlet—my battle cry, my call to arms!"

"Lord above Per. Why do you want to go raking up the past like that? It will do you no good at all."

"So you don't like the idea then? Well Inger, all I can say is—let's see what happens!" said Per, as he snapped his fingers and then proceeded to stride up and down the floor again, his hands behind his back.

"Per, darling. Please listen. I think you should let sleeping dogs lie. I can't imagine what you think you would gain by making some kind of ridiculous protest like that after saying nothing about it for so long. But I know you wouldn't embarrass us all like that darling."

"What I would gain? Embarrass you all? Inger dearest . . . all I'm doing is claiming what's rightfully mine. Besides, you never know what it might mean for us in the future."

"Per. I am only sure about one thing, and that is by doing something like that you will just bring down more upset and annoyance upon your head. You have said yourself that this Anton Steiner is a bit of a rough person who would use any means necessary to bring down an opponent. And then you are not used to speaking in public, and—"

"I suspect my little lady is having a rather premature fit of stage fright on her husband's behalf," said Per buoyantly as he stopped in front of her, lowered his head and gave her his most winning smile. "But yes, let's just see what happens! Watch this space Inger! But hold on. Where are the children? Where is Hagbarth?"

"He's out in the garden with the others, Per."

"We're going to have the biggest game of hide and seek there ever was today!"

"As I was saying Per, I think you should just take little Hagbarth for a walk. Just you and him. He would love that. He walks around most of the day not really sure what to do, poor little thing. Would you not take him out to Kristen Madsen's farm? Do you mind that the farmers' cooperative got a new steam thresher recently and it's being used out there at the moment. He would love that, Per. Anything mechanical has him fascinated."

"Out to Kristen Madsen's, Inger? But you know rightly that the world and his wife will be there at the minute. All going up to see that new machine."

"Aye Per, and that's precisely why you should take him. The more people there are, the more excitement there is for Hagbarth. And I'm sure you can explain how the thing works, Per. You should have seen his excitement the other day when we drove past it in the gig. But of course I couldn't tell him very much about it."

"Yes, yes, Inger of course. I'll take him up there right now."

When Per returned an hour or so later, he immediately began to prepare for his trip to Copenhagen. But when he went up to the attic to fetch his suitcase, he felt stayed by an invisible, ghostly hand. A laming paralysis. But the sensation was fleeting. An opposite, and even stronger impulse, drove him forward—to plunge once again into the maelstrom of life. He felt as if he stood on the last fateful threshold of his existence. If he could not now break free from himself and his seemingly innate melancholy, Rimalt would be the tomb where he breathed his last.

Per had only been to Copenhagen once in the six years since he had fled from the city. Six months after his marriage to Inger, they spent a honeymoon in the capital and stayed there for two weeks; but even at that time Per felt estranged and ill at ease with big city life. The noise on the streets, the clammy hotel beds, the stodgy restaurant food, the endless round of tips and gratuities that had to be left wherever one went, and the large distances that were involved when socializing; there was also the fact that you always had to be "Sunday dressed" and carry gloves, which of course meant constant hair and beard grooming—Inger insisted on no less. All this meant that he simply longed for home after no more than a few days there. Home to his small, tranquil rooms and the informality of life in the country.

It was no different this time round. In the first few days of his return to Copenhagen, his interest in the huge expansion and development that the city had undergone in recent times helped him to settle somewhat. On the very first morning of the very first day, he went straight down to the new port complex that was under construction; then he strolled around the new residential areas in the town and the old quarters of the inner city that had been rebuilt and about which he had read so much in the newspapers. However, once his curiosity and eagerness over these things had been sated, he became the inevitable victim of the feelings of estrangement and loneliness that affect all provincials in a capital city—the very same feelings that had gripped him seventeen years earlier when he had first arrived in Copenhagen after leaving the parental home.

He was also in Copenhagen at its most hectic time—when a departing summer is waiting for winter to arrive and life blossoms to the full both indoors and out. As the rockets and fireworks flew over the early evening sky from Tivoli, the pamp and blare from brass bands could still be heard in garden hostelries; all the theaters were still open and the summer visitors from Germany and Sweden were still about in the bars and cafés. This latter being much to the chagrin of regular patrons who would return from sojourns up the Øresund coast to find that their usual sofa corner had once again been seized by foreigners. Every train and steamship discharged yet more bands of people returning home from holidays in the country or abroad; and despite all the loud complaints about how quickly summer comes and goes, they revealed in their instinctive joy at being home and reunited with friends and family that in their hearts they had missed Copenhagen, even while relaxing in romantic forest-clad hillsides or remote fishing villages. Be they rich merchants and entrepreneurs, or just office workers, shop assistants, artists, and students, all had missed their dear old city with its enchanting array of gas lamps in the cafés and carriages and electrical moonlight on the cobbled streets.

Per felt alienated from all this buzzing liveliness, which to his ears and eyes was nothing more than street racket and grim, hurrying faces. For, truly, as he watched these scurrying hordes of humanity that milled through the streets, risked life and limb jumping on or off the trams, rocked and rolled through the town in hackney carriages, sat down in restaurants as if they were in their living room, ate lunch with a newspaper in their hand, or settled a business deal with a handshake and a glass of beer—none of them ever seeming to grant themselves a moment's quiet he decided for all time that he had seriously misjudged his own self. Not for all the wealth in the world, he swore, could he live such a life again. Indeed, when he occasionally found himself caught up in that human tide, a sort of missionary fever blazed up in him and he would be suddenly be gripped by an overwhelming urge to call out a warning to these people: Stop!

Perhaps for this reason, and after spending five days in Copenhagen, he had still done nothing about arranging an interview, either with the minister of home affairs or the head of the city's hydraulic engineering department. Every time he went to take a step in that direction he was held back by a compelling awareness that he was about to murder the very best elements of his inner self.

"My dearest darling"—he wrote to Inger—"I may as well alert you to the fact that it is more than likely I will be returning home shortly with my mission unaccomplished. I cannot really explain the reasons for this in a letter. I will suffice for now with saying that for each day that has passed over here, it has become clearer and clearer to me that life in Copenhagen suits me no more now than it did seven years ago—quite the opposite in fact. But dearest love, we must not get downhearted about this. There is somewhere in this world where I can work and feel at home and this is only the beginning of my search for that place. Nor can I say that this journey has been a complete waste of time. For I have now been confirmed in my heart of hearts that those feelings I had when I fled from life here in the capital—as rash and emotional as they possibly were— came nevertheless from sensibilities that are deeply ingrained in my nature. Thus, I believe I have gained further clarity and cohesion about my own self and my aspirations and this is a source of great satisfaction to me. Inger, what I have come to realize is that it is not, as I have believed in my more despondent moments, blind chance and fortune that has ruled over my destiny. No, an inner compulsion, which is what I am feeling now, has always steered the arc of my life, even when I was apparently being tossed about and was at the mercy of the wind and waves—I have often felt this very strongly before. My firm resolution, Inger, is now this—if I just allow this automatic steering mechanism to plot my course, I am now in no doubt that I will eventually end up where I am meant to be. So all this is by way of saying that you will all see me back home again. Now you might ask why, given that the original point of my journey no longer pertains, I don't just come back straight away. Well darling Inger, I have to admit that I feel slightly shameful, and it is that which has held me back as I have thought all this through. I left you with great promises of taking life by storm and I now have to return chastened and empty handed. I can only apologize my dearest love. But at least I have the solace that you will not hold it against me."

During his random odyssey around the city, Per very often saw old acquaintances from Philip Salomon's circle of friends. In fact, from the vantage point of the upper deck of a tram and with his heart banging in his chest, he one day watched his former close friend and brother-in-law Ivan as he darted up a street, his little legs working ten to the dozen in the same way they had always done, and as usual he had a document folder flapping under his arm. On other days he saw Aron Israel, Max Bernhardt, Hr. Hasselager, and even Dr. Nathan. He was shocked by the fact that they had changed so little in their appearance. In the same way, he saw several of his old fellow students from the College of Engineering as he walked about Copenhagen. But it was obvious that none of them recognized him. Now they all had the bearing of respected gentlemen with affluent and influential positions. But he knew this to be true anyway because he had followed their progress in the newspapers; but now, as he watched them go by, he felt no envy towards them anymore.

Of course the person he most eagerly, and yet most anxiously, looked out for was Jakobe. He was well aware that she now lived in the center of town and had established a school for disadvantaged children; some kind of part school part sanatorium, which had received quite a lot of publicity. From his Jutland redoubt, he had sought in vain to find out more about this school and its ethos, but the provincial newspapers had said very little about it, other than saying that it was an "admittedly ambitious caprice on the part of the daughter of a wealthy Jew."

Then, one afternoon, when he was sitting in a window seat of a café at the corner of Østergade and Kongens Nytorv, he saw Nanny's husband Otto Dyhring. He too seemed remarkably unchanged in appearance. He was standing on the pavement, talking to a young, beautiful, and very elegantly dressed young lady, who looked to be an actress, and who laughed continually at whatever Dyhring was saying—a laughter that seemed to have been provoked by his bold and forward gaze. There was no doubt that his presence on the street caused no little excitement—well-dressed gentlemen saluted him and passing ladies nudged each other's elbows.

As he took leave of the actress, he pressed her hand warmly before stepping into an open carriage, which had obviously been waiting for him. Hundreds of eyes followed him and followed the progress of his carriage across the square that was bathed in sunshine. Time without number, his golden head was revealed to his audience as he lifted his hat to acknowledge the many greetings from his admirers.

Per recalled that he had read somewhere that Dyhring had just recently returned from Paris, where, as a specially selected delegate from the Danish press, he had attended the inauguration of some public institute or other. Also, while there, Dyhring had been presented to the president of the republic himself and received a decoration. It was clear that he had become Denmark's most obvious and indispensable public representative. He was to be found at any civic occasion of note. Or rather, only when he was there did the occasion take on any kind of significance. Thus, all doors were open to him; all of life's fine and indeed more base pleasures were available to him. Men and women, citizens and aristocrats—all sought to curry his favor. Rumor even had it that the Royal Court used him as an envoy in certain delicate diplomatic situations.

So there was no doubt that there had actually been the stuff of a world conqueror in this man for whom life was just a farce to be played before the crowd. Invincible in his cloak of divine insouciance, he had transformed his life into a series of festivals and bacchanalian delights that were to be enjoyed as he moved along the path of his ceaseless triumphal cavalcade.

But then! Not even this modern Alexander did Per envy.

So whither, then, did his wishes, desires and yearnings lead him in the end? Where was home for Per Sidenius? Right at that very moment in his life, he would begin to grasp the answer to this question.

The preceding day, he had quite by chance seen a public announcement regarding a vacant post as an assistant highways engineer on the Agger peninsula, way out in one of the most remote parts of the Limfjord area in West Jutland, and he had not been able to stop thinking about it since. Here now the idea came to him unbidden once again. It was not so much because he was actually going to apply for the position. Not only was the salary extremely low, but Inger who loved all things that were quiet, comfortable, and luxuriant would never thrive in such a barren waste of sand dunes and stiff marram grass and where salt-caked and icy sea fogs often rolled across the landscape and wild storms from the North Sea could suddenly crash down on the area with a pulverizing harshness. No, the fact that this announcement continually tugged at him was because the location held a strange attraction for him personally and—as he only now realized—this was precisely because of the area's barren and doleful sense of being forsaken—its compete isolation.

It seemed to him that he had never looked so deeply into his own self as he had at that moment. It was as if he had seen the very essence of his own existence laid bare, and he had begun to shudder involuntarily at what was revealed there. For he saw that the reason he had never been happy, despite all the success he had enjoyed in his life, was because he did not want to be happy in the way this concept was normally understood. His longing to go home to Rimalt was not just about Inger and the children, nor was it even the peace and quiet of his own home that drew him back. There was something that went even deeper still. That ghostly hand, which had sought to deter him from making this journey—the same hand that throughout the whole of his life had secretly intervened at all the decisive moments to guide his way—this was nothing other than his own instinctive awareness that it was actually in seclusion and loneliness that his soul was most at home. Deep contemplation, sorrow, and pain were the lodestars of his life's journey.

"Feed me, O Lord, with the bread of tears and give me drink of tears in equal measure."

Now, really now, did he understand the at once alluring, yet terrifying, pull that such strange words could exert over him. That great fortune and happiness he had blindly sought after was in fact a search for the great martyrdom, that irredeemable loss which Pastor Fjaltring had praised so often and had declared to be the divine salvation itself for those souls that had been chosen to bear its cross of stoic affliction.

Per raised his head—and it was with a sense of having woken from a nightmare that he once again looked out across the sun-kissed square and its tumult of carriages, trams, and pedestrians. Shortly afterwards he got up and walked quietly out of the café. In a completely aimless fashion, he zigzagged through small narrow streets in the inner city, until in the end he landed at the green oasis of Ørsted Park. He had been coming here on a regular basis for his morning constitutional— taking advantage of the early hour to make sure that he could be alone with his thoughts. But now, too, in the hour before the city took its lunch, all was peaceful. Children, maids, and nurses had all gone home. The benches were empty. The lawns and pathways were cooled by broad shadows, but the bright sun still shone on the amber and gold leaves and highlighted the many bronze statues with a copper-green glow.

Per sat down on a bench in one of the central paths and while he sat there completely undisturbed, drawing figures in the gravel with his cane, the thought came very strongly to him once again that it would be the happiest thing, both for Inger and the children, if he were dead, or otherwise slipped away from their world. Perhaps especially for the children. He began thinking once again about what Inger had told him recently about Hagbarth. He himself had noticed that his son had been reacting strangely to him—as if the boy was hiding something deep within his soul that he could never share with him. This reminded him that he had one day surprised him in the garden when he was doing nothing more than innocently pretending to be on a hunting trip. The expression that had flashed into the boy's eyes when he saw him had frozen his soul to its depths. For Per, it had been just as if he was watching himself as a child, standing in front of his father on the one hand being terrified and on the other making up all kinds of demeaning excuses for some minor mischief that any child might commit. But Hagbarth's bright brow must never be darkened by the Sidenius mark of Cain! That paternal curse which had cast a shadow on his life, and which had left him banished and without peace wherever in the world he was, must never be passed on to his children. And Inger! Now that he fully appreciated and understood his aloofness and dread of life, how could he possibly allow her to share his fate? Poor child! She didn't realize yet the horrors that awaited her. She still had not grasped that she was shackled to a changeling, an underworld troll who shunned and was blinded by the light and believed good fortune to be a curse. And if her good heart might one day become enthused with love for some other man, she would dutifully conceal her secret as if it were a mortal sin. Then she would wither and die without ever having admitted or known the beauty of true love.

Per straightened himself in readiness to move on, but then his gaze fell upon a statue that loomed over the grass verge on the other side of the path. It was Silenus with Dionysus, when still a baby, in his arms. Using a tree as a support, and with a little smile in the corner of his eyes, the old satyr was bent over the unruly child as it thrashed about. His bearded and epicurean face beamed with all the joy and pride that only a foster father can show.

Per sank down onto the bench once again. He remained gazing at this joyous scene and the carefree beings it depicted until tears welled from his eyes. He could not help but think how things would have been so much different if such faces with such radiant smiles had beamed over him when he was a child and if life from a very early age had not been cast into the realm of doubt and suspicion for him, both at home and at school—most of all by the two people that had brought him into the world. But his baptism had been a kiss of death. Death's burial sign had been branded upon his brow and chest on the first day he ever saw the light of life—in the name of the Father, the Son, and the Holy Ghost.

27

P ER W E NT home the following day. He did mention the assistant highways engineer position to Inger, but more as an indication to her that he had also sought work outside Copenhagen, though without for the present finding anything that might suit them "because settling up there would be impossible for us."

So the days lapsed back into their old, uniform pattern as autumn slipped in over the country with all kinds of temperamental weather. Per had small bits of surveying work here and there, but there was no sign of larger projects on the horizon.

Inger noticed a change in Per. The minute he landed back, it was clear that he was so relieved and glad to be home again. And on the first day, he would hardly let the children out of his sight and had brought presents for each one of them. But at the same time, he seemed beset by a restlessness, and on top of that—towards her—he was now somewhat reticent, almost shy, which was not like him at all. Her very own Per, who would otherwise sit for hours by the window in his study, smoking a pipe or cigar and watching the clouds roll across the heavens, now moved from room to room, went outside and then in again, never settling anywhere for very long. At that very moment, she could hear him going backwards and forwards in his room. It was as if he still carried the agitation of his recent journey in his body. And now he was complaining of restlessness and had set up a makeshift bed on the sofa in his room because little Ingeborg had a cold and was disturbing his sleep with all her night time coughing and sneezing.

Inger reflected quietly on what all this might mean, and, more generally, she dwelled on his recent trip to Copenhagen and what may have happened to him there. One of the reasons that she had always balked at the idea of moving to the capital was that Per's former fiancée lived there. She was mortified at the very thought that her husband might meet with her by accident in the street. Her presumption now was that this had actually happened and that Per himself realized that the situation in Copenhagen would be untenable for all concerned. Thus, she understood the reasons for his change of heart about moving, but also why he would find it difficult to fully explain his reasons.

But that did not change the fact that a solution needed to be found. With each day that passed, she was more and more conscious of this. For the bald truth was that they could not remain in Rimalt without plunging into debt. She was already sitting on a number of unpaid bills—another reason for mortification—but which, for the moment anyway, she had not mentioned to Per. He had enough things plaguing his mind just at that minute, the poor creature. And of course his worries about what the future held for them was yet another torture for him, and it pained her deeply that she could not provide him with some sort of useful advice.

One afternoon, Inger heard the clatter of horses' hooves out in the yard and a man asking to speak to Per. She was just coming up from the cellar and so could not see who the visitor was, but she recognized the voice immediately. It was the young estate owner, Hr. Brück. What does he want here, she asked herself. His sudden and highly unusual appearance at their home surprised her and made her uneasy.

But Hr. Brück too was no less taken aback to find that Per was not at home. When Inger reached the front door and invited him in, Hr. Brück explained that her husband had asked him to come to their house in relation to some surveying work that he had carried out on the Budderuplund estate. Hr. Brück explained that Per had requested permission to compare his measurements with the old ordnance and land survey charts that pertained to the Brück estate and he had brought these drawings and papers with him as requested. Inger apologized repeatedly and had no choice but to bring him in to the sitting room and entertain him, even though she felt really put out by this, partly because she had a small mountain of children's clothes to iron and had only just left the iron on the hotplate to warm.

She could not fathom what had happened to Per. He had been at home for afternoon coffee and the gig was outside near the gate, so he could not have been too far away.

Her immediate source of distress in being left to deal with Hr. Brück was his stammer. This made all conversation stilted and awkward—the more so because he obviously hated being afflicted in that way. This, at least, made her feel sorry for him. She would, she decided, even be able to overcome her long-term aversion to him if it were not for those eyes of his. These were tight and steel gray and even as a young boy carried an intense even violent stare, which had made her uneasy in his presence.

Per did not show up until well over half an hour later. He made many and—as it appeared to Inger—strange and unconvincing excuses for his absence, after which the two men retired to Per's study to peruse the maps and drawings.

Their investigations stretched out over several hours and Per asked Hr. Brück to remain there until evening time and take supper with them. They agreed, furthermore, that Per should go back to Budderuplund to carry out new measurements in an area that was disputed between the estate and a neighboring property. Per then declared that he would do this the very next day after lunchtime as long as the weather gave good sighting conditions. His wish was—as he put it—to get the job out of the way.

"I must also remember to look at your renowned breed of fowls while I'm there. My wife has asked me to look at them a couple of times, but I keep forgetting. She has always had an interest in hens and poultry."

Thus, at the supper table that evening it was the most natural thing in the world for Hr. Brück to suggest that Inger accompany her husband to Budderuplund the next day.

"I do believe Fru Inger that when you see my brood of Vietnamese hens you will envy me."

Inger offered her thanks for the invitation in a way people do when there is no intention of acting upon it.

But the next day when, from behind the bedroom window, she saw the gig being brought out in readiness for Per's journey, she began to regret having told her husband that she was staying at home. The morning promised the kind of sunny early autumn day that can make September so special and she knew that the road to Budderuplund went through some of the most beautiful forests in the region. Then it occurred to her that it might cheer her husband up if she went with him; besides, she really did want to see the old manor house and its grounds once again. She had been there with her parents a couple of times when she was very young and was curious to see how things might have changed. And if, at the same time, she might be able to barter a couple of her Plymouth Rocks for some genuine Vietnamese hens—well, that would be a good day at the market!

In a trice, she had lashed the window up and called out to Per, who was just getting into the carriage:

"Will I come with you, Per?"

Inger got the sense that he had not understood her properly. He stared at her with such a look of utter perplexion that she began to laugh.

"Do you not understand me, Per? You poor child! I want to come with you!"

Per just nodded blankly.

Without complaint, the horse suffered from being unhitched from the gig when this was replaced with the pony carriage. The seats in the best "Sunday" carriage were of red velvet. The harness was also brought out and, a half hour later, man and wife drove out into the lane.

The route took them over the railway tracks and then rose steadily to the crest of a hill that offered a view over the river and surrounding meadows. On the other side of the hill, the ground rapidly fell away towards a wide cut in the land. This was a richly forested valley, and as the trap quickly descended the hill, a riot of multicolored leaves flashed in the sun, as if to greet them. Soon the forest closed about them and the going became heavier. Per pulled up the horse a touch and then allowed it to ease to almost a walking pace.

He simply sat there and said nothing. Inger, on the other hand, was highly animated, and her joy at being out of doors expressed itself in a joyful humming and la la'ing of songs and hymns—she had sat for so long brooding in the house and letting her sorrows get the better of her. Now, as they passed deep into the forest, her euphoria simply overwhelmed her. How lovely it was here! These magnificent trees! This unending profusion of colors! Right over their heads, a solitary bird was twittering gleefully and also seemed to be following their passage through the valley. Try as she might, she could not make out the little creature amongst the leaves and branches, but its song constantly called out to her as they progressed, one moment here, another there; it almost mischievously repeated its refrain—"see here, no, see here!" Inger took in deep drafts of the fresh autumnal air and gloried in the sense of liberation that the day had bestowed upon her. It was as if, at a stroke, all the things that had weighed her down and oppressed her had been expelled from her mind. The culmination of it all was that she was inspired to sing out loud; but then she observed that Per still seemed to be in low spirits and made do with softly humming her favorite song.

Suddenly she gripped Per's arm, dragging it slightly to make him pull up.

"Look!" she whispered.

Just ahead of them in a dense thicket, she had spied a roe deer. With its ears pricked and a quiver in its body, the animal watched them wide eyed and poised for flight. Per kept dead still. The deer too remained motionless, but with its head raised and weighing them almost defiantly with its gaze. Its ears flicked a couple of times and, finally, it stretched its throat forward slightly. But suddenly, as if spooked by its own movements, it switched about and set off in long loping hops into the dark of the forest.

"Hello!" Inger called out instinctively, as she raised her arms in homage. "Hello! Hello there!" she roared again, as the report of snapped twigs and rustling leaves faded to faint echoes, then silence.

The vivid impressions imparted by Mother Nature also began to work their spell on Per. Once more, a faint glimmer of light flickered in his soul. And the touch of Inger's hand had flared through his body like an involuntary shimmer of brightness. His hopes flared into life once again. But the flame was a chimera—a Saint Elmo's omen. And with one single remark, Inger snuffed it out.

"It's such a shame, Per, that you don't go hunting. It must be a wonderful life—all that fresh air and excitement. It wouldn't harm to try it, surely? Just the fact of wandering around in forests and fields, Per. It would have to be good for your health, not to speak of your spirits. Do you not think?"

"I'm afraid Inger that it wouldn't do me much good. You have to be reared to that kind of thing. And, really, I was never encouraged to enjoy nature and the great outdoors. That's probably why it all feels so alien to me. Like some kind of alien force."

"Who actually owns all this forest land, Per?"

"It's all part of Budderuplund estate."

"Imagine! My God. I never realized that it reaches almost to Rimalt."

"It does indeed. A huge piece of property. Hr. State Counsel Brück is rolling in it."

"He is that, without a doubt, Per."

Some time later, they emerged from the forest. And a new vista opened before them, where broad meadows flowed towards raised ground on the other side of a flood plain. But they were soon enveloped in forest land once more and beyond this there were still higher slopes that offered a greater panorama of the fertile landscape all around. Once they reached the south-facing side of the hill they had climbed, a large white building presented itself in the distance. The building was abutted by two tower structures and imposing parkland graced its approach. This was Budderuplund.

Inger looked at it in silence for some time.

"Just think that their gardens and lawns are so extensive, Per. I had completely forgotten all of this."

"Aye, by God. A garden like that would be a wonderful adventure playground for the children, especially little Hagbarth," said Per, in a peculiar, halting delivery that finished abruptly with an ironic laugh through gritted teeth. "He's running out of space at home, dear child."

"What's that large building at the back, Per . . . the one with the raised back?"

"That's the barn. And behind that are the stables and the dairy. Everything spanking new and of the best quality Inger. You have to hand it to those Germans—if they do something, they do it right."

"But Per darling. I'm worried now that they'll find it strange your wife came with you?"

Per reined the horse in. He was ready to stop immediately if need be.

"We can turn right around now if you want to, Inger. There's no harm done."

"Ah no Per. I think they've probably seen us already. There's a man walking up the driveway there. Is that not Thorvald Brück himself?"

"Yes, I think you are right. It looks like the young Hr. Brück all right."

"Well that's that then. We can't go back. And don't forget, Per, that I would really love some of those Vietnamese hens; so make sure that we can get to the henhouse, but don't be too obvious of course. And then I'll take it from there. I know my hens."

It was indeed Thorvald Brück that they had seen walking up the old avenue. This was flanked by linden trees and went from the outside roadway all the way up to the steps of the manor house. And he had indeed seen the little pony trap and had recognized the horse. Thus, as Per and Inger approached the house, he was standing on the stone staircase to greet them.

As a servant, clad in full livery, jumped forward to take the reins from Per, Hr. Brück stepped forward with alacrity to help Inger from the carriage and almost gave a bow in respectfully welcoming her to the manor house.

Thorvald Brück's father, the venerable State Counsel, bade them a formal welcome in the terrace room that overlooked the sweeping lawn. Hr. Brück the elder was a tall, stately gentleman with a silver white head of cropped and vibrant hair. His chin was immaculately clean shaven, his brow severe, and his nose bore the imperiousness of an eagle. In spite of his seventy-three years of age, his posture was just as straightbacked as his son's. It was clear to see that, behind his weather-browned skin, old warrior blood flowed in his veins. Speaking with a marked Schleswig-Holstein tempo in his accent, he passed some delicate compliments on Inger's fresh and appealing appearance and then asked after her parents. Per, on the other hand, he dealt with in a rather superior way.

Wine and fruit was served and a conventional conversation then ensued.

After some considerable time, Per rose from his seat.

"Ah yes, you are going out into the fields, Hr. Sidenius, while the light's still good," said the State Counsel affirmatively. "My son was telling me all about it. Don't worry sir, we shall look after your good lady wife in the meantime."

"Fru Inger is very interested in poultry, father," Thorvald Brück interjected, stammering awfully. "I hope you will allow me to escort you around the hen coops. Perhaps Fru Inger would like to do that right now and refresh her childhood memories of Budderuplund?"

Per walked towards the door, but Inger seemed suddenly to be discomposed at the thought of being left on her own and an objection began to form on her lips. However, at that same moment, Hr. Brück senior gave orders to an attending servant to run the poultry out.

For over an hour, Per tramped along an extensive ditch taking land measurements. He was accompanied by two housemen who carried his tripod and measuring chain. It was impossible for him to concentrate. So torn and distracted was he, that his helpers looked at him several times in utter bewilderment. For he now bitterly regretted what he had done. Was that the action of a man—to leave his wife defenseless? He had even betrayed himself. Oh no. He was not finished with life by a long chalk. He would go back. Reclaim his wife. Reclaim his life. And never let go of it again!

In the meantime, Inger was given a tour of the imposing manor

house and its immediate environs. She was accompanied by Hr. State
Counsel Brück and his son. They went first to the stables and then
moved inside to the dairy. After that they viewed the kennels for the
dogs and hunting hounds. The elder Hr. Brück then led Inger through
the kitchens and the massive pantry. Finally, down they went to the
remarkable ancient cellars in the main building, where Hr. Brück
showed her the remains of a medieval castle, on whose grounds the
new manor house had been built.

By the time Per got back, all three were once again in the terrace
room.

It was clear that State Counsel Brück himself was smitten with
the young and beautiful Inger and invited both her and her husband
to stay for dinner. Inger looked questioningly across to Per, who was
already rising from his seat as he declined the invitation. In an almost
offensive manner—Inger felt—he requested that his carriage be brought
out and the horse harnessed.

Thorvald Brück escorted them by horse for part of their way out.
He rode a tall, long-tailed filly, light ocher in color, which he—clearly
in homage to Inger—pricked on the flank so that it pranced, tossed
its head and reared up alongside their trap, the muzzle starting to
froth in excitement. Hr. Brück sat ramrod straight in the saddle, his
tight-fitting French riding jacket almost provocatively emphasizing
his powerful frame. For this very reason, Inger avoided watching him
and did her best to drag Per into the conversation, but her husband
remained aloof. "All that talk of horses, dogs, and hens is of no interest to me, Inger, and never will be," he told her afterwards.

A short distance before the roadway entered the forest, their
prancing escort bade them farewell and cut off down a side track that
led in a long curve back to Budderuplund. He set off at a gallop and
a swirl of dust, and when he was a safe distance away, Inger's eyes
followed his progress through the trees.

"He's different again on a horse—quite striking," she said.

"Well Inger, he comes from a long line of soldiers and cavalrymen,
so it's no surprise. From what I hear, his own career as an officer in

the army was already guaranteed but that awful speech impediment he has put paid to all that. It's actually quite painful to have to sit there sometimes and wait for him to finish a sentence, a word even."

Inger said nothing for a while and studied the passing trees.

"Yes, the poor dear. But I don't think it was half as bad today you know."

"Did you get a promise of those Vietnamese hens?" Per asked.

Inger's cheeks reddened visibly. She had forgotten all about them.

"No, I can't believe it. What a shame! I am certain I would have got two or three, or four, if I had only asked. Thorvald's father was more than kind and obliging to me."

"Indeed he was, Inger," said Per curtly.

They arrived home just as darkness was descending. Per complained of a raging headache and went into his own room. He lit his pipe and sat by the window, but got up again almost immediately, hung his pipe on the wall and proceeded to pace up and down the floor. His mind was in turmoil and he was simply unable to settle. He felt that he was the most useless person who ever walked the planet—a dismal misanthrope who loved life but shrank back from joyfully embracing it, and then hated it with a vengeance, but was too cowardly to put an end to it.

There was a timid knock at the door. It was Hagbarth who had been sent in to say good night.

On seeing his son's trepidation at approaching his father, tears welled unbidden in Per's eyes. He pulled himself together—even forced himself to smile—and lifted the little boy in front of his face and gave a very soft roar of welcome. There they stood—the child in his father's arms like the spectral figures of Silenus holding Dionysus that he had observed from the bench in Ørsted Park in Copenhagen not too many weeks before.

"My little son is not afraid of his dad—are you Hagbarth?"

"Ahm . . . oh," the boy stammered.

"We are going to be just fine, wee man. Do you not think?"

"Yep," he said, making himself heavy in order to slip down from Per's embrace—it was clear that he felt even less comfortable with his father's attempts at kindliness than with his verbal outbursts of displeasure and impatience.

No sooner had he hit the ground, he was gone through the door. Wracked with anguish, Per threw himself into his chair and plunged his face into his hands.

A week or so after this, Inger and Per drove out in the afternoon to Bøstrup rectory. This was their first visit since Per's return from Copenhagen.

Over recent years, the relationship between Per and his in-laws had developed into a sometimes thinly veiled hostility, which for both sides was only held in check for Inger's sake. Be that as it may, the venom burst out into the open on this occasion.

What inflamed Pastor Blomberg's ire more than anything else was the complete lack of attention, or engagement, that Per invariably showed while he was holding forth on some point or other. This priest, who was otherwise accustomed to a reverently attentive audience whenever he opened his mouth, regarded his son-in-law's obvious indifference as an expression of excessive arrogance and malevolent spite. As far as Inger's mother was concerned, however, it was the drastically reduced financial circumstances under which her daughter had been forced to live in recent times that goaded her inherent animosity towards Per. Now the fact that the much-vaunted trip to Copenhagen had ended in ignominy simply added fuel to the fire of her contempt.

Following a number of minor but highly ominous spats at the dinner table, a vicious row finally erupted once the family had moved to the sitting room.

Per's recent highly wrought state of mind had made him extremely irascible and suspicious of everything. Thus, when his father-in-law began, in a rather reckless manner, to berate him for his seeming indifference to the fact that he could not provide a decent and reassuring standard of living for his wife and children, his anger flared and he told Pastor Blomberg that he would brook no outside interference in his private affairs. His father-in-law then rebuked him for his outburst and, in particular, the dismissive tone in which he spoke—at which point Per lost the run of himself completely, jumped to his feet, slammed his hand down onto the table in front of his father-in-law, and proclaimed that he would no longer accept any lectures from him.

Never had such words been spoken before in Bøstrup rectory. Time stood still as a grave silence took possession of the room. Finally, the pastor rose from his chair with all the indignant majesty his tubby frame could summon and said: "I would seriously request, nay demand sir, that from this day forth you spare us the kind of scene you have just created."

With that, he stepped haughtily from the room and disappeared into his study. His wife followed him dutifully, displaying her most appalled and outraged visage as she went.

Per harnessed the horse and carriage and, shortly afterwards, he and Inger swung out of the courtyard, without Inger's parents showing themselves. While still in the sitting room, the red mist before Per's eyes had cleared momentarily to reveal Inger's deathly pale countenance across the table from him. The very look on her face froze his blood and shattered his defenses. He had not dared to look at her since that moment and not one word was exchanged during the whole journey home. However, despite his wife being well packed with blankets and a muffler, her constant shivering fits were so violent they made the whole carriage rock.

When they got home, she was calmer. Not only did she quietly tolerate Per's help in removing her driving cape, she actually bade him kindly place it up on the hook for her. Inger then went into the nursery to talk to the children and afterwards did her usual evening round about the house.

Per sought refuge in his own room and lit his lamp. Not until he went to set the glass over the wick, did he realize that he too was shaking. He then moved over to the chair at his desk and made a pretense at reading a newspaper as he waited for what was to come.

Ten minutes later, he heard Inger going into their bedroom, and a short time after that she came in to him. To Per's surprise she had undressed and now wore just her negligee and silk neck shawl.

"Have you noticed that your bed has been made up again in here," she said as she straightened the bolster. "Is that what you wanted?"

"Yes—thank you Inger," he said from behind his newspaper.

"Ingeborg's cough is a lot better."

Per gave no reply to this.

She then sat in the rocking chair over by the stove, and the pair of them fell into silence.

"Well, Per," Inger said at last. "Now we really have to make it our business to get away from here."

"Oh? Why do you say that?"

"Per, darling. You know very well why. Because what happened this afternoon did not come just out of the blue. Thinking about it on the way home, I realized that the storm has been building for some time."

"Inger, I am truly sorry for what I did—especially for your sake and also the children's. If only for your feelings, I should have bit my tongue and controlled myself. But just because, where I'm concerned at least, it will now be very difficult to go back to Bøstrup rectory, and it's probably likely that I would not even be welcome there, this will hopefully not mean that you or the children become outcasts as well. And, of course, it would be totally unnatural if you were to keep away from your parents' home because of what has happened."

Inger's head was lowered and she sat forward in the chair looking down at the floor.

"Per, it is amazing how wounding you can be—probably without realizing it yourself. That you could even consider the possibility that I might go somewhere, anywhere, where my husband was not welcome. And with our children—your children!"

"You would turn your back on your own home, Inger?"

"That is the last place I would go, Per, in such circumstances. I think now that staying in this area has become impossible for both of us. Things were going to be difficult even before all this."

"And where have you thought we might go?"

"Well a couple of times now you've mentioned that position as a highways inspector out on the west coast. I think that, at least to tide us over, you should apply for it. And rather today than tomorrow."

"Inger . . . do you actually realize what you are saying? For a start, there's the salary—something I've already mentioned to you—we are talking about less than two thousand crowns, and the prospect of acquiring extra income up there is very slim. It's one of Denmark's most remote and barren regions, Inger, there's nothing but sand dunes, heath and bog—and not a living soul for mile after mile, other than a scattering of smallholders and fishermen here and there."

"But at least we'll have each other Per," she cried with a catch in her voice. "Perhaps more there than we would ever have here."

"My dear, dear Inger! And you, a young woman who is so close to her parents, your old childhood home and all your childhood friends— you who love the comforts of home, with family and friends all about you. No, my darling Inger, it cannot be. That is far too great a sacrifice and a beautiful person like you does not deserve that. If we went down that road, I am sure that you—and with good reason—would never forgive me for accepting that sacrifice in a moment of crisis."

She was now fully bowed and had her face in her hands. She remained like that for a while and then raised her head.

"Oh Jesus help me! If I only knew, Per, what you really wanted!" With that she burst into tears, rose suddenly from her seat and screamed at him: "You are damn well torturing me!"

Without saying good night, she left the room, slamming the door behind her as she did so.

Per just continued staring at the door with a peculiar glazed look. He flinched a number of times but remained rooted. He desperately wanted to rise. To go to her. But he knew the weight of the phantom hand that held him back like an old friend. No. He would never let that happen to her! The clock had run down to its last fateful strike. The disaster was upon them. Her spirit and soul, he knew, were just wakening. And she was no troll woman who cleaved to the netherworld! So now he, Per Sidenius, would hand this free spirit back to life, back to the joyous light. Inger and the children both! As for him. What was to be would be!

*

The following evening, the children had been put to bed and the two domestics were working in the kitchen. Inger had just lit the lamp in the sitting room and had sat down on the sofa to darn some of the children's socks when Per came in from his own room. Though he had remained at home the whole day, they had barely spoken to each other since the night before. Inger had not failed to notice the strange way in which Per had hovered around her and the children all day, without ever properly engaging with any of them; in fact, just after dinner, when little Hagbarth was put up to rest for an hour, she had surprised Per in the nursery. He was standing over the child's cot and was staring at his sleeping son with a queer look on his face.

But it was not just her concerns for the future that had made her so taciturn and reticent that day. She was also very upset by what had happened between them the previous evening. Never in her life had she uttered even the mildest curse. In the aftermath of a new day, she could not understand what had come over her when she had begun to scream at her husband. Hot shame flooded her cheeks when she thought of it.

Per walked up and down and fiddled with different things in the room for a while before finally sitting at the table in such a way that he faced Inger and the sofa. The first word would come to neither of them.

"Now, Per. Have you reflected on our cross words last night and our need to move from here? We really need to discuss it and put it behind us, dear."

"Inger, I have thought of nothing else. But before we talk about that again, we need to clear the air about something else. I mean of course what happened at your parents' home. You yourself said that it did not just come out of the blue and you are absolutely right about that. And now I'm going to tell you why. Because even though my words came out a different way to what I would have said in a more composed moment, if I'm going to be truly honest from now on, I have to say that they expressed feelings that are deeply ingrained within me. It was not just a flash of temper, Inger."

"I've been aware of that for a long time."

"Yes, you said that last night too. But as much as you, dear Inger, have not been completely unaware of the deep disagreement with regard to the life philosophy that separates me from your father and his circle of admirers—and in that sense also from you—is it not strange, indeed quite inexcusable, that you and I have not discussed this as two adults more than we have done? The fault is entirely mine—I accept that. And yes I admit, painful though it is, that it is my own utter spinelessness that has led me to hide the full truth from you. But I was hardly fully aware of this myself until just recently."

"Per, darling. You are completely wrong. Do you think I have not thought about and understood your views? After all, you have never really hidden them from me. I am well aware that you don't have the same beliefs as we do, and of course it goes without saying that this saddens me. But hasn't my father, to be fair to him, always said that he who only sees Christ as a noble and perfect human being, rather than actually being the son of God, may still call himself a Christian and have hope of salvation, if in all other regards he has a true and pure relationship with God and is otherwise honest and God fearing in his whole way of life?"

"But Inger—I don't believe in God either."

"You don't believe in God?"

She lowered the socks and darning material to her lap and stared at him, her face blanched and aghast, just as it had been the previous evening at the rectory.

"No Inger . . . it's true. Really and in truth, that's been my view for a long time. Anywhere and everywhere that I have searched for this God, I have only ever found myself. And for that man who has become completely aware of himself and fully human, a God is not necessary; it is a superfluous thing. For that man, that fully aware man, the idea of an omnipotent superhuman being is neither a source of awe, nor reassurance—regardless of whether that being is portrayed as an almighty father or our final judge."

"Do you know what you are saying? If you are not careful, you are going to end up a wretched and very unhappy man."

"Possibly. But Inger, do you know that there are those for whom misfortune has a curiously captivating and attractive power? In the same way that deep and dark passages on the heath, and murky lakes in forests, are said to affect certain people."

"Well only for those, Per, who have become inured to sin and who can only find happiness when sinning. And that is the Devil's work. It says so in the Good Book."

"Does it? But that's not true of all mankind. They can't all be devils Inger. For there are those who are drawn to misfortune precisely because of their spiritual instincts, which tells them that only sorrow and loss—yes perhaps only utter despair can truly liberate their spiritual and intellectual inner selves. There are, as you know, also plants that only thrive in the shadows and cold air and which even bear flowers each year."

"Per, you can talk about plants all you like but I've never met a human being like that."

"But they are not altogether a rare breed, Inger. History shows that. In brighter times we like to place our trust in superior beings but, on the other hand, in days of hardship and want 'an eagle chick can emerge from a sparrow's egg'—as Pastor Fjaltring once said."

"Pastor Fjaltring? Spare me from Pastor Fjaltring. Has he filled your head with all this?"

"Yes—partly him. All right. Mostly him!"

"Well then I don't understand you at all. Heavens above, Per. He hanged himself!"

"Yes Inger, he did. Unfortunately. I have often had cause to regret that in these last few years. And really, until now his tragic end has remained a mystery to me; no matter how much I pondered it. Now I feel I understand him better than I ever did when he was alive. For his last desperate act is explained if one looks at his relationship with his wife. You might recall that I told you about his strangely subservient behavior towards her—a woman who was, no bones about it, a grim, damaged, and disgraced old hag. Now I believe that originally she was probably the complete opposite of Pastor Fjaltring in her ways—a rich, full-blooded creature whom Nature created for sunshine, joy, and bright days. And that, Inger, is the very reason that her fate preyed on the good pastor's conscience. Because he imprisoned her in the dungeons of his own shadow world, which to him were a blessing and a daily revelation, but for her a slow and terrible strangulation. Who knows, and again if we are being brutally honest, perhaps his sorrow and shame at being witness to her fall from grace held some kind of perverse attraction for him. Sometimes he revealed certain unhealthy and abnormal tendencies that almost gloried in the pain and degradation he felt. Then, of course, when she died his guilty conscience gained the ascendancy. He had destroyed another soul, his wife, by dragging her down to the depths of his despair and that was a cross too great to bear. Of course, not long after she passed away, he hanged himself."

"Per, why are you talking like this and telling me these things?" Inger asked as she looked at him, her eyes wary and full of suspicion. "We were speaking about something entirely different."

Per hesitated and then visibly drew a breath before replying.

"Because I believe, Inger, that their tragedy of a marriage carries important lessons—and clear warnings—for us as well, me and you."

"Me and you!" Again her darning fell into her lap. "Me and you!" What are you talking about Per?

Per looked down at the floor and gave no reply. His face had suddenly gone so white that Inger instinctively let out a sob of fear.

"Per! What has happened to you in this last while? Have I hurt or offended you? Or is it the children? Good God man tell me what is wrong!"

But Per was struck dumb.

Inger rose from the sofa, sat down at the table, and reached her hand across to him as a sign of her concern and tenderness.

"Per darling, please listen to your Inger that loves you dearly! You are not well. You don't even know yourself what you are saying—I know that. Recently, it's as if you've taken the worries of the whole world on your shoulders. Just when I need so very badly to forget all our troubles and just be glad to be alive! Now you're going to tell me, aren't you love? What is it really that is plaguing you so, and has you demented. Is it our money troubles. Is that it?"

"No."

"But what then?"

"It is something far worse than that Inger."

"But then tell me!"

"I can't Inger. Not in the way you want me to."

"Do you feel ill?"

"No. It's not that."

All at once, a glint like lighting flashed across Inger's face.

"Will you give me a faithful answer to just one question, Per?"

"Of course."

"When you were in Copenhagen that last time, did you meet your previous fiancée—her—Frøken Salomon?"

Per looked at her in shock.

"No."

She remained staring at him in clear disbelief.

"You are lying to me!" she cried and jumped from her chair, flinging the darning material across the table as she did so. "Ah! Now I understand everything!" She stormed towards the door, but then turned and stormed back. "You met your old flame and fell head over heels for her again."

"Inger, I'm telling you. You are wrong."

"Well it's some other woman then! Because there's something else behind all this! Now I see it all, Per Sidenius! It's all been one huge sham, a sly deceit! There was I worried sick and all the while you've been getting me ready for this. You want a divorce so that you can marry someone else. That's what it's all about isn't it? Say it right out to my face. Go on!"

Per tried to think things through very quickly.

His racing mind told him that it would be far better for her if he went along with her erroneous assumption and told her a lie. Without some form of compelling reason, she would never agree to a legal separation. He had no choice but to provoke her hatred for him, so that she would despise him from this day forth and banish him from her mind all the quicker. And if he was renouncing so much anyway, his name and honor might as well be included. He spoke softly, but clearly.

"So be it," he said, bowing his head. "It's true."

Inger stood rooted in the middle of the floor. She pressed her hands to the sides of her face, which paled to a shade of its former self. Her eyes held no pupils. Only black coals.

"And like the coward you are, you have kept that from me for nearly a month! So my father was right all along. And I was your greatest defender as usual! And your sleepless nights! Your raging headaches! Ha! I should laugh really. When I think of how night and day I've worried about you and thought of nothing else except how I might cheer you up and make you happy. And all the time, your thoughts and dreams lay with another. Bent over your desk pretending to work when you're only scheme was how best to be rid of us. Disgusting playacting! That you could be so low and mean. Not just to me but your own children! Fie for shame! Truly that is low and disgusting."

In the nursery, "Stub" had begun to whimper. But Inger heard nothing. She had once again begun to pace up and down the floor, talking to herself now more than to him. Only when the child began to scream did she go in to her.

Per straightened in his chair, pushed his head back and gasped. Now it was done! The sacrifice had finally been made! And, through gritted teeth, he swore to see it through to the harrowing end.

Inger came back in. She walked past him twice and then stopped in front of him.

"Have you absolutely nothing to say me? Even now... even now I pray that you will tell me that it's not true!"

He shook his head.

"No, Inger—what help would that be?"

Still she stood in front of him.

Then she turned sobbing from him and fled back to her bedroom.

"So low and mean. So cowardly!" he heard her cry as the door slammed behind her.

Shortly after this, Per realized that the whole house was up. Doors everywhere were being opened and shut, and then he heard Inger giving loud instructions to the house girls. He heard the yard lad's clogs clattering about in the courtyard. The carriage port was opened and he heard the pony trap being pulled out.

She wants to leave this very evening, he said under his breath.

Now all the children were roused from their sleep. Ingeborg was crying and Hagbarth could be heard asking if the house was on fire. From all corners of the house, Inger's harsh and commanding voice was to be heard. One of the house girls came running in to the sitting room. She was in her stocking feet and all flustered as she tried to find something, but turned quickly about in terror at seeing Per. Inger entered the room only once—fully dressed for her journey, in her hat and cape.

"Inger, as it has come to this, it is much better if I leave. Or at least wait until tomorrow!"

She gave no reply. She moved over to the bureau and took her housekeeping money and other small things.

"Will you let me speak to the children?"

"Not tonight. From now on, you may arrange to see us at the rectory."

A half-hour later, the carriage rolled away from the house. Per had not moved. When the last clop from the hooves of his faithful horse and the echo of the carriage wheels had completely died away, he lifted his ashen face away from his hands and instinctively turned his gaze heavenwards.

"Can I do any more than that?"

28

ONCE THE traveler has passed Ydby, with its many somber burial mounds and imposing cairns, on the way from Oddesund to Thisted, and then turns westward towards the quaint little town of Vestervig, which holds the grave of tragic Liden Kirsten—and the lover her brother king brutally denied her—a savage change takes place in the landscape. Further north lies a forlorn and weather-beaten country, where even sheep struggle to find proper nourishment. This is a landscape of sand dunes and bogland, which remains unchanged in the height of summer, or the depths of winter—the blue-green tufted lyme grass and reddish swamp horsetail, or heather, being the only things that can survive the corrosive sea mist in this otherwise scorched terrain. Impenetrable wetlands force the road into large diversionary loops, and on the rare occasions when quiet weather prevails, a heavy mist swirls above these areas like the aftermath of some huge conflagration.

A small farm, or moss-roofed cottage, might be spotted here and there, but there are often several kilometers between any dwelling, and towns are nonexistent. However, one place shows evidence of the first attempts at forming some kind of community. In a hollow, where a meadow of sorts has emerged around both sides of the entrance to a bog, there are four houses. The first one houses a school and the second accommodates an irrigator. The third belongs to a shoemaker. The fourth is empty.

From this last house the remains of a man, who had not reached a great age, had recently been removed, someone who, for many years, had been the subject of much speculation and debate in the area. He had arrived one day as a stranger to the district and had never bothered to reveal anything about his past. That aside, he had actually proved to be excellent company, albeit rather abrupt in his manner, and he had many friends in the area and certainly no enemies, other than the local priest. He was unmarried and had only his housekeeper, an old horse, and some poultry for company. Despite not being a man of letters, he possessed many books. However, he had spent most of his time alone with his thoughts on the country roads as he carried out his official employment, roaming the district in a trap pulled by his coarse-haired Norwegian fjord horse, which was almost blind with age. The man had been an assistant highways inspector by profession, and never had the district's roads been in such good condition as during his time there.

Despite his state of solitude, he always appeared content and at ease with himself. This also belied the fact that he had not been in robust health for many years—something which forced him to observe a strict rectitude in terms of his lifestyle, and especially to renounce all the time-honored enjoyments indulged by the local populace in their search for respite from the unrelenting harshness of their surroundings. His sobriety was a source of great wonder and anxiety for the natives, stoked all the more by his simultaneous abstinence from religious services, not to mention the divine altar, and for this reason he was described by the local priest as a poor unfortunate soul condemned to suffer the horrors of eternal perdition.

One of those upon whom his force of personality had made a great impression was his neighbor, the schoolteacher, a younger man who was of a lively and inquiring disposition, and who had made a joyful habit of slipping over to visit him of an evening in order to debate matters of great import. The teacher was a man who in all circumstances endeavored to live life as honestly and honorably as possible, which touchstones he believed would ensure his hopes of one day being blessed with the glory of eternal salvation. But in spite of these bright hopes and intentions, and although he enjoyed a comfortable family life with his wife and children, he had often struggled through bouts of dejection and lethargy. Yes, he had been forced to face the fact that his godless neighbor, for all his loneliness, seemed happier than he. When he had once worked up the courage to admit this to the engineer, he in turn had replied, in his precise and calm way, that if this was the case, then he had not found his natural habitat, that place where he alone would be able to find his way to the greatest of joys known to man: to become fully and clearly conscious of one's own inner self. But when the teacher then asked him how exactly one went about finding one's own natural habitat, the assistant highways inspector replied that no person could advise another person as to the road best traveled. For here it was a question of each person yielding completely, and without fear, to that innate drive for self-fulfillment that was part of the core of all creation.

On another occasion, the teacher implored him to explain how this "greatest joy" actually felt within a person; but in this regard, too, the engineer refused to be drawn any further. "Ask your priest!" he had replied ironically. However, he did subsequently explain that the key issue for every person was to bond in the most immediate and independent way possible to the things around him, rather than perceiving them through the mediation of others—in the way, for example, that people based their lives on ideas passed from one generation to the next. This kind of truly vibrant approach to life was the necessary precondition for being able to experience the joy of new revelations within every experience, be they modest or spectacular. Yes, the most heartbreaking even. Any human being who has never experienced that joy, which is what it is, when a previously obscure window into the mind, or the reality of life, is suddenly revealed to them, has never truly lived, he explained.

Schoolteacher Mikkelsen would often ponder these words during the assistant highway inspector's final years, when, in spite of horrendous pains brought on by cancer, his spirits remained buoyant, even though he steadfastly refused to call upon external sources of possible solace. Of course, during bouts of severe pain he was in a wretched state and would moan so loudly that the surrounding neighbors were forced to go about with swabs of cotton in their ears; but when they would subsequently call in to him, there he would be with an aspect of one who had undergone a deep and enriching experience. That life was never at any time completely unbearable for him was also confirmed after his death, when a loaded revolver was discovered hidden in a drawer in his bedside table.

In his final days, he lay motionless and refused all visitors. At the very end, the actual process of bodily dissolution occupied his thoughts. When he felt the chill of death itself coursing through his bones, he asked for a mirror.

"It will soon be over," he said rather plaintively to the housekeeper as he gave back the mirror. He had already lost most of his sight.

Shortly afterwards, the final throes of death ensued. It was early evening and a grim gale was rising from the southwest. The wind blew through a crevice in the front doorstep in the manner of a sick dog whining for its master, and the rain rushed in squalls at the window panes. A candle burned near the top of the bed as his father's large silver watch ticked from its vantage point on the bare wall.

The old housekeeper had sent for the teacher because she was too afraid to be left alone with a dying man. But there was nothing that he could do. In his last few hours, the assistant highways inspector had lain quite still, save for some apparent snoring noises. Shortly after midnight, his head slumped to one side. They heard the faintest of sighs, and he was dead.

The following day, a most beautiful October day, with blue skies and hardly a breath of air, he was lowered into the graveyard's sandy earth. There were some twenty people in attendance. A simple hymn was sung, but there was no sermon and the church bell observed proceedings in silence from its tarred and mute gantry. This arrangement had been the express wish of the deceased. The fanfare, however, which he had also requested be played over his grave, had been banned by the priest.

Two of his brothers appeared at the burial service. Neither department chief Eberhard Sidenius nor Thomas Sidenius, the rural dean, chose to wear their ceremonial dress. Following his burial, his last will and testament was opened. To the surprise and consternation of his brothers, he had determined that his estate should be bequeathed to

"Jakobe Salomon's non-denominational school" in Copenhagen. This was an enterprise in which they could see no merit whatsoever. To cap it all, it now became clear that, quite apart from fixtures and fittings and various sums of money in cash, two bank accounts had also existed which when combined amounted to many thousands of crowns. The disciplined, indeed ascetic, lifestyle necessitated by the poor health of the deceased, and which furthermore suited his natural inclinations, had facilitated the setting aside of almost half of his annual salary, not to mention other incomes, which included sums relating to the surrender of patents for some small inventions he had developed. The two brothers were taken aback.

"It really is a tidy amount," the department chief cried a number of times, at first with awe in his voice, and then somewhat suspiciously.

"Yes, it is actually quite a substantial sum of capital," the dean averred, adopting the same shift in tone.

The two brothers looked at each other.

"It is to be hoped that he has acquired it by honest means."

"Of that we can have no doubt, surely?"

When Per's brother Eberhard returned to Copenhagen, a certain curiosity drove him to personally deliver the news of the inheritance, which had befallen Miss Salomon's school.

One day he set out for Nørrebro, where the unmarried philanthropist had established her controversial "child refuge," right in the middle of a very deprived area. A female caretaker led him across a large playground with trees and benches, and as the proprietor was at that moment engaged in teaching duties, he expressed the desire to "have a look around the establishment." A lady teacher then approached him and offered a guided tour of the premises. At one end of the large building, there was a bright and airy dining area with a high ceiling, where one half of the children were just at that point being fed, while the other half attended classes. In a couple of side rooms, there were sewing areas where the children—both boys and girls—learned to darn their socks and mend their clothes and shoes.

Up above there was a series of bathrooms. Every third day, his guide explained, the children had a hot bath. Light, air, water and regular meals were the sole means by which the school encouraged the children's moral sensibilities and these replaced all religious instruction.

"Hmm, I see," the department chief rejoined as he cleared his throat.

The children did not live at the school, as the whole idea was that their clean bodies, well-maintained clothes, and good manners would introduce young missionaries for the cause of cleanliness, order, and discipline into the homes of the surrounding area. The school did, however, open its doors from the early morning when the factory day began and the children received full board for a certain payment, which was not a small fee, but was, in any event, adjusted according to the parents' ability to pay.

All well and good, the department chief thought to himself, but— At the very same moment, he received word that the headmistress awaited him in her office.

Jakobe Salomon was now a woman some forty-odd years of age, and in spite of the fact that she had retained her upright and proud bearing, the passage of time had left its not insignificant mark upon her. It was clear to see that the enterprise she had undertaken here by dint of her formidable energy, and in the teeth of great opposition and rumor-mongering from various quarters, had robbed her of more than just her private fortune. That youthful longing to raise the battle standard for some just cause had now been completely fulfilled. Her face, meanwhile, which her admirers had once described as resembling a proud eagle, her enemies as that of a parrot, was now positively hawk-like. With her prematurely almost white hair, her sallow skin, her large dark eyes, long neck, and simple brown dress, which was plainly decorated with a broad, white-lace collar, she invoked the image of a condor surveying the wide plains from her lonely aerie.

When the department chief entered her office, she rose quickly from her desk to greet him.

"I assume that your kind errand here today is to inform me of your brother's death. I should say, however, that I have already been informed of this by others who saw the death notice in a newspaper."

"If there were no other cause, madam, I would not have troubled you with this visit. Not least because my brother and the question of his ultimate fate is hardly of much concern to your good self."

"In that regard, sir, you are quite mistaken. I owe more to your brother than even he himself could have imagined. From a distance, I have also followed his movements as best I could. Of course, as the years went by, we drifted apart from each other in more ways than one. I know absolutely nothing about the last years of his life. Now, do please tell me what has happened in all that time. Take a seat, sir, and tell me about his sickness and how he left us in the end. It has all been so strange for me not knowing anything of these events."

But the department chief had no intention of making himself comfortable. The rather forward tone, which this somewhat dubious woman had adopted with him, produced an instinctive tightening around his mouth, making his protruding jaw even more prominent.

"As I say, madam, I would not have troubled you at all but for the fact that a particular matter impels me to do so. So I will come straight to the point. Your assumption that my late brother had distanced himself more and more from you, not just literally but also with regards to his views and philosophy, appears not to be completely accurate—you will understand madam that from my point of view this is a source of great regret. For he has, in every clause of his last will and testament, the legality of which is open to serious doubt, appointed your good self, or more accurately your...your...your institution, or whatever the word is you use to describe it, as the sole beneficiary. Now, as my brother leaves behind children, born within a legal marriage, the will is in reality quite invalid; but I have ascertained that neither the rightful legatees, nor their guardians will raise objections to his last wishes being fully observed in this way. This concerns capital amounting to some twenty thousand crowns, the origin of which I am unable to establish. I therefore deem it my duty to inform you personally of this fact. I also require you to state, madam, whether you wish to accept this gift, or not."

*

Jakobe Salomon stood by the side of a chair and leaned against its back, using her elbow for support. She was deeply moved. Reminiscences from her younger days flooded in and overwhelmed her. This woman, who so few people had ever seen cry, was simply unable to hold back her tears.

"Is there any reason, sir, why I should not accept it?" she said quietly. "Your brother and I were very different, and it has often occurred to me that, in truth, I barely understood his particular way of being in the world. But that makes me all the more grateful for the tribute he now sends to me."

"In that regard, Frøken Salomon, may I venture to remind you of a conversation we had some sixteen or seventeen years ago? On that occasion, I used approximately the same words regarding the relationship between you and my brother as you now are using yourself. I think it is now time for you, madam, to accept that it would have been best for all concerned if you had shown more respect for my powers of judgment."

She lifted her head with great pride and looked directly at him.

"Again Hr. Department Chief, you are completely mistaken! I regret absolutely nothing. On the contrary, I feel that it was a great honor for me to have been a part of Per's life. My life really only began to have a meaning after I experienced both the joy and the pain that he caused me. The work that you can see going on all about you is really just as much his as mine. And for that reason, I will always be deeply grateful to him."

"Yes, hmm, well, in that regard, madam, you and I are never likely to see eye to eye. I will, therefore, not delay you any longer. May I bid you good day!"

One evening, a week after the burial ceremony, schoolteacher Mikkelsen and land irrigator Nielsen, who was also the parish clerk, were to be found inside the deceased's abode, which was otherwise secured from intrusion. Their mission was to comply with his brothers' request to draw up an inventory of the remaining physical possessions. The brothers had taken with them all securities, letters and similar things, but in a table, which by chance was positioned with its drawers facing into the wall, a thick bundle was discovered, in effect a little journal, full of notes and memos written in the engineer's barely legible handwriting.

Schoolteacher Mikkelsen could not resist the temptation of studying its contents. Thus, while the parish clerk went around the other rooms with a lamp and noted things down in a list, he sat in the bedroom, by a light that was stuck inside the neck of a bottle, and browsed through the book. It was a kind of diary the highways engineer had maintained during all the years he had lived in the area, and in which he had written down his thoughts and generally kept up a kind of conversation with himself regarding all the things that had happened to him. On one of the book's first pages, the teacher labored his way through the following:

"While we are young, we make reckless demands on life's omnipotent forces. Our desire is that they reveal themselves to us in all their glory. That secret veil, behind which they exert their influence, infuriates us and our only wish is to mold and bend the world's order to our desires. As we get older, and in our impatience, we cast our eyes on man and on the history of man, in the hope that, here at least, we might find some kind of meaning, order, development. In short, to see if the meaning of life is to be found here—the final aim of our struggle and suffering. Until one day, we are stopped by a voice from deep within us, the voice of a phantom asking: But who are you yourself? From that day forward, no other question matters except this one. From that day, our own self becomes the great Sphinx, whose mystery we must solve.

"My true self? That man, who this morning rode out in the driving rain, disheartened, bitter, so incessantly sick of life and its woes, was that my true self? Or he who, in the falling light, sat there at the stove and gave in to the roar of the flames, lulling him into a doze and sweet memories of house and home and laughing children. Was that my true, my real self? Or he who now sits alone by the lamp, neither happy nor sad, neither old nor young, with that quiet heightened awareness of having an inner peace, which only the night and solitude can bestow, is that me, myself, in the form in which I emerged from Nature's hand, unaltered, untainted? Or is all of it the real me, regardless? That entity we call our soul, is it just a fleeting disposition, a result of the dreams in our sleep and newspaper reading, something dependent on the barometer needle and market prices? Or do we have as many souls in us as can appear in our Gnav board game with a lottery of dice, figures, and numbers? Where each time the bag is shaken, a new shape appears: a clown, an old soldier, a night owl . . .

"I must know! I must know!"

Schoolmaster Mikkelsen was shocked. He hardly recognized his former hero in these despondent lines. But as he explored further in order to see the notes written in later years, he came across a letter which lay hidden within the leaves of the book. He looked to see how it was addressed and saw "Hr. Assistant Highways Inspector, P. Sidenius," and from the postmark on the stamp, he could see that the letter was only a few months old. After a brief struggle with his conscience, he eased the letter out of the envelope. It was a woman's handwriting. The sender's address was at the top of the first page— "Budderuplund"—and the letter read as follows:

Word has come to me that you are ill, very ill. For this reason, I must break the vow of silence upon which you insisted. I will never find peace in my heart unless I make you aware of my unending gratitude for all that you have sacrificed for the sake of my happiness. I now understand you completely—that you only wanted the best for me, and I can never thank you enough in this regard. I send greetings from our three children. They are doing well, as are my two younger children. Hagbarth is now a student. He wants to be an engineer and, by everyone's account, he is a strong boy with remarkable abilities and full of spirit. So I am sure he will get on well, wherever in the world he goes. Ingeborg was confirmed last autumn. I have both her and little Lise at home still. They don't know you, of course. That is the way you wanted it, and perhaps it was for the best. Once again, my heartfelt thanks for everything. May God give you the strength to face what lies ahead of you!

Inger

Schoolteacher Mikkelsen nodded conspiratorially to himself and then carefully placed the letter back into the envelope. My word, what a curious man he was, he thought to himself.

The last part of the journal consisted mainly of undated jottings, and several of these ended with the same sentence, which here and there was underlined: "Nature is pure abundance, Nature is wise and merciful!" Here, in these passages, Mikkelsen instantly recognized both the thoughts and expressions used so often by his friend. Just as in a piece like this:

"Without the primordial human drive to grow and develop, that self-creating force which expresses itself in our great passions, be those passions directed outwards towards reality, or inwards to our innermost thoughts, or upwards to the world of our dreams, and without the incredible, indeed mythical, courage to will oneself into that place of ultimate godlike exposure, one will never achieve a state of genuine human independence. Therefore, I count myself lucky to have lived in a time which bestirred this drive and strengthened my courage. Otherwise, I would have remained a half-baked human being, a Sidenius, for the whole of my life."

Or in another place: "In reality, Christ's story and his life teach us nothing other than the fact (which is an ancient truth) that only one thing can overcome suffering and that is man's passion."

On a third sheet was written: "All honor and praise to the dreams of my youth! For in the end, I did indeed conquer the world! The soul of each human being is a universe in itself and the death of that being is the end of the world in miniature."

In another place he read these lines: "The newspapers report today that Hr. Steiner has been appointed as a councilor of state. Really? There's your recompense for a whole life wasted in lies and breathless humbug—just a councilor of state! There is scant reward in the material world. Poor Hr. Steiner! If you only knew how I (in my anonymity) feel myself to be as free as a prince and unbreakable; you would understand, sir, that it is yourself that has been made the fool. But, of course, you are unaware of this and are happy. You congratulate yourself and proudly call champagne toasts to your growing fame. For Nature is pure abundance, nature is wise and merciful."

In another place, the following words could be found under the headline "God": "Voltaire was once quoted as saying that if God did not exist he would have to be invented. I find more truth in the saying when it is switched around. If a God actually existed, we would have to forget him, and not because of fear that our evil deeds would be discovered and punished, but in order to encourage those who will do good works simply for the sake of goodness itself. How can one give alms to the poor with a clear conscience when one believes, and accrues benefit from believing, that God in heaven sits on his throne keeping an account of such deeds and nodding his approval?"

Then, under the headline "More on faith," it said:

"We surround ourselves in this life with so many things, which have come into our possession by pure chance. We might notice one day that we need a new dresser. We go to a cabinetmaker and buy something which just happens to be on display. We look over it with an air of distraction. It is possibly not even really to our liking, but in the very moment we decide to buy it and it comes into our possession, a secret exchange is enacted between ourselves and the object. With tender care, we glide our hands across the French polish; our eyes look on as we lovingly, and with no little fear, follow its transportation up and down stairs, and should a separation be forced upon us in later life, we feel that we have lost a part of our own selves. This is the mystery of possession. But is that not also true of faith?"

There was a note which was written in the final year of his life, which bore the headline "The great phantom."

"Somewhere over in the direction of Mors, the following event took place a few years ago. A local squire had two sons, two small boys. The youngest was a stubborn little tyke whom the father was determined to break. One day, in the tenth year of the boy's life, and when once again he had misbehaved and was therefore about to be disciplined, he sought refuge high up in a tree in the garden. Beside himself with rage and—it is broadly alleged—the consumption of too much wine (for he had just arrived from a post-hunt luncheon on a neighboring estate), his father stood below brandishing his riding whip and demanding that he come down that instant. But in spite of his father's roaring and the impending violence that he promised, the boy remained in his lofty perch and in his trepidation even crawled still higher until, at last, he was to be seen at the very summit. Then came a sudden scream. The branch upon which he had sought a secure footing gave way and the boy plummeted to the ground. He was crippled for life and a guilty conscience drove his father from all reason and he was incarcerated in a madhouse until his death.

"Years passed and the sons grew up. The eldest blossomed into a healthy young gentleman of ruddy cheeks and disposition, what you would call a fine upstanding man, who married a pretty young girl and brought a brood of healthy children into the world, worked the estate up into a model farm and, overall, performed his duties as a man of good standing. In the meantime, his pale and quiet little brother spent his days lying on a camp bed in the park surrounded by his friends and even birds that were happy to eat from his hand. He did not feel in the least miserable, his only torture being the misplaced pity of stupid people and the thought of his father's wretched state. I have seen this boy myself. I suppose at that time he was eighteen or nineteen years of age and I have never been able to forget the transfigured expression in his face. It was as if there was a lustrous aura surrounding his helpless form. In recompense for the loss of his health and wellbeing, his sixth sense, which affords the soul its deepest raptures, had become fully developed. The clumsy boy with the sullen demon in his eye had become—well, a poor creature, neither man nor woman, neither child nor adult—but at the same time a human being whose gaze incessantly reflected the eternal in all its clarity, depth, and harmony. And my thoughts always turned to his father, whose conscience, that hideous phantom, had driven to dark despair because he was not possessed of the faith, the true faith, the faith in Nature, the abundant, the wise and merciful which reveals all and which graciously replaces with on hand what has been lost on the other, which—"

At that point, the schoolteacher was interrupted in his reading, as the parish clerk walked into the room.

"Well that's us done then, Mikkelsen. What's that you have there?"

"It's only the book that we found in the drawer. What will we do with it? It's stuff written down on paper, so it can't go to auction and, really, it's too good to be burned. Do you not think now Nielsen that I might, in all good conscience, bring it with me and have it to keep? Then I would have something to remind me of the roads inspector, may God rest his soul. For—the truth be told—there'll be times when I will miss him sorely, and this has exactly the kind of thing we would sit here and be discussing, like it's all there in front of me again."

"Take it, Mikkelsen. We have no responsibilities where written material is concerned. And, of course, there is no pecuniary advantage involved."

With that, the parish clerk lit a lantern, all the house lights were extinguished, and the two men stepped out of the empty house and closed the front door carefully behind them.

AFTERWORD

HENRIK PONTOPPIDAN (1857–1943) is one of Denmark's greatest writers. His literary production, which would encompass almost
fifty volumes, has made a lasting impression on the Danish literary
landscape and has exerted a significant influence on writers in Scandinavia and beyond. *A Fortunate Man* (*Lykke-Per*), published serially—
a common practice at the time—between 1898 and 1904, would
become a cornerstone in his output. When the novel was first published,
and in particular the key 1905 version on which this translation is
based, there was a general awareness in Denmark that this was a
major literary event. In addition to having certain autobiographical
elements, which commentators did not fail to notice, the novel taps
into some of the major currents and themes that still resonate today.
Pontoppidan's body of work, with *A Fortunate Man* as its most significant literary accomplishment, would earn him the Nobel Prize
for Literature in 1917.

The events depicted in Pontoppidan's oeuvre are bookended by
two wars: a relatively small-scale but historically significant war in
1864 and the so-called Great War of 1914–18. In 1864, the six-year-old
Henrik experienced the occupation of his native town, Randers, in
East Jutland, by Otto Von Bismarck's Prussian troops. One can
imagine the effect this historic event had on a young boy who would
come to understand as he grew through childhood that his country's
territorial area and its population had been cut by a third at a historical stroke. It is worth emphasizing the psychological blow to the
Danes at this grievous loss as it forms an important backdrop and
context for *A Fortunate Man*. The narrow neck of land that separates

the Cimbrian peninsula (Jutland) from what is now northern Germany was guarded by an ancient set of fortifications called *Dannevirke*. These fortifications had never been permanently breached, but in 1864 Prussian and Austrian troops overran the whole of Jutland. It is this conflict that is referred to, with the words "our last war with the Germans," in the first sentence of this novel about Peter Andreas Sidenius, simply called Per.

Even though Pontoppidan's production of fiction continued right up to 1927, his historical narrative space ends with the First World War. Pontoppidan's career as an author began in an 1880s Denmark that bore a sense of hope mixed with defiance against the oppressive Estrup regime, which practiced government by decree and censored anti-establishment criticism. By the end of Pontoppidan's oeuvre, there's a sense of apocalyptic despair right across the artistic and literary community, old and young, in a Europe devastated by war.

However, Pontoppidan was not an author who abandoned all hope entirely, and with the 1918 armistice the prose writer went slightly against his own grain by composing a short poem that endeared him to the Danish people forever—"It's Like a Fairy Tale" ("Det Lyder som et Eventyr"), which begins:

> *Det lyder som et Eventyr, et Sagn fra gamle Dage:*
> *en røvet Datter, dybt begrædt, er kommen frelst tilbage!*

> It sounds like a fairy tale, a legend from days of old:
> a stolen daughter, greatly grieved, is back within our fold!

This poem managed to capture the sense of national joy at the fact that, with the coming of peace, at least some parts of the old national territory in South Jutland were returned to Denmark as a result of postbellum territory realignments—in exactly the same way that Alsace-Lorraine was returned to France.

Like many other of his writer contemporaries, Henrik Pontoppidan was the son of a clergyman. But one of the things that makes Pontoppidan so interesting is that, although he was one of the many intellectuals in Scandinavia at that time who had abandoned the faith in which he had been reared, he never fully embraced liberalism, or laissez-faire attitudes, and never fully turned his back on what he regarded as authentic Christian values.

In fact, as expressed in his literary works, Pontoppidan's contempt is greatest for those within the Church who sought an accommodation with science and technology by liberalizing the basic tenets of their faith—all of course so as to retain their power and influence. We may compare how Pontoppidan aligns Per Sidenius with the "difficult" Pastor Fjaltring in *A Fortunate Man* with his contempt for the liberal, "wishy-washy" Pastor Blomberg. Throughout his life as a writer, Pontoppidan continued to engage with the Christian worldview and its metaphors, and never formally renounced his membership of the Danish state church, or what is known in Denmark as the "Folk Church," or national church of Denmark.

A veritable swarm of Christian ministers populate Pontoppidan's literary landscape—one of them being the principal character in his *The Promised Land (Det forjættede land)* from 1891–1895. And of course the protagonist in *A Fortunate Man* is the son of a pastor. Rather than Christianity as a concept, Henrik Pontoppidan seeks to confront the idea of a fundamentalist Christian upbringing typified by Per Sidenius' childhood. And it is the liberation from the shadow of this childhood that finally gives Per's tortured mind some respite and also brings him a modicum of happiness in the final years of his life.

A Fortunate Man is Henrik Pontoppidan's greatest work. The novel comes at the midpoint of his literary career and was written between 1896 and 1904 when the author was in his forties. However, the roots of *A Fortunate Man* can be traced to his writings a decade earlier, and in particular to *The Promised Land*, another large-scale work that clearly demonstrated Pontoppidan's breadth of vision and dexterity in handling big canvas stories. Indeed, in his acceptance speech to the Nobel Literature Committee, Pontoppidan made clear that his epic novels—*The Promised Land*, *A Fortunate Man*, and the last big novel *The Kingdom of the Dead* (*De dødes rige*)—should broadly be seen as a trilogy. In this trilogy, moreover, the author, as Pontoppidan put it himself, attempted to paint a cohesive picture of modern Denmark in the attitudes to life and the fate of its people.

The Promised Land portrayed a Denmark undergoing major social change and is full of conflicting religious and political movements, all swirling around a well-meaning religious minister who ends up collapsing under the weight of his own blind idealism. This is redolent of Norwegian writer Henrik Ibsen's priest in *Brand* (1866). As a counterpoint to this, *A Fortunate Man* has a main character who is just as widely traveled and has an equally roaming nature as Ibsen's eponymous *Peer Gynt* (1867), and there are many other similarities between the two characters: prolonged immaturity, fierce self-obsession, recklessness, and an abundance of aggressive energy.

The narrative of *A Fortunate Man* posits a range of contrasts. First of all, there's the idea of a young man from the country moving to the capital to seize power and prestige, a classic motif since Balzac; a young man who also experiences not only great victories but crushing defeats because of the familial baggage he has brought with him—impediments from which he can only very slowly free himself. Then there is the contradiction between old and new. In this case, between a fundamentalist, life-renouncing form of Lutheran Christianity and a sensual, hedonistic almost a-religious form of modern Jewishness, represented by the Salomon family. These two worlds are inverse reflections of each other. Peter Andreas Sidenius, with his apostolic forenames (Peter, Andrew), transforms himself into simple "Per Sidenius" and turns his back on his parents and siblings so as to seek fame and fortune in a world of his choosing.

As a marine and hydraulic engineer, Per Sidenius hopes to transform Denmark's transport system, thus making the country more amenable to commercial trade, by the establishment of a freeport on the west coast that was to be linked to a massive network of canals. The utilization of wind and wave energy would also form part of this highly ambitious and sophisticated project. Not only that, the bold Per wins the heart of Jakobe Salomon, daughter of the extremely wealthy Jewish wholesaler and businessman Philip Salomon who foots the bill for Per's sojourn around Europe, all for educational and edifying experiences. In fact, Per Sidenius follows in the footsteps of his creator Henrik Pontoppidan who also traveled to the Alps, Berlin, and Rome. All the way through the novel, Per encounters a broad range of people from very different backgrounds—shipyard workers, finance brokers, civil servants, shipping agents, solicitors, Copenhagen's bourgeoisie, squires of country estates, rotund and haggard priests in their various rectories, and so on.

From a modern perspective, it is undeniable that *A Fortunate Man*, like many novels produced at the time, displays certain cultural, ethnic, or national prejudices; that is to say, making often questionable associations between alleged traits of character and the biological and/or cultural affiliation of the person in question. However, it should be borne in mind that in the author's own time the word "race" did not solely refer to alleged biological traits. For example, people talked and wrote about the German "race" vis-à-vis the French "race" in broader cultural terms, which may or may not have had a disparaging tone. In a letter from 1891 Pontoppidan received the advice to travel from Berlin to Paris because "in spite of all what could be said about racial ties between Germans and Danes, artistic culture as a whole in Denmark has a deeper debt to France than Germany."

One of the most striking encounters in the novel is that between the young Per, newly arrived from the provinces, and the Jewish Salomon family. Per initially puts many of his own prejudices on display, betraying his inherited background. The first member of the Salomon household he encounters is the well-meaning Ivan Salomon, whom Per simply brushes aside, calling him an obsequious Jew. But then anti-Jewish sentiment is rife in the world that Per is trying to conquer. Moreover, his prejudicial bulwark gradually crumbles as he is drawn further into the world of the Salomons. Wealthy, cultured, friendly, liberal, and warm, the Jewish family is everything that his own family is not. Ivan becomes one of Per's most loyal stalwarts, and he later says of Ivan that his "natural disposition was to be helpful, his natural drive was to find things to worship and his only passion was to help ensure that his idols were apportioned their proper place in life's pantheon." And, of course, Per's relationship with Jakobe Salomon can also be seen to serve as a focus lens for further scrutiny of their respective "racial" moorings. It is noteworthy that it is Jakobe who conveys much of the hefty criticism that Pontoppidan levels against the Danish "race," which, in Jakobe's words, is just like the young Per Sidenius:

> In his heart of hearts, Per belonged to a different world that was suffused with a different light. Regardless of how different he appeared, and claimed to feel, from his contemporaries, he was in his very essence a true son of the Cimbrian soil, a natural-born child of the bloodless Danish race with its cold-eyed stare and ultimately cautious mindset.

Pontoppidan further lets Jakobe recount a chilling scene she had witnessed in one of Berlin's main railway stations, "a scene that had a terrible effect on me, so much so that I believe I have never really recovered from it." She describes how a pitiful column of Russian Jews "who for no other reason than their racial origins were driven from house and home, but not before they were robbed, manhandled and in some cases battered and broken. Just like a line of convicts, they had been led under police guard, and accompanied by the catcalls and scorn of the mob, all the way through the heartlands of civilized Europe." In the same letter to Per, Jakobe also relates how, while sitting in a train compartment, she herself was the victim of persecution, a reminder that she too belonged to "the same race as those wandering and persecuted souls." Thus, by portraying Jakobe in a strong and sympathetic light, Pontoppidan assuages much of the novel's latent and at times explicit anti-Jewish sentiment as it is expressed through several characters and episodes such as the above-mentioned one that references the Russian pogroms.

Although their relationship eventually founders, Per acknowledges Jakobe's significance for his personal crusade, and he, in a moment of quiet admission, knows that "Jakobe was a far more well-rounded person, whose importance for his development he would never deny." After years apart, and following the loss of her and Per's baby that dies shortly after an excruciating birth, the final moment of reconciliation occurs when Jakobe learns that Per in his last will has bequeathed funds to the school for disadvantaged children that she has established. Pontoppidan's portrait of the heroine Jakobe, sensuous and intelligent at the same time, is one of the most vivid in all of Danish literature.

It is the huge scale and very wide cultural engagement present in Pontoppidan's novel that has fascinated the Danish reading public for over a hundred years. Add to this the turbulent personal fate of the main character and his fascinating journey of self-discovery. *A Fortunate Man* depicts a whole epoch in its history and culture—the nature and disposition of a whole people and then their fascinating individual traits within that schema. A huge social canvas is contained in one novel. Using irony and radicalism as two sides of the same personal coin, Pontoppidan has managed to delve deeply into his people's inner essence, laid their weaknesses bare and is, at the same time, sparing in his praise.

It is for these reasons that *A Fortunate Man* is the most re-read novel amongst those works officially listed in the Danish classical canon. Innumerable readers, from all age groups and all walks of life, have discovered new angles to the novel. Readers wrestle over these core questions: Is Peter Andreas Sidenius a coward? Or is he a hero? A deeply meditative, sensitive soul, or a flaky charlatan?

It was seventeen years after his debut as author that Pontoppidan wrote *A Fortunate Man*—his coming of age tale of personal liberation. As elsewhere in Europe, this genre was a distinctive feature of Danish literature in the 1880s and '90s and pushing into the twentieth century—another well-known example being *Niels Lyhne* (1882) by J. P. Jacobsen. In the case of *A Fortunate Man*, Pontoppidan created a main character who was younger than him by ten years. Pontoppidan partly grounded his depiction of a younger generation of authors through his ties with them, including Viggo Stuckenberg (1863–1905) and Johannes Jørgensen (1866–1956, subsequently an internationally known biographer of the Catholic saints). With his own personal liberation novel *I gennembrud* (Breakthrough, 1888), Viggo Stuckenberg gave Pontoppidan the key to the father hatred that infuses Per Sidenius, an anti-father feeling that went way beyond the friction that would periodically arise between Pontoppidan and his own father, Dines Pontoppidan. To emphasize this authorial distance, at grammar school in his hometown of Randers Pontoppidan encountered a Lutheran minister and his wife who became the model for Per's parents to a much greater degree than Pontoppidan's own parents in real life. That said, Pontoppidan *was* a diligent raider of his own experience and "life archive" for use in his works—how people looked, their demeanor, and the conditions in which they lived. In this regard Pontoppidan was a strict "realist"; the furniture and fittings of life had to be authentic. So there was nothing strange about the fact that *A Fortunate Man* was long seen as being fully autobiographical. After all, hadn't Pontoppidan himself been an engineering student, right up to his final exams, when he bolted and threw himself into a life as a writer? Hadn't Pontoppidan, as the son of a Lutheran minister, grown up in Randers—the east Jutland town on the banks of a fjord, though this place name is never mentioned in the novel? All these points did in fact contribute indirectly to a change in the novel's timeline as it was being written—so that Per was given the same age as his author and dies at the same time as the year the novel's first edition ends—in 1904.

Pontoppidan faced a number of challenges while writing *A Fortunate Man*, in terms of its composition. For a period of some eight years around the turn of the century, he worked his way through the novel's immense set of components, all of which had to be successfully combined before its hero could be launched into the world—both in terms of the physical, intellectual, and spiritual world and then the constant oscillation between fight and flight that is a feature of Per Sidenius's life story. Thus, it is hardly surprising that midway through this mammoth task, Pontoppidan came to a complete halt and buried himself in studies and revisions of his previous works. He even wrote two new small novels in this period.

Until 1940, when Pontoppidan in the final volume of his first autobiography made a vague mention of "that winter" when he plowed through Friedrich Nietzsche's works, not much has been made of Pontoppidan's, and thereby the novel's, associations with the philosopher. As a student in 1964, I discovered Pontoppidan's library lending list of Nietzsche's works during his "hiatus" years in 1900–1901, and a few years later the literary historian Jørgen Moestrup showed in copious and very precise detail how Nietzschean concepts dislodged Pontoppidan's writer's block so that *A Fortunate Man* could finally be completed. Pontoppidan's interest in Nietzsche is in no small part due to Georg Brandes (1842–1927), at the time a critic known all over Europe, and who, in lectures held in 1888–1889, had been the first to draw attention to the almost unknown Nietzsche. Brandes was by no means just a passing acquaintance of Pontoppidan. The pair sometimes socialized with each other and occasionally corresponded. Indeed Georg Brandes plays a not insignificant part in *A Fortunate Man* in the, somewhat caricatured, guise of the celebrated socialite, arts critic, and raconteur Dr. Nathan.

It is true, and we know from other evidence, that Pontoppidan studied or interested himself in two other philosophers closely. One was Denmark's very own Søren Kierkegaard (1813–1855) and the other was Nietzsche's compatriot Arthur Schopenhauer (1788–1860). However, Schopenhauer might be seen more as Pontoppidan's stepping stone to Nietzsche where *A Fortunate Man* is concerned, in particular because of Nietzsche's book *Schopenhauer as Educator* (1874), which was studied by Pontoppidan. In a more recent work, literary historian and philologist Børge Kristiansen has published a significant work on the identity ethos and recurrent themes, or leitmotifs, in *A Fortunate Man*. Here Kristiansen emphasizes Schopenhauer's idea of "the world as will" and the subsequent rejection of that "will to life" that becomes Per's route to the "good fortune" for which he was destined. To further reinforce the Schopenhauer–Pontoppidan link, in one of his last books—*Et Kærlighedseventyr* (*A Love Tale*, 1918)—Pontoppidan creates a main character who had written a doctoral thesis on Schopenhauer. In the second edition of the book, Schopenhauer is replaced by Eduard von Hartmann (1842–1906), and although there's no evidence, to date, that Pontoppidan read Schopenhauer in the original German, the indirect link via Nietzsche is clear.

Pontoppidan was clearly aware of works like *Thus Spake Zarathustra, On the Genealogy of Morality* and *Schopenhauer as Educator* right from the start of his work on the novel. It is from Nietzsche that the idea of will to power emanates, an idea that, halfway through the novel, sends Per Sidenius hurtling onwards and upwards, only for him to retreat into rural, petty bourgeois mediocrity when he settles down to life in the sleepy Jutland hamlet of Rimalt. Life here is imbued with the liberal Christian ethos of the famous preacher and writer N. F. S. Grundtvig (1783–1872), which stressed folk revival, rural values, and cohesiveness over personal redemption. In his original plans for *A Fortunate Man*, Pontoppidan imagined Per's life journey coming to a stop in his marriage to Pastor Blomberg's daughter Inger. A potential wild stallion hobbled in the end.

Pastor Blomberg is a devotee of the anti-pietist wing of the Lutheran church, which grew in prominence and influence under Grundtvig and discouraged individual flights of religious fervor. However, Pontoppidan's deep study of Nietzsche inspired him to let Per, in personal terms, continue his journey far beyond Rimalt and Grundtvigian folk rallies: just as Søren Kierkegaard attacked Grundtvig, so too does Pastor Fjaltring in *A Fortunate Man*. And, like Kierkegaard, Pastor Fjaltring argues that true faith can only be attained, if it comes at all, through self-doubt and relentless questioning, not only of one's self but the Christian narrative per se. The greatest insights, Fjaltring argues, do not come from cool analysis and reason but rather from divine inspiration gained through deep, passionate meditation. It is from Fjaltring (who himself falters by committing suicide) that Per receives the incitement and courage to make the decisive Kierkegaardian leap towards a healing and fully independent life, which does not win him the world but his own true self. This is achieved by embracing the self in all its facets—warts and all, the good and the bad, the supreme personal attributes and the absolute personal limitations.

But in opposition to Kierkegaard, and in line with Nietzsche, this personal liberation finally happens via an internalization and embracing of the eternal power that resides, as Nietzsche argued, only within man himself—not a conqueror of the great world outside, then, but a conqueror of the hidden human world within.

What attracted Pontoppidan to Nietzsche was his fierce individualism and his positing of the "divine" authority within man himself, as opposed to an overarching God figure posited by Kierkegaard. This new type of modern humanism, that demanded no exterior communal obligations of the individual, was bound to interest a man like Pontoppidan who remained an outsider and shunned all kinds of "movements." Here was a philosophy that spoke to his instinctively rebellious and contrarian sensibilities. Disappointed in his political hopes and expectations after the collapse of young democracies, Pontoppidan was drawn to Nietzsche's ostensibly egotistical philosophy that encouraged people to assert and control their own fates in the same way that a work of art is imagined and then forged. Thus, the respect that must be won is self-respect.

Along an arduous, lengthy, and contorted path, Pontoppidan brings Per Sidenius to his point of self-respect. In other words, he shifts his aspirations for happiness and "success" from external to internal values. Per moves from rapture, both in its material and sensual sense, to the liberating pain of renunciation, stoicism, and simplicity—a lifestyle that has its own rewards and, for Pontoppidan at least, was a better option for the weak and vacillating Danes of modern times. Pontoppidan's enactment of Per's positively "regressive" development—by which the protagonist "barters downwards," sacrificing fame, wealth, and the comforts and security of familial life in exchange for a simpler but perhaps more genuine life—is fetched from the world of fairy-tales, for instance in the Brothers Grimm's *Hans in Luck* (*Hans im Glück*) and Hans Christian Andersen's *What the Old Man Does Is Always*

Right (*Hvad Fatter gør, det er altid det rigtige*). The end of the novel has Per blessing his good fortune in having lived at a time when people were called to will their authentic selves into being in all their own divine nakedness—or according to his diary, found after he has passed: "Without the incredible, indeed mythical, courage to will oneself into that place of ultimate godlike naked exposure, one will never achieve a state of genuine human independence."

The novel's philosophical references are so deftly integrated into the story that they come to the reader as immediate drama without need of explanation. This is just one of the reasons why *A Fortunate Man* has kept its currency and validity through multiple generations of readers and widely shifting times. The work has also effortlessly negotiated massive cultural changes that have seen other once-esteemed titles fall from grace. *A Fortunate Man* possesses the inherent story-telling gifts of its creator— a clear simplicity of language combined with a sophisticated multifaceted depiction of Denmark's physical landscape, social layers, and remarkable individuals, all set in the last quarter of the nineteenth century. Humor, and betimes rough satire, are also regular features in a skillfully and confidently woven composition that adroitly uses particular themes and symbols as narrative waystations.

Pontoppidan's literary production—with *A Fortunate Man* as its crowning jewel—would earn him a Nobel Prize for literature in 1917, which he would share with Karl Gjellerup (1857–1919). A number of Pontoppidan commentators believe that the awarding to Pontoppidan of a "shared" Nobel Prize, rather than the Nobel Committee making an individual award, was due to Pontoppidan's rebellious nature and the radical content of his work, and there is no doubt that Pontoppidan was an inveterate iconoclast from start to finish. Henrik Pontoppidan would hold a similar place in the heart of Danes as that of Thomas Mann (1875–1955) amongst his own compatriots. Pontoppidan never made any public reference to his younger German writer-colleague, but in 1927 Thomas Mann was invited to give an opinion of the Danish Nobel Prize winner on the occasion of his seventieth birthday. Mann wrote the following:

The author of *A Fortunate Man* is a full-blooded storyteller who examines our lives and society so intensely that he ranks amongst the highest class of European writers. As a genuine conservative, he asserts the importance of an expansive style to an impatient world. As a genuine revolutionary, he sees in prose novels, above all, a scrutinizing power. With that charming, indeed captivating, stringency which is the secret of all art, he judges the times and then, as a true poet, points us towards a purer, more honorable way of being human.

A Fortunate Man had already been translated into German in 1906—fittingly titled *Hans im Glück*—and has enjoyed much success in the German-speaking world. In addition to Mann's ringing praise, the influential critics Georg Lukács and Ernst Bloch have hailed the novel as one of the best ever written. Despite winning the Nobel Prize, and despite achieving popularity in Scandinavia, Germany and several other countries, Pontoppidan has, on the whole, failed to resonate in the English-speaking world. It is to be hoped that this edition will spawn more interest in Pontoppidan and will attract new readers across the world who will be able to appreciate and wrestle with *A Fortunate Man*, a truly breathtaking novel by an author who deserves to be ranked as one of the true greats of modern European literature.

A Note on the Text

The three-volume second edition of *A Fortunate Man*, on which the present translation is based, was published in 1905, following a thorough revision and an abridgment of the first edition, which was published as an eight-part series in the years 1898–1904. Pontoppidan had already started work on the second edition of the novel while he was halfway through the first edition, as he was clear that changes were needed. Thus there are features in the last volume of the first edition that can only be fully understood by referring to the second edition. In fact, in a note at the end of the last volume of the first edition, Pontoppidan writes:

> A new, fully reviewed and slightly shorter version of these chronicles relating the life of Per Sidenius will be published early next year. The author would request that this new edition be used as the point of reference in any assessment of the work as a whole.

For this reason, the view that there is actually no such thing as a comprehensive first edition has gained increasing traction.

The third edition of the work published in 1907 was, to all intents and purposes, identical with the 1905 edition. However, in 1918 Pontoppidan once again reviewed the text in preparation for a new version and it is this edition that, since the 1960s, has been used by Gyldendal publishers as the basis for its reprints of the novel in Danish (with the only major difference being that from 1984 onwards the original spelling was modernized in accordance with standard orthography). That Pontoppidan was occasionally plagued by self-doubts as to his ability to make later revisions of his novels is evident from the revision of *The Promised Land* in 1918. He had written to the author Vilhelm Østergaard requesting that he carry out the abridgment demanded by the publishers for a new edition of the novel. Tellingly, Pontoppidan justified his request that Østergaard make the changes thus:

> It's not far off a whole generation since I wrote the book, and the subject—and also partly the way it is treated—seems so distant to me now that I'm worried I'll end up ruining rather than improving things if I start messing with it. Such disasters have happened to me before. Unless I can completely recast the material in question, I'm often quite helpless.

Although there is no direct evidence of Pontoppidan having similar misgivings about the later revisions of *A Fortunate Man*, the quotation voices what popular consensus is increasingly affirming: that Pontoppidan's 1918 revisions of the text cannot be said to have improved the work and that, in fact, the second edition used here should be regarded as the definitive text for the purposes of publication, translation, and text interpretation.

—FLEMMING BEHRENDT
Translated from the Danish by Paul Larkin

OTHER NEW YORK REVIEW CLASSICS

For a complete list of titles, visit www.nyrb.com.

DANTE ALIGHIERI Purgatorio; translated by D. M. Black
CLAUDE ANET Ariane, A Russian Girl
HANNAH ARENDT Rahel Varnhagen: The Life of a Jewish Woman
OĞUZ ATAY Waiting for the Fear
DIANA ATHILL Don't Look at Me Like That
DIANA ATHILL Instead of a Letter
HONORÉ DE BALZAC The Lily in the Valley
POLINA BARSKOVA Living Pictures
ROSALIND BELBEN The Limit
HENRI BOSCO The Child and the River
ANDRÉ BRETON Nadja
DINO BUZZATI The Betwitched Bourgeois: Fifty Stories
DINO BUZZATI A Love Affair
DINO BUZZATI The Singularity
DINO BUZZATI The Stronghold
CRISTINA CAMPO The Unforgivable and Other Writings
CAMILO JOSÉ CELA The Hive
EILEEN CHANG Written on Water
FRANÇOIS-RENÉ DE CHATEAUBRIAND Memoirs from Beyond the Grave, 1800–1815
AMIT CHAUDHURI Afternoon Raag
AMIT CHAUDHURI Freedom Song
AMIT CHAUDHURI A Strange and Sublime Address
LUCILLE CLIFTON Generations: A Memoir
RACHEL COHEN A Chance Meeting: American Encounters
COLETTE Chéri *and* The End of Chéri
E. E. CUMMINGS The Enormous Room
JÓZEF CZAPSKI Memories of Starobielsk: Essays Between Art and History
ANTONIO DI BENEDETTO The Silentiary
ANTONIO DI BENEDETTO The Suicides
HEIMITO VON DODERER The Strudlhof Steps
PIERRE DRIEU LA ROCHELLE The Fire Within
JEAN ECHENOZ Command Performance
FERIT EDGÜ The Wounded Age *and* Eastern Tales
MICHAEL EDWARDS The Bible and Poetry
ROSS FELD Guston in Time: Remembering Philip Guston
BEPPE FENOGLIO A Private Affair
GUSTAVE FLAUBERT The Letters of Gustave Flaubert
WILLIAM GADDIS The Letters of William Gaddis
BENITO PÉREZ GÁLDOS Miaow
MAVIS GALLANT The Uncollected Stories of Mavis Gallant
NATALIA GINZBURG Family *and* Borghesia
JEAN GIONO The Open Road
WILLIAM LINDSAY GRESHAM Nightmare Alley
VASILY GROSSMAN The People Immortal
MARTIN A. HANSEN The Liar
ELIZABETH HARDWICK The Uncollected Essays of Elizabeth Hardwick
GERT HOFMANN Our Philosopher
HENRY JAMES On Writers and Writing
TOVE JANSSON Sun City
ERNST JÜNGER On the Marble Cliffs
MOLLY KEANE Good Behaviour